THE HEIRS

Books by G.Y. Dryansky

OTHER PEOPLE
THE HEIRS

THE HEIRS

A novel about a great European family

G.Y. Dryansky

G.P. PUTNAM'S SONS, NEW YORK

Copyright © 1978 by G.Y. Dryansky

All rights reserved. This book, or parts thereof, must not be reproduced in any form without permission. Published simultaneously in Canada by Longman Canada Limited, Toronto.

Library of Congress Cataloging in Publication Data

Dryansky, G Y
  The heirs

I. Title.
PZ4.D7955He [PS3554.R87] 813'.5'4 78-5222

SBN: 399-11976-0

PRINTED IN THE UNITED STATES OF AMERICA

For Joanne, André and Larisa Dryansky

"Man has to pick up the use of his functions as he goes along—especially the function of Love."
—Mr. Emerson, in *A Room with a View*, by E.M. Forster

FOREWORD

This is an old-fashioned book, about characters who are, in some ways, out of the ordinary. I hope the ways in which they are like all of us are apparent. I have tried to make them faithful to my long observation of persons of their milieu, but I wish to make clear that they are totally fictional—they are in no way directly, or obliquely, based on particular persons who are alive or who have lived. Nor is the Wolfflen family a fictionalized rendition of a real family.

"*Let the dead Past bury its dead* would be a better saying," Galsworthy wrote, "if the Past ever died." Because I think the Past is more than a flea market where a writer can find titillating items of nostalgia, I have tried to follow the current of history during the years described here. But my first ambition has been to tell an entertaining story, and I have gone about trying, taking the liberty with real events which novelists traditionally consider their right.

THE HEIRS

PROLOGUE

The museum is closing—
Your attention! The museum is closing...

The recorded, disembodied voice carried over the grounds, first in French, then in several foreign languages. A married couple in their thirties and their young boy came walking in rapid, crunching steps over the gravel path toward the gate, where the German bus had already recuperated its cargo of tourists. Where the ground grew higher, near the enormous house, Jason Fullerton caught his wife Léa's arm, so that they could look backward at the splendor one more time. At almost five o'clock of the late fall day, the sun was a great ball melting violet into a mother-of-pearl sky, behind the skeletal tops of high oaks which marked the beginning of the forest. Mist had begun to creep over the lawn from the artificial lake where swans fluttered in the moody light. The pink-gray lake, the muffled lawn ... then free-growing meadow, and beyond, the black trees for thousands of acres.

"He gave it away," Fullerton said, with awe that hadn't been dimmed by his intimate knowledge of the story—and with almost personal nostalgia.

This was the first time the Fullertons had been in Europe since Bois Brûlé had changed hands for a second time. The change, not long after the funeral they'd attended in Paris, was achieved rapidly, so rapidly that the present owner, the French government, didn't seem to have had time to install all that appeared necessary for a suitable museum. The guide was as dismayed as they were by the sparse, unfinished air inside the house—Léa realized that museum guides must measure their own prestige by their museums, the way servants measured theirs by their masters'—but the guide confided bleakly that absolutely nothing more was planned.

He had singled them out from the packaged tourists—they were better dressed, they were perhaps even French—and he'd spilled all he knew. No doubt he was also courting the tip he knew was not part of the all-included for the Germans, who trailed after their own expert, prattling like a recording in their own tongue.

"During his lifetime, his was the richest family in Europe," the guide had said, in his preamble to the Fullertons, "if they'd put together all the money in the different branches . . . But *they didn't.*"

"And he just gave all this away," the American husband urged, to see what more the man would say, and how he would cast it.

"He was giving a lot of things away before he died, oh plenty. He had that famous young actress who was helping him to spend. But not on themselves. He was, *monsieur,* a remarkable *seigneur!*"

The old guide's body, under his loose, shiny blue uniform, seemed to come almost to attention, as he raised his voice in praise of the late Baron Marc de Wolfflen.

"The son," he continued, "did not see things the same way." The guide's voice dropped into another confidence: "And there was something, some kind of bad blood between the girl and the son. When the Baron died, his son cut off the running funds for the Institute . . . the Institute had no choice but to turn the place over to the government and hope for the best. So you see the result . . ."

"The Institute?" Fullerton asked.

"It was a place where brilliant people worked on projects for improving things. And then they campaigned to have the government put the changes through. The Baron," he croaked, "was heartbroken by the response."

"His dying word was 'railroads,' " Léa recalled aloud.

"You know the story," the guide said in an offended voice.

"Some of it," she soothed.

The guide became silent as he led them through the downstairs rooms of the château.

Le Musée National du 19ème Siècle:

The National Museum of the Nineteenth Century:

In the ballroom, complicated black machines stood on the marble floor, looking awkward and impoverished, under the Tiepolo-inspired ceiling. The promenade that ran the southern length of the house, recalling the Hall of Mirrors at Versailles, had been filled with mediocre pictures and various mockups under glass. There was nothing else. The machines in the ballroom were arranged crudely, as if they'd just been uncrated: great dinosaurs of technology, cast iron beneath the crystal of the chandeliers.

Perhaps, Léa thought, fighting back a surge of senseless pity for her dead cousin, perhaps it's just as well that "the museum of the nineteenth century" was so unfinished; the so-called century was still unfinished, an epoch conceived sometime in the late seventeen hundreds was still surging forward, two hundred years later, billowing smoke. And the *bilan,* she thought, the ledger of accomplishment and loss, was far from closed.

Above the promenade, she recalled, there'd been the gallery of family portraits. Still there?

"The upstairs is closed to the public," the guide said. "It is still the way the Baron left it. Sometimes visitors interested in the furniture are given permission to go up. But you must apply for that beforehand. Everything is all wrapped."

In one of those rooms, she remembered, one of those bedrooms swaddled in muslin now, the Baron Marc de Wolfflen came into the world unexpectedly early, during a shooting weekend in March, 1914.

Above the staircase leading there, the Wolfflen crest still remained. Léa was shocked to see it, as if she half-expected it would be chipped away, the way old régime things were chipped away from castles and churches in 1789. Was the comparison so absurd?

"His coat of arms," the guide said, who could not see that the design the woman wore on her gold ring was identical. Here he broke into a spiel:

"The crest was designed for Isaiah Wolfflen, a scrap merchant in Mainz, later in Nancy, who became arms supplier and banker to the Revolutionary Government. The family was ennobled (a long story) by Napoleon I, in 1804; its titles were recognized in Austria in 1819 by the Emperor Francis, and by Queen Victoria of England in 1839 ..."

The weak-lunged guide took a breath where no doubt he habitually did. "Note the wolf," he went on, "a wolf rampant, *gules,* or red, bearing a brand with a three-pointed flame (his three sons) in its paw *dexter,* or right, on a field *or.* The crest: a coronet with three pearls. And the motto: *Virtus et Unitas.* Which means—"

"Courage and Unity" the boy interjected in French.

"You know—"

Jason Fullerton comforted the old man with a bill ...

"But why did Cousin Marc name it Bois Brûlé?" the boy asked, in English now, as they drank in a last image of the landscape.

"He didn't," Léa answered. "He didn't build the house, either: his grandfather did. The name existed long before the house. It belonged to the meadow, and it probably went back all the way to the end of the tenth century, when many places in France were named Bois Brûlé."

"Burnt Woods? *Forest fires?*"

"Oh no. There was a moment, you see, in the Middle Ages, when suddenly the future of the world seemed much brighter. The *seigneurs* had ended their private wars which had devastated the land, the coasts were secure from raiders, the Church had become a strong moral force (it was not yet riddled with corruption), and the King maintained a rule of law."

"And so—"

"And so, the peasants were inspired to grow more food. They went into forests, where wolves and wild pigs reigned, and burnt them down to create fields and pasture land. That was a great turning point in history ... "

"Oh history," the boy said. He had inherited a habit of his mother's family to show affection by teasing. *"What's history?"* (His mother taught history to college students.)

The husband, a lawyer, broke in with an answer: "The tricks important people play!" It was a superficial thing to tell the boy, he knew, but it might just silence him long enough for them to get to the gate, before they were closed in for the night.

BOOK ONE

"WE'LL GET EVERYTHING BACK..."

ONE

On the evening of March 11, 1945, a spavined horse was pulling an open, rubber-tired wartime taxi along the Boulevard des Capucines in Paris. Behind the driver were two men in khaki. Their uniforms, of different armies, were not greatly dissimilar, but in other ways they seemed an incongruous pair. A few minutes earlier, the doorman of the Hôtel Scribe had raised his eyebrows and furrowed his forehead as they came out of the revolving front doors together. No doubt he knew war made for strange acquaintances and maybe he knew Major Hoyt, the bigger of the two men, was someone important, and why he was. But doormen, like all servants, are terrific snobs, and by his look he seemed to have thought of Hoyt principally as a freakishly large example of the rustic, oversized Americans living at the hotel since the Germans had left. The other, the short, slight man, was Someone. Despite the surprisingly inelegant droop of his French officer's greatcoat, despite his quiet manner, he was, to anyone who knew something about French society, quite obviously Someone.

He was the Baron Marc de Wolfflen. His father, the Baron

Charles, had been one of the best-known financiers in the country, before he'd fled to exile in London. The Baron Marc had been famous in his own way. In *Images du Monde,* in *L'Illustration,* in all the magazines read by the rich and their servants during the late thirties, his picture had appeared often. He would be in white tie and tails, at one of the season's balls, or in top hat and gray tailcoat, with a set of binoculars hanging from his neck, beside his father at the paddock of Longchamp. Balls and the race course were the favorite backgrounds for photographs in those magazines, and the natural haunts of young society bachelors. The Baron Marc, with his ascetic good features, his velvety gaze, had been considered one of the most eligible bachelors of the Tout-Paris.

During the war, in London, he'd married a fourth cousin, an English Wolfflen. A December, 1944 article in *Le Monde* that had noted his marriage had also mentioned that his wife, Emma, was a talented pianist. The story appeared because the Baron had been named to the Provisional Government's energy committee, and more important to *Le Monde* than the details of his personal life were his credentials as a hero of de Gaulle's espionage service.

Marc de Wolfflen had returned permanently to Paris in December, very much alone.

His wife was being watched through a difficult pregnancy by a Harley Street specialist, and his father, in the eyes of his mother—whose opinion on Charles' health was law—was not well enough, either, to cross the Channel in wartime and suffer winter weather in a city still lacking most amenities. The only other Wolfflens in town were the old Baron Saul, his young son, Léopold, and Saul's wife, Ariel, who was dying of tuberculosis in the American Hospital. At first Marc did his best to see the three of them often, but he soon reduced the contact.

Saul, the Austrian Wolfflen who had moved to Holland just before the First World War and to France in the early twenties, had never been a close cousin to Marc. Early in his youth, the French and English Wolfflens had mocked Saul's business judgment and refused to follow him into petroleum when their backing would have been useful. Despite them, he became richer on oil than the rest of the family combined, and ever since kept his fortune jealously apart from any dealings with the other Wolfflens. Over the years, the family and Saul had argued more than once over whether it was he or they who had broken with the spirit of cooperation in business which old Isaiah, founder of the Wolfflen dynasty, had urged his sons to embrace. A long time ago, the fruitless quarrel had stopped, but Saul continued to exist on the edge of the family.

As if to ease this regret over Saul's right judgment about oil—made at the turn of the century—Marc's father had adopted a certain condescending affection for Saul, who was a small man physically, and superficially too gentle to seem important. But he hated Saul's second wife, Ariel, with uncomplicated intensity—Ariel, the wild Amazon, the Catholic shrew who'd finally disgraced the entire family by staying behind in Paris during the Occupation, while Saul had to flee to Switzerland with their seven-year-old son.

Marc was a young man, though, who had never known hatred in his life; loneliness and pity had driven him to visit Ariel during the first months of his return to Paris and to dine frequently with the grief-stricken husband and son. Saul would often be in tears in front of the boy, who, on the verge of puberty now, had assumed the gray mien of a little old man. Saul complained over and over about the hostility of the family towards his poor wife and made it seem almost as if they and not the Germans were responsible for her illness. The boy, who was growing amazingly fat, ate ravenously, and Saul did nothing to correct his unpleasant manners at table. Watching clumsy Léopold stir his spoon through dripping second helpings of chocolate mousse, Marc couldn't help but ruminate over his father Charles' conviction that Léopold was not really Saul's son, was by no means a Wolfflen.

At the hospital Ariel grew bitchy when she wasn't lost in feeble, half-spoken reveries over great stag hunts she'd led.

The scenes with Ariel, Saul, and Léopold had finally become too hard for Marc to take. He tried to ease his solitude elsewhere by putting together friendships he'd had before the war.

Some of the men he'd known, though, were fighting under Leclerc in Germany, and some who'd turned out to be Pétainists were lying low waiting to be called before the Purification Committees. A mood of the days of the Terror prevailed within what had been the carefree Tout-Paris. Emnities were bitter. People who hadn't taken sides during the Occupation fretted over being thrown in with the collaborators; they were cutting the Pétainists they'd tolerated at dinner tables for years. Everybody in Marc's old circles was calumniating nearly everyone else, and his presence, his Resistance hero's presence, made them all terribly uncomfortable. Marc, who held no grudge against anyone, who'd rather just see all those ugly war years blotted out and the good times of a frivolous society back again, finally went his own lonely way.

On arriving in Paris, he had moved into the Hôtel Scribe which was full of American military people, who had arranged for the best service in town, including hot water twice a week. Marc had no house of his own and his father's great unheated mansion on Avenue Foch had seemed as welcoming as a meat locker. Before long, the bustle at the Scribe became a better-than-nothing kind of company for him. The boisterous voices in the lobby and hallways never asked him anything, never provoked any awkward or painful exchanges over who he'd become and who other people had become during long, terrible years. They were there simply in a vaguely soothing way—a presence of life assuring him that the world of after the war and the world he was about to step into, the world of after thirty, were still inhabitable.

Marc had been about to gather his mail at the concièrge's desk of the Scribe, when Major Hoyt had come up to him in the lobby, with a rather somber "good evening."

"I ... have a matter to inform you about, Baron," he'd said, casting a glance around the room crowded with officers and correspondents who were telling war stories and drinking *fine à l' eau.* "Would it be all right if we went somewhere?" Marc had followed him into the street without a word. Major Kyle R. Hoyt was the ranking U.S. Army Intelligence officer in Paris.

They'd climbed into the cab together looking, from behind, deceptively like Mutt and Jeff. Contrary to what the doorman might have thought as he stared at them in chauvinistic amusement, Hoyt was no coarse funnyman in uniform. He was a gentleman from a noted if no longer rich Baltimore family who'd used his big body to advantage playing fullback at Yale, an extracurricular talent which had helped him win a Rhodes Scholarship to Oxford just before the war broke out. His manners were American, in that they were blunt, precise, but considerate. Marc had learned all this after sitting down beside Hoyt one evening at the Scribe bar. As he had then, Hoyt offered Marc a cigar when they'd sat down in the horse-drawn cab. Marc declined a second time, and waited with silent worry for Hoyt's news, as the Major spent a long moment getting his own cigar lit with a flaring Zippo and keeping it lit against a wind coming up from the Seine.

The cab turned now down the Rue de la Paix. Ahead, night was condensing like mist on the branches of the chestnuts in the Tuileries. Their blurred calligraphy conveyed a sadness. The Baron shuddered, raised the collar of his greatcoat, and fixed his eyes higher on what light remained in a sky smeared with thin clouds like shoals.

Hoyt had begun coughing on the cigar clenched between his teeth.

"Oh my God, hold tight!" he managed to gasp, without losing his grip on the cigar. The horse, which had been trotting in a way that looked like it was fighting to keep all four diseased legs from going off in different directions, burst into a desperate gallop.

"Hold on to your *képi*, Baron!"

Hoyt seemed to be grinning as he shouted with the cigar still between his teeth. The driver stood up, swore, and then fell over onto his seat. Skidding, the carriage hit the edge of the sidewalk and seemed about to either turn over or plow through the window of Cartier. The driver managed to veer the horse out into the road, but by the time he'd broken the horse's gallop, Hoyt was jammed against Marc, who had caught a gust of cigar ash in his eyes.

"Yikes ... I'm terribly sorry, Baron!"

The Baron Marc de Wolfflen, who did not like to be called "Baron," blinked gritty tears. His eyes focused again on the luminous and black-pencilled dusk sky: an Ile de France skyscape full of moody tension, the sky he'd thought of, sodden with nostalgia, during London winters when time had seemed arrested in a swaddle of brown mist. Now for an instant, the sky above the chestnuts was a far ocean, somewhere else he'd rather be, somewhere he'd never been: some bright exotic warm latitude and not here, this evening, in an absurd taxi, waiting for this stranger beside him to say something that already had the smell of bad news.

In the Rue de Castiglione, the horse began to trot erratically again, dodging, maybe, phantoms made of wind and shadow. Hoyt blew great, stoking puffs into his smoke until the end turned bright red. He'd won. He relieved his teeth, put the glowing end close to his eyes appreciatively; then he threw the cigar into the street and dusted ashes from his lapel with his broad palm.

"We've got a problem," he said finally.

"So I suspect."

"It's serious."

"You've bombed the place where Goering hid my father's Rembrandts." Saying this, Marc had an intuition that the news was worse. He closed his eyes and shuddered again, as the wind from the river pulsed over the hack. He was cold mostly because he was nervous, but his English came out in the pleasant and cynical drawl of RAF men he'd frequented, Lysander pilots who'd flown him in and out of occupied France, men who'd practiced the irony of making everything crucial sound routine. "Gone for a shit," the messmates would say, when you asked about one of their number who'd been shot down.

Hoyt frowned.

"It's your cousin," he said. "The Baron Bruno de Wolfflen is in a tough position," Hoyt complained hoarsely. He cleared his throat. "They might just kill him," he said, "as easy as let him out of that castle."

"My cousin's an officer," Marc answered, "he's a prisoner of war." Marc's tone was still calm, but his irony had left him. "They haven't dared touch a hair on his head in four and a half years. There is the Geneva Convention," he went on, but convention wasn't a word that fit this war in any sense. Marc's voice was empty of self-assurance.

"We'll drive up the Champs," Hoyt said. "I've got a proposal to explain to you . . ."

"Today's my birthday," Marc said. He was thinking out loud. "I'm thirty. My cousin will be thirty-two next month—"

"Take it easy, Baron. There's a way we can save him."

The horse trotted into the Rue de Rivoli. Then its gait sputtered and became a walk. The driver, himself a bandy-legged old runt, lost all patience and began to whip and swear. Now the horse stopped with its head between its forelegs and wouldn't budge another step.

"We can walk," Hoyt said. "We can walk back to the Scribe. We don't really have to go any place special . . ."

They left the driver stranded. Hoyt gave him a bill. Behind them, as they walked, the unlit Place de la Concorde was already a field of night, empty and monumental, dour as a graveyard.

Bruno would have made that horse go, Marc was thinking. *Without a whip, just a pair of reins, big, wild, crazy Bruno would have charmed that poor horse into a gallop and galloped it until it fell down dead . . . .*

The Baron Bruno de Wolfflen was a marvelous horseman. At Deauville, in August of 1939, he'd captained the Lilas team through a perfect season, defeating even the team from Buenos Aires that had ridden over the polo fields of Europe like the men of Attila. That afternoon, when Lilas played the Argentines for the Gold Cup, Marc had sat at a table at the edge of the sunny field behind the race course, drinking a watery-sweet Pimm's and applauding every one of Bruno's miraculous near-side backhand strokes. Not without envy. Tall, muscular, quick-nerved Bruno was twice the horseman Marc could ever hope to be. Marc, whose best achievement at sports was dogged, long-distance swimming, took solace in believing he would be twice the financier Bruno could ever hope to be. But up till then, Marc's financial ambitions had been channeled only into vague, inconsequential fantasies. He knew he would have to take over the Banque Wolfflen someday, he dreamed about what it might be like to do so, yet in real life he showed no great appetite for finance. Bruno, on the other hand, was bristling with ambition. In any case, neither had got much of a chance to prove himself at the Banque Wolfflen.

Marc's stern and ponderous old father, the Baron Charles, had had a rough course to steer in the thirties. First there was the Depression, which had spread from America across the Atlantic, and then the socializing government of the Popular Front: Charles responded to events that licked like storm waves at the French Wolfflen fortune by gripping the helm all the more tightly. He held on, he fared forward, although he knew he was condemned to be far from a dominant figure in the long history of Wolfflen moneymaking. Charles' most positive achievement between the two wars was the high reparations he'd managed through sly politics for the nationalized Wolfflen railroads—railroads that were losing money at the time Blum's government took them over. In all of Charles' confidential meetings with his friendly Deputies, his son, Marc, and his nephew, Bruno, were left entirely out in the cold.

The two young men would arrive dutifully all the same, every weekday morning, at the seat of their family's fortune, a marble-faced townhouse in a courtyard of a narrow street near the Bourse. The founder of the Wolfflen dynasty, Isaiah, had once lived with his wife and three sons in that house, built shortly after he'd financed, with two bankers— better known than he was, but whose names now meant nothing—the seizure of power by Napoleon I. On the second floor, up a double staircase, was the Associates' Room, once Isaiah's study, where Marc and Bruno would spend the day with Charles. It was a mahogany-panelled room that smelled of Charles' Havana cigars and of the leather upholstery of the Louis Philippe couches no one ever used.

Charles would sit erect as a buddha behind a Napoleon III desk whose legs were gilded dragon arms. In back of him there hung a portrait of Isaiah with his fingers in a butter colored satin vest— striking a pose dear to his protégé, the first Bonaparte. Further down, in separate corners of a vast blue Chinese carpet, Marc and Bruno each sat at plain office rolltops of the turn of the century. From time to time, Charles would look up from his dossiers or take a halt from his phone calls to summon them to the two chairs in front of his desk. He would brief them on whatever suited him, or give them tasks of execution of the kind a good private secretary could handle.

Bruno would prepare memos full of proposals, and argue often, without avail, to have his way. Marc would study Charles' strategy as best he could, arm himself with whatever he could learn of his father's achievements and mistakes, and daydream.

A complicated history of inheritance had given Charles fifty-five percent of the French Wolfflen fortune. Until 1934, his associate had been his cousin Pierre, Bruno's father. Pierre had had an excessive zeal for airplanes, which had made him an absentee partner, and which finally did him in when the Potez he was piloting from Geneva to Lyon crashed in a snowstorm. His wife was in the co-pilot's seat. Their orphan and only heir, Bruno inherited Pierre's forty-five percent of the Banque Wolfflen only a year after he'd come back from the Wharton School in America. Bruno was the young partner, full of school knowledge of business, anxious to assume responsibility, yet destined to have no more voting power, ultimately, than he had the day he stepped in at twenty-two. Marc was the powerless heir apparent, with no shares at all until Charles retired, or died. Each of the two young men had the leisure to savor frustration to the dregs and there was enough friction built into the setup for them to hate each other. They didn't. But neither felt at any great ease with the other. Bruno was very different from Marc.

Bruno was a tall, strapping blond with jutting features and green eyes that called to mind some Northern English or Scots aristocratic warrior. He was generous and given to anger, loud and openhearted, a gambler, a womanizer, a drinker no one had ever drunk under the table.

The social columns called Marc "civilized, refined." In the family he was called *"Marc l'Enfermé,"* or *"Le Chinois"* (partly because of his dark, almond-shaped eyes). He was the taciturn one, in a clan proud to have pursued both business and pleasure exuberantly for five generations. He was introspective, often moody, and his gaiety expressed itself most often in sensitive wit. His manners were perfect, even if their elegance seemed sometimes a barrier between the world and whatever inner self he seemed to want to shelter. Because he had yet to become vastly attached to anything in his life, Marc was capable of great objectivity.

Physically, Marc was born frail and had grown into a certain spare wiriness. In his height, he resembled Eveline, his mother, more than his father. Or perhaps he resembled most of all Charles' Austrian cousin, Saul—Saul, whom Charles couldn't bring to mind without unpleasant thoughts about Saul's wife and his jealously isolated fortune.

Yes, it was just possible that his son's resemblance to his smaller, richer cousin irritated Charles. Charles was a chunky bear of a man, who had put on a paunch before his majority, in an epoch when girth on a rich man had meant lustiness and good fellowship. Charles would come home on leave from the trenches of the Great War and complain that his infant son was failing to grow. He'd bring in all sorts of specialists to beef up the scrawny child. Instead of getting sturdier under their hybrid care, Marc developed allergies that led to crippling attacks of asthma. He would spend long days bedridden during the pollen season, when each breath was a conscious effort and when he took pathetic refuge from boredom by trying to make tunes out of the sound of bagpipes in his lungs.

His worst attack was in the summer of 1919, when Charles, who had gone on from Verdun after the Armistice to Poland, returned from chasing Bolsheviks to stay. Charles had developed typhus and was down to three-quarters of his normal weight. Eveline—who had gained experience with invalids when she'd turned their country place, Bois Brûlé, into a field hospital in 1917—took direct charge of her husband's convalescence. The family went off to Switzerland. Marc and his gangling adolescent sister, Sara, Nanny, and three chambermaids all sat in retinue behind Mama and Papa, as the cogged railway clanged its way upward toward Zermatt. The mountains below the village were covered with wild flowers: gentian and edelweis. All the way up, Marc kept sneezing, until his nose was spurting blood. Next morning, blue in the face, he went back down the mountain on a stretcher between two train seats.

Bruno came to see him at the hospital in Paris. The room was full of sunlight, which had brightened even the gray stone pillars of the colonnaded eighteenth-century courtyard below. Bruno's blond curls shone like a halo as he stood between Marc's bed and the window. He was already, at seven, quite tall, long legged, well built. That day Marc realized, with a pang of childhood instinct, that there was an easy rapport between his cousin and the physical world that he himself would never have. Bruno was not simply strong and healthy, he was a well-made phenomenon of nature. And Marc realized that he himself was born to approach all simple natural things with a certain awkwardness, wonder, and trepidation. Bruno stayed at Marc's bedside the time it took to play a game of "War." Marc's solace, that day, was to have won the card game and to have smoked a eucalyptus cigaret in front of Bruno.

Marc grew out of his allergies. At twelve he was able to leave home, and the finicky scholarship of a gray-haired tutor. He went off to Croseigne, the smartest pension on the continent, a mini-Eton, set down among the Swiss Alps. Its mock-Gothic cloisters sheltered sons of the European aristocracy, of Asian potentates, and of money men from all over the globe. Switzerland was somewhere else for all of them, and given this potpourri of rank, the boys formed their own hierarchy based on different kinds of achievement. When Marc arrived, Bruno was two forms ahead of him, and a highly esteemed member of the school. He was already captain of the wrestling team, and defeating boys of seventeen.

Marc was twelve and looked ten. For months, he tried to put weight on his narrow frame. He would spend his pocket money buying other boys' tapioca pudding in the refectory. He turned his desk into an ant-infested storehouse of food. He never gained an ounce. From a health magazine to which he'd taken a subscription, he learned about the virtues of wheat germ, and had a jar sent to him by a dietician in Zurich. One evening, he sat swallowing clammy, spoon-clinging spoonfuls in his room, reading a newspaper account of mutilations committed by the Moroccan rebels, the men of Abd-el-Krim, when he was wracked by the worst fit of nausea of his life. Afterwards, it was never clear to him whether the descriptions of torture in the desert or the sweet, grassy paste clinging to his palate was the real cause of his vomiting as he'd never vomited before. In any case, the incident assumed the solemn importance, for him, of an epiphany. In the dormitory toilet, there was a tall, narrow window that looked out on Mount Simon. The white heights shone through the open window in a powdery moonlight. A great chunk of nature. Pale, chill, shaking, Marc turned from the washstand to the window and confronted the broad mountain face to face. Once again, he was pierced by the belief that nature was not his friend. That evening he abandoned all hope of building his physique. He took to reading Baudelaire, who had the same feelings about nature that he had. Baudelaire in a leather-bound volume, lined with water-stained silk. He also wrote away for a manual on something called Ju-Jitsu. From the pictures in the manual, Marc learned all sorts of powerful holds as well as he came to know, by heart, page after page of the *Fleurs du Mal*. He dreamed of tall, black mistresses, and practiced tripping people, using a chair for his victim. He couldn't change his sensitive, frail nature; he would make the most of it ...

After a week of spring rains, a restlessness, an accumulation of pent energy permeated the atmosphere at Croseigne and seemed almost as tangible as the milky fog that blinded the Alps from the valley. The playing fields were swamps. Between study periods, the boys would gather on the narrow slate crosswalks, or under the moss-smelling cloister, and gossip intensely. Two boys were leaving school in midterm. Both their fathers, one a banker in Zurich and the other a Lisbon commodities trader, had been arrested. The parents had been into something fishy together. Impervious to the sensational talk around him, Marc left his French class one midmorning, stepped out from the cloisters, and strode along the crosswalk. The wet air in his nostrils seemed thick with plant smells, the mingled effluvia of rebirth and decay—odor of bark, mold, and new grass. At the far end of the narrow slate walk, a group of older boys were in a long line, playing leap frog. Marc had spotted Bruno's blond head in the group. He went up to his cousin and tapped his elbow.

"I want to show you something."

"What—" But before Bruno could finish an annoyed reply, Marc had hold of his sweater, and then Bruno was flying over Marc's shoulder. He landed in the soggy grass and sprang to his feet almost immediately. Bruno then seemed to leap as far as he'd been tossed;

in an instant, he had hold of Marc's arms. He pushed, Marc tumbled on his back, but Bruno wouldn't let go. He had his knees now on Marc's shoulders and the heel of his palm on Marc's brow, pressing his cousin's head into the cold puddle under him. From below, Bruno's face seemed distorted into caricature: his sharp cleft chin, the great predatory beak of a nose, his salient cheekbones—viewed normally they formed a rugged handsomeness, but from where Marc lay, his cousin's face was a gargoyle's. And then Bruno smiled. The gargoyle's face became an elf's. His eyes brightened with mischief, the smile turned into a laugh, which wasn't at all the gloating laugh of a victor but a laugh tinged with complicity. It seemed to Marc that suddenly his cousin had seen everything from his, Marc's, point of view and knew there was as much victory in Marc's one successful Ju-Jitsu toss—so obviously long prepared, so totally out of character for Marc—as there was in Bruno's easy revenge. Bruno got up and held out his hand. Still laughing, he pulled Marc up and pounded him on the back.

That incident was to be the one Marc's mind would invariably return to when he thought of the complicated rivalry between himself and his cousin. Afterwards, almost as if he'd felt Marc's attack had been provoked by some lapse of kindness on his own part, Bruno tried to bring Marc into his circle of older boys; the daredevil athletic élite of the school. But Marc knew he had nothing to add to the group beyond being a mascot, and nothing really to say to anyone in that number. He broke off the contact, and the cousins drifted apart once again.

Yes, a complicated rivalry. Dosed with mutual admiration and with affection. On the one hand, Bruno's impetuous, volatile willfulness, tempered with an immense generosity and a sense of fair play. On the other, Marc's cool intelligence, generous in its own way—in his willingness to understand, to tolerate, to objectify. Since Marc was to inherit the major share of the Banque Wolfflen, he saw no choice but to assume its management the day power came into his hands. He had no brother to abdicate to, and Wolfflens had no use in business for sisters. Bruno who was destined to a minor share, saw no future for himself unless he could dominate Marc by being stronger-willed. Strategies, schemes, came naturally to Bruno, he saw no success for himself except in seeing his own ideas through to success.

It was clear to both young men that one or the other would have to be the French Wolfflen who would represent his generation in the family's history of financial prowess. One or the other, at the expense of the other.

Bruno was graduated from Croseigne with mediocre grades. Wisely, he skirted the tough French higher education system and entered the Wharton School of Business Administration in Pennsylvania, where the name Wolfflen brought to mind "endowment" to the admissions committee. Bruno went off to America and stayed there two years.

Marc left Croseigne the same year as Bruno, to spend two more years preparing for the Grandes Ecoles at the Lycée Henri Quatre, in Paris. At Henri Quatre, he fell under the influence of Germain Poirier, the poet and specialist in the Romantic period.

Charles de Wolfflen took his son's decision to concentrate on literature for his baccalaureate quite well. Romantic poetry was no training for business, but Charles said it was his conviction that Wolfflens didn't have to train for business, that business was in their blood. He seemed willing to forget that there was a streak of impracticality in the family as recurrent as the family's flair for making money. That, for example, his uncle Yvor of the English Wolfflens had devoted his life to proving zebras could make proper mounts, and that Charles' own older brother, Jean-Nathan, had abdicated from running the Banque Wolfflen and had died in New Guinea (disappeared to be exact, and was presumed to have been eaten) working on his second book on the mores of headhunters. Marc was Charles' only son, and Marc would inherit the majority of the business. Sometime before then, Charles vowed, he would teach Marc all he needed to know about money, so he could hold his own against Bruno. Such was Charles' apparently serene attitude, during those years when Marc went on from his Bac to the very literary Ecole Normale Supérieure. They were happy years for Marc. He was doing what he enjoyed. Reading. Afterwards, of course, he dutifully went into the business. Whereupon Charles showed no sign of wanting to teach him anything.

Now that the war and exile had provided an abrupt, distant, clifflike remove for looking back on those days, Marc could perceive that his literary leanings had for a time been a secret comfort to his father. It seemed to him now that his father might well have feared having another antagonist besides Bruno on his hands, if Marc had showed more impatience to learn the business. An antagonist, or at least a critic. For Charles had been far from invulnerable to criticism.

In '26, Charles had opposed all his fellow regents at the Bank of France in an absurd fight to bring the franc back up to its pre-World War one value. Charles had lent a lot of money during the war; a more flexible man might have realized that getting the money back at its original value had become hopeless. Instead, Charles hooked up with another wild-eyed hard money man, Wilfrid de Reyne, the steel magnate, and lost millions on the exchange bolstering French currency, until Poincaré stabilized the franc—at one-fifth of its prewar value.

The old Baron sought revenge against a government that had treated him so lightly. He began investing heavily outside the country. But many of his investments were ill thought out. He extended a hundred-million-franc credit to the Central Bank of China and signed a contract with Chiang Kai-shek to finance a railroad from Haiphong to Nanking. The Japanese army arrived before the French engineers. The Chinese bank officials slipped into hiding with his funds.

By then, with war threatening Europe, Charles was in a mood to Sum Up, to look backward rather than forward on his career. And it was then for the first time that he began to show concern about Marc's aptitude for succeeding him. For in his summing up, his own mistakes figured small compared with his steadfastness. He saw a place for himself finally in the family's history: as a Wolfflen of great courage. He'd had the grit to hold fast to what he believed and to as much as possible of what he owned, during horrible times for a man of finance. Sometimes, he conceded, his stubbornness had served him badly. But it was just a subtrait, he liked to say, the drawback of that greater quality he called courage. Would his son have the courage to defend the Wolfflen interests when his turn came? History had given Charles a bad patch to hoe. The future might well be worse. War with Hitler seemed inevitable, and after that—God knew. It was up to Marc to be very strong. Charles began telling his son this over and over. He would give Marc lectures on "backbone," the assumption, unstated, behind each lecture being that he feared Marc had none.

At the same time, Charles continued to deprive his son of the chance to make any important decision in the Associates' Room.

The more Charles would worry about Marc's "backbone," the more he could esteem his own achievements. Marc could see this, could see the obsession for justifying himself behind Charles' nagging, and yet Marc couldn't reject his father, couldn't dislike him. For Charles had indeed been brave, during three years in the trenches, and in business; he didn't need to justify himself. And in any case, Marc knew he could never help but love that gruff, proud old bear, his father—love him without any ledger book of faults and wrongs. He couldn't help but want to please Charles. And, at the heart of Marc's tolerance toward his father was something more essentially Marc, that ingrained virtue or flaw—and he wondered if it would take him a lifetime to know which was the right description—his detachment. So far, the events of his own life had touched him so superficially, had inspired him so little, that he was unable to convert the small frustration he'd felt into hostility.

Later, during their exile in London, Marc would look on with awe and pity as Charles, who was becoming more and more constrained by arthritis, would sit beside his fire and talk about starting his career all over again after the war. In exile, Charles had left off Summing Up. He'd become excited by the prospect of a clean slate. He would talk vaguely about forming a re-alliance of power, involving the entire family. For Marc, he was again an admirable and frustrating old man.

As for Charles' relations with Bruno: Bruno had been another sort of problem. Bruno had come back from Wharton full of ideas, full of vocabulary. Charles would insist that Bruno had absolutely no common sense. Bruno would prepare long memos in business-school language, suggesting projects. After summoning the two young men to his desk, Charles would read Bruno aloud in a voice heavy with satire. The memos were mostly projects for absorbing depressed companies, complicated stock operations. Charles favored the Wolfflen's simple, "noble" areas of endeavor: raw materials and pure finance. (Of the three men in the Associates' Room, only Marc had an early intuition that the only thing they could do with their money in the years ahead was to hide it. It wasn't a brave thought, and he kept it to himself.)

Charles and Bruno would quarrel. Charles would call Bruno

"demented." Bruno would storm out of the room. They would make up like lovers. Bruno would ask Charles' advice about personal investments he made outside the Banque Wolfflen. He had a handful of these; he was particularly proud of a cognac distillery he'd salvaged from ruin. Charles would praise Bruno for his "grit" and send long, silent glances toward his silent son.

And so, the thirties rushed toward war while a smaller drama of wills played itself out in the Associates' Room of the Banque Wolfflen ...

Futile. Futile for all three of us. Marc could recall now how pointless those years were, how little anything he or his father or his cousin wanted to accomplish had meant. Beyond the mahogany walls of the Associates' Room, patinaed by the touch, the breath, the rich cigar smoke of their ancestors, history was belittling them. Their fortunes wobbled on a seesaw of events they had no way of controlling; Franco won in Spain and saved the Wolfflen zinc mines from the Socialists; at the other end of the world, the Japanese seized Charles' Central Bank of China. The Popular Front collapsed, the Banque Wolfflen escaped being nationalized, the same year that Hitler annexed Czechoslovakia and seized Charles' controlling shares in the Mokva Bank. *It was if we were three men in a room, disagreeing on how to rearrange the furniture, while the house was burning down all around us.*

The war came, the Phoney War and then the real war. By June of 1940, Bruno had joined an artillery regiment stationed in the Ardennes, where the Maginot Line ended at the "impenetrable forest." Marc, who'd failed his first army physical because of his childhood history of asthma, was waiting to be called up again, when the Germans pierced through the impenetrable forest and the French army went into total disarray.

June 13, 1940—nearly five years later now, years that seemed a century, Marc could remember everything about that evening. Charles in his gilded *grand salon*, stammering at his *maître d' hôtel*. In the hurly-burly of the French rout, Firmin had been unable to find a safe place to ship the four Rembrandts. Charles was implacable. "You have failed my trust, Firmin, you have reneged on your responsibility!" Firmin might have been tempted to lay the failure in trust to the Ministry of War, but instead, he just kept insisting that it was time to pack, sir, the Rembrandts notwithstanding. "Do you think four Rembrandts are something you can turn your back on without a pang in your heart!" Eveline, Marc's tiny mother, shouted down from the landing above the hall: "*Vieil ours!* Old bear! Think of your heart and not your pictures. A little calm ... " Calmly, Eveline had been seeing to the packing upstairs.

Outside: the wide avenue was packed solidly. Cars were stalled in the crowd of refugees that was slowly pulsing toward the Porte Dauphine. The sky orange, grease-brown, and black. The smoke from the burning fuel depots in the suburbs gave off an acrid smell so intense that it pierced the double windows of Charles' salon. Charles had stayed on in Paris until this last day, hiding papers, desperately trying to transfer funds to Switzerland, and to ship valuables south. Now the Germans were already approaching the suburbs of the city.

Marc turned away from the window and said with his characteristic calm:

"No one will destroy the pictures, father. We'll win the war, and you'll get them back. It's time to leave."

Charles raised his eyebrows at his son's tone, but he headed for his bedroom to choose something to travel in. And then Marc showed them the way out.

He had Firmin drive them north, after sundown, while half of Paris was heading south. At Mouligny, only three kilometers from the advancing Germans, a plane Marc had hired with a great sum of cash was waiting in a mown wheatfield.

Tough little Eveline, who had nursed her wounded at Bois Brûlé in 1917, under bombardment by both artillery and planes, berated the pilot for refusing to fly directly to England. "This is a time for courage, *monsieur.*"

"Madness, *madame*, they have big guns all along the way from here to the Channel. Absolute madness."

Marc explained to his mother that the pilot, who had been a daredevil performer greatly admired by cousin Pierre, did not lack courage.

"In any case, my wife is not mad, *monsieur*," Charles blustered. "The moment does not justify rudeness."

Looking back now, Marc could smile at those touches of silliness in the pathetic way they fled that night. Like figures out of Chekhov. Eveline kissed Firmin goodbye on both cheeks. Charles forgivingly shook his hand. Firmin was to be the master of the house, the guardian. For how long? They were leaving for the unknown. Since Isaiah had paid Bonaparte to come home from Egypt, Wolfflens had shaped history, determined the course of wars. Now, in a four-seater Piper that strained with the weight of their luggage, Charles, Eveline, and he were reduced to refugees.

The plane throbbed, tossing in an air current. Charles muttered incomprehensibly. The darkened ground below was something confused, murky, heavy. Behind his father, Marc gazed instead at the stars, buoyed by a strange feeling of satisfaction, a vast ease. In time, he was suspended between a complicated past and a future with no definition. In space, only a sheet of coated canvas that formed the fusillage stood between himself and clear infinity. The plane dipped and fluttered and nearly scraped mountains in the dark. Poor Eveline threw up in her purse. But finally they landed in Biarritz. From Biarritz they managed passage to Casablanca and from Casablanca to Southhampton. Marc's sister, Sara, had gone to London months earlier. War hadn't at all been Sara's preoccupation; she was researching a book on Dante Rossetti. She was waiting for them at the pier with a driver.

When they arrived in London, Marc went immediately to Seymour Place, where General de Gaulle had set up temporary headquarters. He signed into the Resistance. He was, he thought, at last going to do something. Something courageous.

In London, word came of the details of Bruno's capture. Bruno's regiment had been entirely surrounded near Sainte-Agnès. Captain de Wolfflen had galloped off with Lieutenant Emile Cahn-Zalmann, who knew the woods around the village from having shot boar there. They had hoped to scout a weak spot in the Germans' southern lines. They didn't know that by then Hitler controlled everything as far south as Beauvais. The two officers had galloped straight into a line of Panzers.

Captain de Wolfflen, the Baron Bruno de Wolfflen, and Lieutenant Cahn-Zalmann, son of France's wheat king, two prize Jews, were shipped to Kalmbach Castle in Prussia: a medieval fortress for very difficult, or very special, prisoners of war . . .

Four, nearly five years ago . . .
They were once more in the Place Vendôme, Marc and Hoyt. The

Major had his back turned to Marc. He'd halted in front of the empty window of Charvet's famous shirt boutique and had given a disappointed shrug. Without turning, he began the conversation again.

"Your cousin is in good health, last we heard," he said.

Marc stopped next to him.

"When?"

The two of them stood there, side by side, each addressing himself to the faintly moonlit, night-gutted image of the other in the glass. This remove seemed to fascinate both of them, for neither of them budged.

"When did you hear?"

"Someone has made contact from the other side," Hoyt answered obliquely. "He's made a proposition."

"My cousin's a prisoner of war, protected by the Geneva Convention."

Hoyt turned from the window impatiently and touched Marc's forearm.

"Listen, Baron, please don't talk like a cub scout. You know what you're dealing with?"

"Do you? How did he make contact?"

Hoyt shrugged and frowned. His business was intelligence; he seemed to consider the question in bad form. "It's genuine," he finally acceded to reply.

Marc took a few quick steps forward, obliging Hoyt to follow at his heels. "What do you have to tell me?" Marc asked, without looking back.

"It's up to you," Hoyt answered. "He wants to make a deal. He can get your cousin out before the Third Army reaches Kalmbach. He mentioned a precise sum."

"Which was?"

"Three million dollars in Switzerland."

Hoyt looked at Marc full in the face as he mentioned the sum, as if he could not hold back the curiosity which prompted him to capture exactly the look on the Baron de Wolfflen's face that the prospect of paying three million dollars would create. Marc lowered his eyes. He scrutinized, for a moment, the toe of his heavy army blucher. Hoyt followed Marc's look avidly, and then raised his head with a snapping gesture, as if he'd been duped, distracted into looking somewhere other than where the trick was going on. Marc turned his head away entirely.

"What am I to suppose will happen when the Americans reach Kalmbach?" he asked.

"The guard's been changed at the castle. We don't know exactly what all the reason is, except strategically the town is on an important crossroad. It's all SS there now. This person says they've been told to hold out. Period. They don't intend to surrender. Your cousin . . . well, it's logical—"

"Logical?"

"Logical . . . Christ, that they'll liquidate him before they go themselves."

"This person tells you that?"

"Yes sir. I believe him." Hoyt stamped his feet. They might have been cold. Or possibly the gesture told of a desire to run away from the dreary duty he was performing.

"Logical," Marc said with a trace of mockery.

Hoyt answered by holding out his palms. Yes, it was all crazy, but it wasn't his fault.

"It's that kind of ball game," he said.

"Who is this person?"

"Someone small. But he claims he can create a paper to transfer your cousin out of there beforehand. I believe him. I've checked him out . . . You know Baron," he said impatiently, "there are times when little people can get things done that you can't get done by big people, by somebody important. He'll take a risk for money, that's what it amounts to."

"How long will it take . . . for the Americans to reach Kalmbach?"

Hoyt brightened, if only because the conversation was moving somewhere. Finally, Wolfflen seemed to be starting to ask his advice. "Two weeks, three I believe." He coughed. "I've been authorized," he began again, but then he halted, as if he'd made a mistake to lay his authority onto a higher source. "I can render you every assistance that might be necessary," he said.

"He could take the money and simply run away," Marc said. "I suppose you've thought of that."

"Yes, sir, I've thought of that. Of course. We've examined that possibility. It's a risk any way you look at it. My experience, Baron—"

"Colonel, please," Marc corrected finally.

"My experience has been that men who decide to make a deal with the enemy tend to live up to it. I've never thought to understand why. It seems to be a fact—"

"Please do something for me, Major, do me a great favor. Find out everything you can about him. The person. The whole story of his life. Could you call me when you know everything?"

"I've got a whole dossier already—"

"Do you know, my father—"

"I can't say I do personally," Hoyt said.

"Do you know, my father has never given me many lessons," Marc continued, "but he liked to repeat one thing . . .

"Which is?"

"Never go into anything big with someone small. Small people are unpredictable."

As he spoke, the Baron held out his hand to say goodbye. They were at the corner of the Rue Daunou now. Down the street, light glowed through the window of Harry's Bar.

"Where are you heading?" the Major blurted affably. He seemed to have felt, by Marc's tone, that he'd finally pierced this fancy French-Jewish nobleman's remoteness. The Baron had understood that he'd wanted to help.

"To get drunk. By myself, excuse me. It's the only way I can get drunk comfortably. It's my birthday, Major."

And now Marc's voice switched to a tone of discovery—the voice a man might have explaining he'd discovered a suspicious lump on his body:

"I'm thirty," Marc said, nearly bleating.

TWO

Snow had begun to fall on the tarmac of the tiny Swiss airfield. The big sparse flakes had arrived in a curtain of white air that was moving toward the pass in the mountains to the east. It was becoming less and less likely that the German would get through.

"If he doesn't right about now, he's going to have to turn back," said the American pilot, who was standing beside Marc at the edge of the field. As he spoke, Marc could smell the minty-sweet flavor of his gum, a sharp, bright odor on the cold mountain air. The pilot tugged impatiently with the zipper of his reversed sheepskin jacket.

"En tout cas je pense au retour," the pilot said, trying out his French again. "I think we ought to consider having to spend the night here. I'll see about that."

The pilot, whom Hoyt had provided, was a very pleasant, obliging young man. Class of '41, he'd explained, at the University of North Carolina. A major in French literature. Earlier, when their Grumman had reached the Alps, the pilot, whose name was Reaves, had begun talking about Gérard de Nerval's travel journals. He had also read a lot of Lamartine and Baudelaire. The mention of Baudelaire, the sight of Switzerland, had brought back memories of Croseigne to Marc, in a great aching rush of nostalgia. Unhappy years, but how full of ease and sunlight they seemed to him now. His youth. He'd swallowed a lump in his throat as he'd heard Reaves saying:

"What I like in Baudelaire is a certain rich contradiction: that sensuality, that lust for living of a sick man, and at the same time, the self-discipline, his refusal to embrace life at any cost, in an easy, gross way ... "

Yes that was it, Marc had answered, that was precisely it. And so, they'd talked about Lamartine and Baudelaire, while flying over the Alps to meet a German car salesman posing as Superman.

Reaves had his eyes fixed now on the windsock at the far end of the tarmac. *"La Biroute"* he called it, with a note of pride in his French vocabulary. The French airman's term for the windsock was slang for a penis. Marc smiled. *La Biroute* was not behaving in an encouraging way. It kept jabbing, flailing, and sinking over and over. Reaves gave the German half a chance of being able to fly through the pass before the snow covered it, and himself only half a chance of being able to take off again, with the wind pulsing the way it was.

Reaves went off to the shack at the end of the tiny airfield to see if he could telephone a hotel in town. Marc brightened, for a moment, at the idea of a night in a Swiss hotel. Heat. Hot water. Sheets that were not a doubtful gray ...

A throbbing hum, a sound moving on the erratic wind, recalling a swimmer plodding forward, tossed by thick waves, broke off his reverie. Marc thought he recognized the three engines of a Junker 52. A big plane for one passenger. Suppose the German had a squad of armed men with him? Marc was unarmed. Reaves had one pistol in the cockpit. But they were in Switzerland, a neutral place. So what? Too late in any case to think about all that. Marc cupped his hand to the edge of his *képi* vizor and tried to spot the German plane. The snow was falling very thinly on the tarmac now, but beyond it was thicker, and obfuscated his view. By the sound, he couldn't tell which side of the pass the Junker was now. Marc's feet were numb in his little-used stiff dress boots and the cold had got to his bladder. He decided to go inside the shack.

There were soap and hot water in the white tile W.C. Marc washed his hands carefully, and then his face, for the pleasure. He decided not to comb his hair. Reaves would notice when he came out, and he might think Marc had preened himself for this ghastly meeting.

In the mirror, he noticed the bedraggled droop of his greatcoat. His uniform was a half-size or so too big, but Marc knew nothing about sizes and he'd just taken the uniform they'd handed him one day in London and had never bothered to have a proper one made. Before the war, Marc would have all his clothes made by O'Rosen—soberly cut, and flawless. But he'd taken the uniform they'd issued him in London and worn it without even an alteration. He was in espionage. They'd called him a colonel, but he'd never had any troops to command. Doing anything to improve that uniform seemed to him an imposture: he had no desire to pose as a pukkah leader of men. Marc wore the uniform *tel quel,* and he wore it as little as possible. Marc wore it so as not to seem even more out of place, a suspected money-changer, pimp, or black-marketeer, among the crowd in khaki at the lobby of the Scribe. He wore it now because he thought it would have a useful psychological effect on the German.

Marc stared next at his face in the mirror. *My father.* The shape of his face was his father's. The same escutcheon shape, straight sided, flat at the top, rounded at the bottom toward a prominent chin. The nose too—his and his father's were the most refined current examples of the Wolfflen nose: long, but thin and close to the face, looping slightly at the nostrils. "A hawk's bill, not a vulture's" was how Charles would describe that beak. His father's face was without contradictions. As for Marc's own: he was reminded by the toilet mirror that his eyes were radically different from his father's

Marc's were almond-shaped Eastern eyes. Not Chinese, as the family liked to joke, but throwbacks to some place, some time in history way before Isaiah Wolfflen, veiled to Marc's sensibility: Bible days. Or more likely, to the Levant of the d'Alvares Sephardic strain on his mother's side. Charles' eyes were steely German eyes, recalling a nearer past. Charles, the Ashkenazi materialist.

Specious. Specious, easy explanations, Marc told himself. But in any case, Charles used his eyes entirely for seeing the world precisely as it was, and for profiting from his observations. Profiting meaning mainly getting money. Marc knew he used his own eyes to help him get along with people. Sometimes he knew his eyes could seem dull, uninformative details on a face that was a wall behind which he lived. He couldn't help that impression, at times, of indifference; it was that he, everything, on both sides of the wall didn't seem to matter. At other moments, his eyes would shine as he exercised his wit, a wit all the more playful because of his willingness to mock basic things about living others took solemnly. Ambition, for one. Or his eyes would soften as he did little acts of great politeness and gallantry; his eyes then would seem to say: "trust me, like me, I'm not carrying a weapon." No doubt to Charles, his father, his gentle eyes often said, as well, "you are looking at a soft *Schmuck*."

Schmuck was one of about twenty Yiddish words that had been passed on to Charles over four generations. He treated them as if they were heirlooms that were precious but of outmoded taste; he used them rarely and ceremoniously. Among the jabbering Litvaks of the rue des Rosiers, Charles would have felt the queasiness of a tourist who'd taken a wrong turn in the bazaar, he was so totally an upper-class Frenchman, to the subtlest intonation of his voice. But Charles held fast to certain proofs of his Jewishness. The Baron Charles had given many million francs to Palestine; God alone could count the trees his money had planted on the hills above Haifa.

Marc reflected on the ironies in his father's—his family's—Jewishness. Charles could think like a Jew when it pleased him. His manners, all the Wolfflen manners for that matter, their usual habits and pastimes, were precisely those of the rest of Europe's elite. And none of the Wolfflens had been pious since Isaiah Wolfflen himself had left his *kasruth* behind him when he'd uprooted his wife, three sons, and seven daughters from the ghetto of Mainz, to seek a new life in revolutionary France. From a scrap dealer, Isaiah had risen to chief arms supplier of the Republic. Later as a banker, urging General Bonaparte to come home from Egypt and assume a greater destiny than just soldiering, Isaiah was to have written: "great ambitions cannot be fulfilled at the margin of history." Old Isaiah had known, as far as his own ambitions were concerned, being totally Jewish meant being totally marginal. He married his daughters to Christians with titles or great talent and bound the family closer and closer to Europe's ruling circles. And yet he never converted and was proud to see his male progeny hold fast to a certain Jewish identity. Being born Jewish became for male Wolfflens an irrevocable part of their nature, and like Isaiah, they were all too proud to reject a part of themselves. In his generation, the Baron Charles, with his twenty antique words of Yiddish, had become the family's particular champion of nominal Jewishness, a Jewish inheritance more than a heritage, something like property to be safeguarded from loss, maintained with courage. If old Isaiah had not been Jewish, Charles liked to proclaim, if Isaiah had not been delimited by his junk trade in his Mainz ghetto with his unsettled soul battering at the gates, all his progeny would have been nothing. Would have been like everyone else. Being born Jewish was something for them to exult in, because the Wolfflens' strength in history had come in part from exulting courageously in what they were. Making what they were right in their minds. Whether the Wolfflens were always right, and by what criteria they were or weren't, were questions the Baron Charles had never had time to ask himself. Such questions were for soft *Schmucks* ...

Tall, portly, hulking Charles strode through life bent over just enough to keep his face forward of his body, as if he meant to see further ahead than other people that way. His head was like a prow. Marc came up to his shoulder. Marc: Thin boned, slight, compact; the Levantine strain perhaps. In any case, in more ways than one, Marc knew his father looked down on him.

Suspected his willpower. His courage, still? Flying from England to occupied France, over and over during the war, with a cyanide capsule in a tiny pocket under his collar, Marc believed he'd objectively proved his courage.

"What if they catch you?" Charles had once snapped at his son. "Spies don't have the Geneva Convention. They'll want all our money to save your hide."

"It will never come to that," Marc had answered simply, without bravado, "I have a little capsule."

No, it was clear to Marc his father no longer questioned whether he had courage. But it was Marc's kind of courage he still distrusted. For the Baron Charles, the courage of his only son was passive, a courage of suffering and of not much use to Charles.

"Business," Charles liked to repeat, "is also combat." His son had spent the whole war having confronted no one in combat.

"How many Germans have you killed?" Charles had asked on another occasion, with a note of gruff affection in his voice, but not without a trace of disdain as well. (Charles had killed a great many, having led his company in seventeen charges at the Chemin-des-Dames.) That morning Charles had asked, Marc had just returned from a particularly unpleasant mission. His Lysander had failed to appear to pick him up in a field near Rennes, for three straight foggy nights. When he'd finally got back to London, unshaven, still soiled by the sweat of fear, he'd been told the old Baron was sick and he'd headed straight to St. James Park. Charles, who was running a high fever, admitted to a cough. He looked Marc over, curiously, as tea was brought beside the drawing room fire. In his wrinkled civilian suit, Marc must have looked like a derelict.

"How many Germans have you killed?"

Marc had brought back the plans for the German fortifications at La Rochelle. On another mission, he'd walked into the Avenue Marceau apartment of Louis Ducrotelle, with whom he used to play bridge at the Travellers Club, and told him that if he didn't help sabotage his own die-casting plant, it would be bombed to rubble by the RAF. (A bluff that worked.) He'd made all in all twelve trips, by Lysander, in *felouques,* one to Biarritz in a submarine, always in danger, getting there, staying, getting back. And sometimes, during the time there was nothing to do but wait, he would ask himself if he'd kill and how, if it came to that, imagining the scene, the particular murder.

"How many Germans have you killed?" Charles had been talking like a child. No, it was simple. Between the courage of suffering and the courage of doing, Charles had taken an exclusive position in his life.

None, but I would have, Marc's mind had said, but he'd answered his father simply "None."

None, but I would have. He dried his hands. He thought he heard the scuffle of boots outside the shack. As Marc stepped out of the W.C., he saw Reaves coming through the front door.

"They've touched down," Reaves said, brushing a single big flake of snow from his curly dark hair, "they're taxiing in."

Reaves went over to a chair of worn leather and scratched chrome and began thumbing through a copy of *Yank* he'd tucked into his sheepskin. The two Swiss in charge of the airfield had closed the door behind them in their office. Through the door staticky fragments of a radio conversation in Schwyzerdütsch, the funny language of yodelers, could be heard. The gentlemen had provided a pot of coffee before withdrawing, and now the room smelled of coffee. Reaves got up and took the porcelain pot off the stove in the middle of the room. He held a mug up to Marc in an inquiring gesture.

"Please . . . That would be nice," Marc said.

The Junker was roaring outside now. A final flutter of the engines, and then the noise stopped. In a while there were crisp footsteps on the tarmac. Three people? Two people?

"What about getting out?" Marc asked Reaves, as he leaned against the wall near the stove, with his cup in both hands.

"I think it will be all right."

The footsteps stopped at the door. There was a hesitation, as if they were wondering whether to knock, and then the door swung open, and two men came in with a great draft. The tall, younger one was dressed in black leather. The other in a bad, brown melton civilian coat. Civilian German brown. From behind steel-rimmed glasses, his eyes surveyed the primitive waiting room, swept over the pilot, and then settled on Marc's uniform.

"Baron," he began. He pronounced it in English.

"Colonel de Wolfflen." Marc corrected him in English, following him into the no-man's land of a third language. "You are Stahlnecker?"

"Yes." There might have been a trace of a bow in the way the German nodded, sharply cocking his head.

"*Oberleutnant* Ernst Stahlnecker, Waffen SS, serial number forty-seven forty-three eleven-hundred three," Marc said monotonously.

The German furrowed his brow. His eyes ran over Marc's uniform again and fell on the mug Marc was still holding. His face relaxed; he seemed to take the presence of the coffee for a sign of welcome.

The one in leather hovered behind with his hands raised, waiting to help the *Oberleutnant* off with his coat. Marc didn't think *Oberleutnants* had orderlies; he had an intuition that the tall, weak-mouthed blond was Stahlnecker's boy friend, and never mind Ulricka and little Ernst and Ursula, back in Karlsruhe.

Marc's glance went from the tall boy to Reaves. "They can stay here," he said. He opened the door, just as Stahlnecker began unbuttoning his brown coat. The *Oberleutnant*'s head flicked quizzically toward Marc but he stepped out, tightening his gloves.

The snow had stopped entirely. Sunshine mitigated the wind. They walked near the German plane. Marc noticed a pilot dozing over the controls. Stahlnecker had pluck getting himself flown here, but things were obviously in chaos on the German side, and no doubt Stahlnecker had promised a piece of money to everyone along the line. He was a masterful wheeler-dealer. By 1935—thirty-five or -six? Marc tried to reconjure the figure typed in Hoyt's dossier; no matter—by then he'd become quite a big local party man and had turned his gasoline station into the BMW concession for the whole of Baden.

The German followed closely as Marc wheeled away from the plane. He looked down at Marc's hands worriedly, as if he'd expected a briefcase or a satchel to appear the moment they'd left the shack. He opened and closed his gloved fingers.

"I assume you have—" he began.

Marc brushed the windblown collar of his greatcoat from his mouth. "*Oberleutnant,* what kind of power do you have?"

Sunlight flashed off Stahlnecker's spectacles as he turned to stare at Marc. His face was flat, narrow, nearly lipless. My God, *he's* got a real Jewish nose, March said to himself.

"You've been told, I thought," Stahlnecker answered with annoyance. "I can create a paper ..." He gestured with his fist like an orator as he spoke. "With the right signature, that will get them out of there. Cahn-Zalmann as well, if you like."

Another life thrown in for good measure.

Marc half-turned. From Stahlnecker's side, he moved directly in front of him. "Listen to me very carefully," he said in German now. German had been Marc's first foreign language at Croseigne and Henri Quatre. He'd learned English on his nanny's knee, but he'd chosen to study German from the age of eleven. His name, the roots of his family tree, traced back across the Rhine. Before Hitler, the Wolfflens had never partaken in the popular French hatred of the Germans, although once it had been clear to Charles that he'd have to be a war hero, he'd assumed the obligation of killing as many as he could. Long afterwards Charles used to argue, provocatively, that 1914 had been a blunder wrought by French Protestant bankers, who got involved in a stupidly ruthless confrontation over railroads in the Balkans, that the whole slaughter had been a matter of business rivalries that could have been resolved some other way. The Wolfflens had lost a cousin on the Austrian side, Friedrich. Behind all excessive patriotism, Charles used to argue, there's some poor businessman trying to gain advantage. But Hitler had vitiated Charles' principle.

Marc was saying: "I want you to understand me perfectly clearly.

The Führer talks about my family, the power we have, the money, the agents all over doing our will in the dark." He had his hand now on Stahlnecker's elbow. "That's not far from the truth.

"I take you for a responsible person. I expect you to go in there with your paper and get my cousin, Cahn-Zalmann, both of them, out. You yourself. Personally. My cousin is a prisoner of war, protected by the Geneva Convention—"

He looked the German full in the face, as if on those thin, tight-mouthed features, he could decipher how double-dealing, how spiteful or how cowardly he might turn out to be. Marc read only a shocked and dreary tension, but he went on, having bet irrevocably on where the greatest safety lay:

"I will hold you personally responsible for their safety. I have no choice, because it is you and nobody else, you personally, who have come to me and said you're able to guarantee that safety."

He put his other hand on the German's other elbow, and held him there so that he couldn't take a step.

"Then please guarantee it. Because if you won't ... I'll find you. All my family's money will be spent to find you, wherever you go after this war. And if we don't find you, *Oberleutnant* ... we'll find your family. Your wife. Your son. Your daughter. Whoever, whatever, you hold precious behind those beige curtains on Beethovenstrasse."

As if he were listening to another person, Marc heard himself forming the long, tense, German sentences between his teeth, bringing down the terminal verbs like hammer blows.

"I understand how much you love your family, because I love mine ..."

He let go of Stahlnecker's arms. "Afterwards, after you get them out ... come to me. Afterwards," he said. "I can assure you you won't be in need of money to put your life together again. Right now, I'm sorry to tell you there's no way we can negotiate."

He turned heel without looking for the German's reaction. It was all said. He walked a few yards toward his own plane. From knotted glands in his cheeks, saliva was pouring into his mouth; his head felt cold and light. He fought back the sickness rising in his stomach and turned round again, quite deliberately, to shout through the wind:

"Do me another favor, *Oberleutnant*, will you please tell Captain Reaves, my pilot, I think we can get off now."

And then, building that tone strategically close to friendliness, as if he assumed the German was already his accomplice, having understood the unmalicious reasonableness of all he'd said, he shouted again:

"*Auf Wiedersehen, Stahlnecker!*"

Marc managed to reach the other side of the shack before he vomited.

They were landing—a half-hour earlier than Reaves had calculated. The Grumman trembled and sank through a layer of cloud, then came out into radiant sunlight. Below it seemed finally spring. Plowed fields near Compiègne were feathered with pale green; the plumped-out forest stretched southward, looking from above like a huge bunch of parsley.

The forest of Compiègne: Marc knew all the *allées* and lanes down there, hidden from the airplane, where they crossed, where the shortcuts were. As a boy he used to follow the hunt at Compiègne on a bicycle. Later, a few times when he knew Bruno would not be there to show him up, he'd ridden with the pack. His cousin Saul's pack. Marc's memories of those autumn mornings, with mist hanging in the brush and wet leaves crunching under the hooves of the horses, rushed over him, effacing his worries about Bruno, until they suddenly brought on gloom again, as Saul came clearly to mind; Saul—and his wife, Ariel, who would soon be dead.

But he saw Ariel now as she was when he was a boy on a bicycle. He saw her crashing through the brush, riding cross-country while everyone else was trotting on the lanes, her horse held to a very fast trot; Ariel posting sidesaddle, swinging her trim bottom outward, hanging there an instant in the air at the side of her mount, and then on its back again. She was shouting a view of the stag instead of blowing the horn that bounced on her shoulder. Shouting like a red Indian. The hounds were bellowing and racing forward as much out of fear of her riding over them, it seemed, as out of lust for the scent. She rode past the boy Marc, her face all flushed, her lips bright with lipstick and her hennaed hair loose on her dark blue riding coat: radiant, lit up, ecstacized by the chase.

Ariel was forty by then, but still full of wild energy. Saul had bought the Château de la Clarière, near the forest, deliberately to satisfy her love of the hunt. He put together the pack, even though he never once rode with it himself. Ariel responded by refusing to even wear the Wolfflen buttons. She went on hunting in the good Crusader-nobility riding coat of the Duchess de Courceaux's *équipage*, with which she'd ridden since she was a little girl. Ariel had returned all of Saul's loving gestures with the same carelessness. She'd cuckolded him with a score of men, the last of whom was his own chauffeur. And now day after day, in the American hospital, he wept beside her deathbed.

Charles liked to say, charitably, that Saul couldn't be blamed, that a weakness for falling blindly in love ran through the history of Wolfflen males. It would strike then most often, as it had struck the widowed Saul, after a first sane and gentle marriage. They would marry fine Jewish ladies the first time and later fall groveling at the feet of some heathen princess. Fate had spared him the affliction, he'd say. Eveline had shielded him from the call of the wild.

Marc tried to imagine Saul's blinding passion, but he couldn't conjure any empathy. He was sure that he, too, was spared the affliction. That Emma had spared him. He'd first met his wife at Owen Glade, the country house of Lord Vincent Wolfflen, when he was nine. It was during those years when Vincent's son Herbert and he would spend a few weeks of each summer together, alternately at Owen Glade or Charles' place near Paris, Bois Brulé. Emma was down from London for the weekend with her mother. He remembered being seated in the garden, where the children were served tea separately. Across a white table laid out with sandwiches and sticky English cakes was a girl with long blond hair. Herbert was going through another demonstration of his intelligence by explaining in detail just what complicated pattern of marriages had made Emma doubly a fourth cousin to Marc. Marc looked across the cakes at Alice, come to life from his illustrated English storybook. She was beautiful, but she was already twelve, and she was bored by his awed silence even more than by Herbert, who went on displaying morsels of his varied erudition for the rest of the sultry, wasp-plagued afternoon.

Years passed before Marc saw her again. He stopped going to England in the summer. That year Herbert, who was also twelve, had already begun to chafe at playing with a younger cousin who couldn't keep up with his intelligence. A few months later, Herbert entered his teens and left his summers with Marc behind with everything that was part of childhood.

So it was not until Marc had come to London in 1940 that he and Emma crossed paths again. Herbert was the principal brain of MI5 by then, and he had placed "Cousin Emma" in one of his code offices. She'd volunteered her knowledge of mathematics to help win the war. Emma had taken a First in math as well as in music at Cambridge.

Herbert invited her to dinner shortly after Marc had arrived from North Africa. She looked totally different; she was no longer Marc's storybook Alice. Her hair had turned a pale brown, and it was cut short in the wartime bob, which rounded her face and gave her features the full healthy roundness of a Giovanni Bellini madonna. There was actually more youthfulness in that face than the glamorous little blond girl had brought to mind many summers ago. And yet she seemed instantly, totally familiar. It was possible that Marc had fallen in love with Emma that evening, but not as Saul would have fallen in love, not with that sudden attachment to someone remote. It seemed to him that everything that formed her personality—her direct, uncomplicated intelligence, her fresh good looks, her pleasant ease with others—reached out to something alive but undernourished in a dim region of his own soul. Emma seemed what he needed for him to fulfill himself as he was meant to be. To complete himself. And he sensed all that before the dinner was over.

At table, she was nearly as brilliant as Herbert. But where he was brittle, she parried with teasing wit; where he tried to impress with sweeping exaggerations, she poked holes without being aggressive, with a good-humored voice that seemed to say, "Yes, that's an impressive way to put it, Herbert, we know you're not serious, but getting back to where the truth precisely lies ..."

What were they contesting, what was all the talk about that evening? Something about Schopenhauer, about whether T.S. Eliot had a right to be an antisemite, what it did *finally* to his poetry— only just afterward, Marc could barely remember snatches. As he walked home alone that evening through a velvety fog on the Green, toward the rooms he'd rented near Birdcage Walk, he could remember most of all her strong and gentle face, her intonations, the way she shifted her full body to stretch her arm across the table, to halt Herbert in midsentence while she laughed lightly, as if it were then that Herbert had intended her to laugh.

Four weeks and a dozen *tête-a-tête* dinners later she and Marc were engaged. What had she seen in him? She loved him, she said, because he was the one man she'd ever met who seemed so totally ungrasping about life. He let her have her definition of himself; he didn't contradict it, although he hadn't ever honored what he called his dilettantism with that kind of description before. And she told him that his strange dark looks were handsome. "You have the dignified romantic features of a consumptive bullfighter," she'd said, laughing. When she said yes, she'd marry him, he felt more confident in himself than he'd ever felt before.

They made an attractive couple. London looked on them with benevolent envy. They were very smart people to have to dinner. It was Herbert who had the last word, defining their marriage at their own table, raising his glass with good-hearted and funny old-fashioned seriousness: "I drink to the most *symbiotic* couple in London!" Everyone in the dining room actually applauded.

She arranged many bright dinners to distract him, during the long periods between his trips back into Occupied France. When he would leave, they would always say goodbye without any great drama; together they played at making what was fundamentally horrifying natural. One moody afternoon, though, she'd insisted on taking the train with him all the way to Dover. They barely spoke as the train clicked and wailed down to the coast. "Good luck, my hero," she said in a tight voice finally at the pier. A wet, salty, sulphury-smelling night had fallen over the waterfront. The tide had come in with a rush, and the skiff waiting to take him out to a fishing boat slammed back and forth against the legs of the pier. Her voice was full of anguish, but she was trying to sound as calm as a fellow officer.

She was pregnant that night, too, Marc recalled now, she was a few months into her first bad unsuccessful pregnancy, the first of three. He would have liked her to have thrown her arms around him and wept that evening. He'd been seized with a sudden weakness. He would have liked her to have pleaded with him to stay back, for the sake of the child she hoped to give him. Her kiss goodbye had seemed like a handshake. But of course she was right. If both of them had attached any realistic importance to the danger ahead of him that night, they might have both broken into panic. "Good luck, my hero," she repeated. "We love you," patting her belly. She walked back to catch the train that would get her to London in the morning, to the place off Birdcage Walk where, during the next night of bombing, she had probably been in as much danger as he had that night, dodging German patrol boats in the Channel. And of course, she wouldn't hear of moving out of the center of the city afterwards. His father had insisted on staying in St. James Park. They would stay near him, be as brave as he and Eveline were, and besides, the flat was so convenient for her going to work ...

As his plane touched down now, miles away from her, at Le Bourget, Marc reminded himself how much he loved his wife. And with all else, he loved her for something few men had had the privilege to love, something so old-fashioned he knew that he could probably never use the word for it to anyone without drawing a sceptical smile.

Her *highmindedness*.

There was a glare of afternoon sun on the tarmac of Le Bourget, but a chilly wind buffeted Reaves and the Baron as they walked to where a jeep waited.

"I've been authorized to give the Major any message," Reaves said, before they got within earshot of the driver, "anything ..."

"No." Marc chewed his lower lip.

"Anything that we can—"

"Nothing. Well, we'll see ... All right? Nothing more anyone can do at the moment."

"Check," Reaves said, sounding for the first time like an American airman. They rode back into Paris on the pocked and tank-scraped roads, each staring in a different direction.

Marc pushed the matter of Bruno out of his mind. Nothing else could be done now. Nothing. He thought of his wife again. Would it happen this time? She'd had three miscarriages, practically one a year, but she'd kept insisting on giving him a child. His heir. This time, for what seemed to him no special reason, the doctors were optimistic, or were saying so. His heir. The jeep jolted over the edge of a crater in the road. Marc's hands formed fists in the pockets of his greatcoat as he winced with the shock.

THREE

All night, artillery to the west had flashed and rumbled in the room like a summer storm. At dawn, from under a blanket pulled up to his eyes, Captain de Wolfflen had heard the Polish officers overhead being awakened, and marched out, complaining about the cold. It was still silent up there now. They hadn't come back.

Cahn-Zalmann was propped against his pillow, reading Xenophon's *Anabasis*, in Greek, and making notes in the margin with his tight little green handwriting. Bruno got up and began to wash with the piece of Floris soap left from his cousin Charles' last Red Cross package. That was almost three months ago. Since then he hadn't even got a letter from Charles, Marc, or anyone. C-Z had stopped getting mail as well. The disruption in delivery cheered him at first. He understood that the German system was breaking down at all points. But something civilized, proof of *their* being in some way civilized, had been taken out of his life. And since they'd moved C-Z and him, he felt more and more cut off. In a limbo in which nothing was sure, and the worst was as likely as anything else.

The orderly knocked. He came in with the razor, and stood there with his perfunctorily drawn pistol, until Bruno finished shaving and handed back the razor.

Cahn-Zalmann ran his palm over his bearded chin before turning a page. He grunted faintly, reassured himself, it seemed, that he was better off bearded. One of the Poles had taken to calling him "Rabbi." He would say it with such faint mockery in his deference, that C-Z couldn't pin down any certain malice. Friendly, but ever so slightly mocking. Cahn-Zalmann would retaliate by roughing the Pole ever so slightly while playing soccer in the tight courtyard. The Pole was a small version of the archetypal clod of his nation, and Cahn-Zalmann, though he was ten pounds skinnier than he'd been in lycée, was all wire: the Pole would fail to re-retaliate. No one, in any case, was quite in fighting trim, given the rations.

Well, the Poles were gone, taken somewhere this morning, and there goes the soccer. The English would be in a mood. Gone where, Bruno wondered. All through the war, when the Poles complained of something, the Germans had their standard reply: "You're lucky we didn't hand you over to the Russians in 1939." Bruno recalled also a Polish proverb his cousin Charles had brought back from the international Intervention against the Bolsheviks. It went: "Once a German, always a Jew." Charles had been amused. You could laugh at that kind of idiocy before the war.

Yes indeed, the world was one big happy family. Bruno snorted a sour laugh. Cahn-Zalmann looked up disapprovingly from his Greek.

"They hustled out the Polish officers this morning," Bruno said. "Did you hear them?"

"Probably going to shoot them," Cahn-Zalmann answered, yawning. "Can you blame them?"

For the German guards, Bruno and Cahn-Zalmann were *die adlige Juden.* The "noble Jews," said with some merriment. What must now be a month ago, they were separated from the perfect company of the English and locked up together in what had been a true bedchamber of the castle. Just below a big gallery, where all the Polish officers were kept together. Bruno and Cahn-Zalmann now had hands-down the best quarters in the prison, but they could see the other prisoners only at exercise time, and beyond the relative loneliness, Bruno felt something ominous in the segregation.

Noble Jews.

52   THE HEIRS

"We're a noble pair," he said drily to Cahn-Zalmann, airing a stray thought.

"Darling," Cahn-Zalmann said in stage English, and went on reading.

"Not only that, Darling, we're the best-looking two gentlemen in this entire prison."

"What in *Himmel?*"

But indeed they were. They were about the same height, both well over six feet, long legged and long featured. Bruno had a quintessential version of the Wolfflen beak, a predatory and yet full-lipped sensual face. For Bruno, Cahn-Zalmann, with his beard, his velvety eyes (like Cousin Marc's), and his dark skin looked like a Persian out of an ancient miniature. C-Z had no title, but in France his father was known as "The Wheat King." By the twenties, he'd become the biggest grain trader in Europe. He'd saved his fleet from confiscation by sailing every boat he had to Gibralter in June of 1940. Louis Cahn-Zalmann was *the* genius among commodity traders, but his son was interested only in the classics. Emile Cahn-Zalmann had been admitted to the Ecole Normale Supérieure just before he'd been called up into the army.

Since the day they'd been captured together at Sainte-Agnès, Bruno had often tried to get Emile to talk about the mysteries of commodities. C-Z would show just a summary interest. The Wolfflens owned metal mines but they hadn't dealt speculatively in commodities for decades. Pierre de Wolfflen, Bruno's father, had believed that if you weren't born into commodities, you'd better be born the worst kind of pirate to get into them and keep your hide. Pierre would be dead nine years now. The fact that his parents were dead came on like a harsh light in Bruno's consciousness. He was an orphan, if someone thirty-two could still be called that. He was an orphan, and heir to the poorest branch of the family, condemned, in the business, to heed his cousin Charles' say-so. Cousin Charles, of course, seemed to Bruno even more leery of risks than Pierre had been.

But at times, as now, daydreaming—for there was so much time for daydreaming—letting his thoughts and hopes meander, Bruno would imagine a high alliance between his cellmate's fortune and his own family's. And he would imagine himself the *condottiere* of a family renaissance. History, perhaps, had not thrown C-Z and him together by chance. God knew the French Wolfflen family needed a strong man. Someone stronger than good old Marc.

Marc, the family Chinaman. God knew what went on behind those Asian eyes. God knew whether Marc knew what he wanted, and if he were even happy being a Wolfflen. At times Marc would wince to hear headwaiters call him "Baron de Wolfflen," as if they were spilling his secret in public. Marc could be full of charm, or full of a drear inwardness. But for Bruno, in any case, he wasn't full of a will to carry the business forward aggressively.

Of course, if you listened to everyone else in the family, he, Bruno was "Wild Bruno." Crazy Bruno, the family Cossack. Bruno drinks, Bruno whores, Bruno closes the casino every night, Bruno is a rough rider on the polo field. Bruno gets into brawls. All right, but if no one in the family had ever had a taste for fights—where would they be now, did any of them wonder?

Bruno's sour meandering throughts broke off. Suddenly the bedroom filled with the clamor of artillery again. Closer. The Americans had begun an attack in full daylight now. Or maybe the Germans still had a counterattack left in them ...

An hour later shells were still falling, and closer; Bruno couldn't tell how much closer. But After the War couldn't be more than a few days away from Kalmbach. For the time being, he was filled with more dread than joy. He believed the lovely group in black uniforms, whose guest he was, was capable of doing anything to him if they were cornered like rats. Why had they separated C-Z and him from the others? Bruno was far from a coward, but he was convinced that the worst was at any moment a strong possibility. And he hadn't the kind of nerves for contemplating the worst with equanimity. A tremor ran down his back; he jerked his head and found himself facing the door clenching and unclenching his fists.

Two SS came in, an officer and a tall young soldier. The soldier was struggling with two pairs of boots and a pile of clothing. Uniforms.

"Good morning, gentlemen, you will put these on please." The officer's face seemed full of pain, or stress.

"These are not French uniforms. Under the Geneva Convention, we have a right to retain our own French uniforms. I cannot understand ..." He was standing there in his long underwear insisting as calmly as he could on his dignity as an officer, while all the nerves of his back seemed to be rippling.

"This is a matter of your urgent safety!" The officer broke into a rage. "You will put them on!"

"*Schrei' nicht ... Schrei' nicht,*" Cahn-Zalmann soothed, "don't shout," as he threw off his covers. The blond soldier had drawn his peculiar Mauser from its wooden holster with equal calm. Cahn-Zalmann put his Xenophon into a valise where there were some other books. On his hands and knees, a gesture that seemed to Bruno full of reverence, C-Z began to pack in more books.

"You don't need all that shit!" the officer shouted. He looked at his watch. Emile shrugged, stood up. He and Bruno began to put on the uniforms.

The pants were too short for both of them. They must have come out of the officer's closet instead of the soldier's. Yes, the jackets belonged to an *Oberleutnant.* The arms, too, were too short. C-Z looked at the soldier. "Change?" he asked. "Exchange?" The soldier looked away, out the window, from where more cannon noise was coming.

They tucked the short pants into the boots. The boots were too small as well.

"What did you do with the Polacks?" Bruno asked, as he and C-Z were marched down a spiral stone staircase.

"The Polacks?" the officer answered, still concentrating hard on something else.

"He doesn't live here," Cahn-Zalmann said. "He's from somewhere else. What is your name, *Oberleutnant,* may I ask?"

The officer paused a moment on the steps to give his answer to Bruno more import, as if it mattered very much to him that Bruno retain it very clearly:

"Stahlnecker," he said, and dropping his rank: "Ernst Stahlnecker. At your service, gentlemen. Trust me, and please hurry up."

Bruno didn't trust him for one moment. Worry, rage, frustration, whatever bleak emotion or whatever combination, seemed to be rotting inside Stahlnecker and sending poison all through his system. His face was tightened, his eyes glared, as the soldier raced the BMW over a road gouged by Panzer tracks. C-Z sat up front with the soldier and Stahlnecker sat behind with Bruno. He had taken the soldier's Mauser and clipped on the wooden holster stock. It lay on his lap, under his gloved hands.

The soldier tried suddenly to swerve, but the left front wheel plunged over the edge of a bad bomb hole. The underbelly of the car grated against the road surface.

They kept on driving, but after a kilometer or so, when the soldier tried to downshift into a curve, the clutch began to slip. The BMW hobbled along in and out of gear for another kilometer. Stahlnecker ordered the soldier to stop.

They got out. Stahlnecker himself took off his overcoat and jacket and crawled under the car.

He came out from under with his face smudged but somewhat brightened. "I think it can be adjusted." Stahlnecker appeared to know about these things.

Stahlnecker went back under with a screwdriver and a wrench from the trunk. The soldier stood between Bruno and C-Z with the Mauser.

They had stopped near a field that ended in a thick brush of willows. The land was swampy, and the cold had glazed the irregularities of the field with patches of ice. Bruno stood holding the collar of his jacket up around his neck, against the wind blowing across the flat Prussian landscape. It wasn't a scene to inspire joy, but Bruno had spent so much time within the stone confines of a grim thirteenth-century *château fort.* Being out here, smelling a wind full of the odor of plowed earth, cheered him. Cheer mingled with dread in his mind: his nerves seemed overloaded with electricity.

"What do you think they did with the Polacks?" he asked Emile in French.

The soldier understood. "There was an order," he answered in fair French. "There was a concern that if they fall ... into the hands of the Americans, they would eventually be delivered to the Russians. They have been distributed among the civilian population."

"Why don't you distribute us?" Cahn-Zalmann asked.

The soldier frowned. "We are looking after your safety."

Bruno looked at his roommate. Cahn-Zalmann was absurd with that beard in that uniform. But he could pass, perhaps, for someone who'd been a long time up front. They all had much more to worry about than shaving now. They'd lost the war. *They're still fighting but they've lost the war.* The thought turned into an emotion that seemed to swell to bursting inside Bruno's chest. The war, as far as almost all the rest of the world cared, was over in Europe. There was no more hope for the Germans, history had finished with them, all this was crazy anticlimax, but *he* wasn't free, *he* wasn't out of danger. To have got this far—

To have got out, and die somewhere here, absurdly, contributing nothing—the worst; and suddenly it seemed probable to him. The uniforms had a reason. The reason was this: they were to be shot somewhere on this road, done away with, *die adligen Juden,* and the uniforms were to show they'd engineered an escape. That's it! Taking not a second more to check his reasoning, Bruno turned to the soldier. *My age, my height, but more fit (better fed), stronger* flashed through his mind but he went on: "What time?" he asked. The German dropped his eyes toward his watch and that same instant Bruno booted him between the legs with all his might. The German shrieked and fell over on his side. Bruno tried to dive onto the Mauser, but the German, convulsing with pain, all the same clutched it and pointed it toward Bruno. *"Nein nein!"* he was shouting, but for some reason he didn't shoot. *"Nein!"* The gun was under Bruno's nose now, the German on top of him, kneeing his crotch fiercely. Bruno shrieked like an animal and sunk his teeth into the German's forearm. He tore the gun out of the soldier's hand and in one gesture put it to his chest and fired. It was as if the German's back had exploded. Gore splattered over both of them and the German, without even a cry, was just a dead weight on Bruno. Stahlnecker was screaming something incomprehensible. He'd wiggled halfway out from under the car and was about to try to get up when Cahn-Zalmann finally unfroze and kicked him in the head. Blood spurted from his eye socket, but he grabbed C-Z's boot; C-Z was dragging him, trying to move into a good position for another blow with his other foot.

"Barre-toi!" Bruno shouted. C-Z tried to tear away and fell over on his back. Just them Bruno opened up with the automatic pistol full into Stahlnecker's face.

They dragged the corpses into the willows and dumped them there. Coming back, Bruno kicked in the ice on a deep puddle, and they washed the blood off themselves as best they could. The cold water felt like acid on their hands. C-Z brushed his uniform with his palm. His hand moved to a wet spot near his thigh.

"I think I have to pee," he said solemnly.

Bruno sat down on a mossy rock while C-Z turned his back and peed. The wind smelled of tree bark now. The moss under him was soft, live. Sitting there with the Mauser across his knees, Bruno burst suddenly into laughter.

Stahlnecker's adjustment lasted another five kilometers. By then, they were no longer alone on the road. As they continued, twice VW jeeps going the other way slowed down and seemed to want to stop and help, when C-Z could do nothing better than race the engine of the coasting BMW. Bruno, with the Mauser on his lap, simply waved them to keep going. The traffic—jeeps, trucks, motorcycles—was all going east. The Germans were retreating again. Clutching and double-clutching, wrenching up and down the gearbox, somehow C-Z would get the engine to make contact with the drivershaft again, and they'd continue west.

The village of Kleintritt loomed ahead. They decided not to risk breaking down in the middle of the village. Cahn-Zalmann turned into a side road, off which a dirt path led to a patch of woods. They decided to wait among the trees until past nightfall.

Near midnight, they ventured in their painful boots cross-country to the edge of the village. Retreating trucks were still rumbling along the road. But there were no more flashes of fire in the distance. A whole collection of military vehicles stood parked outside a Gasthaus at the edge of Kleintritt. There was a motorcycle with a sidecar whose engine was still warm. Bruno leaped into the sidecar with the Mauser. C-Z kicked the engine back into life, wheeled the cycle around, and headed west.

They drove through the night, bucking traffic. The trucks, jeeps, and later the tanks in retreat were moving as fast as they could, taking both sides of the road. C-Z had to weave and dodge and keep going forward as best he could. The sidecar would bounce, fly into the air, and come down, half the time into a hole that would make Bruno feel his vertebrae were about to fly off in splinters like parts of a burst clock. The vehicles in retreat were using all the lights they had. They seemed more anxious to get away as fast as they could than frightened of strafing. Any plane could have spotted that crowded road anyway; there was a nearly full moon. The best thing was to move as fast as possible. And here were two SS officers tearing ahead in the wrong direction. Drivers shouted complaints at C-Z's acrobatics, but obviously those two were off on something important, do-or-die SS. C-Z drove half-blinded by the oncoming lights, and sometimes as he gunned the motorcycle and plunged into what looked like a space between two vehicles, Bruno would wonder, in the second he had to wonder, whether C-Z wasn't about to splatter them head-on between two headlamps, or whether he'd crash the sidecar where a blackened light seemed empty space. They raced forward. And no one tried to stop them until the whole bedraggled caravan of fleeting troops was suddenly behind them. The cycle opened into a roar, sputtered, then raced like a thoroughbred finally given open field, but at the bottom of a hill a patrol was walking across the road. C-Z drove within a few meters of the patrol. A corporal planted himself in the middle and faced them with his hand outstretched, waiting for papers. Bruno began to shriek in German for them all to make way, and waved his hand furiously for them to advance behind him.

"*Eilen sie sich!*" he shouted, an officer in desperation over being disobeyed. "Get moving!"

Cahn-Zalmann swept the motorcycle into the only hole there was, right beside the stubborn corporal. As they moved past him, Bruno stretched out and pushed his chest gently with a condescending, irritated gesture of his wrist. Behind them, as they barrelled into the open road they could hear shouting:

"*Vorsicht! ... Minen! Minen!*"

There were mines.

They put a few hundred meters between themselves and the patrol, then C-Z stopped behind a blind curve. "Mines," he said. "They said mines."

In the moonlight, they could make out the rubble of Ganzbeck, the village about a kilometer and a half below them. Smoke was rising among the wrecked houses. They could sit here and wait for the Americans to reach them tomorrow. But if there were more patrols tonight, or an artillery barrage from the German side? Bruno's intuition said get out of this limbo. He reasoned that to lay mines you have to dig a hole, and that if they walked carefully on the untouched paved parts of the road, he and C-Z would be safe. He reckoned that the Germans hadn't had much time, nor heart, for ruse.

Bruno pulled his trouser leg out of his boot and ripped as much as he could off the leg of his white, Red Cross package longjohns. They found two pieces of tree branch, and each tied a flag.

Under the moonlight, for two hours and a half, two tall noble Jews in SS uniform, with white banners, played macabre hopscotch along the road to Ganzbeck. At the edge of the village, a khaki soldier stepped out of the shadows with an automatic rifle. Other figures appeared quickly behind him. From among the helmets stirring behind, someone shouted in an American accent:

"Coupla fuckin' killer-Nazi SS. Let 'em have it!"

"Frrrenchhh!" screamed Cahn-Zalmann.

Bruno thought he heard a gun go off close to his ears, as he was wracked suddenly, once again, by laughter. He had just enough time to wonder if the explosion were actually something bursting inside his own head, before he fell to the ground and fainted.

FOUR

    Before her husband and her son arrived, the Baroness Ariel de Wolfflen had been very lively. She'd joked with the nurse the Baron Saul had hired and tipped copiously to insure her every comfort—or as much comfort as could be assured a person incurably ill. As soon as the two of them came in with their faces bulging with unhappiness behind white masks, she fell back on her pillow and stopped talking. Now she lay with her eyes fixed on the ceiling, breathing in a damp, unrhythmic way, which witnessed that her lungs were all ragged. She was feverish again. The nurse got up and wiped her brow with the careful, tentative gestures of someone dusting a precious object. The old woman tossed her head from side to side and laughed softly under her purring breath.
    The boy sat on the window ledge, furtively reading a well-worn pamphlet on tropical fish that he'd taken out of the pocket of his suit jacket. The ledge cut into his thighs. He was chubby and graceless. It had been a bad idea to dress him in grownup clothes, like a midget. The nurse, a *vieille fille*, wondered what her feelings would be toward a son like that; she always found it hard to imagine loving

unlovely children. As for the husband, the Baron Saul, he didn't look like any prince charming. He was short legged and small, too heavy for his slender frame, but he had the gentlest face in the world. Outside the room, when he took off the gauze mask and exposed his moustache, he brought to mind a seal. Even with the mask on, his large, slightly almond-shaped dark eyes projected a gentleness. But when he fell to weeping, it would have a terribly annoying effect on the Baroness. The nurse had taken him aside in the hall one day and chided him, but with no lasting effect. *"Monsieur le Baron,"* she'd said, "when you feel an impulse to weep coming over you, try to consider that it is a very selfish thing to do. As for the Baroness, it just embarrasses her. The Baroness, I assure you, is quite resigned to dying."

She was resigned to dying; death was like her secret lover now, and the last thing she wanted was for the Baron to barge in with his grief. It was as if dying were something exclusive, compatible with her haughtiness. She had lived a full life, and now she knew intimately something almost all other living people didn't know, what it was like to be dying. All the same, dying bored her.

She had lived a full life. Over the weeks the Baroness and the nurse had spent together, the nurse had learned a lot about Ariel de Wolfflen's life. For the public, Ariel, née de Vaunel, was a grand lady who had been sent to Ravensbrück for a spectacular act of heroism. But her nurse knew all the rest. The two women had spent day after day together, during which Ariel would unreel her past in long, wheezy monologues. The nurse would caution Ariel to save her breath, but to no avail: dying bored her; if she couldn't live forward in that stale room, she would live backward in her mind. The nurse had no recourse but to listen, and she listened with pleasure. For the nurse, listening to Ariel's exotic life was like going to the cinema ...

The Baroness' monologues usually began and ended with her father, the one person other than herself to have made a great impression on her. The impression he'd made had been a bad one. The Marquis de Vaunel, her father, descended from Ferry, seigneur de Vaunel, marshal to Philippe-Auguste during the Third Crusade. He had as many quarterings of nobility as any reigning sovereign of Europe, but his honor had been blackened and his life wrecked by an act of cowardice. Ariel was to resent him all his life, not for his cowardice but for his destructive remorse, for what she called his "selfish devotion to disgrace."

The Marquis' great misfortune was to have survived the Fire of the Grand Bazar de la Charité. More than a hundred other gentlemen of his class had also escaped the flames, leaving behind women and children to die trampled on or burnt. As far as anyone can tell, the other men went through a period of sheepish mourning and continued to live their gracious lives, much as before, until the Great War came. But for Lancelot de Vaunel, things were never the same after the fire, which destroyed the great wooden hall the rich had had built to self trinkets, for the benefit of the poor. De Vaunel locked himself away in his room for the rest of his life. He spoke only to the chambermaid, and to unknown persons on a telephone receiver he'd installed beside his desk. For the whole of Paris society, his notorious reclusion kept alive the embers of a shared disgrace. They never forgave the reproach.

From what she told her nurse, Ariel had been a particularly gentle ten-year-old, all the more vulnerable because until that spring of the fire, her life had shone constantly with happiness. But the unpardoning disdain that welled up inside her for her father must have come from some grain of paganry buried in her psyche. At ten, Ariel was pierced with a blood-chilling vision of human behavior. Right and wrong lost their sense for her. She saw the world divided between those who lived with their heads held high and those without pride, such as her father. It didn't matter, she believed, what you did, so long as you did it—in defiance of what anyone else might think— proudly. At ten, Ariel de Vaunel became instinctively a Nietzschean—or more precisely, a plain amoral heathen. She was to live that way the rest of her life, with her head held high.

All the same, she went through a bitter early adolescence. Even her good looks couldn't defend her from ostracism. She'd been born with skin like cream-colored silk and thin, graceful features. As she entered her teens, her breasts plumped out rapidly; her hips and waist formed the drastic curves that were the mark of voluptuousness in women of that era. In bed, strange, vague fantasies of what a nude man might look like kept her awake. She tossed, and stroked her thighs and chest, causing bittersweet pangs of emptyness. She was the kind of young girl who'd be better off married early. But she was ignored by the ladies who organized the mating clubs of the aristocracy, in which girls and boys past puberty were brought together for several seasons of teas, dinners, and dancing parties, after which they were expected to enter adult society as a pool of eligible partners, well acquainted with each other and ready to pair off and marry. Barred from mating within her caste, Ariel wept, as any young girl might, but she dried her eyes and resolutely turned her back on marriage. She promised herself she would have many lovers and no children, that her life would be a flagrant rejection of the life of other women—and a cause of their deep, secret envy. She promised herself, at the same time, that she would never be a *demi-mondaine,* never one of those cake-hatted, overdressed, silk-voiced, walking swamps of pleasure men lunched with furtively in the private rooms of restaurants. Instead, Ariel decided, she would seduce men whenever they gave her the appetite and drop them when they bored her. She would be the foremost female rake of her age. Her daydreams of vengeance were things that could bloom easily in the mind of a miserable and imaginative schoolgirl. But Ariel turned them into reality with gusto.

She lost her virginity at seventeen. She was hunting that day with the pack of her aunt, the Duchess de Courceaux. Despite her ostracism elsewhere, Ariel continued to hunt often, as she had since she was quite young. Her riding was greatly appreciated and in any case, during the day-long chase through the forest, the hunters, caught up in their primitive game of death, would put the scandals of the city out of mind. Anyone who could stay with Ariel de Vaunel as she bolted off the lanes and across the brush, right on the heels of the dogs, was proud to be able to do so. That wet November morning, Boni de Castellane had been riding close behind her since the hounds had been unleashed. The dampness and a shifting wind had blurred the scent, and the dogs were crisscrossing the underbrush, howling with irritation. Ariel followed their every turn, coaxed and railed at them. Castellane finally began to laugh at the noise she was making. She turned her horse around and reined up beside him. He compressed his laugh into a nervous smile, as she looked him full in the eyes defiantly. She held him in her gaze for a long moment; images her mind had conjured and reconjured for years flooded back in a great tumble. It's now, she told herself, and she was surprised by her own total calm. It's this one, he. He'll be the beginning.

Boni de Castellane, blond Boni with his curly hair, his veiled eyelids, and his full mouth, was the Adonis of Paris society. He'd married the American Anna Gould for her millions. She was a plain, humorless girl with hair growing on her shoulders, and he'd kept up his spirits buying precious objects with her money and seducing more palatable women. Boni, for Ariel, was the perfect beginning . . .

Without a further thought, she reached out and put her palm on his thigh. She could feel his muscle shiver under his tightly fitting jodhpur.

Boni was witty but far from deeply cerebral. He had good manners, and a sense of honor when it came to gambling. When it came to affairs of the heart, he let his impulses guide him. He had none of his wife's calculating puritanism—and if he'd once had any, knowing its effects on her disposition had cured him of it. A seventeen-year-old woman, fully ripe, asking to know pleasure, would have her way soon enough. As he reached back and put his own hand on Ariel's knee, where her legs crossed under her skirt and hugged the sidesaddle, Boni might have been thinking, generously, that if Ariel were bound to lose her innocence, there could be no more pleasant way to lose it than with him.

The pack suddenly turned and raced off westward. Ariel's horse trembled with impatience. She reined him through a full turn and rode off suddenly to the east. Boni rode close behind her.

They made love under a rare spruce tree in that forest of soaring, venerable oaks. She kept him on his back to avoid soiling her skirt, which she lifted carefully as she spread her body over him. When she was done with him, she got on her horse and rode without looking back, toward where the hounds were bellowing. That afternoon, Ariel "served" the stag. The animal had fallen on its knees, unable to run any further, in the back lot of a woodcutter. Its eyes were actually full of tears. Ariel took the spear from the houndsman who was approaching the animal with exasperating caution, and ran it through the stag's chest. Boni de Castellane wasn't there. His riding coat was so covered with mud and spruce needles that he had to pretend he'd fallen, and to make his story more convincing, he'd limped off toward the clearing before the stag was at bay.

A year later, Ariel's father died, and his secret debts became known to her mother. Lancelot de Vaunel's private telephone had served as an instrument of self-punishment. He'd used it to communicate with his broker on the Bourse to whom he'd given haywire instructions for five straight years. Ariel's mother was forced to pay off his obligations out of the money that her parents had settled on her own head. All of his fortune and her fabulous dowry was gone.

The money remaining was enough, however, for the widow and her six daughters to live on in careful luxury, even though a husband came along to take only one of the girls off her mother's hands. Ariel's youngest sister married an Australian lawyer and emigrated with him to Brisbane. The other girls might have made more proper marriages, because on the Marquis' death the ignominy that had hung over the family had lifted. Invitations had begun to pour in not long after the notes of condolence. But Ariel's four other sisters seemed to have been already too convinced that life was a shameful burden. Each was to leave her convent school directly to take the vows. One became a nurse in a Catholic hospital in a rural region of Tonkin. As for Ariel, she was soon too far along on her own giddily free way to return to a conventional life.

She abandoned lightheaded Boni de Castellane for the first intelligent man he introduced her to. Enzio Baldeo, the Italian ambassador, was more than a clever diplomat, he was a deeply sensitive writer who complained of the blind smugness of the Belle Epoque in stanzas that recalled Dante. Late at night, after long, repeated séances of copulation, he would keep Ariel fascinated with arguments inspired by his friend Croce proving that the spirit was the only reality. Baldeo was posted to Baghdad just when Ariel had got to know him too well—when she'd stripped him of all the experience, all the understanding of life he had in him to give her. He had also introduced her to a wide circle of fascinating friends. One by one, Ariel went through them. She was young in an age when a woman burning to lead an exceptional life could not hope to be much more than a helpmate to an exceptional man. But Ariel saw a way out: to sample men for her pleasure and to harvest vicariously their exploits. She could not, like the great men she came to know, *do* what they did, but one after the other, she could be close to the events that were important in her time: each man she knew was a way of knowing intimately something important in life. And when she knew enough of one thing she went on to another. Ariel, the innate heathen, never seemed to pass judgments on what she learned from the men who were shaping her time. Or if somewhere she'd found a moral message, she never passed it on to anyone. Certainly not to the nurse at her deathbed, who got from Ariel only little anecdotes, lagniappes about the petty traits of generals, poets, painters, and famous politicians—scraps that Ariel might have offered simply to flaunt how intimate she'd been with greatness. She'd doubtless been privy to enough confidences to stir the envy of an historian. But she seemed to have let all her most significant memories wash away. That's how she'd chosen to live—she'd *consumed* her life as she'd consumed the men who figured in it. What was left in her mind were scraps, and for her it was just as well: all she was interested in by then was her latest lover, who was more than a man, who was Death. As she lay day after day sweating with fever, Death seemed to her overly slow and clumsy.

In all her career of man-sampling, where did the mild-mannered and immensely rich Baron Saul de Wolfflen fit in? Why was he the one man she ever married?

For the nurse, the little man with the features of a gentle walrus and the chubby boy who was or was not his son (Ariel herself couldn't say for sure) were totally different from the fierce old beauty they would come to visit on tiptoe. And yet ... "It was love," Ariel would say, explaining Saul, "I married the Baron because I loved him ... Of course, I never let him know."

Ariel was nearing forty when the Baron Saul von Wolfflen (the "von" would eventually become "de"), recently widowed and childless, arrived in France from Holland. He was short but muscular and sported a clipped moustache. He was past fifty. To the reporter from *L'Illustration,* Saul confided that he was bored living off the immense income of his fortune and that he had no interest, either, in any new money ventures. He hoped that Paris would prove less tedious than Amsterdam had in the two years he'd been living alone there. He had plans to study medicine at the University of Paris.

Ariel by then was installed in a house styled after an English cottage at the edge of the Bois de Boulogne. She kept three horses and rode in the Bois every morning before breakfast. Her afternoons were spent posing in an atelier near Pigalle for her latest lover, Juan Tor, the sculptor. In the evenings, she would give dinner parties at home for celebrities, for all sorts of cultivated, amusing people and bored refugees from High Society. The Baron Saul de Wolfflen was initiated into her set one evening by Professor Hugo Levain, the blood specialist, who was one of Saul's professors and who'd become his close friend.

Ariel stared into the eyes of her new guest across the incandescence of the candles on her dining table. "What do you do?" she asked, knowing perfectly well exactly who he was. The question was one more of those provocations she liked to launch to keep things stirring at her dinners.

Saul answered her perfectly. "I'm a student," he said.

"All my life, I've been a student," Ariel parried.

Saul bid up the exchange by muttering something in Greek. "Sappho," Professor Levain proclaimed, in a voice that seemed to want to help sell his prodigy to the other people at the table. Ariel didn't know any Greek. She turned to the banker at her left, and told him she was concerned about the continuing weakening of the franc. The banker tried to reassure her: Lazard and Morgan had come in on the side of Charles de Wolfflen to bolster the French currency.

"That man is my cousin," Saul broke in. His voice was testy now. Ariel suspected, wrongly, that he was miffed at not sitting at the right of the hostess, where a new and distinguished guest could hope to find himself.

"You'll have to speak up, Baron von Wolfflen," Ariel answered, using his original name with quite deliberate emphasis. "I'm sorry: I put you opposite, so that I could have the pleasure of looking at you all during dinner."

Saul wasted not a moment essaying her tone. The attitude it embraced didn't seem to matter to him. She was to learn later that his indifference to what people thought about him was something vastly important at the core of Saul's personality. She was to learn how much, then, he ressembled her at heart—just as in nature certain things totally opposite can be construed as mirror versions of the same thing. Caring little what people thought of her meant for Ariel a lack of compunction—a license for her to profit guiltlessly from people. Saul, on the other hand, would give of himself entirely, without need of recognition, of sympathy. The extraordinary thing about Saul by the time Ariel met him that evening was that he'd grown past all need of rewards of any sort. He was not just one of the world's richest men, he was a total seigneur. *L'honnête homme.*

The cliché goes: opposites attract. But in physics, mirror existences annihilate each other on contact. In any case, the attraction Ariel felt toward Saul that evening was immense. She sensed instinctively his total self-reliance—that he was the first man she'd ever met who seemed wholly invulnerable. The strength that lay beneath his gentleness excited her.

"That man is my cousin," he said again, a little less softly. "I mention this to show that I weigh what I'm going to say very carefully. He's acting foolishly. The franc will finish at point-two grams of gold or worse. I tell you this, madame—"

"Mademoiselle!"

"Mademoiselle, in case you are involved in currency."

The banker reddened. Ariel proposed a toast "to *le franc dégraissé,*" and turned the conversation toward François Mallet, the gentleman on her right, who was designing an airplane that could carry mail in nearly all weather. Over coffee in the salon, she apologized to the Baron for bringing up the subject of money. Without the least inhibition, with such total ease and naturalness that there seemed nothing lascivious in his motives, he put his hand on her knee, squeezing the warm flesh beneath Poiret's smooth, chilly sequins. Suddenly Ariel de Vaunel saw herself as a girl of seventeen, on horseback on a wet November morning, twenty-three years earlier....

Their courtship was rapid and full of fun. The Baron took a giddy pleasure in pleasing Ariel. For months before they married they romped through Europe, living together, leaving a wake of scandal in the lobbies of the great hotels, and of empty champagne bottles in their rooms. Everywhere the Baron bought her whatever baubles caught her eye and foisted huge *pourboires,* like a Texan on holiday, on every waiter who served her.

What did he see in her? *Her.* The Baron never tried to dissect his love for Ariel. Simply loving her enriched his life; he never *got anything* out of it. He never asked for anything. And so, when she finally cuckolded him, he never felt cheated. Nor did he ever stop loving her.

And how then did things go sour between them? It was inevitable,

Ariel would mutter to the nurse, with a faint laugh which was a sign of ironic resignation rather than joy, and which inevitably sent her ragged lungs into a spate of coughing. It was inevitable, she'd say, and the blame—as much as Ariel could construe "blame" in her heathen world view, the responsibility, she meant—was all hers. It was not in her to love as Saul loved, nor perhaps to ever love at all as other people do. Saul had attracted her. What she found amazing was how long it took for her to sponge up all the interest he held for her: it was a few years before she found him boring.

And then, already deep into middle age, but still lovely as any of the great ripe film beauties, Ariel set forth again on a career of man-hunting.

This time it was plain sex that mattered more to her than anything else—a good, rich variety of sexual partners. And so she took up first of all with her husky chauffeur, a dependable brute who was to serve her periodically over the years. Saul never fired him. Saul never lifted a finger for nearly a decade, never raised his voice in protest, while Ariel collected the most heterogeneous string of lovers imaginable. Saul took up with a few women to keep him company, while he seemed to look on at Ariel's exploits with a passiveness which wasn't at all resignation, which was more like vicarious pleasure of his own, or at least admiration.

"The Baron is the most extraordinary self-sufficient man in the world," Ariel would say, "he loves me but he doesn't need me. He doesn't need anyone or anything. And yet, look how he feels for me ... if he'd only stop weeping *for me* ..."

It was Ariel, finally, who caused the two of them to separate. She could have gone on living with him, side by side yet no longer together, but the Second World War gave her the choice not to. And she chose not to. She liked Paris and couldn't support the dullness of Geneva. It was all as simple as that.

By the time the Germans were marching on Paris, Saul had shrewdly moved all his assets into Switzerland. He'd also bought a beautiful house in Geneva with vast grounds that went down to the lake. Arcadie, the place was called. It had been part of the *heritage* of the man who'd owned all the nerve spas in Divonne-les-Bains, across the border. Saul, who'd dropped his medical studies when he'd taken up with Ariel, thought he could spend the war years in Arcadie quietly learning medicine again. Why medicine appealed to

Saul twice, and each time late in his life, was never clear to anyone. The second time he was nearly seventy.

"I can study medicine again, in Geneva," he said to Ariel, "and you . . ." His sentence faltered. She didn't give him a chance to finish it.

"Go. You go," she said.

"Léopold," Saul began again.

"Take the boy with you. It's time for him to get out from under his mother's skirts. We were going to send him to Croseigne anyway. Bring him back when the war is over. I'll look after the house for you. And the horses."

By then, mainly to please Ariel, Saul had bought a large stable at Chantilly.

Saul kissed his wife once very hard on the mouth and had himself and his son driven to the Gare d'Austerlitz.

Not long afterward, Ariel was given an appointment by the Gestapo at the Hôtel Meurice. A man in a business suit, who looked very much like Himmler but who never gave his name, examined her baptism certificate through thick-lensed glasses, very carefully, as if he knew how to tell a forgery from the real thing.

"You are not Jewish," he confirmed, putting the paper into a drawer of his desk. "You should not wear a Jewish name."

"I have a husband," Ariel explained. Her words echoed in her ears solemnly, like a revelation.

"Your Jewish husband has left you flat. You must resume your maiden name."

"My name is Wolfflen," she insisted. "It's a German name . . . originally, isn't it?"

The man looked up at her icily through his steel-rimmed eyeglasses, while he cracked his knuckles. She noticed that his nails were brown, and that his heavy suit smelled of cabbage, bacon, and tobacco.

Ariel left the Meurice still in possession of Saul's name, but without a house in Paris to go home to. That same day, the Germans confiscated Saul's mansion in the Rue Madame, as Jewish property. Luckily for Ariel, the place in Chantilly was legally hers. She went round to get her clothes, spent the night in the Hôtel Ritz, and took the train up to Chantilly the next morning.

The stables were completely in disorder. Half the help had been drafted and hadn't yet returned. Tending the horses, often with her own hands, Ariel set things in shape in time to compete for the Prix de l'Arc de Triomphe, in which one of Saul's two-year-old mares placed second.

The hunters had packed away their gay coats and their horns for the duration of the war, but the racetracks at Chantilly and Longchamp stayed open. Ariel de Wolfflen became a familiar figure in the paddocks and the owners' section of the grandstands. She took to racing with all the gusto she'd shown for the hunt. She'd be out with the trainers at dawn on the wide, undulating *allées* of the forest of Chantilly to watch her horses thunder past, piercing the morning fog with a spray of dirt off their hooves. Ariel often exercised the mounts herself—it was all she could do to keep herself from being her own jockey at the track. The need to ride gnawed at her until she made the acquaintance of Manuela Bulle, whose family had reopened the Medrano Circus. Mademoiselle Bulle was probably the best performer at dressage in France. Ariel decided to perfect her own style by engaging her as a tutor. In December, 1941, the two of them gave a show for the benefit of the children of French soldiers still not back from the prison camps. The Nazi propaganda office, which was working hard to cement Franco-German friendship, bought up most of the tickets and gave them to the troops occupying Paris. Ariel failed to perceive that her performance had taken on the tinge of Collaboration. She was happy to have done something interesting on horseback.

The German's radio propaganda bureau, the *Rundfunkpolitische Abteiling* run by Kurt Georg Kiesinger, was even more delighted. Kiesinger arranged for Ariel to return to the house in the Rue Madame, as a guest of the occupying forces. He also saw to it that Radio Paris invited the Baroness to give a series of broadcasts on the subject of horse-riding. For Kiesinger, who was shrewder than the Gestapo agent who first interviewed her, it was a coup to have the Aryan Baroness von Wolfflen living under German protection and lending her name to a program on the German-controlled radio. Here again, Ariel, in her fever-wracked accounts, was never to see herself as a collaborationist. "Politics never interested me," she would repeat, "horses did."

Her programs were exceptional. They were totally inspired. Ariel went on with great eloquence and authority about riding, about racing and hunting, about the history of horses, their anatomy, their care and feeding. The use of cars was severely restricted in both zones of France. Ariel's program fell on eager ears. Her name became a household word in the countryside. It seemed to her then that she was going to pass the duration of the war in a very pleasant, constructive way. She couldn't foresee that disaster would strike her before the bitter winter of 1941–42 was over.

Early in March, Hermann Goering arrived in Paris, looking in the newsreels like a bloated vulture; he'd come on another of his pillaging expeditions. Goering had himself driven to the Rue Madame, where he made off with Saul de Wolfflen's collection of Cézannes. From Saul's townhouse, his nose for loot led him to Chantilly. Among the two hundred-odd horses, Goering chose twelve to ship to Germany—the twelve most promising performers. For the others, mostly yearlings and two-year-olds that had never raced, he came up with a solution that made young Kiesinger seem a rank debutante at public relations.

Paris was freezing, and there was little food. The fuel, the trucks, and the trains needed to ship food into Paris had been seized by the Germans—and most of the food as well. The myth of the friendly, "correct" occupation was wearing thin. Goering's idea was simple and dramatic: all those horses, the pampered animals of the idle Jew in Geneva, which were eating daily enough grain to make bread for hundreds of children, would be slaughtered and distributed among the butchers of Paris. Goering had his plan announced for days on Radio Paris. The horses were hers, Ariel insisted. The house and the stables at Chantilly, yes, were in her name, came the word back from Goering. The horses were not.

They were duly slaughtered. Ariel's rage mounted almost beyond control. But she kept silent and plotted her revenge.

On March 14, 1942, Ariel de Vaunel began her regular broadcast on *hippisme*. She was able to speak for a full thirty seconds before she was cut off by a record of Maurice Chevalier singing "Mimi." She managed to say that anyone capable of slaughtering two hundred young thoroughbred animals was capable of far worse, that the honeymoon with the Germans was over—that it was time for Frenchmen to be vigilant!

The Free French radio in London picked up the broadcast and played it back across the Channel all day long. Ariel never heard it.

When she left the studio, a big black Citroën *Quinze-chevaux* was waiting at the curb to take her to the Hôtel Meurice.

Was she tortured—for the names of others in "her group"? Ariel would never say. Her accounts of her life would always end with the broadcast, on a note of triumph. The rest was public knowledge. She was sent to Ravensbrück. For some beclouded reason, through some intervention by one of her many important ex-lovers, or an admirer, she was let out in the winter of 1944. Just as it happened to her father half a century earlier, hands reached into the inferno and lifted her out. But, like his, her life was wrecked ever after. She went back to Paris suffering from incurable consumption.

A ray of late sunlight fell through the thin cream curtains of the hospital window onto her blanket. It illuminated the freckles of age on her hand. Her husband, the little Baron, took the hand in his and drew it up to his gauze mask. In her feverish sleep, she pulled it away and turned onto her side, assuming the position of a fetus.

She was old, the nurse thought. She was of an age to die. The nurse had seen many young people die, snuffed out in the bloom of life. There was no reason, she told herself, to pity this old woman excessively. She was old, she'd lived a full, extraordinary life, she'd been beautiful and loved by great men. Her profile, as she lay with her face just beyond the border of the sunbeam, was still very beautiful. It reminded the nurse of Greto Garbo. The Baroness' beauty made the nurse think of herself—of her own flat, sallow face, her thick calves, and her chunky hands, so unlike the graceful hand that had lain on the blanket. The Baroness was Someone and she made the nurse feel suddenly so ordinary, so much an insignificant bit of human clay, that it seemed to her that it was she, the nurse, who was dying and not the other—dying became transposed in her mind into not having lived. The nurse wasn't moved to envy, but the comparison she'd made depressed her all the same.

People like the Baroness: you mustn't compare yourself to them, you must enjoy their presence on earth by enjoying their lives vicariously. They're so totally another kind of creature that comparisons—

The nurse's train of thought drove her from depression to testiness. "You must go now," she said to the husband and the son, assuming power. "You must go out."

The boy came off the window ledge and stood beside the old woman's bed a moment. Through his mask came words in a voice disturbingly adult.

"I don't think she will last much longer," he said. He went up to his father and kissed him on the hand. "Come," he said.

In the hallway, a tall, bent man with a long face was waiting, wringing a tweed cap in his huge hands. It was Ariel's chauffeur.

The boy, Léopold, who didn't know that that man with a slight harelip might well be his true father, walked past him with a look of recognition appropriate for a servant.

Saul nodded to the man civilly as he paused to remove the mask from his face.

FIVE

In his heart Charles de Wolfflen did not want to attend Ariel's funeral, but for selfish reasons his mind had talked his heart into going. He and Eveline had left for France as soon as they could, to be among the mourners, and they'd run the danger of dying themselves, getting across the Channel. Midway, to the complete shock of all those military people crowded aboard, a U-boat had been sighted. A crazy U-boat. As soon as Charles had made out the snorkel with his own eyes, he had a fleeting premonition that God might be telling him that he, too, had been on the side of Charles' heart. A doubly vengeful Jehovah.

Charles chose now to push the harrowing moments that had followed out of mind. Later when the memory would be fully cooled, perhaps, he could savor it, appreciate his own *sang-froid* and Eveline's; he could dress it up and arrange it into a story worth telling and retelling. Right now he felt very old and tired and happy finally to see land again. The bombed port of Boulogne lay ahead, gray wreckage under gray, gull-specked sky, but to Charles the sight of Cannes or Monte Carlo from the deck of his yacht, on some peacetime afternoon of sunlight, could not be more pleasing to his eyes.

They landed at a ferry dock made of newly lashed yellow timbers. Splintered pieces of the former pier poked through the water, sagged and bobbed in the turbulence the ferry's prow had made. Beyond, a few yards along the rubbled waterfront, a building had received a direct hit; suddenly Charles recognized the gay flowered wallpaper that lay exposed through broken walls, indecently, it seemed, like underwear. The building had been a restaurant he'd greatly loved. A good, simple place. Motoring up for the Dover ferry before the war, Charles used to like to time his trip so as to arrive there for lunch. He and Eveline would eat the excellent sole with a bottle of corked farm cider. They would eat at the same table with Firmin and the patron would treat all three of them with very simple and comfortable hospitality. Charles recalled that he and Eveline were capable of greatly enjoying simplicity, but it was very rarely that anyone who knew who they were would let them have it.

"That was Chez Albert," Charles said between pursed lips, as he pointed to the wreckage for his wife.

"Ahh ..." little Eveline said in a grieved voice. She looked stunned by all the wreckage. She'd seen plenty of it in London, but that wasn't at home, that was in a temporary nightmare; this was the France she'd known before. Her small face was strained and weary looking. Simplicity aside, Charles was glad he'd wired Firmin to be waiting for them at the pier with a car full of gasoline, at all costs. After that ferry full of soldiers, the last thing Charles would have wanted to do now was to pack his wife and her nine parchment suitcases into a crowded train. Firmin had wired back that the Germans had made off with the Rolls and that he was trying to repair the engine of the Renault. Sell the Renault, Charles had replied, or burn it, lay hands on something else, and not another Renault, either. Charles was determined not to go home from exile in a car bearing the name of a Pétainist.

A shiny Buick was witting on the quay, an old thing out of the twenties, which gleamed all the same, as if Firmin had spent hours waiting for the boat polishing it. Firmin's gray uniform, his jodhpurs and boots, were equally impeccable. He greeted Charles and Eveline as if they'd only been to London for the weekend.

"Madame la Baronne, Monsieur le Baron ont-ils fait un bon voyage?"

"Marvelous," Charles griped, "we were nearly sunk."

Eveline was shaking Firmin's hand. She looked so tired to Charles he wasn't sure she knew who Firmin was. She looked like she was sleepwalking.

Firmin's sleeves gave off a smell of camphor as he helped two dockmen load the Buick with the baggage: two steamers and two cases on the rack above, three cases strapped behind, a valise in the rear leg-room, another on the front seat. The springs bowed out into strained arcs. He got in beside Firmin gingerly, and sat down on one of his wife's cases, leaving her the rear seat to stretch out on.

"Try to sleep a little," he coaxed.

"I'm very confused," she answered as she obeyed. Like a child, she drew her feet up on the seat and curled her small body into a fetal position. In an instant she was giving off a purring snore.

The Buick seemed to bear the weight well, except when it lost speed uphill. It even had a heater. Charles relaxed as they drove smoothly through the bald northern landscape of sugar-beet fields. In a few minutes, Eveline coughed and awoke.

"When is the funeral?" she asked, raising her head from the seat and then letting it fall again. Her eyes were closed as she spoke, and her voice blurred with fatigue.

"Try to nap," Charles soothed.

"When?" She was trying to get things straight in her mind before she would allow herself to surrender again to sleep.

"Tomorrow, of course," Charles snapped. "Rest a little." He corrected his harsh tone. He hadn't meant to be short with his wife, but thinking about the funeral had irritated him.

They were burying Ariel the Terrible. Charles had always hated her. Perhaps he was wrong to have hated her, perhaps he should have been simply awed, as most people were, by the phenomenon and not even have thought of her as a person you could hate or love. But she had been too selfish for Charles to have been able to stomach. Charles knew that he himself was strong willed. Yes, he admitted, he had a strong ego—which made it hard for him to be awed by anyone, which explained, maybe, why Ariel's black magic didn't work on him—but Ariel was nothing else but ego, an ego like a sharp-toothed maw that had wanted to consume everyone else. Even the Germans weren't able to put up with her finally. Her friends, the Germans. Charles' anger mounted as his mind turned to the chief reason he'd hated Ariel—for what she'd done to the family. The years during which she'd henpecked Saul and had cuckolded him were nothing in comparison. She had refused to follow her husband and son into exile. She had even turned her back on her own little son. She had run around and no doubt slept around (though she was well into sixty) with the worst scum of the Pétainist aristocracy. And now, as if the Devil were taking care of his own, she was being given a heroine's burial. A single incident, when she'd opened her big mouth on Radio Paris, had turned her into a heroine of the Resistance.

Charles' face flushed with indignation, but his head began to reason with his emotions again. The family was playing the whole thing perfectly. Saul's insistence on a great fancy funeral had given them no choice. They would all attend, they'd go along with the ruse, look grieved for the photographers, and let Ariel be the family martyr for the newspapers. Jehovah, if he saw fit, could settle the true accounts with Ariel in private, afterwards. Yes, they'd bury her as one of their own, with the dignity Wolfflens owe themselves. For appearance's sake. For Saul's sake, since Saul despite his blinding infatuation had never veered from being a basically decent man. For the whole family's sake.

During four years of exile, Charles had thought a lot about the family, about how the Wolfflen ties had frayed in his generation. There had been a time when people in finance would say "Wolfflen is up to something." By Wolfflen they'd meant a single power making its will known all over Europe. Since then Saul had gone his own way into oil; Vincent and his son Herbert had made themselves into public servants whose first loyalty was to the crown of England. And Charles was left now with a fortune that was a shambles of what he'd escaped with, what he'd hidden and what had been stolen from him. In exile, fighting back fits of depression as he'd sat idly beside an alien-smelling brown coal fire, Charles had constantly turned over in his mind the last great role history might offer him: to be the Wolfflen who restored the family alliance.

Saul was the person he would need most of all to help him. Saul had taken more money with him to Switzerland when he'd gone into exile than the rest of the family had put together. And Saul was a basically decent man. Ariel had been a noxious influence on him, his love for her had increased the distance between Saul and his cousins. But now that she was dead, now that she'd left him with a weak son to rear, whom better could he turn to than his family? They would have to welcome him with open arms.

And so it pleased Charles now to think that all the family was going to bury Saul's bitch, his succubus, together, with their heads high. The funeral would be the family's first reunion since the war had started. All the Wolfflens would be there, except Emma, Marc's wife. Even Bruno, he recalled, thank God.

Eveline yawned and stretched across the back seat of the old Buick. She'd barely slept, but was not at all exhausted. She felt just a mellow drowsiness now. Had they passed Beauvais while she'd slept? She would have liked to have stopped and had another look at the cathedral whose whole structure always seemed stretched, pulled toward heaven as if by some taut, invisible chains.

It was Charles who was nodding off now, in the seat beside Firmin. Two gray heads. Charles' just a hair below the roof because of the valise he was sitting on. She sat up and leaned forward, asking Firmin in a whisper:

"Have we gone through Beauvais?"

"Yes, *madame la Baronne.*"

"Ahhh..."

She stretched out again and closed her eyes. The frantic moments of the ferry came back to her now, but free of any terror. They came back as if they were something acquired, achieved. The incident would be something to tell her grandchildren.

She'd been on deck with Charles when all the bells had started ringing and the life jackets were being passed out by seamen at a run.

"There it is!" Charles had said, passing her the binoculars an English naval lieutenant had let him peer through. She couldn't see it. How could anyone make out a thin black periscope against all those oily-looking black waves? But she confessed to herself that she was past sixty, and didn't have her eyes checked often enough for fear of having to wear glasses.

"My guess," the lieutenant said, "is that he won't surface and fire." The wind stole half his smoke as the lieutenant sucked in a gust from his cigaret, open mouthed. "I reckon that if he's mad enough to be in the Channel these days, he wants to make a run for it. Spain, Portugal, South America, perhaps. There may well be somebody big down in that boat."

There's somebody big right on this boat, Eveline answered, but to herself, of course. The someone in question, her husband of thirty-five years, seemed outwardly not at all nervous.

"You were right," he said; he shrugged and smiled comically.

He meant about the yacht.

When they'd decided to return to France for the funeral, she'd suggested that they hire a yacht at Dover. But the Admiralty said it would not ... ah, be a pleasant way to travel. There was a war still on. Something about unauthorized nonmilitary craft crossing the Channel. Something about mines, in any case, a danger still of mines. So there they were on a ferry crowded with soldiers, heading for Boulogne as bedraggled as steerage passengers bound for the new world. And in a Channel supposedly long cleared of Germans, a U-boat was moving closer and closer to their stern.

Obviously, the best thing to have taken was not a yacht but an airplane. Marc could have got them onto a Dakota. "I've grown afraid of flying," Eveline had said, and had known immediately that Charles knew she was not telling the truth. The true reason they hadn't taken a plane was that whoever would have loaded the baggage would have likely taken one look at Eveline's nine suitcases and laughed in the Baroness' face. And Eveline was not prepared to part with any of them. Eight of the nine cases had miraculously been freighted down to her at Biarritz, after they'd fled Paris. With those eight valises and the one with which she'd left the Avenue Foch she'd traveled from Biarritz to Casablanca, Casablanca to England. Since then, their contents had become no longer a wardrobe but an important part of Eveline's life. Once she'd read of immigrants to America who clung to little bags of earth from their home countries. Her cases and their contents were for her, in her more splendid way, her piece of "home," relics of a world destroyed like a manor that had caught fire. The material presence of those things and their enduring splendor were more than proof her world had existed, they encouraged her to believe it could exist again. There were Paquins, Schiaparellis, Lelongs, and Patous in those suitcases, with effluvia of powder in the silks, traces of perfume. And all the dresses, in her memory, were so many happy events. So many: evenings with funny people, poets, painters at the Boeuf sur le Toît, with Charles laughing his head off at Cocteau's tight-mouthed little *bon mots*, ordering champagne for everyone; the sequined Lelong brought to mind a ball *chez* Arturo Gomes; the mad Schiaparelli silk print was a dress she'd worn to a dinner *tête-à-tête* with Charles *chez* Florence, and another time simply *"pour égayer,"* to bring gaiety to a late September afternoon they'd spent talking in the garden, on Avenue Foch. She clung to the whole lot, the dresses and the images of the past each evoked—as if brilliant scales of time were fastened to the rich cloth by invisible strands joining one form of being to another. She clung to them, finally, not because she was frightened to be without them—Eveline was a woman too strong to need emotional crutches—but because she had always and would always hold fast to what she loved. Just as for thirty-five years she'd held fast to Charles.

"No, I wasn't right," she said, as she took his arm on the bridge of the ferry, "I should have left behind the goddamn valises and got into a plane."

Charles laughed to hear her swear.

She took his arm and led him away from where people assured her they could see the snorkel of a submarine toward where she'd heard the laughter of others. In the deck room, some GI's, having put on their life jackets, were clowning, performing a mock wrestling match. The crowd of soldiers on the benches and all over the floor reminded her of the people packed together in the Underground on the one night she and Charles had slept in a shelter.

The air inside was a fetid broth; they stepped out again very quickly.

"There you are," said the lieutenant, who knew who they were.

"Tell me what exactly we must do if we're torpedoed," Eveline replied.

"You'll follow me. Right now, we've picked up some company. Would you care to see?" The rail was crowded three deep, but the lieutenant brought them up to the bridge.

Two British submarine chasers had turned up. They seemed to have popped out from behind the fog, as if "from offstage." Two little gray boats. They sped toward the snorkel. The ferry began to rock when they began throwing over depth charges.

"He's finished," the lieutenant said. "He'll never shake them. Now if he wants to commit suicide, he'll torpedo us, but if he knows what's good for him, he'll show his face like a well-mannered chap."

Slowly a lozenge of black metal began to grow on the surface. "You see," said the lieutenant. Finally Eveline could see it: the turret now, and then the deck. The hatch clanged open. Then a sailor came out of the turret with a white flag ...

In the Buick now, with her eyes closed, Eveline relived that incredible moment: suddenly the entire ferry burst into a cheer, joy swept over the boat like a rainstorm.

For Eveline, it was as if something inside her unknotted. Her lungs swelled with briny air. For an instant in her mind, the surrender of the U-boat was transformed into The End of the War ...

The sailor on the German boat turned, white flag in hand, toward the ferry, and took a deep bow.

Eveline knew that she and Charles had suffered far less during the war than millions of other people. Nonetheless, the past half-decade had been the worst in their lives. It was not just the danger that had made it so—although during the bombings of the fall of 1940 they'd known easily as much danger night after night as they had on that ferry—it was the alienation that weighed on them, that belittled them. They had not merely been in an alien land, but had been alien in time. No matter how kind people were to them, no matter how much their social position had been insured by their name, they felt totally out of contact, because they were two old people who could do little about the war going on all around them except endure it, outlast it. It wasn't Charles' nature to do little in adversity, nor was it Eveline's.

During the first autumn, when the bombs fell nightly, they compensated their frustration in a small way by refusing to be perturbed. Instead of heading for shelter in the Underground, they played poker in the cellar of their house in St. James Park until the all-clear sounded, and then walked out to watch firemen struggling in burnt houses with crumbled cellars. The bombs fell fifty-seven nights in a row, and only once, very early in September, did Charles and Eveline go down into a shelter. That evening they'd been motivated by an ingenuous zeal to do what was done in the host country. They thought it might increase their feeling of belonging. It was after all a way of taking part in what was going on. The next morning, though, as they separated from the damp crowd where the blue Underground lamp was still glowing through dark fog, each read in the other's bleary eyes that they'd never go down there again. They would live together privately and take whatever risks of dying together, privately.

It had been a *Shelter for Fifty Persons*. There were mattresses, pillows, faint lamplight beside a radio. Someone began a round of introductions. "Monsieur and Madame de Wolfflen ..." There was a special politeness for the French visitors, although no one showed the bad form of drawing attention to their famous name. Women with alcohol burners made tea and began offering round biscuits. The warden in a leather coat took bets on the number of Messerschmitts and Heinkel-III's that would be shot down. The winner would get half a crown, the rest go to the Airplane Purchase Fund. Later, the radio announced the figure for the first raid, played "God Save the Queen" and even the "Marseillaise," while they all rose solemnly. Then each bid all a good night and bedded down.

Eveline and Charles had felt like interlopers. They couldn't help it, they hadn't been moved by snobbery; on the contrary, in a special way, all that communion down there had proved too *rich* for their blood. They'd been born and bred in high privacy. There'd been more promiscuous friendliness down there than they could cope with comfortably. And they'd noticed how the special politeness the others had accorded them had also made the others uneasy.

So they stayed home night after night in the house they'd rented in St. James Park. The neighborhood was declared a high-danger area, but Churchill himself was staying put, at the Annex, not far away. Eveline and Charles made a specious calculation to encourage themselves to remain in their house, a lovely early-nineteenth-century building whose windows seemed almost to suck in whatever sunlight there was during that London fall. They calculated that the worst night of bombings had produced two thousand victims out of a population of eight million. Their chances of being bombed, anywhere in town, were not much greater than of being run over by a taxi—by one of those taxis that kept driving calmly through the worst raids, stopping at red lights, getting people wherever they asked to go.

"Why don't you take a place where it's safe, in the country?"

Emma, Marc's wife, had asked Eveline one afternoon when Eveline had spilt tea all over the bosom of her dress, because her hand was shaking. The night before, she'd seen firebombs in a nightmare that had sundered her thin sleep, hours after the all-clear had sounded.

"Don't be foolish," Eveline had answered. She'd popped a little watercress sandwich into her mouth and licked her fingers, miming contentment. "Don't be foolish. Charles must keep in touch."

Charles had to "keep in touch." France's future was being haggled over by a variety of factions. The community of exiles was teeming with intrigue. De Gaulle was opposed by the Gombault clique. There were also people in the embassy who hated "the Jews and Communists" surrounding the General. In the Gaullists' own camp, the right wing was quarreling with the left, and there were the people grouped around Jean Monnet, reporting to the Americans. And all the while, the English kept pinning their hopes of putting down de Gaulle on one cracked notion after the other: that Herriot would leave France, that Admiral Darlan would quickly see the light, that Giraud would prove himself a leader of men.

Charles had been more astute than the English. He went to the General's cramped quarters at Seymour Place the day his son, Marc, had enrolled in the Gaullist Resistance. People were offering the General what they could. Someone had given a diamond ring, someone had even given a barrel of wine, which stood in the cramped hallway of the first floor. Charles handed the General a blank check.

De Gaulle had held the check between his thumb and forefinger for a long moment—so long that Charles had wondered whether the General's cigaret, held by two fingers under the check, was going to burn his fingers and the check as well. Finally, he took the check in his other hand and put out the cigaret in an ashtray on his scuffed desk, staring all the while, wordless, into the eyes of Charles, who was nearly the General's own height. Then he sat down at the desk and filled in the check for what Charles guessed would amount to a month's expenses. He offered Charles his famous limp handshake and a flowery expression of thanks and goodbye. A month later—as de Gaulle must have calculated and confirmed to himself while the cigaret burned close to the Baron de Wolfflen's offer of patronage—the English assumed the General's expenses. They had no more likely French leader to back.

For the rest of the war, thinking he was "keeping in touch," Charles wandered through the community of French refugees, feeling out where he could establish power. Everyone was anxious to take his money, but the old Baron was too conspicuous a figure of the Old France of Privilege to adopt as a clear ally. Among all the factions, people were extolling or paying lip service to the New France that would come into being after the war was won. A France more "fraternal" and more egalitarian. The General himself had said on the radio in 1940:

"One thing is certain, France will not consent to go back to the political, moral, and social situation that existed beforehand ... This war is a revolution—"

The Baron Charles de Wolfflen was in no man's eyes a revolutionary. And so he made his way through the expatriate community, alternately flattered (for money always risked turning into power) and gossiped against, admired and cold shouldered. He would buy lunches at L'Ecu de France or Le Coq d'Or for people who came to him asking for money for a magazine, a pamphlet, or a paper they wanted to put out, and over coffee he'd write out a check. Or people would come to see him at St. James Park, with the names of Vichy politicians full of important secrets who could be bribed into fleeing to England. And Charles would pay for the bribes. Or Charles would pay for little morale-building dances at the Free French Club, where, among the posters of châteaux, there would be a gramophone playing Charles Trenet, and the young French soldiers would do a "boogie woogie" to *"Boom—quand mon coeur fait boom!"*

Charles' son, Marc, had many close friends among the young men of brains and talent surrounding de Gaulle. But to Charles' dismay, Marc had shown himself totally allergic to politics. Instead of staying close to Seymour Place and later St. Stephen's House, where de Gaulle was making plans for the entire next decade, Marc had insisted on repeatedly risking his life in the Resistance. He'd even turned his back on a regular army commission, after the Free French had taken part in the liberation of North Africa. A spy was a glorified messenger in Charles' eyes. The only time Marc had shown any interest in politics he'd started a quarrel with his own cousin. Herbert, the family genius, was just about running MI5. Marc had gone to see him to protest the efforts by the English to buy away, outright, some of the best men in the Gaullist resistance organization BCRA, and attach them to British Intelligence. Herbert had refused to listen to his cousin.

"I know nothing of what you're mentioning," he'd said coolly, "but in no case can you ask me to do anything that might obstruct the best interests of Great Britain."

Marc stormed out on Herbert and didn't speak to his cousin for months. Now they were still on a cold footing. England, France, what did all that matter, Charles thought, between two Wolfflens. They were Wolfflens for God's sake, they were first of all Wolfflens.

Charles had never told himself it was the role of Wolfflens to buy their way into power. In his own mind, he hadn't offered Charles de Gaulle a bribe with his blank check. It had simply seemed natural to him that a Wolfflen's true place was close to power. That his role was to use money to promote the power that would run things the right way. In this notion of "the right way," Charles included thoughts of decency, fair play, and widespread prosperity, although all these generalities were never very clearly defined in Charles' mind. To Eveline, whom Charles knew wouldn't laugh at him, Charles would sometimes bare a simpler and clearer postulate he harbored deep inside him: that Europe had been a far happier place for everyone when the Wolfflens, pulling together, had run everything. Before his time.

SIX

"We're home!" Charles said. He was sitting beside his wife now, as the Buick swept out of the Bois de Boulogne onto Avenue Foch.

"Thank God," she said. Her voice rose from the lethargy of after-sleep, like someone surfacing through water.

"Thank God, we're home!" she said with energy now. As she squeezed him he could smell the Shalimar in her hair; it excited his lungs like smoke, and the sudden boon of the odor heightened the pleasure of the image he had all at once of his own house.

Avenue Foch looked drear. A convoy of parked army supply trucks lined the side alleys. The wide central lane was empty all the way to the sooty Arch of Triumph.

"Nothing has changed," Firmin said reassuringly.

But Charles recalled that except for Firmin all the servants had scattered in any direction they could find a job.

General von Kreisampt, who had moved in, had found his own staff, and they of course were gone now. Firmin had insisted on staying, to protect what he could. He'd been a walking reproach to the occupants, but they kept him. He knew how everything worked.

"I've tried to find the new people you asked for, *monsieur le Baron*. I've found no one, that is, no one you'd be happy with. Other than Xavier, the cook, who's come back. Hugo found a job as sommelier at La Rue. He shipped half the cave to Berlin. I understand they're holding him out at Drancy now. They have a whole camp full of collaborators. I understand they had Albert, from Maxim's ..."

"Are you all alone then?" Eveline's voice was full of sympathy. In London they'd managed with three servants. But Avenue Foch was so huge ...

"I and my wife, and of course Xavier, *madame la Baronne*. I had thought that Catherine would be with you."

Catherine was the Baroness' chambermaid.

"Catherine," said the Baron, giving the singularity of what he was about to say an opening note of drollery, "has left the Baroness' employ. She's driving an ambulance, I suspect somewhere beyond Strasbourg by now."

"Ahh ..." Firmin said drearily. The back of his thick head reddened below his carefully cut gray hair. His face disappeared from the rear-view mirror. "I see ..." Firmin was a stout and arthritic Auvergnat of fifty-eight, of an age when the prudence of knowing your body won't say yes to certain high adventure is still tempered by a guilt over giving in to getting old without a fight. Firmin had stayed behind, supplying a cell of the BCRA with whatever tidbits he could pick up in the house.

The house: Charles was surprised at how accustomed he'd become to the proportions of that narrow row building off St. James Park. As they drove uphill through the gate, his own house looked to him like some public edifice. He felt, suddenly, an unexpected coldness toward it.

It was not a beautiful house, and it was too imposing to be charming. But it had been his father's wedding gift. He and Eveline had grown to love it, as they had come to know years of loving each other in it, loving each other and rearing children. The house was like someone close who'd always been good to them. They loved it without introspection, with the indulgent respect you hold toward a stuffy but kind old aunt.

Thirty-five years earlier when the Baron Francis de Wolfflen,

Charles' father, had ordered the house to be built, the inebria over Art Nouveau had ebbed; in the arts, pampered melancholy and free fancy began to give way to a clenched seriousness, as Europe entered the decade in which armed peace turned to war. Many people's taste turned classic again. They groped for a permanence as if they sensed that things were soon bound never to be the same. Francis, who had the Wolfflen gift of intuition as much as any of them, might have even sensed he was building the last house the family would build for a long time. It was to be the last up to that very day in March, 1945, when Charles and Eveline returned from exile.

Francis wanted a sense of permanence and he looked for it in the classic. Unfortunately, the solid and sure architect he hired, a man covered with honors, turned out to be too dull a workman to count beyond the blandishments of his contemporary clientele. By the '30s, few people could remember Adolphe Verroust. But Charles' and Eveline's house was his masterpiece.

The proportions were as certain as the steps of a music box waltz. Palladio's reason without his grace. There were half-columns, instead of columns, in relief on the facade of the first floor, along with a lot of carving whose distant inspiration might have been Mantegna. Verroust's great stroke of imagination was to do the facade in a rose-hued marble.

Francis had ordered a hill for the house to sit on. He'd brought in tons of earth, so that the square block of ground sloped toward the house, making it visible above the iron fence that followed the corner of Avenue Foch and the Avenue Raymond Pousseguin. Below, the gardens were sheltered by the fence and the chestnuts Francis had planted fully grown.

Firmin drove up to the main door.
"There will have been workmen today—" he began, as he rang.
There came a shriek from the other side of the door.
"Marthe!" Firmin shouted. "Marthe!"
Marthe was his wife. It sounded now as if she were groaning.
Firmin pulled out his keys. He unbolted and pushed open the door a quarter of the way, then slammed it shut.
Something had smeared into an arc on the marble floor as the

door had moved open. Charles, pushing himself between Eveline and the door, realized that someone had shat, not on his doorstep, but inside his house.

Firmin's wide face was flushed brick red as he turned toward the Baron with his hands open, imploringly it seemed.

He turned his body and gestured toward the side entrance.

"We've had in workmen," he was saying drearily, "for a last-minute cleaning ... Strangers—all of a sudden they're all Communists!"

The Baron led his wife, whose face seemed drained of blood, inside their house, through the servants' entrance.

Marc came by a quarter of an hour later, apologizing for not having been there when his parents arrived. He'd been called into a meeting of his energy committee, and when he'd finally got out there was no taxi to be had; he'd walked from the Rue de Grenelle to the Avenue Foch.

Eveline noticed that her son seemed less thin, less fragile looking. His face had lost some of the hollowed look of the "phthisic poet" she'd used to tease him about.

"You're getting fat," she teased now, as they headed for the library. "It's my age, Mother," he parried. "I'm over the hill."

"He's stopped running," Charles bantered. Another of Charles' references to Marc's way of going to war.

Marc was pondering a nonaggressive reply when his mother, who was walking ahead of them from the salon into the library, gave a little gasp.

The men rushed up to her where she stood, staring with one foot as if frozen on the threshold. The library had been ransacked. What could be saved had been stacked carefully, probably by Firmin, into meticulous piles, like artifacts at some archeological dig. There were torn books, pieces of the walnut molding, and fragments of the mantelpiece lined near the hearth. The remnants of carved marble recalled broken gravestones.

"It could have been worse, it could have been everything," Eveline said, smiling wanly at her husband. She rang for Firmin to serve them tea among the ruins.

"We've found your Rembrandts, Father," Marc said. There could be no better time than now to tell him. "They were locked in a boxcar on a railroad spur near Mainz."

"We'll get everything back," Eveline said. "You'll see Charles, we'll get everything back . . ."

Marc talked about the meeting he'd attended that day. Someone close to the General, a man with no staff title, had briefed the members of the energy committee about what was going to happen to the coalfields that had been exempt from the nationalizations of the past December. The man's name was Gaston Robinet. Marc had never heard of him in London, the man hadn't even been in the Resistance, but now people were saying that the bushy-browed Robinet, who'd spent the war teaching history in a *lycée* in Nice, was de Gaulle's closest confidant. When the General was appointed head of the provisional government, Robinet had managed a small office job at the Rue de Solferino and he'd climbed rapidly in importance ever since.

"Sounds to me the kind of person we could use on our side," Charles interjected. "What is his secret?"

"I don't know. I have no idea. It would take a lot of doing to have him 'on our side,' judging by what he spelled out."

"Nationalization—more nationalization?" Charles ran his palm over his chin fretfully as he spoke.

"Oh yes." Marc explained that the provisional government's takeovers in the Nord and the Pas de Calais were not to be construed as a compromise. After the elections, de Gaulle intended to nationalize the third of the nation's coal resources that remained in private hands, including of course the Barville mines belonging to the Banque Wolfflen. If he wanted to remain at the head of the nation, the General would have no choice but to form a tripartite government with the powerful Communists and Socialists, who were crying for widespread nationalizations. To blunt their thrust, the Gaullists would have to give ground in certain areas unconditionally. Energy, Robinet had explained, was one of them.

The ex-schoolteacher had gone on in a pedantic, almost chiding voice, to the committee full of Gaullists. If private industry would survive, it would have to be flexible. The mood of the nation was increasingly leftist—

"To hell with coal!" Charles burst impatiently into Marc's account of the meeting. "What will they pay? Do you want to know what I think, Saul was right about coal fifty years ago. Coal is *démodé*. We scratched the best out of Barville when my father was alive. Money, my son. Money is what our business is. Pure money!"

"I don't know what they'll pay," Marc answered quietly. "Most likely the reparations will be in the form of bonds, redeemable after, say, seven years."

Charles had got up and walked into the salon before Marc had answered, and now he was pacing there, looking at the four light rectangles on the walls where his Rembrandts had hung, peering with a concentrated gaze as if he could see the paintings once again in place.

"Bonds are money!" Charles called to his son. "We'll get it all back. We'll get everything back!"

Marc winced. "Anyway, I've resigned from the committee," he said quietly to his mother. "It's just a lot of people squabbling for advantages, for allotments. Could that really have been what the war was for, Mother—Monsieur de Wendel's steel plants, and the Baron de Wolfflen's coal mines?"

"Your father will be glad to have you fulltime in the bank," she replied. "He'll have great need of you . . ."

"I think he's less sure of that than you are . . ."

"Money!" Charles shouted from the other room. They could hear his fist slam down on his Boule commode.

Once again Eveline avoided the gist of what her son was saying: "How is poor Bruno?" she asked. . . .

The Mass was over. After the chauffeur and the handful of Ariel's relations had come foward for their wafers the Wolfflens filed out of the Cathedral looking like soaked birds. They shook themselves a little and seemed to gather height from the fresh air.

In the Rue du Cloître-Notre-Dame, a line of black carriages waited behind a hearse drawn by six dark horses. The gasoline shortage justified an old-fashioned horse-drawn procession, and Saul was pleased by this chance for added pomp. Besides, Ariel had always preferred horses to machines.

Saul sat alone with her son in the foremost carriage, as the cortège clattered and squeaked slowly over the cobbles of the city, northward toward Père Lachaise. Neither of them spoke. Like someone watching far activity on a mirror of water, the boy kept staring at the misty images of the city that crept across the side window. Saul was evading his grief in ruminations about fate. He believed that he'd had more lessons from fate than anyone else in the family. The ultimate and global lesson, which he believed the whole family had yet to learn, was what it was to be a human being. In his eyes, everything they did somehow came back to a matter of pride. They'd pinched their lives into the narrow roles of standard-bearers. Their flag was their name. In Saul's eyes they'd ironically diminished themselves. For all of Charles' vaunted Yiddish vocabulary, Saul had never heard his cousin pronounce the word *Mensch*. Like the others, Charles seemed to think fate was just the force that had predestined Wolfflens to be the Chosen of the Chosen. But all men, Saul knew, had to respect fate as a sailor respects the winds and currents of the sea. And to respect one's own heart, the source of all real skill in navigating through life. Of all the family, he believed he was the one who could be the most serene, the least self-protective in his judgments about living. With all else, he'd been the family's most daring example of a moneymaker since Isaiah. Fate had even turned him into a kingmaker. Only it had happened without his knowing, and his king had been a tyrant. The worst one the world had ever known:

Fate had seen to it that Saul had been strolling, on a particularly windless day for the Mariahilfer Strasse, past a kiosk with foreign publications. It was the end of May, 1891, and the twenty-one-year-old Baron Saul had gone out for an aimless "airing" which he'd hoped, without great conviction, would relieve the boredom of a Vienna Saturday afternoon for a young man with a great name, much money, but neither close friends nor passionate interests. The closest thing he had to ambition was a diffuse longing that someday he'd be seized by an inspiration that would turn him into some kind of artist. He paused at the kiosk to browse for something to read at a café and his hand fell upon the May fifteenth issue of the *Revue des Deux Mondes*.

An éclair and a chocolate torte later, von Wolfflen had read twice, in that intellectual French review, an article signed by an employee of the Russian oil company Mantacheff. The author, C.S.

Gulbenkian, urged the financiers of Paris to invest in the Baku petroleum fields. Oil, he pointed out, could be very useful in wartime. It could replace coal as a fuel for battleships.

Sunlight glinted on the porcelain of the young Baron's half-finished cup of French-style coffee. The nickel filter that had muzzled the cup lay beside it, looking all at once like a miniature of some important piece of industrial equipment. In the hot light that fell on his table, Saul's imagination carried to him guessed-at images of Baku: baked plains with enormous steel elements, as if from some giant laboratory, pumping liquid coal out of the ground. A shiver passed over him, which he recognized, without ever having known it before, as the mystical current of inspiration. Then his imagery dissolved, leaving in his mind an abstraction, an essence, a message. He hailed a cab and had himself driven home, where he woke his father, the Baron Sigismund, from his afternoon nap.

The Baron Sigismund would have preferred being allowed to sleep. He was an even-tempered gentleman who regulated his day carefully according to a nearly unchanging schedule. At four-fifteen, after lunch and his nap, he would have himself driven from the Wolfflen mansion in the Inner City to his bank nearby. At the bank, his principal interest was in staying on the right side of price fluctuations in the bond market. The major achievement of his life had been to finance the growth of railroads in the Austrian Empire, through underwriting and through taking strong positions in bonds on behalf of the Austrian branch of the Wolfflen family. Sigismund had been convinced that railroads were a necessity in modern times, but it had been his father who'd made the first important commitment—to a form of transportation which, at the time, was primitive and undependable. Sigismund had brought to fruition his father Franz's risky initiatives, and since he'd succeeded marvelously through careful management without great risks, he was never in his life tempted to succeed further by doing anything that might be dangerous. He did what he did well because everything he did, everything he was—down to his physiognomy—was so totally consistent; nothing about him was extreme. He wore well-trimmed muttonchop whiskers, instead of a beard, on an even-featured face. He was neither tall nor overly short, just a shade thinner than the portliness that characterized men of his age and class, and neither fashionable nor out of date in his dress.

When Saul arrived home flushed, stuttering about oil, Sigismund gave him the courtesy of fifteen minutes of silent reflection before saying no.

That same day, Saul wrote to his French and English cousins. Had they read the article? Would they? Would they then convince his father to join with them in what he believed would be the most promising family venture since the heirs of Isaiah had founded banks in the major financial centers of Europe? An impetuous letter. After many weeks, replies came from London and Paris, patronizing, thinly indulgent letters of rejection. Young Saul might just have something there, one ought not discourage the boy from thinking like a financier, but they were very occupied with what they were doing. All very prosperous, backing railroads, financing mercury-mining in Spain, copper in Africa, lending money to the profligate Khedive of Egypt, who was paying them back in Nile bottom land, miles of it, which would need managing. Everywhere their money was bringing in enormous returns. For France, it was truly the Belle Epoque, and Victoria still reigned over the greatest empire the world had known. Why did they have to take risks in Russia? Francis de Wolfflen wrote back that he would never invest in Russia so long as there were pogroms. A good excuse. Saul was tempted to argue that if the Wolfflens got a good grasp on the economy of Russia, there would be no more pogroms. But he didn't. He didn't write back. He knew what he was up against. Lassitude. Decadence, he hissed to himself. Having no other recourse he bided his time, but biding time to realize an ambition was different from having no ambition at all.

Five years later the Baron Sigismund von Wolfflen died, leaving control of the Austrian Wolfflen fortune to Saul. Once again Saul wrote to London and Paris. Once again the family wrote back that it wasn't interested in petroleum. Why petroleum? That summer the Khedive had defaulted on another loan and the Banque Wolfflen had taken title to forty thousand more acres of cotton fields. Shares in the Wolfflen Telegraph Company had just nearly doubled, after it had laid its second underwater cable from London to New York. The English and the French Wolfflens had more than enough business on their plates.

Saul brooded at his desk where the dossiers were brought in daily, bulging with memoranda in the careful script of underlings navigating their careers as they made a point here and a point there moving vast sums in and out of bonds. Two weeks after his rejection from the other Wolfflens, Saul was seized with vertigo. He lay his spinning head on Sigismund's desk. The blood surged at his temples, saliva rushed into his mouth, nausea swept over him. He fainted. When the attack had subsided, his head felt light, chilly ... and calm. It came to him with full authority that he would die young, and maybe by his own hand, if he had to spend the rest of his days with memos. Next morning he packed and headed for the Caspian Sea.

Vienna to Budapest, Budapest to Belgrade, Belgrade to Sofia: the young Baron's private carriage on the Orient Express bore him over the rail lines his father's money and talent for fund-raising had built. The train clicked over the rail-joints relentlessly, until the sound became the noise of a clock. Saul had time, time, time on his hands: time to get cold feet. Near Constantinople, eating his morning croissant, he took a white rose from the cut-glass vase on his table and plucked the petals: "yes ... no ... yes ... no"—like a lover asking fate if he were loved. But he was only passing time, asking for confirmation. He was committed, unalterably, to his "yes."

He took a steamer that hopped up the far coast of the Black Sea: Kerasan to Trebizond, Trebizond to Batum, where at last he got another train. At Tiflis he was able to rent a private car. From Tiflis to Elizabetpol, the train hugged the feet of the Somketian Mountains, while to the north and east the high Caucasus glared like a wall all the way to the sea. But the steppe widened and from a channel between the two ranges the world became a place less harsh as the train clicked along smoothly over the last two hundred miles of flatland to the port of Alyat. The way snaked north again, and as the train followed the shoreline, sometimes Saul could make out a spur of land through the sweaty lake mist that stunted the Caucasus—Baku.

Baku was, of course, not as he had envisioned. No clean, well-defined plains and shining machinery. Derricks clustered among gray board shacks on the misty flats beyond the town, which rose in the form of a rough ampitheatre around the bay. The town was rife with the imprint of dead epochs: the eleventh-century minaret, the cramped streets around the fortress of Bad-Kube, palace of the Khans—little leaders who were vassals to the Shah, and whose splendor was provincial, done on the cheap.

C.S. Gulbenkian had left long ago for London, where he'd

obtained the capital he'd needed for the Russian company and collected a huge commission. Baku had become pawed over and parceled. A dozen companies were working cheek by jowl in the flats. But in a bar where the riggers gathered, Saul learned of Albrecht Heller, a German Jew, an engineer from Berlin who had the rights to the most promising wells, and who was doing very badly. Heller's company, Brittania, named by the Englishman he'd bought it from (an adventuresome clergyman who'd abandoned a Yorkshire parish on inheriting, and who returned to the cloth a few years later, leaving Baku for a leper colony in Kenya) had its office in a rickety building with a lacelike facade near the waterfront. Heller's problem as he explained it, offering a breakfast of vodka, blackbread, and smoked sturgeon on his scuffed desk, was simply money. Cash-flow, as accountants of the future were to call it. Heller was pumping great quantities of crude, but the delays he suffered shipping on erratic tramps and the long delays in getting paid were making it impossible for him to meet his running costs.

Saul got out his checkbook, and for a sum that no one was ever able to learn, but which was known with hindsight to be astonishingly low, he bought seventy percent of Brittania. That afternoon, Heller and von Wolfflen strolled the port of Baku looking for an Englishman named Cyril Halstead.

"My bank will cover our running costs," Wolfflen had said, "and finance the purchase of a fleet."

Halstead had five steamers in need of repairs, running irregularly under the name of the Moon Steamer Company. Saul took out his checkbook again, and Brittania Oil became Brittania-Moon. At the end of the month, while the Brittania-Moon fleet was being scraped, refitted, and painted in gold and crimson Wolfflen colors, the Baron Saul went back to Vienna and got out of railroads.

The ascendency of von Wolfflen and Heller, two partners perfectly mated in their foresight, their taste for risks, their natural love of honesty not only for its own sake but as a stimulating handicap, would be a story long in telling. To be brief, on January 11, 1912, Heller was freshly dead of a coronary thrombosis, and Saul von Wolfflen, his sole heir, was sitting at a table set with loukum and other Turskish sweets while Calouste Sarkis Gulbenkian sipped thick coffee and murmured blandishments to the Baron, who had most of Baku in his pocket.

The scene was a huge wooden summer house on the Bosphorus.

Gulbenkian had rented it, opened it in the winter, and installed himself with thirty servants who saw to it that the villa was a total pleasure dome for visitors. Most of these were a number of young officers who'd taken part in the overthrow of Abdu-el-Hamid, and who were now more interested in politics than in combating the Italians in Libya. Gulbenkian was representing the Anglo-Dutch Oil Company, whose money came from London but which was based in Holland, a country which had already made clear that it would be neutral in the coming European war. Von Wolfflen had arrived in Istanbul with his late partner, anxious to expand out of Baku and do business with the Young Turks. In Saul's pocket had been an offer to exploit the Mossoul oilfields, which concession would have made Brittania-Moon the dominant crude producer on the Caspian. But Gulbenkian was already on the scene, as were agents from a half-dozen other petroleum companies.

All of those companies had decided on the same ruse. Instead of asking the government directly for a franchise, as Saul did, they'd each bought the claims of one or several of the many heirs of Abdu-el-Hamid. Each petitioned the new rulers with the same argument: the oilfields of Mossoul had been the Sultan's personal property. Even though he was deposed, they remained the personal property of his heirs. Each foreign company contended that in buying the rights to the oil from a legitimate heir, they were *bona fide* property holders under Turkish law. The Sultan had been stripped of his power, but his personal property had never been taken from him.

For weeks on end after Heller and von Wolfflen had arrived, a vicious struggle had been continuing among the patrons of the heirs. The two partners had looked on, aghast. They had had to quarrel for advantages in Russia, they'd driven hard bargains, but Baku had never been like this. The smell of impending war had driven the conflict among the oil people into a frenzy, like blood on the water among sharks. While officials high and low were being plied with conflicting bribes, company agents were being physically attacked in their hotel rooms by other agents. Heller suddenly cracked; he took to drinking heavily. Heller was completely disoriented; he was at heart an engineer, a man who liked simple, mechanical rules. He had a German Jew's fear of disorder, and he was in no way up to crime. Nor, of course, was Saul. The weeks they spent powerlessly waiting for the government to answer their attractive, straightforward offer were the worst in both their lives. Heller failed to survive them. He collapsed and died the evening an agent for Shell was stabbed to death in a fish restaurant on the Golden Horn. Saul had decided to pack and leave when the bellhop brought him a message from Mr. Gulbenkian inviting him to take coffee at his villa. Gulbenkian liked to "globalize" his problems. He wasn't just interested in Mosscul, he wanted Baku as well. He seemed nervous as he pecked with a little spoon at the paste of powdered coffee and sugar at the bottom of his cup. He explained that Anglo-Dutch quite obviously was very much aware of the Baron's great importance and prestige. No one, he said, would be foolish enough to underestimate the network of power the Wolfflen family represented. "Obviously the Baron's offer . . ." And here Gulbenkian's voice rested its weight on the word *offer* until it sounded like the hallowed term for something dear beyond the measure of this world. "Obviously the Baron's offer was of the kind that dashed the hopes of all the contending legacies . . ."

Would the Baron, all the same, accept to consider the problem "globally" and seize a brilliant business opportunity: an alliance with Anglo-Dutch, the most experienced petroleum people in the world, motivated and directed by a genius, Lord Norbert Netterling?

The deal was concluded in Vienna. Netterling himself came for the signing of the papers. Saul knew he'd gone as far as he could as an active competitor in the world of oil. He handed over his Baku holdings and withdrew his beleaguered offer to exploit Mossoul. Brittania-Moon became Brittania-Dutch, and Saul von Wolfflen became an inactive shareholder of the new company, with twenty-three percent. No one else, not even Netterling himself, had anything close to twenty-three percent of what was to become the largest petroleum company on earth.

The following year, Saul abandoned Vienna for Amsterdam. He foresaw that the war coming on was going to be an immense immoral carnage, a conflict of greed, and he wanted no part of it. The hatreds of nationalism were straining the bonds of the Austrian empire, and Saul could see that the Jews, the one Volk with no piece of land to set a flag on, hadn't a bright future if the empire came apart. Without the least nostalgia, he quit Vienna—two weeks, as fate had it, before the Archduke, who'd gone to Serbia to inspect railroads, was shot riding in his carriage. Saul was to spend the First World War in Holland, reaping profit from his holdings of Brittania-

Dutch, which made enormous sums supplying the allies from tankers flying the neutral colors of the Dutch Antilles.

Holland was a dull, smug place after the balls, the salons, the social intrigues and intellectual infighting, in short the feverish decadence of Vienna on the brink of war. But Saul hardly gave himself time to be bored. On the Sunday his ship docked in Amsterdam, he took a quick stroll through the damp stillness of the Herrengracht, where he'd rented a house, then escaped on the first train for the Hague. It would be a long time before he'd see the capital again. In his pocket that fateful Sunday was a confidential letter from Dr. Sigmund Freud to the Baroness Edwina van der Poel. The Baroness was a patient of the doctor. Possibly the letter, to which he'd attributed an urgency expressed with considerable anguish, contained some sort of instructions for survival, as if he knew the war would separate him from his patient for a long time. Saul was an acquaintance of Freud. The doctor was far from a socialite, but his reputation as a poker player was greater among the upper circles of Vienna than that of a healer of minds. Freud and von Wolfflen would often play a two-handed game together on Saturdays. Once, out of curiosity, the Baron had offered himself for analysis. After a few months of what Freud described as "running limpid water through a sieve," the doctor pronounced the Baron von Wolfflen the sanest person he'd ever encountered. "Dangerously sane," he later clucked, as he wiped his stuffed nose with a fretting gesture before cutting the deck.

What Freud wrote to the Baroness van der Poel Saul never learned. Once, much later, he asked Edwina whether it was simply a letter of introduction aimed at throwing the two of them together, since Freud knew how much Edwina needed someone to lean on, and how much Saul would enjoy being that person. The Baroness, by then the Baroness von Wolfflen—Saul's first wife—simply blushed and gave a gentle laugh, which quickly, pitifully, became a cough resonating in the depths of her corrupted lungs . . .

Saul had never met Edwina before that day he arrived for the first time at Zarn, ten miles from the Hague, where her castle overlooked the North Sea from what in Holland would pass for a promontory. He knew that she was a patient of his learned acquaintance who would come to him in Vienna for months of analysis and then leave and return again, much in the way other women of her time observed the season at the spas. Saul hadn't known what kind of help the doctor had been giving her, what her "hysteria" was, why Freud accepted treating her in that periodic way.

One look at Zarn Castle told Saul that the Baroness was probably insane to be living there. Zarn was a mid-nineteenth-century Dutch version of the French middle ages—faithful to a variety of precise models in a variety of details, but totally wrong in its chunky ensemble. Facing the dune-road that ended at a moat, there was even a Roman Catholic chapel with stained glass. At first, Saul couldn't think what use it had, since the van der Poels were a family of Jewish bankers serving the Protestant crown of Holland, and a Catholic probably couldn't be found for miles around Zarn.

Von Wolfflen arrived in time for dinner, which was at the high table of an immense, empty hall lit with kerosene lamps. He and Edwina were alone. The oak table went on for yards from the corner they occupied. To relieve its emptiness, the Baroness had had an arrangement of shrubs, flowers, and a great variety of tall potted plants set out. The table gave Saul the distinct feeling of being at the edge of a forest or a jungle. The feeling, and the spicy green odor wafting on the drafts that rose and ebbed and rose again through the great hall, was disorienting, disarming. For miles, Saul had passed nothing but dune-grass and rare twisted willows, as the Baroness' carriage had borne him from the railroad station to its kindred spirit, Zarn Castle.

They dined on fat white asparagus, larks, and mocha éclairs. Saul followed Edwina's example, attacking everything with his fingers. Between courses, the Baroness' muscular woman servant kept changing the little crystal *rince-doigts* in which orchids floated. An engraving of a chipmunk from a book in his childhood came to Saul's mind, while Edwina nibbled at the little bacon-bandaged fowl, clenched as if in a fine vise, some jeweler's tool, in her tight, spidery fingers. Her rapid mouth was a small oval with close, sharp teeth. In the chiaroscuro of the lamplight, Saul found her far from beautiful, but "interesting," some rare, fragile improvisation of nature. He intuited a strained adolescence, during which she must have grown like a strong-willed plant out of earth poor in nourishment. She was an orphan, but rich of course in money; her poverty was something thinned out in her biological inheritance, some frailty, the aftermath and retribution in her blood of the nineteenth-century male van der Poel's rumored debauchery.

As he bit into the marrow of a bird, Saul suddenly recalled the history of Zarn. "Holland has need of this kind of thing," had been Edwina's father's public justification when he'd built it. He'd talked about an exposure to the "spirit of an age," having been greatly moved by what Viollet-le-Duc had accomplished with the restoration of Pierrefonds. He made the place available at appointed times to picnickers—a custom, Saul was to learn, that continued after his death, for every Saturday, while Edwina took refuge in her bedroom, tow-haired children in *sabots* would scamper all over the ramparts, playing knights in armor. Whatever else old Poel had meant by "the spirit of an age" was ambiguous: there had been talk that Poel and a handful of other worthies would leave their families in Amsterdam to conduct sex parties in the castle and black masses in the chapel. Poor Edwina, Saul thought. She seemed all too delicate to shoulder the enduring scandal. How old was she? She looked just out of puberty, but he guessed that she was twenty-three.

"Under what circumstances," she asked, "did you encounter the good doctor?"

"Poker" was all Saul could express. The Baroness had posed her question just as he was crunching into the other thighbone of his bird.

She didn't ask him to explain. "I have delivered my soul into his hands," she sighed.

Thereafter conversation came awkwardly. The Baron asked about the plants, and the Baroness was finally able to fill out the quarter-hour of éclairs by enumerating the species, origin, prescribed care, and state of health of each green creature on the table. The Baron declined coffee. He was greatly tired from the voyage and wanted a good night's sleep. Edwina explained that her nerves never allowed her to take coffee. The woman servant brought two lamps and gave him one. She led the way upstairs, while Edwina walked between the beams of his lamp and the servant's. There was a narrow turn on a landing, a passage leading away from where they stood. Suddenly the two women were gone. The passage lay in darkness. He heard Edwina's high, tight voice echo "Good night, *monsieur*."

On the next landing, he found his bedroom, where a fire was panting for life on the hearth. Despite the smoke, he was soon asleep between a fluffy eiderdown and a gentle feather mattress.

A week later, twelve people came to lunch. From the rapid introductions, Saul understood that the tall, very white man was the local pastor (whom Edwina referred to as "Doubting Thomas"). Present also was the schoolteacher, a round, bearded fellow with the glare of a cutthroat; a horticulturist in tweeds; an old woman who wrote music; and a medical doctor in his thirties, beardless and near bald, who gave off a smell which Saul identified unsurely as formaldehyde.

The Baron failed to quite catch what the others' occupations were. He gathered, though, that the guests and Edwina were the thirteen intellectuals of Zarn township, and that the group united regularly for Sunday lunch at the castle. He soon learned that the meeting was more a seminar than a lunch. The platters of roast pork and apples were taken away rapidly while half the company tried to control their furtive glances of regret. Edwina was expounding on her last meetings in Vienna with Dr. Freud. For each luncheon, Saul learned, there was a single topic of conversation, which the members of the set took turns in preparing. The zeal with which Edwina attacked her subject, and with which the others joined in the assault, led Saul to believe that The Good Doctor was a number Edwina repeated often among the Zarn thirteen.

Saul was shocked. Doctors were obliged to keep their rapport with patients totally confidential. Shouldn't patients feel morally bound to be equally discrete? Yet there was Edwina, flushed, radiant for the first time since Saul had arrived, describing how she'd led poor Freud on by faking through a maze of arbitrary associations so that he and his theories would eventually butt against a wall.

"I just tell him any old thing—"

"I should think," Saul interrupted, "that that in itself tells him a great deal about you—"

His interruption went unheeded, except by the pastor, who flicked his wrist in Saul's direction, a gesture which clearly meant "shut up."

"I mix shit with chocolate—"

Saul was to learn that it was hopeless: whenever Edwina's turn came to present a subject at Sunday lunch, there would be no real discussion; there would be a gathering for the kill. Edwina, the only member of the group who did any traveling, would regularly bring back, like prisoners bound and trussed, bits of what was new in the world. Dr. Freud was only one of them. Always, the Thirteen, with her guidance, would gleefully do to death whatever she gave them, safely behind the ramparts of their smug provincialism, the double provincialism of a backward place in neutral Holland. Thus Edwina held sway as the regent luminary among twelve cheap minds. It seemed to Saul that Edwina was worthy of a better role in life. Why did she need them? There was something there that seemed pitiful to him. Was Freud on to her game? Was she perhaps a double agent with her soul, confessing what went on in Zarn to the doctor in Vienna? In any case, Saul realized the Baroness needed help. Freud's anxious hand-squeezing as he entrusted his letter to Saul had not been unwarranted.

The schoolteacher and Saul were the only ones who managed a decent crack at the food, that first Sunday of Saul's. When the schoolteacher noticed that Saul, too, was blatantly eating, he assumed an air of complicity with the Baron. Unlike Saul, the schoolteacher had also drunk a lot of wine.

Edwina's voice had risen sharply. She was describing the doctor's dull choice of bow ties. "Ever since her divorce," the schoolteacher whispered to Saul in appreciation, "she is absolutely inspired."

"Her divorce?" Saul said. "The Baroness has never been married." He was surprised by an instant pang of jealousy.

"Elle est divorcée de l'amour, mon ami," the Dutchman answered. And then, with his heavy accent in English, the language imposed on the luncheon: "She is divarrced fan love." With that he actually put his hand tenderly on the fly of his trousers and rolled his eyes upward with a burlesque look of melancholy.

Saul turned his head away quickly from the tipsy professor and faced Edwina again, whose radiant features seemed more "interesting" again than those of any woman he'd ever seen before. Such was the message of his eyes; he was incapable of censoring it with the reasons to belittle, distrust, and dislike her that her luncheon party was thrusting upon his mind. "She needs help," he heard himself think, again, in the tone of the good doctor, his poker acquaintance. Freud's voice rode in his mind like a leaf on rapid water, over the clacking of the guests' footsteps as they quit the dining hall to take infusions in a small smoking room with a machinemade tapestry on the walls, a scene of Noah lying drunk, hung perhaps by Edwina's father. The pastor took Saul's elbow at the doorway. "Hans is a boastful liar," he hissed through big, wide-spaced gray teeth. His breath smelled like fresh cowdung. "He has never had her. No man has known her."

Saul was soon convinced that the pastor was right. His belief in her virginity proved all he needed to make his muddled attitudes toward her yield to an obsession. He lusted after her, telling himself "she needed help." His idea was *énorme,* preposterous—what way to health could he clear for her, where Freud's genius might have stumbled into a maze? And yet he pursued her, not thinking for an instant that vanity might be the force propelling him, urging him to *accomplish* some supreme act of sexual prowess beyond mere acrobatics of the body. He believed there was a love for her welling inside him in the form of a great current of benevolent energy, and that if his body penetrated hers he could make her as strong and as sane as he was. As if in deflowering her he would drain her of demons.

Von Wolfflen decided to remain at Zarn until Edwina either yielded to him, or had him physically forced out of the castle. (Her woman servant, so irritatingly ever present, was quite up to accomplishing that task.) At the same time, Saul knew that a frontal attack, anything resembling roughness, would doom him to failure. He steeled himself for a gentle, slow seduction.

Edwina showed no impatience to see Saul leave, as weeks passed with her visitor still settled in his smokey room overlooking the chapel. Never once, from the very day he arrived, did she ask him how long he meant to stay. The life she couldn't seem to open wide enough on her own must have been essentially very lonely for the Baroness. He stayed. By the end of the month, the word was rife in Zarn that the Baroness van der Poel and the Baron von Wolfflen were "living together," although, over meals brightened by talk of music, painting, books, they'd barely explored the civilized outposts of each other's minds. Saul smouldered, but bided his time.

One afternoon he returned from the post office with a packet of seeds. He announced to Edwina that they'd arrived from Java and that they belonged to a rare form of the castor plant, one with a particularly viscous oil content. He hoped to "experiment" with them in the castle hothouse, which housed Edwina's orchids and the orange trees that lined the walks of the castle gardens in summer. Later, Saul produced a whole batch of other seeds he had had mailed to him.

At Sunday lunch, where Saul had unavoidably become the fourteenth member of the club, Edwina announced that the Baron von Wolfflen was staying on at Zarn to perform "biological experiments." She made a little rustle in her throat—a habit she had—and waited for responses, which did not come. "He is turning my hothouse into a garden of Eden," she said with an edge of nervous laughter in her voice.

A sour grin played on the pastor's lips. Saul pretended not to notice. His seeds would begin to sprout the following fall. He had, in effect, a six-month visa to remain at Zarn. In the smoking room, he took the horticulturist aside and begged him for advice on what care would be needed during the dormant months ahead. But neither Saul nor Edwina were to witness the artificial springtime in the greenhouse of Zarn.

April was a month of relentless rain. On the fateful morning of the sixth, Edwina, who had been pacing the long winter parlor reading Rilke aloud, suddenly threw her book into the fire and raced out into the wet without a coat. Saul, who'd been eavesdropping in the drawing room, drinking the harsh music of her German on the echo of her footsteps, spied her moving across the lawn toward the sea. He ran from the window and hastened out after her as she sped on her long legs, her dress billowing behind her like a black sail. Suddenly she caught herself on a hawthorn and fell down on her face. He walked up to her silently, turned her head around, and kissed her, for the first time, on her mouth. He pulled his head away as fast as she did hers: blood was running through her lips. Saul realized he'd been a fool. A fool not to have noticed what was happening when the Baroness' habit of constantly clearing her throat had developed into a plaintive little cough. Stunned for a moment, he watched the thick red of her blood being pinkened and consumed by the rain on her chin. He lifted her up, carried her into the house, and sent the woman servant for the doctor.

Dr. Piers Wolters, the most laconic member of the Sunday club, came out of Edwina's bedchamber and pronounced only one word: "Switzerland."

But Edwina became even more feverish as she contemplated having to cross through Germany. Finally, she absolutely refused to go anywhere she could "feel the conflict taking place." Saul wasn't sure of what she meant. There were forces in her mind, and in her lungs, he realized, imbuing her with distorted, blurred motives. He didn't try to understand; well-meaning craft prompted him to answer the bizarre with the bizarre. "I'll take you on a boat to Italy," he said, hoping that through the prism of her ailments that odd suggestion would strike straight home. A boat trip would be long, but Edwina seemed determined to languish at Zarn. "We'll make a cruise," he said, grinning like a salesman. "How beautiful," she answered. Her eyes gleamed, with disease, surely, and maybe with an image of the sea.

From Amsterdam, Edwina, Saul, and the woman servant had no trouble sailing to Genoa on a neutral Dutch steamer. But by Genoa, Edwina had a boiling fever and was all worn out. More than a week on the boat had had a particularly bad effect on her. She'd been seasick most of the way, and had alternately spat blood and vomited. The ship, which was not plying the most lucrative of routes, was ill run, and no amount of Saul's tipping had been able to get Edwina's bedsheets changed quickly enough. Her room had taken on a nauseating smell, which the sea air had accentuated. During the two days' train ride from Genoa to Grier, in Switzerland, Edwina vomited again, frequently, and the compartment smelled worse than the cabin on the ship. Saul reached the end of the journey full of guilty disgust. From the moment he'd tasted Edwina's blood on the lawn of Zarn, he'd been fighting back a repulsion toward the woman he had been lusting after unrequitedly. It had happened that fast—and he couldn't put down the disgust that had seized him as suddenly and as unreasonably as his passion, any more easily than he had been able to quash the passion. As he left the train, a horrible ache attacked his face and head; he thought of the events fate had thrust into his life.

He had hastened to Zarn out of boredom, to deliver a message whose contents were a mystery to him, and he'd wound up smitten by a passion whose motives were more complicated than any he'd ever known himself to have. And here he was in Switzerland with the object of that passion, a sick woman he'd rather now have never met. And soon he would be all that poor person had in the world to comfort her. The Dutch servant had given notice and bought herself a train ticket to Geneva the moment she saw the immense mountains walling in the plateau of Grier. "They will give me nightmares," she'd announced. Saul too felt a panicky urge to get away.

He wondered if there were any chance Edwina would let him go, once he installed her in a chalet on the grounds of the Sonnfeld Clinic. But putting the question to himself that way, poisoned with guilt, was simply telling himself he couldn't leave her. His face ached. He felt depressed for the first time since Istanbul.

As they rode a horse-drawn carriage a mile up-mountain to the sanitarium, Edwina clutched his hand. "We'll be a club of two now," she said, smiling wanly but roguishly. "We shall have to carry, intellectually, the weight of fourteen." Edwina's pointed joke at her own expense—for he'd mocked her and her country luminaries once, in a fit of frustrated lust—failed to move Saul to the slightest merriment. As he felt her thin, cold fingers gripping his under the sheepskin throw, he thought of the thrill he would have felt, the euphoria of achievement, at that same gesture only weeks ago. Now he suspected bleakly that she was in love with him.

Professor Sonnfeld told Saul he gave the Baroness three months to live. Saul promised himself to stay on. He felt compelled to prove to himself that he was "a human being." (Incorrigibly, he identified being human with being kind.) He took a suite at the Grier Adler and visited Edwina every moment he was allowed. Three months passed and turned into four, then five. Edwina rallied; his solicitude filled her with a courage to survive. In a dark corner of his mind—a place not so dark as to be hidden to him—Saul wished she would pass away. And then things changed between them.

They turned into fast friends—but that's a very paltry way to describe what happened between the Baron and the Baroness. Even "Platonic lovers" falls short of what they became to each other; for there were moments of ecstatic understanding when to both of them their minds seemed in some way actually to copulate.

The shadow of death and Sonnfeld's strict metering of the visits had imposed an urgency on their conversations which made it possible for Edwina's mind to seduce Saul's. The Baroness seemed to sense that total success or total failure were the only possibilities in their singular relationship. As soon as she was sure she was going to live, she brought forth her greatest ammunition, opening her mind to him like some great lady who until then had sheltered her most precious jewels from the eyes of the vulgar. Over those paltry, stilted lunches at Zarn, where she'd never been urged to intensity, she'd taken up the lazy role of a queen bee among intellectual drones.

She'd lived as if time were not precious, as if any attitude toward life might do, since there would alway us be time later for another. Now she'd come back from despair with a gift of time running through her hands like water brought from a difficult spring where there'd been no dipper, no bucket, one had to drink what one could how one could. Before, Saul had never been able to perceive that Edwina was a genius. Now he knew.

Her mind was an encyclopedia of knowledge and an unfailing instrument of perception. She seemed aware of everything. Saul felt that she could even read his soul, fathom, understand, and pardon his abnormal revulsion toward her sickness—of which he was quickly cured. Soon each visit to Edwina became a stop-off on a great journey of the brain: famous men came forward like innkeepers—Freud, Nietzsche, Hegel, Husserl. Together, Saul and Edwina's minds entered their bright establishments, supped, and slaked their thirsts before traveling on. And on this heady fare, somehow Edwina's body flourished too.

As the lesions in Edwina's lungs gradually began to scar, Dr. Sonnfeld allowed the two of them to walk for several minutes over the lawns of the clinic during each visit. A year from the day she and Saul had arrived at Grier, Edwina was still alive. That afternoon, Saul summoned a hassidic rabbi from Zürich. The three of them stood through the marriage ceremony with tears in their eyes. Sonnfeld, a beardless, bald, cold fish, suppressed his usual love of prohibitions and offered everyone, even Edwina, pear brandy afterwards.

Saul stayed on his magic mountain with Edwina for five more years. His rooms at the Adler filled up with so many books the chambermaids had trouble moving around. When he wasn't visiting the Baroness, Saul would read or paint in watercolor. Each Saturday he would take the train down to Zürich, where he would spend the weekend, always in the same brothel, but each time with a different girl. His life was compartmented, but it didn't seem to him incomplete. He considered himself a contented man. It hardly occurred to him that he was approaching forty, that his youth was receding with his hairline . . .

Edwina's lungs were no longer in danger of failing her, and yet they never healed entirely. Her disease would flower and wither in cycles. Sonnfeld refused to let her leave the clinic for fear that one of her relapses might take a truly dangerous turn. Before long, the Baroness had become the doctor's most inveterate patient: others moved in and out, died all around her, and she lingered without impatience, nostalgia, the *doyenne* of the sanitarium.

One day when Edwina and Saul were jumping from rock to rock on a brook near the main building of the clinic, Edwina experienced a terrific pain in her arm. She was dead of a heart attack before Saul could carry her to Sonnfeld.

Five years of Saul's life were dead with her. What regrets? That he'd never *known* her? They say consumptives crave sex abnormally, but "from the neck down I'm all withered," she'd warned after the rabbi and Sonnfeld had left them alone in her chalet. Her voice had been so full of fear and latent reproach. That, and his esteem for their very special idyll—for the fragile fact that it had escaped everything banal and rude—caused him to strangle his passion. No regrets. Instead he felt a remorse, paradoxically, throughout his body. It ached in his stomach. All of him mourned a friend such as his mind, he knew, would never encounter again.

On returning from Switzerland to the Herrengracht, Saul found that a letter had followed him: an invitation to attend an emergency board meeting of Brittania-Dutch Oil.

For five years, Saul had given little thought to his investments. After becoming the largest shareholder in B-D by selling his Baku holdings to the company, he'd put implicit faith in the celebrated business acumen of Norbert Netterling. Throughout the war, Netterling's cool, canny management had made B-D prosper. He'd outplayed the Rockefellers of Standard Oil in a race to build the world's largest tanker fleet. B-D ships were afloat constantly on all the waters of the globe, serving Brittania-Dutch refineries in such far-flung places as Siam, Trinidad, Venezuela, the Dutch West Indies, Malaysia, and the Philippines. The one black spot in the picture for Netterling was Baku. For shortly after the Revolution in Russia, Lenin had nationalized the Baku oilfields. Netterling's influence in the British Foreign Office had enabled him to riposte quickly by inspiring the occupation of the Caucasus by an expeditionary force, which set up an autonomous regional government. But on the day before Netterling had called for the emergency meeting of the B-D board, Trotsky's Red Guards had reconquered Baku.

Saul von Wolfflen accepted the news with equanimity. Once again, he thanked fate. Saul had had no idea who Lenin or Trotsky was when he'd sold his holdings in Baku, but had he by chance held onto them, he would have been nearly wiped out financially. Instead, the shares he'd acquired in B-D, thanks to Netterling's adroitness, had multiplied in value. Baku was now just a drop in the bucket for Brittania-Dutch. Von Wolfflen thought B-D could well live without it. Netterling, though, was of a totally other turn of mind.

Saul's acquaintance Dr. Freud would certainly have found Lord Norbert Netterling a quintessential example of the anal personality. Netterling was an obsessive collector—he saved coins, paintings, oriental rugs, matchbox covers, cigar bands, and medicine bottles. He'd even established a pig farm in Surrey, because the anguish of throwing away the garbage of his Mayfair townhouse had become too much for him—particularly since he kept one of the most elegant tables in London, for wining and dining useful politicians. The good fare he provided did nothing, though, to change Netterling himself, either in body or soul. He remained thin, muscular, hard as a rock, and dour as a convict. Losing an umbrella could set him to chewing the carpet for days on end. The loss of Baku, for Norbert Netterling, was totally unacceptable.

At the board meeting, Saul yielded to Netterling's bitter rhetoric. After all, Saul, who owed his fortune in B-D stock to Baku, could hardly plead for writing Baku off as a loss. He knew he owed Netterling gratitude. As for the other board members, they were all well disposed to follow Lord Norbert wherever he'd take them. The Bolsheviks were a band of revolutionaries whom no decent government had recognized. Saul kept silent when they sent the stenographer out of the room, and raised his hands with the others to vote a secret war chest for Norbert Netterling. A few years later Saul would realize, too late, the immoral consequences of that vote. But how could he have foreseen the complicated outcome of having unbridled Netterling's evil soul on that fatal afternoon in 1920?

Netterling began pouring money into White Guard adventures. At the same time he was buying up, for his own account, all the shares he could get of the small Russian petroleum companies whose stock had fallen close to zero in value on the Western exchanges. His hopes flared, sputtered, and died with the fortunes of General Wrangel and Admiral Kolchek. Finally, Netterling realized that the

112   THE HEIRS

hope of liberating Baku lay, once again, outside Russia. The chance he decided to take—the one hope he saw—seemed such a longshot that he kept it to himself. But he had only himself to answer to for the way he spent his war chest. Secretly he boarded a train for Munich.

When Adolf Hitler got out of Landsberg Prison, where he'd spent nine months for his aborted beer-hall putsch, he was a very depressed young man. Through a French journalist, he let it be known to Philippe Berthelot, general secretary of the Quai d'Orsay, that he was willing to stop making trouble in Germany and would emigrate to South America for seven million francs. The French foreign ministry didn't consider the money a necessary investment. Soon afterward, Sir Norbert Netterling offered Adolf Hitler much more to stay. Hitler took heart.

Faithfulness to history requires mentioning that Netterling was not the only important industrialist to encourage Adolf Hitler, thinking he could use the Führer's charisma as a front for his own ambitions. Sir Norbert's scheme was simple and ruthless: the West would send Hitler off to seek *Lebensraum* among the Bolsheviks. Hitler would bleed Germany to free the Russians of the Soviet yoke, but just before he could install his own colonial rule, the Western powers would step in and chop him down to size. Baku would be part of the booty. Hitler, however, had another way of looking at the chessboard.

In May of 1941, Norbert Netterling, deprived of Baku and much else, died a broken-hearted man in occupied Holland. The Führer, who was not totally immune to gratitude, sent a uniformed emissary to the funeral, with a wreath bearing a ribbon in the Führer's personal colors. By then, Saul von Wolfflen had fled into Switzerland from France . . .

Saul had learned of Netterling's conspiracy very late in the game. The truth was he'd once again abandoned the lonely boredom of Holland, this time for France, where at a Parisian dinner table fate had prepared another encounter. Another obsession. Ariel, his huntress. Netterling's foul dealings did not, in any case, become blatant until he began accompanying Hitler on his electoral campaign of 1932. From a newspaper photo, Saul recognized Netterling sitting in the back seat of the open car in which Hitler was barnstorming the countryside, speaking at every crossroad and flailing a rhinoceros-hide whip into hostile crowds along the route. When Netterling returned to London shortly afterwards, Saul von Wolfflen was waiting for him. He caught up with Sir Norbert on the steps of White's Club and attacked him with a cane. Netterling, who was much bigger than Saul, fought back vigorously. The two of them, rolling at the curb, had to be torn apart by a bobby. The fight made the newspapers and so did Wolfflen's second attack. After a hot bath at his hotel, he picked up the phone and sold every last share he had of Brittania-Dutch, driving the value of the stock to the floor. Brittania-Dutch suffered its blackest day. The board fired Netterling, not for what he'd done with his war chest, but for what had happened to the stock. As for Saul, he took his money and put it into the widest spread of safe securities possible, most of them in Switzerland. He realized, with great bitterness, that he'd been wrong not to see that a concentration of money imposed the exercise of power, for the better or for the worse. His sin, he knew, was to have failed to exercise his power until it was too late. But of the many things the Baron Saul von Wolfflen had tasted in his full and varied life, power for him had had the dullest taste of all...

A full and varied life...
Ariel's hearse became visible from the window of Saul's carriage as it turned, leading the cortège east. A shiver passed over him. His blood seemed to run out of his members into his entrails, where an ache stronger than the pain of grief now was swelling. Suddenly, he felt alarmed for himself. For the first time, ruminating about the past had made him feel so fragile. He'd never before given more than a moment's thought to his health. Yet after all, he told himself, he was seventy-four. He'd been an old man for a long time, and had known it, known the slowness that had crept into his gait, the chill of his extremities at night, and the feelings of wear damp days brought to his joints. But now, for the first time, he was seized with the truth that this old body was likely to break down suddenly, be seized by some violent disruption. Getting old: it was more than wearing away, it was getting closer to some moment when the tidy balance of the body's sensitive machinery turns into chaos. He was astonished that he'd never cared to look at the future that way before—never consciously, lucidly, as now when his thoughts seemed currents circling a pole that was his awareness of the pain in his chest.

Nerves, he told himself, breathing deeply to relax. And the pain gave way several notches in intensity. Yes, nerves.

A diagnosis which, if true, still changed nothing essentially, he thought. The great loss of age was the loss of future, not in the plain sense of the nearness of death, but because old age was hollow: emptied of the energy and time needed to begin adventures.

Full and varied. Yes, he'd had all sorts of experiences. He'd loved twice, intensely—two women with the same disease. (For an instant that coincidence caused him to wonder if he were, metaphorically, a carrier, one of those people whom fate wills never to be stricken, but to corrupt others. It was a stray reflection he discredited; he couldn't sincerely blame himself for many things.) He'd hated once. He'd hated a man enough to want to cane him to death. He'd gambled and won, struggled and succeeded, built a fortune greater than he'd inherited, and turned his back on struggling to store up all the learning he could. A full life. *To no end.* Then where was the flaw? Specifically? His answer came in a rush, not specific but insistent: he told himself that what he missed and now would never have was a *wholeness*. The word dominated his awareness without satisfying his understanding. Somewhere among the Greeks he'd read in Grier, there might have been some equivalent term, enlightened by some rich dialogue. His memory had frayed and he'd lost it. As for his own epoch, the word didn't exist with any satisfying meaning.

That was the trouble!

But we understand only faintly what it means because we know the lack of it, he thought. Other men suffer that deprivation when they're squeezed by singular obsessions. All the Netterlings. His own life had been built up in compartments, had gone from one thing to another, a lot of experiences, accumulating no worthwhile shape. If it weren't for love, his life would have been chaos, he realized. And now all his future was the boy of thirteen beside him in the carriage who bore his name. What example have I provided him, Saul asked himself. Chaos? What advice—what advice can a father give in our time? How can I tell him what to be, without having found the answer for myself?

Léopold was lost in his own thoughts. His round, pimpled face wore its usual impassiveness. Saul loved the poor boy, and the boy seemed to love him, but neither could say much to each other.

The boy was totally inward. He'd built a little world of little preoccupations—his tropical fish, his coin collection—built it like a tent around himself. From a chink in the tent, he occasionally peered out with those glazed eyes.

I couldn't tell him the one thing I know, Saul realized. I couldn't tell him because he'll have to know it by himself. I could talk around it, I could say: watch out, love isn't someone or something you want, it's what you bless for simply being there—

But all that he'll have to know himself. Poor boy, Saul loved him, yet he heard himself reflect: "You'd think Ariel would have made someone comelier"—just as years ago he'd felt himself repulsed by poor Edwina's blood and vomit. He couldn't help it.

Poor Edwina. Poor Ariel, he thought. Poor Ariel... Poor flesh.

I couldn't even tell him loving would do him any good.

The horses strained as they headed uphill to where the gate of the cemetery of Père Lachaise overlooked the Boulevard de Menilmontant. Soon, Saul realized, the burial would be over. Her body would be sent down to rot, and for the rest, all she'd be would be little bits of thought flickering now and then in other people's minds.

A wholeness. Did someone really have the word, the point of reference whose definition gave a place in the whole to everything? He couldn't remember. His memory was not what it had been. My memory's gone moldy, he said to himself, and the pain in his chest flared again.

SEVEN

The Rue de la Roquette became at its fag end a narrow, cobbled lane bordered by rotting houses whose facades stonecutters had embellished to resemble Renaissance manors. Plumbers and ironworkers had since taken over the street and the alleys that snaked off on both sides. The lane was sloppy, a grimy accumulation of workshops suggesting all that was make-do and vulnerable to erosion. Beyond, at the mouth of the street, late sunlight illuminated the Boulevard de Menilmontant like a goal. A symbolist painter of Ariel's father's time, depicting accurately the cortège of black carriages being drawn up the steep hill of that ugly street toward the radiant cemetery entrance, would have had no trouble creating his saleable message.

The carriage stopped at the large, broken hemisphere of wall that was the entrance to Père Lachaise. The mourners got out to follow the hearse on foot inside the cemetery, as was the custom. Beyond the ivy-covered walls, a wide avenue led to where the plateau yielded again to hillside, a hillside covered with narrow tombs close to each other, most of them in the form of midget Roman or Greek buildings. All in all, they gave the necropolis the look of some bustling ancient Mediterranean city—Knidos, say, as it had been—rising above the plateau as if above a lively port where merchant vessels from all over dropped anchor.

At the gate, the hearse driver from the Maison Henri de Borniol presented a paper to a guard who had come out of a little *loge*, a man in a blue uniform like a policeman's which hung on his old body. He drew a pair of steel-rimmed eyeglasses from his handkerchief pocket and read: Ariel's document was in order, she had been duly assigned to an authentic plot. The guard touched the brim of his *képi* in a regulation salute. The mourners followed Ariel's body across the frontier. The cold made their footsteps clatter on the tarred red gravel of the graveyard's *avenue principale*. Their breath formed puffs of steam as they advanced toward the ecumenical Monument aux Morts, Belle Epoque stone nudes at the entrance to a cave that shored the elevation on which the Maison de Mont Louis had once stood. In that house, dedicated during the Enlightenment to the rest and recreation of the city's Jesuits, Father François d'Aix de la Chaize, confessor to the Sun King, had established a mini-Versailles: a court more merry than the king's, a palace of feasting and fornication, with formal gardens, *orangerie*, and fountains. All gone.

Ariel's mourners wheeled right slowly in rough double file, following the hearse away from the dead end formed by the monument. They entered L'Avenue du Puits. A little further ahead, where this lane lined with chestnuts became the Avenue Casimir Périer, lay the graveyard's old quarter, with its Jewish section.

Charles de Wolfflen's stomach rumbled. The carriage ride up from the Ile de la Cité had been slow and chilling. His body had spent his lunch keeping him warm. Now his stomach felt hollow and his chilled joints ached. He looked forward to the end of this whole business, to some tea and toast, and later a good dinner. His mind had begun to conjure images of what he'd most like to eat—a rack of lamb with pink flesh, sauced with drawn butter and chopped tarragon—when he brought all his thoughts to attention. This was no time to lose discipline. He remembered that the burial was of important political use to him. His arm slipped out from under Eveline's. He hurried his stiff joints forward and put his arm around Saul's shoulders. The first reaction in Saul's eyes as he felt Charles' weight was puzzlement.

They were close now to the Wolfflen family vault, a discreet narrow temple whose only external markings were a W in the iron grillwork of each of two small windows. From across the narrow lane that ran through its division of the area, the tomb faced a slab erected to the memory of Tobias Koen, pedicurist to Monsieur, the brother of Louis XVI, and to the Empress Josephine, the Emperor Napoleon I, and Charles X. To its right were neighbors of still greater note: Héloise and Abélard, star-crossed lovers who'd suffered a destiny worse than that of Romeo and Juliet. They lay now, side by side, under a Gothic-style porch. As Charles sighted the peaks of their monument, a shiver passed over him. He recalled the story: how Pierre Abélard, the most celebrated scholar in Paris, founder of the city's university, had been set upon by thugs hired by Fulbert, Canon of Notre Dame. They cut off his testicles. Abélard had given a baby to the Canon's niece, Héloise, "a most learned and most beautiful lady." Later, Abélard, who'd become a powerful abbot, had Héloise made an abbess. All his life, he'd fought with the church bureaucracy, defending logic against mysticism. A follower of Aristotle, he believed in dialogues—that people could achieve truth by talking to each other, posing questions. "A moderate realist" was how the church classed him now, precursor to Aquinas. "A moderate realist" who'd lost his testicles with his heart. All that, Charles recalled—as his grip on Saul became more a crutch for his own stiff legs than a comfort to his cousin—all that happened nearly nine hundred years ago.

The remains of the abbot and the abbess had been brought to Père Lachaise when the necropolis opened for business in May of 1804. The graveyard's promoters had decided to use the relics of the two lovers as a lure to induce fashionable people to buy plots. About a dozen other celebrities were transplanted here, including Molière and La Fontaine. The great dead were given the role of "locomotives," as Paris society was to describe that function a century and a half later. "Locomotives" were people sufficiently envied or adored to turn whatever they did into the fashion, to draw the whole *beau monde* behind them. The reburials served that purpose; Père Lachaise became *the* place to be buried, so much so that the cemetery soon spread up the hillside, congesting acres with stone, way up to where in 1871 the troops of Versailles had to hunt exasperatingly among the crowded tombs for the last Communards, whom they slaughtered against the walls. And now there were so many crypts that old people of note, seeking proper company for their bones, spent years of anxiety waiting for the lease to run out on some plot, or for plots leased "perpetually" to become free, when families fell short of being, as regulations required, perpetually interested in keeping neat their forebears' last property on earth.

A sexton was working with a sledgehammer on a decrepit, once perpetual leasehold, as Ariel's cortège reached the edge of the Seventh Division. The hearse kept moving uphill. Saul didn't even slacken his pace. Eveline, who had moved alongside him and her husband, failed to hold back a sigh of surprise. Saul frowned at her for a second before fixing his eyes toward the higher plateau. Charles looked toward Bruno, who, with Marc beside him, had actually stopped walking. Bruno's eyes glittered with malicious humor. Awareness of the surprise Saul had dealt them spread over the faces of the other mourners:

Ariel was not going to be buried in the Wolfflen crypt.

Charles' arm moved off Saul's shoulder. His first reaction was a keen feeling that Saul was in the midst of dealing a huge insult to the other Wolfflens who'd followed him, indulged him, through his whole ceremony at the cathedral. But then very quickly Charles' umbrage gave way to relief. It was just as likely Saul had been motivated by tact, he thought. Keeping her out of the family's most private territory, he'd bury her with her own. In any case, Charles could not help but feel relieved that her bones would not be mouldering near his someday, where the Wolfflen dead were shelved in intimacy, one upon the other, under the marble floor of the crypt. Charles preached patience to his stomach as he prepared his legs for the steep climb that remained up to the de Vaunel plot.

They reached the plateau. The congested hillside gave way to a lawn, which sloped back down from the chapel to the rear of the Monument aux Morts. The lawn had been settled during the last part of the nineteenth century and beginning of the twentieth by large individual tombstones, well spaced among the aucuba and low junipers, and embellished with moody hack sculpture, all very sentimental, new-rich, and extravagant.

Still higher, beyond a temporary corner crypt where plot-owners caught short by death were stored namelessly until their tombs were finished, was the de Vaunel plot. It lay to the right of the chapel across the lane, amid a huddle of old tombs, but was distinct from them. A fence of stone pillars connected by iron chain marked de Vaunel land, where instead of a crypt there was a tall, thin pyramid surrounded by small stone half-ovals poking through the sparse grass. The pyramid was a monument to Etienne de Vaunel, Duke and Peer, *"Défenseur de Louis XVI."*

The hearse stopped on the gravel between the lawn and the chapel. The driver got out and, opening the rear door, released five hired pallbearers cramped inside. Having lifted out the long mahogany box, they hesitated a moment, sampled its weight on their shoulders, then wheeled about slowly and turned their backs on the road that continued across the Avenue Feuillant, where the de Vaunels lay.

Once again, Charles and Bruno exchanged queer looks. Bruno's face was more than puzzled, there was a certain air of arrogant satisfaction in his glance, an air of pleasure that things were happening in a totally irregular way. Saul was walking by himself now at the heels of the pallbearers, with the boy a step behind him. The hired men paused and strained again, scuffing their soles as they wheeled with the coffin once more, this time turning onto the narrow steps that led down the green hillside. Saul stopped short. He flinched. A cat had come out suddenly from the skirts of a spruce tree. It crossed between the other mourners and Saul. The others had stopped too, surprised not by the cat but by the discovery of where Saul was leading them. Midway down the lawn, black mounds of earth marked a new grave, ready beside a large porphyry slab. On the slab, covered with fresh flowers, were the black marble bust of a handsome man and the large, deep-lettered inscription: "Sydney Swarc, Founder of the World Society for Ethereal Communication."

As the pallbearers paused to note the best way between the bushes to the monument, it became clear to all the Wolfflens that Saul had brought them out to bury his second wife where she'd likely asked to lie: beside a parlor mystic, high society's mini-Rasputin of *Les Années Folles*.

Swarc was practically unknown to current generations, but once he'd written a book that had stirred the salons and dining tables of Paris. It had been called *L'Ether est Eternel*. In it he'd contended that nothing one did on this earth was of any great importance one way or another, since the world was only a temporary playground where ethereal spirits passed in and out to relieve the intensity of Eternal Contemplation, a state which he perhaps inconsistently described as one of vast peace and immense concentration of energy. There might have been further inconsistency in his advocating a technique of meditation to make contact between earth and the Ether. Having set down on paper the ideas he'd expounded for a decade in a salon that was actually a meeting ground for paying members, Swarc allowed his diabetes to kill him. He passed on, leaving behind a cult whose surviving members still kept his grave constantly embellished with fresh flowers. He'd also left behind two mistresses: the film actress Paula Rosier and Ariel de Vaunel. Mademoiselle de Vaunel was to become, after six months of blatant competitive mourning, the Baroness Saul von Wolfflen. All of Paris had been aware of the whole story.

The hired men were still muttering over how best to get to the hole, their promise of relief. Saul began to weep. He gave forth sobs that were barely audible, but his chest was working up and down under his tailcoat like an asthmatic's. Behind his father, Léopold began wringing his thick hands while tears streamed down his face. His father's grief had set him off, and it was clear that Léopold, whose eyes were fixed on Saul instead of the coffin, was weeping for Saul, who'd been father and mother to him for years, and not for the wild woman in the box who'd been no mother at all.

Marc de Wolfflen felt moved to step forward, to do something for his cousin, for the boy. But what? They stood there, father and son, a gray-haired, whiskered man and an adolescent weeping, both of them, over the old man's final loss, or his liberation—the end of an infatuation beyond reason, a devastating folly. Pride, cuckoldry, humiliation—the ponderous words came into Marc's mind, as they had, no doubt, come into the minds of the other mourners, restless to explain this disconcerting phenomenon, this mad happening Saul had staged. For a moment, Marc thought he had pierced the comedy and had understood that Saul was experiencing something Beyond, some tortuous but seigneurial emotion. But again, he lost contact. He reasoned then. He reasoned that Saul had *outbid* calumny, carried his indulgence toward Ariel to the exaggerated height where it had become a monument to his own will. A height of pride. This funeral was then something he'd *achieved*. He'd got them all, the whole family, to follow him through the hocus-pocus at the cathedral, to put up with the caravan across Paris, and, finally, with Swarc's flowery presence. He'd made all the Wolfflens accomplices in his self-indulgence. Saul had *loved* Ariel, but what had he meant? Once he'd confessed to Charles: "I love to see her live." Marc's mind fell back into a muddle. He had no more than a glimpse of understanding about Saul and Ariel. He was sure of one thing—with all else, Ariel would go down in the family's annals as Saul's great folly, a folly among many Wolfflen follies, sharing a meaning with Cousin Yvor's dedication to making polo ponies of zebras, with Samuel Wolfflen's unflagging pursuit of four-spotted ladybugs across all continents throughout half the last century. Marc recalled that a wild streak of *self-indulgence* ran through Wolfflen history like an inherited disease . . .

A pack of men in bulky coats and sad fedoras, who seemed at first to be all cripples, came hurrying up the hill. Photographers. Each with a big Speed Graphic strapped to one hand, which caused him to lower one shoulder and hobbled his gait. They'd all been let in together, and now they seemed to be racing each other to get to the family before Ariel was lowered into her grave. They reached the lawn just as Saul and the pallbearers had begun to move forward again. They swept over the lawn and began to fire rapidly, but in a deferent hush. The glare of their flashbulbs sputtered in the damp, wintry air as they took picture after picture, pulling black magazines of film out of their sagging coat pockets. All at once, there was an explosion: a flashbulb had fallen from the hands of one of the newspapermen and burst on a monument. Then calamity happened very fast:

Another cemetery cat, a fat black one, leapt from the roof of the last tomb the pallbearers had passed, and, with a frightened shriek, ran across the back of one of them, then onto the coffin and away into the bushes. The man bolted. The coffin tipped. The man caught it before it tumbled over, but he fell to one knee and the corner of the box dug into his thigh. Ariel's chauffeur rushed forward, as the other pallbearers struggled off balance, each with his own end, unable to come to the aid of his suffering colleague.

"Ah merde! Ah merde!" the fallen man wailed.

"Ahhhmerde!"

Just as the chauffeur grabbed the corner of the box with his big hands and lifted it in one sweep off the pallbearer's thigh, a funny sound came from among the mourners: a sort of giggle.

Saul wheeled about, crouched like a boxer. He waved his way through the others until he stood in front of Bruno. He seized the sleeve of Bruno's uniform.

"What?" Saul was saying, "what ..." All he seemed able to say. His teeth were bared and his moustache was twitching.

Bruno's face, as he looked down at his furious old cousin, was a confusion of embarrassment and mirth.

"What!"

Bruno appeared to bite his tongue, but it was hopeless. A shrill laugh escaped him. He seemed as helpless as a man with hiccoughs as he covered his face with his hands.

Charles stood between them now, as Saul's hands formed fists. Charles looked like a cook whose kitchen had caught fire. He took Saul's arm. "Listen—" he began, but then he just stood there with his mouth open. Everyone's eyes were on the cat, which had for some crazy reason returned to the scene and was now meowing angrily a few feet away on the grass. Bruno, who'd managed to shut up and put a serious look on his face, seemed about to laugh all over again.

"Apologize!" Saul hissed.

"Witch," was all Bruno said. Between his teeth.

"Nazi!"

It was Saul who said it. But now Charles was between them again, pushing Bruno toward a safe distance. "Fool! Fool!" Charles spat out, as he turned to Saul. But all at once something happened to Charles. What looked for an instant like a smile flashed across the side of his face, but it wasn't a smile at all. His mouth twisted, blood began to spurt from his nose. He flailed his arms out as if he'd suffered a terrific blow to the chest. His cane fell. He sagged to his knees, rolled on the grass, and lay at Saul's feet twitching.

"A doctor!" Saul wailed, as he kneeled to grapple with the stud of

Charles' starched wing collar. Bruno was racing across the grass, back down toward the entrance.

Somehow below he found a taxi, a wheezy Citroën, in which he appeared a few minutes later in front of the chapel. He got out and came charging down the lawn, where Marc and Ariel's chauffeur met him halfway, carrying Charles by his arms and legs. They hurried back to the cab and spread Charles across the back seat as best they could. The taxi spun gravel backing up, before racing downhill with Marc and Bruno crammed beside the driver. Ariel's chauffeur stood on the plateau with his hands thrust into his black overcoat. He stood there a long moment, scowling. No, he decided finally, he would not go back down and join the other mourners ...

Below, the pallbearers had set the coffin beside the grave and were waiting for order to be restored. Eveline was weeping a few yards away, with her back turned on everyone. She had run up the hill as fast as her old frame could carry her, but she'd failed to reach the cab in time to go along. Sara had come up beside her and gathered her mother in her long arms.

Saul was incoherent. He stood at the head of the grave, biting the knuckle of his thumb and mumbling something that sounded like: "Never. Never ..." The pallbearers became distraught. No one seemed to intend to give them their cue. For some reason—who knew: perhaps in deference to Swarc?—Saul had not planned formal rites at the grave. So there was no outsider, no priest or whomever, to get everything over with.

"Not one of you knows a thing about living!" Saul cried out as he continued to stare into the empty grave.

No one answered. The silent embarrassment seemed bound to last an eternity, until Léopold, the boy, spoke up. He had Charles' ivory-tipped cane in his hand, and he rapped it against a stone.

His gruff puberic voice was pierced, finally, by the shrill plaintiveness of a child as he urged: "Everyone! Please! We have to finish this."

With great relief they all obeyed him, lowered their heads, faced the hole. The pallbearers set their burden on the ropes they'd prepared, and slowly finished the job.

Herbert struck a deal with the photographers, took out a wad of English pounds for them to split among them. Later Sara made calls to a number of publishers. There were no pictures of the funeral in the press next day. Just brief articles recounting that the Baron Charles de Wolfflen had suffered a stroke at his cousin's wife's funeral, and had been hospitalized in critical condition.

EIGHT

"I did it," Bruno kept repeating as they walked against the gusts of wind from the exit of Lariboisière Hospital toward the Boulevard Barbès. The overhead *métro* in the Boulevard intensified the gloom of the dying winter day. Bruno walked with his palms thrust into his armpits, his thumbs stiff, in a way that recalled pistols tucked into shoulder holsters.

"It's finished. I screwed up everything. That's what I've got a talent for. Charles wanted to play up to him. We needed him."

Marc wouldn't answer.

"I'm not like you. I don't have a gram of tact."

"What a family," Marc said at last.

"Marc . . . will you ever forgive me for your father?"

"Shut up Bruno, for God's sake. It just happened."

"Saul's a fool," Bruno answered, inspired by what he might have taken for a reprieve. "I just couldn't help it. He was too much a fool to be true."

"Saul's no fool. He's a Wolfflen. He does what suits him and he expects everybody else to consider it all very natural. The trouble is, we're all Wolfflens."

Bruno halted and took his cousin by the elbow. "Marc," he said, "let's not be fools. Let's you and I never be fools toward each other."

The rumble of the train passing overhead consumed Bruno's last few words. In the time it took Marc to be sure he'd heard right, his mind had already raced backward two decades. It brought him to Switzerland, Croseigne. His rival's face was glaring down on him. His shoulders ached from the weight of Bruno's knees and the puddle was chilling his scalp. Then suddenly young Bruno was standing with his hand outstretched, his eyes full of good humor, a smile irradiating his face . . .

Marc took Bruno's hand. As he did so, he had a feeling that his cousin was totally insincere, that Bruno always played with people to suit some strategy—erratic, harebrained as that strategy might be. Yet Marc felt ashamed to think so. He held onto his cousin, tightening his grip, until Bruno let go.

"Charles is very very tough, Marc, you know that. He'll be all right. I—"

"Oh, yes. Don't you worry."

"So odd, did you hear what he said, just as we were leaving?"

"The name?"

"Yes, he kept talking about some person named Robinet. Does that mean anything to you?"

"Don't you know?" Marc answered. "He's that little fellow close to de Gaulle."

"He said something like having to make contact with Robinet." Bruno shrugged.

A cab advanced along their side of the boulevard.

"Hey, Robinet!" Bruno shouted at the driver as if the name were some password.

The cab screeched to a halt. They ran up to it. Bruno pulled open the rear door and pushed his cousin in ahead of him.

When Marc got back to the Avenue Foch, there was a telegram. Emma had given birth—to a healthy boy.

BOOK TWO

MEN OF AMBITION

ONE

"Who? I'm sorry..."

Marc pretended they had a bad connection. He couldn't for the life of him place the name the man was repeating in English—or Dutch?

"Kyle Hoyt... Kyle Hoyt."

The Baron gave up. "I'm sorry I don't remember..."

"You remember the imbroglio involving your cousin—"

The American officer. It all came back: the horse-drawn taxi on a cold night. Bruno in bad trouble. Cigar ashes. The war was two years over, and that desperate fix had become an "imbroglio" in the language of the American who had offered to help Marc save his cousin's life. Now he remembered everything.

Kyle Hoyt said he was calling to invite Marc and the Baron Bruno to meet with John Foster Dulles. Dulles had quietly arrived in Paris from London to deal with what Hoyt referred to as "your insurrection."

"I told Mr. Dulles we knew each other," Hoyt warned when Marc arrived at his hotel room. His voice was uneasy. Marc sensed that he and Bruno were being led to a meeting with Dulles by Hoyt like a couple of Hoyt's trophies. Bruno, who'd arrived at the hotel first, sipped his drink with a waggish air. He was enjoying the treatment.

"I said if anyone is *au fait* about what's going on, it ought to be the Wolfflens."

Marc looked assayingly at Hoyt. He remembered a heavier man. The face had got ruddier, and noting the ruptured capillaries at Hoyt's nostrils, Marc wondered if he were looking at a drinker. Hoyt hadn't told him what his current work was. Marc assumed he was still in some form of intelligence. He'd been in London with Dulles at the Four-Power Conference on Germany, which Dulles, in the face of the Russians' bottomless capacity to say "nyet," had just abandoned to part of his staff. "France is a bigger headache than Germany," Hoyt had said, reproachfully.

Marc let Hoyt's judgment of the Wolfflens' importance stand without comment, but he asked: "Will my father be at the meeting with Dulles? Frankly, I haven't yet mentioned it to him for fear he wasn't asked."

"He wasn't ... asked. Sorry. Your father, Baron, is—in our book at least—an out and out Gaullist. Mr. Dulles will be talking to the Gaullists separately."

"And in your book, you don't lump my cousin Bruno and me in with my father?"

"Come on, Baron," Hoyt teased, "I don't even think *you two guys* see eye to eye—on everything. I mean everybody knows ... everybody knows, Baron, that in every family people have differences of opinion ..."

"My father will have a memo on this meeting."

"Shall we go?" Hoyt asked. "Shall we go? You know, Baron, it's a great pleasure for me to see you again. You look in fine form."

"Christ," he added, "can you tell me where I get a shirt done? They're even on strike here."

As they made their way through the long corridor of the hotel to the elevator, Bruno checked his cousin, letting Hoyt, who hadn't noticed, get several feet ahead.

"He told me about your epic meeting the last time," Bruno said. "You never said a word."

"What did it matter? You got out on your own."

"If you were I," Bruno challenged, "how would you have taken it?"

"Well? What would *you* have done?" Marc parried.

"Marc, you old bastard, I would have told the Germans to put a bullet in you." He laughed.

Hoyt, who'd reached the elevator, jerked around suddenly and scowled. He appeared to think the joke was on him.

In the elevator, he took revenge on these two Frenchmen. He said—and it sounded as if he were pretending to think out loud accidentally—"My God, this goddamn government better hold up. We've already put three hundred million dollars into it!"

On the way to the Avenue d'Iéna, Marc wondered how much Foster Dulles would resemble his brother Allen, whom Marc had met a few times during the war.

Allen Dulles had a gentle face for a ringleader of spies: roundish, professorial with the spectacles and pipe. The delegate to the United Nations who greeted the two Wolfflens in a salon of the residence looked like a banker. Behind steel-rimmed glasses, his eyes were slightly crossed; the touch of convergence in his cold gaze gave it intensity. His eyes weren't his fault, obviously, nor was the fact that the slight hook of his nostrils and the upward set of the right side of his mouth combined to give him an embittered look. When he spoke, his jaw wagged forward—another gesture that fated him to seem disagreeable. His features all suggested a man who could explode into rage, but his manners were impeccable.

He didn't waste words on empty amenities. He addressed his guests with great formality, but succinctly.

"You were very kind to agree to this informal meeting. I'm sure it is clear to you as it is to my government that the events in France at this moment are of capital importance. Naturally we are in very close contact with the government of your nation. Our meeting today fits into a number we are having with responsible people outside the government.

"May I begin by asking you to evaluate the gravity of the situation."

Marc said: "We haven't any exclusive knowledge."

"Give me your assessment." Dulles leaned forward, grasping both arms of his chair. As he looked at Marc, he seemed to be making an assessment himself.

"Personally," Marc said, "I don't think the Communists have any intention of starting a civil war. And if they did, they'd have no chance—unless, of course, the Russians come rolling through Germany, but then we're talking about a general war, in which the French situation would be—well, do *you* have reason to believe the Russians, in the state their country is in now, would begin another war?"

Dulles squinted. "Please continue."

"Well, the whole country's on strike, isn't it? The strikes will keep hurting the nation very badly until the strikers have to go back to work to stay alive. Most of them, I believe, want to go back to work now. It's up to the government to keep the others out of their way. If the Socialists are firm with the strikers—something hard for a Socialist to do—then the coalition between the Socialists and the Centrists will hold. Which is simply to say that the government, if it acts with strength, will survive."

Dulles' face took on a look of satisfaction.

"Yes, you have to be tough," he said. "Now what about General de Gaulle?"

There was silence.

"Since he walked out of the government, we find him very difficult to deal with, quite frankly," Dulles said at last. The sour look of the right side of his mouth shifted into a smile. "Actually we always have."

Dulles seemed to feel the need to strike a note of affability.

"Our government," he said, "is committed heavily to the economic recovery of a free and friendly France. The aid will be considerable, and of course the dollars will have to be properly channeled. I'd venture that you gentlemen will have a good share in handling that."

There wasn't a hint of *quid pro quo* in what he said, not the barest suggestion that if Charles de Wolfflen turned his back on de Gaulle so that the current government, which had already made its deal with Washington, could prevail, there would be excellent commissions for the Banque Wolfflen. But neither Bruno nor Marc needed a hint.

The two cousins left the meeting together in Bruno's car. Bruno plunged his shift lever back and forth, speeding through the empty streets, downshifting with a great blare at every turn.

"He's right," Bruno said.

"Ah?"

"What do you mean, 'ah'? For God's sake, Marc, he's right! Anyway, they're coming down on the side of the government with all their money, so we might as well get the whole thing straight with Charles."

"He's right about what?"

"Marc, it doesn't matter what he's right about; to me the man's a zombie, all right? But they've got the weight, Marc. De Gaulle is finished without them. We've got to get it clear to Charles. He's making a mistake playing around with the General, and he's going to get us cut out of everything. He's going to get us cut right out of the whole future of this country unless he watches his step."

"You tell Charles to 'watch his step.'"

"Marc, you tell him, for God's sake! You're his son. You, in principle, are going to be running everything when the time comes to undo his mistakes. ... You're the heir ... for God's sake."

"What do you mean, 'in principle'?"

"I mean ... who knows? You don't even seem to *want* to handle anything ..."

"I don't want to tell Charles what to do. He'll just do the opposite."

Bruno puffed his cheeks and exhaled.

"It's a pity," he said.

"Ah?"

"I mean it's just a pity there's no way you ... can prevail on him. You're his son. ... Marc, I wonder sometimes if you know what you really want."

Marc didn't answer. Just then they came to the gate of his house, and he got out and slammed Bruno's car door shut behind him.

TWO

Later, as Marc downed an aspirin in his bathroom, it came to him who it was John Foster Dulles resembled: Woodrow Wilson. The face, and from what he knew of Wilson, the manner. Wilson had been a rigid man—rigid, and highly principled. At Versailles, the others had turned his principles into a smokescreen for their conniving. Dulles, though, seemed an even more dangerous person: a rigid man playing at *Realpolitik*.

Toward the end of the meeting he kept going on with his lesson about the Communists. He couldn't understand how a civilized country such as France had let them into the government, and why France had taken so long to kick them out. And now the country might have to face a civil war.

"We must never lose sight of the fact that we are facing an enemy devoted to world domination, addicted to a doctrine whose goal is the enslavement of men's minds."

Yet, from all Marc knew of Benoît Franchon, the Communist union leader, he seemed to be basically a decent Frenchman, even if a wrong-minded idealist. Dulles was too rigid himself to see more in the man than Stalin's robot. Or was he, Marc, he asked himself, too naive, too self-satisfied about his "objectivity" to see evil intricately at work?

The sound of his son crying broke into his thoughts. He headed for the nursery, where he found Emma holding Gilbert against her chest. She had tried to get him to walk, taking one hand, and he'd fallen.

"He isn't hurt," she said, "he's humiliated."

Marc took the boy into his own arms. Gilbert brought with him the trace of Emma's musky perfume mingled with his smell of sour spit and cereal, a corruption of Marc's wife's presence, more intense now as he kissed Gilbert on his pink cheek. Husband. Father. In the two years he'd been a father, Marc still handled the boy like a fragile and precious gift someone had just thrust into his hands. He was still all thumbs at parenthood.

"The little Jesus," Emma said, with pride and humor mingled in her voice. She was mocking a woman, some maid who had stopped, frozen in admiration, in front of the swing in the Tuileries on which Gilbert had been sitting dreamy eyed and lazy, as was, it already seemed, his nature. "The little Jesus!" His governess had reported the story with great pride indeed. Perhaps Gilbert did look like some sentimental version of the Christ Child with which maids were familiar. Cherubic, but with authority. Not anybody's baby face. Gilbert already had well-structured features. His eyes were his father's, heavy-lidded, but they were more variable. Gilbert's gaze could shift through moods like a sky of moving clouds. Behind those eyes, behind all those variations, there had to be a great sensitivity, exceptional intelligence at work. Marc thought so. He was proud of his heir and loved him quite spontaneously. He just didn't know what else to do with him but kiss him, and the bigger questions— what kind of father did he have to be, what right lessons, from now until the end of his own life, would he have to pass on—baffled him even more disconcertedly.

"I want to know about the Americans," Emma said as she prepared tea for the two of them downstairs in the small salon. Emma drawing tea always reminded Marc that his wife was a pianist. There was never a stray gesture, not a motion that seemed out of place, as she poured water out of her silver kettle into her silver pot, in and out of her china cups membraned by light, never seeming to pay any attention to her hands at all. Finally she poured the tea, whose smokey odor mingled with the smell of the alcohol flaming under her kettle, and with the deep bitter-sweetness of the marmalade, a blend of odors which meant teatime with Emma as it always had been as far back as London, which seemed to Marc—now that a jumble of old images came to mind—so very far back, only a few years but another continent of time, an ocean of meaning away. *He missed them.* For all their hellish uncertainty they had a certainty he missed greatly now: a certainty of what he was trying to do and why. His nostalgia began to taste of gloom.

"You want to know about the Americans . . ."

She'd noticed his eyes had been drinking her in. "If you take me apart too often in your mind," she warned, "one day you'll lose a piece of me. You'll find a piece missing."

"I met the man named John Foster Dulles," he said.

"I like the name."

"You might not have been delighted by the man. He seems forceful enough. Maybe it's good to know the Americans are full of resolve. We're so befuddled here, to say the least. Mr. Dulles asked for our appraisal of the 'insurrection.' He's very agitated. Things got worse instead of better with the Russians when they met in London. Molotov said he did not like the Marshall Plan. What could you expect? I think Dulles was courting their rejection."

"What did he tell you?"

"He gave *us* nothing. He said he wanted to have evaluations from important and influential people. We let the compliment stand, even though he didn't ask to see Charles. We let the insult stand, to find out what he was up to. I still don't know. He seems indeed disturbed that my father still hears the 'Marseillaise' when you mention de Gaulle. Mr. Dulles obviously wants to make a ledger, first-hand, of the forces at work. Who is what. In case Mr. Truman might have to send in the Marines to protect American lives and property. Who knows? As one of his compatriots put it in a manner more blunt than Mr. Dulles, his government has made an investment in the current government. 'The Third Force.' Mr. Dulles seems, in any case, a gentleman."

Emma watched her husband bite into a scone in a way that marked his irritation.

"Bruno gave him to believe all we want to do is do business," he said. "I didn't contradict him..."

"It's good to have you home for tea," she said, at a loss for anything else to say, but wanting to comfort him somehow.

"I've nothing else to do," he said.

Emma rose and poked the fire. With her back to the mantelpiece, she could see straight out the window to the garden, where snow was beginning to cling to the hedges. She was pleased that the sleet had turned to snow, that the cold weather had pushed itself beyond mere nastiness and in becoming still colder had become something beautiful. Was that a lesson about extremes? Her mind formed the question and quickly erased it. Her nature wasn't receptive to extremes and that was that. She was lucid enough to know that her playing, to mention a crucial example, might be a good deal better if there were a touch of frenzy to it. But frenzy isn't something you can force, you don't have it willfully by jumping up and down. She never had it. She was not miserable without it. She was an Apollonian person, she told herself, choosing a technical word that brought an authority of learning, a certain fatality, to her definition. For example, she had had quite a simple, sane, and wholly pleasing day by practicing at the piano in the morning, lunching with her mother-in-law at Maxim's, teaching the baby to walk in the afternoon, and then, seeing her husband now, home early, over tea. For another example, she would get a simple, sane, and wholly satisfying feeling by just walking through the rooms of this house. She loved this house, not passionately, but with a serenity that glowed inside her smoothly like the bed of embers fallen and evened out under the andirons of the fire.

It wasn't a large house. It had no gilded ballroom like Marc's parents' place on the Avenue Foch. Its style was much less "hussy" as she thought of it, more sedate, rugged, and of course, much older. She and Marc had bought this house the day they visited it. It was a compact, lozenge-shaped manor without wings, with a gravel court out front, the chaste gravel court which, as with the older, eighteenth-century townhouses, kept secret the luxury of the rear garden. The garden was long, covered with healthy grass, and lined with hedges. A stand of ancient chestnuts hid the far wall, which separated the property from the rear of an apartment building on the Cours Albert Premier. The house was a Restoration manor, built in the "country place" spirit that appealed to the rich foreigners and Empire celebrities then out of grace, who founded a smart set, a wealthy bohemia, on the Right Bank from the river to the Champs Elysées. Henri Falk, the textile magnate, had inherited the house through his mother's family. When he died at the age of ninety-three, the oldest member of the Jockey Club, his heirs had put it up for sale. All the rooms still smelled of sickness the day Emma and Marc came to inspect; there were bottles of opium syrup in Falk's bedroom closet. A half-dozen empty vials, and one still half-full. The old man had succumbed, finally, to cancer of the spleen.

His furniture had also been up for sale: furniture as old as the house, with the vertical, self-consciously classic lines of the period. Emma would have been happy to have bought it all, it was all very "pleasantly plain" she thought, and she liked its "appropriateness." But no sooner had they put a deposit on the place than a great, *gazogène* Peugeot truck pulled up—full of Charles de Wolfflen's housewarming gifts. Inside there were down-cushioned gilded chairs signed Jacob, tables, commodes, and desks inlaid with whole gardens and bearing carved brass garlands, all in the delicate proportions unmistakably Riesener. Before the war, this lode of Louis Seize treasure had been under muslin in the attic of Charles' country house, Bois Brûlé. It had just been repatriated from a *Schloss* in Bavaria.

Those splendid pieces invaded the dead man's mock-pastoral manor like ghosts of the beheaded king's court. Brilliant. Frivolous.

"I feel like Marie Antoinette," was the only comment Emma could muster the day they moved in. When they stepped into the principal salon, she took Marc's hand in hers and raised it, as if they were about to join a room full of people dancing a minuet. Then she stopped in front of him, blocking the way, and looked with narrowed eyes directly into his. "Does this mean," she asked, "that the only place I can go from here is the guillotine?" He snorted a laugh and pulled her against his chest. She broke away and smoothed her fine brown hair back into order. "I'll have to get all sorts of rare silks for the windows," she said. "It will cost you a fortune." With her last sentence, she tried to imitate the voice of a *cocotte*...

Since then, she'd more than got used to all those things, she'd come to love them dearly. She'd broken the ice with them, come to understand them. Where others might have seen mere splendor, she saw now the quality of line, the perfect harmonies of volume. Underneath, there was always a rightness in those pieces, a rightness that was quiet but self-assured. And, finding in them this element which spoke the most clearly to her, she had in a way tamed, domesticated these overpowering objects, in her mind. Now everything seemed to fit exactly where she'd placed it, every chair, table, painting, every swelling commode. And the whole house spoke of balance, comfort, and ease. The one flaw in her Apollonian love nest was that Marc didn't seem nearly as comfortable here as she did. Marc didn't seem right in his own skin anywhere. Not since the end of the war.

THREE

Gaston Robinet, a soft, indolent man, not yet fat, had a more-than-usual antagonism toward getting out of bed that morning. Nine o'clock winter light gave the curtains of his room the color of mouse fur. The radio was droning with insipid and tactless self-assurance about rain again ... and the continuing bad news.

On November twenty-ninth, the government had brought a bill to parliament, asking for power to imprison summarily those who "obstructed the right to work." By the morning of December third, the assembly had been meeting night and day. The debates vacillated between a Communist filibuster and a riot...

In his mind and body, Gaston Robinet felt awful. When he got up to look into his mouth in his bedroom mirror, he was shocked by the ugliness of what he saw. His bright red tonsils were nearly touching. He lay on his belly and took his own temperature. The thermometer registered 38.5 degrees centigrade. A fine infection. But he was home, in his bed, in his own apartment, with a good supply of coal in his bathtub thanks to the gym teacher across the landing who was going skiing for the school holiday, and who'd bartered his month's coal ration for some *foie gras*. Robinet's mother had sent him crocks of *foie gras*, homemade. To compensate for his not being able to spend Christmas in Périgord with his parents. Gaston had written home that it was impossible for him to leave Paris. Too much work. While writing, he could hear his father's hollow, mocking laughter at the word *work*. His father despised the General.

Lucien Robinet was a well-off farmer whose family had always owned its own land, but his heart had been with the Socialists since '36.

Lying in bed with the newspapers the housekeeper had brought with breakfast, Gaston Robinet wondered what words his old father would have for the Socialist Minister of the Interior and his antistrike bill.

This morning, the debate was getting only second billing on the front pages. There had been a catastrophe in the middle of the night. The train from Paris to Lille had been derailed and there were at least sixteen people dead, a great many more badly mutilated. Robinet's feverish head swam as it imagined, against his will, the scene of the wreck: the carnage, the screaming, the blood, gore, and twisted metal. He was a man with the deepest revulsion toward violence. He often wondered how he would have endured if the war had lasted longer for the French Army, and he'd been obliged to experience combat. The thought would always fill him with dread, although he was certain he was not a coward, that if the moment came for him to risk his life because he had to, he'd do so. But he couldn't help his nature: he was not one of the death-obsessed young men of his time, no brooding Malraux; he hated violence, he liked life—a comfortable, sane, sunny life.

So the news of the wreck upset him very much. The rails had been severed, it was a clear case of sabotage. Who? The Communists? Yet the Communists must know that the disaster would only serve the government's case for its antistrike bill. Now there were martyrs, blatant victims of "the insurrection." The government then? That was a chilling supposition, but he let his mind reason it out. The first necessity of any government is to remain in power. Governments, like human beings, sometimes kill in self-preservation.

A hideous thought, but history confirmed it. This was a statement of fact like a biological observation. His father could never make peace with that kind of truth, he retreated from any contact with it. But it existed, as real as he was, and more enduring. Christianity had got nowhere with it in nearly two thousand years. Viscerally, by his basic nature, Gaston Robinet could not make peace with murder, either. He could never numb himself to violence. But yesterday in Rouen, when the metal workers charged de Gaulle's jeep while he was giving his speech, Robinet had grappled with a striker, giving blow for blow, kick for kick, with a man much bigger than he was.

Robinet had his revulsions, but he also had acquired one vital compulsion—to lift himself from obscurity. To be "nobody" for him was not to have lived at all. At thirty-seven, single, intelligent, level headed, he had, he believed, an excellent chance of rising in life. He was no green youngster, yet neither were others of his generation whose careers had had to wait out the war. His career had started late, but he was well placed. There was nothing to hold him back but those visceral scruples, stronger within him than ideals. Yet there was no certainty that he'd have to try them. He told himself he would face whatever problems they might raise when and if the time came. There was no need for him to torment himself by projecting abstract moral dilemmas onto his conscience. Would he, if he were Monsieur Schuman, the Premier, or Monsieur Moch, Minister of the Interior, derail the Paris-Lille Express? Had they? He brushed those questions aside and concentrated on the here and now: he had a fever, he felt awful, and he had a luncheon appointment with the Baron de Wolfflen he couldn't afford to miss.

"Rabble!" Charles had said. Eveline could not help but agree. Nothing the Baroness had ever known in her life had ever seemed so ugly. Grown men, educated men, lawyers, the elected representatives of the people, screaming the cheapest insults at each other, literally going for each other's throats.

"I told you," Charles had said, "this country can't be ruled by the Assembly. There aren't enough decent men in French politics to constitute a parliament."

The Baron and Baroness Charles de Wolfflen had been to the morning session at the Palais Bourbon. The smell of that enclave where hundreds of Deputies had been sitting for six days straight was overpowering, even high up in the visitors' boxes. A smell filthier than mere sweat, gassy and sour. In the corridors, the air was gray and stale with cigaret smoke. Greasy papers caught your shoes where men stood, their ties undone, vests hanging open, stooped over sandwiches. Totally engrossed in chewing, Eveline thought, tired but ferocious, like beasts come upon carrion.

And high above the Assembly, Eveline had felt she was looking down on some circle of hell Dante had failed to describe. Ugly, middle-aged men in disheveled suits were sleeping or reading, while others shouted insults at each other across the floor. The Communists had monopolized the lectern most of the morning, taking turns reading Jaurès to rile the Socialists, who replied with a continual volley of catcalls. Then, when Jules Moch began to speak, the Communists all began to chant "Heil Hitler!"—to Moch, the Jew whose son had been killed in the Resistance—whereupon a whole gang of Deputies swept out of their seats at the far right and came down on the Communists, swinging their fists. The ushers charged, as nervous and ineffectual as waiters at some gangster wedding in Marseilles that had turned into a riot.

Eveline and Charles had left early.

The vote on the government's "right to work" bill was expected to come up by the afternoon. Charles called the bank and asked someone to sit in and phone him the results. He'd had his stomachful but he was very anxious to know if there would be a decision before the Bourse closed. Despite his personal repugnance toward the Third Force, he'd taken some bullish short-term positions. He was convinced that the Paris-Lille train wreck had been a boon to the government.

"A pack of ruffians who will vote for order," was his final comment on the session, as he and his wife stepped into the Boulevard Saint-Germain, where Firmin was to meet them with the Buick. A vast crowd had gathered in front of the police, soldiers, *Gardes Mobiles,* and gendarmes deployed, with their different uniforms and varying reliability, like the separate corps of the army of some emperor. The crowd was picturesque and pathetic. They hadn't come with placards. Instead, each of the demonstrators was wearing the clothes of his trade. There were miners with goggled helmets, *metallos* in leather aprons carrying tongs, waiters in black tie. A whole crowd of blond young girls from an Alsatian biscuit factory were wearing the dirndls, long black skirts, and starched white headdresses of their region. Wet snow was falling, but none saw fit to cover his identity with some ordinary coat. They were chanting:

"Nous voulons voir nos élus!" We want to see the people we elected!

"You've seen them," Charles said to Eveline. He made the face of an idiot. But his expression changed quickly into a serene look of appreciation as he gazed at the ruddy visage of his wife. Snowflakes were turning into glistening drops of water on the white hair protruding from her beret. What a sport, what a good companion she was, he thought. Since he'd come back from the hospital two years ago, she'd become more his companion than ever. He confided in her more and more.

"Now you must meet my young man," he said.

The Buick was idling on the quay, a few yards from the shuttered bay window of the Nouveau Cercle. A trail of vapor was pulsing out of the exhaust of that tall old polished car, as distinctive in its own way as the dress of the workers.

Charles moved forward, raising his cane to signal to Firmin that he was crossing over. The demonstrators drew away with a deference so immediate it seemed a reflex, as the trembling old man crossed through them on the arm of a small but upright and intense-looking gray lady.

Robinet felt particularly elated over having been invited *en famille*. This would be the first time he would meet the Baroness and their daughter. He still didn't know the Baron very well at all. The first time he'd seen him was two years ago, a peculiar encounter. Wolfflen had summoned him to his room in the hospital. Robinet hadn't known why, precisely, but when someone like that takes an interest in you, you don't turn your back on the opportunity.

"People have been telling me about you," he'd said, lying there propped against a crowd of pillows in a room full of plants and flowers from what must have been all sorts of important men.

"I crave knowing worthwhile young people."

The Baron had had Robinet come back four times to prolong their conversation on the future of France, on the economic situation. At the time, neither one of them could have predicted that de Gaulle was going to quit the government suddenly a year later. They'd met twice again after that shocking day in January of '46. They talked about a vast number of things. It turned out they loved the same painters with the same intensity, but Robinet had to go to museums to satisfy his passion. Before the war, he'd scrimped to make a pilgrimage to the Rijksmuseum. He'd never made it to the Hague; that would have meant another night in a hotel. The Baron had four Rembrandts at home. In Robinet's mind, that fact more than any other put Charles de Wolfflen in an entirely different world from ordinary mortals. For Robinet himself, it was a great lift to come into direct personal contact with a real Wolfflen; merely knowing one of the illustrious barons, just as merely knowing de Gaulle, put Robinet on a plane above the anonymous crowd. But his mind could only conceive dazzling approximations of what it was like to be Charles de Wolfflen and live intimately, privately, with four Rembrandts. To hang them where he wanted, to *own* them, to *destroy* them even, if he wished. He couldn't fathom all the giddy self-esteem he'd feel if he were in the old Baron's shoes.

"You must come to my home when I'm out of here, and see my four portraits . . ."

That was at their next to last meeting. But at their last meeting, the Baron had offered Robinet a job. And Robinet had refused it. So the invitation was never repeated. Now it was Robinet who had asked to see the Baron, for a precise reason. The Rassemblement du Peuple Français was badly in need of money, and the General had given Robinet the task of raising thirty million francs. "Two hundred six thousand dollars," he'd added, and since nothing de Gaulle said was said lightly, Robinet presumed that if worse came to worse, he would have to go and pay court directly to the Americans. An unpromising prospect. But so far he'd done quite well. He'd seen Marcel Dassault, the airplane manufacturer, and had managed to talk that steel-cold man into putting up nearly a third. A handful of other businessmen had brought Robinet's figure to nearly half the goal. If Wolfflen could account for the other half . . .

Robinet had been ushered into a salon, where at last he came face to face with the Rembrandts. He calculated that he had only time enough to communicate with one of them before the Baron would receive him. He chose the self-portrait, whose rich and subtle lighting had never been faithfully rendered in the books he'd seen. Suddenly, he found something oddly intimidating in the great painter's expression, something supercilious. It struck Robinet that a man must have enormous self-confidence to be able to stare into a mirror often and long enough—with that pursed mouth, knitted brow, one hand perched on his hip—to create a portrait such as that one. *He knew he was someone reverential. That he would last forever in history.*

Robinet turned heel on the picture and sank into a downy chair facing the fireplace, where he tried to fix his thoughts on how precisely he would bring up the question of the money. He was sitting there stiffly, with his heavy forehead tensed, when the Baron came in. As Robinet got up, he noticed in a flash how sick his host still looked. His heart sank for the proud, courageous old man who'd gone out of his way to befriend him. But Robinet couldn't suppress a blunt calculation: he was glad, for his own sake, that he had turned down the job.

Lunch was served on a table set in the library. "Wolfflens have no dining rooms," the Baron explained amiably, "we eat wherever we feel like. My ancestor, Isaiah, founded the custom. He used to eat in the kitchen." The Baron pointed Robinet to the chair at his wife's right. "He didn't see fit to keep a room with a big empty table in the middle . . . useless except when company came."

The Baron, Robinet mused as his hand embraced a crisp, crest-embroidered Porthault napkin, could shoulder that kind of homely explanation. Nearly two hundred years had gone by since Isaiah Wolfflen ate in the kitchen of the townhouse that was now the seat of the Banque Wolfflen. And if he'd eaten in the kitchen, he'd also— as the Baron had no need to mention—broken bread with Bonaparte "when company came." And Charles de Wolfflen's own father had been close enough to the second Emperor to shoot with him all the time on his own immense estate, Bois Brulé. Just one of his châteaux. All of this anyone could read in the history books. As well as something else the Baron hadn't felt the need to mention: the great lords before the Revolution had no dining rooms either. They ate wherever they felt like . . .

Years later, at the height of his power, Gaston Robinet would remember this luncheon for important reasons. He would also inevitably recall that it was the first time he had eaten on Compagnie des Indes porcelain, *famille verte*. Waiting to be served, the daughter absently traced the rhythmic patterns on her plate with her long fingers. She seemed to him as awkward as a little girl among strange adults, although she was well past thirty. She was older than the Baron's son, Marc, Robinet recalled. Upright in her chair, she towered over the other three at the table. The Baron, although stooped, was a tall man, but his daughter was even taller than he was. Angular, her long face sharply defined—my God, she's a living Modigliani, Robinet exclaimed to himself. She spoke in a hoarse voice: "Father will have the results of the Assembly. He left word to be telephoned." Her tone was considerate, as if despite her own awkwardness she saw the need to put him at ease, and assumed the duty of doing it in case her mother hadn't yet noticed. So she'd reached out to where he lived: he was a politician, perhaps he had the vote heavily on his mind. But at that moment Gaston Robinet was thinking entirely of Sara de Wolfflen. Would he, he wondered, have been as fascinated by her looks, in no way conventionally beautiful, if she were some other, anonymous woman? He couldn't honestly answer himself. She seemed to him so totally *racée*, thoroughbred. Even her awkwardness bore Robinet a message of paradoxical cool self-awareness. She *allowed herself* to be awkward. She could. He thought she was precisely what he'd sensed a Wolfflen woman might be like. With that realization, a fantasy surged irrepressibly into his mind. Suppose this luncheon served to revive what might have been the beginning of a true friendship with the Baron. Suppose he got to know the daughter. And then ... he'd marry her. She was roughly his age. Suppose he would take the Baron's unmarried daughter off his hands. No, not *take her*. *Bring himself*, into this family. What a fantasy. He flushed. Glancing sideways to his right, he saw that she had reddened, too. Some current had passed between them. With all else, he realized, he found Sara physically exciting. But prudence intervened to put his fantasy out of mind.

She barely spoke throughout lunch. Her mother was equally terse. Robinet could perceive a complicity in the silence of the two women. He'd come on business. They seemed to have adopted the discreet role of witnesses, while offering at the same time their presence as an amenity, a favor, a privilege that distinguished him from business acquaintances the Baron chose to keep wholly business, at a lower level of contact. Robinet knew that after he left they would turn into a jury. They would render the Baron all their impressions of the guest newly-admitted to this higher level. Meanwhile, in a congenial voice, the old Baron kept asking Robinet questions about himself.

"You're still with the ministry?"

"Ah yes ... as ever, sir." Robinet's smile, as he paused from scraping his oyster, contained measured self-deprecation, a debonair modesty.

"Yes, I'm still discouraging alcoholic Breton mothers from putting calvados in their babies' bottles to make them sleep—with pamphlets they cannot read."

When Robinet had refused the Baron's offer to have him enter the banking business, he'd taken a sinecure at the Ministry of Health's information service. It allowed him to pursue his work with de Gaulle, which had become more and more important in the last year. He'd got the post thanks to a closet Gaullist in the ministry, and at the time he'd cherished getting it. It was a toehold in government, a way of breaking out of his academic past. Now that the rise of the RPF had brought him a precocious importance, it bothered him to wear the label of a little functionary as well. But that was his "real" job, in the sense that it was the one he needed to live. He wasn't born a Wolfflen, for example, and at the moment, with de Gaulle still out of power, he was still the aide-de-camp of an ambition. Yet de Gaulle was de Gaulle and time would tell. So if the Baron, with his question, had meant to chide Robinet for his choice two years ago, Robinet *for the sake of his mission here* would play him along with this self-deprecation. But Robinet never regretted his refusal. Time would tell, and he was sure now that there was a longer road ahead for him in politics than in business—at least than there would have been at the Banque Wolfflen.

"I need to keep the people under me from going at each other before I retire," the Baron had confided, but Robinet had been far from sure that that was exactly what the old man wanted. No matter what conflicts might exist between the Baron Bruno and the Baron Marc, one thing was sure: the old man couldn't tolerate anyone else's having any power around him so long as he lived. The top of the mountain could never have been more than the position of a glorified private secretary. And—and here Robinet had viewed the matter with brutal clarity—the moment the Baron Charles died, he, Robinet, would have been kicked down the mountain and likely kicked out of the firm by those frustrated young men who took over. Oh no, so far he regretted nothing.

Robinet felt his fever come over him again. He was sweating. His shirt was stuck to his back. He hoped he didn't smell. Come what may, he went on with his job:

"But my life is not entirely lacking in excitement," he added, keeping his ingratiating smile. "I'm still with the General as well."

"Who doesn't know that?" Charles answered. "Who doesn't know that you're a very important person?" Charles took the sporting tone a distinguished old man might take in praising a young man, but Robinet was irritated by what he took to be patronizing. He didn't answer. He helped himself very slowly to the wild boar and the jelly, while the hand of the Baron's *maître d'hôtel* began to sag with the weight of the platter.

The Baron continued in a slightly more direct tone: "Since you are so close to the General, you must know everything. You must tell us everything—"

"No one, *monsieur*, knows everything when it comes to the General," Robinet corrected, reverting to that tone of his, which was a balance between ingratiating and ironic. His irony wore authority.

"Ah, but tell us what he will do. Suppose the government can't cope..."

"*Monsieur*, we are not talking about General Boulanger," Robinet said, with full authority now. "If the government asks de Gaulle to save the country, he will accept, but a *coup d'état* is out of the question. On the other hand, he will save the country if called on, but he will not save the government. There would have to be an entirely new constitution."

"And outlawing the Communists? You'd have a civil war."

"The General has never specifically said he'd outlaw the Communists. Unless of course there's another world war—"

"Do you believe there will be another world war?" the Baroness interjected anxiously.

"Ah, *madame*, you must ask the Baron. His analysis of the situation would be better founded than mine. He's closer to the source, in the sense that he's closer to one of the potentially aggressive sides. I would like to ask him, for my information, whether John Foster Dulles is counting on another war."

"Mr. Dulles met with my people, *monsieur* Robinet, to warn me to keep away from you." The Baron chuckled. "He didn't know that Paris is a village and that if someone happens to cross the street at the same time as a Wolfflen, the next day the whole village will have them negotiating something."

The boar was passed again. The Baron, noticing the look of regret in Robinet's eyes just after he'd shaken his head, insisted that his guest have more.

"We've been teasing each other, *monsieur* Robinet," he went on. "Now I will tell you something in a very straightforward way. I'm a Gaullist. I was a Gaullist in 1940, when any decent Frenchman worth his salt was a Gaullist—and we weren't many at first. I was a Gaullist all through the intriguing in London. I daresay I like the General more than he likes me. I don't know what he's all about with his labor-management cooperative system or whatever, or if he'd ever seriously try to do something like that. Or whether it could ever work. I think he's sensible enough at heart to leave economic matters, in the end, to those who know about such things. What counts at the moment, *monsieur* Robinet, is that he is the only one. That there is no one capable of bringing order to this country short of delivering ourselves up to the United States and becoming a forty-ninth star on their flag."

"No one has answered me about the war," Eveline insisted. But just then the Baron was called to the phone. In his absence, Robinet offered an answer:

"Probably, *madame,* no one responsible on either side wants war. But each side is going at it as if the other did. There lies the danger..."

The Baron was back again very quickly. His face was bleak as he sat down. He looked into his nearly empty glass, swirled the last drop of wine absently, and with irritation.

"Ask him for more wine," he said to his wife.

Eveline rang. The man in the black tailcoat reappeared.

"Nobody has any wine," Charles protested.

The *maître d'hôtel* shouldered Charles' carping tone without reacting, other than to pour out more wine.

"Shall we drink to the government?" Charles said. "Let us drink to the 'Third Force.' That was the vote. The government is out of danger. The law was passed."

"It's a transfusion for a dying man," Robinet said heatedly. Charles looked at him with appreciation.

There was silence for a long while. No one seemed to want to touch the newly poured wine until Charles finally took a ruminative sip.

Robinet's rear molar encountered something hard. He debated swallowing, then shifted the foreign object toward the front of his mouth. As he dropped it into his plate from his fork, it broke the silence with a high *ting*. It was a ball of shot.

Charles smiled wryly. "Our lunch comes from Bois Brûlé, *monsieur* Robinet," he said. "We have been reduced to living off the land. Do you shoot, *monsieur* Robinet?"

Robinet answered frankly that he'd never done any hunting of any kind.

"You must shoot with me at Bois Brûlé. You have to take up shooting. Anyone who wants to get on in politics or in business, *monsieur* Robinet, must shoot. In America, they have the same sort of custom about golf. They settle their affairs on the open green, while we do the same thing tramping around the underbrush with shotguns. Do you think that says something about our respective cultures?"

Robinet seemed to feel the conversation risked diffusing into aimless melancholy. He attacked directly, returning to the problem that was now a hovering *malaise*. "The vote was unfortunate," he said, but with a confident smile.

"What will you do?" asked Charles.

"Let us suppose they break the strikes, which they likely will. All it will give them is a reprieve. What will we do? We will prevail, *monsieur*. Even if in four years' time. In four years there are the legislative elections. The General will go on talking to the people all over the country. Forty percent are with us now. In four years we'll be assured of a majority."

"And then, would you take the Americans' help if they offered it? Realistically speaking, *monsieur* Robinet, there may be no other economic alternative."

Robinet raised his eyebrows. His smile was just a trace left at the edge of his lips, but his eyes were bright and engaging.

"The Rassemblement du Peuple Français, *monsieur*, will accept help from whatever friendly quarters and repay friendship with friendship. But there is no one in France except the General who is capable of befriending his benefactors without becoming their vassal. The Americans need us as much as we need them—"

"At present, how much money do you need?" the Baron interjected. Suddenly, it was he who was putting the "subject" of the lunch blatantly on the table.

"We need forty million francs, *monsieur*," Robinet answered, with a figure ten million above his target.

"How much do you have?"

"I have half, *monsieur*."

"When you have tried to raise the rest, come back. We'll have lunch again," the Baron said. "I'll give you all that's missing. Is that satisfactory?"

"Right now, you're my last stop, *monsieur le Baron*."

Charles laughed appreciatively. "Ahh. That was a brilliant answer, *monsieur* Robinet."

The Baron sipped his wine, allowing a long pause before he spoke again. "You know, once I offered the General money and he all but refused it. He accepted a pittance. He was so shrewd, he seemed to know the English were about to pick up his bills, because they had no one else worth endorsing, and he must have felt it would be easier to tell them to go to hell when the time came, afterwards, than it would be to tell a French banker. Do me a favor, *monsieur* Robinet, when you take my money to the General, say to him that the Baron Charles de Wolfflen has taken the precaution to fill out the sum this time. He'll know what you mean."

The *maître d'hôtel* came in with a high, precarious soufflé for dessert. When it reached the Baron, he broke the remainder of the crust with a sharp rap of the serving spoon, which made Robinet think of an auctioneer striking his gavel.

"You are really ... exceptionally bright, *monsieur* Robinet," the Baron said cheerfully.

After their guest had left, the Baron and his wife and daughter went back into the blue salon and had more coffee.

"You notice," the Baron remarked, "he wasn't at all sure of himself, but he didn't fawn. Ah, he was strong, in the end. He didn't fawn."

"He is unusual," Sara offered. "That is, he strikes you even just by his looks as someone unusual. Which is not to say he's extraordinary *looking*, but there's something—it's in the animation of his face, the changes of weather more than his features. And under it all, I get the sense of a profound lethargy. A lazy hedonism he has to fight against, perhaps. Maybe it's just those heavy brows..."

"He heaped his plate," the Baron said. "Did you notice? He was trying not to, but he wound up heaping his plate. And the way he looked at you, Eveline, watching on which side you would put the finger bowl before he removed his own from his plate. He's come from nowhere. But let me tell you, he will go far."

"With you?" Sara interjected.

"He'll go wherever he wants to go. Me? He already speaks to me as if I were his equal. I intimidate him, we intimidate him, it's what we have, our manners, this place—all that's clearly better, quite blatantly better than what he has. But when it comes to—what? More *active* things, more consequential things, consequential in the sense of having an effect on what will go on in this world, he's not at all scared off by the Baron and the Baroness de Wolfflen. Perhaps *you* scare him, Sara." The Baron gave his daughter back the amused tone of her question. "Perhaps you. He looked at you..."

"*Il m'emmerde!*"

There were often moments when Sara enjoyed overruling her good breeding that way, with a good, strong filthy word. Yet a keen-eyed expression, something like fright, had crossed her face. Her mother noticed her hand pinch her coffee cup tightly. The Baron skated away from his failed jest.

"I want to hear your opinion, Eveline."

"I don't know. You would like to have him work for you?"

"I need someone. Not just anyone. I have a feeling about that young man. I've never misjudged anyone..."

"You have a son," Eveline said quietly.

"That's precisely, my dear, why I need someone. Marc will need a Colbert, Eveline. To put it bluntly, Bruno will eat Marc alive if he has no one on his side. Now there is me. I can prepare someone who will stand beside my son."

Eveline stared pensively at the silver sugar bowl next to her coffee pot on the tray. The young man, who was not all that young ... he was older than Marc ... she thought his eyes had flickered when he'd seen all those lumps of sugar heaped in the bowl.

"In any case, he's chosen to work for de Gaulle," Eveline said. "How much money will you give them?"

"I might give them fifteen million francs. I think that's what they need at the moment. Dassault gave them ten. I have that on good authority."

"I have two things to say." Sara had recovered from her moment of difficulty and was speaking to her father with a careful, persuasive gentleness. "One is that it is not at all sure that de Gaulle is going anywhere. The second is that you've misjudged your son."

"You needn't worry," Charles said. Lifting his cup with his good left hand, he took another sip of coffee. He tried to sound nonchalant: "We will manage to do business no matter who is in power, you needn't worry. And I intend to be around, myself, for a good long time."

He smiled, but wanly. A faint shiver passed over Eveline as she saw the intense but gray look in her husband's eyes.

"Sara is telling you you don't know Marc," she chided.

"Marc? Marc? Who, my dear, knows Marc?"

FOUR

He would try to bring to mind, as best he could, the man of whom there was no picture...

At Bois Brûlé, Marc's father's country house, in the wing known as "the gallery," there were portraits of Wolfflens dating from the early nineteenth century to Charles' generation. Only one Wolfflen male was missing: Isaiah, founder of the dynasty. Isaiah Wolfflen had never seen fit to pose for a painter, to set down his exact features for posterity. Bonaparte's gift of a baronship failed to move him. He'd been a man without vanity, who'd taken his meals in the kitchen. He was reported to have once said he was no one, "personally," nothing more than what he'd done. He had ridden the current of history, had never set his will against it, and he'd mastered it.

During those confused years that followed the Second World War, Marc de Wolfflen would think often of Isaiah. He was drawn to his ancestor's variety of pride, a confident self-effacement—not self-effacement, really, but the extinction of all the glitter of self—a serene confidence in the enduring legend of his accomplishment.

158   THE HEIRS

Isaiah had all Marc hoped he might someday have, as a person, and saw no way yet of achieving.

The founder had left no precise image of himself, and no one living now had seen him in the flesh. But what he was like, beyond what he'd accomplished, was family lore, and also in the history books. In the ghetto of Mainz, where he was born and had spent half his life, Isaiah Wolfflen hadn't stood out in any way. He was a middle-sized man with rather a strong face. Generations later, people would talk about the "Wolfflen nose"—a beak ("an eagle's, not a vulture's," the Baron Charles would boast)—and the sensuous Wolfflen lips. But any number of Isaiah's neighbors might have had those features, later called distinguished. Many of them were his cousins; intermarriage was frequent in the ghetto. Isaiah's wife, Hannah, daughter of Elihu Heine, wine merchant (no relation to the banking family of the poet), was Isaiah's fourth cousin. Her dowry had helped him to shore up a junk business that had gone first static, and then shaky.

At times, Marc de Wolfflen found reassurance in the fact that his great ancestor had spent half his life doing nothing that would help him to accomplish his great destiny. But when Isaiah made his move, he made it with instant decisiveness. He had heard a rumor. Later it seemed to be fact. Then, in the rear of his *Schul'* where businessmen gossiped while the rabbi prayed, he heard it from a man who'd traveled back from where it had actually happened: that Sabbath in August of 1789, Isaiah Wolfflen was convinced that the Assemblée Générale in Paris had forced a document on the King called The Rights of Man.

He had a wife, a widowed mother-in-law, seven daughters, and three sons, and he told them all to pack what could be packed. He sold his business, and a few days later the Wolfflens had paid their last florin they'd ever pay of Jewish Voyager's Body Tax, as they hurried out of Germany on the road to Nancy in a mule-drawn wagon.

Not long afterward, the Revolutionary Government was to proclaim Jews in France citizens of the Republic. Isaiah had sensed that what the Assembly had been saying about liberty and equality would have a profound effect on the lot of his people. But, despite the fact that he had no learning beyond the Hebrew he needed for his prayers, he'd understood that even bigger changes were taking place in the world. His understanding was a feeling, a visceral awareness of the way energy was flowing. The idleness of the aristocracy and its extravagant spending were the raw material of all manner of anecdotes recounted by ghetto merchants who dealt with those lords. Isaiah saw beyond the humor. He perceived that history was a movement of energy from the hands of one group of people to those of another, and he believed that it was moving then into the hands of those who were working. Those who were working, for Isaiah, were men such as himself, entrepreneurs, who gained strength by expending themselves, like gymnasts. Men living for a future from which they expected more. In contrast, any definition Isaiah tried out for the aristocracy had to do with its past. For Isaiah, France had become the country where men would be free to work to have more.

He was inspired, and when Isaiah settled in Nancy, he applied himself with new vigor to his commercial endeavors. He decided to specialize in scrap metal, and invested the money he'd got from his business in Mainz riding up and down Lorraine on horseback, buying old items of steel and iron. He came upon small-town dealers, and instead of competing with them he offered to take what they had and sell it where it would fetch the best price, if they were willing to wait to be paid. In a year, Isaiah Wolfflen, with little capital outlay of his own, had turned all the local dealers into his suppliers and was making the price of scrap iron in Lorraine. Keeping a small margin of a great volume for himself, while working with other people's goods and money, he had developed a strategy financiers generations later were to call leverage. And he was to exploit it with more daring and foresight than would anyone else of his time.

In August of 1790, the military garrison of Nancy mutinied. Isaiah was able to witness close up the fever that was pushing the nation toward violent upheaval. He came home from the Place Stanislas, where the soldiers were running about shouting "liberty," with a bloody nose. He hadn't been struck, he'd had a fit of emotion. Legend was to say that he'd been profoundly inspired by the cause of the Revolution, but later events invite caution toward this simplistic bit of lore. No one knows what precise justification Isaiah gave to his wife that day, when he told her he was investing their future and the future of their children in a feeling he had about where events were going. No one knows her answer either. One can only try to imagine those two former ghetto Jews, born at the edge, in a subprovince, sitting down in the kitchen to talk about how they would fit themselves into history. But history was in their veins—knowing who they were wasn't possible for them without their projecting imagination across a continent, and history was with them daily in their prayers, the story that went all the way to the Beginning.

Apparently, Hannah said yes; and Isaiah Wolfflen addressed himself directly to the Assembly, offering to sell metal in exchange for its promissory notes, which few men would accept, at premium prices.

The Assembly needed scrap to melt into cannon, for the possibility of a foreign intervention was becoming more and more likely. On August 27, 1791, the Emperor of Germany and the King of Prussia met in Pilnitz to draft an open threat to the French, insisting that Louis XVI be released from imprisonment. All that following fall and winter, Isaiah worked desperately to get together as much scrap iron as he could, but he soon realized that the supplies in the northeast were becoming exhausted. Isaiah had a contract to deliver a large quantity of iron in May of 1792. By the twenty-eighth of April, when the Austrian Emperor attacked Lille, Isaiah had got together just enough iron for his delivery. But he didn't deliver.

Pretending to be short, he wheedled and pleaded for three months' grace. In exchange, he offered to supply the Assembly with rifles. He had learned from his village dealers that agents of the government had been scouring the countryside for useable rifles of all sorts. It was apparent that the French now needed rifles more than they did cannon.

Shortage had driven up the Paris price of iron, and Isaiah was easily able to borrow gold on the value of the scrap he'd collected. By now he knew that the price of scrap would go even higher, and that if he could manage to hold onto his iron he could make a killing. But he'd promised rifles, and he had more than a killing in mind.

With half the gold, he sent his eldest son, Noah, riding far south of the Seine to buy up all the iron he could. With the other half he rode to Calais, where he boarded a fast vessel to Amsterdam. He placed an order with the Dutch arms merchants for 43,000 rifles, using his gold as down payment. On returning to Paris, he discreetly sold the scrap Noah had bought cheaply in the south for more than double the price at which he had originally agreed to deliver scrap to the Assembly.

He could now easily repay his loan. Instead, Isaiah returned to Amsterdam and covered the delivery of half the rifles he'd ordered. They arrived in France in time for the major conflict, which broke out in August. For his rifles, Isaiah accepted the Assembly's promissory note, and at the same time he delivered at the contracted price the scrap iron he'd pledged to deliver, accepting again a promissory note in payment. He now had an outstanding loan equal to the June value of his scrap, a government note equal to something less than that, plus another promissory note equal to the value of some 21,000 rifles. Isaiah's future depended on the government paper he was holding.

From August to late in September, the French armies kept retreating. At Verdun, where Beaurepaire had surrendered, the Prussians began a march on Paris, aided on September eleventh by the Count d'Artois who brought with him six thousand horsemen. On the fourteenth, the French abandoned Chalons-sur-Marne, a hundred miles from the capital. The hopes of the anti-Monarchists sank, but six days later Kellermann defeated the Prussians at Valmy, and the following day the jubilant Convention proclaimed the Republic. The French army took heart and poured into Savoy. The Prussians were harried and outfought, until by October twenty-second they were driven completely out of France, and a week later they were pursued all the way to Frankfurt. By mid-November the French occupied Brussels, and all the financiers who'd been unwilling to extend credit to the revolutionary government were clamoring to do business with the victorious Republic.

Isaiah had no trouble selling the notes the Convention had assumed from the Assembly. He repaid his loan, and used the rest to pay for and ship the final lot of rifles, which arrived well before Holland joined the coalition against France in the spring of 1793.

After final payment by the Convention, Isaiah's profit, for all his risk and effort, was not much more than a comfortable margin on the rifles. He'd provided the badly needed rifles, and he'd kept to his agreement to deliver the iron he'd promised at the price agreed on, even though the market price had doubled. His gamble seemed a vast display of faith in the Revolution, and from then on the Republic was to put faith in him. Isaiah's dealings in iron, gold, and rifles had graduated him from scrap. Historians would see, in his understanding of leverage, his nimbleness in different markets, his adroitness in international transactions, the beginnings of modern finance.

Isaiah Wolfflen, the Patriot Banker, had become the principal money-raiser for the army marching victoriously through Europe by the time the Terror came in the spring of 1794. He was safe from reproach, and prospering, but he was far from a tranquil man. The execution of the Royal Family a year and a half earlier had troubled him profoundly. Now the bloodthirsty crowds chasing the tumbrils gave him nightmares. The Revolution had turned into a heathen festival of blood: unreasonable, destructive, unpredictable. Like Mirabeau, Wolfflen had come to prefer a constitutional monarchy. He looked toward England, where the king assured a stable government while his subjects enjoyed the free pursuit of wealth.

Shortly before the fall of Robespierre, Isaiah put his oldest son, Noah, and a shipment of gold aboard a small boat that left under the cover of night from Saint-Vaast-La-Hougue to Southhampton. Noah was barely twenty-one, and Hannah took his leaving very hard. England was at war with France and God alone knew how long the conflict would last. She might never see her son again. Hannah was a simple woman, by all accounts. She'd been content in Mainz, delighted by Nancy, and was living a fairytale in the townhouse full of liveried servants in Paris. Probably she would have been totally happy to see all her children grow up and prosper close to her. But, dry eyed, she packed Noah bread soaked in beer and beef sausage—the rations she used to pack him for a night's ride from Nancy—knowing that he might never ride home again. The Wolfflens' private diaspora had begun. Bread soaked in beer and beef sausage. But Isaiah was already dreaming a dynasty.

Noah used his gold to found a small bank in Lombard Street. He and his father quickly set up a system of payments for trade between England and France, which functioned under the noses of both governments despite the hostilities. Instead of risking having to smuggle gold into France, English customers could pay Noah, who ordered Isaiah to make payment to French suppliers. In the same way, French merchants could pay Isaiah for their English imports.

Isaiah and Noah collected a commission at each end, while operating a simple ledger book between them, and using a corps of messengers to note their transactions.

To the French Committee of Public Safety, the Wolfflen messengers seemed dangerously like a network of spies. Isaiah was questioned by the police, and finally even jailed once. His reputation as the Great Patriot had worn thin with the *Directoire,* but the banking services he offered saved him from deep trouble. In 1799, however, the *Directoire,* having made a mess of the nation's finances, was in danger of reneging on its credit and was secretly envisaging heavy taxes on capital. Isaiah got word of the situation, and used his information to form his first alliance outside the family. Wolfflen had never spoken to the haughty Protestant bankers Le Coulteulx and Perregaux before that day he went to see them each, without an appointment, to tell them what he knew and what had to be done. He needed the prestige of their names, although years later their names would mean next to nothing to anyone while his would be legend. How precisely he pleaded his cause was of course never recorded. Almost none of Isaiah Wolfflen's words have been preserved, but when he left them he sent a messenger to General Bonaparte in Egypt. Bonaparte, on learning that the three bankers would underwrite his ambition to the extent of two million francs, turned the campaign against the Turks over to Kléber and headed for Paris, where on the eighteenth of Brumaire the well-armed Bonapartists proclaimed him First Consul.

As a younger man in Mainz, Isaiah Wolfflen had asked life just for freedom; he had a feeling for where history was going, and he wanted to be there, with his sleeves rolled up, to exercise his ambition. But the *Coup d'Etat* of the eighteenth of Brumaire, which he engineered, and Napoleon's inexorable progress toward coronation, matured his thinking. It became clear to him that being on the right side of historical pressures was far more important than being totally free, and he acquired the deep conviction that nothing important could happen without financing. He sharpened, clarified his goal; set for himself and his progeny the simple, sure task of raising money to help the inevitable come true.

When Bonaparte conferred a baronship on Isaiah, Daniel, his second-oldest son (who had an artistic bent that was to turn up in the family several times again), drew a coat of arms. Daniel was also a dandy, and appreciated lavishness. But Isaiah rejected his first design, and insisted on something sober, almost stark: a red wolf, rampant, on a gold field, with a triple-flamed brand in its right paw. His motto: *Virtus et Unitas.*

Isaiah's escutcheon was to give competitors an excuse to call him predatory. But there's no proof in history that he ever preyed on any man. He simply put his money in the right place, or in the hands of the right person, at the right time, ahead of other people. The worst that Bonaparte, after his second exile, could say about Isaiah de Wolfflen (in a letter to his former General Burin) was that he'd been "ungrateful." But had he a right to expect Isaiah to follow him blindly in his bad judgment? The week Bonaparte led his army into Russia, Wolfflen sent his second son to Austria. By the time, two years later, Napoleon had bled the nation with defeats, Daniel von Wolfflen had done wonders with Metternich's personal fortune, which he'd buttressed first of all with a 650,000-guilder loan.

Isaiah was on less good terms with Louis XVIII, the Bourbon whom Metternich put on the throne of France when Napoleon abdicated in the spring of 1814. Isaiah seemed to the King an obvious Bonapartist. Yet during the Hundred Days, after Napoleon's escape from Elba, Wolfflen was to prove what Napoleon called his "ingratitude" and what Isaiah considered his loyalty—not so much to the new ruler, but to history.

Bonaparte marched through France, gathering at every crossroad the elements of an army that followed him to Paris and caused the King to flee into exile. The Hundred Days were one of the headiest moments in the story of France. Isaiah de Wolfflen, however, studied what he knew of the strength of the nations united by the Treaty of Vienna, and saw that period for what it was: a moment, a last flurry of panache on the part of the ingenious little Corsican whose courage he appreciated greatly, but less than he did his own judgment. Like the King, Isaiah viewed Napoleon's return from afar. He "took sick" and went into the mountains of Savoy to care for his lungs. From his retreat, he sent a secret message to Louis XVIII, offering whatever assistance the deposed king might find useful. Three weeks after the Battle of Waterloo, in July of 1815, Isaiah returned to Paris on the same day as the King. He was Louis XVIII's most trusted financial counselor by September.

* * *

Was he a cynic, an opportunist, or a lucid realist? Trying to understand the man to whom he owed all he had, Marc de Wolfflen could get no further than the historians. Even in the family, the exact details of Isaiah's character, the full texture of his motives, were no more known than the exact details of his face. He'd left his imprint on great events; he was also a great philanthropist in an age when charity was niggardly and rare; he built hospitals, and on feastdays he would send his liveried men into the streets of poor neighborhoods, distributing pieces of gold. He gave more to the wretched than did the governments of his time. Perhaps, Marc thought, he felt simply that history had offered him no choice: he had either to assume what power he could in the world, or yield to the power of others whom he believed were profoundly inferior to himself. But again, he never showed any vanity.

When he was well past eighty he died placidly, without remorse, without regrets, accepting death as an inscrutable necessity, just as finally, perhaps, he had viewed his life as an inscrutable necessity, as naturally ordered as the events to which he'd married it. His will had no pious or philosophical chapters; it was just an inventory of who was to get what. The evening he knew he would never again leave his bed, he summoned all his children, and he waited weeks to die until both Noah and Daniel had arrived. Before expiring, he gave a short lecture. He exhorted his descendants to follow his example of philanthropy and he talked to them about the Industrial Revolution. In their lifetimes, he said, they would see rural Europe develop into a continent mechanized beyond anything he could imagine. The world would become far more complicated and competitive, and it was in the interest of the Wolfflens to work as simply as they could, strengthening their hold at the base of Europe's industrial economy. He advised his children to leave the intricacies of manufacturing and commerce to smaller people, to care for their friendships with men in power, and deal massively in what all the others would need: first of all money, then raw materials. To these he added transportation. The Baron Isaiah de Wolfflen's last word, as he expired near midnight on the twenty-sixth of July, 1830, was "railroads."

They listened to him, and they prospered. In banking, mining, shipbuilding, and railroads, and in the delicate financing of governments, they paid for the future and the future paid them back. Their money multiplied their power, and their power gave them more money. But Isaiah's ambition had its limits, of which he may have been aware. He'd begun his last and only lecture with "My poor children..." Perhaps he had indeed foreseen that the Industrial Revolution would burgeon beyond any one family's hope of domination, that a startling variety of needs and temptations would cause hungry competitors to spring up, and that some of them, too weak on their own, would join hands to take on the Wolfflens, that the years ahead would be full of battles. They were, and the Wolfflens won most of them, but they lost enough to see their power decline. And perhaps it was historically inevitable, too, that some of the Wolfflens, rich as they cared to be, would turn their backs on the conflict, developing other interests. Already, in Isaiah's lifetime, Daniel was spending much of his energy on lavish entertaining, a habit Benjamin, who was to inherit the French bank, was to ape.

In Reinhart Weil's *History of the Austrian Empire*, there is a brilliant description of one of Daniel von Wolfflen's dinners, taken from the letters of the Duke von Aschenbühl:

"The splendor of the ladies' silk gowns and their jewelry was nearly outmatched by the care the gentlemen had shown in their grooming and attire. The house was full of uniforms. There lacked only the decorations to make you think you were at a ball given by his Imperial Majesty. But the most splendidly dressed of all were the Wolfflen footmen, in red regalia, standing two to each step, on the staircase leading up to the first floor. Above, the heady commingling of the guests' perfumes suddenly encountered another gust of sweet effluvia. The great mirrored hall that led to the ballroom where tables were set had been planted with flowers. A path of mown grass led across this delightful lawn to the tables, on which the vermeil candelabra and plates shone through thick beds of orchids. At several places, among the tables laid for two hundred, blocks of ice had been placed. Not mere blocks, to be sure, but ice sculptured in the form of dryads. Behind the Baron von Wolfflen, there had been placed an ice sculpture of the goat-footed Pan. The use of ice to cool the room is something done in Russia, it seems. But I cannot imagine that the Russians have sculptors such as those of whom Wolfflen availed himself; nor would anyone in all of Russia, if not the Czar, have had the money to have given that memorable dinner of July 8, 1840."

The Wolfflens had the money, and never before in history had the future seemed to belong so clearly and simply to money. Aristocrats curried the Wolfflens' friendship for a chance to get into business. Perhaps it was inevitable that some of the family would pick up the manners as well as the unstriving world-view that some of their new friends could only half-heartedly discard. By the time the nineteenth century was three-quarters of the way over, Wolfflens had financed and built railroads in nearly every country of Europe, but Vivian Wolfflen of the English branch was riding year-round on all the lines, in his private train, hooting and whistling his life away at the controls of his locomotive. The younger sons of other rich families went out into the colonies, into the army or the church. But younger and older Wolfflens alike became artists, scientists, and daft eccentrics. Vivian with his choo-choo, Yvor with his zebras, and Charles' own brother, Jean-Nathan, martyred for dubious knowledge about maneaters. Vincent had probably cared more about the Crown than his bank, and neither of his sons, not Ian the biologist nor Herbert the brilliant public servant showed more than passing interest in perpetuating their wealth.

Perhaps it was all written into history, as Isaiah might have put it, from the Beginning: that a waning of common interests would cause the family ties to fray, that those Wolfflens who did their best to persevere in finance would not have the network of support their ancestors had. *"My poor children..."*

They were rich. They were, by Marc's generation, all as rich, perhaps, as anyone sane could ever care to be. But neither they nor the world of money was what it had been. Put together, their money might make them the richest family in Europe, but it had been a long time since they'd thought of putting more than a little of their money together. The ties were frayed, the interests dispersed; there were painful jealousies.

All that was Marc's legacy. And if Isaiah's wisdom still held, he'd have to make something new of it, to be on the side of history again. Yet the times were unpredictable, his way wasn't clear to him, nor were even the impulses of his own heart. Who knew Marc? Not even Marc. He was a man of facets, with whole sides of him still undefined. One thing seemed clear to him in the tenebrous, yammering bazaar which was the France he'd returned to from a Manichean war: he was a Wolfflen. That definition was inescapable, it formed a context and a scale of measurement for whatever he would accomplish. It offered a game of high stakes to inspire him. All right, he'd play. But how ... with what strategy ... when?

So, as the confused year 1947 drew to a close, Marc de Wolfflen's personal uncertainty matched his country's. He knew moments, even, when the wild hope of another war would flash through him uncontrollably. War would give him once again the patent enemy faint regions of his consciousness craved, but in the daylight of reason, he didn't want war, nor could he look on his father as an enemy. He let each inconsequential day at the bank take care of itself.

In any case, war didn't come to France. Though there were skirmishes in the colonies, Madagascar, Algeria, far off in Indo-China, there was neither war nor civil war. The day after the government obtained its right-to-work law, it sent tanks to the occupied mines, factories, and railroad stations, and dislodged the strikers. A few people were shot, but no uprising followed. Within a week, the Communist leaders of the CGT union called off the strike. Soon after, a large portion of the union, financed by the American Federation of Labor (and as time would reveal, the Central Intelligence Agency), seceded. Another tremor of labor unrest passed over France a year later, but the French calmly plodded forward, inspired by nothing more exalting than the promise of prosperity through the Marshall Plan.

Half a lesson was there for Marc, though he'd need a few years to see it. Meanwhile he plodded forward, more vaguely than most people. But there were to be moments, as the century moved towards its midpoint, when Gaston Robinet, advisor to General de Gaulle, felt even more uncertain of his future than the Baron Marc de Wolfflen.

FIVE

Midway through his stroll in the village of Zermatt the Baron paused, as he'd often done in the past, at the little cemetery. He turned off the packed snow of the roadway and poked his way with his cane and his clumsy fur-lined boots, on a crust above inches of powder, each step a tiny plummeting, until his foot found both support and resistance. This trekking through the unplowed snow with powerful, deliberate strides made him feel like a giant. His health had been improving, and he enjoyed those few yards of fantasy more than any exercise he'd had in a long time. They took him to the part of the graveyard that interested him, where the village buried people who died attempting to climb the Matterhorn. The ends of the dead climbers' picks poked through the snow beside some of the little markers. Once Charles had thought he'd offer Zermatt a monument to these dead, something more impressive than the modest graves and rusting picks, but he'd changed his mind. He'd realized that these low stones and little tools were precisely what was fitting. They preserved the scale between the dead who'd enacted, in their beautiful vanity, life's essential story, and that hostile peak of ice and granite. Like an enormous tooth, it stood blatant in the sunlight, snow blowing in a powder where the thick base was capped by the final, deadly spur of granite. Did they die hating it? If they were the men he believed they were, they surely did not die hating it, he thought. True horsemen never hate a horse that throws them. Men who try to master their lives are not men who hate the world that gives them their chance at mastery. He himself loved nature as a horseman or a mountain climber loves nature. These dead, whom Charles could not pass without paying homage, had known the one kind of failure he could admire.

Back on the road, he felt mellow, content. The sun was good, the air pure and lightened by silence. Then, as if in a fairytale, a horse-drawn sled came jingling by, bringing some people up from the electric cog-railway station. The horse slowed to defecate. The golden manure steamed and sent a rich, fermented smell into the air. Charles smiled, for even that event was something that pleased him; everything natural was right. We've no other standards to guide us. Nor did he mean just tooth and claw nature, for that was a pinched view of the world, a reasoning for nastiness. No, he thought, kindness was natural too, and charity. What was unnatural, then? What was corrupt? Ah, we know that, he answered himself, just as we know spoiled food. The world didn't need new morals. It needed more courage, and charity that wasn't given out of guilt, like amends. But now the Baron wasn't happy with the little ontological deliberation that passed through his mind. He wasn't happy, at the moment, to generalize. He breathed deeply, and hungered for the apple tart he was going to eat in the Konditerei at the crossroads.

And the tart was everything he'd hoped it would be. He swept the sweetness of the glazing from his tongue with hot sips of tea. Charles was no *gourmand,* but in this world there was a perfect time for everything and now, at eleven in the morning after an hour's walk in the cold, dry air, it was the perfect time for a sweet little reward. Smells of buttery *Weinachtstollen* being baked wafted through the doorway of the workroom. Here there was cleanliness and light and warmth and peace. How happy he was to be in Switzerland. There were newspapers hung on varnished rods near his table, but he didn't stir himself. He could see the dark headline of the *Neue Zürcher Zeitung.* One hundred five thousand American troops and ninety-eight-thousand civilians had been evacuated at Hung-nam. The Chinese were still pouring across the Korean frontier. There was also an analytical article about the chances of the new French High Commissioner, General de Lattre de Tassigny, for pacifying Indo-China. But Charles let his temptation to reach over for the paper recede. He would be reaching to the other side of the world, and he was happy to stay where he was, gathering strength and joyful courage, even during this little moment of pleasure, for a winter of hard work at the bank. The Americans would manage. As for Indo-China, he recalled that certain of his rivals had rubber plantations there. It was for them to worry. He'd paid for his lesson about investing in the Far East before the war.

Think of something else. And suddenly the tart in front of him, the thought of investments, brought to mind his cousin Saul. In an interview, Saul had once recounted that he'd decided to go into petroleum while eating a pastry in a café on the Mariahilfer Strasse. Madcap Saul. Poor Saul, poor fool. It was now five years since they'd spoken to each other. Poor Saul was afflicted with the gene of headstrong eccentricity that ran through the family, was afflicted—no other term seemed right to Charles, as a way to explain the unending feast of hostility Saul had made of his estrangement, since that crazy burial of his awful second wife. Of course, Bruno had behaved just as madly. But think of all the young man had gone through.

Since then, the family had come together again to bury Vincent. Saul and his joyless little boy had spoken to no one that day, but each other, Ian, and Herbert. Charles could see them again now, the rain soaking the bright green lawn, and the two of them against a background of chalky and coal-black English gravestones, in *yarmulkas* instead of brimmed hats, water all over their faces, outsuffering the other mourners. Poor, stubborn Saul. And then, once again, in February of '49, he and Saul had crossed paths on the steps of the Cercle Interallié, where fate had it that Charles, who almost never frequented that club, had accepted some other member's invitation to a business lunch. They walked in nearly side by side. Charles had tried to catch his cousin's eye, but Saul deliberately turned his head away. Charles had been tempted to take his cousin's arm, but by the way his face had reddened and his moustache seemed to have tensed, who knows, he might have made a scene. Our differences are our own business. He thought "our differences" in a way that gave them a certain dreary, institutional finality. Ah, but sadly, the whole world knows of them. No help, perhaps. The next day Saul had withdrawn his membership in the Cercle Interallié.

Help what can be helped. Forget what cannot. Finish your pastry, he told himself, and your tea, delicious tea, and use today well.

Eveline was back at the hotel under an eiderdown, with a heap of books all over her bed. She'd begun sniffling the day they'd arrived from Paris. "Delightful," she'd said, dabbing her inflamed little nose with a handkerchief, "I'm getting a cold. I can lie in bed for a week and do nothing but read." Since the children weren't coming it didn't much matter. Tonight they would finesse the Christmas cheer by having a splendid rogue and kept-woman's bedside dinner. Eveline would recount *Sodom and Gomorrah*. She was a rapid and highly sensitive reader, and hearing her describe a book was almost reading it and sometimes better. "If my cold holds up, I will get through all of Proust. All the way to the letters to the Countess de Noailles. I'll have conquered heights!" She'd ordered dozens of books to be sent, express, from the Avenue Foch.

"Get some oxygen," she'd urged when he awoke this morning. Her room had the bitter smell of medicine. "Don't languish with me."

He'd submitted his program for her approval: "First I'll walk around the village, I'll have some tea, then take the *Zug* up to Sunegge where I shall eat lunch, watch the skiers, and be back."

"Just go gently," she'd cautioned, assenting.

It was eleven-thirty. He had a half-hour to stroll down to the cog-railway station.

There were only a handful of skiers going up at midday. The nearly empty train advanced with a steady clang and got him to his destination five minutes ahead of the timetable. On the terrace of the restaurant, where the sun was strong enough for him to sit with a grog outdoors, he watched a handful of skiers come down from the run that ended practically at his feet. The tiny figures would grow and grow as they zigzagged down the last slope then poled themselves across the flat, blurred and radiant in the sunlight like visiting gods, until, big as life, they were before him in a wheeling rush of snow. One by one. Two by two on the flat. They left their skis at the edge of the terrace and went in to eat. He followed them, his head full of memories of this run and others. He partook of the same menu they did, alone in his corner of a rough wooden table. Sausages and a great mound of warm potato salad. But, not having worked up the appetite the others had, he picked at his food. The day was not turning out quite right. He realized that he was bored.

Afterward, he decided to walk alongside the railway tracks. Except for where the Matterhorn towered with bleak sovereignty, all the other juts of the landscape were rounded and made gentle by the thick snow. It stretched, shadowed blue, in all directions, from the thin track. Charles thought of the moon. Ten minutes later, a path went off to the left, cleared and beaten with prints. He turned off and followed it toward a precipice. He knew the place. There was an exceptional view. He was happy to spy another walker at the end of the path, a Swiss with one of those greased and weather-worn haversacks, a man about his own age, Charles judged, but thin and wiry. He was wearing leather knickers and just a sweater.

"Good day," Charles said, in the accent of his school German.

"Good day," the man answered, in soft, homely Swiss-German. He did not turn around from his view. "How small," he said, after awhile. awhile.

"How small, sir?"

"How small we are."

Since there was only one rock to sit on, the man politely rose and turned to leave.

"Praise God."

"Praise God."

The old Swiss set off briskly. A few yards down the path, his curiosity got the best of his politeness, and he flicked his head round quickly to get another look at the tall, heavy man in the fox-lined city coat.

Charles sat on the cold rock and took in the view. He was just at the edge of a drop that went off sheerly to the right and sloped to the left a long way down to a plateau. The mountains on the other side were in Italy. It was peculiar, he thought, to conceive of Italy as a cold place.

The Baron rose to stretch and breathe deeply. Height bothered him in the city—he could recall getting dizzy on someone's eighth-floor terrace—but here at the edge of a great natural precipice he felt totally at ease. He stretched again, stood there with his arms out, like some savage invoking his god, until something seemed to rush along his cold left leg, hot as a flame. Then the leg went numb, it buckled and he fell. He tumbled to the left, rolling while his cane skidded past. He rolled until he hit with a thump that sent a shock through his back, like the shock of a drill hitting the nerve of a tooth. He couldn't get up. All his limbs felt numb, and, as he tried to shout, he could only moan lowly, in no language. Somewhere above, voices passed and faded in what must have been Schwyzerdütsch, but as they reached him across the blue-white, muffling expanse of snow, space seemed transfigured into time, and it was over a long stretch of time that he believed he heard voices, or a voice, calling, coaxing, in what he took for Yiddish.

SIX

"Marry me . . ."

"What?"

She was far ahead of him on the dike, and the wind was blowing from her to him.

Now she strode toward him, heedless of puddles. It was very early in the morning, no one else was stirring out; she advanced, a lone figure on the gray dike. Watching her, he felt like a ghost luring one of the living. He felt something resembling guilt. Everyone took him for a reckless roughneck, and no one knew the *holes* that could suddenly appear in Bruno's life, moments when he would begin to plummet: his spirits, his hopes, his self-esteem, all falling . . . On both sides of them, sparse snow lay like a counterpane of lace on the putty-colored sand. The tide was coming in fast and the racket the gulls made sounded as if they were egging it on.

"You walk like a boy," was all he could say when she came up to him. She slipped her arm onto Bruno's and wheeled them both around to gaze, once again, on One of Man's Great Wonders, Mont Saint-Michel.

"I'm bored," he said.

"I die for a cup of coffee," she said, and pulled him toward the island.

"You know we're so very alike," he said.

"What are you trying to sell me?"

Had she heard? He flushed.

They had been seeing each other for a month. And now they were in Normandy not to admire monuments but to get away to somewhere they'd be anonymous. Paris was talking.

Bruno had met Edmée at the tennis court of the Polo de Paris, and he'd dared play against her. She'd whipped him three sets in a row, during which he'd scored a total of three points. But off the court, things had gone better for him, he believed. He'd been her lover for a month, and yet he feared that if he'd *ask her,* she'd bolt like a half-tamed young mare and run from him forever. If he asked her to marry him.

He loved her. He didn't care to *diagnose* why. She was straight waisted, and perhaps when she got older—she was only twenty-three—she might put on too much weight above her hips. Her athlete's arms were rather too muscular to look well poking out of a ball gown, and her hands were far from elegant. Her little upturned nose, freckled face, and thick red hair had once made him tease: "You look like a Breton cowmaid, Edmée." He didn't care.

They had coffee in their room at the Mère Poulard, and sitting there fully clothed on the bed that had served well his cause that night, he found courage, but not enough to say it right:

"Look here," he began, "let's make a commitment..."

"Don't talk business! We'd better move on..."

When she stood up he slipped his hands under her skirt, all the way up until the cold smoothness of her stockings turned into the warmth of her thigh. He drew her backwards onto the bed with him, and they tumbled through a flurry of kisses. She pulled away and got up.

"What do you want?" she asked.

"I thought it was obvious," he said.

"No, I mean ... all told," she said, straightening her hair, "I mean I don't even know what makes you tick."

"When I'm all wound up, I tick."

"Yes, you're so full of energy."

"Don't mock me, Edmée. If you don't want me, just tell me to go to hell, that's all."

"I want to know you better."

"I want," he said abruptly, "to be a king!"

"You're already a baron, isn't that enough?"

"I want to be king of the barons!"

"You love a fight, don't you?" she asked.

"A good fight."

"I suppose you'd like to fight your cousin, people say that."

"Marc?"

"Yes, you know exactly what I mean."

"We had a fight once. We were kids."

"Who won?"

"The way I see it, we both did."

"That didn't satisfy you—did it?"

"I can't say it did. We've got a problem, though, you see. Essentially, we're very fond of each other."

"I don't understand. I love to win. I go into a tennis match and I can kill the other girl, but after it's over all I want is a shower. I don't want to win at everything. I love the game, winning gives the game a meaning, but when I'm too old and slow I'll get just as much pleasure out of knitting for my children."

"You don't understand a man's life."

"And you do."

"I'm a man."

She didn't answer.

"I'm a man!" he shouted." He beat his chest like King Kong, then he seized her and covered her face with kisses. "I'm your man."

She was silent, withdrawn, as they drove along the shore eastward, he didn't know to where. The sky was clear, the sun shone, and it seemed to have enforced an unusual calm on the wintry water. There was no wind; it was as if they'd driven into a strange envelope of clement weather, in which the growl of his speeding MG was an aggressive intrusion.

"I feel a slack," he ventured.

"Uh . . . hmm."

He drove until they reached a promontory where he pulled up on the grass. He didn't know what town this was. Behind, mock-Tudor nineteenth-century summer houses stood out, in erratic lots, their windows blinded with red shutters. He wondered how they'd survived the invasion five years ago ... Perhaps there had been more of them, destroyed, traceless now. He brought his mind back to his own cause:

"Marry me," he said. "Let's make a vow, all right? If not it will be all too easy between us, and what's easy gets slack. Take a chance with me, Edmée ..."

He'd said it, just standing there apart from her, blocking her view of the blue water, both hands at his sides.

She looked at him with her arms folded, like a child about to accuse another of cheating at a game.

And she said "yes," as if he had just said "no."

They came to a fishing village built of granite, and they stayed there a week in a pleasant little hotel which had been converted from a railway station. The train no longer stopped at Barfleur, it hadn't for years. The hotel, converted in the thirties, was called L'Hôtel Moderne. A week, during which they waited for birth certificates to arrive and papers to be done. He forbade the posting of bans, as was his right as a citizen according to Section 169 of the civic code. He'd read all that in secret before they'd left Paris. He'd prepared an elopement like a burglar studying his next job. Quite as nervously. No one would know until afterward. They wasted time walking along backroads and drinking in the café beside the granite church with an arthritic old sailor. His name was Edouard. They bought him "bogneaus" as he called his mixture of *pastis* and *cassis* liqueur. *"Bonne eau,"* sweet as a child's drink. He knew songs from the Franco-Prussian War, and had served on a submarine chaser in 1914—a disguised sailing vessel, fitted out with guns to fire suddenly on U-Boats surfacing to attack it.

Edouard had seen only one submarine.

It had surfaced, and an officer had come out with a camera and taken a picture of the sailing boat.

"Did you fire?"

"How could we have fired? He was taking our picture!"

A week later the sailing vessel was blown in half by a torpedo.

Edouard said *"j'avons,"* the way they did in the eighteenth century, and once he asked, autographing a photo of himself for Edmée, "what year are we?"

Bruno and Edmée's room at the Moderne was all floral and rustic.

He found it strangely familiar, like a room he'd known in a dream. He wasn't sure whether a dream or a nightmare. The seafood was delicious in the dining room downstairs, which was hung with nineteenth-century amateur paintings, seascapes.

When the papers were all ready, Bruno brought Edouard and a half-dozen of his friends from the café to the town hall, as witnesses. Two by two, he crammed them into the MG and gave them the hair-raising little ride they'd been dying for.

It wasn't until they were at the town hall the Bruno and Edouard each discovered exactly who the other was. The mayor pointed out to the Baron that Edouard Boisard, Chevalier of the Legion of Honor, had captained the life-saving crew credited with rescuing more sailors and airmen out of the Channel than any other crew.

"Twenty-two, not counting Germans," Edouard confirmed.

Bruno treated everyone, the mayor, his wife the witnesses, their wives, to a festive lunch at the Moderne. He ordered lobsters and everything else that was expensive.

No one was rude enough to tip off a newspaper. That summer, however, when the tourists came, the marriage of the Baron Bruno de Wolfflen to Edmée Carrières the amateur tennis champion of France, was recounted to any stranger who cared to listen. The Wolfflen wedding had entered the annals of Barfleur. And on a table in her bedroom in the Rue de l'Université, Edmée de Wolfflen was to keep always an antographed photo of the life-saving champion of the English Channel, dated December 23, 1950.

"You've married me," he'd said, triumphant, on the steps of the town hall. "I've won."

"That's exactly what I wanted to do," she'd parried.

"Call it a draw," he'd said.

He'd kissed her—for the crowd, for himself, for her—several times, and she would always remember how his mouth tasted sweetly musky, a little like clover.

SEVEN

For the village doctor, it was a miracle. The man was seventy years old. It was his second stroke, and he'd lain out there until nearly nightfall before they found him. But along with, perhaps, the angels, he'd had a fur-lined coat to protect him. The weather was unusually clement, and his will to survive was obviously made of iron.

They brought him down from the mountain in a coma, but he came out of it almost immediately with an injection of procaine. His left leg remained paralyzed. The village doctor, whose great expertise was fractures, found no bones broken and advised the Baroness to send him to Zürich as soon as he was strong enough to be moved.

Charles stayed on at the Steg Clinic in Zürich for two months. They did everything to his leg—all sorts of baths, massage, exercise. They gave him cortisone, and on his strong insistence they allowed the famous chiropractor from Geneva, Dr. Illi, to have a look at him. But the Baron came out, when crocuses were popping through the grainy soil of the clinic garden, in a wheelchair. Beside the lake where the grounds ended, he sniffed the trace of juvenescent sweetness in the mist, and wondered whether now that part of his body had already gone dead to his control, he was entering his last springtime on earth. But Charles didn't like to persist at questions for which, either personally or by delegation, he couldn't come up with an answer. The matter was outside his own expertise, and he'd already delegated the director of the clinic to reply. "You can live ten more years or ten more minutes," the doctor had answered, a guileless Swiss. "It's like that, apoplexy."

As Firmin wheeled him to the Rolls for the long drive home, the Baron put the question out of mind for good.

He spent much of the gentle Paris spring in his garden, Avenue Foch. He discovered that he could go on doing business from home, but long meetings would tire him and he judged, coldly, that his effectiveness in affairs was reduced by roughly the same proportion as the movement of his body. He consoled himself by repeating to Eveline the adage of mistresses: that part of a good man was better than all of a bad one. Eveline became the arbiter of his appointments. She quickly got to know who was worth how much time, and she had no compunction about breaking into meetings she felt were going on too long for the the person and the subject. She could chase people with the gentlest admonitions—firm all the same, but which would come out sounding to the visitor like flattery. Charles never tried to mitigate her judgments. He knew that, caught up in the details of business, he would lose his awareness of the pace his health made necessary. If it weren't for Eveline, he'd end every day as he did the few days she happened to be absent: trembling with fatigue. He was proud of his wife's efficiency and proud that it did nothing to spoil her manners. The world was getting rougher, as he could well judge by the parade of people passing through his own house. Not all the businessmen of 1951 knew quite how to enter rooms such as his, how to sit in them, how, simply, to talk to a man like himself. Eveline's good breeding was a moralizing force on the days he berated himself secretly for having turned his home—and hers—into something like a doctor's or a lawyer's office, where people seemed to exude with their nervous hopefulness an unhealthy effluvia, and a grit they carried in from the world outside.

The one visitor she accorded great indulgence was Gaston Robinet. Eveline would let Charles' meetings with Robinet go on without interruption, since her husband seemed actually to gain strength from being with that man. Robinet had accentuated something in his manner: the certain humor his eyes revealed, which saved his deference from obsequiousness. He *was* deferent, but wore the ease of a man confident that anything short of being precise would do neither his listener nor himself any good at all. "He treats me as an equal," Charles had said three years earlier, appreciatively but not without a certain probing wariness. Now he liked to repeat: "Robinet is solid. When you speak to him, things never go out of focus."

"Solid," Eveline had echoed with a wink the first time she'd heard that comment from her husband. For the gentleman had put on weight. He'd recently been married, and she presumed his sudden girth came from his having married a woman whose dowry afforded him a good cook.

"Ah no, she hasn't all that," Charles said, savoring gossip, "her father is still looking him over. You see it's an *occupational* thing. He's a politician. He eats all that heavy lunch at the Brasserie Lipp, and he has to stand around absorbing canapés at two, maybe three, receptions every evening, before dinner. You see what private persons such as you and I are spared. If I showed up to eat *cassoulet* with someone at the Brasserie Lipp, all those deputies and editors at the other tables would presume that Wolfflen is plotting another eighteenth of Brumaire."

What were Robinet and the Baron plotting in the privacy of Avenue Foch? No *coup d'état*, but Charles was very anxious for a Gaullist victory in the June parliamentary elections, even though the General, who had his own list of compromising places to be seen, never came himself to the Baron de Wolfflen's townhouse. But Robinet would make Wolfflen aware, step by step, of the election strategy. In a sense, he was accounting to the Baron for how his money was being spent, but of course Robinet never couched things that way, and Charles was not the General's sole patron. There were a handful of men, old men for the most part, who like Charles felt deprived of high adventure. Romantics. Backing a candidate is always an investment, but those Gaullists surely knew they'd find a safer, more efficient return for their money by putting it in the hands of the right functionaries. Modern financial life was a daily crowd of events. And in the government, no one was better able to shine the brief light of approval, or discreetly to nudge forward one or another event in the crowd, than a *chef du cabinet*, a permanent secretary. Ministers were worth buying for rare grand projects, but Presidents risked becoming white elephants. Yet these old patriots fed on ancient dreams. No doubt they told themselves their business would be better, their personal power greater, under a Gaullist regime. But de Gaulle had never made quite clear, in details, what regime he foresaw. He talked about France's destiny as A Great Nation. No doubt, finally, in the minds of those old gentlemen such as Charles de Wolfflen, Charles de Gaulle's cause was the struggle of important souls against trivia. Yet in his conversations with the Baron, Gaston Robinet avoided any lofty cloudiness. That wasn't his forte. He knew specifically what was *wrong:* the Fourth Republic was a concatenation of incompetence; there had been ten bad governments in five years. When Robinet mentioned vigor and *élan,* Charles' face would gain color.

Robinet would often come to lunch, at which times Sara would arrange not to be at home.

Months before he had married, Robinet had telephoned after a lunch at the house, and invited Sara to accompany him to a dinner at the apartment of Pierre François-Lancet, the corporate lawyer who'd achieved celebrity in the high circles of Paris for his brilliance at work and the refinement of his table. Sara took the invitation for a bit of bad-mannered pluck on Robinet's part. They didn't know each other well enough for him to invite her anywhere. They saw each other only at her father's for lunch, and they had nothing else in common. She felt it must have been ambition that obscured in his mind the fact that Sara de Wolfflen could not show up at a dinner with someone presumed to be a stranger to her, unless she wanted to make a point by it, to *declare* she was seeing that person. Her usual dinner partners were childhood friends or safely homosexual, which meant in both cases she was *seeing* no one. Indeed she was seeing no one, and in no way intended to have people think she was seeing Gaston Robinet. She didn't think she was snubbing him. It was simply a fact that he was not the kind of man she'd enjoy being with, because for her he had nothing, not a shared background, nor any particularly novel talent. He was a politician. Her father's lunches with him weren't a matter of friendship. He should have seized all that, but he'd pushed himself where he had no right to intrude, and when he responded badly to her polite refusal, she was chilled by the perception of something cheaply cynical in his invitation. The hard, offended tone in which he'd said "very well, *mademoiselle,*" turned ironic as he repeated his *"mademoiselle."* She'd sensed that he'd dare ask because he'd desperately wanted to turn up with Someone at that dinner. At times since then, she wondered whether she had judged him harshly or too simply, whether she'd denied a certain romantic complexity that dwelled behind those bushy-browed sunken eyes. She was oddly relieved to hear that he had married François-Lancet's daughter, and troubled by something like guilt to learn that Robinet's new wife resembled her physically.

In any case, she stayed out of his way as he came and went at Avenue Foch, all spring long.

Sara, like Eveline, was happy for the cheer Robinet brought her father. Charles was in a heady mood for months. On June 21, the day of the elections, he voted early with his wife and daughter and took them to the Brasserie Lipp for lunch. He sat unself-consciously in his wheelchair and allowed no one at the neighboring tables to catch his eye; he managed to look rather boyishly arrogant. That evening the results began coming in over the radio and they sounded rather bad. He had the lights turned on in the garden, ordered dinner for midnight, and sat out alone in his chair, listening to the spring birds who year after year found a haven in his big garden. The sweet night fell, and then the chirping was pierced by the sound of the telephone in the house. It was Robinet, calling from the Ministry of the Interior, where the results were being tallied. They'd lost. By now it seemed clear that de Gaulle would not get much more than twenty percent of the vote. The Communists might get more than twenty-five percent. But it was apparent that the existing coalition would be able to put its factions together, and go on ruling.

"The people will have the government they deserve," Robinet said.

"They always do, my good friend," Charles answered. "But don't worry for the General, his time will come ... Don't worry for your own future, either, Monsieur Robinet."

When he hung up, he wheeled himself close to the fireplace of his library, where lilacs had been placed on the hearth. He stared at the flowers a long time, like a man gazing at embers. At dinner, Charles had them finish the bottle of champagne he'd ordered and asked Firmin to bring another.

Next morning at breakfast, he told Eveline that their lives lacked amusement and that he'd decided to give a ball.

EIGHT

The ball that the Baron Charles de Wolfflen gave at Roquebrune near Monte Carlo in July of 1951 was a milestone of social history. It was the first ball of any importance since the war, the first time in more than a decade that people of social prominence from all over the continent and even from America came together. In its splendid decor and preparations, it outshone the great balls given by Count Etienne de Beaumont and the Duke de Doudeauville in the thirties. Few of the high socialites invited knew beforehand just how many people there would be, and some of these "best people" were not happy, finally, with the crowd they encountered. They failed to realize that the Baron de Wolfflen was not simply reviving balls that evening, he was altering the tradition, gearing it to the age. His *Bal du Roi Soleil*, the Sun King Ball, was the first party in European society that American columnists could call a "blast." Henceforth that term, later prefixed by the words "jet set" would be a viable cliché for more than twenty years.

The Baron allowed in every photographer who asked to attend, and there were perhaps forty of them. He required them only to wear the powdered wigs, breeches, and brocaded frock-coats that the other "nobles of the court" were wearing. Some of the photographers came with their women, who, although they obviously couldn't afford the period gowns the other female guests had had made at the couture houses, did their best to fit in with faded theatre costumes. A few of the photographers, unused to the hospitality extended them, got quite drunk; on this score, they were indistinguishable from many other guests. There was a definite mood of license by the time the party abruptly ended.

Life had the best pictures of all, in color, over four pages. But the most thought-provoking record of the event can be found in the mémoires of Albert de Feuillière, retired chief of protocol at the Quai d'Orsay, who was one of the most indefatigable socializers of the half-century following the First World War.

"Each time I have looked back in tranquillity at that strangely impressive event—its strangeness having since faded, of course—I have been troubled by the old Baron's motives," Feuillière writes. *"I hope that I am not doing a disservice to a great gentleman's memory, in noting, finally, that I cannot help but believe the Bal du Roi Soleil was a supremely artful act of contempt. But what art! What art ... a splendor flawed only in memory by that horrible accident that befell the Baron's daughter—I, for one, believe it was an accident.*

"Consider what reasons the Baron might have had to celebrate: he'd been living in a wheelchair for months, his health was poor. True, the Banque Wolfflen, pillaged by the Germans during the war, was well on its feet again, but its hope of gaining more power was greatly restrained by the implicit privileges of the handful of banks that had been nationalized. It was obvious he would be a handicapped competitor in any business in which the government of France had any influence—and in what important business had it not? Here we come to another of the Baron's great chagrins: All of Paris knew he had been strongly backing General de Gaulle in the legislative elections, and de Gaulle had failed to come to power. In many ways, the old Baron must have come to look up himself as an 'outsider.' His rather noble response was to invite everyone who was not, to a ball! The ball. The eccentric way he brought that huge party to an end, and the fact that he was never to receive again except intimately (his infirmity had already confined his social life to his own receptions) were to confirm my appreciation of the Baron's motives that night—

motives intensified, later, by the grief that was to strike him. I think, in short, that he had decided to pay the piper, so that a society gone decadent by his standards would dance for his bitter amusement. He held up a mirror to a world he himself refused to gaze on thereafter. But thanks to him, to his truly poetic règlement des comptes, how that world did sparkle!

"*But before I linger on descriptions, permit an old man who has seen much history with his own eyes to emphasize that this ball, this festival of frivolity, which the world has come to call futility, was in a serious way prophetic. If I were a moralist, I should use the word* symptom, *but the reader will pardon me for not presenting myself as anything more than a diplomat and a careful, albeit now weary, observer of what people who call themselves 'worldly' call 'the world'*—le monde des mondains. *Shoemaker, stick to your last. What I saw for the first time at the Baron's beautiful villa in Roquebrune I was to see many times again over a period of roughly twenty years, those years of postwar ebullient prosperity. The principal figures would change, some were to fall into various sorts of disgrace, or— what was to be considered worse—to fall out of fashion. For fashion was to be the supreme arbiter of the time. The figures would change, some of them, and some would prevail, as nimble at fashion as a Jesuit with his texts. But there at the Baron's party, for the first time, they were all assembled: the* new *set, so many they were quite literally a herd.*

"*Old regime nobles plying some successful trade, publicists with and without dubious titles, real estate speculators who entertained, diplomats such as your humble servant, politicians, high-living industrialists, photographers, journalists, film-makers, decorators. Yes, and the Baron had even invited the hairdressers responsible for the spectacular coiffures of the women. Here they were, for the first time consecrated by a stunning feast, the new court without a king, the new prosperity's restless* seigneurs, *the vassals of Fashion.*

"*A herd. And a herd with herd instincts. That love celebrities had of being packed together in an enormous crowd, as they were that evening, was to be one of the curious features of the period. From America, there came the slang expression 'making the scene.' For these people, the importance of the 'scene' was to be measured by the mass of scenemakers present, the number of names considered suitable for photographs on pages four and five of that inexplicably feared* franc-tireur *and arbiter of fashion and social prominence, the* Women's Wear Daily, *whose editors with the lint of the garment trade on their heels peered hungrily into the bakery window of every 'scene,' camera, pencil, and metaphorical machine gun in hand.*

"*Among 'scenes,' I can recall an evening with New York friends at a night club known as 'Arthur's,' a 'discothèque.' Outside, a line of humble people in degrees of finery stretched the length of the street. They were waiting to be allowed eventually in to the 'bad room' of this establishment vaunted by all the newspaper columnists. From the packed bad room it was nearly impossible to make out any of the celebrities in the 'good room,' who were also crowded* derrière *to* derrière. *I was told by my hosts that those people trying to find room to gyrate where there was none were the cream of New York City, but I am obliged to note there was an effluvia in the 'good room' more frankly animal than the musk of perfume. How could it have been otherwise? I think also of the ball given many years later, in 1972, by Giovanni Volpi in his palazzo on the Grand Canal in Venice. All along the canal, the Old Guard of the city had bolted its windows shut in disdain, but the gondolas kept coming until there was an immense traffic jam at the quay of the palazzo, and on the quay, in the hall, on the staircase, and in the ballroom not a person could move among the thousand or so people in black tie and evening dresses, not a person could literally take a step. The newspapers called it the party of the year.*

"*In 1951, Charles de Wolfflen, in all the fullness of his irony, had imposed the minuet for the early part of his evening. (In tribute to the old-fashioned, careful, and stylized pursuit of play that characterized the most interesting of those people, it must be said that at least a hundred of Wolfflen's guests had bothered to learn the steps in the three weeks since his invitations had gone out.) Afterward, a Negro band replaced the chamber musicians, and hell broke loose. But I am getting ahead of myself in the description.*

"*It would be best to begin by pointing out that for those guests who weren't already on the coast for the month, the ball actually began in Paris. At the Gare de Lyon. The Baron had hired a train, as tastefully furnished as the regular overnight* Train Bleu, *now, alas, no more than a legend. The fittings, the paneling inlaid with mother-of-pearl, the plush of the train the Baron had rented were as lovely as they'd been when the wagons were constructed, just before 1914 I* would judge. In the smoking car, the dining car, the sleepers, everywhere, there were fresh garlands of fleurs-de-lys. In the compartments, magnums of champagne stood in ice buckets, and there were hampers containing foie gras and beluga caviar for midnight snacks.

"I, who was not on that train, was told that bachelor guests found themselves sharing sleepers with beautiful young girls whom no one had seen before in society. I have never heard this from a source serious enough to trust. Adhering strictly to the fact that may have provoked the rumor, we may note that the Baron had invited the entire cabine of mannequins of the House of Dior. Since the collections were only two weeks away, the invitation sent Monsieur Dior into a panic. He put the danger to his work schedule in the balance with the publicity his house would accrue, and boarded the train with his troupe of beauties. He was said to have eaten his way through two hampers before retiring in the single reserved for him. Mere rumor again, perhaps.

"On arriving in Monte Carlo, the guests from Paris were driven to their rooms in the Hermitage Hotel. A subtle distinction was thus established between the quality of the guests who normally spent July on the coast, many of whom were at the Hôtel de Paris, and those who were brought down on a free excursion. It was most chic that evening to say one was staying at a villa, one's own or a friend's, or on a yacht. It was second best to say one was at the Hôtel de Paris, or the Old Beach. The Hermitage was a poor reference, for the time of those great commercial 'launchings' had not yet come, when the most noted people and often the richest were to be invited, all expenses paid, so as to garnish the publicized openings of hotels, communal resorts, and the premières of one kind or another—when, in effect, it had become more chic to be bought than to pay.

"The house in Roquebrune, which the Baron had acquired from the Princess Irina Bobrinskaya after the revolution in her country, stood on a steep hill (more craggy and abrupt than the hillock his father had created to set off his manor on Avenue Foch). It was, of course, the largest villa in the area, but not overdone, not too far along in fraud, so to speak, as were so many of those mock Renaissance, Belle Epoque houses on the coast. The first floor, all in stone instead of woodwork and gilding, was almost entirely one vast room; you came in and saw just the great staircase and the row of

'French doors,' as the Americans say, which gave onto the terrace. To the right, there was the Baron's study. Above there were chambers. Cleared of most of its furniture, the first floor's great hall was an ideal ballroom, and when all the doors were opened onto the terrace, the star-seeded Mediterranean sky was all there, a stark bichromatic fresco, framed by the thin doorways and the delicate marble balustrade of the terrace. Nature enveloped in art. That evening, the Beauvais tapestries of the great hall were garlanded with fleurs-delys (art framed by nature), and illuminated by hundreds of candles set in the vast crystal chandelier.

"The Baron, bewigged and in a gold-threaded frock-coat embroidered in Persian motifs, sat—far from self-conscious of his infirmity—in a chair of the period of Louis XIV, not a chair such as one sat in, normally, but one of those tooled leather-covered chairs in which noblemen were carried through the streets. Beside him to receive, his wife stood erect and dignified, that tiny woman who was such a source of strength to him, looking, in her period ball gown, like some perfect antique doll, were it not for her animated grace. Beside this pair, whose natural stateliness spoke of the theme they had chosen for the evening, the enormous boyeur—he seemed at least two meters tall—all in blue silk with a white wig, pounded the floor with a staff a half-meter taller than himself before and after calling out the name of each guest.

"The guests flowed through the hall onto the terrace, where, during the early part of the evening, only those who dared minuet lingered. The best people, they were, who had been bred to know that a ball was an ephemeral work of art, and a communal one, doomed to endure but an evening, yet demanding the finest contribution of everyone—servants, host, and guests—so that each detail would make the whole totally memorable—for everyone. The best people had taken great care with their costumes, each a fine bit of embroidery in the total tapestry, just as the cooks, the pastrymakers, the graceful footmen in exquisite livery had all outdone themselves. And so also, the best people had spent three weeks learning the minuet, to offer the beauty of the dance to their host. The others looked up from the formal gardens, accessible from the terrace by wide and elegant marble steps. They peered in curiosity for a little while, most of them, before attacking the cold meats set out on torch-lit tables. Fortunate it was, too, that they preferred the caviar, the lobsters, and the pheasant en ballotine *crammed with truffles to the dance. The terrace could never have held everyone.*

"*But the grounds were vast and so they absorbed 'the flow of humanity'—what other way to put it? Beyond the torch-lit formal gardens, divided by boxwood, hedge, and orange trees was a marble balustrade recalling the terrace, broken by another set of steps that led to a wide lawn, empty except for a few eucalyptus and a grove of lemons, which sheltered the swimming pool. Guests gathered around the pool or wandered over the dewy lawn, inhaling the air of the Midi, that unmistakable and unforgettable potpourri: sage, verbena, lemon, and whiffs of a warm sea. Beyond the lawn, there were no more torches; high rocks overlooked an inlet and glowed in patches under the moon, as if their light were welling outward from within. The sea was present as an odor, an expanse of gleaming, and a rhythmic insistence against the cliffs.*

"*At one point, wandering to the edge of the lights, I heard the tide shift, I think. I heard a rush of sea over the gravel between the rocks, which—in my still young enough, still romantic enough imagination— I associated with a burst of applause. As if there were a host of mysterious hands, hands of sunken extramortals who weave the pattern of the tides and of history, reaching up through the surface of that sea, the Mediterranean, kind, warm, and yet temperamental lake on whose banks we had pitched our civilization—hands applauding: us.*

"*Later, when the jazz band assembled on the terrace, all the flow of humanity rushed the other way. People came forth as if out of the trees and hedges and attacked the steps of the terrace for the opportunity to dance the 'be-bop.' There was great confusion* . . ."

Something was happening to the weather. Clouds had hidden the stars and a strange wind, not the mistral, was coming off the sea in a pulsing way. The torches smoked and gasped, their flames now straight and slender, now flattened, nearly horizontal. The sea could be heard raking the edges of the inlet with a strong undertow. Yet the air was light and crisp. Sara de Wolfflen sensed that these were the rare dry heaves of a storm that would pass without bringing rain.

The guests seemed to take little notice. The terrace was a bedlam now, the house jammed with dancers as well, and the steps to the garden made her think of a moment of Eisenstein's in Odessa run backwards. A while ago, someone on the steps had trod on a woman's gown, and it had torn as she pushed her way upward. There had almost been a fist fight, since the offender, who was likely drunk, had failed to apologize. The woman—who was she? Sara didn't know—had gone on about the cost, until someone piped up insolently from the rear, suggesting that the dress no doubt had been borrowed from the house whose name the woman was throwing around, instead of bought. "Enough, enough publicity!" he'd shouted finally. Sara thought she'd recognized the satirical voice of a friend since childhood, Pierre de Lussac. Sara had taken her distance. Here on the lawn, there was room and calm, and still the horn of the black musician could be heard without the faintest blur. Yes, the air was crisp. And the music was beautiful. There was no doubt that it was beautiful. As she passed the lemon grove, she heard people splashing in the pool.

"*A moi! A moi!* Come on, we're playing polo!"

"*A moi, chéri!*"

"Could you stay still a moment please sir, I'm using color..."

A light flashed. Something went *swock* on the water. An article of clothing, she guessed, or a wig. Sara turned and headed toward the dark, farthest edge of lawn.

The evening was filling her with confused emotions. There was a headiness to this party she could not put down simply to vulgarity. In some veiled, indomitable way, all this bacchanal was right and meaningful. Although God knows the vulgarity was at the same time shocking. That man Robinet. He'd come upon her as if he'd been stalking her, and had asked her to dance the minuet. She couldn't of course just say no. But the look his eyes shot forth was *triumphal,* as he moved that fattened frame of his with gestures that were positively mincing. He knew the dance. He was inflicting her with his self-satisfaction. Consciously, perhaps vengefully, inflicting her, it had seemed. She shuddered now, thinking about him, and yet he didn't seem to her a *bad* man, not evil really. There was just something in his *wanting,* his ambition, so almost childish that it imposed, on what sometimes seemed a total void of consideration, this pathetic, awkward, stiff crust of comportment. And yet all the intelligence seemed always there, active. Robinet made her think of some tragic play during which you could see underclothes peeping out of the hero's period costume. She couldn't laugh at him because of pity, because of a measure of respect even, but she didn't enjoy her feelings toward him one bit. They, as well as he, were somehow unseemly.

Bruno had saved her when the dance was over. Robinet was about to hunt down his wife to present to her and she might have been stuck with the two of them, for who could say what she was like? Sara didn't like her father's reputation. He was one of those expensive lawyers who constantly had their hands in things. Politico-business. A doer of deals. Bruno had come up, nodded to him—had Robinet noticed, as she had, the irony in that slow, decorous nod? He had beamed back, and before his smile had dissolved the two cousins were gone.

"Your suitor."

"Mon Dieu," she'd sighed.

"Bruno, where is Edmée?"

"Making up. Peeing, I actually suspect."

"Bruno, you know, it's so nice to have true romantic lovers in the family. Perhaps we all profit, perhaps even against our wills. Our own blood circulates faster, commanded by yours."

"Keep making fun of me, Sara, I'm capable of slapping, you know that."

"Oh no," she'd said, "oh really no. I really do mean it. Bruno, I really did so admire your eloping."

He'd flustered. "Well I had no choice, really, Sara. Here was this beautiful lady who, in a moment of weakness—madness?—was suddenly willing to sign a paper that she would put up with me. When you have a contract like that staring you in the face, you have to act fast."

He'd shrugged. "I suppose there are some trick clauses I failed to read."

"Bruno," she'd urged, "you really aren't as mad as we all think. You ought to like yourself more."

Then Edmée had appeared and slipped her arm around her husband's. A red-haired, freckled, frank girl. Healthy and pretty. Sara had liked her gesture; it wasn't possessive, she hadn't claimed Bruno, she'd linked up with him. The two women kissed each other on the cheeks.

"I haven't told anyone, but I'll tell you, Sara," Bruno had said. "I have shouldered, so to speak, my obligation to our great family." He patted his wife's abdomen. "Edmée is preparing us another of us. An heir."

"Ahhh!" Sara had taken both of Edmée's hands and kissed her warmly again. She kissed Bruno, but in a moment her two favorite lovers had melted away into the darkness and Sara had been once again alone.

The strange wind had stopped, but the sea was still noisy, and the jazz had just hit its stride. No one but her, on the grounds below the steps of the formal gardens, except for gigglers splashing in the lemon grove. She looked for an instant at the packed terrace, a flickering glow in the darkness, and turned toward the sea.

She saw the luminous rocks and it was as if memory struck her hard in the face. The light of summers long before the war made her squint. Here they had liked to bathe. They'd go down the "steps" as they called the natural path from rock to smaller rock, and walk into the sea from the narrow half-oval of beach, coming suddenly on the coolness, the gentle pain of the gravel. Then they'd bake themselves again on the granite, until the salt dried on their skin and prickled.

There had been one particular moment. They were both fourteen. Emilie, whose body had changed from a girl's to a woman's that winter, was lying facedown. Sara cast a sidelong glance at her, taking in the flattened rounds of her breasts, the curve of her back flowing down to her high, round buttocks. She reached her hand over, impulsively, and ran it along the fine down on Emilie's spine. Her friend's buttocks quivered, their salt-flecked skin puckered into gooseflesh. Then she rolled slowly over on her side, and smiled at Sara.

The memory of her leaning on her elbow in that sunlight made Sara's heart beat faster now, decades later, on a dark, confused night. She had reached out her arm and placed her hand behind Emilie's ear, as if she would draw her towards her, but instead she lay stiff-armed, and in an instant she burst into tears. Emilie bounded up and scurried down to the water. Her smile, Sara would always believe, had been an invitation. To what? What might have happened? Nothing could ever have happened; Sara would never have allowed anything to happen. What she wanted, not even allowing herself to *see it* in her mind, was unnatural. What both of them perhaps wanted. And she knew that if she had it all to live over again now, she would still do nothing. It was not something moral, not a question of *sin*. What she'd wanted was ugly, she believed, because it was a deforming, a corruption of the natural. What was natural frightened her, but between being *a freak* and being celibate, only one choice seemed honorable to her. Nature seemed to her a stern, cold parent whose ways were all the same just, a parent she would not dishonor herself by dishonoring.

Afterwards, she and Emilie never let themselves play with fire, although she was sure now they'd loved each other more than any other two friends ever had. Next day, Sara came to the rocks in a bathing suit. By implicit agreement they drew a curtain over a part of their lives. Yet after Emilie was married, she took care to say very little about her husband to Sara. The subject made them both ill at ease. Sara thought her friend had married a totally banal man, but perhaps she was very happy, as far as that side of her life went, perhaps Emilie and her husband had drawn great pleasure from each other.

Sara shuddered again. Emilie had married a short-legged Dane with a prominent rump, a pale, blond, even-faced man, heir to a shipbuilding fortune, who'd gone to Winchester and was more English in his hee-haw mannerisms than any dry Englishman. An image came to her of the two of them dancing together—at whose party?—Emilie in a gown cut very low, revealing her lovely back, her gentle shoulders. In the front you could see her belly distended from bearing children . . .

She'd gone with her short-legged Danish stallion most of the way out of Sara's life, and then, a few years later, she was dead of her tumor in the head, snuffed out, and it was likely that she'd died happy.

Sara stepped out on the rocks. She felt suddenly quite miserable. She didn't know where to turn now, who to look for. And after tonight, she would wake up, feeling again the inexplicable cheer that came naturally to her with the simple presence of morning, and subsided as the day slid towards noon, wondering who to see, who to call—and should I think a little more today about Burne-Jones? She was alive and had days and days and days and days to cross through, to fill . . .

On impulse, not wanting to think of anything any longer—not just now in the dark harboring memories—she raised her skirts and made her way down the "steps," leaving her pumps behind her. The gravel gave her feet its rough pleasure. Then the sea licked at her toes and stole tiny eggs of stone from under them, making her wobble. The water was very warm. She hiked her skirts higher and began to walk out. She walked until the sea sloshed at her knees, and then suddenly a swell came in and struck her hard below the waist. She reeled and then another wave struck her. The undertow sucked her legs. Stumbling, she turned her back on the water and ran as best she could back toward the rocks. Danger. But what danger was there really in dying? Oh no, no, she wouldn't ... unnatural ... a question of honor. And now her heart swelled with sudden optimism. Her chest seemed to unbind as she breathed the wet air. She had, in any case, little to lose: this life. Everything was easy then: she'd live, find the place she could trade this little—and live, somehow, more rightly. And it would be far from here, far far, far from the crowd on the terrace, all that, and from the house too, and memories, far. Far from the family.

She knew a path that ran between boxwood at the edge of the property. She saw herself alone there now, there already, flanking the revelry, on the path that led to a servant's door, and backstairs. She moved forward, holding her ball gown out of the water like a cumbersome banner, until, realizing it was not really precious to her, she let it fall. It hit the water at the same time that an enormous wave struck her from behind. She tumbled and was battered. Her face slammed into the gravel. She felt herself lifted in a high surge, then battered down again. Then, in a swirl of cloth and water, she was moving, backwards it seemed. But she was no longer sure of backwards or forwards, nor of up or down. She was underwater, and a flowing and a stinging at her temple made her feel she was bleeding. Her head reeled. She opened her mouth to scream, and the sea burned in.

Among all the bright costumes, Firmin's worn black summer suit looked strange. He could have brought to mind the guard in a museum, if the mood in the Baron's house were not so totally unlike that of a museum. "The place was rollicking," to quote the cable Nancy Farrow, the society columnist of the New York *Daily Mirror,* filed the morning after. Firmin made his way through the resplendent euphoria feeling in no way out of place. If the Baron had wanted him to dress up, he would have said so. There had been apparently no need. These people, Firmin thought, were *figurants,* mere extras in the Baron's life. His own place was more permanent and serious. Firmin had been sent among them to deliver a message, and he threaded his way surely, touching them just as much as he needed to.

The Baron Marc was leaning against the railing of the terrace, smoking.

"*Monsieur le Baron: monsieur le Baron* Charles would like to see *monsieur le Baron* in his study."

As Marc got himself into motion, he noticed Firmin's eyes were still searching among the guests. He looked at him inquisitively.

"*Monsieur le Baron* Bruno," the servant explained.

Marc shrugged and headed into the house.

The electric lighting was a shock. All the objects in the room seemed oddly brittle. The varnish glared on the Baron Charles' Empire desk, where he sat with his hands folded, sweating under his wig. Marc, tossing his own wig onto a chair, made the gesture of a worn and disillusioned soldier throwing away his helmet. He heard steps behind him, and turned to see Bruno assaying the scene with a restless glance before stepping closer. Bruno threw his wig down beside Marc's.

Charles felt moved to defend himself. "I haven't entertained on any scale for twelve years. Would you expect me to give a tea-dance now?" He ran his palm over his eyes, then made a little impatient movement with his wrist. "We can't hibernate, you know. We're going to have to see a lot more people we've never seen before. We're going to have to go with the times, gentlemen. And I tell you what else we need in this family, we need to have a little more amusement." Neither of the other two answered him, or showed any reaction at all. "Personally, I intend to enjoy myself more—"

Behind them, Firmin had just shown another person into the room. It was Gaston Robinet, who advanced briskly from Wolfflen to Wolfflen, giving the rote French handshake. Noticing that Marc and Bruno were wigless, he seemed to reflect a moment, then removed his own; he found a place for it carefully on a lamp table strewn with bibelots. Firmin went out, closing the door behind him.

As the men he'd summoned found seats, Charles rolled a pencil between his fingers ruminatively. He stared at his hands and when he looked up his eyes wore a distant look, as if once having made these three men appear before him, he'd shut them out of his consciousness, thinking of something that didn't concern them. Finally he said: "I've decided to restructure everything." His eyes flashed from face to face, settling finally on Marc's. "The times require better organization." He looked at his hands again and seemed about to say more, but instead he cleared his throat nervously and drew a paper from the top drawer of his desk. "It will be easier if I read," he said. And so he began in the flat, formal voice of a man reading to an assembly:

"Henceforth, all the Wolfflen-controlled companies and all the shares of companies owned by Wolfflen in the fields of mining and metal extraction will be grouped under a single holding company, to be known as Wolmetal. The president of the Wolmetal holding company will be Marc de Wolfflen. Henceforth, all the Wolfflen-controlled companies and all shares of companies owned by Wolfflen in the fields of transport, excluding the real estate holdings remaining from the nationalized Wolfflen railroad companies, will be grouped under a single holding company to be known as Woltrans. The president of the Woltrans holding company will be Marc de Wolfflen.

"Henceforth, all Wolfflen-controlled companies and Wolfflen shares in similar companies dealing in construction and real estate, including the real estate holdings of the former Wolfflen railroad companies, will be grouped under the holding company to be known as Intermobil, the president of which will be Bruno de Wolfflen.

"The various other wholly owned or Wolfflen-controlled companies will be grouped into the holding company hereby created under the name of Intervest. The president of Intervest will be *monsieur* Gaston Robinet.

"All the long- and short-term investments of the Banque Wolfflen not included above will remain under the management directly of the bank.

"The presidents of the holding companies will be responsible for the expansion of their groups, but all access to capitalization, other than self-financing, will be through the Banque Wolfflen, subject to the approval of the bank."

For the first time, Charles looked up from his text. "As for myself," he said, "I am taking my distance from day to day business while keeping control. I am resigning as president and general manager of the bank and taking on the position of chairman of the board, on which I retain the majority of votes." He looked at his pencil again. "I hereby name *monsieur Gaston Robinet* president and general manager of the bank." He paused a moment, but did not look up. "*Monsieur* Robinet will report directly to me. The presidents of the holding companies will report to the president and general manager of the Banque Wolfflen ... *monsieur Gaston Robinet.*"

He began rolling his pencil again, head down. He seemed very tired. Marc tried to catch his father's gaze, but gave up, as he rose from his chair. And so he spoke not to his father's head, nor to Robinet, whose look was a cliché of composure, of imposed gravity, as if for some political reason he was at the funeral of a man he barely knew. Marc spoke instead to Bruno while his eyes turned away from Robinet's satin pump, where they'd settled absently for a moment.

"I refuse," Marc said. "This is totally unacceptable."

He walked out without waiting for anyone's reaction. The blood was pulsing so loudly at his temples that he didn't know someone was walking beside him until he felt an arm go round his neck and rest on his shoulder.

"Don't look fierce," Bruno said. "Smile, for God's sake. Smile, and we'll just collect the women and go."

He had something in his other hand. "You forgot your *perruque,* old man."

Marc actually accepted the wig Bruno handed him. He held it absently; his mind was a jumble of memories. Bruno was wearing a smile.

"Well, we're each on his own," Bruno said. He looked positively radiant.

"So it's up to the best man," he said.

Marc didn't hear. His mind was still years in the past, when he'd last seen Bruno smile down on him that way.

The Viscount de Feullière ends his account of the *"Bal du Roi Soleil"* with the following:

"It was some time past two in the morning, quite early on for a ball, when the chamber musicians set themselves up again, in the hall this time, to give the jazz orchestra a respite from its strain. Now all sorts of people, inhibited at the beginning but inspired by the Baron's endless flow of champagne, attempted the dance. They filled the house and the terrace, hopping about, applying the reflexes, if you will, of a lindy to the minuet. But suddenly the dancers in the hall were in total confusion; the music broke off, and the room buzzed with whispers.

"The old Baron had emerged from his study. He was in his steel wheelchair, propelled by a manservant out of costume in a black uniform. The Baron had removed his wig, and his face was bright red. He looked at no one as the servant wheeled him through the crowd, the servant looking at no one it seemed, either, but moving surely and rapidly, until they reached the staircase, where the man helped the Baron out of his chair and up the stairs.

"None of the family was visible anywhere. Slowly at first, and then in great haste, the guests made their way out on their own—with the exception, I'm told, of a party who'd gone into the pool in their underwear and who had to be informed by the Marquis de Lussac that the Baron had gone to bed, and that decorum, which, all things considered still applied, required them to understand that the ball was over.

"Next morning, as anyone who read the papers at the time will recall, the drowned and battered body of the Baron's poor daughter came ashore among the rocks near the Old Beach Hotel. What might have inspired her to have a midnight bathe in her heavy ball gown no one has ever been able to explain. Bad tonques have said the worst. For me, nothing bizarre on the part of a Wolfflen would ever come as a surprise.

"That was, as I said, the grief-stricken Baron's last party. He barely saw anyone in the years that remained to him. In business, as in Paris' social life, he lowered his profile entirely. The Banque Wolffen, because of the Baron Charles' unfortunate political position was to remain, as the English say, in Coventry, for some time. But thanks to the adroitness of its president, Robinet—whose acumen for handling people already presaged his greater destiny—it pursued a modestly prosperous course. As for the careers of the Baron's son and nephew, for several years the less serious people had to say, the better things seemed."

BOOK THREE

CASTLES IN SPAIN

ONE

Probably no more than one out of two men who caught sight of Thérèse (or Tereza) de Flandres (born Nielsen) from across the front room at Maxim's, as she lunched invariably with just one other person in the far alcove among the plants, would consider her physically compelling.

Her odds of pleasing didn't get any better until you were right up close, at eye level and within her reach. She had in her gaze and fingers a magnetism even those insensitive to her looks could perceive, sometimes with a faint chill of fright. Probably very few men would be brave enough to drop their defenses against her high-energy waves and fall in love with her. But when it comes to love it might be said that the strongest people go about unarmed. And if contained energy is a measure of strength, Marc de Wolfflen was a man with a lot of inner strength on the day he met the newlywed Duchess de Flandres.

He had only recently turned his back on his father's bank, and hadn't found himself any vast new project. Having added up his holdings outside the bank, mainly a portfolio of assets inherited from his maternal grandmother, he'd concluded there was enough for him to live on if he did not abandon himself totally to extravagance. He also had his house in Paris and stables in Chantilly belonging to a property called High Cottage, which had also come down to him from the Baron Francis' wife, Chloé, née Lazard. Marc had never kept horses there, his interest in racing having been limited to the pleasure he would get from a Sunday in good weather at Longchamp. Yet recently, he'd had another look at High Cottage, a great mock-Norman house built half a century earlier when his sporting maternal forbears had amused themselves bringing English jockeys and trainers to France. The house had been damaged by the Germans who'd bivouacked there. It was boarded up and musty, with moldy roofbeams. But the stables were nearly intact. And on impulse Marc had decided to reopen High Cottage for racing.

He'd come to Maxim's to have lunch with a man who knew a lot about horses, and as he followed Albert, the *maître d'hôtel*, through the doorway of the front room, his mind was on trainers and grooms and the amount of mash a horse cost you in a year. He noticed the woman because she was directly in his line of sight, at what was soon to be called *la table de la Duchesse*, the best table for two, and where years later the Greek billionaire Aristotle Onassis would lunch *tête-à-tête* with his wife, "Jackie," who had the same Helen of Troy quality as Thérèse de Flandres, but less intensely and more publicly. Marc saw a porcelain-skinned female with dark hair, narrow eyes over a long narrow nose. Her marked hips and full breasts made him think she was Brazilian, and he was half-right.

Since it was he who had invited his acquaintance, a man formerly active in the Society for Encouraging Racing in France, he'd arrived early and had a few minutes to sit alone, nibbling on the cold shrimp set out on his table near the middle of the room. He looked at her discreetly one more time, as she talked in an animated, Latin way, touching, touching, touching the hand of the woman sitting with her. She smiled a lot, and he could see her eyes shift sideways and take in the rest of the room. He couldn't tell whether she was checking to see if her presence was being appreciated or was wary of eavesdroppers. By the relish she seemed to take in explaining whatever she was explaining, Marc surmised it could only be choice gossip. Her half-glance, which caught him watching, made him turn to ask for the menu. He liked her face, liked above all the vitality in it as she talked, although the sunlight, rinsed gray by the front window before it fell on her table, did little for her complexion. Marc recalled that the first time he'd been to Maxim's, when he was nineteen, there'd been a terrace where she was sitting, which was smashed in the 1934 riot at the Concorde not long afterward. He'd invited a girl three years older than he was, and stuttered all through lunch for the first and only time in his life. He closed his mind to nostalgia and studied what he would eat.

When Marc's guest arrived, he went straight to the table of the dark-haired woman and kissed her hello on both cheeks. People were beginning to do that in public instead of shaking or kissing hands.

"Excuse me," his friend said, returning to Marc. "Flandres," he explained.

Marc de Wolfflen knew the lady's husband, the Duke de Flandres as two people in the same thin social stratum, two members of the Jockey Club, can more or less know each other. They were not in the same social set. The Flandres were typically "Faubourg Saint-Germain," part of a little in-group of aristocrats who never "went out," who saw little of anyone except each other, who considered frugality more of a virtue than elegance—an oddly puritan lot for France, speaking well-formed French but with an English-sounding accent that matched their tweeds. Closet monarchists many of them, heirs of anti-Dreyfusards, they considered themselves the topmost crust of Paris, but were provincial to the point of spending as much time as possible in their unheated country castles. The current Duke's father had lived most of the time on his vast sugar-beet plantation in the North, leaving his son to acquire his education in Paris in the chilly shadow of the old Duke's second wife, a withered lady who had been a zealous member of the Mutual Aid Association of the French Nobility. For eighteen years until her death she'd chaired, incorruptibly, the committee that verified the genealogy of applicants for membership. Friends of Marc who'd attended Lycée Condorcet remembered Hervé de Flandres as an ingrown, sad, cautious young man even though he was very well built and startlingly good looking in a blond, Siegfried sort of way.

Scandal came into his hallowed family when the father died. The young Duke mustered his courage and muffled his sense of propriety to challenge the widow in court over a very one-sided will. After all the fuss in the newspapers, he came out relatively badly, with most of the sugar beets still in the hands of the Duchess. She died soon afterward herself, leaving her property to her daughter by her first marriage. The Duke had inherited his father's house in Paris, with little money, though, to reciprocate dinner invitations and no place in the country to hide. He'd gone into the Foreign Ministry, a haven for cases such as his so long as they aspired to be serviceable and not to an ambassadorship, and last Marc had heard, the Quai d'Orsay had posted him to Brazil. So that explained—

"The new Duchess!" his friend said enthusiastically. "She has recently arrived ... flashing her diadem, in Paris, for the first time. You've heard of her: Nielsen. Paper. Timber in Norway. Her mother's a da Cunha."

Yes, Marc had heard of her; perhaps—he tried to remember—he'd even seen her when last she was in Paris. Her father had taken a house in the Rue du Faubourg Saint-Honoré. It was before the war; the family was in Paris for several springtimes. And then the war— they must have gone to South America. Yes, some dark girl of sixteen or so ...

"Yes, she came out in Paris," Marc said, "with a whole troupe of other girls at the Cours Victor Hugo."

"She had a sister at that same school I fell in love with," his acquaintance said. "Who's become a fat matron in Brazil. That race of woman doesn't preserve well ... ah, but Tereza ... I think Tereza is very ... very special. I chose the wrong sister." He gave a little worldly chuckle. "But I was too young, too unsophisticated to see it. Her sister was a perfect doll ..."

"Hervé de Flandres ... " Marc said, as the waiter handed another menu to his acquaintance.

His acquaintance was one of those not very rare experts among well-born people on the genealogy of their entire caste, worldwide. When he and Marc had ordered he did a rundown on the Duchess, *sotto voce*—not, perhaps, so much out of discretion. He seemed, instead, to want to make what he said sound utterly crucial.

"Her father made a lot in newsprint. Her mother, Mathilde da Cunha, was the daughter of Vasco da Cunha, cacao plantations, and Hilda Kreuzer, whose family still has the monopoly on brewing beer in Brazil." The man's voice was oddly chiding and full of awe, as if he thought Marc *should* and did somewhere in his own mind have all this stored, and at the same time as if he were giving very choice information. Marc listened patiently; so many people in his life had been like his acquaintance. Patiently, for after all, *he'd* invited the man, whom he really didn't know that well at all, to learn how he could reopen High Cottage for racing without losing his shirt.

Over lunch the man gave Marc some names and addresses of trainers in France, England, and Ireland, as well as a warning: the horse world liked nothing better than skinning a stranger who tries to break into their group. They're all very charming and hospitable, but never buy a horse from a man who invites you to dinner. The thing is to get a good trainer, even if you have to pay him more than anyone else pays their trainers; indeed pay him much more. With luck, you'll find him loyal and honest, and for three years you do everything he says. After which, there's a chance *you'll* be able to tell whether *he* has any talent. After which, you keep him, or get a trainer who's good and with whom you can now have a meaningful chat or argument. Marc was at an advantage: his family already had a past in racing. They're all very clannish, and as in any club, it helps to have your name in the annals ...

"But it wouldn't incidentally, do you any harm to talk to the Duke ..."

"Hervé de Flandres?"

"He knows horseflesh. He was a gentleman rider when his father was still alive." The man had that faintly chiding voice again.

"Well then, introduce me to the Duchess," Marc replied.

His acquaintance, much of whose pleasure in life was knowing a lot of good people and having them all know how many he knew, gave a happy nod.

She was still eating dessert when the two men came up to her table. Marc would always recall it seemed so perfect: she was eating what is called a *puits d'amour,* a "well-of-love," which was a pastry gorged with custard and glazed. One of the things Marc was always to adore about Thérèse was her frank, sensual enjoyment of food.

Her friend at lunch was Liliane Picard, a woman in her sixties, an ambulatory warehouse of gossip, one of the Paris social world's noted *concièrges*. Although she and Marc knew each other—there was no one she didn't know—Marc's acquaintance, her soulmate, introduced her to Marc ahead of the Duchess. This gave Thérèse a chance to give the Baron a long look before speaking to him.

"Of course I know the Baron. I knew him when he wore short

pants—*n'est-ce pas?* How is your father, how is the Baroness Eveline?"

"And Thérèse, do you know Marc de Wolfflen? La Duchesse de Flandres: Le Baron de Wolfflen." Marc's acquaintance beamed with pleasure as the titles rolled off his tongue.

She fixed him in her look again, her direct, face-to-face look. Norwegian eyes, he thought, on that Brazilian face. Latin, yes, but recalling any number of hybrids long before her parents' exotic match: a presence of the Indian in her cheekbones, of the Negro, perhaps, in her taut lips.

"Marc is going to reopen his family's place in Chantilly. Shouldn't he talk to your husband about horses?"

"High Cottage," she said.

"Oh, you know it?" Marc said.

"We've just bought a place nearby. The Helfenberg stables . . ."

As they waited on the sidewalk for Marc's car, his acquaintance was positively excited by the new piece of information he had to spread. "Helfenberg sold out. She must have offered him a fortune."

Aloïs Helfenberg was a man who for tax reasons lived a little bit everywhere. He carried a Mexican passport, although he was born in France, and he spent enough time in America to be considered one of their own by New York society. In France, he owned—until Thérèse de Flandres came along with what must have been an irresistible offer—one of the most successful stables. His business was great works of art—a profession begun by David Helfenberg three generations earlier.

"It had to be *her*," Marc's guest went on, "Flandres doesn't have the imagination to go after Helfenberg. One thing sure, *he* doesn't have the money."

The doorman arrived behind the wheel of Marc's Jaguar.

"Extraordinary weather," Marc said, looking up at a porcelain late-September sky. He spoke as if were thinking aloud. "Indian Summer they call it in America . . . You know . . . I wish I could put the roof down on the car . . . Suppose we drive into the Bois?"

But the car was dark as they got in and Marc said "Perhaps not." The other man didn't seem to notice that a decision had been taken and rescinded. His mind was still buzzing with his Duchess.

"She's got money," he said, "she's got a name and a title, her table every day at Maxim's, and now she's got her stables at Chantilly. She's going to have her stall in the owner's stand at Longchamp. She's going to do *everything*. Now she's a Duchess, but she's got her sights set on becoming queen of Paris."

"She has quite an appetite," Marc said. His hand still seemed to feel the imprint of the lady's fingers as he thought about next weekend, when he and his wife were invited to have lunch in Chantilly with the Duke de Flandres and his future queen.

It was obvious that the Duke had been running, in his stiff, pained way, very hard to catch up with his wife's lightning campaign through Paris society. They'd just got back from São Paolo, where he'd been a vice-consul. He'd barely had time to settle into his new post in the Latin American section of the Quay, and here she was, getting about, putting forward rapidly all her artillery, buying all sorts of new things for his house in Paris *and* suddenly the stables; plotting out her future court with that hag, Picard. And now she'd invited the Wolfflens to lunch, who'd never really been *his people* in the days he saw next to no one, in the days when he could afford to see next to no one. The Wolfflens had always been people who "went out." And the Flandres were not. Not that the Duke seemed adverse to changing his social category—now that he had the means—to descending from where the Faubourg Saint-Germain *gratin* looked at the world, more a cracked and dusty shelf than a pedestal. No, he was anxious to go along probably. To have fun. He was just still very awkward about it. And being a diplomat in the second most important station in Brazil hadn't increased his worldliness. He was, however, a very pleasant man to look at, distinctively handsome, with big even features and a tall sturdy body; and to his credit, if he couldn't conceal his effort, it was a sincere effort he made to receive the Wolfflens well in the house in which the odor of Aloïs Helfenberg's chain-smoked Havanas still persisted. Perhaps Thérèse was still too new to understand all the nuances of her invitation: that bringing her husband and a Wolfflen together at the same table was in itself making a tiny bit of social history.

They were both in the Jockey, but Marc had rarely gone there since the war, and Hervé was a pillar of the club. Marc suspected, unfairly perhaps and without evidence, that antisemitism still lingered in the Flandres way of looking at the world. He didn't particularly admire the Duke's war record. Flandres, having failed to be admitted to the Ecole Polytechnique, attended the cavalry officers' school at Saumur. He was to be one of those colonels who turned a deaf ear to de Gaulle in the impotent stump of an army Hitler allowed Pétain. Very near the end of the conflict, though, he made his way to joining Leclerc in the recapture of Alsace, and came out on the right side, with a *Croix de Guerre*. But since Marc had said yes to the young Duchess, he too did his best to make the luncheon pleasant.

For a man who bought and sold some of the world's greatest works of art, Helfenberg had furnished his house in Chantilly with surprisingly mediocre taste. He had a lot of worn furniture all through the big rooms, which the overhanging eaves of the second floor kept from getting decent sunlight. Everywhere on the dark, wood-paneled walls, there were nineteenth-century English lithographs with racing themes. No doubt the old dealer had insisted on selling the place lock, stock, and barrel and had managed a high price for his "furnishings." Thérèse apologized for the look of the house, which they were of course going to change soon, but the Duke didn't seem at all embarrassed. The poor light and the fustiness, as well as the lithographs, recalled the Jockey Club, and Flandres seemed to feel very much at home.

Not long after, Thérèse was going to turn her—and Marc de Wolfflen's—table into International Society's most elegant canteen; her settings as well as her chef would be photographed by American, English, French, and Italian *Vogue*. But that afternoon Marc and she first ate together, her sensual mouth twisted in anguish and her eyes struggled to give cues, as a heavy woman with gray hair yellowed for want of washing, Helfenberg's housekeeper no doubt, passed awkwardly and at times precariously, dry partridge and a salver nearly overflowing with greasy sauce. It was true Thérèse had a great appetite—as Marc had sensed when she'd attacked her *puits d'amour* at Maxim's—but she barely touched that lunch. Emma ate precisely what was needed to be polite, Marc followed her example, while the Duke scraped at his bones. He then helped himself largely to a *brie* that was chalky for want of proper ripening. The young Duchess' lips parted for an instant as she looked at him, showing her fine, sharp white teeth, like baby teeth, then she caught Marc noticing and lowered her eyes. When she looked up, he was still gazing at her; she answered his regard with a smile that made his throat tighten. He would remember that everything had begun with that smile.

Emma was talking to the Duke about English gardens. How they loved the English, his caste; their ancestors had, after all, conquered that country in 1066. They were cousins of the English nobles. Coffee was served at table, after which the Duke assigned Emma to his wife, whom he cautioned to "note well" her advice on the neglected roses behind the house, while he took Marc on a tour of *his* stables.

In a long building, quite unlike the rustic courtyard around which the gabled stalls of High Cottage had been built, there stood, twitching and ruminating on immaculate cement, 120 mounts. The Duke explained that Helfenberg had built, at huge cost, the most modern and healthiest stables in France.

"A little like a factory," the Duke offered, "not much charm."

Marc nodded.

"But you can't quarrel with the results. That little ... fellow knew what he was doing."

They talked horses. The Duke, who by the end of lunch had loosened up drinking his own wine, repeated that he'd do everything he could to help Marc reopen High Cottage.

"When you think of what life Chantilly had in the time of our grandfathers ... and now these properties all boarded up. But it can all be brought back. It must." He began to talk like a diplomat: "France is the most elegant place in the world for racing. I have seen how they race in America. On dirt, and no one dresses. The crowd is unimaginable. No, racing is a great asset to the reputation of our country."

They rejoined the ladies in the rose garden, which was sad indeed.

"The Wolfflens and the Flandres are going to revive this town," the Duke offered. He was now thoroughly congenial. *"Monsieur,* at the next sale of yearlings in Deauville, I'll bid for you, if it suits you."

Thérèse took Marc's arm as they headed back into the house. "You're so ... elegant," she said in a half-whisper. Before he could muster a reply to what sounded to him a remark made with the guilelessness of a child, she wedged her heel in the stone of the shabby steps leading to the terrace. She began to fall; he caught her by her shoulders and she gripped his biceps to steady herself. They stood there for an instant looking ridiculously like a couple doing an exhibition of the tango. He was close enough to her face to smell her mouth; a deeper sweetness than her lipstick.

He held her for what seemed to him a long moment in front of the other two, who stood with their faces twisted in dismay, apparently at her fall.

Something is going to happen, Marc told himself—he knew what—and there's a good chance it's all going to be ridiculous ...

Before driving back down to Paris, Emma and Marc stopped at High Cottage. The house was locked and shuttered as they'd left it last, as it had been for decades. High Cottage: a high cottage, a tall, rambling, funny version of a Norman farmhouse, built when that brick and beam style was the rage in many parts of France for the manors of city people. Named when the racing world of Chantilly still had a weakness for things English. The swollen cottage had replaced a much smaller house, to accommodate the huge family of Marc's maternal grandparents. He was led now to recall that his own generation was far less prolific ...

The caretaker, a one-legged invalid of the First World War, came limping out of his gatehouse. Would the Baron like the key again? His wife peered at Marc and Emma, thinking she was unseen, from a corner of a window. They'd been let alone for years, and what now?

"Do you want to go in again?"

Emma shook her head. She'd seen it all the last time: the overstuffed furniture smelling like urine, the dusty floors where there had been what looked like rat droppings.

Instead of going in, they walked all around the house, looking at it.

"It's quite a project," Marc said. He grabbed in sudden irritation at the high grass, not noticing the nettles. He pulled his hand away fast, shaking it.

"You've burned yourself," Emma said with great concern. She took his hand and did, suddenly, something he'd never known her to have done before; she kissed his palm. She drew away rubbing her lips.

"That was imprudent ... you've picked up the sting."

On the way back to the car, Emma said: "She's very pretty."

"Who?" The hypocrisy of his "who?" was another little step toward betraying her.

"My last duchess."

He chuckled deliberately. "Not many men would think so. Pretty, no."

"How would you describe her?" Her voice said the question wasn't innocent.

"Different," he said.

"We shall have to invite them back," she said, settling next to him in the car. Her place there, beside the driver, and her "we" seemed to bolster her with a comforting feeling of proprietorship. "In Paris."

"Oh, there's no hurry," he lied.

TWO

They saw each other again at a party. The Duke had been sent on a trade mission to South America, and his wife had come alone to the twenty-third birthday party of Godwin Laver. Laver was the *Wunderkind* of European finance, and many people, such as Marc de Wolfflen, were accepting his invitations simply for insight to exactly who he was. As for Thérèse, though she was more than five years older than Laver, she had an essential thing in common with him. If old Charles de Wolfflen, back at his Sun King Ball, had heard the flute of Dionysus before others of his caste, both Thérèse and Laver knew the right steps to dance to it long before most people. Laver was a pioneer among the European rich of being With It. He was an Englishman born into Non-Establishment money, heir to a good shoe factory, who'd spent his nineteenth and twentieth years passing through America. Early on, in New Orleans, he'd fallen in with a group of roaming poets who, when their time came to be marketed, were to be called "Beatniks." On inheriting control of his dead father's factory at the age of twenty-one, Laver came home, bought a suit, and decided there was more pleasure being With It with a lot of money than in sleeping in the back seats of old cars, eating peanut butter and lettuce, and drinking pee-weak American beer. He also decided to have fun playing with his fortune.

He sold his majority share in the prosperous shoe factory to the husbands of his sisters, and began to speculate, principally in real estate. In two years, he'd left the gentlemen of the City breathless with awe, resentment, and in some cases admiration: he'd proved himself one of the shrewdest men with money in England and was extremely rich. Recently he'd come to Paris to begin investing on the Continent, and he was willing to listen to all sorts of imaginative schemes; he'd become a kind of Pied Piper for Walter Mittys of the Money Establishment, who came to him with dreamed-up projects they hadn't dared bring to daylight among their peers. He might have made an excellent partner for Bruno de Wolfflen, but the Baron for some reason had taken an aversion to the mention of Laver's name—possibly because the Englishman had done so well so young. It was not at all unlikely that Bruno simply envied him, and many less proud gentlemen were to encounter each other in the private elevator of the Neuilly apartment Laver had rented—one of the rare penthouses in the Paris area, with a garden overlooking the Bois de Boulogne.

On the evening of Laver's birthday, the apartment and the garden contained a heterogeneous mixture of guests. There was a sprinkling of people such as Marc de Wolfflen, who thought it would be fascinating to encounter The Phenomenon. There were a number of Laver's suppliants, as well as some people whom Godwin had met at other parties and had apparently found pleasant company. He seemed to have invited a great number of people out of no self-interest other than pleasure, and among them, too, were a handful of people such as Thérèse de Flandres, who knew that God Laver really knew how to have a good time.

Naturally, the people didn't mix. They occupied the enormous apartment in zones. With their reflex for choosing the best place to be in any situation, Marc's kind took over the center of Laver's wide-open living area, an expanse that gave out on his garden on three sides, encompassing a bar, a corner where you dined and where a buffet—a great *couscous* with a whole roasted lamb—was set up, and several sitting areas. The furniture was new, fifties stage-and-screen exaggerations of the swank of the thirties. Where the distinguished set had gathered, there was soft leather and bearskins on the floor.

Laver and his three houseboys in blue jackets doted on the center group, on the one hand offering conversation—mainly about business—and on the other, all sorts of *hors d'oeuvres* preparatory to the *méchoui*. The North African tidbits on the trays prompted Laver to explain that he was a friend of el Glaoui, ruler of Morocco, one of whose sons was expected that evening. In the outer zone of the room, where sparse clusters of people had formed, there were already two lone men in *djellebas,* whom some people took for Arabs, but who—as Marc was to learn from Thérèse—were two homosexual decorators who knew beforehand what the theme of God's party would be.

The other people grouped here and there on the fringes of the room were chiefly those who, with a polite awareness of rank, had hesitated before gravitating toward the center, and who'd found no places left. Some of the men had been inciting Laver to do business with them. They exuded a certain nervous glow in their corners, as if they believed being here was a favorable omen for their projects.

The third zone of life at the party, the third circle, was in mysterious movement—young men and women were drifting back and forth from the terrace, through the far end of the apartment, and into the long, cork-paneled hallway that led, presumably, to bedrooms. They moved in a titter of giggles.

Marc's eyes followed his host as Laver came off the terrace, giggling also lightly for an instant, but breaking away from the others to head back toward the center of the room. It was hard for Marc to get a good idea of the man from his features. Laver was tall and slender, but his rounded shoulders and the mound of abdomen below his belt were not at all youthful. His curly blond hair, which seemed never to have been healthy, was already receding. His nose was flat, his eyes, Marc had already noticed, could shift like skies through ranges of opacity or brilliance. His lips, a little carplike Marc thought, were heavy but more comical than sensual. But he had a habit, when he seemed to think he wasn't observed, of setting his teeth into a look of sternness, which might have even stemmed from a certain cruelty.

Before he had got far across the room, the Duchess de Flandres had left the terrace and caught up with him, taking his arm. They advanced together on Marc and Emma.

"He looks rather piggish," Emma observed. Emma had been moody from the time she and Marc left their house for the party.

"You know each other," Laver said as they came up. "You both know Tereza, our ex-Princess of São Paolo."

"Have you given more thought to horses?" Thérèse asked. Her eyes flashed, bathed Marc's face in a greeting, and then looked at the rug.

"I expect we'll open High Cottage next fall," Marc said.

She turned to Emma. "Ah ... well, then ..." she began to say. Marc noticed that the nails of the fingers of her right hand were dug into her palm, curled into a fist.

"We'll have lunch again soon," Emma said without enthusiasm.

Laver looked at the two women and seemed to sense static building in the air. "Tereza, I present you to—"

He left with her so quickly they seemed to vanish.

"I'm not at all comfortable here," Emma said. "Let's ... oh let's get some air."

Grass was growing healthily on the grounds of the penthouse. And flowers. There were chrysanthemums in full bloom. An English garden, but lit up in an un-English way with bright spotlights. Just out of the light, a thin man with a moustache and sunglasses was smoking a cigaret. His smoke reached Marc and Emma with a strange pungency, like the smell of burning rope.

"We're in Morocco, Hollywood, Paris, and Surrey at the same time," Marc said lightly, trying to improve his wife's mood. "It's extraordinary."

"Marc, frankly, I'd rather be at home just now," she said.

"We'll go."

"No, you want to stay. You might even want to get to know this man. He's become very interesting in the business world. Hasn't he?"

"Oh, come on, Emma, I'm not courting that man."

"Stay. You'll regret leaving. All this is *interesting*."

He looked at her but she lowered her eyes, and though it was quite dark where they stood, he thought he could see her shudder.

"All right," he said.

He started to escort her back into the room.

218   THE HEIRS

"No ..." she said, "I'll just disappear. It will be better. I'd rather not handshake my way out of there. No incident. I'll slip away. If he asks, tell him I had a migraine." She looked off at the cloud-smirched October Paris sky. "Oh, I don't care what the hell you tell him!" she said.

"I'll call the chauffeur to let him know where I left the car ..."

"I have my keys," she said, "I know how to drive ... I'm chilly." She squeezed his hand, kissed him lightly, and hurried away.

He stood there, half-rueful, half-excited by a sense of liberation, rueful, guilty over the odd way his blood seemed to be pumping faster since she'd left. The man smoking on the chaise-lounge got up slowly and shuffled towards him. As he moved fully into the light, Marc recognized who he was. His name was Max Mieger. He was a Hollywood producer in his sixties who'd gone to a dress collection at Jean Patou, had fallen in love with a twenty-year-old mannequin on the spot, and had married her in three weeks. Now he produced second-rate movies in Paris and kept a yacht at Monte Carlo. Marc had seen him and his wife at a number of public places, but they'd never spoken.

"Hi," the man said. "I'm having a smoke ..."

"Hello."

"My missus is back there ..." he went on, moving his arm in a very slow arc toward the rear of the apartment, "I'm having a smoke." He chuckled.

"Are you *hep!*" he asked.

"What's that you say?" As if he'd unconsciously meant to take distance from the man and his language (which was also Marc's wife's) Marc's "th" was imperfect.

"I *know* you're French," Mieger said, "but I'm asking if you are *hep*."

Marc shrugged

"Take a chance," the producer said "Try my brand ... Live a little."

Marc took the hashish cigaret.

Mieger clicked open a Zippo lighter, which flared in the light wind. He lit Marc's smoke and then put the closed lighter under Marc's nose. There was some kind of crest on it and an inscription.

"Douglas MacArthur," Mieger said. "General Douglas MacArthur gave me that lighter. In 1944. We were making a picture about The Philippines, and he gave me the fullest cooperation. Marvelous man. Marvelous. The war was on. Do you remember that war, sir?"

"Yes, sir," Marc said, taking leave of Mieger by touching his arm gently.

"I wouldn't give a fart for Truman . . ." Mieger's voice trailed off as Marc receded toward the edge of the garden. Below: the woods, all inky, and further on, the gray gleam of the Lac Inférieur, a long loop of water with two furry islands. The cigaret was strong and bitter. Marc sat down on a white bench and sucked in the smoke until it took effect, and it was as if the pull of gravity had become greatly reduced. In its place, there seemed to be a viscosity to the air.

He peered one more instant at the city's domesticated parcel of nature, then turned toward the house with a smile spreading all over his face, a smile out of nowhere. Inside, he didn't head for the center, but shuffled toward the hallway. When he got to the door of what he presumed was the "master" bedroom, he asked himself what the "master's" lair might be like. He chuckled, and entered. There was a great bed covered with fur, and he moved toward it with uncertain feet. He sat down, and then he lay down. His sense of time was too distorted for him to know how long he had been lying there, it seemed quite a long time, when the door opened. He heard a rustle of taffeta. A very young blond girl had come in. She went into the bathroom, where she turned on the light and came out again quickly, leaving the door partly open. Through the opening there came just enough light for them to see each other. She didn't say anything as she bent forward to reach a zipper and then shrugged her shoulders, causing her dress to fall at her feet. She pulled off her shoes, and quickly took everything else off, except for her bra. She jumped onto the bed, still without a word, took his head in her hands, and kissed him . . .

He made a poor job of it. The cigaret hadn't exactly helped his libido. She was eager and panting but when he was done, she slipped off the bed quickly and began to dress again. He was, although still fuzzy minded, quite ashamed. He opened his mouth to speak to her at last, and out came any old thing: "Why the bra?" he asked.

"Not your fucking business!" she shot back. When he laughed uncontrollably, she left, slamming the door.

It might have been very much later when his mind began to focus normally again. He got up and dressed.

As he tied his shoes he shrugged to himself, feeling like a man who'd been waylaid, shanghaied, but who was about to make an escape.

In the hallway he came upon his Duchess, who had just come out of another room.

"I'm leaving," she told him with blunt familiarity in her voice.

"It must be late ... I'll take you ... I'll accompany you."

Almost everyone had left, and God Laver was nowhere saying goodbye.

When they got to her Bentley, her chauffeur, who was slumped over the wheel asleep, didn't budge. She opened the rear door with her key and they got an enormous whiff of cheap red wine. She began to pound the man on his shoulder with her fists, swearing in Portuguese. "You're fired!" she said in French. He mumbled in some language. She opened the door, pushed him out of the car, and took the wheel. The man straightened himself and smoothed his wrinkled uniform, shaking his head as if he were awakening from a nightmare. By then, Marc was beside the Duchess. She sped away, leaving the man lurching in the middle of the street.

"He'll find his way home," she said, "I'll take him in. What else can I do? I brought him over with me. I can't let him sleep under the bridges."

"I'll drop you off," she offered.

"We can drive a little."

She flashed him a smile. At the Mare Saint-James, a little pond, she stopped the car.

"We can walk a little," she said.

His head was now quite clear, but he was shivering. He went round to open her door, and before she had straightened up from getting out, he put his hands on her shoulders, drew her against him, and kissed her neck. She kissed him back, she covered his eyes, his face, with kisses.

They stood there on the wet grass, with the new taste of each other on their lips, and the gassy mud of the pond in their nostrils. He could feel the warm shape of her body against him through their clothes. They had nowhere to go for two people decently to make love. On the Paris side of the wood there were little hotels where men and women pulled in at any hour of the night; he remembered ads in the entertainment sections of the newspapers, featuring "champagne suppers." But it was all too cheap to take her into a house full of furtive copulators. Impossible tonight, he told himself. They would go about it as lovers ought to, the first time. He foresaw a lifetime with her. He was completely smitten. But as he led her away from gazing at the threads of mist on the pond, suddenly he couldn't keep himself from pulling open the rear door of the car. "We'd better wait!" he warned himself aloud. But she drew her dress over her head in one quick shake, as if she'd been impatient for his move.

"Why did you marry him?" he asked later, as she drove aimlessly through the lanes of the Bois, having made several circles.

He spoke motivated by jealousy.

"He was beautiful and he was French," she explained, "and I was a little girl in Brazil. . . . It took me three weeks of marriage to realize he was made of cardboard. . . . But at least he got me out of the clutches of my mother. For you, I suppose, South Americans are charming—*hot blooded*, yes?" She smiled and took his hand. "But our kind, our class, in my country they're made of steel. The most ungenerous people in the world. Not always with money—they'll throw it around under *your* nose. They like to impress the Europeans—and they'll throw it around with the best of taste. But they are the world's most ungenerous people with their emotions . . ."

"You—"

"I escaped."

"Why did you marry her?" she countered, a moment later.

"She belongs to a part of my life . . ."

"*Belonged!*" she coaxed.

"Belongs. But as far as . . . a man and a woman goes, it's gone between us. She knows it's gone."

She didn't answer for a while, but then she said: "I think I'm in love with you . . . I've thought of you a lot—"

He lifted her hand to his face and kissed it.

It was dawn, and a café near a bus stop was opening on the Paris side of the Bois. A waiter was taking straw chairs that had been piled one on top of the other in a corner and setting them out on the glassed-in terrace. They sat down and order coffee and croissants.

"My husband has a family motto," she said "under his crest. On all his writing paper. Do you know what it is?

"*We persist.*" That's what they do, they hang on. They've hung on since the Crusades. A very old family ... but I think basically they're very small. Very petty. They're hangovers. I think he has all of that in him—petty and persistent. You can expect that he will hang on. He will make trouble. He is also very Catholic ... *pour la forme.*"

Marc didn't reply.

"It's absolutely silly, disgusting, how they love money, too. They think they *deserve it* more than the *upstarts* who've made it. But they'll do the lowest things to have it. They'll humiliate themselves."

The coffee came and she dunked a corner of her croissant through the head of the foaming milk, like a child.

"I'll give you an example," she said. "The Duke said he would bid for you at the yearling sales, yes? Well, he'll go and bid for you and do very well. He knows horses, he knows the people, he knows that world, and you'll think he's become your very best friend to help you in that way. Then, afterwards, you see, he'll mention his commission. Just like that. You see, that race doesn't feel humiliated by anything they say to people they consider born irremediably inferior to them. He thinks your lot are just a bunch of sheeny money-lenders. Oh ... he admires much about you, envies. He'll say he admires your brains. You're a smart people—that is his kind's way of telling themselves they are not prejudiced. But they've got a slot for you in their minds, and it's far below them."

"You're telling me all this—"

"Because ... he's my husband. And you know as well as I do that you're going to be ... *my lover.*" She pronounced the old-fashioned word with a twist of humor in her voice.

"I don't have a slot for people like your husband. I have a limbo I cast them into."

She laughed gently. "You have a motto, too," she said.

"My family? Yes ..."

"Tell me what it is."

"*Virtus et Unitas* ..." he said awkwardly.

"*Courage,*" she teased. He frowned.

"I have a motto of my own," she said. "I'll tell you what it is: '*Il vaut mieux des remords que des regrets.*' Better remorse than regret."

After her coffee, she asked for a glass of water. She found a pill in her purse and swallowed it with the water.

"I have a heart," she explained when they were in the car again. "I remember reading a book in English, *The Good Soldier*, and that was how it was put: There was a character, or there were two of them, who had 'a heart.' I've had it since I was a child. I can drop dead at any minute."

"I will treat you, always, with the greatest delicacy," he said.

"That would kill me," she replied.

Emma was up when Marc came in. She was writing a letter in her dressing room.

She'd sensed everything already.

"I would have thought," she said, before she went back to her letter, "that when *you* inevitably went wild, *you* would at least have done it with taste."

THREE

So there never was another *déjeuner à quatre,* luncheon for four, between the Marc de Wolfflens and the Hervé de Flandres. Thérèse abandoned the Flandres townhouse in the Faubourg Saint-Germain and moved across the Seine into an apartment on Avenue Montaigne. The Duke fell back on his religion. Solitary in his pew in the Eglise Sainte-Clotilde, he affected a dignified sorrow; he went often to confession, but his confessions took the form of complaints. His priest counseled resignation. His lawyers, too, advised him against divorce. The Duchess had a heart; she could take leave of this world at any moment, and as her husband he had a right to much of all she'd leave behind.

Emma, too, though she couldn't bring herself to wish the death of anyone, at first spent a lot of time hoping that the Great Romance of Paris would be short lived. Then she fell back on the solace of her legitimacy. She was born a Wolfflen and married to a Baron de Wolfflen. She would not *abdicate*. In those days in her stratum of society, where love-marriages were far from the rule, divorces provoked by love were even more rare. To have a mistress or a lover was a normal event of civilized living, but to cast off one's legitimate partner, to destroy an alliance, to amputate a branch of the family tree because of a love affair was a form of punishment and self-punishment, a form of insult reasonable people rarely sank to.

And so Emma and Marc settled into one of those marriages of friendship that were reason's complement to the public and unofficial liaisons of passion, following a tradition in French society since the days of the court. The custom required that Marc should not abandon Emma, so long as she didn't choose to divorce him, and so he continued to respect her and to enhance her honor with his title, his name, and his publicly known affection. When it came to affairs of the heart, nothing in France at the time was scandalous if it were done in a civilized way. And so Emma, too, by the unwritten rules of the arrangement, was free to see whomever she wanted. She began to go out with a number of men, none of whom was able to earn the reputation of her lover. She settled after a while on one social partner, the fifty-year-old bachelor son of General Arthaud, one of the heroes of the First World War, whose volumes of military history and high friendships had won him a seat in the Academy. Philippe Arthaud, who had a post at the Quai d'Orsay, was a brilliant conversationalist and one of the most cultivated men in Paris. He was far gentler than his fierce old father, rather shy and nervous. His personality and his bachelorhood led some people to consider him a secret homosexual. Marc at times would wonder whether Arthaud and Emma were sleeping together. Wishing guiltily for Emma's happiness, he would wish that they were.

Marc half-moved-out. He and Emma rearranged the rooms upstairs so that he had an apartment of his own. He would be gone for days to Avenue Montaigne, yet he and Emma were very concerned that he maintain a presence in the house to exert an influence in the life of his son. Gilbert must have perceived, as children can, all that was essentially absent in his father's presence—or the presence of something withered in the atmosphere around him. Marc would seek occasions to be alone with the boy, would help him with his lessons and run with him in the Bois, but Gilbert was growing up very close to his mother. He had become the little man in her life; she drenched him with affection. When Gilbert wasn't with his parents, he was the bane of the existence of his governess and often the other servants as well. Marc couldn't help but notice that his son was becoming very self-centered and narcissistic. He had a way of looking into a mirror that revealed he already knew how much his looks were superior to other people's. He was indeed extraordinarily handsome, in a surprisingly mature, square-featured way. But all in all, he wasn't a happy child. Alone with his parents, he was dutiful and well mannered. He was a careful student. Yet he lacked spontaneity and he was seldom given to mirth. When he was eleven, Marc suggested to Emma that the best thing might be to send him right away to a boarding school. Yet Marc wasn't insistent, his own memories of Croseigne weren't all rosy, and Emma absolutely balked at the idea. There would be a time for him to go off.

Emma clung to the child, to her responsibilities to her name, and to whatever else was left of her marriage. A friendship. And Marc, though he sometimes perceived guiltily that the life he'd chosen for himself was injuring his son's, could see no other choice. From the day he laid eyes on Thérèse he knew, as perhaps he knew without telling himself he knew long before then, that his marriage to Emma was condemned to wither. And so he played his life as it lay.

In the eyes of a handful of gray women in Paris, Thérèse da Cunha had made a blunder in social strategy, abandoning her legitimate place beside the Duke de Flandres for the sake of becoming the Baron de Wolfflen's mistress. They were wrong, wrong first of all about Thérèse's character. It was certain that she was socially ambitious, although her ambition went beyond a need to promote herself. She didn't suffer from that kind of insecurity. Instead she was one of those women born with great intelligence and no talent, who all their lives feel in painful exile unless celebrated people of power and talent accept their company—and more than accept, pay homage to *their* special attractiveness. She was in short a born Hostess, born to reign at a dinner table, ambitious to reign at the most celebrated table of all. But first of all she was a woman born for loving men; she had a strong appetite for men—not just a sexual craving; she loved the constant presence of a man in her life, the intimacy of living with a man, the presence of his voice, his touch, his odor, his will, his reasoning, and his own strong lust. But not just any man. So the misguided gossips were wrong not to understand that when the Duchess de Flandres fell in love with Marc de Wolfflen, she would have left with him for a desert island if he asked her to. (How long she would have remained there before casting out bottled messages for help is another question.) They were also wrong not to know that Thérèse could have her cake and eat it. She knew. She knew that the Duke had nothing but an old name and title to recommend him, whereas Marc was the most profoundly elegant man in Paris. He had a name honored by far more accomplishments than the Duke's over the decades since Flandres' great-great-grandfather had lost his head out of loyalty to Louis Seize. And Marc was heir to a powerful fortune. Married to him or not, she would reign beside him. There were, moreover, many precedents to encourage her, reaching from beyond du Barry to the present. When Thérèse began outfitting her apartment in the Avenue Montaigne, the most notable table in town belonged to the Mistress of the Viscount Alfred de Flins, the champagne and steel heir. In less than a year, Thérèse's table outclassed hers.

There are still some old men alive who can recount what it was like to meet Thérèse during the early days of her "career." Though at the time she never flirted, the moment she fixed her attention on men she made them deeply aware of her womanliness—not simply of her obvious beauty, of her dark eyes and her porcelain skin, nor of her eccentric mixture of perfumes, nor the velvety touch of lithe fingers in your hand. There was something else, like *duende* in a flamenco singer's voice, ineffably diabolic or godly, an archetypal seductiveness, in her total presence, It was as if with all her refinement, she embodied the energy of a certain life-force, and that energy in her was charged "female" the way an electric current can be charged "positive" or "negative." In those days she had a benevolent effect on everyone she liked, and she liked a great many people. "People who profited from being alive," as she put it. She sought them out and charmed them all. Her admiring voice when she spoke to a man she'd placed far from her could make him feel like a guest of honor. There was a lilt in her Brazilian accent that could sound touchingly childish—and it wasn't a studied ruse; she was, in some measure, still a provincial child fascinated by the world of urbane adults. But she had a natural and sure taste for embellishing that world, for enriching it esthetically. And if she lacked ruse, she was short on neither intelligence nor self-protective instinct. She could take the hand of a friend or an enemy in a way that could make him feel sexy, without her revealing any coquetry. She learned to talk to writers about writing, to politicians about politics, to actors about directors—and she did her best to make businessmen stop talking business. When she found out that by some quirk of fate the Belgian ambassador had the best cook in Paris, she stole the man away by doubling his salary. And then, huddling with him over menus, and in long exigeses of what had gone right and wrong after every dinner, she forced him to show twice the imagination and far more zeal than he'd ever shown in his craft. Her food, her flowers, her table settings, her iconoclastic "mixture" of guests—who were either deeply involved in influencing the world or just deeply enjoying it—spread her renown not only through Paris but throughout all the haunts of what was beginning to be called the International Set. *"Elle nous exalte,"* she *enhances* us, the Austrian symphony director Richard Wolper once said about her way of making people seem to glow, not with her light but their own, near her. But in her soul, Thérèse walked a tightrope between her lust for excitement and her more serene love of all forms of beauty. As the social world she knew reached beyond Paris to every city and resort where there were people who cared intensely about splendor and pleasure and who could afford a rich share of both, she changed from a queen to an empress. But after a while, the notables of her court became more superficial, and the fun became more shrill. Perhaps built into every sort of empire is its inevitable decline.

Not long after Thérèse and Marc began living together, he bought the desanctified ruins of a Carmelite convent above Marbella on the southern coast of Spain. The convent was the first project they were to undertake together, the first marriage of two exceptional tastes. They rented a house in the village for June and July, and hired a Spanish architect without great pretensions who would execute what they imagined. They would awaken early in the cool of morning, their heads teeming with designs—there wasn't going to be a detail, from the patterns in the tile of the floors to the proportions of the rooms, from the placing of the windows down to the hardware, which would escape the mark of their creative taste. Beginning at breakfast they would draw and redraw wings, apartments, rooms, and corridors, here following, there improving the plan made by the foundations of the ruins. In the afternoon, the architect would arrive with finished drawings based on their sketches and half the time, at the end of the afternoon, he would tear up what he'd brought, and go home to begin again. When they weren't with the patient Señor Almeda, they were with the numerous houseguests who filed through the house week after week. The guests rose late and drowsed their days away at the edge of the pool, having arrived extenuated and heavy with gossip, exuding the hectic presence of some far-off capital or other. There were dinners outside in candlelight under an immaculate sky and lots of heady *sangria*, beginning with lunch.

The guests would tease Marc and Thérèse about the ever-changing plans of their "castle in Spain." Among the summer residents of Marbella, the convent was rechristened simply "the castle," and the term was seldom pronounced without a note of awesome expectation.

One morning while Thérèse was sunning on the great patio of her bedroom, which overlooked the steep hillside, a dusty Rover appeared on the winding road to the rented house. Three persons in khaki shorts got out of the car when it stopped at the great wooden gate to the courtyard.

The sound of the bronze bell ringing brought Marc out on the patio.

"Why—it's Herbert," he exclaimed.

While she dressed, he hurried down to greet his cousin Lord Herbert Wolfflen, Lady Vanessa, and their son, Raphael. Three tanned and perspiring tourists.

"Well, we couldn't practically drive past your door without stopping ... or so *Vanessa* argued," Herbert bantered, as Thérèse led her husband's cousins toward a shaded table near the pool. Herbert's tone was congenial enough, but Marc could still believe his wife really had to talk him into stopping. Herbert was very fond of Emma, and had consequently grown less fond of Marc since Thérèse. From the corner of his eye he gave a barely veiled, cold, assaying look at his hostess, while she instructed her houseboy in what everyone wanted to drink. She caught his look and repaid it with a condescending smile, and then her eyes panned all three of these people who'd barged in. Herbert, who was a few years older than Marc, was not an unattractive man, she thought, distinctive in a Prince Philip sort of way, and would be even more so if his long, hairy legs weren't poking out of floppy shorts. Because of her shape and her sagging face, Vanessa reminded Thérèse of a ripe old tomato. The teenage boy was stout, like his mother, and swarthy.

"Actually, we've come to use your shower!" Vanessa chirped a little defiantly, in answer to Thérèse's gaze.

"Yes, and fill your cantines!" Thérèse replied.

Dinner was worse than awkward. Thérèse offered to let some of the Spanish gentlefolk on the Herberts' route know they were coming. Herbert wanted to have nothing to do with Spanish gentlefolk. He was happy that the relaxation of the Chancellor of the Exchequer's austerity program was allowing him to spend money in a country he'd never seen, to see the Goyas he'd never got round to seeing before. But socializing was something different. Socializing was like diplomatic recognition.

"When you think they're talking of letting Hitler's friend into the UN—"

"Your attitude is senseless," Thérèse said.

"It's senseless if you mean to say that I'm a rich man, but that doesn't make me—the people who run this country with an iron hand, Thérèse, are criminals."

"If those people were not still here, Herbert," she shot back, "this country would be run with an iron hand by Communists. Franco at least prevented that."

"You are not well informed, Thérèse," Herbert said coldly.

"Herbert, don't be a *bore*," Vanessa pleaded. "Let's talk about something less *exciting*. Oh hell, let's talk about religion."

But Thérèse hadn't finished with Herbert.

"If the rich are uneasy being rich," she said, "they ought to give their money away and be done with it. If they're not willing to stand up and be counted as part of their own class, when they have to, then they'll be pulled down. And then where will you be? The poor, Herbert, have never got beyond destroying when they've tried to destroy. Then the rich come back—the same ones, or *others*, worse—"

Raphael, the boy who'd said nothing, who'd been shyly eating his soup, suddenly perked up. "That's absurd," he said authoritatively. "All my father means to say is simply that in the Spanish Civil War a democratic government was brought down by an unpardonable ally of Hitler. All my father is trying to say is simply that in this country the rich have helped themselves to everything."

Thérèse was about to reply, but Marc stayed her by reaching across the table and taking her wrist.

"Herbert," Marc said, "tell us the latest Churchill story."

But Herbert simply went "Hmm . . ." and it was a long time and much forced talk about gardens, pictures at the Prado, garlic, and Spanish olive oil before Herbert warmed up enough to bestow upon his fellow diners his inside information on the latest of the aging Prime Minister's social gaffes.

The Herberts decided to press on in the morning. While their bags were being packed, Herbert and Marc walked together through the lemon grove between the house and a wood of pines.

"I saw Emma in Paris," Herbert said.

"Oh don't look so awkward. . . . You know I always see Emma in Paris. We're best friends."

"She was not in the best spirits."

"I can no longer help that, Herbert."

"Are you really serious . . . about this?" Herbert waved his hand to take in the landscape. This place. But what he very obviously meant was: this life. *That woman.*

Marc looked toward the house. His manservant had pushed the Rover (which he'd washed) through the narrow gateway to make it easier for Herbert to drive off. A maid came running with a last khaki satchel, which had almost been forgotten.

"Well, I see you're all packed," Marc said, turning his gaze to the fig tree beyond the gate.

At the end of July, Marc and Thérèse went up to Monte Carlo, where their arrival caused a stir which all the same took second billing to the resort's great piece of gossip: Godwin Laver had just run off with the adolescent daughter of Luis Fuertaga, the Chilean nitrate and Guana millionaire. It seemed that the old man had caught on to Godwin's infatuation and hauled up anchor on his yacht. To no avail: Laver caught up with the boat in Venice and eloped with the girl. The lovers were last seen leaving the lobby of the Danieli, but they were rumored to be living like Robinson Crusoe on some beach in the Baleares.

When Marc heard the story he understood immediately that Laver's elopement was also a defection. A strange melancholy came over him.

He was to have that same peculiar feeling now and then at brief moments over the years, and in particular one evening at the end of August, 1960. They were at the Normandy in Deauville, he and Thérèse; they'd gone up for the yearling sales and to watch Bruno's polo team, Lilas, compete for the Gold Cup. Among the tables at the match, Marc had come upon his son, who'd arrived on his own.

It struck him quite suddenly how grown up Gilbert was. He was taller than Marc, and he spoke with a rough voice as he shook his father's hand to say hello awkwardly. That evening, before dressing to go down to the crowd at the bar for a drink, Marc lay on his bed with his eyes half-closed. That special melancholy swept over him more intensely than ever before. He recalled that at thirty he'd considered himself old and that half again that number of years had passed since then, and almost as many since he'd hungered to do something of great importance. He tried to laugh at himself, but loneliness chilled his blood now. He wanted to take Thérèse in his arms. She was making up in her bathroom, and so he went out the door of his room, which gave onto the lawn. From the grass ringing with crickets, he could see a fuschia sunset over the Channel. He took a deep breath and told himself how splendid it was simply to be alive and able to perceive that beautiful end of day. He took heart.

Sitting in his wheelchair in his garden, Avenue Foch, Marc's father, who was eighty, watched at more or less the same time the same natural phenomenon, thinking much the same thing.

FOUR

"Bruno is going to do us all in," Léopold said. "The man is a crook..."

The man responsible for Léopold's distress, as he tried to relax with his feet in his father's swimming pool, was named Francis R. Goodfriend. At the vortex of Léopold's worry was the news that Mr. Goodfriend have invited Bruno de Wolfflen to join the board of his new company, and although they were still talking money, Bruno seemed about to accept the position.

"Bruno is absolutely no match for him. I took one look at Goodfriend the first time he came to me and I knew right then that he was crooked. And he had the nerve to come back. Bruno is asking for—"

Léopold was distracted by his father's gesture. In what might have been meant as some form of answer, Saul von Wolfflen had wagged his head as he went into a last sprint on his exercycle. Pedaling furiously, he fixed his look on the instrument whose needle flashed toward an analog of speed high enough to create a pleased glint in his eye. Having reached his goal, he coasted with his hands at his side.

"Five kilometers," Saul said, sitting down at the edge of the pool happily winded beside Léopold.

The Baron Saul was eighty-eight years old. Sitting there bald and naked, with his long testicles hanging like an *aumonière,* some medieval wallet, in the warm water, he looked reduced but exceedingly hardy, a yew tree in February. His limbs had lost almost all their fat and only a droop in his belly betrayed that he had once been a rather roundish man. Saul had devoted himself very seriously to exercise and clean living in recent years.

In 1955, he'd had a thirty-yard pool dug in the middle of the great crystal palace of a greenhouse that stood on the grounds of his place in the Rue Madame—one of those properties on the Left Bank, in the Faubourg Saint-Germain, where you enter a door in a banal, cream-colored rear wall and find yourself in Eden on the other side. The greenhouse was Saul's inner-Eden. He would spend hours working with his own hands on the numerous tropical trees and bushes he'd put in, muttering to himself—reliving, who knows, a precious moment of his life years ago in Holland. His pool was the only private pool in Paris, but neither he nor Léopold were moved to boast about this; they preferred to keep it their secret. Religiously, or rather like two awed boys deliciously trespassing, they made their way along the humid, spicy lanes of the greenhouse every evening, and swam naked together.

Léopold's body, too, had improved as he'd grown older. He was a bit thick in the trunk and heavy in the thighs, but he'd grown tall enough to carry his weight, none of which was quite flab. His round face had taken on more definition, so that his large eyes no longer seemed the only sign of life on a plain landscape. His acne had healed, leaving a few scars whose presence, recalling adolescence, made him seem younger than his twenty-eight years. Saul was gratified to notice that something about the boy had become identifiably Wolfflen: his lips, which were now quite full and sensitive. When Léopold spoke, Saul also thought he could tell that Léopold had the instinctive intelligence that—for all their flaws—the members of his family seldom lacked.

"*Monsieur* Goodfriend has absolutely no substance," Léopold began again, "because even if I may be the only one to have done so, I have checked him out . . ."

"Imagery . . . that's what he wants," Saul interjected. "He wants to buy our image—that's the word they have now. Substance is not the main thing, my son."

"He's a crook," Léopold persisted. "I know it. You know it. Why doesn't everyone else know it? Why doesn't Bruno?"

Saul tugged on his moustache and once again gave that little wag of his head. Léopold wondered if somewhere in his father's vast travels he'd encountered a people for whom that gesture was part of the language. Now Léopold thought he knew what it meant. He thought it meant the world is crazy.

Léopold had spoken to his father with the even tone of a man who wasn't boasting, who knew—he too—enough about other people's stupidity, but was not motivated to make any case for himself. At twenty-eight, having run the Baron Saul's group of investments for seven years, judiciously if not imaginatively, he talked like an old professional. Saul had given Léopold total power, sink or swim, the day of his majority. Instead of trying to be a boy wizard, he'd begun by consulting the old Baron more frequently than it interested Saul, and by calling, in flattering homage, on all the great gray heads of the *quartier de la Bourse*. Léopold had aimed straight out for respectability; and he'd earned it.

When Ronnie Goodfriend attacked the "Old Guard Plutocrats of European Finance" young Léopold von Wolfflen was one of the men he had in mind.

Once, in a pep talk he'd given in Geneva to his sales force, Goodfriend, the president of World Investors Representatives, actually contrasted himself with Léopold directly, calling the young Baron a "constipated, hibernating little bear." Those words, purportedly for internal WIR ears only, came back to Léopold and confirmed to him the grudge Goodfriend held against him. Why not? Léopold had said no to the man whom *Fortune*, in a cover story, was to call "the Bubbly Genius of Offshore Mutuals." Having made his famous remark about Léopold, Goodfriend all the same came back, with the magazine story faceup in the attaché case he opened on Léopold's desk, and tried once again to do business. Obviously, as some men believe Everyone has his price, Goodfriend, the supersalesman, believed everyone had his weak moment. But Léopold had agreed to receive Bubbly Ronnie again simply to tell him what he thought of him eye to eye:

"Mr. Goodfriend, it is my informed opinion that you might well do something that will put you in jail someday."

"Has he broken any laws anywhere?" Saul asked now, rubbing his right calf under the water.

Léopold shrugged. "Maybe not yet. But no one will touch him in America."

Léopold's words to Goodfriend had been harsh and vengeful, out of keeping with his usual equanimity. For so far, Ronnie Goodfriend appeared to have done nothing very illegal. When Léopold had checked on him five years ago, he'd learned that he'd been fired from the first and only Wall Street brokerage house he'd worked for. From a good source, Léopold had learned that Goodfriend had been speculating for himself in the over-the-counter market, extending himself credit. He was well ahead in his gambling when his firm caught on, and the company simply forced him to sell out and sacked him without a scandal.

By the first time he'd approached Léopold, he'd become the head of a large team of semibohemian expatriate Americans roaming Europe in old used cars, offering shares in the Urquehart Mutual Fund, which had had a spectacular success with small investors in America. They were selling by putting their feet in the doorways of the huts of noncommissioned officers on U.S. Army bases.

Goodfriend had asked to open an account in the small, exclusive, private bank Léopold controlled in Lausanne. He'd called Léopold for an appointment saying he was a friend of Hugo Sellier, of the Crédit Lyonnais. Léopold took what he said on the phone at face value and agreed to see Goodfriend personally, but when he checked afterwards, he learned the friendship with Sellier had no substance beyond the fact that Goodfriend had come across the old banker at the bar of the Relais Plaza and introduced himself, flashing some blandishments about Sellier's reputation.

"All he wanted the first time was an account in the bank," Léopold said to Saul as he rose from the poolside and headed for the humming towel-dryer. "He sounded almost as if he thought we'd be flattered." As Léopold turned back toward his father, the hot towel he'd extracted caught in the palm tree beside the cedar door of the dryer. "I'll cut that," Saul apologized, looking sidelong at Léopold's irritated struggle with the leaf. Léopold was not good with his hands. Perhaps not with the rest of his body, either, although he had in Saul's opinion all he needed there. He was awkward physically . . .

Léopold continued: " 'I believe, Baron de Wolfflen,' he said to me, 'that a man's check is like a calling card, and I want to have the name of people of your station on my personal checkbook.' " Léopold couldn't suppress a wry laugh now at what Goodfriend had said before he began taking his phrases from hired speechwriters. "He told me he intended to be one of our best customers in a short time."

In five years, Goodfriend had increased WIR's sales in the Urquehart Fund to the rate of $68 million annually, and he was selling not only to crop-headed G.I.'s in Europe but to hundreds of thousands of people all over the globe who had access to U.S. dollars. Except, of course, in America itself. The "front-end load" of charges WIR took from investors was much too high for the Securities and Exchange Commission.

The second time Goodfriend had called on Léopold, a month ago, it was to offer Léopold's Lausanne bank the role of depository of cash for the mutual fund Goodfriend had decided to found on his own: the Public Capital Institution. After Goodfriend left Léopold's office, red faced, blinking in nervous rage, and shooting his cuffs under the sleeves of his tight Cardin suit, Léopold had called Gaston Robinet at the Banque Wolfflen and advised him to beware. But Goodfriend lowered his sights. He found another Swiss bank anxious for the large amount of cash the PCI was expected to bring in. He then addressed himself not to the Banque Wolfflen but to the Baron Bruno, who was still fishing without anchor in the financial world. Goodfriend offered Bruno a place on the board of the Public Capital Institution. He was a long way past needing a good name along with his own on his personal checkbook. He was paying notable men to sit on the board of his "Institution." He already had a former finance minister of Belgium.

"Imagery . . ." Saul said just before he plunged into the water. He did a rapid crawl across the width of the pool and back, then frog-stroked to the ladder. As he abandoned the water in his turn, his wet, bald crown glistened like a precious object.

"Imagery," he said again, "a form of capital invented, in case you

238   THE HEIRS

didn't know it, by Marcel Boussac, the financier of Monsieur Christian Dior. Monsieur Dior made luxurious clothes for very rich women. Monsieur Boussac sells a little piece of that 'image' of luxury to housewives and secretaries by putting Monsieur Dior's name on stockings and girdles. Most of the consumers aren't even aware that Monsieur Dior died of overeating three years ago. His image lives on . . ."

Saul chose a warm towel; it hung on his small frame like the robe of a bedouin. "Our image lives on and on," he said with a provocative smile. "People see us as the mythic *haute couture* of finance."

He got the response he'd teased for: "We're by no means dead," Léopold replied evenly.

"Ah yes . . . of course, but for Mister Goodfriend the name Wolfflen is a large chunk of underexploited capital."

"The first time I called Bruno, on Wednesday, I told him as tactfully as I could that each of us wore the responsibility for the entire Wolfflen name," Léopold said, "that none of us had the right to get into anything that even risked smelling bad . . ."

"As tactfully as you could . . ." Saul was a trifle amused.

"Yes, and he snapped at me," Léopold said in the tone of a child offended by injustice. "He said: 'What do you expect me to do, change my name?' And then he went into a long defense of Ronnie Goodfriend. I had the feeling I was reading a glossy brochure on PCI I'd been shown, called 'Popular Capitalism.' 'Goodfriend is the kind of man who's going to save people like us'—he actually put it that way—'Goodfriend realizes that the capitalist system is being challenged all over the world, and that unless the little man is encouraged to have a stake in capitalism, the system will go under.' "

"Yes, the little man in the black hole of Calcutta—" Saul interjected wryly, "Mister Small-investor."

"You see . . ." Léopold said with a sense of frustration, "the man is shameless. You see. I see." And he shrugged.

They dressed in an alcove where Saul had planted orchids beside a curved wall of sandlewood. A smell of wild places—jungles where white men tread in fear—and at the same time suggestive of elegance, recalling candlelight and the shoulders of women in silk, suffused through the hot, wet air.

"I told him—" Léopold said, cupping the heel of his stockinged foot with a long shoehorn as he slipped on a thickish Lobb blucher. Léopold walked in a heavy way, and had his shoes made accordingly, to take the punishment. "I told him I don't know anything about our eventual salvation, but I do know that Ronnie Goodfriend is tacking something like a thirteen percent front-end load on the WIR monthly investment program, and that I assumed he was inventing his own fund so that he could pick up the several more points Urquehart is taking from the investor on the other end.

"Can you imagine that? The way he's got it worked out, some of those little people would come out with nothing if they cashed-in in a year."

"His hour is in the future," Saul said. *"Caveat emptor."*

"*Caveat* Bruno. But Bruno said: 'The investor knows all about it, his contract is in black and white. How else can he have top experts investing for him for the centimes he puts in every month. Anyway, PCI is going to give them much much more than it takes in fees. It's going to give them real growth for their money, for all these people who've been nothing more than docile milking cows for the savings banks. The market is booming in America, and Ronnie knows where to go with it ...'

"'Then, why,' I asked, 'does the Public Capital Institution have its Depository of Cash in Switzerland, its Depository of Securities in Luxembourg, its Transfer Agent and Registrar in Lichtenstein, while the fund itself is incorporated in Curaçao? Why, if not to keep the whole operation beyond the control of the laws of each of those places, as well as beyond the view of the Securities Exchange Commission?'

"You know what he answered? He said: 'Because, Léopold, in each and every one of those places, including the Security Exchange Commission, and in my own family, there are Establishment reactionaries very anxious to shoot down the whole new idea.'

"'Listen, Léopold,' he said, 'I am getting into something very very big. You haven't a clue, Léopold, about how enormous this is going to be. You ask me what I'm putting my name on, Léopold—I am putting my name on a very big future. *The* future.' "

"You know, Léopold," Saul said in a soft, reasoning voice now, "I try to see Bruno for what he is. If I don't talk to him, it's because I can't bring myself to talk to him. But I won't calumniate him. And yet—knowing the man—I consider it quite natural that he will shoot off his mouth saying bad things about us. He does it with a certain *righteousness*."

Saul paused to be able to form in words exactly what he felt.

"Bruno is indignant. You see? He's the indignant orphan of the family. He's got a lot of energy and he's flailed around a lot, and what with Charles, I suppose he is indignant that he hasn't had his right place in the family somehow. Bruno has nothing crooked in his nature. I am positive he's totally honest. But Bruno needs very badly to do something 'with a very big future.' You see? He needs to very badly."

Léopold grunted—a grudging signal that he'd understood, but was skeptical.

"What did he say when you phoned a second time?"

"The second time he wouldn't even take my call. They said he was in conference. He didn't call back ... of course."

"I consider that his natural reaction."

Saul's comprehending pessimism didn't settle anything. They both assumed a perturbed silence now as they made their way through the long greenhouse. Their path wound among date palms and banana trees and many low plants Léopold's father had put in, whose names he could never remember. Saul paused at a guava plant with a ripe fruit. He picked the fruit and squeezed it in two, baring the bright, sticky seeds. He nibbled ruminatively, appreciatively, on one half and offered the other to Léopold, who declined with a shake of his head. Léopold put his palm to his abdomen. He was trying to lose weight.

"Did you ... take this up with Charles?"

"With Robinet."

"Ah ..." Saul's "ah" had a note of relief to it. Léopold was Saul's buffer between himself and the rest of the family. Léopold kept up thinly-cordial contact with all of them; he went occasionally to their dinners, but he'd never quite broken the ice with them. An awareness of separation had turned into a reflexive way of thinking on his part and on theirs. An uneasiness had never been overcome. It was as if Léopold still wore the alien presence of his mother among the other Wolfflens. As it turned out, he was less polished, less "worldly" than they, and in his big, stocky physique they could not help but recall the build of Saul's chauffeur. When it came to business, Léopold stayed as far away as he could from the rest of the family, partly because he considered himself a much more astute businessman than any of them, partly because Saul would have it that way. Saul took a measure of relief in the fact that Léopold had not gone to Charles but to the president of the bank that bore the Wolfflen name, the official man in power. The less he had to do with Charles directly the better he felt. He couldn't explain to himself clearly why he resented Charles even more than Bruno. Perhaps it was somehow because Charles was of his own generation, because in a dim way he begrudged Charles' *having also survived,* reaching the narrow enclave of old age. As if he saw in Charles a threatening rival in the race against death. It was not all clear to the reasoning part of Saul's mind. Maybe he held Charles responsible for Bruno's being the way he was, held Charles chiefly to blame for the episode at Ariel's funeral. The reasoning part of Saul's mind would have pardoned that injury a long time ago—he was a wise, mellow, charitable man. But his guts wouldn't give up their antagonism, their revulsion at the cynicism of the others, which had caused him to suffer. And with all else, something in Saul's region of instincts confirmed the repugnance of his viscera, told him that he and his son had better stay as far away from the other Wolfflens as they could when it came to money, because—and here again he couldn't conceptualize just how or why, but he *felt it*—they were *heading for a fall.*

Saul and Léopold found their coats in a closet near the entrance of the greenhouse, and prepared to go back into winter. Saul wrapped a long cashmere scarf around his neck and tucked it into an old loden shooting-coat. His pants were thick carpenter's corduroy. Saul rarely stirred out of the grounds of his huge property in the middle of Paris, and he dressed with the casual practicality of a man in the country. To cover his bald head, he put on a multicolored crocheted skiing bonnet.

Outside it was dark and freezing. Saul tugged at the earflaps of his bonnet. "Bruno is honest," he said again, seeking cheer. "Maybe he is right. What *will* preserve capitalism . . . in the long run?"

"Human nature," Léopold answered with total certitude.

The cold gravel of the pathway rasped under their shoes. They walked, both of them, in the same wide-stepping, hard-heeled way, and from behind in the dark, it looked as if the little figure in the

242 THE HEIRS

pompon bonnet and drooping coat were the son, and the tall, bulky man in the chesterfield, bare headed, thick haired, the father. Ahead of them Saul's white house gleamed like an ocean liner: a long rectangle, set on a still longer one. Round windows near the top formed yellow circles of light. Saul paused with his hands on his hips to look in satisfaction at the house, as if he'd only just had it built. Actually it had gone up more than thirty years ago, not long after he had moved to Paris. He'd bought the property from the Marquis de Serres, whose eighteenth-century house had burned to the ground. The Marquis, who hadn't much money, had been reduced to living at a privileged monthly rate in a little room under the eaves of the Hôtel Claridge. Saul had been glad to find such an excellent lot of land with no house left on it. He'd wanted to live in something definitely his own. He had his architect, G. T. Rietveld, plan the new house right on top of the gaping, vaulted cellars of the old; Rietveld was one of the Dutch de Stijl group, contemporaries of the Bauhaus, but men who could give more charm than could the Germans to geometry. Wolfflen had seen Rietveld's masterful house in Utrecht, built for the Schröder family. "Please do me something twice the size," Saul had said, "with less glass and as much lightness and harmony." It wasn't an easy task. Looking now, again, for the Nth time, Saul was once again certain that Rietveld had succeeded.

The greenhouse, in which the Marquis's grape and melon plantation had died of neglect, had been an early work of the man who designed the Grand Palais. Rietveld, less fanatic than his peers, had urged Saul to spare it; and so it stood far off on the grounds, a bright, arid ghost, until Saul took up horticulture again in the 1950's.

Inside Rietveld's house, the open rooms seemed to float on a rhythmic arrangement of four levels, with the main room reaching from the ground to the very top. There were several paintings by the architect's friend Piet Mondrian. The furniture was also of the epoch—that last period when original things for the home were made by hand in precious materials; there were chairs and chaise-longues in palmwood and leopard skin by Pierre Legrain, tables covered with lacquered sharkskin, and—looking forward to the totally machine age—geometric ensembles in chrome tubing by Robert Mallet-Stevens, along with Le Corbusier's famous undulent lounge chair in the original chrome and ponyhide, which stood in what had been Ariel's dressing room. Ariel had loved the iconoclasm of the place. It was the only modern house in the entire Faubourg Saint-Germain, the most hallowed of upper-crust neighborhoods. But at times she used to complain, unreasonably, that she could perceive the lingering bitter stink of fire seeping from the cellars through the sheepskin parchment walls and the ebony and cork flooring. Ariel . . .

Saul cleared his throat. "What about Marc?" he asked. He had not cleared away the melancholy that had come over him; he spoke with a certain plaintiveness. "Can Marc reason with him?"

"Marc. Marc hasn't been able to reason with his own crotch for these many years . . ."

FIVE

The Duke was drinking heavily. In his cups he was accusing Marc de Wolfflen of having "driven" him "out of Chantilly." The truth was that Thérèse had stopped paying the enormous running costs of the Helfenberg stables. At a sober moment, the Duke had countered by selling the place, which she had paid for, and pocketing the money. He'd found an excellent customer in a colossally rich Swiss, and among his horse-world friends he'd made a lot of the good price he'd got. His boasting had been hollow, though. For a brief while, he'd been one of the great owners of France, the man who'd taken over the Helfenberg stables. After the sale, he'd had to retrench on his old reputation as a prominent gentleman rider of the thirties; watching the Baron Marc de Wolfflen's ascension as a horseman had done nothing to assuage Flandres' overall bitterness toward Marc.

Marc had rapidly become more and more of an expert in the ways of buying the best horses and getting the most out of them. He'd filled his life with racing, spending days on end at High Cottage; often, when he had a dinner in town, he would make the hour's drive to Chantilly from Paris the next morning after only a few hours sleep. By the fall of 1960, the stables of High Cottage had been profitable for several years running, and Marc had the particular satisfaction on the first Sunday of October to have one of his mounts competing for the Prix de l'Arc de Triomphe, the most important race in France, the final big race of the season.

The Sunday of the Arc was a rite, and the mood of that autumn afternoon was charged with a sense of the ultimate and the quintessential. Families with little children lolled on the lawn that bordered the lusher grass of Longchamp's track. A racing day in France was a day for unbinding, a willful consecration to leisure: life was compressed into a beautiful afternoon, during which all other striving, like mist in sunlight, melted away, leaving the rituals of Chance and The Contest, the contest played out as art, by elegant thoroughbreds and jockeys in gorgeous silks. For many Parisians of all classes, the track was their *corridà:* life and theatre, both at once, life made simple and crucial symbol as well. Yet the symbolism of Longchamp, unlike that of the bullring, was bravely comic. It spoke of a joy that could renew itself eternally. The Prix de l'Arc, enacted in a slanting light predicting winter, by the best horses, the best jockeys, and a crowd, rich and poor, in its best finery, was the ultimate affirmation that the world the Impressionists had painted could come back to life at certain magic moments.

The sun was strong on that day of the Arc in 1960, but a cold breeze would sometimes rustle through the surrounding Bois de Boulogne and sweep over Longchamp, causing a flutter among the veils and scarves of the women. The portion of the grandstand set aside for horseowners was a thick bouquet of those ladies in delicate *toilettes.* Among the owners everyone was in his most careful ritual dress. The women wore wide-brimmed floral hats and couture dresses, over which some of them—the most sensitive to chill or the most ostentatious—had draped furs. The gentlemen owners had on putty-gray tail-coated suits and gray top hats, and their male guests were in light flannel or pinstriped worsteds. Some of the visitors— mainly the English in town especially for the Arc—sported their slouched brown racetrack fedoras and their *boutonnières.*

The box belonging to Marc de Wolfflen was full of people close to him, whose presence together gave him a sense of well-being. Thérèse, first of all—she'd been feeling weak that morning but had perked up, and was now playing the occasion to the hilt in a costumey, big-flowered dress. Emma had come with Philippe Arthaud. Bruno and Edmée were there with Iris, their daughter.

Marc didn't feel like ruining the day by mentioning the Goodfriend matter to Bruno. But it was there all the same, in the silence between them. What could Marc tell Bruno, from what vantage could he send down advice? He knew there wasn't any. Bruno had been flailing around, trying desperately to do something big, for years. And Marc's own life had taken on the sunny indolence of a day at Longchamp. That perception fled across his mind while he passed his binoculars to his cousin at the start of the second race. Along with the perception that he was happy. Yes, he was happy...

Bruno took the glasses, and then, pressing his daughter against his chest, he reached over her shoulders and put them to her eyes. Bruno was a very affectionate father, even though he'd been terribly disappointed that Iris had not been a boy, an heir. She looked like a boy, already gangly like her father, and bony. Bruno had wanted a boy and Edmée hadn't given him more than one child, so far. He and Bruno, one child each. The race is thinning out. Thérèse didn't want any children, motherhood just wasn't her act. Well, I have a son, Marc thought. I have a son.

Marc was particularly pleased that Gilbert was with him. The boy had worked hard to get free for the weekend from Croseigne, and he'd even gone to the trouble to get his hands on a gray tail-coated suit like his father's. Marc felt that in putting on that uniform Gilbert had made a gesture of adoption, a movement closer to the father with whom he had communicated so little over the years. He is *assuming* being a Wolfflen, Marc told himself. It was a moment's imprecise intuition, more than a measured conviction about where he stood with his son, but that moment cheered him more than the fact that his horse, Carabine, stood a good chance of winning the Arc.

Carabine might place second, maybe third, and maybe not at all, as Hervé de Flandres saw it. Wolfflen's horse had a problem and his problem was Lancelot. There was even a chance that they'd wear each other out and neither would finish in the money. They were two headstrong speed horses, three-year-olds with plenty of stamina, and neither jockey might want to give the other much of a lead for fear of never catching up. Yet if they fought it out hard enough too early, there was a good opportunity for Nescafé, who ran well "under cover" to burst out of the field and steal the race in the homestretch. A lot depended on what position they'd draw at the gate. Flandres estimated a starting position close to the rail at Longchamp was worth a ten percent advantage; a thousand of the track's twenty-four hundred meters were in the turns, and Longchamp's long, gradual turns put a bad strain on outside horses. If either Carabine or Lancelot drew an outside position, his chances would be badly compromised, and if they both did, so much the better for Nescafé. Particularly since the even track made picking your way through the field a relatively smooth business. And yet Lancelot, the favorite, was very very fast. Very fast. Flandres knew that favorites arrived first only three times out of ten, and he'd sooner not bet than put his money on Lancelot with meager odds. On the other hand, Nescafé looked good... He decided to suspend his choice of whether to bet or not until after he'd had an eyeful of the horses in the paddock.

Flandres had begun the afternoon very pleasantly. He'd lunched with friends in the Bois, at the Cascades, and they'd set him down, next to a rather eager young American girl, very pretty, whom he knew he had impressed. Her family was in oil and cattle. Everyone had drunk a lot of wine, and Flandres had had a cognac as well after his coffee, and a good cigar. He'd left the table with the name of her hotel, feeling the rush of optimism he always felt after a lot of food and wine. Now his mood was falling, he felt drained. He knew there was something purely physical at work, that the meal and the alcohol had set glands spurting tonic into his blood, and that now his system had come down from its high. All that was understandable, but understanding didn't improve his spirits.

From where he sat, at the low, far right-hand corner of the Jockey Club's section of the grandstand, he could see the owners coming and going among their boxes to the left. The people around him were older and in more sober cloth. He felt an impulse of disdain toward that flashy lot in their boxes, but he knew at the same time that it was a self-protective emotion he felt. That lot he would have gladly joined, as an owner himself. He would have joined them today and would have worn among them, at the same time, the distinction of being who he was, born better. He would have been something special among them.... He'd been willing ... he'd been willing to eat with Thérèse wherever she'd wanted, with whatever dubious "amusing" people she would have liked. He responded to fun as well as the next person; he hadn't been brought up to make it the object of his life, but so long as he didn't have to make himself ridiculous, he'd been willing. Yet this afternoon he'd declined to accompany his friends at lunch to the owners' boxes where they'd been invited by Ali Khan. "I'll join you later," he'd said, "I've someone to meet . . ." But now he was sitting by himself. He realized that he'd fallen back on a grim line of defense, that although it was very proper to be sitting where he was sitting, it certainly wasn't very amusing. And now, though he could just about make out her face in profile, he could hear distinctly the loud voice of the woman he'd married. Laughing. Amusing, no doubt, all the people around her—where he couldn't hold his head up anymore. *The object of his life . . .* The words came back, dangled in his mind a moment and faded, leaving no message behind. The third race was over; he decided to go down to the paddock early to avoid bumping into *that lot* on the way. On the other hand, why had he come here today? Go where I like, he told himself. But he didn't really want to hear a clear answer. He had time to drink something at the little bar under the chestnut trees.

The promenade before each race of the starting horses with their jockeys, around the green paddock of Longchamp, is beautiful to look at, but for the trained eye, the paddock is as instructive as it is showy. There are first of all the obvious physical defects of the horses, which become clear at close view: the faintly hollow thighs and low-slung bellies, the palpitating shoulders—all the failings of nature that may be ever so slight, but reduce the horse's chances of defeating a more perfect animal in a highly competitive race. And then there is the matter of a horse's state of mind. Hervé de Flandres had no quarrel with people who contended that a horse was the stupidest animal going; all the same, the mental condition of a horse before a race was one of the most important factors in his chances of winning. A horse daubed with white sweat, particularly at the belly, was an overwrought horse, and one that skittered or dropped turds when his jockey mounted him was a horse frightened of the track, from having, perhaps, been whipped hard his last time out. On the other hand, a horse with taut but untwitching muscles, with an eye neither rolling excitedly nor gone dull, a horse walking with long, even, collected strides, was a horse anxious to go out and do his best.

Such was a good description of Nescafé, as his jockey, Willy Beck, led him past the portion of the rail where the Duke was standing. It was an equally exact description of a horse Flandres hadn't given a thought to: Easy Money. As for Lancelot and Carabine, they were both in a bit of a lather ...

The odds posted against Nescafé were fourteen to one when Flandres left the paddock. Beck had drawn sixth position from the rail in a race of seventeen horses. Byron Fuller, Lancelot's jockey, had drawn eleventh, but was still riding the favorite at three to one. Carabine had drawn the best starting place, number one off the rail, and the odds on him were nine to two. Easy Money was running second from the rail, at thirty-two to four. She was being mounted by Yvan Golles, who was a hot young jockey. Flandres was tempted for a moment to bet Nescafé to win and Easy Money to place, but he had a second thought; he was leery of Golles' inexperience. He walked quickly to the nearest large-stake betting counter and put five thousand francs on Nescafé to win. Having downed a split of champagne and three whiskeys at the *buvette* before entering the paddock, he was feeling much more up ... in a winning mood.

No sooner had the race begun than Flandres could hear his wife shouting like some common woman at the rail from the Wolfflen box. Carabine, profiting from his favored starting position, had taken a large lead. She was screaming, the woman he'd married, actually screaming with excitement over the man's horse ...

Carabine was well ahead, riding alone, before the first turn, and Tim O'Brien, his jockey, was wondering what Lancelot might be up to. Fuller had dashed out of the box and then checked Lancelot for a split-second by edging closer to the inside; several horses charged ahead of him, and in a moment he was no longer in the open, on the outside, but riding covered in the field. O'Brien realized that Fuller was riding an entirely different kind of race from the one he'd expected: holding back, instead of fighting for the lead Carabine had taken with ease. Suddenly, just at the turn, O'Brien thought he perceived one of the reasons for Fuller's strategy: Easy Money was in the clear, right beside Carabine, and charging ahead. Fuller must have realized that before Easy Money gave out he would have drawn the best out of Carabine, after which Fuller would come forward on Lancelot in the homestretch.

Golles' motives, as he rode Easy Money, were less clear to

O'Brien. He couldn't understand why Golles was asking Easy Money for all he could give so early, unless he had far more of a horse in his hands than anybody knew he had. But as Golles' face flashed beside O'Brien's, O'Brien understood all there was to understand: Easy Money was running away. Once he'd seen daylight there was nothing in Golles' skill as a jockey to hold him back. Golles was running with his face twisted and his tongue out, and his hands were all over the place. O'Brien dropped his own hands slightly and moved his thumbs forward, loosening Carabine's grip on the bit and shortening the reins at the same time. Carabine slackened, and O'Brien held him inside at Easy Money's tail. He'd let Easy Money set his pace.

The other horses were not far behind now, and Nescafé was running deliberately last. Beck felt like he had a twelve-cylinder engine in second gear in his hands as he and Nescafé went into the straightaway again. Just then, though, the horse ahead of Nescafé, Noonday, began to fade, and Beck knew that if he didn't overtake him he risked falling too far behind. He swung out to pass Noonday, but as soon as Nescafé saw nothing but daylight ahead of him, he took off as fast as he could gallop. The field was running tight now, and Beck had no place to find cover, no choice but to let Nescafé give what he had and hope that most of it would last to the finish line.

When they came into the homestretch, Nescafé was running third, behind Carabine and Easy Money, but a hundred meters from the finish, Beck felt a sickening slackness between his fingers. He began to flail with his crop, furious, yet knowing full well that all he was doing now was punishing the horse . . .

By then, Carabine had made his bid. It was said of Tim O'Brien that he "had no arms," that he failed to apply a crop in tight moments when one was needed. But what he lacked in arms he had in hands. As he flashed ahead of Easy Money, he shifted his wrists to give Carabine the bit to lean on hard, and, riding so high he was nearly standing up, he put almost all his weight just over the horse's shoulders. He dug his heels into Carabine and concentrated on letting his own body catch the rhythm of the horse. Now it was all up to the horse . . .

Golles began swinging his crop high in the air on Easy Money, but the mare had given more than anyone might have hoped. The finish was only a few meters ahead, and now Golles could see Lancelot charging forward with incredible acceleration. Lancelot moved between the rail and Easy Money's rear, and Golles knew just then that if he fought for second place he might just make it. He pointed Easy Money closer into the rail. Fuller came slamming against him on Lancelot, flailing his crop, and from the look on his face he seemed about to plant it on Golles' neck instead of on Lancelot. They rode jammed together that way, even after they'd followed Carabine over the finish line.

Carabine the winner. Lancelot second. Easy Money third.

Nescafé finished sixteenth. . . .

The Duke's enthusiasm had died a sudden death the moment Nescafé fell apart in the homestretch. And then his disappointment bloomed into anger; he felt *outraged* by an injustice, and because it wasn't his own horse he felt for now, he fed his anger with righteousness. If Lancelot had been able to get through he would surely have won. Flandres' mind conceived the worst: Wolfflen had bought Easy Money to lead his horse and then to keep Lancelot back.

The Jew bought the race, he thought, hearing his wife's voice once again, stridently joyful. He headed back down to the open-air bar.

The photographers were all over the paddock, and Thérèse was doing nothing to stay out of the picture. She kissed Marc, she kissed O'Brien, she kissed Carabine, and there were twenty flashbulbs going off with each kiss.

"Who's the lady?" one of the photographers asked another, as they pushed forward beside Emma and Arthaud. The man who asked had to be from some provincial newspaper.

"His partner," Emma volunteered evenly, turning to go.

"Can you tell me her name, *madame*, please?" It struck Emma as peculiar that there were people whose lives had been untouched by any awareness of Thérèse's existence.

"Her name is Flandres," Arthaud answered. "Moll Flandres . . ." He led Emma away on his arm.

"Extraordinary race," Arthaud said as his Peugeot bore the two of them through the Bois. Chestnut leaves crackled under the tires and flashed like scared fish through the gusts made by the car ahead. There was a faint, stomach-tickling odor of gasoline. For the sake of a breath of oxygen, Emma rolled down her window and exposed her fine brown hair to the punishment of the wind. The woods smelled of sand, dusty exhaust, and bitter plant decay. Although she was not a country person, Emma thought she could perceive the scent of nature's death pangs, of a dying season, which seemed to call to her plummeting spirits, like calling to like.

"Oh the race!" She started. "Absolutely incredible."

Arthaud gave her a long look. He touched her wrist as he turned away to steer into a curve one-handed, with what seemed conscious jauntiness.

"Emma," he said, "must you ... must you really stay on and endure all that?"

"All that?"

"Her *reign*."

As she gave a little hollow laugh, the wind blew her hair into her mouth. With a child's sensuousness, she held a fine strand between her teeth a moment, before she let the wind take it again. Then she rolled the window up.

"Well, you know I'm not a prisoner in the castle dungeon, Philippe," she insisted. "Marc and I ... love each other—for what we are, not for what we give each other. That's an aspect of love—it's not *the whole thing*, obviously. If tomorrow someone came and *swept me off my feet*—" she waved her hand to emphasize the irony in her voice "—then maybe I'd just go off—but you see I *don't* really crave that at all."

"What do you crave, Emma?" he asked gently.

"I don't crave."

They drove on in silence until a red light brought them to a halt near the Parc de la Muette. The grounds were crowded with children and mothers with baby carriages. Arthaud noted the scene with a pained, alien regard.

"If I ..." he began, "if I were capable of being that person—" his voice was half-defensive, half-apologetic, "You know I would have tried long ago. You're so ... You're too—"

She squeezed his hand. She knew his secret, the wreckage strewn in a dark side of his life. Once, even, a young man had beaten him very badly and walked out of his apartment with the Academician's sword that had belonged to his father, the old general.

"Emma, live your life!" he urged.

"There comes a time, Philippe," she said evenly, "when you know you'll never change your shortcomings, your lacks, your aberrations, and you have to stop being remorseful over them. You have to live with them openly then, openly in sin in a way, and try to make something constructive out of them, something virtuous, in that sense. The question is always how, isn't it? The answer is never the same for everyone. *The answer may not be there for everyone.*"

The light changed, and he drove on without replying.

The remaining races were anticlimactic, and as Marc and Thérèse left the paddock, Marc urged her to take the car and return home. "I'm going back to have champagne with the grooms. . . . You needn't. You were very tired this morning. You weren't really well, Thérèse."

"Oh no," she pleaded, "I'm going to have champagne. I'm going to have champagne with the grooms."

It struck him that she'd answered like a spoiled child. But he didn't insist.

Injustice . . . was what it . . .

Flandres had seen the light of the flashbulbs from where he stood at the *buvette*. All that excitement at the paddock only served to heighten his indignation: an injustice had been committed. He was into his fourth rapid scotch now, and he no longer was sure of what the boundaries of that injustice were; he was oppressed by a feeling of having been personally wronged. Perhaps it would be better if he collected his . . . thoughts. Better clear . . . clear up. How beautiful, how beautiful.

His perception of the weather broke through his anger, and he remained rapt in contemplation of trees and grass and bright human figures for a full quarter-hour. "Good," he finally said, after which he nursed another scotch, gulped down still another, and headed for the stables.

The area behind the paddock was reserved for owners and those who worked for them, but the old man at the gate was hardly inclined to turn away the Duke because he'd sold his stables. He was tempted to say something pleasant and servile to that High Gentleman who had always deigned to be pleasant with him when he passed. The gatekeeper wanted to form some greeting that, while still respectfully distant, would let the Duke know that he could always feel very much at home here. But when he noticed the pink glaze of the Duke's eyes, his instincts made him contract his greeting into a muffled *"m'sieu' le Duc."* The Duke went by him without uttering a word. The gatekeeper realized, not without secret gratitude, that a Duke's life wasn't all joy. *Monsieur le Duc* seemed sullen and full of pent anguish; and he was not walking straight.

Marc and Thérèse spotted him as they left Carabine's stable and turned into the aisle to head towards their car. He hurried up to them with a disjointed stride.

"He's drunk," Thérèse whispered, and she pulled Marc back with her into the shadow of the stable to let her husband pass.

The Duke turned heel and stepped into the stable. He tasted the coolness of the place, and the smell of straw and horses. They brought back the indistinct but sharp essence of a mood he'd known over and over in his life, a residue of emotion drained of precise time and place but vivid in its own concentrated way. It buoyed him for an instant.

"I'm sorry . . ." he said, in a blurred voice, but almost congenially, "I saw that you cheated." He was smiling. His smile was like a scar across his tight, bleary face. The Duke turned away from Marc and eyed his wife with the gaze of a streetcorner idler watching some strange lovely go past. Then his eyes seemed to retreat into his head.

"Thérèse . . ." he said vacantly.

"You'll leave right now," Marc said.

The tall Duke leaned forward over Marc as if he were going to fall on him. He put his long arm out slowly and took hold of Marc's starched collar. Marc's hand flashed out. With his palm on the Duke's face, he flung the man backward. Flandres reeled until he hit the wall behind him. Then he straightened up. His face was as red as a wound. Behind him there were reins hanging on a peg; he'd felt them as he fell against the wall. Suddenly he reached behind and then began to flail the long strips of leather like a whip. He caught Marc just under the eye with a buckle. Blood began to run down the Baron's cheek. O'Brien and Marc's trainer lunged forward, but Flandres held them off by flailing the reins in a great arc, until he stood facing Marc.

Thérèse shrieked something at her husband in Portuguese. He wheeled. The reins made a splattering noise as they struck her neck.

She sucked her breath in with the pain as she reached out and caught the reins, holding them just long enough for Marc to snatch them in both his hands. He moved under them and his hands made their way along them, until he stood toe to toe with the Duke. Flandres dropped his weapon and reached for Marc's neck. Marc's hands flashed out again, palm open, but instead of hitting Flandres, he caught his jacket and pulled him toward him in what looked like an embrace. He pulled him close, and then he pulled him down, down, until the Duke was on his knees in what seemed a stupor.

"Kill him! I hope you kill him!" Thérèse shouted. She shouted something else in Portuguese. Just then the Duke's fist blazed into Marc's face. With the pain, there came something like the splatter of acid in Marc's mouth; he was conscious just long enough to judge that it was his own blood.

When he came to, he saw the Duke sagging in the arms of O'Brien and the trainer. Flandres had his eyes pinched closed, as if, if he held them closed tightly enough and long enough, he might open them to find that what had happened had not really happened—and that maybe all that had happened to him since he'd met that woman, heard her voice, had never happened. Marc put his hand to his numb mouth. His lips felt like they were stuffed with nails. He touched raw, cold gum where two top teeth had been.

The Baron and his mistress were silent as the car bore them back to her apartment. Finally she shrugged impatiently, and took a pill from a little gold box in her purse. She spoke, blurred by an effort to hold the medicine under her tongue.

"I'm sorry," she said huskily. "You see, he's my husband." Her distorted voice kept him from knowing whether there was loyalty intended in what she'd said, and to whom. Marc stared at his chauffeur's hat for an instant without replying, but then he shrugged and took Thérèse's hand.

As if somehow he could be physically cleansed of the incident, Marc stood under his shower a long time. The whole day had gone badly wrong, beginning with the race. He'd won, yes, but he'd been cheated of a clean victory. If Lancelot had had a chance to break free ... Marc's lone satisfaction was with O'Brien, O'Brien's subtle but firm mastery. ...

Thérèse was in her dressing room, taking off her makeup. They had planned to dine at Bruno's that evening, but Marc couldn't go anywhere now with his mouth in the state it was in.

"You must telephone," she called across a row of open doors. Marc came out of his dressing room and went to the phone beside his bed.

"Will you talk to him tonight?" she called again. He shrugged to himself, but in a moment she was there beside him, sitting on his bed, with her legs parting the slit in the skirt she'd chosen for their dinner alone at home. Her new makeup was just a touch of color, but looking at her he realized that she never really needed any makeup at all. That special skin. Her fine legs suddenly made him think of unsheathed knife blades. He became ashamed of his face.

"About Goodfriend?" he said. "All right. I'll tell him what I think of him. My objections will probably encourage Bruno to go in with him."

"Well, then, why did he advise you he was seeing him?"

"To prove to me how important many people think he is. Do you understand?"

"Call."

She sat there with her back turned while Marc telephoned his cousin. A sudden fit of flu, Marc alibied.

"God, your voice sounds like you've had your teeth kicked in," Bruno said. Did he already know? "You'd better stay in bed for a while."

Marc went straight to the matter of Goodfriend, testy over the suspicion that Bruno was mocking him.

"Listen, Marc, I'm tired of hearing all sorts of people who aren't up to much themselves telling me to say no to the way the world is going."

"What?" Marc wasn't sure he'd caught all Bruno had compressed in his angry sentence. But Bruno just said, "I'm sorry we won't see you. Take care of yourself." And hung up.

Marc put down the phone, drenched with a feeling of being totally ineffectual. Thérèse stood up and slipped her hand onto his chest through the opening in his dressing gown.

"My poor Marc."

He drew away and turned his back so that she couldn't see his mouth as he spoke. He said: "I'm going to marry you."

"How?" she laughed.
He shrugged in an irritated way.

But the Duke had convinced a Miss Beverly Henry, whose family was in oil and cattle, to stay on in Paris, and after a few months of consulting his mirror as to his future, he made known that he was open to a friendly settlement regarding his current marriage.

SIX

"He paid?"

"He paid," Léopold answered his father, "five hundred thousand dollars. A perfect sum. Not enough for the Duke to be able to consider himself rich afterwards, too much for the Duke to have turned down."

"And the Duke ... Did the Duke bargain for more?"

"Oh there was no chance of bargaining. . . . Marc sent his chauffeur with a paper guaranteeing the Duke de Flandres payment of the sum when a divorce became final between the Duke and the Duchess. He instructed the chauffeur to tell Flandres personally that this would be the Baron's only and final communication with him on the matter. You see, Marc wanted his *chauffeur* to tell him; he wouldn't even write him a letter. You know Marc; but his chauffeur told mine."

"Is that where you got it? And Marc told his chauffeur what he was doing? Come—"

"Oh no. The chauffeur didn't know what the 'communication' was. He might have guessed. But you see, *the Duke* told someone. He told one of his horse friends. And of course it got around. It's all over Paris."

Saul rubbed his eyes and then opened them in an incredulous stare, as if instead of having heard this strange piece of news he'd spotted something strange behind the palm trees facing them, some interloping little beast from nowhere, which had made its way into his home-grown, domesticated jungle, this hothouse he had planted with his own hands. He traced a circle in the water of the pool around his knees and said:

"I told you Marc's a Wolfflen."

"The Duke, you see," Léopold went on, "feels that his honor has had satisfaction. *Reparations*. He appears in no way ashamed. . . . People knew he wanted to be paid."

Léopold had had his full of the subject. He slipped off the side of the pool into the water, making a great *thwock!* with his heavy body. He turned and began a slow crawl toward the far end. He bobbed his head from side to side inefficiently. Watching his son swim, Saul wondered what kind of aquatic creature he resembled. *A porpoise* he thought.

Léopold came out of the pool and headed for the dressing area. He had a dinner it town.

"You're staying?" he asked his father.

"I have five more laps to honor my schedule," Saul answered, "and then I'm going for a bike ride."

Léopold looked at the exercycle and smiled.

"Not too far," he teased.

The pool was warm and coddling as Saul sidestroked, in light thrusts and glides, from one end to the other. The water brushed past his cheek. He felt like a child in the arms of its mother. He did five laps, and then he decided to do one more. He left the water by hoisting himself over the side of the pool instead of using the steps; it took him two tries, but he made it. And then, still dripping wet, he mounted his exercycle.

He pedaled for five minutes steadily, and then he built up speed. Sweat mingled with the water on his chest. The dial in front of him said ten kilometers an hour when he felt a terrific explosion, a burst of pain at his throat that brought to mind instantly a moment when, as a young man, he was accelerating in a powerful Daimler coupe and suddenly the gear box burst apart. And now his mind, though the pain in his body wouldn't let go, was riding free; in a great glow of light it was reeling scenes before his eyes as if he were moving in a rapid open touring car through all his past. He saw Mama and Sigismund. His vision zoomed onto a piece of chocolate cake. Then he was in Baku with Albrecht Heller observing the wooden frieze outside Halstead's office. Now he saw Edwina, young Edwina ... now, Ariel the evening he first met her. All those people appeared, one after the other, and then all together, all around him, wheeling, wheeling, he and his past were on a Ferris wheel. On the ground below he saw Netterling and Gulbenkian fighting over the control lever. Beyond the parched fairgrounds he could see thick woods. Then the wheeling stopped—or had gathered such speed that at last he felt no movement at all anymore, like the Russian who'd gone whirling through space. The woods—and now he was back just a while ago, that evening, when he'd seen—had he seen?—something live flash among his rubber trees. Now he saw it yes now a figure like a gargoyle the day they'd buried Ariel ... on a buttress—the cathedral. Here it was flesh, alive, dancing a taunting jig, insolent, waving a tail with a mouth and an enormous penis. If he pedaled harder, he could run that execrable creature down. His vision held steady, and the pain seemed to flow behind him like a splatter of liquid in the wind as he moved at enormous speed. He was going to run that thing over—.

His feet fell off the pedals. The pedals whirled and banged against his calves, but he no longer felt them.

Léopold's dinner was spoiled by bad news.

"I've attended a briefing with your cousin and Mr. Goodfriend," another guest informed him as the party chatted in little groups before being seated for dinner.

"My cousin."

"Bruno. Dynamic person! Not to speak of *monsieur* Goodfriend."

The man was in advertising. He talked very energetically. He explained that Bruno and Ronnie had come to the agency he presided over to have it create the campaign for the new company the two were involved in, the Public Capital Institution.

So it was done. Bruno had definitely teamed up with Goodfriend.

"We've decided on something very nice, very institutional for them, for the first ad," the man went on, "a half-page in the *Herald Tribune,* here and in New York, with just a picture of the board seated as if at a meeting, with everyone's name on a plaque in front of him. You get the flavor of the United Nations—"

"Where will my cousin be sitting?" Léopold asked wryly. The man seemed to perceive that Léopold was not happy. He may have wondered if he should have revealed his meeting. "Oh ... we haven't laid it all out yet," he said, as if he could take back the information he'd already given. But then he seemed curious over Léopold's dissatisfaction. He seemed to smell gossip. He prodded:

"They said they're getting something else together. A breakthrough. The first French Mutual Fund. Wolfflen Opportunités. I suppose you're involved ..."

"No," Léopold said in the most neutral voice he could muster. "I have nothing at all to do with it."

Léopold and his wife, Françoise, left the dinner party early. Françoise was what everyone called "a sweet person." Her good nature was her greatest asset, since she was rather plain in a short, thick-set way, and had no particular talent, not even for conversation. For Léopold, she was not merely "sweet" but one of the world's few profoundly good people. All love for him, and charity for the rest of the world. Her love prompted her to comfort him as he sat stiffly behind the wheel of his Mercedes with his lips pursed in anguish. She put her small hand in the crook of his elbow. He showed no reaction.

"You talked about Bruno," she ventured.

"Yes. Soon the whole world will be talking about Bruno. About 'Wolfflen Opportunités.' God, Françoise, that man will drag us all into the mud."

"Speak to him," she coaxed.

"I *spoke* to him," he answered with irritation. "It never does any good to speak to Crazy Bruno."

"What good can it ever do," she asked gently, "when you only speak to each other when there's a crisis?"

He didn't answer.

Françoise was a Vollkorn. The Vollkorns were a small Alsacian-Jewish banking family, very reserved, very respected. She'd approached her wedding with fear and awe of the great flamboyant clan she was entering. But she hadn't been a Wolfflen long before she'd discovered the envies and jealousies that divided the Barons. For her, all that was a pity, and beneath them. She wished she could be closer to the other Wolfflen women; it seemed natural to her that they should stay together, take a social stance together. Sponsor the same causes. But Edmée's friends were not Thérèse's and Léopold had the bitter knowledge, although he never told Françoise, that both of them considered her *sans intérêt*, of no interest.

Suddenly a great blue police van swept around the Mercedes and nearly forced Léopold to mount the curb. As he braked in shock three more vans went by him.

"Something is happening," Léopold said drearily.

Françoise flicked on the radio.

They recognized the voice of the Prime Minister, Michel Debré. As he spoke in what they later learned was a rebroadcast of a speech earlier that evening, they were able to make out that Paris was in danger of being invaded by paratroopers loyal to the generals who'd seized power in Algeria.

"Crazy," Léopold said, "the whole world is going crazy. My father's right."

So by the time they arrived at the house they shared with Saul, Léopold was already very upset. In the front hallway, they found the whole household in tears.

"They've landed?" Léopold asked.

Sobbing too much to say anything coherent, the chief housekeeper led Léopold out to the greenhouse. Françoise followed at their heels, her face drawn with distress. Perhaps *she* already guessed what had happened.

The housekeeper had gone to the greenhouse to look for the Baron Saul, having been sent by the *maître d'hôtel*, who couldn't understand why the Baron had failed to come to dinner a full half-hour after his usual time.

A doctor had come, but something in the housekeeper's agitated state of mind had made her insist that the Baron Saul not be moved until the Baron Léopold returned. As if she, the servant, were a child, and the Baron an awesome parent who had the power, which neither she nor the doctor had, to right what had happened, to repair it.

Saul was still there on his cycle. The doctor had closed his eyes, but his jaw was set, his moustache bristled, and his arms were fixed hard on the handlebar. He seemed not only still alive, but full of vigor and determination, steeling himself to tackle some high hill he saw in his mind.

SEVEN

Deauville, August, 1961
The tide was out. From where she sat with Marc, Emma could see hundreds of yards of putty-colored beach patched with foam, running flat as slate to the Channel. The long stretch between the gray water and the dry sand was lifeless but below their table on the other side of the boardwalk people with cabañas and beach chairs were packed together. The boardwalk was crowded, too—there were innumerable crisp old women in linen and gray-haired men with blazers, skimmers, and carnations. Deauville in August: the rich and would be rich were sharing a month of idleness and the favors of a fickle sun.

"Is it all right?" her husband asked.

To be obliging, she said yes, and picked at it: a white wedge of turbot, much too big, that lay on her plate. She stabbed the skin, and it followed her fork like a long black ribbon. He reached across the table and served her more *sauce mousseline*. He refilled her glass with champagne.

The Baron and the Baroness Marc de Wolfflen were having a late lunch together at Ciro's. The Baron's mistress had returned to Paris, where her lawyer had returned from the Midi.

"Will you buy it finally?" she asked, freeing her fork with the splay fishknife.

"Oh no ... no, the price is too high. Too high! They thought a Wolfflen, well you know. But not on your life."

He sipped his champagne. "Anyway ... I'm not impatient for a stud farm. After all, I'm not. And Deauville is getting terribly crowded."

In confirmation, they both looked with rueful silence at the mass of flesh in bathing suits below.

Marc had come close to buying the Haras Fresnay, a stud farm a few miles outside of town. It had seemed to him a sensible extension of his racing activities, and it would have given him a pleasant place to live in August.

"Perhaps you would only have found yourself more encumbered," she offered.

He didn't answer. He reddened. She had found a way to come to the subject at hand.

"The divorce is done?" she said.

"Yes ..."

"Well then," she said brightly, "what do *I* have to sign?"

"Whatever." He flushed again. "I don't know. Whatever *the lawyers* say. I want you to have—"

"I have all I need."

"Well, God, Emma, I want you to at least keep the house."

"Too big for me. I honestly would not find it pleasant."

He shook his head. He seemed about to stammer something.

She said: "She's free? You're free. I'm free. Marry her for heaven's sake. See the thing through. We mustn't any of us think about what the papers might print."

He rocked his glass slightly, staring at the bubbles he'd stirred up. "Emma," he began, "I'm sorry—no, listen to me, I can't say I'm sorry about—Thérèse. What I mean is I'm ... I am really sorry about ... *the waste*. You ... see? Because you are such an extraordinary human being, Emma—"

She stood up. "Waste!" she said. "Marc ... you, my poor Marc, you are the waste."

"I meant the waste between you and me," he flustered, "not you, but no, what? The wasted chance, the *miss—*"

"Your life," she insisted, "you risk wasting your entire life. Marc, do you think *this* is all you have in you? My poor Marc."

He didn't answer. She sat down again in silence. And all he could do was set his face in a grim try at composure. As he tightened his jaw, he felt his new teeth wiggle.

She wouldn't stay to have dessert. She'd come up to the Hôtel du Golf for a weekend's breath of air, and had promised her cousin Bruno she'd give up golf that afternoon to watch him play polo. In her mind, as she kissed her husband goodbye, she already formed an image of Bruno on horseback with his mallet and helmet. It brought to mind some condottiere, and in that same instant, with that same metaphor, came a flash of fantasy: she imagined herself married to the other cousin, to Bruno. The instant of absurdity passed. Flushed, and with her temples throbbing in confused emotion, she found herself at the restaurant door with Marc, where she bounded into a taxi alone.

As the cab drew away, she thought she heard her husband shout something. It sounded like "You'll see! . . . My turn!" But she let the driver keep right on going.

EIGHT

On a quiet Easter holiday morning in 1964, a beeping and flashing ambulance raced through suburban Neuilly, bearing an important patient on the verge of death. The Baron Charles de Wolfflen was rushed to a room prepared for him in haste in the Intensive Care section of the American Hospital, one of the most up to date in France. The room had all the equipment in the current arsenal of medicine for postponing certain death. But none of the doctors—assembled from the best of those who weren't away enjoying the last of the year's good skiing in the Alps or the first strong rays of sun in the Midi—gave the old gentleman more than a straw of a chance of pulling through.

The Baron had begun his breakfast in bed cheerfully that morning; then, all at once, pouring himself another cup of the Darjeeling tea he drank every morning by the litre, he slumped over and squeezed the service button on his night table in a convulsive grasp.

By the time the ambulance got him to the hospital, he was almost entirely paralyzed, and his ability to communicate had been reduced to blinking his eyes and uttering an occasionally comprehensible slur.

Next day the Baron's room began to overflow with flowers from all sorts of people, many of whom he'd barely seen in recent years. His grandson Gilbert, who happened to be the first Wolfflen to accompany Eveline that day in her vigil at her husband's bedside, began to sneeze the moment he entered the room.

"I—" he sputtered and started another fit of sneezing.

As he blew his nose, tears poured down his cheeks.

"He's not ... going to ..." Eveline insisted, mistaking Gilbert's tears for a sign of desperate grief. But as he wiped his face with his handkerchief, she understood his distress. In a moment, before he could begin to speak again, his breath was coming noisily. Asthma, she thought. Like his father. Memory welled up in her; her mind went back decades, to when her son was a sickly child and the man now motionless on his back was a hardy officer. The stranger who'd become her lover, her husband, a true half of her own existence. She saw him now in his uniform of horizon blue. Horizon blue, her mind repeated; the words had the furry evocativeness of poetry. Horizon, time receding behind her. Blue. Blue death. Time runs one way, people try to stand in the rushing stream. Two people hold onto each other, until—it can't be helped—one or the other is torn away. Gone like foam. She bobbed her head up like someone fighting off sleep, some sentinel.

"I'll call you the nurse!" she said to the wheezing young man.

The nurse Eveline summoned led Gilbert down to the out-patient department. Just as they left the room, Eveline called back to her, gesturing at the flowers with a wave of her hand:

"Get them out, please, give them away," the Baroness hissed. "This isn't ..." Her voice plummeted, went slack like a kite in sagging wind. "No, this is not a funeral."

Gilbert made a point of coming back after his injection, peering into the room first to be sure the flowers were gone. Without them, the room looked desolate. There was the huge man, his grandfather, lying still as stone on a bed surrounded by ugly instruments, and at his feet in a small steel chair, the tiny woman, his grandmother, erect, composed, and miserable. Gilbert had come back for her sake. Eveline hadn't accepted the fact that her vigil was no longer much different from a wake. She was still hoping, and so it was now she who was in danger—of going to pieces.

"Come," he said softly, going up to her, "will you stretch your legs a little?" He led her into the hallway, motioning to the sick man that they would be right back. Charles acknowledged his grandson's gesture with a twisted squint.

"He's very alert," the Baroness said as Gilbert put his arm around her and led her into the pale hallway smelling of alcohol. Eveline looked up at Gilbert's even-featured face. Her grandson was now a handsome, well-built young man of nineteen. As they walked, she felt the book stuffed into his coat pocket brush against her. He'd been reading, no doubt, in the taxi. It was Easter recess, but Gilbert was wasting no time ... still cramming. A year ago, he'd been graduated from Croseigne with excellent grades, and he'd entered the Lycée Louis-le-Grand for a year more, to prepare for the highly elite Ecole Polytechnique. It was already rather certain that he would be admitted.

"He seems comfortable," Gilbert ventured. With reflexive tact, he stepped into her line of vision. A nurse had just then come out of a room where there was someone who looked like the victim of a fire. She'd left the door ajar, and Gilbert had had a chilling glimpse of the mutilated and bandaged patient.

But Eveline had seen him too. She thought: you see there are worse ways of going. But immediately she reprimanded herself for giving in. No, Charles had come through twice before ...

"He's better than he was yesterday," she affirmed.

She looked up at her grandson to gauge his reaction. Maybe Gilbert, too, had noticed he'd looked better. But that instant she read on his face that his mind was elsewhere. *His books*. Oh yes, she was alone, for nobody knew but she—not this solicitous and absent boy, nor any of them, no one dared hope but she alone, no one seemed to believe—

He is going to live!

She bit her lip in desolation. And now it was as if a shadow fell on her hopes and she was no longer quite sure, herself ...

The chauffeur had arrived to pick up Edmée and drop her at the tennis courts of the Racing Club. Bruno drove away from the hospital alone in his Lamborghini. Seeing Charles again, and in that state, had filled him with a confusion of nostalgia, guilt and regret. Bruno had an important appointment, and anyone coming up beside the specially built open-roof sports car at a traffic light could notice

270   THE HEIRS

that the man lucky enough to be driving that long, low, maroon beauty, a man craggily handsome, with gray-flecked hair yet still beaming good health, nonetheless did not look happy. Bruno's appointment was with Antoine Stirne, partner in Vauclaire and Stirne, the auditing firm that served Wolfflen Opportunités, just as it had served the private business affairs of Bruno's father and grandfather. Bruno found Stirne's telephone call, asking for an appointment that same day, worrisome. Stirne had been going over the Wolfflen Opportunités' annual statement.

"Any particular dossier to have ready?" Bruno had asked, fishing.

"It has to do with the revaluation of the North Sea leaseholds," the accountant had answered in a voice, which, though it wasn't unfriendly, seemed too deliberately neutral, as if Stirne for some reason was defensively taking distance. Bruno had known Antoine Stirne since they were both quite young. Why, he was a friend. . . . This last thought cheered Bruno; whatever the problem was, it was surely something he and Stirne could work out.

As he blared at high speed through the empty streets of Neuilly, Bruno thought he should have taken Ronnie's advice and gone away for the week instead of simply offering Ronnie the keys to his chalet in Gstaad. He wouldn't have minded some skiing. Maybe old Stirne ought to have given himself a rest as well . . .

In the Avenue de la Grande Armée, empty but dotted with traffic lights, he kept his engine wound tight in second. The Arch of Triumph loomed over the stretch of vacant street. At its feet, cars were going round, no doubt mostly the cars of tourists turning into the Champs Elysées. Approaching the mêlée slowly, pacing himself to avoid all the red lights, Bruno let the whole matter of Wolfflen Opportunités uncoil itself in his mind.

Goodfriend and Bruno's mutual fund company had begun buying on the Bourse in 1962, when the market was low. The French exchange had followed the 1961 slump on Wall Street, but it had been expected to turn upward again rapidly. Wall Street stubbornly failed to make a significant rally, however, and the Bourse declined even further. By late spring of 1963, the Bourse seemed chronically depressed. Sales had increased the volume of the Wolfflen Opportunités holdings dramatically, but the value per-share picture was quite another story. The value per-share of Wolfflen Opportunités had fallen thirty percent in the company's first year and a half of operation, a drop not much less than the average decline in the value of shares on the Bourse. Wolfflen Opportunités had failed to prove its prowess, and if there was not yet a rush of contract-holders seeking redemptions, sales in the mutual fund were dwindling drastically. Portfolio managers at the banks seemed to have given up on the Bourse entirely and were scouring the financial scene for better placements than securities. It became clear to Bruno and Goodfriend that a trend toward redemptions of Wolfflen Opportunités' monthly contracts might rapidly set it, in which case not only would the redeeming customers take big losses, but also Wolfflen Opportunités would soon find itself in a severely tight position for cash to cover the redemptions. Wisely though, as the market remained dead through the winter of 1963, Goodfriend and Bruno had begun holding incoming cash from sales in the form of short-term paper, instead of putting it into more securities. But this money was earning less for the customers than they would get in a savings bank. The important question was whether the company should continue to take a defensive position, hoping that the stock market would turn up, or whether Wolfflen Opportunités should take its cash and try to save the situation by finding some promising investments outside the Bourse, the investments other money men in France were already desperately hunting.

For both Goodfriend and Bruno, the choice was obvious. Neither was willing to prepare for defeat when victory was a live possibility. Bruno in particular was determined to go on the offensive. After the first annual report of Wolfflen Opportunités, *La Vie Française,* the stock market sheet, wrote that "The Baron Bruno, having taken up and let fall numerous enterprises, has yet to display the Midas Touch for which his family is famous."

Not long afterward, Ronnie Goodfriend came to the Baron with "the opportunity of the century in North Sea oil."

The Lamborghini lunged into the Place de l'Etoile, but the traffic, as Bruno had predicted, was largely foreign, and he found himself quickly trapped within a host of timid fumblers who knew nothing about navigating the confluence of twelve big streets. By the time he reached the mouth of the Champs Elysées, his mood of pentup worry was riddled with irritation ...

The opportunity of the century. Well, it wasn't exactly what it had seemed, but it wasn't as bad as it had seemed to be later either. Ronnie had saved the situation. ... *Hadn't he?*

Landco, an American natural resources conglomerate, which had owned the leases on the offshore drilling sites, was in trouble, Ronnie had explained, and hadn't the capability nor the time to exploit the leases. The company was mainly in the business of selling tax shelters and had all sorts of immediate problems, in particular a problem of cash. The leases could be had for $10 million in ready money. Ronnie produced geological surveys showing the composition of the sea bottom, and he had inside information that Shell had just verified the presence of oil in three places whose geological data was almost identical with the sites Ronnie had in mind.

"And another thing," Ronnie said, "they pulled up rocks from down there and when they broke them open they smelled like goddamn hi-test."

Wolfflen Opportunités bought the leases from Landco. Bruno insisted they begin exploratory drilling immediately. Ronnie favored holding on to the property and, for the sake of the forthcoming annual report to the contract-holders, simply revaluing it upward as soon as the Shell strikes became known. But doing nothing didn't make sense to Bruno, and so on his insistence the drilling began.

Ronnie's inside information was correct. Shell had indeed made three good strikes twenty miles away in similar shale, but what wasn't obvious in the geological reports Ronnie had shown Bruno was that even Shell was not ready, technically, to tackle the North Sea in a commercial way and that the currents at Wolfflen Opportunités' sites were such that bringing up oil over a sustained period would be particularly problematic. This became painfully obvious after the exploratory drilling company's platform had collapsed and three workers were drowned. The accident managed to get beyond the local English press and make two paragraphs in the *Financial Times*. Bruno and Ronnie had had to halt drilling before any oil was struck.

The annual report was looming, and Bruno and Goodfriend were in a dilemma as to how to evaluate the leases into which they had put $10 million of their customers' cash. At least Bruno was in a dilemma, that is. Ronnie was glowing with optimism.

"The state of the art is changing every minute," he insisted. "There's oil down there all right, and sooner—I don't mean later—somebody with a head on his shoulders is going to have the apparatus to bring it up. Look, there's only so much petroleum in this entire world."

Ronnie said he was convinced that Wolfflen Opportunités had bought the leases for one-third their current value, and he proposed that they should be revalued in the annual report at three hundred percent their purchase price. Here was the one-stroke way of redeeming the company's bad performance on the Bourse that they'd been after.

Bruno knew it was difficult for an auditor to judge the value of an asset not publicly quoted, but one way to do so was on the basis of the sale of a significant portion of the asset. An accountant could safely presume that all of the asset could fetch, at the time of the sale, proportionately the same price as the part sold. Ronnie stubbornly defended his position on what the leases were worth, and Bruno had to take his hat off to him: he came up with a buyer for a one-tenth share at three million dollars. They revalued the rest at twenty-seven million and drank a bottle of champagne together after they'd finished the annual report and sent it off to Vauclaire and Stirne for their signatures.

"This is just the beginning," Ronnie had said, clinking glasses . . .

From the Champs Elysées, Bruno turned into the Avenue de Marigny, where Wolfflen Opportunités had its offices. The company had purchased a townhouse that used to belong to La Belle Otéro, the turn-of-the-century *demi-mondaine* (as the highest-priced prostitutes were known in those days). Bruno's office was her former upstairs sitting room; Ronnie had cheerfully accepted the former main bedroom, saying it would "give him inspiration." Downstairs, he'd filled the floor with secretaries each of whom had the looks of a cover girl. The art directors of *Vogue* and *Elle* were periodically sweeping down on the WO offices, raiding it for new faces. It was good public relations, Ronnie argued.

The uniformed doorman saluted before pulling open the huge and ornate green-lacquered portals for the Lamborghini. In the courtyard, Bruno noticed that Antoine Stirne's snub, square and *sérieuse* gray Peugeot was parked where Ronnie's Maserati usually stood. Yes, Ronnie and his current three girlfriends were in Bruno's place in Gstaad. In *his* bed. An image of naked bodies rushed into his awareness, while his mood fell once again, plummeted now; its nagging uncertainty had been pierced by an intuition: *I've been suckered*, Bruno thought in English, calling on one of Ronnie's favorite words . . .

Antoine Stirne hadn't gone to Swiss boarding school, although his old Jewish family, a branch of which was important at the Bourse, was upper class enough for his father to be received by Bruno's father, the Baron Pierre, as a friend, and for Bruno and Antoine to have played together before Bruno had gone off to Croseigne. The younger Stirne, like his father, lacked flamboyance, and ambition as well. He'd gone to the lycée Janson, a good government-run school not far from his father's apartment in the Sixteenth Arrondissement, a neighborhood of well-off and self-contented families full of children, and he'd assumed, after the Sorbonne, the task of helping perpetuate the presence of Stirne in Vauclaire and Stirne, accountants. Such had been the task of the eldest sons in his branch of the Stirne family for generations. It was the least eminent branch, but it was eminently respectable. Antoine Stirne had married early a plain girl whose family was well known to his and she'd given him five children. From the time Bruno had gone off to that cosmopolitan school for the children of the world's motley millionaires, Stirne had followed the career of his former playmate with a certain amused tolerance, the kind of tolerance good-hearted and enlightened bourgeoisie sometimes show for artists and their like. For Antoine Stirne as much as he was for anyone, Bruno de Wolfflen was Wild Bruno.

Bruno asked one of Ronnie's secretaries in the skeleton crew present that week to bring up coffee. Stirne began the conversation cordially, remarking, as he'd done on other visits, on the splendor of the Belle Otéro's gilded, molded walls. He was a man not immune to splendor, and had a weakness, even, for the gushy renditions of Louis Seize that represented the most conservative side of Belle Epoque taste. The apartment he had inherited from his father off the Avenue Mozart had similar if less splendid fakery on its walls, as Bruno remembered. Half the furniture there, Pierre had once felt obliged to note, consisted of copies. Stirne's love of splendor was like that:

respect from a distance, through the filter of imitations. But he knew what he talked about, knew all the styles and signatures, even if his enthusiasm somehow wore the smallness of a furtive weakness for pastries. As for his own presence, he was the most plain looking person imaginable. He wore black broadcloth suits, ready-made but expensive for ready-made, maroon jacquard ties, and thick soled black bluchers. His hair was cropped short on a large head with small features. Under his little, wide nose, he sported, out of perhaps a hidden vanity, an old-fashioned molted moustache, which, while he would have cringed at the comparison, recalled the moustache of Pierre Laval, the Vichy premier executed after the war. The similarity stopped there, for there was nothing sinister about Antoine Stirne. He was honest, dependable, worthy at his craft, and a humane, if narrow, person.

Bruno brought the conversation quickly to its purpose.

"Yes, the North Sea leases, Bruno," Stirne said. Stirne called very few people outside his family by their first names, but Bruno was one of them. The way he said "Bruno" now, he assumed the slight tone of authority, close to paternalism, of someone's doctor. Well he was, in a way, the company's doctor. But if he examined, his job wasn't to cure.

"I might as well tell you as directly and frankly as possible, Bruno, what is *not* possible, in my opinion. I am not sure that you are totally aware of all the circumstances of the revaluation. In any case ... the figure ... will not work."

"Why not?" Bruno was irritated. Suddenly he'd snapped at this drab man so unlike himself, though he knew by now his rightful target was far away, over the Alps.

Stirne's tact fell back a notch at Bruno's tone. "All right," he said, "I propose we go over ... the difficulties one by one. First of all—"

"Yes, first of all?"

"First of all, Bruno, are you aware that the Landco Company from which you bought the leaseholds is run by a man who has done numerous transactions either buying or selling, in which Mr. Goodfriend, your associate, has been closely involved?"

"I know who the man is; I don't know him intimately."

"Do you know that Mr. Goodfriend's mother, who wears the name she acquired in her second marriage, owns twenty percent of Landco ... a little old lady in an apartment on the West Side of Manhattan? I'm not a detective, Bruno, I'm an accountant ..."

He cleared his throat, a gesture of nervous embarrassment. "But I've had these things researched," he continued, "I had to, because of my initial ... reticence, over the revaluation. Bruno, you must understand, this is the sort of thing I could not look at in a superficial way."

There was a faint, musky odor of sweat in the office. Both men were flushed as they sat across the desk from each other, Bruno in the seat of authority, Stirne in a chair set for those who come for instructions or to solicit. But those conventions didn't apply now. The desk divided Bruno from the person who, with a simple act of approval, could raise him from deep trouble, like someone raising a drowning man up through the blackness of cold water into sunlight. The desk stood there, a bulky embodiment of the separation between Stirne, the impeccable Stirne, and the man out of the wild and colorful life of affairs where men sinned just as in some splendid bordel. Stirne might have envied Bruno, but that murky and complicated emotion would not stir him to sin as well, to sin without any of the adventure, any of the pleasure, simply to save not Bruno's soul but his reputation.

Bruno's upper teeth flashed over his lip a moment. He looked down at the thick, creamy carpeting of his office. Perhaps he felt pleasure in feeding his eyes that luxury again, but his face had gone gray. He spoke without looking up: "Go on," he said. "No ... I was not aware ..."

"In a very approximate manner of speaking," Stirne continued tactfully, gently, but without mercy, "Mr. Goodfriend has bought the leaseholds from himself, or rather, Wolfflen Opportunités has bought them from him."

Bruno flailed his arms out impatiently. "All right," he insisted, "but the revaluation was based not on the price at which we bought but the price at which we *sold—*"

Stirne leaned across the desk to make his point. "To the Hugger Corporation.

"From what you just said," he continued, straightening up again, leaning back in his chair with the undefensive attitude of a reasonable man sure of his ground, "from what you just said, Bruno, I can only assume that you were not aware that Hugger is controlled by a third company, of which Landco holds forty percent of the voting shares. I suppose that was not obvious. Hugger is registered in the Bahamas, and Landco in Maryland."

"I never thought—"

"That your associate would, in a rough way of speaking, sell his own company leases at ten million dollars and then buy back a tenth of them at three million. The net effect, however, is that his mother has acquired seven million dollars of Wolfflen Opportunités' cash. For some leases. Well, as for the leases, there is another way to have some idea what they are worth, other than the test sale you made. Let us concede that the evaluation of an expert can only be very more-or-less—"

Bruno simply nodded, as if impatient for the blade to fall.

"But I have taken the liberty to consult one regarding the thirty-million-dollar figure for the revaluation we are discussing."

Suddenly the Baron rose and stepped away from his seat, as if not being there when the blow came, he might escape harm. Stirne kept talking evenly.

"Considering all the uncertainties at the present moment, considering that even Shell has little hope of having viable equipment for drilling the sea commercially before five years or so . . . considering all that can change in the future, the estimation I got for the value of your leaseholds was something in the neighborhood of two million dollars."

Bruno sat down again. He began to bring his fist down onto the desk, but in midair his palm opened and his gesture turned into one of defense.

"You refuse to endorse the revaluation?" he asked lowly.

Stirne swallowed hard and nodded.

"If you refuse to endorse the revaluation," Bruno went on in a dull monotone, "then our name will be . . .

"All right, Antoine," he shouted suddenly, "so I've picked up a bad hand!"

Stirne came close to wincing. He turned his head. He replied as gently, it seemed, as he could:

"It's very bad, Bruno. . . . I know it's very bad. But you see, Vauclaire and I . . . we also have a name to uphold."

NINE

On the third day of his attack, the Baron Charles de Wolfflen's only sign of life was a pearl trailing light across a gray-green cathode tube. It moved from end to end, vanished at the right-hand margin, and reappeared at the left. Once, when the bleep disappeared at the edge of the screen, Eveline's mind revived something she'd learned far back in childhood: that before Magellan, seafarers believed if they sailed too far they would reach the edge of the world, and fall over into the void. Eveline sat before that screen for hours on end, as if her being there could somehow keep that spark from vanishing forever—could save her husband from the void. The pearl kept returning, and sometimes when it moved faster or changed the shape of its sweep, she even believed that Charles' system was about to rally. She was the only one who believed it. The doctors had reduced their role to assuring that he would go out on his own painlessly.

"They're not allowed to do anything that will kill him," Marc explained in a voice in which grief blended with a sense of absurdity. He was speaking to Gaston Robinet, whom he'd encountered in the hospital hallway. When Robinet had last come by, the day before, the old Baron had been able to blink a greeting.

His son and the director of his bank stood just beyond the dying man's door, shifting their feet awkwardly, not knowing what or how much they had to say to each other. Marc continued bitterly:

"The doctors' premise seems to be that if Charles lasts in that state for a few more years, something might be invented that will save him ..." He shook his head.

Robinet knit his heavy brows and took nervous, pecking puffs of the cigaret he held in his lips.

"How ... long?" the man finally asked, his voice husky with smoke and sadness.

Marc shrugged. "He's already gone beyond their predictions. It can't be long! But he apparently has a very strong heart ..."

"The Baron is a very strong man," Robinet said with bleak respect. "And his heart was in everything he did ..."

Marc studied Robinet's tightened face. "You ... ah ... are kind to—"

"Ah no, *monsieur*. Don't say that word. Can I tell you something outside of any question of polite sympathy?"

Robinet looked Marc full in the face now, and his eyes seemed to glare with emotion.

"He is your father," he said, "and no one can know the grief you feel now. But can you understand what it can mean to have a stranger stretch his hand out into your life, a benevolent hand, and offer you the chance to realize that life. You'll excuse me if I sound impertinent, but I cannot help but think of the Baron as a foster-parent."

Marc sensed that Robinet was "shooting his wad." It was as if he wanted to make clear "for the record," for whatever record of objective truth men kept in the baggage of their careers, that his relationship with Charles had meant more than banal opportunism, that it had had, for him, a noble awesomeness. He'd spoken with emotion. He'd obviously seen no point in fawning, as if he were certain that once the Baron Charles was officially dead, he could expect no quarter from his son.

"Well, I must return to ..." Robinet said, letting his sentence trail. He didn't say it: to the bank. But Robinet had taken *the first step*. And although his father was still "clinically" alive, a strange feeling of excitement moved Marc suddenly to step out on that ledge of sincerity to which Robinet had lured him, to stand there with him toe to toe, and blurt the truth of where they were in life, *vis-à-vis* each other, and where they would be.

But as he began, he could not get beyond that stiff, formal language to which Frenchmen who are not intimate with each other are so often condemned, the cold diplomacy of *"vous"* opposite *"vous."*

"Monsieur Robinet," he said, "one moment." He halted to catch Robinet's mood in his glance, but the eyes of his father's director seemed almost closed under the weight of his heavy lids and thick brows. *"Monsieur* Robinet ... you know my father ... has been ... exceptionally impressed by the job you ... have been doing ... in the bank. Of course, you don't need me to tell you that. You don't even need *my father's* praise. What you've accomplished is a fact known to everyone. You are one of the leaders in your field. But you know that you have my father's deep gratitude. And I ...."

Robinet's eyes had widened into a pained and defensive glare.

"I ... Permit me to add my own gratitude. ..." He swallowed. *"Monsieur* Robinet, I want to make clear to you that your post at the Banque Wolfflen ... will ... still be there ... after. As far as I am concerned I shall be most happy to work with you—"

Now Robinet flashed Marc a look of intense curiosity.

"This is an inappropriate time to talk," Marc continued. "But perhaps it would be the fairest thing if you had as much time as possible to ponder your options." Marc paused. "I have to make clear to you that I shall be far more active in the bank than the Baron Charles was. So by necessity, in the context, your title cannot have the same meaning. ... I am obliged to be actively in charge."

Robinet's cigaret had burned down and there was no ashtray in the hall. Finally, conscious of the crudeness of what he was doing it seemed, but without a choice, he let it fall and ground it under the sole of his shoe. He put his hands into his jacket pockets.

"Thank you, *monsieur,"* he said, "I have already been turning my options over in my mind."

"I can understand—"

"I have been tempted for some time to return to politics ... to government."

Marc took his father's manager's hand in his.

"Well, you will decide," he said.

Robinet's face was a mask of dignity now. Marc held him a moment longer, before walking with him to the elevator. *"Monsieur Robinet,"* he added, "there is a detail, also, perhaps worth making perfectly clear now. No one who has served the Wolfflens as well as you have will be permitted to part company with us empty handed."

Robinet replied only by tightening his hand on Marc's. Neither spoke as they continued down the wan hallway. After Robinet's intense, flushed face was obliterated by the sliding metal doors of the elevator, Marc was overcome by a sense of shame. It seemed to him he had said nothing right, and that the time had been terribly wrong as well. And now his last sentence sounded so vulgar in his memory that his ears burned. Of course Robinet could expect to take something with him. He'd been no little employee. Full of remorse, Marc tried to tell himself that what he'd finally said might have all the same been taken as a kindness. That, after all, Robinet or his wife might have appreciated being reassured on that point. They were living on a scale far beyond what anyone could afford on a government salary.

Yet Marc recalled that he'd spoken, "shot his own wad" not out of kindness, but because of a curious, indomitable agitation within himself.

When Bruno came to the hospital the following evening, Marc was able to tell him that Gaston Robinet had phoned to say there would be a revision of the cabinet before the end of the month and that the General had decided to name him Minister of Finance.

Bruno showed barely any reaction to the important news.

"Ahh . . ." he said absently.

Bruno's face was gray and agitated. He began to pace the hallway.

Marc suggested that he and Bruno go down to the hospital garden, thinking that it would do Eveline no good to see Bruno in the state he was in. Marc sensed deep trouble. As they walked toward the far end of the garden, Marc bluntly urged Bruno to tell him what was wrong. In five minutes, Bruno unburdened himself of all there was to say about Ronnie Goodfriend, Antoine Stirne, and North Sea oil.

Bruno looked at Marc now, bracing himself with what seemed gritty defiance, in case his cousin would dare add criticism to his already heavy burden of humiliation. But Marc was silent while his excited mind sifted, like a rapid machine, the facts Bruno had just explained. Then he said:

"How much do you own of the management company?"

"Fifty-one percent."

"Still?"

"Yes, of course . . . still. The rest is Ronnie and some other people from PCI who take orders from him."

"The bank . . . the Banque Wolfflen will be able to propose a solution. If he won't accept . . . you'll have to tell him, Bruno, we'll do everything we can, we'll spend every penny we have to put him in jail. Lawsuits, private detectives, everything we can. If our name gets smeared, his name is going to be a number. . . . We'll make him rot behind bars. Can you tell him that?"

"I think it is pretty clear by now that I don't consider him my best friend," Bruno said drearily. "What solution, Marc?"

"How are the management shares worked out?"

"They can't be traded. There's a provision allowing shareholders to be bought out by any of the others; the price is based on the performance of the mutual fund."

"Per share?"

"And the volume. The volume counts less."

"All right, we'll buy them out. The Banque Wolfflen will buy everyone in the management out. Looking at the performance at the moment, I'd say that the shares of the management company are nearly worthless."

"And then it will be the bank's problem entirely. What will—"

"The bank will offer seven million dollars for the rest of the leaseholds, which means the fund's ten million dollars in the North Sea will be converted back to cash. That takes care of Stirne's evaluation. As for the customers, the new Wolfflen management will offer to redeem any of their contracts at thirty percent above today's market value. We'll keep the offer open for six months, at the end of which we'll close the fund, we'll turn it into a closed-end fund and we'll try to do the best we can for the pile of other people's money we'll be handling. No more automatic redemptions, no more running after more cash to be able to pay out, no more salesmen, Bruno, no more feet in the door, no Ronnie—"

Bruno stared at his cousin in disbelief.

"How much do you expect the Banque Wolfflen will lose on all this?" he asked finally.

"Outside the North Sea? How many customers will redeem? I hope that if we make that kind of offer, explaining our intention to get into long-term capital commitments after the six months, most of them will stay with us. *We* have a *name*. We don't have the reputation of deliberately losing money. I hope that they believe that their shares are worth at least thirty percent more than current value, because *we* think they are. I think most of them will ride along with us. We have to count on our name ..."

Bruno didn't answer. He looked away toward a thin layer of fuschia cloud that was piling up on the horizon of the dusk sky. Judging by his anguish-distorted profile, he might have been wishing he was dead.

"We can do all this in the bank, together," Marc said quietly.

Bruno turned and faced his cousin, wearing the saddest of smiles.

"There you are," he said, "it's the second time ... you saved my life."

Marc flushed. He realized he didn't, he didn't want Bruno to have so totally lost—

"No I didn't," he blurted. "You know I didn't even—" And then he tried to give shelter to both his cousin and himself behind a gentle irony. "Anyway, there's probably a lot of oil down there," he went on. "One of these days they'll invent a way for us to get it. Isn't it about time the French branch of the family did something about oil?"

"Congratulations," Bruno said huskily; then he turned and went away.

Marc continued to pace the garden. Night had nearly fallen, and the reddish clouds appeared to have been absorbed by the buildings on the skyline. The edge of Paris glowed gray-pink under the most peculiar night sky. It was cream-colored. Neither moon nor stars were visible, but light suffused over the landscape from horizon to horizon. On a nearby balcony, one of those *"terrasses"* all French city dwellers cherish but none use, a blackbird stood out sharply against the sky in profile. It was trilling exquisitely what Marc had learned in some book was a nasty warning to other birds not to trespass into its territory. Crickets whirred in the lawn. Marc recalled again, vaguely, something medieval scholars might have written about listening to the wheeling of the planets, about some state of grace in which one could hear "the music of the spheres." He couldn't hear it, but he was all at once intensely aware of the enormous hurly-burly of the universe, as it went through its earnest business of existing; energy seemed to be seeping through that peculiar sky. It seemed burdened with energy.

He felt it because he felt burdened with energy, too. Nervous, and oddly euphoric; although in a room overhead his father was dying, his conscience couldn't suppress his euphoria. He could sense his life changing. He felt like a bear coming out of winter. Imagined instants of his future sparkled one after the other in his mind. His conscience tried to douse them, he thought again of Robinet and Bruno, and how he'd *handled* each of them. He tried to shame himself, but the euphoria prevailed. And now as he thought of Bruno once again, his mood soared still higher. He couldn't help it. It had happened. Though it hadn't come about in a way he might have thought it would, he'd won, he'd won, in the most unexpected sense he'd won, yes, but he'd definitely won and now he knew with total certainty that he'd never have to worry about Bruno as a rival—not ever again.

There came a cry from one of the rooms overhead. At first it seemed to him the shriek of a woman in childbirth. But in an instant he knew that the voice was his mother's, and that his father was dead.

BOOK FOUR

REVELATIONS

ONE

There were women in those days when youth was everything, who crossed into their forties like ungainly worn vessels rounding the Cape of Good Hope: reeling in distress and floundering in despair. Not Thérèse de Wolfflen. She was forty-three in 1966, but as she looked into the three-sided mirror of a dressing booth at Courrèges, one afternoon of the bright fall of that year, she could honestly congratulate herself that her figure had barely changed in ten—no, fifteen years. She had slipped into a dress from the collection tailored to the body of a mannequin. As always, her hips were wider than the model's; they pulled taut the skirt, and her full breasts caused the armholes to strain against her skin. But her belly was flat and she could pinch empty cloth on both sides of her waist. Smiling into the mirror, she noted that her face had not betrayed her any more than her body. It had thinned in recent years and gained intensity, but not tension. A certain puffy bloom had vanished, leaving the essential grace of the structure of her bones. Her mouth had retained its fullness, without turning downward. Happiness, she told herself, was the best cosmetic in the world...

From the changing booth beside hers, a voice broke into her thoughts. Mrs. Kyle R. Hoyt was crying: "Oh my Lord! ... Oh Lord—"

Sally Hoyt, the wife of the President and Chief Executive Officer of the Dynamerica Corporation, was in Paris with her husband during his important meetings with Marc and Bruno de Wolfflen concerning copper.

That morning Thérèse had rapidly learned that Mrs. Hoyt was a Wisconsan, that she had a master's degree in psychology and was preparing, in what spare time she had, a doctoral thesis entitled "On Conditioning Optimism: A Behaviorist Approach," and that she presided over numerous charities involving children. Despite all of Sally's achievements, there were moments in the short time she and Thérèse had spent together when Thérèse had been moved to pity.

Rushing into the changing booth next to hers, Thérèse experienced another of those moments.

Mrs. Hoyt was still repeating "Oh my Lord . . ."

"Lord," she exclaimed, spotting Thérèse in the mirror, "is this me?"

"Let me see," Thérèse said, stepping back to assay Mrs. Hoyt.

"Why not?" Thérèse lied.

"Oh no. *Know thyself.* And I know me. You could wear this. *You* could carry it off . . ."

Mrs. Hoyt had tried on a bright orange stiff wool coat, in the shape of a cone, with a little collar and patch pockets. The coat stopped at midthigh, and Sally Hoyt had taken her dress off and pulled her half-slip up under her armpits to get the true effect. It shocked her, but being half-naked under "that thousand-dollar cloth coat" must have titillated her in some other way. Her voice came out a bit giggly.

"As for me," she continued, "let's just say I've had my kicks for the day."

She was right, Thérèse knew, she couldn't carry it off. As Sally removed the coat, Thérèse's eyes settled on the flat backside beneath the woman's slip. Mrs. Hoyt was a plain, not ugly, woman, with a strong chin, a sharp little nose, and an unassertive body. She looked to Thérèse any age between thirty and fifty. If she happened suddenly to go gray, she would look a healthy sixty. Thérèse thought of her as one of those people whose physical selves were strangers to them all their lives, strange presences, like misadopted children, which made themselves known most often at moments of disappointment—over illness, ugliness. One of those people with no sensuality. "My kicks for the day," she'd said.

Thérèse would never think of her own pleasure as something due to her in doses, rationed. She was willing to concede she lived for pleasure. She did not have, as Mrs. Hoyt had, a master's degree, but she believed she had a joyful mastery with people, a beneficent touch for bringing out the best each had to give each other in the form of wit and gaiety. And she'd known how to put her fun to further use. So much of her entertaining had served her husband's business since Marc had inherited control of the bank.

Today, she thought, was a case in point. But as she quickly steered her guest away from the middle-aged French lady in white leotards and a white sweater, who'd fluttered into the changing booth all greedy eyed, Thérèse realized that this was no longer fun. Today was work. She was already tired. And the only thing that was going to save her from Mrs. Hoyt today was a worrisome appointment.

She told the saleswoman she'd be back to order something another day, and that Madame Hoyt had found nothing to suit her. All hope of a new customer gone, the woman in white pressed a buzzer, the doors swung open, untouched, as if in a horror movie, and the two visitors stepped out of that world of white-coated plywood and white vinyl flooring, onto the drab hall carpet of a nineteenth-century French apartment building.

In the car, Sally laughed into her hand.

"I'm sorry," she said, "I can't help it. To me it looked like she was wearing long underwear. I thought I'd burst out laughing ... and that man ... he looked like he worked in an asylum. He's got such funny eyes ..."

Courrèges had greeted them coldly after they came in, and had given Sally a thirty-second onceover before retreating back into his studio. He was capable, these days, of suspecting that the Baroness was trying to sneak his nemesis, an American manufacturer, in on him. He'd showed funny eyes, and of course Sally did not expect to meet a man as muscular as a masseur, wearing a white tee shirt, white ducks, and white shoes, in a business premise, and in the middle of the fall.

Thérèse felt vulnerable now. Something in the world she took for granted, frivolities, pretensions, and all, was being laughed at from the outside. But what bothered her more was the taste of failure.

She had set forth with Hoyt's wife to where few mortals were now allowed. Courrèges had barricaded himself against all but a handful of private customers, since the copies of his look had flooded the Western world with no profit to himself. Mrs. Hoyt was to have been entertained and duly impressed. But now Thérèse realized the visit was a flop: she had failed in something she'd undertaken to help Marc.

To help Marc with his business. She realized that like Sally, she too might well be in some people's definition first of all The Wife of A Highly Successful Businessman. Marc de Wolfflen was the name the international financial publications invariably reached for when they wanted to name someone "heads up and savvy" in France. "Heads up and savvy"—Marc loved to repeat that epithet of *Business Week* every time he did some little thing at work that pleased him. It gave him a great laugh each time. "Heads up and savvy! *N'est-ce pas*, Thérèse?" And yet doing things well at work genuinely pleased him. A lot. And he'd done a lot of big things well since he'd succeeded Charles.

At one time, Thérèse had suspected that the role of a man of affairs would fall on her husband like a cloak too loose for his narrow, poetic-looking figure. But he'd worn it with surprising naturalness, with ease, and confidence. He had made one of the most important decisions in the history of his family's fortune: he'd completely restructured the French Wolfflen interests into a holding company quoted on the Bourse. While keeping control of the Holding in the family, he'd opened the Wolfflen fortune to a transfusion of new money and spread the group into new ventures. Bruno, who'd been scarred by his own rashness, had gone on loudly against making Wolfflens answerable to people outside the family, but Marc had prevailed. He'd taken the family fortune, as he'd said at the last shareholders' meeting, "out of a solid, but cramped fortress."

The projected accord with Dynamerica would be the first partnership between the French Wolfflen group and a major non-French company. When Thérèse first heard of the negotiations with the Americans she immediately brought up the name of Ronnie Goodfriend.

"A crook is a crook," Marc had answered impatiently, "no matter what his nationality. There've been enough big crooks in the history of French finance to fill a telephone directory. Goodfriend could have taken lessons from some of them."

The important thing to keep in mind, Marc had pointed out, was that in almost every way The Current was flowing from the States. "You don't get in the way of The Current, Thérèse. The European companies who can't cooperate with the Americans as equals will become their vassals."

In her own day-to-day life, Thérèse greatly enjoyed Americans. She wasn't French, had none of the French self-satisfied chauvinism. Her social life brought her to a vast number of places close to where a jet plane could land. Everywhere, and even in Paris, a goodly number of the women she saw regularly were American. Women who, she thought, resembled her: unjaded and vigorous, aware of all the subtleties but never so rigid as the damned Europeans often were. At their best, she believed the Americans were the patricians of our time. But the Hoyts ... she had never quite met people like the Hoyts. She hadn't encountered their category. She didn't even know quite what their category was.

Kyle R. Hoyt figured greatly in Marc's thinking these days, although when Marc had first met Hoyt in the dreary winter of 1945, Hoyt hadn't seemed to him a person he'd ever have to think about one way or another. At that distant time, Hoyt and the government he served had offered to help Marc buy his cousin's life. Hoyt had been sympathetic, obliging, but remote. When two years later he turned up in the retinue of John Foster Dulles, he seemed to the Baron a proud man diminished, harried, and off balance in the service of a man as proud as he was and vastly more high ranking. Marc had had no contact with Hoyt since then, until a year ago, when Hoyt had wired the Banque Wolfflen, having learned he could do some low-cost financing in Eurodollars. Over a period of three months, Dynamerica had acquired an insurance company, a publishing house, and a large copper mine. Hoyt was very much in need of cash. He was thinking of forming a financial subsidiary in Lichtenstein and placing a public issue of its securities on one of the European exchanges. His bank had advised him to see the Wolfflens first.

After checking Dynamerica's credit thoroughly, Marc had told Hoyt that he didn't need to found the company, that the Banque

Wolfflen could place Dynamerica twenty-year convertible debentures privately, without all that trouble.

Hoyt, who was also in the executive jet business, got a plane from his Paris sales office and went on a four-day tour of London, Geneva, Zurich, Frankfurt, and Milan with Marc and Bruno. By the time they were back in Paris, Hoyt had placed $43 million in five percent securities. He'd borrowed at a third less than what it would have cost him in the United States. Bruno reflected, not without an edge of bitterness, that the Wolfflens could never have moved paper for one of their own companies that fast.

Thérèse remembered Marc's account of the trip vividly, not only because of the financial coup involved, but also because it was at that time she bothered to get a definition from her husband of debentures ("a bond issued without security, whose value depends in large part on the reputation of the issuer").

Now Marc was hoping to interest Hoyt in investing $95 million in the Cofra Copper Company, which extracted and refined ore from a mine long part of the French Wolfflen holdings in Nouwanda, a former part of French West Africa. In exchange for the money needed to modernize the company, Marc was offering Hoyt's Dynamerica forty-five percent of the shares.

While the gentlemen met over business, the ladies were expected to enjoy each other's company about town. Such was still the custom in 1966.

Their next stop was lunch.

They went to the Relais Plaza close by, where Thérèse had reserved a table because it was more amusing than Maxim's for a stranger, and less intimidating. They settled into Thérèse's habitual table, near the mirror in the nook between the bar and the door, the good nook. Here the whole room was visible: the bar where tall young men sipped bloodies with older women or mannequins in their teens (they would nurse a drink all through lunch, some of them, catching the hand of important people coming in, then leave and eat at half the price in the Bar des Théâtres across the street. Thérèse had long ago noticed the game and blessed those poor, well-dressed rascals for their pluck); the other little tables where women of her caste served each other gossip and displayed their wardrobes, and then the general brouhaha of the people all the long narrow way to the far platform, a mixture of all sorts of wealthy names from everywhere, all but working businessmen. The Relais was not a place for business lunches, as every other restaurant in town had become.

They had barely looked at the menu when a whole troupe began appearing before them, to pay homage to the Baroness de Wolfflen. Dark young men wearing closely tailored suits, in town from Rio, getting an early start on the season that drove them from the muggy heat of their own country to Paris. Others with similar mien, from Buenos Aires, Rome, and Milan, old Frenchmen with red ribbons in their pinstriped lapels, women in Courrèges, and some in Saint Laurent's luxurious mock-hoodlum mink and leather jackets. The Beautiful People, as they were being called, beautifully groomed, bustling with panache. They came and kissed the hand or the cheeks of the Baroness, depending on their sex and what degree of intimacy she'd consented them, and vacant eyed, the men made the motions of kissing the stranger's hand, the women of shaking it, as Thérèse introduced *madame* Hoyt ... *madame* Hoyt in her knit dress that would have passed for fashionable in a less exigent milieu. Nearly a dozen people came up to their table and departed, looking as if their acquaintance with Thérèse were something precious they were carrying off with them, to boast of, elsewhere.

"Oh this is wonderful," Sally finally said, when the parade was over and she'd tasted the lamb chop that had arrived after the usual immoderate wait for service. Thérèse knew that it wasn't wonderful, that people did not go to the Relais for the food but for each other, to gossip and eye and salute each other, for which they gladly put up with unexceptional food, slow service, and the intense din of their aggregate chatter. Perhaps Mrs. Hoyt didn't really think the chop was wonderful either. She had left off picking at it to smile at a Shih-Tsu lapdog, eating the *plat du jour*, lentils with pork, on a little rug at its mistress' feet a few tables away. Affection radiated in her eyes for her fellow innocent.

Thérèse was relieved that Sally passed up the pastries. They had coffee and left.

"We'll drop *madame* Hoyt at Alexander's," Thérèse told her chauffeur.

"I've ordered him to take special care of you. No one else but he will put a comb to your hair."

When they reached the hairdressers, Thérèse kissed Sally goodbye on her cheeks. Perhaps the day had been saved.

"It will be a small dinner tonight," she said. "We want to keep it intimate."

The day had been saved. She fell back onto the spicy leather of her car, composing herself for her next appointment. It was with her doctor, who'd invited her to look at "the pictures."

He was a man of sixty who played a lot of tennis. His hands were freckled and dry, but under his long, straight-falling white smock, you could sense a thin, youthful body. He moved in a crisp way. He was visibly a happy man, having made his mark as one of the revered names in his field. There were also silver cups on a shelf in his office: amateur championships of some kind, which he'd won— Thérèse had never bothered to read the engravings. Perhaps he kept the trophies there to remind his poor patients that people who exercise a lot seldom get heart trouble. But by the time they were in his hands, it was too late for advice: the cups shone like a gleeful reproach. For Thérèse they had no personal meaning. Once, as a little girl, on what she'd thought would be a wonderful trip with her father to Mexico City, she'd come down with a fever, and she'd had to live as if a knife were pointed at her heart ever since.

"*Voilà,*" the doctor said. He flashed on a light panel on the wall and there she was, her own insides. She looked at the X-ray with unsympathetic fascination. So ugly: a blob of muscle going its own way, enlarging itself, threatening thereby to kill itself, and her. She hated her heart. It was as if it were some parasitic organism inside her.

"*Voilà,*" he said again. He traced the swollen curve with the tip of his horn-rimmed eyeglasses. Beautiful frames, she noticed. Something was engraved on a plaque inside one arm. He put the tip of the frame into the corner of his mouth now, and he stood facing her in silence, looking, for some reason, very proud of his picture.

"*Voilà quoi?*"

"You must live more quietly."

"You said that years ago, and I haven't got any better."

"I'm afraid . . . you've gotten a little worse."

She shrugged. "So what the hell good does it do?"

"Well, you must be more careful than ever. Perhaps there are activities you can eliminate. You must spend more time resting. Even if you just sat down for once and decided to eliminate from your life a few things that you'd find futile on reflection anyway. Doesn't anything in your crowded life seem futile?"

"Yes," she said sweetly, "seeing you."
He frowned like a wounded father.
"I'll have a nap before dinner," she said. "Word of honor."

She rose and took a little pad from the table beside her bed. On it was a circle with a line drawn down the middle: the map of her round dinner table.

Once again, Thérèse confirmed the wisdom of her keeping the party small. After her day with Sally, she was convinced that a large dinner would find the Hoyts oarless and floundering in a maelstrom of Parisian repartee. On the other hand, if she'd invited no one of note, the Hoyts could rightfully consider themselves insulted; they could presume that the Wolfflens had considered them unfit to be shown to society. Thérèse had decided to invite three couples in addition to Bruno and Edmée. She wanted people the Hoyts could immediately place as important—not just socialites revered in Paris with halos invisible to Kyle and Sally. She wanted people "international" enough to make suitable conversation in English, people intimate enough with each other not to spend the dinner fencing for the brilliant role, who would instead help Marc, Bruno, Edmée, and her make the Hoyts feel comfortable.

With all these considerations in mind, she'd drawn up the following list:

"Monsieur et Madame Gaston Robinet
"Monsieur Godwin Laver et son invitée
"Emma de Wolfflen et Monsieur Philippe Arthaud
"Bruno et Edmée de Wolfflen."

The presence of Robinet, the Finance Minister, was an obvious honor to the Hoyts and a suggestion of Marc's power, since in all dealings with foreign companies the blessings of the Ministry of Finance were necessary. Emma, beyond being still another Wolfflen, was a pianist known to anyone who knew music, and no doubt Mrs. Hoyt did. She was also, like Laver, a fellow "Anglo-Saxon" who could make the Hoyts feel closer to home. Arthaud, more than simply a minor diplomat, was an obliging gentleman whose talent for small talk could charm an aborigine about to cook him. Laver was a star of international finance, an old friend of Thérèse (and she was convinced Marc should be seeing more of him.) He could talk and keep his mouth shut as well as anyone in the business world. In the years since he'd come back from his island, since that shocking death, in childbirth, of his child wife, Godwin Laver had become a reserved man. Except on one count: he always dated gorgeous young girls, rarely the same one twice. Thérèse, who had never envied any other woman, felt unmitigatedly happy that the face of the lady who'd accompany Laver would embellish her table beyond anything she could accomplish with her flowers.

Thérèse was pleased with one more aspect of her table: she had placed Emma well, to Robinet's left. She was Marc's enduring friend. It was hard for her and Emma to be friends, too. But this was once Emma's house, and she would always find an honored place in it when she returned.

"It's right," Thérèse whispered to herself. "It's perfect." If all went well, as it should, the Hoyts might know and yet not be aware that two of the people at table had lived together here unhappily for years, and that one guest had occupied the host's rightful place in his family business for nearly as long. And in enjoying their dinner while failing to see the seams of the event Thérèse had stitched together, nor any sign of tension from old oppositions, the Hoyts would have experienced a quintessentially Parisian evening, after all.

It proved too much to hope for. Hoyt seemed absent to the point of insolence. Thérèse sensed that he turned his energy on and off depending on whether or not there was business at hand. It might have been his way of conserving himself, of staying bright when he had to. Over dinner he answered all the pseudo-questions a hostess draws on to get talk going, but he put nothing in the pot, so to speak, himself. The conversation was indeed like a cold pot full of something congealed and bland, sitting there in everyone's imagination while the best beluga from Petrossian, the most delicate rack of lamb, and a soufflé of prunes, airy and delicious, an extravagant sweet hussy of a dessert, were passed. Hoyt barely touched the La Garne '45, '28, and '06. At one point Thérèse noticed he was bringing his glass to his lips but only pretending to sip.

Sally was somewhat more accessible, but Philippe Arthaud seemed for once at a loss for inspiration.

"And does your wife enjoy your being in government service?" she asked him, revealing that Hoyt had not done a thorough biographical dossier on his intended partners. They were Wolfflens. Perhaps that had been enough for him to know.

"Ah, *madame* is not my wife—"

"Oh I'm sorry! I thought she just used her ... other name ... for her career."

"Ah no. Ah no. But you, *madame* Hoyt. Did you enjoy your husband's career in the government?"

"I liked it better some places than others. I liked Washington better than Karachi, for one good example. For a while, we were all over the place, countries I can't even spell anymore. Unfortunately I was never with Kyle in Paris. That was before my time—I mean before we were married. I confess, *monsieur* Arthaud, I've been the happiest of all in Rochester. Not the city—not the city—it's not Paris, you know, but it was settling down to a real home base. The children's schooling had been a kind of revolving-door affair. No, I confess: I've been happiest of all from the day my husband decided to manufacture semiconductors in Rochester."

"Your husband is a genius of technology from what I understand." Arthaud, for his part, was a bit shaky over Hoyt's background, but a compliment never hurt.

"Oh no! He's smart, but he doesn't know anything about those little things. That's why he has engineers. *Monsieur* Arthaud, if my husband had to know all there was to know about all the things he's into now, he'd be a walking encyclopedia twenty-four volumes wide. No, Kyle's background was intelligence. It was a publicly known job, so don't you think I'm ripping off his cloak and exposing his dagger. Of course, he's sensitive about it, all the same. All that's got such a bad reputation, now. But tell me, *monsieur* Arthaud, do you happen to know a country that has no spies?"

"Tibet," he ventured.

"Maybe that's why they're part of China now."

Arthaud laughed. Hoyt, who had taken advantage of a dead spot in his conversation with Edmée to take out his pen and note something on a little card, looked their way. His brow was still furrowed with the intensity of the thought he'd noted and underlined on his card. Illegible to Edmée.

"We're talking about government service, darling," Sally called across the table.

"Oh yes. Oh yes," Hoyt said.

Gaston Robinet glared at Arthaud as if he were capable of spilling government secrets for the sake of a *bon mot*.

Coffee was soon brought into the next room.

Thérèse took her place on the sofa and began to serve. Emma stood nearby. Poor Emma, all flushed. "Emma," Thérèse said gently, "you take—"

"No sugar."

She served her first. She was closest, which was a good enough excuse for the favor. Having passed the cup, done the favor, Thérèse couldn't think of anything to say. They were civilized people, and since Emma was so much older than she was it came naturally to Thérèse to treat Emma with the consideration due a pleasant but distant aunt. Yet Thérèse and she rarely said much to each other, rarely anything beyond meaningless pleasantries. Both knew, in the end, that both their lives had been marked indelibly by one man, the same one, but in ways too different for him to bind them, either through affection or antipathy, to each other.

Emma gazed now, feeling suddenly very estranged, at the man in the red gold-buttoned coat who had set the silver coffee service down in front of Thérèse. She recalled that "in her time" Marc had been content to dress his servants in white jackets. Now she conceded that the man did look better in the Wolfflen colors, and that for a Wolfflen that sort of thing was not at all ostentatious. Unconsciously she bit her lip, confessing to herself that she hadn't been expansive enough in the way she'd run this house. Too withdrawn. Her thoughts broke off as she overheard Bruno asking the blond actress who'd come with Laver "where she could be reached." Well, there was an expansive Wolfflen . . .

The girl was all in white Courrèges, in a stiff dress exactly like the one in pink Thérèse was wearing, except that they were heavily seamed in different ways. The same white booties. They both recalled Alice in Wonderland. Emma thought that at best both dresses were inappropriate for dinner, but she didn't care for Courrèges at all. She saw something cynically twisted in that mixture of children's wear and space clothes. Emma could recall Courrèges when he was an assistant at Balenciaga. She remembered an intense, insensitive face. Emma never thought much about fashion, even if she had an eye for clothes. She dressed almost entirely at Balenciaga. The poor man was old and repeated himself these days, but he was still the best. The times, she felt, had got worse, not his talent. She thought little about fashion, and yet she could not help but note how disparate the fashion was at Marc's table tonight. The two Courrèges—vulgar and conspicuous—the luxurious sportiveness of Edmée's red Chanel suit, the inanity of Madame Robinet's black crêpe dress from Guy Laroche or someplace like that, her own stark Balenciaga black crêpe. And to boot, Mrs. Hoyt's multicolored silk print by Pucci, the dress that never wrinkles in a suitcase. What a jumble of taste it all was! Mere fashion yes, but she knew that fashion was one of the languages an age uses to describe itself. Well, it was a motley age. A frenetic age of indiscriminate mingling of contrasts. And the most vulgar ways were the most in fashion. Emma made her deduction automatically, and although she assumed it could be confirmed by the general state of things, she realized a second later that she had only a very vague notion of the state of things.

Out of touch. She bit her lip again.

She traveled greatly now. (She had even played Chopin at Carnegie Hall that spring, and even Mrs. Hoyt, as it turned out, had been in New York then and heard her. "When I read what Glick said in the *Times*, I absolutely had to have a ticket at any price!") And yet, she simply moved her hermetic world from place to place. From one concert hall to another, all with that same bitter smell. Hotel rooms and concert halls. The loving warmth of applause followed by late meals alone in a room full of flowers. Was she unhappy; no, she told herself. No, she was sad only once in a while to discover herself—out of touch. At times, as this evening, that made her feel inferior. Would she be happier still Marc's wife? She raised the question lucidly to herself; being here made the question seem natural. No, she answered herself lucidly. All that was history. And when things weren't right between two people, being alone with someone else was far harder than being alone with oneself.

Arthaud came up to her. "I was not very brilliant," he apologized.

"Oh, it's not your fault, you silly."

No, she couldn't blame him for another man's crudeness, nor for the fact that although he was the finest of friends, he was incapable of being more to her than that. Did she want more? What disturbed her most was that she didn't even know if she wanted to desire more.

"Will you have a cognac or a fruit alcohol, Mr. Hoyt?"

Thérèse had searched for the English word for *eau-de-vie* and had been obliged to invent "fruit alcohol." Beside her the red-jacketed servant was holding a tray heavy with bottles: cognac, *poire, framboise, kirsch, vieux calvados.*

"I'll take another *fruit juice,* if there's some left."

Hoyt had had an orange juice before dinner, and as Thérèse had noted he'd barely touched his wine. He showed no inhibitions now in explaining why:

"A drink for me is like a company, Thérèse. If I have one I just have to have another. And then another. But you see, the two habits are mutually exclusive, so it didn't take me long to decide which was the one doing me more good."

"Kyle's been a teetotaler for years," Sally Hoyt confirmed. Marc's eyes took on the remote look they sometimes did when he'd had a glimpse of something he'd have preferred not to have seen. Hoyt accepted a cigar, and as he lit it, Marc suddenly recalled the wind that had blown the Major's cigar ash in his eyes more than twenty years ago. Well, times change, and people change, he told himself, and those who don't move forward are as good as dead.

The after-dinner guests were arriving now. Late, for they'd all had important dinners elsewhere. This was no crowd of B-list figures extended what the French call an invitation to pick their teeth with those invited for dinner. It was the continuation of all the best dinners in town that evening.

The guests settled in clusters throughout the Wolfflens' vast salon, on the Louis XVI chairs covered with colorfully embroidered silk, muted velvet, and suede. A second footman paused at a few lamps, dropping Floris scent into cups heating above the light bulbs. The air took on a delicious headiness. Thérèse led the Hoyts from group to group, introducing them to Countess X and Le Prince Y, Monsieur and Madame A dash B; the names would surely remain a jumble in their heads next morning, but they would have retained that there'd been a quantity of titles. Thérèse didn't keep the Hoyts long enough with any group for a conversation to begin ... she moved them about deliberately quickly and brought them safely back, leaving Hoyt to talk business with Bruno and Marc in the adjoining small salon, and Mrs. Hoyt with the Robinets, Emma, and Arthaud ...

Once, as she passed, she could hear her husband talking like a salesman. Marc was summing up the presentation he'd made that afternoon.

Marc had pointed out that the ore coming up from the Cofra mine in Nouwanda was down to 1.3 percent copper, somewhat below the world average. But there was still an enormous amount of ore coming up. What was needed was to get rid of the outmoded Wolfflen smeltering and refining plant near Marseilles and replace it with a modern plant at the minesite. That way they'd save enough in shipping costs, by shipping electrolytic copper instead of ore, to compensate for the relatively low quality of the ore. They could also avoid the highly costly antipollution requirements they were likely to face in Marseilles in a few years. (Hoyt had confirmed that the American copper people were already trembling in the shadow of coming legislation.) They would employ a lot of Nouwandans, and appease the government, which, since Nouwandan independence, had made noises about being "exploited for raw materials."

Thérèse came into the little salon before Marc could explain the figures he'd placed that afternoon on the various investments. "So," she said, rousing the men like a cowmaid rousing a part of her herd that had found too distant shade. "So," she said in English, "Marc de Wolfflen I presume ... are you ready to return to civilization?"

There was annoyance in his eyes as he looked up from the huddle of bulls and faced her, but she just locked her gaze onto his and gave him back a frown.

When all the other people had left, the Wolfflens, Edmée and Bruno, Marc and Thérèse, took the Hoyts for a quick look-in, at Castel's and New Jimmy's. They didn't go down to the dance floor at Castel's, but had a drink at the ground-floor bar with the *patron*. Hoyt, who'd played college football, enjoyed meeting Castel, who'd been a rugbyman, although there was little they could say to each other. Sally Hoyt enjoyed seeing, from a few feet away, Marcello Mastroianni. They left early, but by the time they arrived at New Jimmy's, the dance floor was packed. They sat at their *banquette*, sipping Dom Perignon, watching the dancers like people at a show. The music was too loud for any conversation. Finally, when the crowd thinned out a little, Marc invited Sally Hoyt to dance. They danced to "You've Got to Hide Your Love Away" and when the music shifted to the frantic "Satisfaction," they kept on dancing. Thérèse noted, a little surprised, how efficiently Mrs. Hoyt followed the music. Her motions were precise and fluid. And soulless, but she managed a certain brave dignity, faced with the frenzy of the Rolling Stones. She managed it with a composed and absent look.

Thérèse's eyes moved over all the dancers. She almost never danced herself—a question of her health—but she could sit for hours at New Jimmy's, freed of the need to talk, looking at all the sleek people perform, refined by the dance into something other than all the roles and appurtenances of their lives, transformed, reduced to human bodies in motion. Yet never quite totally changed, for their lives clung to them all the same, their movements suggested histories, who they were to the world between the lines of their mention in *Who's Who* or the *Bottin Mondain*. They remained, fatally, attitudes in motion. Thérèse's great secret amusement was to try to imagine from the way each person danced how he made love. She was of the opinion that there were very few good dancers in this world, and her not too extensive experience told her there were few good lovers as well. She looked at Marc now, as he moved with a limber, loose sway, a faintly ironic smile on his face. Marc was a *sweet* lover; he made love with the same sort of gentle patience his smile revealed now...

Suddenly she drained her glass of champagne and stood up. She slipped forward through the crowd of people leaving the dance floor, past her husband and Sally Hoyt. Hoyt, rising to his obligation, followed her, although she moved onto the floor without even taking note that he was there. She began to dance.

She danced in a way no one at that time was dancing. The *discaire*, peering out of her little cabin, might have been struck by the rare presence of the Baroness on the dance floor. She put on "Satisfaction" once again, as if to egg her on. Thérèse planted her feet and didn't lift them. Her body danced, swayed, and writhed. Her hands flew up over her head, palms outward as if in supplication. Her fingers danced. People melted away around her. In a moment, she was alone out there with Hoyt and the whole room was watching, from the tables or standing at the fringe of the dance floor. Hoyt tried to catch her style, but he was floundering, adding gusto where only grace could have saved him, stamping his feet. For her, he wasn't there, was no more there than anyone else in the room.

"I try—and I try—and I try..."

The *discaire* swept Mick Jagger's voice away. An old *slow* came on. "If you were the only girl in the world..." Hundreds of years old. Perry Como. People began appearing around her again. She felt a hand on her shoulder. It was Marc's. He held her against him for a minute and swayed to the music, and then led her off the floor. She was in a sweat. She was still damp with perspiration when he undressed her an hour later. He peeled away her clothes and they made love clinging to each other.

Next day, Marc, Bruno, and the Hoyts left for Africa. As she kissed her husband goodbye at the doorway of her bedroom, Thérèse couldn't judge whether she could possibly miss him more than she was relieved the Hoyts were going.

When they got back to Paris, it took Hoyt and the Wolfflens only another day to work out the details of their joint venture. That evening Bruno and Edmée took the Hoyts to dinner in a bistro. Marc came without Thérèse.

"Thérèse is very disappointed, but she's not feeling at all strong this evening," he said, making himself—for she'd given him no choice—an accomplice in her lie.

TWO

When his manservant knocked at his bedroom door with breakfast on the morning of June 28, 1967, the Baron had already been up for several hours, tossing about, hoping to go back to sleep. Marc would have liked to have been able to sleep through the whole summer's day rather than go through the two unpleasant meetings he had on his agenda. Thérèse was away: the person he really wanted to be with. Instead he had to spend time with Godwin Laver and Gaston Robinet, and the nature of his business with each told him in advance that his time would be spent unpleasantly. He looked at the tray being propped in front of him, laden with juice, croissants, and coffee, as if it were some device for restraining a prisoner.

"No, please," he said to the man in the red coat who wore his habitual look of reserved but ingratiating morning cheer.

"No, please, tell the Baron Gilbert that I'd like very much to have his company at breakfast this morning."

Gilbert came down to the table set up hastily in the library in his pyjamas and dressing gown.

"Are we having a meeting?"

"I asked for the pleasure of your company ... You were out very late last night."

Gilbert shook his head and puffed out his cheeks. "I'm wiped out."

"Was it worth it?"

"It was very strange," Gilbert answered, "but we won't go into that."

A mannequin Gilbert was sleeping with in a nonserious way had taken him to a gay discothèque that whole group of hers was frequenting. Which was all right, he thought, except for the photographer who took his picture.

Marc shrugged. The clock beside his bed had said four-fifteen when Gilbert's steps, as he went past Marc's door, had woken Marc from his thin sleep. (For the past year, Gilbert had been living in the apartment Marc had made for himself in the days he and Emma had turned their marriage into a friendship.) Marc examined without disapproval the morning-after, vulnerable look that had come over his son's handsome features. Marc at twenty-two had been just as much the young bachelor about town; of course the haunts had changed.

"Where'd you go?" he asked.

"Oh ... let's not go into that," Gilbert said, as he passed across the table the copy of *l'Aurore* he'd unfolded.

"Look." The page was turned to a story about a toast President de Gaulle had proposed to the President of Turkey over dinner at the Elysée the night before. Marc read: "... the dominating and opposing ambitions of Washington, Moscow, and Peking ..." The General was on his high horse again, flailing his rusty lance, following up his shrill attack on the United States in the cabinet meeting of a week ago. ("The War in Vietnam begun by the Americans ..." had caused, as he put it, "a psychological and political process which ended in the struggle in the Middle East.") The General was now refusing to supply even the spare parts the Israelis had ordered for their Mirage jets before the war.

"The General's all lathered up again," Gilbert said. "Do you honestly think there's any use in seeing Robinet?"

"I don't relish the idea of asking him to plead our case, but I feel it's my duty. What would you do?"

These days Marc frequently asked his son what he would do in his place. He was trying hard, perhaps, he sometimes admitted, too *consciously* hard, to get closer to Gilbert. Closer than he'd been since the breakup of his marriage with Emma. By now, Gilbert had matured enough to see things objectively, and Marc had been deeply pleased when he'd accepted the offer of the apartment in Marc's townhouse. ("You're a Wolfflen," Emma had told him—as Gilbert had dispassionately recounted to Marc afterwards—"Your future is at your father's side, and you needn't fight any battles for me that I don't choose to fight myself.") Shortly after Gilbert had moved in, Marc had reduced his own shares in the Holding Wolfflen to give his son fifteen percent.

"I suppose I'd do what you're doing," Gilbert replied, "but I wouldn't have great hopes. Would it make it less painful if I went with you?"

"I'll go alone, don't bother, it will be better *man to man* . . ."

"And with Godwin?"

"I'll see him by myself as well. There's no use in anyone's being there. Bruno's gone to Luxembourg. I've slept, or rather tried to sleep, on what we talked about yesterday, and I come up with the same solution. I'll tell him he can have the whole company."

As Marc took his final sip of coffee, he peered over his cup at his son's face for a reaction.

"Of course," Gilbert said. Yes, Marc thought, Gilbert was level headed, he didn't let emotions flaw his thinking. "But Bruno's right of course too," Gilbert added, "we can never do business with the man again."

"Of course, Bruno's right," Marc murmured absently as he got up. "I'll check the mail," he said, leaving for the front of the house. There'd been nothing with the newspapers that morning, but Marc still hoped a letter from Thérèse might have arrived.

Of course Bruno was right.
Was he?

It was indeed possible, Marc thought, that Laver had behaved rather slippery, even if people were saying it was the Wolfflens who'd tried to pull a fast deal. The story went back to a year ago, when the Holding Wolfflen acquired forty percent of Bison, a supermarket chain with good locations but a backward management. While the Wolffens were looking hard for a completely new management team, Godwin Laver came forward and offered to cooperate with the Wolfflens in the company by taking twenty percent. There was no question of a takeover; he wanted no more than to buy up quietly twenty percent of the company on the Bourse, and along with his financial presence he was offering some of the best supermarket expertise in Europe, since he already owned chains in Holland and Great Britain, chains he'd rescued from heavy losses in the few years he'd controlled them. The deal had seemed very promising to the Wolfflens, and indeed, Godwin had limited his participation to twenty percent. A month ago, he acquired a chain of department stores with a subsidiary in supermarkets and he suggested that the subsidiary be merged with Bison. Again, Laver's proposal made good sense. Laver, Bruno, and Marc agreed that the merger would take place through an exchange of three shares of Bison for seven shares of Godwin's subsidiary. The deal was all signed when suddenly a small shareholder in Godwin's company filed suit, contending that the exchange ratio was unfair. The commissioners of the Bourse came in, examined the assets of both companies, and ruled that a proper ratio was three shares for five. With the new arithmetic, Godwin Laver, who had twenty percent of Bison and controlling interest in his subsidiary, would gain control of the merged company.

"He put that little guy up to it," was Bruno's immediate reaction. "He knew we wouldn't agree to a merger if we lost control and so he feinted by striking a deal with us. Then the bastard went round the back door with the little guy and his lawyers and challenged the deal."

Laver was pleading innocent. "There are a lot of things you can't measure in all this," he'd insisted, "namely what it means to tie in with the Wolfflens, God, all your access to credit, your prestige, your image of quality. Honestly, Marc, I believe there's a lot of hard-to-measure good will there, but go tell it to the commissioners ..."

Well, if we were outplayed we had ourselves to blame, Marc thought now, as he entered the elevator that went directly to the Associates Room in the new Holding Wolfflen building, across the cobbled courtyard from the eighteenth-century townhouse in which Isaiah had lived and worked, and where every French Wolfflen, up to now, had had his office. The new building, of tinted glass and chrome, fitted into the program of expansion Marc had undertaken since he'd succeeded Charles. They'd needed more offices. They'd also needed to look more up to date. Marc was still proud of his building, but as he left the elevator that brought him to the fifth floor with a rapid hiss, he noticed a small crack in the slate that covered the hallway walls. He'd have to have that looked at.

Ourselves to blame, he thought again. We should have had a more realistic idea of what was worth what before we wet our feet. The commissioners are no fools. And they have nobody's ax to grind.

Godwin was already waiting outside the Associates Room. His long body was slouched in a leather chair, his paunch peered through his open jacket—a homely, ungainly presence, which seemed to spite the youthfulness that still radiated from his intense face. He left off scratching his head nervously and stood up as Marc approached. The Baron offered him a hasty greeting.

The furniture of the Associates Room was exactly as it was in the house across the courtyard, but the old, fusty, ornate paneling had been exchanged for smooth Honduras mahogany, and the worn Chinese rug was gone. Marc did not lead Laver to his desk but to a corner where there were leather armchairs. He offered neither a drink, coffee, cigars, nor small talk.

"We've thought our position ... in this mess ... through, Godwin. We are not interested in a minority role, particularly since neither Bruno nor I ... nor Gilbert agree with you on your plans to expand into Belgium ... particularly since all the market studies we've asked for say no—"

"You've asked the wrong people—"

"Godwin, I don't want to sidetrack the issue, I'm sorry. What I want to tell you is that we're not interested in a minority share of your company, in any case. We've decided to clean up the whole matter by getting out entirely. We intend to sell all our shares in Bison, and we'd welcome an offer from you—"

"Marc, *this isn't my fault.*"

"Godwin, I'm not here to lay any blame. I can't argue with the commissioners. We've looked at the facts, as they stand now, and we're responding to the facts."

"All right." His voice fell as he added: "I'll give you ninety million francs for your shares, and if it suits you, I'd like to purchase them in three installments over the next eighteen months."

Godwin's figure was twenty million francs higher than what Marc would have offered if he were in Godwin's shoes.

"That's a generous figure . . ."

"I'd rather you'd kept your shares. But that's my honest judgment of what they're worth."

Godwin rose. He stood with his characteristic slouch and ran his hand boyishly through his sparse, unhealthy blond hair. Then he began to pace with his hands in his suitcoat pockets.

"I want you to understand," he said, "I want you and Bruno . . . and Gilbert to understand that what matters to me most in this whole hulabaloo is keeping your friendship."

Without rising, Marc gazed at the tall, harried-looking man in front of him. By the expression on Godwin's face, he seemed sincere. Marc realized that young Laver was a very complicated person.

Thérèse was away and Gilbert had said he had a lunch in town with some friend in advertising. Marc decided not to go home for lunch as he usually did, not to go home to the empty house, but instead to have lunch brought to him in the little salon off the Associates' Room, where he and Bruno sometimes took lunch with their top staff. It would have been pleasant if Bruno were there to share lunch with him now but Bruno was meeting with the directors of the branch of the Banque Wolfflen they'd established in Luxembourg. Marc ordered a steak and salad and a good bottle of La Garne, and asked to have the early edition of *France-Soir* brought up with the food.

Marc brushed past the headlines to turn to Lucille Tortet's gossip column on page five. Lucille Tortet was in the Algarve for big festivities, and that was where Thérèse was.

Suddenly a photograph of his wife loomed at him. "The Baroness Marc de Wolfflen, Back from the Beach." Thérèse had on a bikini and a big straw hat. Her incredible body, on page five of *France-Soir*, and far away in the Algarve, where the Duke de Caramon was giving a ball, preceded by a week of parties given by his guests. Thérèse had urged Marc to go with her but it was ridiculous, in the middle of everything, in the middle of all he had to do, to face up to—

Ridiculous. She'd gone alone. Often, now, she went alone, or rather without him, to social events, even in Paris, escorted by one of her new handful of *chevaliers servants*. Even in Paris, he couldn't keep up with five or six nights or seven nights a week of going out, to dinner and then to Castel's or Régine's with a full schedule the next day. She would sleep until late in the afternoon, but he couldn't, and he owed his full energy to the people he worked with and, well, to his stockholders, and finally, with all else, he didn't enjoy seeing the same faces six, seven nights anyway. Thérèse did; as for her health, it miraculously seemed to thrive on all that. She reigned over those people and her social power seemed to feed her with physical energy. Perhaps it was not a very *serious* form of power, but he could understand her exulting in it; anyway he loved her. Loved that body he looked at, again, with regret. His eyes froze on the picture. He could make out now, dark but definitely present a few steps behind Thérèse, a man in a bathing suit of about thirty, judging by his trim body. Who? He felt the blood drain from his face. But then he reasoned with himself. He doesn't even belong in the picture. It's just somebody. Nobody, nothing to do with her, somebody in the background. But since it was the first time during one of her trips without him he had not had a long, daily letter from his wife, he was vulnerable to jealousy. He read Tortet's column hungrily for some news of her, but she wasn't even mentioned. She'd been given the picture that day. It had no doubt been, in the manner in which Tortet measured out presence to her people, top billing, and enough. And now Marc wondered suddenly if any of those light-footed escorts of Thérèse in Paris could be up to something serious with her. Preposterous. Weak jealousy. But his salad went down with difficulty. He skipped cheese and dessert and decided to take a calming walk around the neighborhood of the bank before having himself driven to the Louvre.

In the wing of the Louvre that lodged the Ministry of Finance, a great marble staircase led to the first floor, where among heavily gilded walls, the Minister worked behind a long, ornate desk. Gaston Robinet rose from his desk when a *huissier* in a black tailcoat ushered in the Baron Marc de Wolfflen.

Robinet looked in fine form. He had recently come back from a tour of the former French colonies in West Africa, where he'd proposed new measures for economic cooperation in the Franc Zone. He'd also, as Marc noticed from his photographs in the newspapers, taken time to make a three-day sail in the South Atlantic on the yacht of the President of Nouwanda. He was tan and hale, and his eye had the confident, bright look, as well, of a man whose work is his pleasure.

"Ah," he said with a note of bonhommie, "you've come to talk to me about another enormous deal you've put together with the Americans."

"I don't make those kinds of deals every day," Marc parried. "Today is not one of my enormous-deal days."

Robinet's heavy face took on a greater seriousness.

"You'd like to hear how things stand with the Nouwandans," he said.

"Yes, that would interest me," Marc said, "but my reason for coming doesn't concern business. . . . You know I'm the chairman of the CFI . . ."

"Yes, of course," Robinet replied. His heavy eyebrows seemed to sink over his eyes. His look was suddenly like that of a medical specialist about to tell his patient he needs an operation.

Being chairman of the Comité Français pour Israël, the French Committee for Israel, was one of several nonbusiness activities in which Marc had followed in the shoes of his father. Like Charles, Marc gave a lot of money to Israel, but the chairmanship had never taken much of his time; it had demanded less of him than, say, the Wolfflen Hospital for Crippled Children which needed the presence of a keen business mind to face rising costs and to plan modernization. For years, Marc had been happy to think of the CFI chairmanship as an honorary thing. The Wolfflens were Jews and were in no way interested in muffling the fact that they were Jews. But Marc had always thought that beating the drum too loudly for Israel carried with it a danger for the Jews in France, the danger of falling prey to the old antisemitic arguments that Jews were not really French, that their loyalty was elsewhere. The crisis which had produced the Six-Day War had altered his thinking.

"Israel," Marc began, "is far from out of danger. I don't think the Arabs have changed their minds about destroying the Jewish State . . ."

"It's obvious," Robinet answered, "that the Israelis haven't made new friends of the Arabs by attacking them."

"Gaston," Marc began (since Robinet had become a familiar figure at Thérèse's table, he'd become "Gaston" for the Wolfflens), "I don't think you have the time for the two of us to debate the situation in the Middle East. I've come to ask a service, not for myself, but for a great number of French citizens. . . . I asked for an appointment with the General, and he has refused to see me. I'd be grateful if someone who has his confidence could explain to him why I wanted to see him. I'm not asking him for the moon, Gaston; I don't even expect him to change France's policy in the Middle East. I want a simple, precise thing. A very small thing. There is a contract signed, there is a shipment of planes and spare parts for which the Israelis have already paid. I am asking simply that France honor its signature and deliver. It could be done in total secrecy."

Robinet toyed with a gold pen on his desk. He sat, a spectator of his own fingers. He didn't raise his eyes as he said: "I don't think there can be an exception to the embargo. The General warned the Israelis not to strike the first blow."

"Gaston, are you aware of the fact that our government deliberately failed to deliver this equipment *before* the war? The embargo existed against Israel *beforehand*—"

"There was some rumor printed in *L'Aurore*."

"It's a fact. There's proof. Gaston, de Gaulle is a General—if he were in the Israelis' shoes three weeks ago, would he have struck the first blow? That was their only chance. Now he's put an embargo on all arms to the war zone and only last week he decided to give more money to the Algerians. Who are shipping arms to the war zone. What kind of neutral policy is that? Up to now, Israel has counted on France for ninety percent of its arms. Who does the embargo hurt, the people who are being supplied by the Russians?"

"The only hope for Israel, Marc, is to make peace with its neighbors, it can't go on forever as a fortress—"

"Gaston, you're not giving a press conference now. How can you make peace with someone who won't recognize you're alive? No, Gaston, the French position, if it comes to you and I having to argue about it, is simple. It's simple hypocrisy. France isn't giving any lessons to the Israelis about peace. France has looked at the figures and decided there's more of a future in dealing with the Arabs than with the Israelis. You know the figures, you know what can be sold and what we have to buy. You're the Minister of Finance. I didn't come to argue about policy, I came for one specific thing, but I'll tell you something. For the first time that I know of, the General is thinking like a businessman, but he's making a mistake. Because even in business you have to listen to the heart; if you don't, you lose respect, and you lose your self-respect. You lose some very important capital for the long-run functioning of a business."

"If he has refused to see you ... I don't know what I can do."

"If he has ministers, it is to counsel him."

"Foreign affairs, Marc, are not my domain."

"Goodbye, Gaston. I hope that I may hear from you."

But as Marc returned to the car waiting for him in the courtyard of the Ministry, he held no hope of getting help from Gaston Robinet. Well, how much could he be faulted, Marc thought—there isn't a minister in the cabinet who can stand up to the General. Well, we'll probably be seeing less of old Gaston, he realized. And less of Godwin Laver. And perhaps he'd be seeing less of his own wife: three people for different reasons moving away from him, he thought, moving away, each of them with a totally different meaning from the others in his life; and yet, all three had influenced his day, today, in the same manner: they'd given him a feeling worse than loneliness, a sense of estrangement. *Listen to the heart* he heard himself saying. *Meaning—what?*

He decided to dine with his mother, poor old Eveline, whom *he'd* abandoned for several weeks. And then he was unhappy once again, to recall that he hadn't waited to hear what Robinet might have told him about how things stood with the Nouwandans, in whose country his company and Dynamerica had made an enormous investment in copper.

THREE

Eveline was sitting in the garden. The summer night smelled green there, as Marc went out to join her. It called to his emotions, making him suddenly giddy and melancholy at the same time; there in the middle of Avenue Foch, on a civilized street, it announced the presence of things that parenthesize the unobservant, busy man: the realm of dumb life, of plants which suck in the sun and charge the air with oxygen, of stars and time and inexorable beginnings and endings, the whole belittling mechanism.

Firmin was setting up a table. Limping about. His rheumatism.

"We're about to lose our Firmin," Eveline said. "He'll be 'going home,' as he put it."

Firmin broke into the conversation, something he'd never dared do in his years in the household. "Everyone must know when it's time to give up, *monsieur le Baron.*"

Firmin explained that over the years he had managed to purchase a farm in his home town, in Auvergne. He and his wife were going to retire there.

"But everything has changed," he said. "Everything has changed, *monsieur le Baron*. They no longer cut the grass."

"They no longer cut the grass?" Marc smiled indulgently.

"No one has the heart for it anymore."

Firmin pointed out that the pastures in his area were all on steep mountainsides. In the past, the lush grass that grew there, yielding only at the last few meters to rock, moss, and gentian, used to be cut by bands of peasants working patiently with scythes. Now no one wanted to do that kind of work anymore. The young had left the farms to work in Clermont-Ferrand, or Paris. The old were on Social Security and rented their pastures to cows from the sparer flatlands of Charentes, who wallowed in the tall, rich, aromatic grass all summer. But there was no hope of winter fodder. A good machine to cut those mountainsides had yet to be invented. So there were few local herds now.

"What can you do, *monsieur le Baron*? One must learn to live with one's own time." Firmin sounded only formally sad.

"He's sold his flatland for a trailer camp," Eveline whispered as the *maître d'hôtel* went back into the house to get the silver. "He's the richest man in his town."

But Marc had noticed that Firmin had got quite thin lately. His face, once robust and hard featured, had thinned and paled.

"Is he ill?"

"He has been to see a specialist for his liver," Eveline answered, and then she tucked her nose into her fist, in that comical French gesture for a tippler. She sighed.

"How is Thérèse . . . these days?"

"Completely active," Marc said brightly.

"She is extraordinary." Eveline had never been really intimate with her son's second wife, but she admired, sometimes incomprehensibly, Thérèse's dynamism.

"Yes. Extraordinary," Marc said with nostalgia.

"I saw the *France-Soir*," Eveline said.

"Yes. Yes." Marc didn't know what his mother might have thought of the picture.

"People do go about a lot these days," she said, without going into it. "People are always getting on and off airplanes." She seemed to say it without reproach, with a certain charitable serenity.

Marc's only reaction was to recall that at times nowadays his mother's mind would fray, and that things she said that seemed charged with innuendos were sometimes really just simple impressions, like those of a child.

"It's a difficult way to live," she went on.

"I said, it's a difficult way to live," she insisted.

"One must live one's time," he imitated, trying to be evasively witty.

"There are things one must never do at any time," she said, her voice darkening with seriousness now. "One must never put a trailer camp in one's front yard."

"Mother, are you being reproachful?"

"No. Not really. We can live without that kind of publicity. . . . But that's superficial. Wolfflens are not puritans. Wolfflens have the authority to shock. Why not? I mean, Marc, for you and her, it must be a difficult way to live."

She was retreating from her first reproach, leaving another behind like a landmine for him to trip over.

"Your father and I," she went on, "always did everything together."

"Thérèse, and I, in the most important ways, are as close as any two people can be."

"Your father always said you were too cerebral, Marc. Sometimes that can be very dangerous. Sometimes you must look at things in a simpler way."

"Dangerous?"

"People who are together are together."

He didn't answer. He suspected his mother was being hard on him to punish his long absence from here. She was taking revenge perhaps for his having neglected not Thérèse, but her. He didn't answer, and he was saved from the need to change the subject when Firmin reappeared.

"*Madame la Baronne est servie.*"

"It's actually a little chilly tonight," Eveline said, "I should have asked you if you minded dining outside." She spoke in an apologetic voice, taking his hand in both of hers as she rose from her chair.

"No," he said, "no, it's perfect. It's perfect."

* * *

Thérèse came home tan and fit, bubbling with gossip.

"Can you imagine," she was saying over lunch, "the woman arrived without an invitation to the ball, and camped there for a week ... and trailed after everyone begging them to—put in a good word!"

She was talking about the well-known widow of a cosmetic king. Marc listened, gray faced.

"And then she offered to buy a card for ten thousand dollars!"

"Who was that other person trailing after you?" He couldn't keep himself from asking.

"And then when that didn't work, she just *showed up*, dressed to kill, without a card. ... And *they turned her away!* I mean how can someone be— What?"

"Some fellow ... in a bathing suit."

"Oh my God, who? Trailing me?"

He'd actually saved the newspaper. She burst out laughing when he showed her the picture.

"That—that's Lucille Tortet! That's one of her flunkies, her 'leg men.' Oh—Marc, you're jealous ... that's so marvelous, you're jealous!"

"It is not marvelous for me."

His voice came close to being hostile. Her eyes narrowed.

"What do you want of me?" she blurted.

He shrugged.

"What do you expect, a geisha for your business entertainment?"

He broke a piece of bread to do something with his hands, which were shaking.

"What the hell do you mean," he said.

"I won't waste my time on people you have to waste your time on. I will not, for example, have the false, eager faces of Mr. and Mrs. Kyle Hoyt at my table again. Sitting there beaming with some foul inner light, like a couple of pioneers aglow with the idea of stealing a great piece of land from the Indians!"

"I just ask you never to make a fool of me," he said, knowing he meant more but could not say it. What he wanted, he knew, you couldn't get by asking. Devotion. "That's all!" he said angrily.

"Marc, just don't ever ... don't ever if you love someone try to clip her wings."

It was her way of putting it, of couching it as if she were some third party giving advice, that proved too much. He banged the table and his wineglass overturned. She drew back in her chair, while the stain flooded the tablecloth in her direction.

"Darling, if it comes to that," he said, "I won't clip your wings, I'll shoot you right out of the goddamn sky." The ugliness of what he heard himself saying filled him suddenly with shame.

But she could almost believe he meant it.

"Disgusting," she said.

In any case, their conversation changed nothing.

FOUR

"There are too many yachts in this world," Max Mieger realized, aloud. Mieger's *Ladykiller* had been plying the Mediterranean every summer for years, and never had its owner seen a jamup such as the one that addressed his eyes that late morning in May, 1968. The season hadn't even really begun, and there wasn't a bit of dock space in the port of Saint Tropez.

"There's the garbage scow," Mieger offered, as *Ladykiller* drew close to the wide yacht of Herbert Lanin, the retired building tycoon who had sold his company two years ago to the Dynamerica Corporation. "There's Nick the Greek," he went on, pointing to the end of the breakwater, near which the low, black three-master of Plato Stavropolis lay at anchor. "And yoo-hoo, there's Mrs. Nauter, the cold cream queen, and there by the grace of God is the *bateau* of *monsieur* Charlie Revson. The fleet is in, *Cupcake*."

"Max," Thérèse de Wolfflen protested, "stop calling me *Cupcake*."

"Why not, it's a nice name, and you're a sweet lady."

"Now I know," she spat at him, "you get this way when you're drunk. . . . And you've been drunk since we left Monte Carlo."

"Max, please," cried Mieger's cabinmate, coming out on deck. A thin blond. "Stop calling Thérèse *Cupcake* and stop calling me Eva Braun!"

"He gets this way when he's bored," she said, turning to Thérèse, "he tries to squeeze a little amusement out of people. Out from under their skin."

"Max is drunk," Thérèse said sullenly.

Mieger left the deck without answering. He went back to his cabin to hunt for a cigar.

"We should go somewhere different," the blond said to Thérèse. "Eva Braun" was a gentle young girl with a beclouded background from West Berlin. She had married the Baron von Ludhofen, and had been soon afterward divorced, but she'd hung on to his title as if it were part of the alimony. Mieger, who was separated from his wife, had considered meeting Eva von Ludhofen in the lobby of the Hôtel de Paris a stroke of good fortune. Sharing his cabin now was a young, good-looking girl who was a Baroness. All his wife had to show for herself at the moment was a fortyish *Paris-Match* photographer. What else Mieger, the expatriate movie mogul, failed to number consciously among Eva's qualities was her endurance for putting up with tyrannical old men, a knack of low-born German girls. He came back on deck now, coughing from the smoke he'd just lit.

"Thérèse, I apologize."

"What are we doing?" he asked both women. The captain had killed the engines, and *Ladykiller* was drifting several hundred yards from the quay, where rear deck beside rear deck, high-masted English crafts lay alongside the motor vessels of Italian "refrigerator millionaires," new-rich Milanese, wealthy from things such as kitchen equipment, textiles, and clothes.

"We're in your hands," Thérèse said wearily. In answer to Mieger's question, she had also formed another in her mind: what am I doing here? She'd accepted sailing with Mieger on impulse because she was bored. They'd dined together in Monte Carlo at the Hôtel de Paris as the guests of Marianne Chrysler, and he'd seemed a civilized man. He had always seemed to her reasonably civilized. Now he was bored and it was as if a mask had fallen from his face. He was incredibly cheap. And she was bored and answering him cheap for cheap. And his girl friend, sweet as she was, "Eva Braun," was cheap and servile. The only people aboard who weren't acting cheaply, aside from the crew, where the Bartolinis, whose presence aboard Thérèse had accepted as a kind of seal of approval, encouraging her to join the cruise. Now the Conte and the Contessa, their two grown boys, and a tutor were staying to themselves as much as possible, as far away on the boat as they could be from their host. At the moment, they were sunbathing on the foredeck. On second thought, Thérèse realized, they had behaved cheaply, too, in the total sense of the word: they hadn't much money and were making the best of a free ride. They liked yachts, they liked to swim, they liked to sunbathe, and they liked what Mieger's cook could whip up. It was as basic as that. *What,* she asked herself again, *am I doing here?* If Marc had given her some of his time—if he hadn't left her alone in Roquebrune—

"What do you say we have a drink at Felix?" Mieger said.

"Maxey," Eva said, "you're the only one who drinks at this hour."

"Well, c'mon to Sennequier," he answered, "I'll buy you a *café liègeois.*" He wrapped an arm around each of them, and suddenly he seemed to Thérèse pathetic.

Thérèse, Eva, and Max went ashore in a *vedette* and sat on the terrace of Sennequier in the port. The dry side of the quays was even more crowded than the water. Between them and the strangers from Italy playing gin on their gladiola-laden rear decks was a thick bustle of humanity, driving minis, on motorbikes, on foot, the same people going back and forth from one end of the port to the other, in and out of the boutiques, back and forth, intent on showing themselves on this stifling Rialto.

"I get claustrophobia in a situation such as this," Mieger said. He had ordered a double *exprès, bien serré,* and the strong coffee seemed to be at least rinsing away his bad comedy routine. He took Eva's hand affectionately in his. "Tell me a place and we'll go there, dear," he said.

"Turkey," she said, as if it were a guessing game.

"Yeah. Yes. All right. I mean it."

"For how long?" Thérèse asked, half-yawning. She felt the breezeless sunshine baking away her energy. Wisdom, she knew, dictated jumping ship. She should have her bags sent for that very moment but she felt like being somewhere far, and she'd never been to Turkey. A long way to go with Mieger, and yet she lacked the energy to resist; she knew she would let this whole stupid adventure run its course; it would be an *experience;* she felt up to new sensations, even irritations, and she just didn't have the energy to up and go anywhere alone, least of all home.

"Three weeks out and back," Mieger said.

Marc was in the middle of a meeting when Thérèse telephoned.

"Yes, you told me you were staying on," he said. His voice had the indulgent reasonableness people use to handle children.

"I won't be back for a month. From *Turkey.*"

"A month ... well ..."

There were people around him. They were close to him, physically, and close to him, she could tell, in his thoughts. She'd interrupted something. He was in a hurry to get back to his business and here was his wife announcing she'd be gone for a month. Thérèse got a secret thrill of pleasure from the undercurrent of irritation she perceived in his voice. She'd hit him when he wasn't looking. Now what. *React.*

She gave him a chance to tell her something better than "a month ... well" but he was silent. She heard his hand cup the phone while he had a word with one of the other people in the Associates' Room. It was as if he'd put his hand over her mouth.

The sound of his silence became unmuffled, clear again; he'd removed his hand, but he was not saying anything yet.

"Thérèse?" he began.

"Take care, darling," she said.

"Yes ... take care, darling."

Mieger and the two women had lunch without the Bartolinis at Felix's. When they got back to the yacht, they struck anchor.

As the yacht churned south, Mieger's attitude improved. The idea that they were going someplace, not just sloshing around off the coast of France, seemed to have lifted his boredom, which had driven him to drink too much. They were going very far, and Mieger, who'd seen the world, who'd seen war, assumed the virile air of a man who can take charge of things; he affected the air of supreme commander of the vessel, and spent much of his time consulting maps with his captain. They had powerful diesel engines, and were going to make as few stops as possible before Bodrum.

Mieger's *Ladykiller,* though it wasn't the newest, most eye-catching yacht in the Mediterranean, was comfortable, spacious, and well appointed. Carpeting and teak trim everywhere. Thérèse had a large cabin to herself, the most luxurious accommodations of all, since both couples were sharing cabins and the tutor and the two boys were all three thrown in together. Her bathtub had gilt taps in the form of human breasts—a bit trashy, but over her bed there was a fine Carlo Crivelli madonna, a cartoon for a celebrated painting.

"Yours is the Virgin's cabin," Mieger joked. It was barely morning in the port of Bastia (they'd made Corsica overnight) and both of them were already up. Mieger was seeing to his vessel, and Thérèse had been unable to sleep in the damp heat that invaded her cabin. The sun, luckily, was beginning to fry away the mist, as Thérèse sat in a deck chair facing the quay where inactive fishing skiffs bobbed below a landscape of white buildings abruptly crowded into the mountainside, green above the town.

"Well, I'm not moving out," she parried.

He laughed knowingly, as if what she said were a private joke.

She wondered what people did think of all her going about without Marc. *No doubt they believe I'm a totally* free agent. But no one had ever been able to dredge up anything juicy about her.

One of Mieger's crewmen, unfolding more deck chairs, roused her from her thoughts as she pondered an answer to her host's laughter. The Bartolinis were up. At last night's dinner, they had come into the fold. The adventure of sailing far was now something that everyone shared. Dado, the Count, had opened up toward Mieger by asking him all sorts of questions about navigation. The boredom that had frayed everyone's civility was gone. The Bartolinis were no longer sleeping until eleven.

"Buon giorno!" Dado sat down beside Thérèse with a mug of coffee in his hand. He was a dark, long-legged man with big, floppy hands and a great, thin nose, which accented the length of a face crowned by curly gray hair. *Racé* was the word the French would use for his distinctive good looks, thoroughbred. Thoroughbred? It was true you didn't see men who looked like Dado waiting on tables. His wife, who was also from a very old Sicilian noble family, could be taken for his sister. But their two boys were blond and blue eyed. The Vikings had left their seed where the Greeks, Romans, Goths, Visigoths, Saracens, and who all else had bred, on that island. The

Sicilians were no more thoroughbred than the Brazilians, and in both cases, Thérèse noted with satisfaction, the mixing had done wonders. The Bartolinis in particular were four extraordinary-looking human beings.

"Coffee ... *Cupcake?*" Dado asked.

"He's stopped that," she said.

"He's not such a bad sort. It's like with everyone else; you have to make contact with them in the part of the imagination where they think they truly exist. There's something like that in Tolstoy, if I remember, something about getting on with people by treating them as if they were what they pretend to be. A knack of Vronsky's. No? But Max doesn't pretend. He believes in his greatness. After all, he was the man who produced *King Solomon.*"

"In 1953."

"Elizabeth Taylor still sends him presents on his birthday. You heard him."

And what, after all, had Dado produced, Thérèse asked herself, other than two beautiful sons? Dado knew a lot about how to treat others. He and his wife had an ancient house in Palermo, described by one of the few people she knew who'd seen it as "needing restoration," and a house in Cap d'Antibes, which Marina Bartolini had inherited and which was in a frankly sordid state. They never invited, but had a vast choice among invitations. They charmed when they had to, were withdrawn when it seemed the best policy, treated the world exactly as they needed to to burnish their image. And under it all: a mediocre income from tenant farmers, a close eye to the slightest expense, and laziness. And above it all, the noble attitudes: a Catholicism as purely formal as Marina's perennial crucifix was decorative. Despite both their philanderings. And the tutor who went everywhere with the boys, assuring an unbringing such as they would have had had they been born when the Bartolinis were related to the kings of Sicily. Their fundamental *indifference* made Thérèse compare the Bartolinis to her first husband. But they played better with others than the Duke did, even if they were cynical about it. They were much more secure in their secret alienation. And they got more pleasure out of others that way.

And they were beautiful, truly beautiful to watch in action. So full of the sunny self-confidence which obviates nastiness. Looking at the grace with which Dado kissed both his sons good morning, Thérèse felt that people like that ought, after all, to be paid to live.

The boys were wearing only Bermuda shorts. The older one was nineteen and the younger sixteen, and they both had fine, strong bodies with no adolescent gawkiness. That one, Thérèse thought now, watching the older boy climb over the side to take a boat to shore, that boy looks like Michelangelo's Young David. Exactly.

"Be back for lunch. We're leaving," Mieger called after them. Thérèse watched Dado's eyes. She thought she could see them brighten a little, as if the Count were relieved that they were not eating ashore, that he would not have to pretend to fight Max for the check.

"Hey and put something on!" Mieger had stepped out onto the deck now. "The Corsicans are a very chaste people," he said to Thérèse and Dado. The tutor appeared quickly with two blue polo shirts, which he threw to the older boy.

"There's nothing to see but let them go," Mieger said with a tone of authority almost paternal. He went in again to talk to the captain. How blue were Mieger's veins on his thin calves, blue as his bathing suit.

Thérèse decided to stretch her legs. She walked back to the rear deck where the tutor had settled. He was wearing a jacket, as he always did, a jacket and an ascot; in his careful clothes, he looked more like a yachtsman out of the twenties than anyone else on board, but his thick glasses and the constant presence of a book in his hand preserved a professorial mien. His short hair was graying, although he seemed barely thirty years old. Thérèse noted that he was reading a worn copy of *Anna Karenina* in Italian. It struck her that Dado had come upon the tutor's book and that it was there he found the reference to Count Vronsky he'd felt well worth remembering.

The tutor smiled a greeting. She thought at first that his smile showed gratitude that someone had bothered to come back where he was and break his solitude. But as his smile remained fixed for what she thought was too long, she saw a certain condescension in it, as if he were crediting her with having understood the value of his presence aboard.

The sunny days followed one another rapidly. They stopped at Porto San Stefano and Capri, but only for the needs of the boat; they all knew those places well enough, and not even the boys went ashore. They slipped through the narrow straits of Messina into the Ionian Sea.

They could see Greece on the morning of the eleventh, when the news on Radio Monte Carlo revealed that there'd been a full-scale riot in Paris, that about one thousand people had been wounded in confrontations between the police and students who'd built barricades of cobblestones, cars, and sawn trees. The astonishing news swept over everyone at breakfast like a breeze. It stirred them into clichés about the times they were living through, an uncertain, bizarre, baroque age of assassinations and unrest. But all that was miles of sea and land away and becoming more and more remote as the *Ladykiller* moved across empty water toward more primitive parts.

They passed the green side of Greece and came upon the bald Aegean islands. Turkey loomed with the lushness of a promised land. They had sunbathed and swum, played cards, read, and even fished; in the end it was mostly the abstract promise of getting somewhere that kept them from being bored. They anchored opposite the white town of Bodrum, and everyone hurried into the *vedette*, hungry for land.

The town was quickly visited. A whitewashed fishing port, with the usual narrow, dank streets smelling of cooking and primitive drains. Eva took a photograph of "native women," as she called them, in colorful "harem pants." The Bartolinis bargained skillfully for some *kilims* in a carpet-dealer's shop. At noon, a loudspeaker resounded throughout the town. The owner of the café where they'd stopped for sage tea explained that the people were being exhorted to be clean and patriotic, and warned that all stray dogs in the streets the next day would be shot on sight by a police patrol organized for that purpose. Everyone tried hard not to laugh while the owner was still talking.

Mieger made an effort to root out points of interest in Bodrum from his guidebook. "You know," he said, "this little place was once very important. It was where Heroditus came from." No one seemed impressed.

"I know what we'll do!" He had a burst of inspiration. "We'll rent some cars and drive to Ephesus, the dead city."

* * *

They drove in a caravan of three old Fords, the best cars to be had. Mieger divided up the party at random, skirting any problem of protocol, and Thérèse wound up in the lead car, sitting in the rear beside Mieger, while the tutor sat beside the hired driver.

"I've been checking out the guide," Mieger said. "This is one of the most interesting places in Turkey a person can see. It was the number-one town in Asia in the days of the Greeks."

The tutor spoke without turning around: " 'Is there any city larger than this? Those who have ships at sea become rich through it. Its merchants are the richest in the world and its magic arts fascinate all nations.' "

"Who said that, professor?" Mieger asked in a patronizing voice.

"Saint John. In his Revelation."

"I told you," Mieger said to Thérèse.

The sun was beating heavily on the delta of the Meander, into which they'd driven. To the right, it gleamed on granite juttings of the tough mountainside; toward the sea, it refracted on haze, through which, here and there, the bright print dress of peasants stooping over tobacco plants garnished the pale greenery and dust of the plain.

"I'm sorry I couldn't get us any air conditioning" Mieger said, as he wiped sweat from his weathered, freckled neck with a handkerchief. He sounded humiliated; it was the second time he'd failed them on that score. The *Ladykiller's* air conditioning had broken down just after they'd left Italy.

Mieger was in a light Lacoste shirt and ducks, and Thérèse had put on a tee shirt and a pair of jeans, but the professor was still clad in his perennial blazer, even though its back was soaked and wrinkled.

"Well, what happened?" Thérèse asked.

"They were the only cars they had," he answered.

"No. What happened to Ephesus?"

"Bad news. The port silted up and people began getting malaria. After a while the whole place became a ghost town."

"What will we see?" she continued.

"What's left," he answered, impatient with her for the first time.

They stopped first on the road outside the center of the town, to see what was left of one of the seven wonders of the ancient world:

the temple of Artemis, the Earth Goddess. As they left the car, the tutor attached himself to Thérèse, in honor, perhaps, of the curiosity she'd made apparent.

"The Greeks considered her fanatically chaste," the professor offered, "but for the Ephesans she was much more . . . earthy."

"She—"

"Had many lovers."

Thérèse laughed. "You know everything."

"I read the guide before Mr. Mieger did."

"And Saint John?"

"Ah . . . that sort of thing I had drummed into me, long beforehand."

"If the figs were ripe," said Mieger, coming up to the two who'd shared his car, "we could say we picked figs. Right now, all we can say is that we've seen a pile of rubble."

Bits of broken marble, remnants of columns poked through the grass amid the fig trees. The tutor led Thérèse closer to the ruins, to point out what was left of the design of the temple.

"Your husband would be interested to see this," he said.

"My husband, why my husband especially?" Her voice backed away from the hint of intimacy the tutor had taken on in referring to Marc.

"You are looking at the seat of the world's first bank," he explained. "There was a special office for banking, in the temple. Aristeides called Ephesus 'the universal bank of Asia . . . the refuge for those in need of credit.'"

"Well, yes, you know everything."

"The guide," he insisted, with heavy humility.

The others were already back in their cars. Mieger honked.

"Come along, lovebirds," he said.

Hollyhocks and tall grass poked through the rubble. Bees sizzled in the sunlight that blanched the remnants of columns, friezes, and arches.

"If you go by weight," Mieger said, "I bet there's more history standing here than in the forum of Rome."

He talked as if he had to defend the place finally, since it was his idea to come here. The godlike sons of the Bartolinis hunted around for something small enough to carry off, until Mieger warned that they could "get us all locked up in a Turkish black hole." Eva had brought her camera, and was taking pictures of everybody. The Bartolinis put on an air of cheerful curiosity. It was beneath them to act either tired or bored, ever; that would be, Thérèse assumed, an admission on their part that they couldn't *faire face,* cope, or that they'd allowed themselves to have been taken advantage of. As for Thérèse, curiosity was one of her natural appetites. After several minutes during which the party was dispersed, Thérèse and the professor, the two obviously interested visitors, assumed the role of leaders. The others followed yards behind, too languid from the heat, perhaps, to tell their feet where to go on their own.

They passed the grassy amphitheatre, and lingered with a certain prurience at the brothels, noting how the rooms were laid out. Mieger rested on a seat in the long row of public toilets. They passed the Temple of Hadrian, the Emperor Trajan's Fountain, and the Temple of the Emperor Damitianus. And then they hiked the long way under the heat, up to the hillside where a more recent edifice stood, the house where the Virgin Mary was said to have lived and died, having come to Ephesus with Saint John, after the persecutions of Herod Agrippa had scattered the Christians of Jerusalem.

Below the house, there were Turkish women gathering water from a fountain set into a stone wall.

"They believe it will make them fertile," the tutor said.

"Who drummed the Bible into you?" Thérèse asked abruptly.

"All my teachers since I was a child.... And until I left the monastery."

"Aha..." She smiled. "Do the Bartolinis know that their sons are in the hands of a defrocked priest?"

"Oh there was no scandal. I left on my own, for a personal reason."

"I see." She would not ask.

"Personally," he offered, "I had lost all belief in all of it."

She shrugged. Nothing she could say. No balm to lay on, if that was what his wounded voice asked for now. Yes, belief, she thought, was definitely a personal thing. Although she'd been taught by nuns, she had no longer any formal creed, either. She avoided intuitively any behavior she held unworthy of her, and she believed no one was perfect. As for the other side of the veil, she had no idea ...

"Do you believe in some of it?" she asked.

"I believe there is an answer, but that no one has found it yet," he said.

"You believe in the Apocalypse," she said lightly, in a teasing way.

"'But in the days of the voice of the seventh angel,'" the tutor answered, smiling, "'when he shall begin to sound, the mystery of God should be finished, as he hath declared to his servants the prophets.'"

He removed his thick glasses and began to wipe the mist of perspiration that had begun to form on them. She looked at his face, and it was as if he'd suddenly, in a way, undressed. For the first time she saw his face entirely. His vague eyes seemed to peer with an endearing and youthful vulnerability over his flaring nostrils and the hard set of his thin lips and large teeth. It was a face not lacking in interest . . .

"Well," she said girlishly, "I'm disappointed. I thought you knew everything."

Mieger led the way downhill with Eva. She had her arm around him, and from behind it looked as if she were holding him up. He walked with a sad roundshoulderedness, and his hips in the low-waisted ducks showed the wide, pathetic flatness of an old man's body. Mieger didn't take the last walk with the others—under the ruined arcades of the avenue leading to the meadow where the harbor once lay. When they got back, they found him leaning against a fender of one of the Fords, hunched over.

He looked up. "Christ, I've been sitting here trying to imagine it," he said. "The whole place full of people. Sheep and goats going at each other in the streets, camels and donkeys. It says in the book that when Marc Antony showed up, there were so many lutes and guitars going you couldn't hear yourself think. . . . Doesn't it make you sick to look at it?"

No one replied. "He's overtired," Eva whispered to Thérèse. She got in beside him in the lead car, drawing him close to her in a motherly way. And Thérèse rode back with the Bartolinis.

"Yes, he's an interesting young man, isn't he?" Marina said. They could see the graying head of the tutor, upright and stiff, where he sat with the others in the rear of the car ahead.

Having turned what she said into a question, Marina hung fire for a long moment of probing silence, before she added "And very proud, did you notice? For someone who isn't *anyone*, really at all. ... But he's marvelous with the boys."

"Ah . . . ?"

"They're ahead of everyone else in school."

"And he's always with you?"

"Dado's family has always had tutors living in. It's a great tradition. Dado's father would have sooner done without servants than without his sons' tutor. *N'est-ce pas*, Dado?"

Dado grunted. He made it seem as if talking to him about the tutor or about his family or both was like calling attention to some beautiful object he owned of which he'd grown tired. "And my grandfather, and his father, and his father, always there was a tutor," he said, "you see how brilliant it has made us. I can't even do long division anymore." He drew a cigaret from his case with a faint air of displeasure.

"He may be very bright," Thérèse said, returning to the man whose head bobbed stiffly beside Eva's fluffy coiffure as the car ahead passed over a hole. "But he's a walking failure. God knows what he may have tried to succeed at . . ."

There was pasta for dinner and everyone ate ravenously, as cheerful over the food as children at a party. Fettucini *al pesto*. Mieger's Cambodian chef, who cooked beautifully in any language, had found fresh basil in the market. Afterwards, the boys and the tutor went off to the foredeck to practice reading Greek. Thérèse was tempted to retire to her cabin and read, but she recalled that the air conditioning was broken. She sat out listening to mosquitos and to Max, who tried to engage Dado in a discussion of the moral and philosophical limits of pleasure. What had got him started? Dado did little more than grunt. Only Eva helped Mieger with his monologue, asking all the obvious questions. Mieger was giving a rambling account of what he would not do. He would have sex with two women at the same time, but he would not do anything with another man present. His limit in dope was cocaine. Eva prodded him for a yes or no answer, pill by pill, covering a whole pharmacopoeia.

"I'm going in," Thérèse said.

"You'll suffer," Mieger warned.
"I'm dead tired."

She was tired and worried that her fatigue was serious. She felt the same strange lightheadedness she'd known each time she'd had an attack of rheumatic fever during her adolescence. Twice, only, but each time there'd been a little more damage to her aortic valve, and over the years since, her left ventrical had gradually grown larger from working too hard to pump the blood leaking back. Now she remembered her last X-ray; a great awareness of vulnerability came over her.

The evening was so sticky. ... A smell came up from around the yacht, not the filthy smell of French and Italian harbors, but a deep, salty redolence. A flock of mosquitos played with death around the globe of the overhead light. She tried to read the latest Sagan, but she hadn't even the strength for empathy, for dipping into those lovers' lives. Someone knocked just as she put the book down.

The tutor knocked again and then came in.

"I wondered if you just wanted some tea."

He stood there in his shirt with his sleeves rolled to his elbows, holding a cup and saucer in his hand.

"Don't you think you'll catch cold all undressed like that?" she said.

"It's been unbearable," he said, "but there's a breeze up now; if you went out you'd feel it."

"No ... but I'll take the tea, thank you."

"Hot tea is cooling," he said.

She exhaled loudly through her lips. "I can't sleep, I can't read, I feel as if I can hardly keep on breathing. ..."

"Distract me," she challenged.

He left and returned with his cup. "Thank you," she said again, repairing the tone of insolence with which she'd thanked him before he'd gone out.

"There is a doctor in town, surely ..."

"Oh no. ... I mustn't exaggerate to myself. When I think of it now, I realize that all my fatigue is just a revolt in my mind—against a great accumulation of boredom."

"I'll go," he said.

"No ... I asked you to distract me. I didn't mean you were

boring." She sipped some tea and sat up, drawing the sheets into her armpits.

He made a confused gesture with his palm. "Where shall I begin?"

"Talk," she coaxed.

"Talk about you," he dared.

"Heads or tails," she said, brightening, "either about me or about you."

She reached beside the Cartier watch that lay with its gold clasp spread open on her night table. She found a small silver ashtray. "Heads," she said, "you speak," tossing the object on her sheet. It landed on its back. "*Voilà.*"

"Let's not be absurd," he said with a certain hardness in his voice now. "Can it possibly be of any interest to you who I am ... and where I've come from?"

"Well, what do you intend to do," she said, laughing at his serious regard, "stand there and recite from The Apocalypse?"

She knew after she'd spoken that there was a dangerous ambiguity in the way she'd taunted him. She let it stand. She felt light, but chilly and light, at last. The breeze was blowing through the portholes of the cabin. She felt peculiarly alert now, and could feel the blood going faster in her chest.

"Well ... sit down ... at least," she said, pointing to the armchair.

He sat down on the bed, at her feet. He removed his glasses, and once again she saw the face she'd seen at the ruins, vulnerable and brooding.

"I should make love to you," he said. Just like that, abruptly, dispassionately.

"What?"

"There's something there. You know it. I know it. You know it to keep me here. We just have to go a little further. To find out where it will take us."

She tried to laugh. "I can't see where we can possibly go," she said.

"Then ... it will be as if nothing had happened, anyway. Since I am no one."

She opened her mouth to shout at him to go, but in an instant his mouth was on hers. She tasted his breath, his tongue. His hand reached under her nightshirt. He moved gently. She could have thrown him off, but instead she shuddered, half in fear, half in anticipation, and like an insomniac yielding at last to sleep, she yielded to his wraithlike gentleness, until her breath came so fast she thought the pleasure would suffocate her.

Wraithlike. Now it seemed she'd indeed made love with a ghost, and not the stranger heavily present beside her. The tutor was smoking. She hated the smell of his cigaret in the close cabin, but she wouldn't tell him, because she did not want to say anything to him.

"Please go," she finally said.

He dressed without replying. As he reached for the cabin door, she called after him.

"*Monsieur*," she said, "it's taken us nowhere. I'd thank you to forget it."

"Well, I hope you thought it was worth finding out," he said in a wounded and insolent voice. "No regrets." She threw the ashtray at him as he passed through the door. She missed, and he took no notice.

Better remorse than regret.

Once she'd called that adage her motto. She didn't feel either now. Just a vague awareness of having somehow set herself adrift. The sour and almost fecal odor of Turkish tobacco continued to abuse her nostrils. She pulled the sheet over her head, and lay there in the stifling darkness a long moment, smelling the remnants of her own perfume. A womanly smell—and now an image of the barren women at the spring above the ruined city flashed into her mind. Would children have made a difference? She didn't think so. She saw clearly now that things were ripe for this to happen, that she was ripe to have herself made love to by some no one, to make love to herself that way. She'd reached out for a taste of intimacy with a stranger ... and a taste was more than enough and would be more than enough, now and then. She hadn't the—what? strength? courage?—to want to fall in love, although nothing could be the same as it once had been with Marc. Regret? Remorse? She'd lost what she'd lost before now. She couldn't even remember exactly when. She hadn't wanted to take notice. Now she couldn't even formulate what exactly she'd lost.

But now her mind became crowded with images of what could still be the same. She imagined people all around her.... She remembered that in Paris she was envied, she was adored. She reigned. There, it was as if she were the star dancer the chorus carried through the air night after night. It buoyed her, uplifted her to think of her court. She decided that when she'd return, she would reign even more brilliantly, even more arrogantly. She was terribly anxious now to be back in Paris, because there her life was bright with purpose.

A little while later, the sound of a resonant, undulant voice roused her from sleep. Mieger's radio was on. The breeze had fallen, and the wet heat in her cabin provoked her to try the air-conditioning button again, as if, with all else, she might experience a miracle tonight, for she knew the system had been broken, and there was no chance of getting new parts until they docked at Rhodes. The fan was going above her bed, but the rubber blades seemed to cut their way through the thick air without stirring it. She rose, put on her dressing gown, and went out on deck, where the air was cooler, although full of mist.

Mieger was sitting in a deck chair with his big Zenith portable propped on a table, alongside a bottle of whisky. The voice on the radio was French.

"The General was on," he said glumly, without greeting her. "They just had a replay on Radio Monte Carlo.

"The poor beggar," he muttered, before sipping from a glass of neat whisky. "He sounded like he had one foot in the grave. The whole of France has become a looney bin. Strikes, riots, what the hell, what the hell for? He got on the air and he sounded half-dead, and when he got off the students went and tore the hell out of Paris all over again. It's still going on. They're burning cars again, they're tearing up streets. What the hell do they want? They tried to set the Bourse on fire. Sheeee ... "

He took a fast gulp from his tumbler.

"You know, it may sound pretentious on my part, but I can feel something personal for de Gaulle. I made his acquaintance once. We had a conversation during the war, when I was producing a lot of pictures to show the Free French were still in there fighting. I saw him in London, and actually I was at a dinner FDR gave for him in Washington, I think it was in July of '44, right after D-Day. But we didn't have an opportunity to talk then. The first time we had a real conversation. We ... Jesus, I can't even remember what he said ..."

Mieger's voice was slurring as he rambled. He jerked his hand in the air in an irritated way, as if he were trying to catch what his mind was searching for.

"Anyway," he said, "anyway, I have a strong personal feeling for the man. He's got balls, pardon me. He's got 'em. That's my generation I'm talking about, pardon me.

"We put our balls through the mill. Christ, we went through everything. Depression, don't tell me about it. You know what it is to eat dinner on a pear for two, a pear and a piece of bread, in a room in Boyle Heights? My poor goddamn first wife, rest her soul. She didn't have a dime for, Christ what, when we were struggling. Two kids. But I'm not talking about me. You see. I mean all of us. Then the war, for Christ's sake—not counting the First World War. We were up against it. And we pushed. We pushed and we pushed, for Christ's sake. What the hell do they want? They got everything, these kids. Christ, *everything*. And what they don't got they just have to work a little. . . . What the hell could possibly make them so destructive?"

He sipped again. He raised his bottle toward Thérèse in invitation, but she shook her head. He looked at it in the moonlight and saw that it was empty anyway.

"Well, no matter what happens, my dear, I don't think the poor General has long to go.

"Out of touch," he muttered. "But who can be in touch, nowadays? What's there to touch? Sheee ...

"Christ," he said, "there are too many goddamn spoiled people in this world." His face was contorted with frustration as he reached for his empty bottle of Chivas and flung it over the side of his yacht.

The voyage home was melancholy, as they often are for explorers. When they stopped at Corfu, Thérèse found an English and French bookstore up in the old town, and carried off a bundle of Agatha Christie and Simenon thrillers. With which she holed up in her cabin much of the time. The professor intensified his lesson-giving with the boys. When he wasn't prodding their recital of Latin declensions or dates in the history of the Roman Empire, he was at his retreat on the foredeck with a book. She didn't know what he read. They stayed out of each other's way. The Bartolinis got browner and browner. Mieger stopped drinking under the doting care of Eva, who went around hovering behind him, ready to massage his neck or pop a candy in his mouth whenever he seemed vulnerable to such a move. Thérèse suspected that the woman was grooming Mieger to divorce his wife, a little *salope*, no longer the lovely young mannequin from Patou but with a fierce power over his heart all the same. Strange how people choose their misery, she thought once, watching Mieger post a card covered with puppy-love X's, from Messina to wherever his wife was—with whomever. Thérèse let the thought leave her mind before extending it ... to her own life.

When the *Ladykiller* docked at last in Monte Carlo, Thérèse decided to give a party. She rented the restaurant Le Pirate not far away, which Aristotle Onassis had made famous with his plate-smashing feasts, and from the concièrge of the Hôtel de Paris she got a list of everyone in town who was remotely interesting. She hired a Brazilian orchestra and ordered fish cooked Brazilian-style. Along with the champagne, she had the barmen serve *batida*. She packed the restaurant full of people—the concièrge's list—some of whom she'd never met, and that night she didn't meet them either. They were her show, all of them, surrounding her with life, filling her ears with the laughter and music she'd craved intensely, the way a seaman gone for months finally craves land. She sat beside Dado Bartolini, watching samba after samba, watching, as she drank more and more, the party getting drunker. It was inevitable that someone among those strangers, taking himself for a Greek shipping millionaire, would begin throwing plates around. The crockery began to fly. When a stuffed crab splashed onto her dress she wanted to get up and throw everyone out, but Dado put his hand on hers, squeezed it, and held her seated.

"Just leave," he cautioned. "It's out of control."

She let him find the way out over the debris. Marina followed at their heels. Outside, all three took deep breaths. As she inhaled, staring up at the brilliant sky, Thérèse felt her head spin. She had drunk two or three of those sweet, chocolaty *batidas*, imprudently mixing them with all that champagne.

"I'm . . . I'm going to . . ." Saliva rushed into her mouth. She felt her face grow cold and her knees weaken. She took a step that became a lunge forward. She was falling ... but with both hands she grabbed at the chrome bumper of her gleaming Rolls. Dado ran up beside her, but she waved him back, and half-straightening herself, she felt her way across the front of the car and to the other side. Now she expected it: a great blow of pain in her chest, an explosion of pain, and then maybe everything would be over. Would be resolved. But it didn't happen. Instead she felt a conclusive tickle; safe from view where she'd dragged herself, she threw up, holding onto the fat, bitter tire of her car.

As she straightened herself, the sound of music coming from the restaurant that had ben whirling through her head stopped abruptly. Dado and Marina were standing hunched over, looking away from the car. She had a few moments to arrange her hair before a man came running toward her from inside the restaurant.

"*Madame*, the musicians!" he said. "Don't forget the musicians!"

"What?" she mumbled.

"If you are leaving you must pay the musicians," he said.

She looked at him, a spindly, wiry-haired man of her own country, wth deep pockmarks on his dark face. Her own country. He was the bandleader. He had spoken sweetly, oilily to her before the dinner, promising, in Portuguese, that she "would have a sensational time."

"Of course they will be paid," she said in Portuguese.

"You don't understand," he answered in French, as if her speaking Portuguese now had placed him as an inferior. He wasn't green. He knew his rights. "You don't understand, the custom is to pay the musicians on the spot, in cash. I thought you were aware of the ... procedure."

"I don't carry money," she said evenly.

The little man turned toward Dado.

"*Monsieur*, you understand. My name is not Wolfflen. I can't pay them myself."

Dado never carried money either.

"*Monsieur*," Dado began to reason in a cynically congenial voice, "*monsieur*, if you and your colleague expect to play music on the coast again, you will permit the Baroness to go home now, where in the morning she will write you a check."

Dado didn't wait for the man to respond. Avoiding the other side of the car, he slid across the leather of the front seat, leaving the door open for the two women. Marina nudged Thérèse inside, and they drove away.

"Where is my chauffeur?" Thérèse asked.

"You told him to leave the car at the restaurant ... you remember," Marina said in a soothing voice.

"I don't remember ... I am not well. I don't understand. I just don't understand all that aggressiveness. All of them. *Him*. What low manners." She laughed weakly. "He promised me a sensational time," she said as her laughter trailed off. "I just do not know what is happening."

Her head began to go giddy again as the car descended and climbed the snakelike coastal roads. She felt Marina reach over to pull her head onto her shoulder. She felt Marina's fingers moving through her long hair.

She awoke not knowing what in particular had happened from the time she fell asleep in the car until that moment she found herself in a room at the Hôtel de Paris in bed between Marina and Dado. She remembered nothing and considered it better not to insist on retrieving whatever had happened. The three of them were naked under the bedsheet. The other two were still asleep. She climbed over Dado, who lay on his back with his arms above his head, asleep exactly as he'd used to lie sunbathing on Mieger's deck.

Thérèse sorted out her own clothes from the pile on the floor near the bed. Her keys. She dressed. She was gratified to find the Rolls packed near the entrance as she stepped out into the oppressive sunlight of a new day.

FIVE

Edmée was going to have a baby. Bruno prayed for a boy—prayed literally, awake with his hand laid gently on the belly of his wife. He'd taken to lying beside Edmée in her room night after night, a kind of guardian, keeping an absurd kind of watch. And he prayed, so help him, unabashed. He would whisper while his wife's breath came long and furry through sleep: "Dear God," adding "God of my fathers" for extra help, "Dear God, God of my fathers, give me a son."

They were no longer young, neither he nor Edmée. It was a last chance. And Bruno badly felt the need of a blessing. His life ... his life had become nothing he'd dreamed it would become. He'd dreamed vaguely, and beyond the margins of the probable, given what he had to go with in life, which was so much and yet not enough. Not the magic number that meant control of something big. He'd dreamed and later he'd tried, and had had what seemed his chance, but under pressure—and even under pressure of their own ambition men can get a bad sight on things—he'd lost touch with what was really possible and made a mess. And that was an old story now, bitter, yet a little less bitter each time in the recalling, like an old romance gone wrong. Now he was a responsible man. Vice-chairman of the Wolfflen Holding Company. Number two, and there was no way on earth, it seemed now, to be anything else. He could shout at Marc when Marc seemed to him to be heading wrong, but Marc seldom seemed to be heading wrong, truth to tell. And shouting was of no use, Marc held up under it, as he should, bless him. Yes, bless Marc too. Bruno couldn't see it any other way, in any viler way: bless Marc, who is fulfilling his life as he was destined to fulfill it, cousin of my own blood. And anyway, shouting was not deciding. Bruno was bitter, but not ready to wear the attitude of a man hopelessly and ridiculously bitter.

A son, if he saw it clearly, was not an answer to his life. Another chance—but not really a last chance for him, himself. How many people who engender heirs see their own hope in them clearly, that is, reasonably? Heirs inherit and bury you, the voice of reason said to him once, and he was not looking forward to being buried. And yet, there was the other voice, the stronger voice whose urgings continue to make men see a specious extension of themselves in the children who will bury them. He had a daughter, he was a Wolfflen and Wolffens leave sons. He wasn't just a man with two feet in the time of this world, sinking, he was, yes, even physically, as he saw it, a piece of a tradition. Men, particularly disappointed men, live by myths, drugged in a way by the beauty of them. He told himself that, he knew it. But knowing it didn't make any difference. What was more natural than wanting a son? Than Bruno, orphan since he was young, wanting after all a boy to father?

Edmée's time came. And Bruno had just enough, just the grain of remove to be able to see himself as a little ridiculous in all his nervous agitation, but not enough removed to do his fluttering stomach any good. His memory gave him Levin, in *Anna Karenina,* when Kitty's moment had come. He preached calm to himself, but his stomach would not listen.

He sat waiting, for what already seemed an eternity. The room he was in had become so familiar from the idle roaming about of his eyes, so familar that it seemed to him a *huis clos* he'd lived in forever in some distorted dream version of life, the boundaries of some other form of existence he'd assumed—forever. He hated each detail his eyes had scrubbed over and over. Yet Edmée had chosen this place, with this waiting room all in chrome and foam rubber covered with purple jersey and the Martial Raysse and the Andy Warhol attacking you from the walls; she'd chosen this place because it was the newest maternity clinic in Paris and "had the best service." She was looking at it as if it were a hotel. *She* was calm.

What was in reality no more than a few hours ago, she'd woken him.

"I think we'd better go," she'd said.

It was six in the morning. Bruno took the wheel of the Rolls himself and sat her in the back with her precious burden. She found the chauffeur's hat on the front seat and popped it on his head, giggling. He tore it off.

"You must be careful while I'm driving!" He protested. Levin. Well pregnancies, yes, were not the crises they were in Moscow before the turn of the century. But *his* wife's case was special, was particularly delicate. Having deposited her in her room at the clinic, Bruno got on the phone to the doctor, who was of course asleep.

"It's time for you to come!"

"Who . . . what time is it?"

"You promised to be there before the midwife." No such promise had been made.

"Oh . . . Wolfflen . . . Is the midwife there?"

Was the midwife there?

"For God's sake, get on over here!" he shouted into the phone, and then he bounded into the elevator to make sure that the midwife had arrived.

The midwife wasn't there. There were nurses.

"Where the devil is the doctor?"

"It's not time yet. You go downstairs and wait." The way she'd given him back his rudeness had calmed him.

Edmée called from inside the room they'd put her in:

"Du calme!" She called in a laughing voice.

She was calm. On the way to the hosital she had made him stop at a café that was just opening up.

"I'm starved. I have a feeling they won't give me anything to eat."

"We can't take a chance."

"Stop or I'll scream for help."
They ordered café au lait and croissants.
"Uhmmm!' she exclaimed with her head lowered, as she dipped her croissant greedily into the foaming head on her coffee.
"Ai!"
Another spasm came over her, and he hurried her back to the car. Like a child she wouldn't leave behind her half-eaten croissant. She was still nibbling at it in the back seat.

Like a child. Since her pregnancy had begun to show—had become already something *present*, no longer a veiled fuctioning of her body, known only to itself—Edmée had become its servant. And in reducing the bustle of her life to serve *it*, to protect *it*, and insure its healthy progress toward a life of its own, she'd become, herself, childlike. Childlike in the simplicity with which she went about her singular role. She was hungry. She could assume that *it*, although about to kick free of her needs, was hungry too. He'd discovered another Edmée, or rather they'd discovered her together.

Now he saw the doctor coming in. The man passed through the glass hallway doors, which whished open as he crossed an electric beam. He headed for the chrome elevator. His clothes looked like he'd thrown them on hastily—a chino Italian suit, still bearing the wrinkles of a previous day. Turning toward the elevator, he caught sight of the Baron, and he seemed to hesitate between pretending not to have noticed him and saying good morning. He turned toward the waiting room, and his face betrayed what might have been a weakness for being indulgent toward celebrated customers.

"Good morning," he said, and came into the waiting room to shake Bruno's hand. Bruno wondered whether to apologize for his tone on the telephone; he realized it would be least humiliating for the man if they ignored what had happened. But he couldn't keep himself from shouting:

"The midwife . . . hasn't come yet!"

The doctor looked at the sunburst clock on the wall of the waiting room and compared it with what the Roman numerals of his tank watch said. Nine-thirty.

"I'll go up and see how things are," he said in a conciliatory tone. The elevator arrived. The doors flashed open, and he turned and disappeared behind them as they flashed closed again.

Bruno was all alone again.

The fool, Bruno thought, the she-ass. You trust your life to people like that. Well, maybe in the end they don't have to be any more clever than auto mechanics, so long as they know what they're working on. Edmée's gossip about her gynaecologist came back to mind. He'd married a cover girl, she'd said, and she'd run around on him almost from the day they were married. They were divorced in three years, and now he was a great gay blade of the discothèques. His real passion, she'd said, the thing that mattered to him for its own sake and not for the sake of impressing anyone else, was golf. Golf. How did she know that? Edmée can get anyone to give himself away. Servants were always unburdening their hearts to her. But maybe she had to be fairly intimate with *him* for him to have told her the secret meaning of his life. Golf—ha! He tried to laugh to himself but did not succeed in stifling a pang of jealousy.

The boredom of waiting was corrupting, he realized. He asked the receptionist, for some silly reason, whether she thought "it would be long."

"Oh, some time," she said, as if she knew. Perhaps she knew by a sort of rule of thumb, based on what she'd seen, sitting there. Well where, by the way, were other expectant fathers? If there were someone, he might even make conversation, but it struck him that the clinic was empty of patients other than his wife. It must not be a very good place after all. *She'd taken the choice too lightly.* He felt a chill of fright.

"Oh it will take some time," the receptionist repeated, with an ungenerous, official tone to her voice. As if she wanted to warn him to behave, and not be impatient. She was a hefty lady of Northern mien, this one. Maybe, he thought, she was a lesbian, who hated all the expectant fathers who hung around piously wringing their hands after what they'd done to their wives.

"Do you think I could go out?" He tested her.

"Bien sûr." Yes, she had some Nordic accent.

"Why will it take a long time?"

She didn't answer.

"I'm going out for a newspaper," he said, as if to ask permission. She didn't reply. She just looked at the gold and chrome sunburst in the lobby. Perhaps *she'd* been there all night and was counting the minutes now before leaving. Having said he would, he left.

He began walking fast, hunting for a kiosk, as if he had to come back with a newspaper at all costs to justify his leaving. But he didn't want to waste any time. It was a Sunday morning, late in May, and the streets of the Seventh Arrondissement were empty. Everybody's got a country house, Bruno muttered to himself uncharitably, because the kiosk he came to on the Boulevard Saint-Germain was boarded up. He saw a café on the corner of the Boulevard and the Rue Montalembert. They might have the *Journal du Dimanche*. When he got there, hurrying uphill, he found a kiosk was open just opposite, at the Rue du Bac *métro* station. When he got back, there was a different receptionist, an Indo-Chinese.

"I'm Bruno de Wolfflen," he shouted, "has anyone tried to reach me?"

She looked at the flustered Baron with a gaze more uninterested than tolerant. The inscrutable East.

"Has anyone asked for you?" she finally said.

"My wife is upstairs!"

"Oh no. No, it's all right."

He read the entire paper in five minutes. It was full of nothing. An excuse for movie and real estate ads. For a moment, throwing the paper onto the purple-covered foam chair beside his, he thought he heard a baby crying. Straining his ears, he realized that he hadn't heard anything.

He waited for an hour more; the Sunday silence of the neighborhood and the silence of the empty clinic weighed on his ears like water at the bottom of a pool. He never heard a baby crying.

The gynaecologist came down first.

"Your wife is doing fine," he said. He was a coward, Bruno realized afterwards.

"What is it? ... Is it *over*?"

"Yes. Your wife has come through excellently."

"*What* is it?"

The doctor had already changed out of his operation uniform. He was back in the summer suit in which he'd arrived, sporting that new-fashioned thirties cut, scrubbed and smelling of cologne.

"There's a problem with the child, *monsieur*," he said with his head down and his hands in his jacket pockets.

"Certain ... abnormalities."

Bruno's eyes widened. He felt as if he couldn't keep them from trying to burst out of his head. His stomach seemed to tighten like a fist.

"My wife!" he cried. "Does she know?"

"Yes. The anesthesis was local. She ... saw."

He headed for the elevator and hit the command button with his fist. He turned round for an instant, looking for the doctor, the mechanic of human bodies. But the gynaecologist was already hurrying, with a roundshouldered, long-legged gait, toward the exit of the clinic. Bruno was tempted to chase him, but the elevator hissed open, and stunned, as if he were obeying it, he got in and went up.

Another doctor was in an office talking to nurses. He saw the Baron enter the hallway, and called to him. Bruno halted. His spirits lifted, unreasonably, again, as he took the man in pale green for a beneficent presence.

"What ... ?" Bruno blurted.

"It's all right," the man soothed as he came up to the Baron. "She is all right ..."

"What is it?"

"I ... don't think ... it will live," the doctor said hoarsely, almost in a whisper.

"I said what is it!"

"It's ... a male."

"Well doctor, you're GOING TO DAMN WELL SAVE MY SON!" Bruno had his hands on the doctor's lapels and he was pulling the man towards him. The doctor simply fixed Bruno's biceps in both his hands.

"Look ... it would be better not to."

"What's the matter!"

"It's not an uncommon occurrence, in pregnancies late in life."

Late in life, Edmée.

"I want to see my wife!" Bruno blurted.

"She's all right," the doctor repeated. Perhaps he expected a compliment. "Don't upset her."

Edmée was lying propped up with pillows. Her face was drained of all color except for where the skin seemed to have darkened all of a sudden around her eyes. She took his hand as he came up to kiss her. As he tasted her lips, she began to sob. The tears swept down her cheeks and onto his. It came to him that he had never before seen his wife weep, an extraordinary thing in a marriage ... She was extraordinary ...

"They've told you," she said. Her voice was dry, almost crackly.

He nodded as she reached for the box of tissues beside her bed. She blew her nose slowly, and carefully; she wasn't going to weep anymore, she was mopping up all that uncontrolled grief with the calm process of clearing her nostrils.

"I don't want you to see it," she said slowly, imperatively. And then, her voice went hollow: *"What a mess."*

He could see anger in her face; through the grief and fatigue, it seemed to give her face a hardness that kept it from sagging into an ugly look of shock. It gave it its dignity. He understood that she'd uttered a judgment on herself. A judgment of failure.

"I have to," he blundered, as if that would be a way he could better share the calamity, shoulder it, with her.

"No ... it's going to die! What good will you get out of it? It's not even alive ... as we understand being alive."

He sat down beside her.

"No, you will not see it," she said. "Promise."

"All right." He was calm now. He had regained his strength. He blotted out his own feelings and tried to conceive a strategy for helping his wife. A strategy. But none came to mind and so he sat there in silence, until a nurse entered and said that the gynaecologist had called and asked to have the Baroness given a sedative, and that the other doctor, whatever purpose he served, had approved it. She came in with some pills and a glass of water, and Bruno ceded his wife to her and her drugs in impotent silence. He kissed Edmée again, after she'd downed the pills, acquiescent, but with silent disgust. He left her.

In the hallway, he saw the long, gray-haired doctor where he still sat in the office. A strange creature in a uniform, who lived with calamity from day to day. Other people's, yet he knew intimately that there were mistakes on this earth that could not be repaired, and there were losses beyond normal experience, with no compensation at all. Today was Bruno's worst taste of that kind of calamity. He told himself he was lucky, for there were even men whose lives were strewn with these misfortunes, one after another, from which you could recuperate nothing, not even a meaning. In any case, now there was nothing for him here. He went up to the doctor, shook his hand to say goodbye, and signaled for the elevator to take him down.

The child died in three days. "Hydrocephalic" read the notation on the gynaecologist's file for the Baroness Bruno de Wolfflen. The file ended soon afterward, with the results of a routine examination. The Baroness was all right. And her husband, faithful to his promise, had never gone in to look at their failure.

SIX

    Conversations would die as he approached, at parties, at the Jockey or the Travellers, at the premieres of plays and films to which he still escorted his wife—it seemed to Marc he was preceded always by a sort of invisible herald, blowing not a trumpet but something like a kazoo. No one laughed, they were all too worldly for that, but at times he didn't like the way people smiled in his direction. He knew people gossiped, and he did nothing. And after a while, they stopped. Thérèse's carryings-on and his complaisance became, in a manner of speaking, fixtures of the social scene they inhabited, simply part of the way people defined the two of them. Yet sometimes people would still speculate on why he "put up with it." She was so blatant.
    Thérèse had come back from Monte Carlo feeling as if she'd gone through an operation, as if something had been cut out of her—some organ that had stopped functioning and without which she could now keep on going, but precariously. She'd become, literally, preoccupied with her health, had a long visit with Bern, which resolved nothing, turned up nothing new.
    "You can bury me ... if you live right," he said.

"You've just given me a reason to live," she said.

Then she spent a lot of time looking into mirrors, watching for lines to grow or appear on her face, which she treated to a variety of new creams, convinced that a grayness had got into her skin, that age was after her, like a mugger on a dark street, about to pounce and disfigure. This siege of depression lasted a month, after which the young gym instructor she'd hired to teach her rejuvenating exercises at home touched her in a provocative way. She didn't bother to ask herself if the palm that grazed her breast might have been showing a customary solicitude; she took it and held it there. He responded by kissing her ear, and the next day they were in bed, by appointment, at his studio apartment upstairs from the Café de Flore. Just like that. That was the start of a lot of reckless, indiscriminate experiences with men. Something had stopped functioning, and something else flared into life.

Marc didn't clip her wings. He didn't even upset any wineglasses again. Stunned but taking all the blame, Marc retreated into his own fastidiousness, and into the winter of his life, while Thérèse turned hers into a continuous feast of random pleasure. His failure to reproach, his silence, goaded her into more and more flamboyant infidelities—as if she were unfaithful not to him, but to the place he'd chosen to inhabit; she was calling to him, waving the flimsy trivial lovers she took in his face, like a savage waving gaudy signals—calling him to jump the breach, come over to her, leave his own arid place.

She took up, for example, with a man named Jacques Lurel, a noted real estate finagler, half-bald, with a Marlboro ad air of virility, whose usual fare was Nordic nymphets in pairs and threes. She went down to Saint Tropez with him to his house, which was already full of little blondes. He called in some of his friends, a bar owner, a local land dealer, the owner of the busiest boutique for jeans in the port. All three very inside Saint Tropez, very locally important. He treated them to what he had, Thérèse included, and the party went on for days. Naturally, it got around the tables of Sennequier; men like that don't let their promotions go unnoticed, even if they have to let them slip out in the form of secrets. Lurel never minded. The party culminated when the sculptor, Vignon, was called in to do a mold of Lurel's penis as he lay on his dining room table, surrounded by candles and the encouraging crowd of houseguests. To help out, Thérèse was said to have performed "the works" on Lurel in front of everyone. That was a lie. Of the kind she'd let herself in for.

She left the party with the sculptor, and stayed with him nearly a month. He was in a period of his career when the number of times he appeared in *Vogue* had fallen off, and the gossip did him good. She left him to be back in Paris for a dinner at the Marquis de Sayre's, and he went around the port getting a week's more mileage out of the affair by saying he'd kicked her out, the rotten-rich Baroness. In Paris, at the Marquis's party, which she attended with her husband, the Baroness found a visiting Brazilian, who took her to the discothèques and his hotel for seven nights in a row.

People wondered how Marc put up with her. He suffered, but told himself he'd asked for it: that there was no helping the fact that reason was the master of his character and that only by allowing himself to go mad could he have kept up with Thérèse in her labyrinth of pleasure. Allowing himself to go mad, and to leave his whole life there. The master of his character had wanted much else. The situation was beyond help. He told himself that sort of thing, building a peculiar wall around his feelings. But sometimes, in his sleep, the wall would disappear; he would shake and stutter into wakefulness, recalling how like nothing else in the world loving Thérèse and being loved by her had been. A part of him, too, seemed to die. And he got old.

People wondered why they didn't divorce. What happened was that as Marc became less and less a husband to Thérèse, he became more and more a father. Sheltering her, giving Thérèse the base of secure affection behind all her foraging, he also delegated part of his own existence to her. She lived that part for him, while he lived for his career as a man of affairs, which gave him another sort of pleasure.

And in her way, Thérèse became more and more devoted to Marc. Once it was understood between them that one part of her life was in another orbit, she drew closer to him, as far as the rest was concerned. She became a watchdog of his little comforts, scolding the servants into a fanatic coddling of the Baron. She would choose his clothes for his business trips, saw them packed with no bother to him, and would send the butler out to the airport along with the chauffeur to be sure the Baron never had even to look at a piece of luggage until he was at the other end of his flight. Little things like that, to make his life easier. And when she ate with him at home, she always had the cook do something he liked especially well. She gorged him with *oeufs à la neige*. Once during a lull in their outside lives, he gained four pounds in a week. When she left for Mexico City, he lived on salads and rye crackers until he'd taken it all off. For he'd grown very careful about being physically fit. A strange kind of cramp would bother his stomach at times, for which the doctor could find no physical cause, but otherwise he held up under the grueling schedule he'd set himself in business. Since he'd regrouped the French Wolfflen assets in a publicly held holding company, he'd been working doubly hard. He would open his newspaper to the day's quotation for the Holding Wolfflen—the evening paper, brought him sometimes while he was still at his desk—and he'd accept the figure as a kind of personal grade.

For Marc believed that he'd found his way as a Wolfflen, that he'd set the family fortune moving with the current of history again. It had become clear to him that the hope for amassing more money for the Wolfflens lay in controlling other people's money, that the vast capital needed to do anything important in the modern world had to come from outside the family's own resources—from the stock market, where already in America the expanding middle class was pouring back its increasing share of the wealth. What was happening in America was destined to happen in France. And so, over Bruno's objections—Bruno seemed to want always to have all the advantages and no disadvantages in any situation, to have Wolfflens ask nothing of anyone and somehow be as powerful as the most levered conglomerate—over Bruno's objections, Marc had gone public, and made the bank a subsidiary of the Holding. Yet, unlike the Rothschilds, who turned their bank commercial and entered a costly fight with the big government-owned commercial banks for the small customers' dribs and drabs, Marc had kept the Banque Wolfflen an investment bank. The little man interested Marc in another way, for the little man was living better and better and spending more and more. Marc had begun to acquire company after company dealing in consumer goods and services. And in all Marc did, he saw himself not simply as a man apace with his time, but a leader in a movement toward more and more economic democracy in the Western world. That vision helped him to exult in his work.

He'd acquired holiday camps and clothing companies, motels and furniture factories and, he prospered, "heads up and savvy," as the sixties zoomed ahead. He prospered and he was more and more busy, and soon he was too busy to take to heart the disappointing Bourse—for, after an early flurry of interests in glamor stocks such as Holding Wolfflen, stagnation had set in, and the little investors, on whom Marc was counting to come in as they had in America, never forsook their prediliction for gold Napoléons and real estate. He went on acquiring, although it became clear to him that the buoyant market wasn't there, to boost the value of Holding Wolfflen with each acquisition. He redoubled his efforts, addressed himself to getting more and more revenue out of his companies, to the problems of making factories run right and to building management teams. But results were slow, and working away at ailing companies as if at broken motors lacked the drama of big financial operations. There were always frustrations—you were dealing always with people, their shortcomings, their disorder, their unreasonable way of making decisions.

He became a harried, irritated man.

One evening, he was up with the books of a carpet company he'd bought. He'd bought it with a brand new loom, a great investment that had driven the previous owners broke—they'd lacked the cash to pay for it—and he'd thought he'd got a bargain. Now, as he tried to figure his costs to build a new price structure, it seemed to him impossible to compete in any market with the Belgians. Unless he could rapidly achieve the volume the Belgians already had achieved, he could never get his prices down low enough—and to reach that volume, his prices would have already to be competitive. A vicious circle, a serpent biting its own tail. He figured and he figured on his little solid-state calculator, a plaything he used to enjoy, and all he could come up with was years ahead of losses.

He flicked off his machine, and as he sat there at the desk in his bedroom, aimlessly wiping his glasses, he heard a car door grunt shut in his courtyard. And he realized that someone had brought his wife home.

The wallclock said two. Ten past. He got up with a cracking sound in his knees. His feet were cold. He stirred, went downstairs in his slippers and dressing gown. Descending, he saw his wife's shadow, motionless on the marble of his front hall; then he saw her with her coat on, with her collar up, as if she were in a windstorm, there in front of the mirror not moving. He sensed that something had gone wrong for her that evening, out where he had no share in her life.

"Ah," he said, as he reached the foot of the stairs. She turned to him with glassy eyes. "What—" he began gently, "what is—" But then suddenly he trembled and he seized her by the arms and began to shake her.

She broke away. "It's not my fault!" she cried. He gripped her face in his hand. "What?" The way he squeezed her cheeks made her so ugly it chilled him, and he let go. She began to sob.

"It wasn't my fault," she said, heaving like a child. She lunged at him, and he flinched, but all she wanted was to throw her arms around his neck. She caught him and held him for a moment, before he broke loose and turned away. He stood a moment with his arms close to his sides, and then he mounted the stairs, went into his bedroom and closed the door behind him.

But that early morning she was with him in a dream. They were at a spring ball, and dusk had not yet fallen around the country house filled with guests. The orchestra was already playing, but some of the guests had gone out on the lawn with hunting horns they had taken from the walls of the study, where they were hung among the heads of many-pointed stags. The men in their tailcoats were blowing the horns and the sound seemed to fray into a special harmony, before it died in the fog of the forest beyond the lawn. Marc realized that this was his house, Bois Brûlé, and it was for him and his wife to open the ball. But there was not another soul in the room as he took her hand in his and began a waltz. And so they swept and turned across the whole empty ballroom, until he held her and turned and turned with her under a great crystal chandelier.

The chandelier fell. The room went dark and the crystal shattered all around. In the darkness he could feel a cold stinging and he knew he was covered with cuts. He felt himself bleeding. Bleeding and bleeding: it was as if all his blood were running out of him and his flesh were shriveling on his bones. In the dark he could no longer see Thérèse. Then, as he surfaced from sleep just enough to know he was having a nightmare, a thought penetrated him. I'm an old man, he thought. Worse. I've never been young.

BOOK FIVE

THE LEGACY

ONE

On a morning early in March of 1974, the Baron Marc de Wolfflen awoke believing for the first time that life's motive was not the pursuit of happiness but a blind will to survive. Going to bed the night before, he'd felt indifferent to the prospect of getting up. He was quite willing to join all the dead who'd passed through his life in eternal sleep. But here it was morning, his eyes were open to the teeming world, he was hungry and his legs itched to stretch and get about. His body refused to believe that all that might not be worth the effort. He noted, with his usual objectivity, that physically he showed none of the clinical signs of depression. Even though he was in serious trouble.

Trouble. Now the word seemed to materialize into something, gas or liquid, fighting the current of peristalsis, somewhere either in his large or small intestine—which was as close as he could come to knowing what was where deep inside his body. (As for his mind ... for one thing he was forgetting more often than he used to.)

He strained his abdominal muscles as he stood up, trying to crush that bubble, or whatever it was. Something in him was still fighting hard to keep him whole and happy. So for the moment an illusion appeared plausible: he believed that if he could get through the crisis facing him now, he'd find peace in age. Rather that he'd make peace with age. Once he was past this threshold ahead—in a week he would enter his sixtieth year on earth—sixty was old, period— something in his bloodstream would collaborate with the poisons making his cells old, and would bring him acceptance.

Ah, no, but he still wanted more out of life!

And now he found his thoughts depressing ... and specious. He knew nothing about those things, biochemistry, the body, medicine. For the sake of his wife, he paid others to know and they didn't know enough. He wondered if he might have made a good doctor, a good biochemist, or something like that, had he set out in life in one of those directions. Hadn't. Too late.

Money was in his blood . . .

While shaving, condemned to a mirror, a moment came back to him, almost repeated itself. A moment rose from his memory like a little chip of mica from a bubbling spring. But instead of seeing the traces of his father's features in the mirror as he had thirty years ago in a cold Swiss toilet, this time he saw the Baron Charles' actual face flash in front of him, as if Charles' ghost had suddenly come up from behind and wiped away his own presence.

Charles had made a lot of money from Cofra. *Charles would not have made the mistakes I made with that company. Anyone, in my time, might have made the mistakes I made with that company.* The ghost was gone. Unfortunately, he had not come with any advice.

Charles had given little advice. What advice he'd given, had always sounded more like predictions. For example, when Marc announced to his father he intended to marry Thérèse, the old man had replied:

"She is absolutely sensational! Hold on to her, yes, but if you *tie yourself* to her ... she'll cut your legs from under you."

More a prediction than a warning. All of life was like business, Charles believed, fools will act like fools, advice was wasted breath. Failures were bound to follow their wrong lights and fail.

Charles, Marc reflected glumly, must have died believing his son was a born failure. Yet, at the time, Marc had felt full of brilliant destiny. Thérèse was a marvel, the Helen he'd seized from another man. And when they'd lain Charles under, and the whole family was bending over the graveyard grass, washing their hands in that ritual of grief, Marc had grieved, felt the loss, not of someone close and affectionate but of a part of his own life like part of a house fallen away—grieved sincerely, in his entrails and yet—

And yet, yes, a wall had fallen. And the world gaped in front of him and he was free and virile and would master it. And that day he became the head of the Banque Wolfflen.

And he'd made of it a far greater thing than it was. He'd made the family holdings grow far more than Charles ever had. He'd made crucial changes, run the family's fortune energetically, in the way most appropriate for his time. He hadn't tried to counter history—

All the same, now that the Holding Wolfflen was a public company, the value of the Wolfflen fortune was measured by what other people thought of it, and Wolfflen shares were plummeting on the Bourse.

All the same, he had made, wrongly or rightly, an objectively disastrous decision regarding Cofra, one of the most important companies Charles had passed on to him.

Now in the light of a bad March morning, with the barometer in his bathroom falling—a gift from Thérèse, a recent gimcrack—it came to him, yes, that his father must have died believing that he, Marc, was born to fail. And that all that lay ahead of him, no matter what victories brought him there, all he was free to do was to situate his defeat. What realm, what battlefield. Life, ah yes, was war, Charles knew. Marc had never wanted to believe it, and now he'd marched Cofra, and the French Wolfflen fortune, into a kind of ambush.

Poor Robinet! Suddenly, that exclamation reverberated in Marc's mind, all out of context, for no reason that profited him.

Marc dressed quickly. He had the Sunday morning to himself. Thérèse and her decorator, Pérou, were out at Bois Brûlé, the country place Marc had inherited from Charles, twenty miles from Paris. They were measuring the walls for her folly. For the decorations of the Pop-Op Ball.

"I can't call it off," she'd said. "I can't, Marc. You can't do this to people. They've already ordered their costumes. They've spent considerable sums."

"For God's sake, Thérèse, who else but you could conceive of a ball at this time?"

At this time: for in the fall, using the occasion of the Yom Kippur

War, the Arab oil suppliers had first cut off oil to the West, then rationed it out at enormously higher prices. Europe was still in the grip of "the energy crisis." Houses had been ill heated all winter, gasoline was scarce, companies were failing, the Bourse was sick, and the shares in the Holding Wolfflen, because of its own particular problem, falling even faster than the others.

She was giving a ball.

And he'd let her back him into a crazy compromise. They would go on with it, but they would bar the press. Not even *Vogue*. That way, the Pop-Op Ball, she reasoned, could take place for the people concerned, and as far as the public went it would not exist. There would be no publicity, hence no bad publicity. No resentment. He was hardly convinced by this harebrained reasoning. But he'd let her talk him into it. She had more than willpower. She had strange powers . . .

The morning for himself. But what could he accomplish? He had taken the Cofra financial dossier home with him yesterday. Pages of figures, adding up to no solution. Three years ago, the modern refining plant the Holding Wolfflen had built with its partner Dynamerica had begun operating. Since which, the ore they'd begun hitting at the minesite had fallen in copper content to as little, at times, as one percent (Charles had seen pyrites coming out of there half-copper!), the market price had fallen abruptly, and the Nouwandan government was showing no mercy.

What the figures added up to was losses running $25 million a year.

Marc sat down a moment at the huge desk in his study, a fine late-eighteenth-century piece, with gold beasts on its legs, figures which brought to mind the lair of some heathen potentate. Between two candlesticks, facing him, Thérèse had placed a bronze figure of a bareback rider. She lavished him with gifts. The way the bronze man was perched, arms wide apart, knees high, it seemed to Marc the horse was out of control. He turned his back on the desk, the dossier, and went up to his rose marble fireplace.

What *would* Charles have done? Charles might have shut the mine down and watched the market. But Charles, in his time, would not have had to account for that to President Alexandre Kumbi, The Warrior Whose Glance Chills the Coward's Heart.

The clean and perfectly cut logs in the fireplace seemed suddenly perfectly vulgar. Artificial. There was not a smokestain on the bricks inside. Marc realized he was not responsible for this situation. Nothing in view, nothing in his library was there because he put it there. Years ago, he and Thérèse would do extraordinary things together for their houses. But it had been years since he'd had time to get involved in that. When the library had been redone, he'd asked her to handle the whole thing. And this was it. Over the years, Thérèse had become impatient with fine taste. Her heart wasn't in it anymore. No one's heart was in this room. Anymore. But from this minor carping, his mind, as if opening onto a door where a balcony had fallen, opened onto real damage again and true danger:

The point is, Charles would never had made the Wolfflen fortune vulnerable to the will of outsiders. And at this point Marc seemed to hear his cousin Bruno's bitter laughter.

Yet—and putting the larger question of not going public aside—Charles on his own would have had far less chance than a holding company of making $95 million available for a single investment. Charles, or anyone, would have looked for a partner. If Charles had been operating then. But perhaps Charles, with better Wolfflen instinct than Marc, might have given Kyle R. Hoyt a thorough look and shown him the door, instead of offering him 45 percent, as Marc had done.

But Charles had been long dead, and times were different. And in all fairness, who in those halycon days just a few years ago could have foreseen Hoyt's weaknesses? The storm that would wreck him? And the Wolfflens floundering in his whirlpool as he headed for the bottom?

The books, he recalled, were after all still his. He reached down a paperback copy of *The Diaries of Franz Kafka,* which he'd bought at Kennedy Airport on a business trip to New York. He opened the book to anywhere and began reading. He was still reading by the now faint light of his desk lamp when Thérèse arrived.

The late end of the morning had grayed out. March light. Rain coming. At the door she switched on the table lamps immediately. That gesture matched the way she had bounded up the stone stairs that led from the hall of their townhouse to his library. She broke in on him full of energy, flushed, with a touch of sweat on the faint down above her lips.

Her lips, her lips, her mouth. They could still astound him. The way her upper lip kept her mouth half-open, showing a trace of its underside.

"Lovely ... but somewhere some kind of aborigine, some Caliban crept into her family," Charles had said.

Cut your legs. Yet there she was in his life, something totally natural and inexplicable; at one time, she'd reached into it like lightning, filled the very air around him with energy; his world had been like some thick, tropical place, soaked, saturated with the power to sprout. Was it her fault, he asked himself, that he hadn't responded the right way?

Which was—?

"Kafka," she noted in her husky voice. "Will you have a drink before lunch?" she asked.

He looked at his watch. He'd been reading until past noon. A doomed young man's hypersensitive complaints. "Coitus as punishment for the happiness of being together—" His eye caught the sentence before the paperback flopped closed on his needlepoint couch.

Poor drab Franz.

If anything, Thérèse had brought Marc happiness in bed. Confidence. He had always had a vast appetite for women, but shyness had troubled his rapports. Emma, his first wife, would have sided with Kafka on the matter. He recalled that with Thérèse, he'd learned what a mindless feast sex could be. Nowadays, though, he couldn't bring himself to enter her bedroom. Her lovers, current and past, stood guard in his mind. That kind of contact between them was over, but still at times she could stir his blood with a look, a gesture of her body. And oddly, more than regret, he continued to feel pleasure in having her in his house. He looked on her as a self-justifying phenomenon. As if she were his spoiled daughter. Was it a fallacious way he'd found, unconsciously, for solving things? This dreary day was all too propitious for self-probing.

"Scotch?" she asked. "Have you been reading that book all morning?"

"Reading," he said, "thinking ... I've been going over in my mind ... our difficulties—" He didn't know how much there was any point in saying, but her mind was already there:

"In Nouwanda," she said.

"Cofra. Yes," he answered. Conceded. The ice whined against the insides of his glass as he brought the drink to his lips. She was straightening her rinsed-blond hair with her fingertips in the gilded mirror over the fireplace. She looked at him through the mirror.

"What is the latest from Mister Koyt?" she asked.

"Hoyt," he said. "No latest ... from him. The latest, perhaps, is that the United States government has decided to look into him over there. His whole house of cards is a shambles. Dynamerica ..."

Marc took a swallow of scotch as if to wash the taste of that name, the name of Hoyt's mythic conglomerate, out of his mouth. He tasted phenol now. *Drink, disinfectant, or poison, depending on the dose. Life, like business, was a matter of dosing your danger. Your risks. Hoyt should have known.*

He said: "I'm afraid our Mister Hoyt definitely has to get out of Cofra to patch together what he can in America. There'll be no more latest from Hoyt on this. It's a divorce."

"You'll be well rid of him!" It was all so obvious to her.

"Our contract gives us first option," Marc said patiently. He swallowed again. "In other words, we have the chance to take or find someone else to take his shares. If we find someone suitable, we'll be well rid of him." He cleared his throat. The taste of phenol had thinned out into a mellow smokiness in his mouth. "If we find someone ...

"Do you know anyone who wants forty-five percent of a company losing twenty-five million dollars a year?"

But when Marc had turned to Raphael, Herbert's son, at the Wolfflen Bank in London, he'd believed in the case he'd made. Copper was a sound long-term investment. And Hoyt's original price of $95 million was now considerably less than forty-five percent of what it would cost anyone to prospect, to buy new mining rights and build equivalent refining equipment elsewhere. Marc still believed Cofra was a sound investment. The new refinery was operating smoothly. The losses could be expected to go down considerably this year. Copper prices had shown signs of rallying ...

"This particular project is one in which I would not consider our cooperation useful," Raphael had answered. To which he'd appended in longhand: "England: no energy except in the workers' enthusiasm for strikes, no brains in government, except my father's, and don't expect Labour to listen to him, too many politicians, too much inflation. Our hands are full." And he added: "I wonder what will eventually happen to white investments in Africa."

Raphael talked and wrote like a smart-aleck. He'd been full of himself ever since Herbert gave him the whole show to run, with no one to answer to in the family but a lot of uninterested artists and eccentrics.

Marc heard himself thinking something mean and envious, and he checked himself. All the same, Raphael was wrong. But nothing could change Raphael's high opinion of his own judgment.

"Let Hoyt find his own buyer," Thérèse said. She was facing him directly now. He lowered his eyes. "If he wants to get out."

"Do you think things are that simple? It's a total mess over there. The man is a pariah. Nobody knows what he owes and what he might have felt obliged to steal. Nobody wants to touch him . . . Except, he's borrowed from some very funny loan brokers, apparently. The money apparently came from pure gangsters. Yes, criminals . . . Yes, *they* may take his Cofra stock . . . Anonymous bearer stock—" Hoyt, Marc recalled, had stipulated bearer stock; for the Wolfflens, it had seemed a detail—"they'd take his stock rather than his worthless hide, if it came to that. And at least they'd get their money out of the United States. Laundered, they call it. Well, we couldn't accept—you understand?—we couldn't even think of sitting in the same room with those people."

With hindsight, Marc now realized that he didn't relish sitting in the same room with Kyle R. Hoyt again.

"It's hopeless if we don't find anyone," he continued. "If we have to fight, it will all end up with lawyers. Lawsuits. The company will be paralyzed and the lawyers will have a great feast. Hopeless . . ."

"Léopold will help you," she said. "You'd do him a favor. He likes to think of himself as the family's golden boy."

She laughed, and Marc took her laughter badly. He suspected she was making another joke about Cousin Léopold's clouded parentage.

His eyes were on the horse and rider, and a part of his mind was trying to judge once again whether it was a good piece or not. No doubt about it, the sculpture, Thérèse's gift for his last birthday, was a fine example of late-eighteenth-century bronze. Yes, he thought, Thérèse *had* taste. But she allowed it little power over her life. Knowing that this was not an age for the predominance of taste. She had the strength of being perfectly at ease with her time. And she wouldn't hold back that strength. Knowing that taste was passive. And that people concerned about taste, in her time, spent their lives renouncing more than enjoying.

As for Léopold, in Thérèse's way of thinking he had neither good enough taste nor enough gusto for life. He was a fuddy-duddy, and his wife, she'd repeat around, was *molle,* a bore. Edmée happened to share Thérèse's feelings about the Léopold de Wolfflens, although Marc knew she also shared *their* feeling about Thérèse, the whole family's feeling about Thérèse: that she'd become very vulgar in recent years. So *public.* All her parties—the photographs in the popular press with dubious people. So Edmée and Thérèse talked about Françoise, and Françoise and Edmée talked about Thérèse, and they talked enough for Paris to know, alas, that all was not harmony among the Wolfflens. Thérèse cared little what anyone ever said; she kept steaming ahead, knowing that Edmée, outside of Bruno's polo friends and her own sporty lot, had not much of a social sphere of influence. Thérèse was queen bee of the jetters. She was queen of *something,* something alive, she could argue. And now, again, Marc could see how her deliberate, untrammeled "vulgarity" was a consequence of her energy . . .

And after all was said, Léopold and Françoise might well envy her fame. Everyone knew that the people they saw were nobodies socially. Heavies. Léopold and Françoise had no flair, and after all was said, they knew it, and for all their money, the knowledge did not sit easy with them.

Some time, perhaps, years ago, there might have been an opportunity to draw Léopold closer to the French Wolfflens. To bury Saul's resentment. But it hadn't happened . . .

What had Marc meant to say? "I can't go hat in hand to Léopold now," he said. "It won't work."

He thought of Thérèse, still, as he spoke. Charles, you didn't see the future teeming in her. She's more natural for *now,* more authentic than any of us. And I'm the one who found her.

Helen of Troy, he thought, recalling the man he was twenty years ago . . .

"Godwin Laver can raise all the money he wants," she said.

Probably. Godwin Laver was more than ever the star of the European financial scene. Not much past forty, balding and a little porcine though—but teeming with energy. Responsible people were saying that the enormous Unigam international chemical company would back Laver in whatever he went into. But there had been *l'affaire* Bison, the famous abortive supermarket merger. The whole business with the Bourse commissioners defending Laver's shareholders' against the Wolfflens' evaluation of the shares. Marc had walked away from the merger with Laver, and Bruno had sworn never to speak to Godwin Laver again.

"Bruno can't stand him," Marc answered. "He thinks that if ever we got involved with Laver again, he'd try to swallow us up in little pieces."

"Bruno!" She was behind his desk now, looking at the closed Cofra dossier, as she spat out his cousin's name. "Crazy Bruno." She opened the folder, fluttered the pages, and slammed the cover shut without reading. Only a gesture. Which seemed to speak of an instant of boredom. Something to do with her hands. Thérèse's nervous energy could understand Laver's.

Suddenly the bizarre thought came to Marc that Thérèse might have slept with Godwin Laver at one time or another. Before Marc had met her, or perhaps more recently. At some point in his climb to fame and power, Laver might have got a great charge of self-esteem from sleeping with a Wolfflen's wife. No. No. But looking at the messed-up supermarket merger as objectively as he could now, Marc thought of something similar but more plausible: Godwin had wanted badly to go into business with the Wolfflens.

"Well, Marc, you're the boss," she said. "You're the one who must make the decisions . . . and who will have to bear whatever blame. You don't want people to say behind your back that Bruno is deciding everything."

"Bruno is my cousin," he protested patiently, "I can overrule him on any number of things, but it would be particularly distasteful for me to oblige him to sit down to business with a man he cannot stand. . . . Besides, as for people . . ."

For a tiny moment Marc had the strange feeling of having escaped this room, and the problems that seemed ready to condense like horrible chimera in its stale air—each problem crying, ugly mouthed, big ones and little ones he'd stuffed away, a roomful of monsters that were the invisible furies of his life, big ones and little ones, a whole pack—of having escaped his past, his history, his name, his responsibility. He was staring at a cloud that was slowly escaping the margins of his window.

"People," he went on, "have always found nasty things to say about the Wolfflens. For a century and a half. Let them talk. Our strength, in the face of calumny, is sticking together."

His voice trailed over the last sentence, as if he were distracted again. His voice had no conviction.

"Bruno is a total and absolute wild madman, and everyone knows it, because it's true," she said.

He didn't come to Bruno's defense again. Perhaps it was true. Perhaps Laver was in the right, as far as the merger went, and Bruno had reacted wildly. Godwin had been foxy, perhaps, but the Wolfflens had been wrong about what the stock was worth. Objectively speaking, they'd been wrong, and the Bourse commissioners had confirmed this. Realizing this, Marc realized at the same time his *weakness* for objectivity. Bruno, Laver, Thérèse—their subjectivity made them better fighters than he was. Other people's opinions were other people's fortresses and their armies on the march. I might have made a good scientist, he told himself. But in business, too, the exact facts count first, for any strategy. I might have been a good businessman. I *have* been a good businessman.

There were problems with Cofra built into history. Charles died in time to look good. And things are not hopeless yet!

Thérèse was holding the Cofra dossier in her outstretched hand. "Is it hopeless?" she asked. Could she hear his mind? She smiled at him now, and for an instant, things seemed to him as they once were, when he and she were so close they could sometimes hear each other think.

There were footfalls on the stairs. Marc recognized the graceless gait of his son. As if the stone were being kicked step after step. Gilbert popped his sleepy, movie-star head in the doorway, looked vacantly for a moment at his stepmother, then at his father, and went on to his rooms without greeting them. He seemed to presume there was a quarrel going on.

Gilbert had been to the outdoor stamp market that morning. At lunch he will bore Marc with the arcane details of his purchases. Thérèse will simply tune herself out of the conversation. And Marc will be victimized by Gilbert's spiel, aimed at proving what excellent dealings he had done. Since Marc knew nothing and cared not at all about postage stamps, Gilbert will have, as usual, an easy mark for his boasting. Once Marc had spoken to Beauchamps, the head currency man at the bank, about Gilbert's stamp collection. Beauchamps' collection was internationally reputed. He was embarrassed talking to Marc about Gilbert's stamps, but since Marc pressed him, he allowed as diplomatically as he could that Gilbert's collection was of no interest.

Gilbert was nearly thirty and he still had a child's collection. That was what Marc had retained from the conversation. But the stamps gave him other gratifications. Once, when Gilbert was barely out of his teens, Marc had accompanied him to the open market at the Rond Point. He'd watched the boy bargain. Haggle, and tease those gray old men who needed to sell a few stamps to get them through their week. His prey. What mattered to Gilbert most was to impose himself as Someone. But deep down, Gilbert kept working against himself Marc realized, knowing, at the same time, that his objective thoughts about his son could never efface the love he felt for him. He loved Gilbert the way a mother would, with total pardon, and he pitied him. Gilbert wasn't comfortable in his own skin. All his petty self-aggrandizement might have to do with his not knowing quite what he was. If he was a closet fairy, as Thérèse had it, presumably from her decorator, he was also a closet many other things. Whatever he really was was still in the dark, anguishing in the dark, Marc thought, and although Marc wasn't wont to think in psychological clichés, he believed deeply that poor Gilbert's failure to come forth as a genuine person had much to do with his parents, Emma, himself ... and Thérèse. He wasn't sure how precisely they'd failed the boy, but they'd been, he realized dimly, a kind of trampoline for his manhood that had given way. There was more to all that than he cared to understand at this moment, but as usual, Marc reserved for himself the weight of the blame, whatever precise blame there might be in the eyes of an expert on human souls and what they do to each other. Souls, he'd said to himself. But the experts don't use that word.

He thought: the plain fact is that Thérèse and I are a catastrophic combination. It was almost *hubris* for me to have taken up with her. All that followed was a consequence of my mistake ...

"I suppose he spent the morning with his mannequin," Thérèse said. Marc hadn't answered her question about Cofra. Assuming, perhaps, that he'd rather not, she'd switched the conversation to Gilbert.

"Cynthia Ashe?" Marc smiled deliberately, as if his smile might color the topic with a goodnaturedness absent in his wife's tone. "Come on now, don't be catty, Thérèse. Cynthia is no simple little mannequin. She's not a mannequin at all anymore. I think he said he was going to the stamp market."

"She's ambitious . . . I suppose she went with him," Thérèse said, as she ran her fingertips along the tail of the bronze horse. "I don't know what else they could do together." She smiled into her hand.

"You listen to sick people," he snapped.

Gay or not—and Marc still held out for not—handsome Gilbert was not without arms in life. His little stamp collection was just one symptom of his acquisitiveness. Marc felt a strange satisfaction as he recalled his son's appetite to possess—well, but it was a weapon in life. And he was a Baron de Wolfflen, that was another. Providing it all doesn't go to pieces. If we had nothing, they'd all spit on us. Two hundred years of envy.

Sixty: that figure for the year he was entering came into Marc's mind again. He felt an instant of panic. He could not leave Gilbert a mess.

All this crossed Marc's mind as he waited for Thérèse to defend herself.

"Forgive me," she said with a half-yawn.

He brightened. "No, it's not hopeless," he said now. "I am going to try everything."

"I know you will, my darling," she said as she took both his hands in hers. "Well, I've been out to see about the decorations! And we've got a whole new idea. I can't tell you!—"

Clearly there was no hope whatever of calling off the Pop-Op Ball.

"Can I have a hint?" he answered with indulgence.

"Marc, your birthday is going to make history."

He held out his glass for another scotch.

"I'll tell you—I'll tell you what I'm going to be. A complete work of art," she said, pouring. "It's *dément!* It's incredible. Have you given any thought to what you'll be?"

Before he took the glass again, he raised his palms in front of him in a clown's gesture of uncertainty. She paid back his endearing gesture with a loving smile. She kissed his cheek. Those lips of hers. "Marc," she said, "I want you to come up with something that will make everyone else envy you."

Have you given any thought to what you'll be echoed in his mind. She'd meant what costume for the crazy ball. But the question came back rinsed of her voice, echoed, himself to himself, in fearful solitude.

An old man, he answered himself. *In his sixtieth year on earth.*

She kissed him on his lips now. She might have seen something ghastly on his face.

"Courage, Marc," she said. "Darling, I know you'll do what you have to do." That same moment he decided he would go to Cousin Léopold.

TWO

As for courage, he allowed himself the opinion that it was courage now, of a sort, a blindly energetic will to go forward, which was driving him to see Léopold; he had no strategy. Their appointment was three-quarters of an hour away; Marc decided he would walk from his office in the Rue Feydeau near the Bourse all the way to Léopold's house in the Faubourg Saint-Germain. Walking would fill his brain cells with oxygen and help his nerves. He whished down the chromed elevator of the building he'd built, the monument to his era at the helm of the French Wolfflen fortune. His stomach fluttered as the elevator sank to the ground floor, and just then Marc recalled the story in *Les Echoes* that had come out of his interview with the little dwarf who'd come to see him two days ago. The man had written:

"Marc de Wolfflen, coming late to the head of the French Wolfflen dynasty, was obliged to modernize, to seek new directions. Except for some mining interests such as Cofra, nationalization before and after the last war had absorbed the industries that had been the fiefs of the celebrated barons—railroads, coal, electric power. The Baron Marc restructured boldly, even made the legendary Banque Wolfflen a stepchild of his new holding company, and he spread the reparations his father had amassed and much of the family's other wealth, as well, across a broad table of industries in which he believed the future lay. Unfortunately, the Wolfflens' 'know-how' as the Anglo-Saxons say, was not always up to the challenge of the industries they entered, where competition was already strong. They lacked infrastructure, and their acquisitions, in the recent recession, have in many cases, fared even worse than the general economy. Their acute need of an outside partner to help bear the burden of Cofra—and perhaps to provide the brainpower to see the company through to a solution—illustrates how, through the forces of history and perhaps bad choices, the once all-powerful Wolfflens have become an investment group as vulnerable as many others."

It was probably crazy to see the hand of President Gaston Robinet—waving goodbye to the family—in the article. Yet the dwarf, the journalist whom Robinet had used to send out selected leaks when he was Minister of Finance, was considered still very close to the President. And Marc's dossier on Cofra, asking for some quite feasible measures of relief, had gone to Robinet's Finance Minister weeks ago, and there was still no word.

President Robinet. Who would have ever thought ... But Robinet, stepping from the shadows of the finance ministry, had suddenly revealed an "infrastructure" as the man put it, of fervent followers. They'd brought the Centrists as well as the old Gaullists solidly behind him, and carried him to victory in the elections two years ago. And now, inside the Elysée, at the height of his strange career, he was dying. Suffering an incurable disease and trying to sift out a succession from the ambitious men around him, trying with lucid remorse to find his heir. Marc could grieve for him, for the ill blow fortune had struck him in the end, even though over the years he'd clearly grown more and more chilly to the family. The Wolfflens were rarely invited to dinner at the Elysée, and never to anything intimate. And Thérèse's invitations to the private film screenings given by Robinet's wife had begun to dwindle.

What did he owe them? After all? Robinet had made a lot of money for the Wolfflens. And in his two years as President of France, he'd kept the nation fat, happy, optimistic, until the Arab oil crisis swept over the Western nations like some black wave on the sands where they all lay vacationing. Now he was dying, and his page in history—it could only really be a few paragraphs now—was still uncomposed. Marc could feel for him. And Marc had always admired his intelligence, his shrewd way of measuring people.

But even he, Marc recalled, had been taken in by Kyle R. Hoyt. When the Ministry of Finance was informed of the Cofra merger, Robinet had been favorably impressed. Here was the kind of deal with the Americans the Gaullists could bless: it gave the French company new strength, a stronger presence on the international market, and it was not a subjugation of the French, for Hoyt was taking a minority share.

Hoyt was an adventurer, but he could see, as Marc saw and could still see, that Cofra had a solid long-range future. As for the short-range:

The price of copper fell twenty percent the year after the new refinery became operative. And ten percent more the year after that. And the dollar, in which Cofra's prices were quoted, was devalued twice. And on Nouwandan Independence Day, two years ago, President Kumbi, the Enlightened Man of Africa, head of the most stable and most pro-Western government on the continent (as the *New York Times* had put it) gave his New Policy speech. It was time to get tough with those who sought to preserve the vestiges of imperialism.

There followed a new tax on operations instead of on profits. The Western imperialists were too clever at concealing profits. So for two straight years, in a terrible market, with prices down, no hope of profit yet in sight, Marc had to pay heavy taxes on every ton of ore he extracted, heavier taxes than he'd ever paid when Cofra was making money.

And Hoyt, Hoyt had trouble at home that made Cofra only a small part of his worries. There had been a moment of truth on Wall Street during which Dynamerica shares had gone through the floor. All Hoyt's masterful bookkeeping had begun to unravel and he needed cash. He was holed up in a hotel suite in Las Vegas, where the press reported he was meeting all sorts of dubious people.

And he'd written, in a language that at this point in the evolution of the man he might have even deemed a credit to his education, that Cofra was "too distant and too exotic in terms of our home-base structure and data digestibility for us to sense sufficient operative contact with the situation." Whereupon, he begged Marc to "find a suitable substitute entrepreneurial equivalent" for Dynamerica.

If not? If not, he had "encountered potentially interested parties."

Nowadays, now at a more sober time, perhaps anyone who'd seen Hoyt in Paris the last time he was in town, who'd watched his reflex of apprehension at the customs gate at Orly, who'd noticed that his graying red hair had been died shoe-polish brown and that his craggy features looked suspiciously fixed in place, suggesting a lift that had produced something frozen and perhaps about to shatter, who saw Hoyt in his new Lapidus suit—his flare-legged Now Generation tie-salesman's suit—carrying his fetish, a scuffed Samsonite attaché case: anyone, were then now, might be disinclined to buy, as the American saying went, a used car from that man.

Yet Hoyt had sold and bought enormous companies before all his levers began to crack. And right now, Marc supposed, there were maybe four or five Hoyts slouching toward fame and ultimate disgrace in currency and commodities.

The financial world was a casino. All sorts of people were being allowed in to play, as if these were to be the last throws of the wheel before the house caved in. Hard times for a Wolfflen to be old and hard times, poor Gilbert, for a Wolfflen to be young. They were still standing there, so to speak, in their black ties, while the *salle privée* kept filling up with rough strangers . . .

He entered a colonnade of chestnut trees. A rainstorm the night before had flailed the leaves and left a whole carpet of them splattered on the sidewalk. The chestnuts brought to mind a similar double row, lining the *allée* that led to the front of the house at Bois Brûlé, an *allée* much wider than this street. *Bois Brûlé,* that enormous property his grandfather had built—where, Marc recalled now, as a child he had never seen fallen leaves. The gardeners would be up before dawn after a night of rain. They seemed to have a magic talent for collecting every leaf heading for the lawns and *allées* before they even landed. Magic . . . there were sixty of those men. Marc had let all but ten gardeners go. Sixty . . . what might the press have done with that titbit? And yet, when a man could spend his money as he liked and be admired for it, Marc had lived in a wonderland. When he was a little boy, there'd been huge dinners at

Bois Brûlé with a footman in silk stockings behind every chair. He realized that among the old rich, his was, after all, the most difficult generation. They'd known wonders, lived in a way no one would likely ever live again, and were now a little like *émigrés*, refuged in a land of less. Well, was it not to his credit, Marc thought, that he hadn't chosen to live in the past like some exiled Hungarian prince? That he'd faced the present and based all his investment strategy on what he saw for the future. He'd placed his bets on consumer products. If the rich were poorer, there was far more money in the hands of the masses. And later, he'd even sold both his Rolls and bought a Mercedes and a mini. Even Thérèse, now, preferred to ride beside her chauffeur in the mini. "Thank God we've got rid of that fossil," she'd said, the day they'd sold her Silver Cloud.

Fossil. The word reverberated in his mind. And the fallen leaves underfoot, too, made Marc think of fossils. And a man of sixty nowadays is practically a fossil, he thought, a remnant of an age that seems as distant as a stratum of geological time. And now he thought of the chunk of pyrites the size of a fist on his desk in the Associates Room. A paperweight that symbolized the Compagnie Africaine de Cuivre, Cofra—

What could he say to Léopold? After all the years of petty friction, would he turn out, finally, to be an enemy?

Frayed contacts ... cracks in the escutcheon.

Virtus et Unitas ... Courage and Unity ...

The words flickered in his mind, and then he recalled the portrait of Old Hannah, in the gallery at *Bois Brûlé*, Isaiah's wife who'd seen her sons pulled in separate directions by destiny. *"Bleibt zusammen!"* she'd urged, not in Latin but in Yiddish, the old woman from Mainz, with a weakness all her life for salt herring and boiled potatoes. She was lucid to the end, and burning with wonder as much as pride. Her love was a center that held them, as they sold and cornered markets all together. *Zusammen ... Virtus et—*

Suddenly he had an image of his own mother. She was roaming the pink marble hallway, Avenue Foch. Empty now, but for her and two servants. Firmin gone, retired in his village in Auvergne. The servants kept changing; she was hard to deal with. "I'd like to go to *Bois Brûlé!*" she'd insist, when the sun shone. And once, he learned, he couldn't remember how, once they'd packed her parchment valises and walked her around the garden. "I'm so happy to be back in Paris," she said when they led her inside. And they unpacked, hiding snickers . . .

"The once all-powerful Wolfflens . . . the once all-powerful Wolfflens."

"Courage," his wife had said. And then on a day in London long buried in the past, his father was saying, in a voice depreciative and ironic:

"How many Germans have you killed?"

THREE

It was still said of Léopold de Wolfflen that he could reinvest most of his interest every year, and that he lived, royally, on the interest from his interest. The Baron Léopold was probably the richest non-Greek in Europe. The investment bank he'd inherited from Saul still had only one client, its owner.

Léopold was now a round man of forty-two, who looked ten years older. He had had his first heart attack a year ago, since which he'd been spending a day or two more a week at home, under the cajoling of his doctors and his wife, Françoise. The latter was the sun of his life. And the moon was his only child, Léa.

When Marc arrived, Léopold was doing something with some orchids in his greenhouse.

Françoise led Marc through the house to the garden. When they'd kissed hello at the door, Marc noticed that the flesh around her neck had begun to thicken, but in general, aging had brought out her best features—her cheekbones and her fine nose—and changed her from someone rather plain to what is called "a handsome woman." A handsome woman from an honorable family—but, as Thérèse liked to repeat, she had no *chic*. Thérèse depreciated her by calling her "the cosy type." Yet the kisses on both cheeks Françoise had exchanged with Marc were formal and without warmth. She knew where she stood with his wife. As Marc followed her to the edge of the garden where she left him, they didn't exchange a word.

From the far end, where the greenhouse lay, Léopold began to approach very slowly.

The sun on this unusually warm March day was finally receding. In the moody afternoon light, Léopold's garden seemed under a spell of calm, as if it were some paradise sealed away in time.

It was the largest private garden in Paris. The greenhouse was at the end of a gravel path, half-hidden by maples. Inside that immense birdcage of iron ribs and glass, Marc recalled, Léopold had a good acre of jungle and his pool. Behind, the lawn sloped gently toward more trees that masked the tennis court. The garden of Marc's townhouse could all fit in a little corner of Léopold's. What rankled Thérèse as much, comparing their lot with Léopold's, was that she and Marc could not have a pool. If they dug, they'd find themselves in the *métro*.

Léopold came closer, along the gravel (which in summer he would line with potted orange trees). He seemed to have a touch of a limp, as if his flesh were a burden he couldn't quite balance properly. He dressed for the country at home, the way his father had. He was wearing canvas shoes, a loose sweater, and a pair of baggy corduroys the color of tobacco. His moon face, whose soft mien was challenged by his bristling moustache, wore an unattractive smile. Marc judged it to be a superior smile as Léopold took his hand and pressed him into a deep white garden chair.

"Let's take advantage," he said, waving his hand in a gesture that spoke of the weather.

As he sat down, Marc recognized a square white envelope, lying torn open on the table between them. It was an invitation to the Pop-Op Ball. Although Thérèse never invited the Léopolds to her dinner parties, they had to be on the list for a ball, expecially since the ball was Marc's birthday party. Léopold noticed Marc's glance. He picked up the envelope, held it a second for no apparent purpose, then dropped it on the table.

"Françoise has ordered some kind of costume," Léopold said almost sorrowfully.

"What will *you* be, Léopold?"

Marc smiled. His voice had made a try at banter.

"You know me, Marc, I'll come as I am. People will find that amusing enough."

Françoise came up with a tray heavy with bottles and glasses. Léopold's servants always seemed to disappear in her presence. She liked to wait on him personally. He took the heavy tray from her and set it down on top of the envelope. He beamed her a look of adulation.

"No, don't look so troubled, I'll think of something," Léopold said, as Françoise went off the way she'd arrived, without opening her mouth. Marc watched her disappear into the house. He recalled that one of the things that Thérèse could stand least of all about Françoise was her "geisha act." Safely a baroness, rich beyond most people's conception, Françoise played a servant to the man fortune had sent to give her all that.

Or why not simply believe they were in love with each other? Marc realized he'd been thinking in a way conditioned by Thérèse. For an instant Marc tried to imagine being married to Françoise. But what a bore she'd be. He'd leave her without a second's hesitation for Thérèse. Thérèse was a Phenomenon. Yes, and it struck him now that even her ball was a majestic act of impudence. And they'd all come. He'll come, they'll all be there, decked out. And Thérèse will have a laugh ...

"You'll be fifty-nine, that's so?"

"That's so."

"I know. Ask me anyone in the family's birthdate; I know them all. March eleventh, nineteen—"

"That's so!" Marc cut him off before he could finish the figure.

"I know marriages, too," Léopold went on, "both of yours ..."

"You should be the family historian, Léopold."

"I could. Tell me about business, Marc."

"Not fantastic. Cofra ... is still a great problem."

Léopold shifted the weight of his buttocks. "That's what you had in mind?"

"I wanted to have ... your feelings."

Léopold opened his palms and gave Marc a quizzical look. "My feelings." A gardener was approaching with a potted plant in his hand. Léopold called to the man:

380   THE HEIRS

"Back in the greenhouse!"
The man reversed his direction.
"We'll have an engagement party soon," Léopold said to Marc, "it'll be Herbert's turn. Léa. Léa's decided to get married. Jason . . ."

Marc wasn't surprised. He'd predicted the marriage in his mind, the first time he'd seen Léa with Jason, a year ago, now . . . Herbert's turn:

Since the time when Isaiah's sons had left home, it was a family practice to celebrate important family events in rotating order, each time in the house of a different Wolfflen. "Hannah's Rule," they called it. Her device for bringing her brood together. For keeping it together. All Wolfflen children were the children of each Wolfflen. It was the turn of Lord Herbert Wolfflen. He would give the party for Léa's engagement at Owen Glade, his place in Devon.

Jason, Marc remembered, was Jason Fullerton, a Jewish boy from Pittsburgh whom Léa had met at Stanford. He was going to be a lawyer. His grandfather had changed his name and become a Pittsburgh worthy, after doing well in the linen supply business. Léopold had explained all this to Marc last June at Longchamp, where Marc had come upon Léa with Jason in the paddock. Jason had got himself a bowler and a pair of binoculars. Marc was suspicious of that pale, blond, featureless American. He certainly wasn't marrying Léa for her looks.

Léa was only nineteen, and a brilliant student, but she had a face like a gargoyle. Or rather, with her Golda Meir-Mona Lisa counterpoint of eternal *Zuriss* and exhilarating pride, she greatly resembled old Hannah as she appeared in the gallery of *Bois Brûlé*. Léopold had borrowed the picture and had a copy made, which he'd hung above the fireplace of his library. His daughter's homeliness was in one sense a godsend for Léopold.

"They'll both be back from America at the end of the school term," Léopold was saying. "We'll have the party then." But Marc was only half-listening. His mind was conjuring out of memory an image of Léopold's own mother. There were no portraits of *her* in Léopold's house. Ariel, that tall, lean, wide-mouthed woman.

Marc's father used to say that her lovers had been a quiver of arrows, to balance psychologically her power against his cousin Saul's. Saul's power was charm and money and being a Wolfflen in a world in which Wolfflen meant more to most people than the nearly broke descendants of crusaders; with Ariel he'd wanted to use his power to please, not wound, but that tall, grand, fair *Shiksa* had warrior's blood. Charles had always insisted that Ariel was a pagan, a barbarian who needed to hurt to be healthy, and probably an antisemite.

In the end, her real victim had been Léopold, who grew up being called "the chauffeur's son." People repeatedly scrutinized his features, hunting for the true mark of the chauffeur. No one in his official family was sure that he had a drop of Jewish, let alone Wolfflen, blood in him, yet through all the years Léopold had borne his cross valiantly. From his twenties on, he'd given enormously to Israel. He'd built a hospital in Tel Aviv and paid for the physics department of Haifa University. He'd vacationed often at Ashkalon. He'd learned to use a lot of Yiddish, and told wise stories recorded in the ghettos of Eastern Europe. And Saul had loved him. Saul had left his entire fortune to Léopold.

"Léopold, son born to my wife, Ariel," read his will, with an ambiguity there that might have been a final and first reproach to Ariel.

But by then, Françoise had borne Léopold Léa, from birth the living image of Isaiah de Wolfflen's wife, co-founder of the dynasty.

Marc believed now that Léopold's story had a fine Talmudic flavor. It was possible Léopold was no true-born son of the faith, and by the rules of the Orthodox he was not, since his mother had not been Jewish, no matter who his father had been. But he'd walked with such zeal in the ways of Jehovah, honoring and loving Saul, that the Lord at length sent him Léa, the image of the matriarch of his line. To prove his lineage? The best way to believe the story, Marc thought, was to believe that Léa's birth was a message, that through her, God had grafted upon Léopold, the bastard, holy parentage.

The best way to believe—

The best way to believe the story—Marc caught himself in mid-thought—was a way of deforming Léopold's life into a joke. "Léopold's Story." It had gone through his mind again, now, as he recalled Ariel, a tale, another family anecdote like all the hellzapoppin accounts in the Wolfflen biographies. A joke nearly drained of what was most real in it: the conflicts of the heart. But there was a real man beside him now, who had worn the same name as he, in any case, with honor for forty-odd years . . .

Léopold coughed. Marc brought himself back into the present.

"I'm very happy for Léa," he managed to say in the wrong voice, whose gravity puzzled Léopold.

"It's her choice," Léopold said. He set down his glass. There was a leaf pattern traced in the silver of the tray. Marc's walk came back to him. Here he was; something might be settled. What? Well he wouldn't beg.

"You mentioned Cofra," Léopold said. His voice shifted moods, dropped its emphaticness.

"Yes... well, you know—" Marc began.

"I've heard all sorts of things," Léopold said.

"That company will be an excellent long-term investment for someone," Marc started to say. Léopold broke in:

"What about Hoyt? Whom does he have, does he have anybody?"

"If anyone, the worst people. Impossible people."

"Who?"

"The worst. Murderers. God knows."

Léopold bit the flesh beside his thumbnail.

"Godwin Laver is a gambler," he said very quietly, almost as if he had spoken accidentally before he'd committed himself to say what he'd been thinking.

"Bruno won't have him. Bruno thinks he'd love to swallow us up, if he could. Maybe Bruno is right."

"Godwin was in the right. In Bison, Marc, Godwin was in the right and Bruno was wrong. And you listened to Bruno." Marc thought there was something like grief, just then, in Léopold's voice.

"Léopold, what point is there in the two of us talking about Godwin Laver?" Marc regretted immediately the petulance in his tone.

"You asked for 'my feelings.' Listen, Marc, I don't say it to hurt you—"

"That company is a good investment. Anybody who buys into it will be getting a chance to produce copper for a little more than half—in pounds of metal capacity per dollar of investment—half of what he'd pay anywhere in the world. All we have to do is hold out, Léopold. All we need is a good injection of money. To carry us over."

"Listen, not to hurt you, Marc—" Léopold was running his hand across his brow with his head lowered. Finally he looked directly into Marc's eyes.

"But face it, Marc. Face the facts! You've lost your credibility. If you went tomorrow into the market and tried to raise that money, they would laugh Marc, excuse me . . . You've lost your credibility. You're losing what? Twenty million dollars a year. Thirty? That means you're not credible anymore. If you found a buyer, do you think he'd agree to let you keep the majority? Do you think they'd let you keep running it? There'd have to be a whole new management, a whole new strategy. If one is possible! Before you do anything face the facts. I'm your cousin. I'm giving you my feelings. Excuse me."

Marc closed his eyes. Then, looking straight at Léopold, he said patiently: "I happen to think there'll be someone who'll look at the facts, Léopold, and realize that getting into Cofra is the kind of opportunity that won't be around in the coming years. My credibility aside, Léopold. I mean the facts."

"The oil problem," Léopold said. "Would you include that in your facts? Production is going to go down. People are going to use less copper. For I don't know how long. Who can see daylight in this thing? Copper prices, Marc, are going to fall again—"

"I'm not sure . . . I'm thinking of the long run. There is only so much copper in the ground—"

"You're not sure. You're not sure!" Léopold had stood up and was shouting now. "Do you think I'm a fool?"

"I'm asking you, Marc," he began again, "do you take me for a fool?" He was indeed asking. He wanted an answer.

"No," Marc said quietly, "I invited your opinion. Don't excite yourself Léopold. We can drop the subject. Forget it."

"My opinion. My feelings! Who in this family is sincerely interested in my feelings, Marc? You want me to help you—"

"Forget it, Léopold, forget it! Sit down!"

"I will decide myself what I choose to forget and not to forget!" Léopold smiled for an instant at his crazy sentence, but then his face fell: "There are a lot of things impossible for me to forget."

"I'll go now," Marc said.

"Marc!" It was Léopold who'd taken a few steps, but he called to Marc now as Marc rose out of his chair. "Don't talk crap to me. I'm your cousin, but talk to me like we were two intelligent people. Any stranger—any stranger you went to would ask to see your plan. Show it to me. Show me a *plan de redressement*. Let's not talk about the long run, show me how you're going to save that company from going under before there's a long run. Show me how you're going to keep whatever money goes in now from going where the rest went. Talk to me like we were two intelligent people!"

"I believe in copper, Léopold. For me it's very simple. I believe we've got an important mine. We've got the best equipment in the world. Let's forget it. Forget it. All right?"

Léopold came up beside him.

"You know who's hurting you Marc?" Marc lowered his head and looked toward the house. Léopold took Marc by the arm and stopped him from moving. "He's hurting you because he's not helping you. He has no sense of gratitude."

"That's not exactly a way to put it," Marc said in a dry voice.

"He's worse than de Gaulle," Léopold insisted. "He's afraid to help you. To even touch you. Wolfflen! Wolfflen! You understand? Money! Jews! ... Have you heard anything?"

"I expect a dossier takes a little time these days."

"Always the gentleman, Marc."

"Take care of yourself, Léopold." He took a step. Léopold still had hold of his arm.

"Show me a way, Marc. Forgive the way I put it. I'm not *fin*. I'm not the subtle one in the family."

"It's nothing for you to get upset about, Léopold."

"Get back to me. I mean it. Show me a way."

There was a way. Both of them knew it. Marc had explored it, as always, as a gentleman. Now he knew there'd have to be a confrontation. Because he had to keep advancing. He had to try everything.

At the front door, out of rote, he kissed Françoise on both cheeks, and as he did so he realized he and she hadn't exchanged a word beyond hello and goodbye. He hadn't even asked her about Léopold's health.

FOUR

They drove into the courtyard of the Elysée in a gray company Citroën, all three Wolfflens in the one car, looking a little like detectives, or gangsters, or minor officials. Instead of a chauffeur, Bruno had taken the wheel.

As they trotted up the steps, Marc looked at the plate-glass doorway fitted onto the eighteenth-century facade and decided that it made the presidential palace seem like some historic house turned into a restaurant.

Pompadour and the Duchess of Berri, he recalled, had lived here. Louis Napoléon made it the home of the elected leader of the French, then plotted his *coup d'état* in the *Salon d'Argent*. De Gaulle had put in the glass. It must have had something to do with protection, with keeping the courtyard visible. No doubt it was bulletproof.

Two men in tails took their coats. A third usher led them upstairs to the *Salon Doré*, a vast square room over the rear hall with high windows giving onto the gardens. Was it a token of intimacy that the President invited his former employers to wait for him in his office, not the *antichambre*? Marc wondered.

The room was furnished in a mixture of Louis Seize and Regency. The gilded walls, which gave the salon its name, were done during the Second Empire. Robinet had added personal touches of modernity. A large acquamarine Hans Hartung, thin lines shaved with a knife on thick oil, covered half the mirror behind his desk. There was a Bram van Velde on the opposite wall, a small Brancusi white marble on the mantel of the fireplace.

"Modern classics." Robinet's interest in what the common man still considered *avant garde* was thin, and pragmatic. Marc knew how little Robinet knew. But he had begun life with no money, no old name. So he'd looked for prestige in the unconventional, the artistic, yet no further than his simple awe and conventional respect for where he found himself in life—so far beyond his early dreams— allowed him. Madame Robinet had exaggerated once, when she'd redone part of the private apartments in the latest of what Marc called "contemporary baroque." Undulant foam covered in candy-colored jersey.

L'Express had questioned the change. But about that same time Gaston Robinet contracted cancer of the marrow, and the furniture became of very remote importance.

He was heading out of history full of pain and drugs, before he'd had a chance to lay de Gaulle's ghost and stamp his own mark on the affairs of France.

Now, since the Arabs had multiplied the price of oil, he had to face dying in the middle of a crisis. Until now he'd held things together, there'd been order and prosperity. He'd overseered a minor moment of well-being, during a time when, to the entire West, inflation had seemed a remotely poisonous tonic, a habit, like smoking, that everyone enjoyed and decried. Now it was a cancer. Seventeen percent: the unions were screaming for more money to meet the ferocious cost of living. They were hungry, and he was sick and tired.

An odor of cologne in his empty office recalled Robinet's attraction to fine living. Marc remembered Robinet's *bonhomie,* his lust for good food, his eye for young girls. He'd bought his father a small vineyard in Burgundy. There was a photo of Robinet and his wife in the country beside the little Brancusi. Perhaps it was taken on his father's land. But then Marc realized that the landscape didn't at all resemble a cramped vineyard. The picture had been taken at Bois Brûlé.

There were voices in another room. A woman's voice in firm tones and the low grunting of assent. The door opened. Robinet took a few stiff steps and held out his right hand. In his other hand he held a dossier. He looked horribly puffy. He brought to mind a molting owl.

Each of them shook his hand.

"Comment allez-vous, Monsieur le Président?" Gilbert said. He earned a pursed smile from Robinet, and a twinkle of the eyes, as if Robinet were teasing him for his formality.

"Est-ce que vous allez bien . . . ?" Marc seemed to be trying to place where on the scale of familiarity Robinet had shifted for him.

"Gaston," Bruno said.

The woman who had been standing behind the President with a blue portfolio clutched to her chest looked at them all with a placid assaying glance, and closed the door behind her before they could decide whether to greet her as well.

She was Chantalle Chevallier. A round, plain-faced woman of forty-odd. Chantalle Chevallier. She'd been a lawyer in Toulouse and a workhorse of the Gaullist party before she was appointed to the Elysée staff. She'd come in to handle welfare questions and moved closer and closer to the President until now the political reporters called her his chief nurse and advisor. His enemies said she was running the country.

"Messieurs?" Robinet sat down behind his desk with the tentativeness in his movements of an old bather testing cold water. He put his elbows on the desk and held out his palms toward the Wolfflens.

They seated themselves facing him. Marc crossed his legs and hiked his trouser cuffs.

"We would like to bring to your attention," he began, "a dossier we've presented to the Ministry of Finance. Cofra—"

Robinet patted the dossier on his desk, the one he'd come in with.

"We'd like to review the situation with you."

"Nouwanda," Robinet said. He pushed himself back into his chair, experimenting with the distribution of his vast weight as if he were seeking a solid position to entrench himself. "Right now, a very different sort of country."

"Very much," Marc said. "Yes, but they're still in the Franc Zone. Their imports would bankrupt them if they got out, if they ever had to worry about their own balance of payments."

Robinet shrugged his shoulders. "Raw materials are the future," he said. "They have all those natural resources."

Bruno frowned. Why was Robinet smiling then? Their eyes met. The President frowned. He seemed to pause a moment to rally breath, or patience.

"The President of Nouwanda is a former nightclub bouncer," he said. "He was a tough captain in the Foreign Legion. A cruel man. Not educated, not intelligent, perhaps. But tough. Wily. We made him out to be a hero when he cooperated with us, when he obeyed us, is what I mean. He's the same man, but now ... but now we think he's different." Robinet shrugged again. "He manages to keep ahead of the Leftists by killing them as fast as he can lay hands on them. The same with all his opponents. (There are days I find that enviable.)

"The people are poor. The government did little for them when it depended entirely on us, and it still does little for them. But when Kumbi makes fun of the foreigners the people enjoy it. He could break all ties with us if he liked. The people would enjoy it. Their payments situation would be a mess, but Kumbi would see to it that there were so many transistor radios and so many motorbikes and for the rest they can live on manioc root ... Or he'd nationalize the foreign interests. He'd take your mine."

"They wouldn't know how to begin running it," Marc said quietly. "I would have thought," he went on, "that the influence of France in that country is considerably greater, still, than you seem to suggest."

"I'd love to see the figures on all the aid we pour into that country," Bruno interjected.

"All the better if they leave us," Robinet said. "France can use the money."

"Our problem," Bruno said, and now his voice was testy—"Our problem is that we have a business in that country."

"If you came for my advice," Robinet answered—and there was no shade of irony in his voice, he was serious. Was his intelligence failing now?—"I'd say you'd be wise to get out of that investment."

"Will you buy it from us, Gaston?" Bruno asked in a raised voice.

Robinet flushed. "What are the particular issues we might take up at this time?" he asked stiffly.

"We have a problem with that man you mentioned," Bruno began. Bruno was excited. Anything could happen now. Marc shot him a concerned look, raised his palm slightly off his knee, held it up discreetly but firmly toward his cousin. He broke in:

"We want to review our tax situation with you. Cofra hasn't been profitable for a few years, but every time we move a shovelful of ore our taxes go up. We're putting in something that greatly adds to the local economy. We refine on the spot. But the harder we try, the more we're taxed."

Robinet closed his eyes. He trembled slightly for an instant, as if a tremor of pain were passing over him.

"Yes," he said. Yes, he knew all this. What difference did it make to the cells gone wild in his marrow. "Yes. But at this point I don't think we can exert much influence over the policies of President Kumbi."

"Copper is a strategic metal," Bruno said. "You can pressure him to change his tax structure ... You have the power to get us subsidies, to get us a rebate, here, on the taxes we pay that gangster. That's about a quarter of our turnover now. With that kind of cut in our costs we could see daylight. Copper is going to be very scarce. A rebate, a subsidy, a loan, for a couple of years. We're going to make money if we stick it out, but right now we're taxed on every move we make and we're not getting any profit out. We're losing our shirts!"

Suddenly Bruno went white. He seemed to realize that he sounded like a desperate beggar. "France is going to need copper," he said in a new, cold voice.

"Cofra isn't a French company," Robinet said petulantly. "You're incorporated in Luxembourg and you're operating in Nouwanda."

"The Cofra holding company, with all the Wolfflen shares in it, with more than half the shares of the mining company is French," Marc said. "Surely you remember ..." he said, knowing Robinet of course remembered.

Gilbert suddenly perked up like the Dormouse. His face became animated with indignation.

"The Wolfflens," he said, "have never tried to escape French taxes. And we have nothing hidden in Switzerland. No one in France is as immaculate about this as we are."

Robinet grunted and shifted his weight again. His cortisone-swollen body seemed so much barely animate flesh attached loosely to his bones. His bird's face, which had once been softened with gaiety and ruse, was bloated so that his famous energetic eyes were nearly forced shut. The Wolfflens were talking to a dying man. He'd already crossed a border and it was as if he was in the process of forgetting the language of the living. What did all of it mean—honor, the loss of millions of dollars, or the gain, or power—when all of it was happening on the other side of the border?

"Luxembourg," Robinet said, as if ruminatively, but the word might have just been echoing for no clear reason in his mind.

What does Luxembourg have to do with anything, Marc was thinking, but he said with great patience: "Luxembourg is the natural place for an international company, it is one of the few places that attract a lot of capital for large bond issues—"

Robinet knew all this, any half-informed person knew this. The conversation was fraying. Or Robinet was going out of his way to carp. His illness. Lately, in cabinet meetings, he was said to be insupportable when he wasn't drugged.

"Tax advantages," the President said.

"Yes, there are no taxes withheld on the bondholders' coupons," Marc said, "but . . . in any case, we're in no position to put anything on the bond market." Robinet didn't need any of these explanations.

Gilbert cleared his throat. More noisily than he seemed to have intended. Everyone looked at him. Gilbert brushed his hair back with a rapid gesture of his palm. "As for our being an international company, *monsieur le Président*," he began, "we are, uh, faced with a great problem on that score."

Marc took up his son's initiative. "We're in a crisis with Dynamerica," he said bluntly.

"*Monsieur* Hoyt," Robinet said. He pronounced the name in French, with a rapid puff of breath that made it sound ridiculous.

"He has to get out," Marc said. "He is under investigation. The only people who'll do business with him now are very bad people. If the transfer of shares depends on him—"

"*La Mafia*," Robinet interjected. In a mock Italian accent now. The Great United States was at the mercy of a handful of Sicilian killers, and at the mercy of a few little yellow people in the jungles of Indochina. History was turning into burlesque. And Robinet hadn't lost his sense of humor.

"The time won't be far off," he began seriously now, "when they'll be the only ones in America with money. The Mafia. And maybe the Arabs. I wouldn't be surprised if Mr. Nixon . . ." His voice trailed. He'd dropped a hint of knowing something, but he wouldn't say it. He was President of France—their ex-employee was—and he was privy to a lot of things to which they weren't. But presidents don't reveal things, offhand, about other presidents.

"If Hoyt sells those people his shares," Bruno broke in, "our Cofra holding will go through the floor of the Bourse. But the point is, in no way could we deal with them. We just could not do business with those people!"

Robinet rapped his thick fingers on his desk. "Yes," he said. His yes said nothing.

"There are four hundred nationally owned companies in France," Bruno said, "there are a dozen nationalized banks and all of them bigger than we are. We're offering a partner a stake in the future of what will be a very rare commodity."

"Yes," Robinet said again, exactly the same way.

"Then there can be a purely French solution to this—?" Bruno went on. His assertion had turned into a question at the very end, as if he'd lost nerve somehow, or faith.

Robinet cocked his head back. He waited to answer.

Purely French Solution. That had been a catchword with Robinet since the time he was Finance Minister. By the early sixties, the Americans had begun buying European companies as if they were moving down the aisles of a supermarket. They were everywhere on the continent, they had thirty percent of the industry in Belgium and about ten percent of the industry of France when Robinet took action in the Finance Ministry.

Robinet blocked all the American dossiers. At the time, there was an interminable list of sleepy, naively managed family companies lined up to sell out control for the comfort of a portfolio paid for in dollars.

Robinet invented Purely French Solutions to the distress or the decadence of these companies. He promoted all-French mergers, trusts, joint ventures. He straddled many strong businesses with weak ones in the process. When there'd been grumbling he'd argued that national interest came ahead of profits, and at the same time he would arrange ample credit from the nationalized banks, and offer subsidies and high-profit government contracts.

Robinet could arrange a Purely French Solution for Cofra. In the long run, he might well be proved right for holding the company up by the armpits for three, four, how many years? But the cost would be enormous, and the long run had become obscure, the day that no one could yet see at the end of the tunnel. And somewhere in that darkness, he would die early. And the opposition had only recently sapped his popularity, by revealing how much the Gaullists had spent trying for a French answer to IBM in the computer industry.

The French consortium had spent years reinventing what IBM already had on the market, and their salespeople had been offering beggars' terms. In the end, they hadn't shaken IBM's grip on the European market. Even their own air force had fought hard not to switch computers.

But beyond all this simple understanding of Robinet's options, based on common knowledge, there was something that seemed to descend on all of them now through his long, heavy silence at that moment, like something invisible tracking its way through a cloud chamber. All three of them, waiting for the President to say something, could detect it: They were Wolfflens. They were the bankers in striped pants and top hats on the posters pasted to factory walls. Mimeographed under the caricatures was their name, not de Wankle, Croulle, or Paradin, nor the names of any other inconspicuous Christian gentry who had grown as rich as they were.

For the auto worker at Billancourt or the Breton artichoke farmer a solution for the Wolfflens was not a purely French solution. It was a deal for the profit of International Capitalism. Myths die hard among the people. Robinet, the politician, knew it. And the Wolfflens knew it. And prejudice dies even harder.

The Wolfflens had changed Robinet's life. Lifted him out of obscurity, but for years, whenever he'd speak to the Assembly on economic matters, there'd been a claque among the Communist seats, shouting "Wolfflen! Wolfflen!"

For *Humanité,* the Communist daily, he was "President Robinet, of the Banque Wolfflen."

The Wolfflens could argue—but they'd never do it—that he owed them Everything. But he was dying, and maybe, cynically, he simply counted on death to cancel his debts. And after all, he'd already given them good value. He'd done a lot at the bank. Charles had chosen him to run it because he expected him to make money for him. He had. You could argue that he'd given them more than good value.

In any case, none of them had breathed a suggestion of his debt. They sat there and watched him shudder for an instant. He had no time left for great deeds of destiny. But he could try to go out popular, widely loved. The Wolfflens were not widely loved. And the Left had Robinet with his back to the wall. The times were getting darker, and he wasn't sure of dying, even in a limited way, happy.

He flattened his palms on his desk. "I'm afraid," he said, "that I can offer nothing constructive at the present moment."

Bruno's face filled with blood. "We—" he began, and then he halted for breath enough for what he seemed ready to shout. His cousins fixed him looks of horrible moritification, as if they both suddenly knew that he was about to say it. What never should be said: that Robinet owed them something. For a moment Bruno stood in front of the President's desk with his mouth open, while his eyes moved from face to face among the others of his family. His eyes rested on Marc's face. Marc's features were composed now, hard, serene. His almond eyes were elsewhere. Somehow, Bruno caught his calm. He finished his sentence as best he could, as quickly as he could.

"We don't have that much time," he said.

"I understand," Robinet said.

It was hopeless. And Bruno had humiliated himself saying anything to avoid saying what couldn't be said. He sat down, smouldering.

Robinet raised himself from his chair quickly, as if a sudden swell of energy had come over him. As if to counter the guilt he might wear in their eyes, to counter-reproach them, he said to Marc:

"You are still giving the 'Pop-Op Ball'?"

Bruno was on his feet again. His anger now seemed condensed, controlled, like a coiled spring, and it came out of him with a knife edge of sarcasm as he said overpolitely:

"By all means, *monsieur le Président*, we are indeed giving the ball. Balls are part of our way of living. Everybody likes a party, especially when times are bad. Poor people give little parties. Rich people give big parties. Wolfflens give balls. They are part of our tradition, and without tradition, people, rich or poor, are very poor indeed. But more important, balls are very beautiful—"

Who would have believed it? There was Wild Bruno on his feet, arguing for Thérèse, as if his own wildness had touched base in this instant of great stress with her folly and had revealed in it something that had struck Marc when he'd first fallen in love with her, something still breathtaking that raised Thérèse's extravagant ways, all of them, her lovers, her balls, beyond lust and pomp, to a defiant, existential grandeur of panache. Worthy of a Borgia, or a Wolfflen.

Bruno's anger was uncoiling too quickly for him to hold back now. "Balls are beautiful, as you know, having attended several of ours." His voice was gaining volume. "Maybe, nowadays, if we stopped giving balls, there would be none, they would vanish from the history of this country. That would be a loss. And bear in mind," he said, and now he was shouting, "that when we spend money on a ball we give it to somebody. We put money in the hands of a number of hard-working people. The decorations, for example, require artisans. And it is in the interest of France that those people and their crafts survive. We pay the best caterers, who maintain our nation's proud art of cooking, yes? What I mean is, we don't just stash the money away in Switzerland! The way other people are doing every day, right under the nose of your Minister of Finance!"

Robinet might have pressed some button. The Chevallier woman was in the room in an instant. She glared at the Wolfflens like a housekeeper who had come upon burglars.

Marc took Bruno by the arm and extended his hand to Robinet, murmuring goodbye. They all got out of there in a hurry. That might have been the last time they'd see Gaston Robinet.

". . . Thanks," Marc said in the hallway.

"Cousin . . ." Bruno answered. Nothing more. His face was still upset. He walked ahead to catch up with Gilbert.

"How is Cynthia?" he asked.

"Sorry?"

"How is Cynthia Ashe?"

"She's left for California," Gilbert said, fixing his eyes ahead of him on a Gobelin tapestry, keeping his face in profile. "To make a picture."

Then he faced Bruno bleakly. "Have you been talking to my stepmother?"

"No . . . Oh no." Bruno shot a glance back at Marc, who, watching Gilbert pass onto the steps, observed half-consciously that there was no trace of femininity in his gait.

Marc took the wheel of the car on the way back. His stomach was killing him as he nodded to the salute of the Elysée guard in nineteenth-century dress. He gunned the Citroën through the entrance. Then he made a note in his mind to do two things: he would check to be sure Godwin Laver had been sent an invitation to the Pop-Op Ball, and he would have a talk as soon as he could with Beauchamps, the head currency specialist at the bank.

Suddenly, he felt like a man who had to come back off a ledge. He was in terrible trouble, and yet, up there, the whole world seemed so small and far, he couldn't help but relax. Something in his abdomen unknotted, the pain smoothed out into a dull throb. He would try every move possible. And finally, all that out there, to some remote objective Eye, couldn't be really any bigger than it seemed now, from his desperate perch.

Across the street from the Elysée, a crowd had gathered on the sidewalk. For a second, Marc flushed with anger, thinking that for some perverse reason, Robinet had made their visit public. Then he recalled that the morning news had reported an invitation, for four o'clock, from Robinet to the heads of all three labor unions, who were threatening another day-long general strike.

It was ten of four.

FIVE

Godwin Laver sat in a beach chair outside his cabaña apartment at the Beverly Wilshire Hotel and watched his eighteen-year-old daughter, Alice, breaststroke almost silently, with cat grace, back and forth across the pool.

She'd swum all morning, gluttonously, while he was talking with his American partners and their Los Angeles bankers, getting the last funding details straight for what his partners had originally—ludicrously, he thought—wanted to call Open City. The name was dangerous, he'd argued finally. It was the argument that had worked. What could they call it? The name would matter . . .

Alice could still get excited about swimming in the winter, though she'd been all over the world with him. She's unspoiled, he told himself. Even though he treated her with a widower's indulgence—and that of a man with enormous means. Unspoiled? On reflection, he wasn't sure, and he wasn't a man to fool himself to make himself feel good. She hadn't really been tried by anything, by any important experience. Naïve might not be the word, either, for her frank, primitive enthusiasms. She was like her mother on that score. More than her rearing, he thought, it was probably her Indian blood revealing itself.

Alice had jumped at the chance to go with him to the United States. And Godwin was making this a very pleasant, useful trip.

The terms of the financing of the real estate project were falling nicely into place. Money was scarce in America, but his name carried weight even out here.

His partners were young hotshots who'd got an option on an unspoiled, wooded piece of coastland at an incredibly good price. They were in their early thirties or late twenties, all three of them, and hadn't quite understood what he meant when he said Open City brought to mind Anna Magnani being abused by Germans in uniform. He'd convinced them with his second argument: "Call it Open City and you'll have the Hell's Angels fighting with the guards every night to get in."

The project was a village of private houses with maid service, maintenance, pools, golf and a clubhouse-nightclub, for rich "raised consciousness" people of all sexes, living separately or in whatever version of plurality they chose. The only important ban was on children. Children, all the partners agreed, would make for all kinds of problems.

The name Open City was supposed to suggest "the sense of freedom and adventure that characterized the community," but the more Godwin thought about that name, the worse it sounded to him. The place was going to indeed be heavily protected, and any newspaper reporter who came along would have fun with the suggestion of hypocrisy. And Godwin didn't like hypocrisy in any case. He had, he thought, certain clear and open ways of looking at the world and if certain people called him a Fascist, it was, he thought, because he was not hypocritical about his opinions.

After the morning's conference, he'd dropped in unannounced, celebrity to celebrity, to say hello to Billy Sterling at the office of Ultimate Pictures. Billy, the Chief of Production, had been introduced to Godwin by Harold Burwine, who ran the conglomerate Ultimate belonged to now. Burwine was just about the last conglomerate-juggler still keeping his dumbbells in the air, and Godwin considered him a genius. Billy was flashy but entertaining and very kind toward other people's egos, untypically "nice" for Hollywood and probably insincere, finally. He was Godwin's age but he looked ten years younger, while Godwin looked any age from forty-five to fifty-five.

Billy always rounded up good-looking girls when he came to Paris, and Godwin liked to join Billy's restaurant dinner parties to sop up a little cheap glamor. They were fun. Billy Sterling's flashiness was acceptable to Laver because he was natural, he was Hollywood.

Godwin had left a note with Sterling's secretary to find out at what number he could reach Cynthia Ashe at about seven this evening. Sterling was producing the picture Cynthia had told Godwin about when he'd last run into her at Régine's discothèque in Paris.

He'd be in Los Angeles in a week, he'd told her, and they'd have to have dinner together. Godwin had never had dinner alone with Cynthia, but they were both part of a group of a hundred-odd Parisians who were all on at least a small-talk basis with each other. It was the group more or less defined by fame and money, and you could fill out its roster by going through the party photo captions of *Vogue.*

Cynthia had been at Régine's that evening with Gilbert de Wolfflen. Gilbert had looked at him with a trace of hostility when he'd suggested dinner. She was about to become engaged to Gilbert, so people said, but Godwin didn't believe in that match for a minute.

Gilbert's stepmother, Thérèse de Wolfflen, was dead set against it, and Thérèse had a long record of having her way in this world. "Wolfflens are not destined to marry actresses," she was going around saying. "Fucking and marrying are two different things," she'd say (bad words had become chic), and she'd simper: "but I can't imagine what Gilbert is doing . . ." Thérèse, of course, feared Cynthia's youthful chic like the plague. People were also saying that Cynthia had left France with an ultimatum to handsome Gilbert: formalize things or forget it. People were enjoying the whole drama.

The whole thing is a can of worms, Godwin thought, and it didn't concern him at all. He and Cynthia would simply be two Parisians from the same group, both in the same foreign city, and it would be quite natural for them to have a pleasant dinner together and compare observations of the strange local ways. If things got beyond that—and he brightened to suppose for the first time, now, that they might—well, they'd be two consenting adults.

Just then, one of the hotel's Mexicans in a red tunic brought him a message that seemed an omen: Miss Ashe could be reached after seven-thirty at KL-5-4563. He drew a cigar from the Hermès leather case on the table beside his chair. A Cuban Larrañaga he'd smuggled past American customs. He clipped the end with the gold clip that had lain by the cigar case, and lit his smoke in a carefully sensual way. All in all, as his new partners would put it, he felt "very good vibrations" about this entire trip.

Before going to Los Angeles, Godwin Laver had stopped in Las Vegas. He'd had a little fun at the roulette tables and he'd had a long conversation with Kyle Hoyt. Though they'd never met before, they'd huddled together, at ease with each other, over a series of drinks, like two men who knew the same secret hand grips. Hoyt was a man at the end of his rope, but he hadn't at all been urgent or obsequious with Laver. He was obviously drinking a lot, but the three or four scotch and sodas he'd downed as they'd talked had in no way befuddled him. They'd seemed almost to give him a harder, more monumental presence. He'd sipped and grown more and more—almost Buddha-like, Laver thought. His movements were spare and slow, his voice measured, sure—*sure*. He was tough and faintly ironic. In that hotel suite, Laver felt he'd entered Hoyt's bunker. A dark, Mediterranean-looking man in shirtsleeves and brown sharkskin pants sat in a chair facing the door. His—bodyguard? My God . . .

"What are you into over here, Godwin?"

"Oh . . . property . . ."

"Ah uh . . . That's the coming thing . . ."

Hoyt had sounded like the old pro, giving his benediction to the neophyte. Laver had accepted it gracefully, knowing he was, indeed, a generation ahead in his thinking compared to Hoyt. Hoyt, who'd had his cover of *Time*. ("The clout of energetic acumen" was the wordsmiths' word for him.)

At the end of his rope . . . sitting there like a gentleman . . . with the shifty-eyed greaser picking his teeth near the door.

"There's only so much copper in the earth," Laver had got around to saying.

On the table near the couch there was an envelope that had contained a letter from Hoyt's wife, sent from an address in Wisconsin.

"You understand . . ." Hoyt had answered. Something flared in his glassy eyes. "Ah huh . . . you're the kind of man to understand."

Godwin Laver understood. Raw materials. The coming thing . . .

People who did not like Godwin Laver liked to call him a gambler. He had a taste for speculation. And the courage, he told himself. He was a heavy better at Deauville, Monte Carlo, or wherever he found himself near a gaming table. He was a ferocious backgammon opponent, he was hard to beat at poker. Except for one brief interval in his life, he'd gambled a lot (but never compulsively) since he'd inherited the base of his fortune. He had also, a little later on, borrowed at great peril for some land dealings that were, as others saw them, very risky. They'd brought him more money than he'd been heir to.

But all in all Laver didn't conceive of himself, of his essential self, as a gambler. All his business thinking now was based on some very simple and solid long-range principles. Godwin Laver was an early example of the doomsday-minded capitalists who were to grow in number as the last quarter of the twentieth century steamed toward its finish, throwing off an immense cloud of pollution.

The planet was finally showing clear signs of wearing out. The West had lost its will to dominate the world, and insure itself cheap raw materials. In twenty years, Godwin figured, Paris and London would look like Calcutta. You had to have claim to things everyone needed, and be willing to fight to hold them, if you were to avoid the horror for yourself.

Godwin had had some projections done on copper, and Cofra interested him. The Wolfflens interested him. By the time he'd met with Hoyt, he'd thought of an answer to the company's current problems. It involved a gamble. But he'd calculated the necessary stake to be no more than $3 million, which he could well afford to lose. And he hadn't had the pleasure of a big risk in a long time.

Aside from soybeans, whose situation he'd learned intimately, Laver had steered clear of all the will o' the wisps in commodities, the cocoa bonanzas, the sugar killings—he wasn't involved in any of the markets that for an outsider had more than two green numbers on the wheel.

Instead, in a large, exceptionally modern warehouse in Düsseldorf, under optimal atmospheric conditions, there was several million dollars worth of cowhide in the name of Godwin Laver. Once Laver had read that the current world herd-count was such, that if some time in the next five years the Soviet citizens were to reach the level of consumption of one pair of shoes per year, there would be a drastic world scarcity of leather. Godwin knew leather.

Godwin recalled that the year of his father's death, he'd inherited enough shoe money to be able to live on just the interest of sure investments, without ever having to get involved in business at all.

And during one short interlude in his life that followed, he thought he could live that way. It was possible that his terrible luck then was fate telling him he'd strayed onto the wrong path. He could believe in fate. He didn't know of anything better to believe in.

But that had been such a fantastic moment. But—

His mind suddenly got caught on a worn bit of verse, two lines from Webster that T.S. Eliot had dredged up. (Godwin read poetry, for he considered himself a "basically romantic person.") The lines took hold of his consciousness and he heard them, like it or not.

"But that was in another country—"

He managed, just in time, to alter the cruel bite of the second line—for *her* sake, for his own—

And besides the woman is dead.

She'd died giving birth to Alice. *The Spanish doctor.*

He stubbed out his cigar, half-consumed, before it became bitter. And he called to his daughter—that perfect image of her mother—to come out of the water at last and have a late lunch with him.

SIX

After he'd dropped Cynthia off, Godwin had his driver take him all up and down Sunset Boulevard. It was an impulse he couldn't explain, beyond the certainty that he wouldn't be able to sleep if he went straight back to the hotel. It was 3:30 in the morning, the dregs of a not too pleasant night.

It had turned out that Cynthia was staying on a hilltop above Santa Monica with Bill Summer, the fashion designer she knew from her cover-girl days, and his husband or wife, a philosophy professor at Berkeley. When Godwin came to get Cynthia, they offered drinks. Hal, the mate, had made Godwin uneasy from the start. Godwin asked what he did and he got a long, drawn-out explanation of logical positivism. It sounded like a lot of crap. "We *know* what you do," Bill sneered, and what was that supposed to have meant? When Godwin and Cynthia left, the two men were going on to another round of bloodies. When they got back, all the lights were still on in that house, which was nearly all glass and built, in confusing levels, into the hillside; Bill and Hal were having a bad row, and there was a third man there with them. Godwin gathered very quickly that the third man, a Frenchman who'd married an old American mannequin Cynthia knew and become an ad man in California, had been seduced by Hal. Hal had apparently suggested, after several bloodies, that they all three talk the whole matter over sensibly, without the mannequin of course, who'd left for the East with her kids. But when the Frenchman arrived everything had gone wild. Hal was very drunk and was threatening alternately to jump over the edge of the mountain or put a chair through a glass wall. All three of them were shouting obscenities, and the Frenchman was also weeping.

Cynthia ran in and moved around from one to the other, hugging them, kissing them, calming them down. They stopped shouting and Hal, at last, with the voice of a dowager offering tea, asked Godwin if he'd like a drink for the road. Godwin kissed Cynthia on her cheeks and got out, waving a vague farewell to all.

Cynthia had many homosexual friends, a fact that didn't help Gilbert de Wolfflen's cause, Godwin reflected. Before him, she'd frequently be escorted around by a faggot. This was actually a habit among girls her age, he'd noted, girls in their twenties, in the fashion-social milieu. They were said to enjoy the boys' looks, their way of dressing, their wit, and the fact that they didn't make any aggressive demands. But Godwin considered this habit, and his observation that the number of fags around was growing geometrically, to be another sign that the world was sick and getting sicker.

Cynthia was also said to have liked Older Men. And he, Godwin realized, as he sat slumped sullenly in the back of his hired Continental, was an Older Man now. It hadn't helped. Neither had he made any demands. He hadn't sensed an opening. Maybe she liked older men because they, too, didn't often make demands. What did she really like?

Should he have hired a sportscar? Gilbert had a Ferrari. The idea of setting himself in competition with that cow-eyed young man—his train of thought, he discovered, had really come to that—seemed suddenly ridiculous. Anyway, Gilbert wasn't that young either, he was about thirty, over the hill. Forget it!

Godwin snorted at his own foolishness. The driver cocked his ear.

"Nothing," Godwin said.

But the driver had taken the stirring of life back there as an invitation to communicate.

"She's breathing easy now," he said.

"Uh?"

"Yeah . . . she's breathing good. I can always tell when there's less pollution. She accelerates in a whole other way. She's a completely different car."

Godwin snorted again. But his laughter was pleasureless. He was in a black mood.

His mood had fallen the moment they entered the restaurant. He knew it was the place to go with a young girl, but when they walked in he recalled that he loathed the place. The Bistro. Fake. Nothing really French about it. He hated the gloomy light, the smoked mirrors, the crowding of the tables and the stupid slate menu the waiter pushed around with idiotic pomp from table to table. His lamb chop was cold, fatty, muttony, and he had to send it back to be heated, whereupon it came back overdone. He looked at the sleek and cheap Hollywood people at the other tables, for whom this was really the place to be, and he reminded himself with added unpleasantness that here was more proof that the world was getting sicker.

Cynthia ate a salad and a platter of cooked vegetables. She "took," she said, "as little meat as possible into my system." Meat produced aggressiveness.

She went on to say a lot of equally silly things. A jumble of white magic, gurus, and fetishes.

It didn't help his evening for him to learn that she was "not feeling very up."

Sterling had neglected to tell him that Cynthia had just been dropped from her picture. She'd come over for her first important role, after having done several big parts in Europe. James Gaetano, one of the important new young men in Hollywood, had been fascinated by her looks. He'd decided he wanted to direct her in a mystery movie patterned after the Bogart movies of the forties. She was to be the mysterious leading female, who didn't have much to say.

But whatever she'd said apparently didn't please Gaetano. He was bringing in Lee Remick to take Cynthia's place.

"Bad luck," Godwin had said, sipping his thick California wine, much vaunted by the *sommelier*, which might have been better if it had been opened two days ago. What could he really have said? She'd shrugged, and pulled at one of her necklaces.

As for all that stuff, her modish superstitions, Godwin didn't quite know what to say either. He believed vaguely in fate himself, yes, but he never *relied* on it.

Her superstitions seemed to dangle from her conversation like all that hardware from her neck—and most of those items, too, were full of powers, she assured him. She wore an ebony ear from the Seychelles on a leather necklace, to absorb all "the bad vibrations" sent into the air by people saying bad things about her.

"You know who," she said, smiling, then hurried to explain that when the ear could absorb no more of that kind of poison it would crack, and she'd have to journey back, halfway and more across the world, to get another.

Yes all that sort of nonsense was in fashion in these strange times, Godwin thought, and yet she seemed so childishly sincere about them. Childish. And again, she was far from a child. At eighteen, she'd lived for nearly a year with Nicky Fallan, a fashion photographer. After Fallan, she'd moved to Rome with Giancarlo Testa, the moody young Apollo of intellectual Italian movies, who was supposed to be bisexual, and from there, from Testa, who'd seemed physically the answer to any teenage prayer, she went on to Gilbert de Wolfflen. Godwin realized that he didn't think much of any of her lovers. Apparently she was ambitious. Apparently, all her superstitions had something to do with the anxieties of her ambition. And yet there seemed to be more. At dinner she'd kept bringing up the term "good values." So and so, had "good values." He forgot who, barely listening as he studied her face. She seemed to have a childlike anxiety that there might be too many things in the world unexplainably unfair. With her superstitions, she seemed to tinker with the unknown, in the hopes of insuring fairness. And luck. Which, finally, weren't all that compatible. A child.

Her face even had an adolescent gawkiness to it. Her famous huge eyes seemed out of balance with her long features. She was photogenic, all right. Pretty in her funny way, but her face seemed to be going through a stage when everything on it was not exactly developing at the same pace. Someday it would all come into harmony. But no, she was already past twenty-four. Those features were there for life. They could grow on you.

He took her to The Candy Store after dinner. At the door when they arrived, someone unacceptable was having a punchup with the bouncer. Fighting seemed to have been in the air that night. Maybe he was lucky not to have parted with Cynthia on worse terms. At worst, the evening might have bored her, although he'd kept her on the floor for nearly every dance. But in retrospect, he might have danced like a fool, too frenetically, compared to that stiff, cold, new thing that she and a number of the others were doing.

She'd just given him her cheeks without kissing him back when he'd left her. It hadn't been a successful evening, and now he decided that, if he were more superstitious, he'd suspect that this city spooked him. He decided he didn't care for it at all. It made him almost physically uneasy—there was no real city here, it was all road, as everyone invariably remarked. But he, Godwin, sensed he needed more, an enveloping presence, not to shelter him exactly, but to put him at ease—he felt like a man who couldn't sleep uncovered.

And here on Sunset Boulevard, heading back toward La Cienega now, he was in a quintessence of the place, not its heart—there was none. Just this Strip. And he'd immersed himself in it with a certain defiance. But it continued to spook him. And all across America, he recalled, in the suburban and exurban sprawl, there were strips such as this one, arteries that lead to no heart but were themselves elongated centers, arraying all a man needs to consume. Somewhere attached to the strip stood a man's house, somewhere else his job, in between he lived as a spender. Sign after sign called out the presence of something to consume. Here was a fast food place, Steer Inn, here beyond it the billboard of a mortician, here there was a bar with a "live show." Signs of almost equal size; size of sign meant nothing, had no relation to the importance of the need they called to, as if here a man were so totally *serviced* that a scale of values didn't matter, all needs were equally stated. Casuistry.

Put a man through this trough of stores and showrooms, over and over, strip him of his manpower, then his spending power, then his lusts, his orgones or whatever, put him through like a battery calf who'd never seen daylight from womb to destruction, and drop him off, finally, somewhere on the strip, at some mortician, "Funeral Director" or whatever. His wife could settle with a credit card, the sign said. And now, after years of "consumer democracy," of more and more for all, the people were going to have to go the same road for less and less.

This strip was America. And Europe was turning into something not too different. They called Godwin Laver a Fascist, but one thing he knew he wasn't: he wasn't any Samuel Smiles of the Consumer Society. He hated it, saw through it, and he believed that all the counterculture business, the "organic" business and the hippy business and the cults and the drugs did nothing to change the fact that the setup gave a man only one choice: between being powerful or having the power act upon him. What now seemed a long time ago, Godwin had made his choice. For himself and for his progeny, if that were at all possible these days. Hopefully, at least for Alice.

He made his way unsurely through the long empty corridors of the Beverly Wilshire; at each corner he hesitated, to confirm in his mind the direction of the pool. He'd stayed here many times, and each time he'd taken a cabaña apartment, but he'd never quite mastered the hall scheme. Now the maze seemed exceptionally unpleasant. At last he recognized the right door.

The pool fountain had stopped working. There were streaks like grease in the Los Angeles night sky. Here there was a moist stink in the air. He wondered absurdly if those guests they were accepting had been peeing in the pool. His daughter went in that water . . . He sat down, still wide awake, even if his mind had become vulnerable to absurdity.

He thought again—as he often did—about the Wolfflens. Their financial power was no longer anything like what it once was. Godwin didn't consider himself a boor, he knew enough about music and painting for most dinner conversations, but he had no truly brilliant friends outside of business. The Wolfflens were close to all kinds of people. Along with all her clothing designers, decorators, rich Americans, and international hangers-on, Thérèse de Wolfflen's guest list for the Pop-Op Ball, Godwin ventured, would include all the best-known painters in Paris, Rudolf Nureyev, and at least Herbert von Karajan. They will have all accepted. Going to a Wolfflen Ball was taking part in history.

Godwin had his invitation. He was glad the Bison thing had been settled in a civilized way. But it rankled him, nonetheless, that his partnership with the Wolfflens hadn't materialized. It depressed him to wonder why Bruno had felt compelled to get the best of him on the stock. Afterwards, Godwin had turned the company around, had fired all the people who had to be fired, the people Marc had held onto admirably but catastrophically all the same. He'd changed the supermarket group's whole advertising strategy. He'd opened a highly profitable chain of stores in Belgium. The Wolfflens, Godwin thought, could have shared the advantages he'd brought in.

Yet with all their befuddlements and eccentricities he couldn't help but admire them. The pity was that Bruno never understood what Godwin had really been offering in Bison: friendship. He wasn't just a money-grubbing businessman. He, too, had lofty motives. Maybe even Bruno could be made to understand that now. Now, in Cofra. He could save them . . .

The canvas of his chair was damp. What time was it? His watch said four. Nearly four in the morning. He rose and stretched. Yes, and there was only so much copper in the earth.

Inside, through the faint hum of the air system of his cabaña, Laver thought he could make out the sound of Alice breathing next door. His mind welled again with sentiment. She was like her mother. In her grace, her manners, which stood out in an age of tough, vulgar women. And like her mother, she had that remoteness, a side of her he was too shy or fearful—or insensitive, he asked himself—to understand fully. Yet that remoteness, which at times could seem so cold, could fill him with awe. It was something outside his own familiar desires and hopes, inexplicably attractive and admirable.

Alice was a girl of great quality. Godwin was too wise to believe that he could totally control her life, given the times they were living in, but he wanted very much for her to find an enclave of quality equal to her own, to harbor her. The sickness of the times was likely to be nothing compared to whatever turbulent mess lay ahead for the world. He wanted her to live among the important and brilliant people of her epoch, at a safe height; without ever having to struggle socially and be false or cunning as a consequence.

Several times, at a number of parties, it gave him pleasure to notice her in conversation with Gilbert de Wolfflen. After all, Gilbert was handsome and he was very gentle. And Alice was far better looking, far more appropriate a match for him than Cynthia Ashe.

But in this last moment of rumination, Cynthia's face was the one that formed most clearly in his mind, dominating it finally. That funny face.

"Thérèse would like nothing better than for me to sit out in

California and not show my face at her ball," she was saying, cramped beside him at that little restaurant table in the half-dark. Their knees had been jammed together. "But you see," she sighed, "there's nothing here now to keep me ... and I wouldn't miss any show that she puts on for the world. Give her her due.

"I won't hide," she'd said, "she can't count on me for that. It's Gilbert's father's birthday ..."

Tough old child, he thought.

Like me, he realized, and decided not to give that thought any clear examination. He headed for bed, for sleep, he hoped. He looked forward to checking out before noon.

SEVEN

Through the double glass front of Hubert Beauchamps' office, the scene in the next room resembled a silent comedy. There were four men with four phones each, each man rushing from phone to phone. The glass muffled their rapid talk into pantomime.

Marc de Wolfflen looked out for a moment, with his back to Beauchamps. Out there was his bank's foreign exchange operation, a small currency department as currency departments went. The Banque Wolfflen hadn't been very active in exchange for some years. Even before Marc had taken over.

"Three hundred million dollars," Beauchamp was saying in a neutral voice, that nearly absent tone of a man who had sought the right tone and failed to find it.

Beauchamps was a solid, conservative man. He favored interest arbitrage—the hedged pursuit of currencies paying the highest interest at the moment—over speculation. He was a rare figure now in his field. Most good currency men had developed a taste for risks, and if you wouldn't let them gamble, they'd leave you, and you'd be left with people not sharp enough to follow the market. Beauchamps was sharp, but old fashioned.

He said again, as if coming to a sum of numbers: "That makes a three-hundred-million-dollar forward position distributed over less than a month."

Marc turned. Beauchamps had heard correctly. "Yes," Marc said quietly, "twelve contracts two months forward, a few days apart each, as of today. Twenty-five million dollars each." He crossed his arms and stared at the photo of his father beside his own on the wall behind Beauchamps' desk. He's worked for both of us, Marc thought, he's older than I am, even. Sixty-what? Beauchamps was a heavy little man with black hair on either side of the wide stripe of baldness that ran across the top of his head. Always the same anthracite wool suit. The same one or one of several identical ones, it was impossible to tell. White shirt, dark tie. And in this total look of absent or hidden personality Beauchamps' age was also hidden. You never thought of his age.

Beauchamps, Marc knew, had two hobbies: stamps and cooking. And that was all Marc knew about him as a person beyond his function at the bank. Marc thought about those photos behind the desk, and became conscious of his dislike for them. Not the particular photos, but the idea. There was something feudal or Fascistic about it, he thought. He recalled the photos of Gaston Robinet in his tails and presidential sash in all the public buildings, and he didn't like those either. But people always had to have people to follow, not just ideas. It bothered him to think of himself tacked up there, as Hubert Beauchamps' Leader. For a second, he felt a tinge of guilt.

"Dollars for Deutschemarks," he said.

"At?"

"At two-eighty to the dollar. Each contract."

Marc was making an enormous bet against the consensus of opinion in the market. That morning the dollar was worth 2.85 Deutschemarks. There was a strong feeling the dollar would soon rise to three. Europe was in a hole for dollars to pay for the multiplied costs of its Arab oil imports, and the United States depended on Arab oil for less than ten percent of its needs. The dollar was expected to rally against all European currency, and Marc was betting that in two months it would be worth less against the mark than it was today.

He could explain his opinion, but he wouldn't explain the reason the bank, which had never gambled, was gambling now. Why, that is, Marc de Wolfflen was gambling. He could try to tell an intimate, but he realized that he had no one intimate enough to tell in his life. Beauchamps was a stranger, despite his years of service; all Marc could hope from him was tact.

Beauchamps was silent. It was his silence that prodded Marc to say: "The Germans will never let their payments balance deteriorate, Hubert. They'd go into recession first, they'd burn the Black Forest for fuel." He added, for credence: "I happen to know they have a number of heavy machinery export deals practically assured, which will keep their payments situation well ahead. The mark is solid."

"And the dollar," Beauchamps said with a note of complicity now, "is rotten at the core."

Maybe Beauchamps agreed with Marc about the Deutschemark. Certainly, he must not have agreed on a three-hundred-million-dollar bet. But as their eyes met then, Marc felt the contact: Beauchamps seemed to understand at least that some profound, lonely decision had brought Marc to his office, some decision taken beyond commonplace calculation. And he wasn't going to violate that decision with an opinion. Marc felt an impulse to grip Beauchamps' hand with both of his. Hubert was profoundly a gentleman.

"We couldn't do it in France," Beauchamps said. "The bank of France would notice our ... extreme position. They wouldn't allow it to go on past the month."

"The branch in Luxembourg," Marc said, "is under local laws. They can do it. You can send them instructions."

"Yes."

For a few seconds Beauchamps wore a look of distress, but he turned away to make a note on his desk calendar. Three hundred million dollars was a large amount of trading, although, of course, Marc didn't need three hundred million to play the game, a game being played by important financial groups all over the world. All he needed was the good name of The Banque Wolfflen. He was ordering contracts to deliver $25 million for Deutschemarks on each day of a given number of days, starting two months from now. When the contracts fell due, the bank would borrow the dollars that had to be delivered, and the people on the other end of the contracts would borrow the marks. It was easy for a respected member of the financial community to borrow the money just for a few days. The borrowed money would be exchanged, at the rate agreed on in the contract: 2.80 marks to the dollar. When Marc would get his Deutschemarks, he would have to change them back into dollars to repay his loan. He would change them at that day's rate, and the difference between that day's rate and the rate of 2.80 to the dollar, plus his interest costs, would determine how much he won or lost on his transaction. If he lost, he'd have to come up with more money than he got in changing his marks to repay the loan. If the dollar went to three, and stayed around three during the period his contracts fell due, the Banque Wolfflen would be out roughly $20 million.

"Telex Luxembourg before lunch, will you Hubert? No. Telephone, and confirm by mail."

"Right away." Beauchamps stood up. Marc rose from his chair beside the desk. They shook hands, as they always did when Marc left Beauchamps' office. Marc held onto Beauchamps' hand. He felt that the revelation he was about to make was a weakness; Beauchamps might well prefer to know nothing personal at all. He was discreet, gallant, but he wasn't a friend, and yet Marc sensed that saying at least what he was going to say was in some way also a kindness—not so much because it would reassure Beauchamps of his own safety, but because it would affirm that what was going on was something beyond the game-playing and money-grubbing of speculation and the ledgerbooks of business. He said, human being to human being:

"You know, Hubert, if I could do this myself, in my own name, I would. . . . But there's the law; I couldn't. But you mustn't have the slightest concern. If we lose, I'll make it up. I'll make it all good with the bank. Personally."

Beauchamps tightened his handshake. "Yes . . . I understand." Marc looked at him a second and then lowered his eyes. They fell on the little ribbon of the Resistance that brightened the lapel of Beauchamps' coal-gray suit.

"Thank you very much," Marc said.

On his way back to the Associates' Room, Marc thought again of what he stood to win: maybe as much as $40 million if his feeling about the mark was right. A lot of money. And yet he couldn't place its importance. It wouldn't be enough to do what had to be done with Cofra. If he lost, he'd sell Bois Brûlé, he'd already decided that. He'd sell the land. There was enough there to build a good-sized town—only a half-hour's train ride from Paris. He would give the château to the government. They could call it the Wolfflen Museum. It was a perfect example of Second Empire architecture. But as Marc saw it in his mind now, it looked like one of those great railroad stations Charles' father had built for the lines the Wolfflens no longer owned.

He thought: And if there were really someone intimate enough in my life to tell, I still couldn't tell it. I couldn't explain it so that it could be totally understood. All the pending business of his life seemed so totally absurd to him now. He would go on, he would do all he could to save Cofra, but for him it had all gone beyond desperation. It had gone beyond meaning. And now it was as if he'd jumped off one ledge onto another. The world out there seemed no clearer, no closer to him. But now at least he would satisfy in a very stern, cleanly defined way one point of great curiosity that remained: this adventure, which in a way was extraneous, merely parallel to his life, might tell him whether or not he was born to lose. He laughed to himself dryly. At himself. He was— He realized that, where he stood now, *he* wasn't yet clear to himself, either.

EIGHT

The subway, gas, and electrical workers had gone on strike the morning of the Pop-Op Ball. It was a wildcat movement: the bargaining sessions with the ailing President had dragged on for more than a month, far too slowly for the young extremists in the rank-and-file.

The route out of Paris toward Marc de Wolfflen's château, Bois Brûlé, was jammed with cars full of people who'd been trapped in traffic hours past the end of their working day. The streets of the lower-class suburb, Noisy-le-sec, were black. Papers carried by the wind flashed in the beams of headlights and flapped against the cars like crazed bats. Edmée de Wolfflen, sitting beside her husband, Bruno, in Bruno's Rolls, jumped back in her seat, startled, and shielded her face with her forearm.

"Just paper, *madame la Baronne*," the driver said without flinching. He worked his windshield wiper until it was gone.

Edmée's nerves were raw. She pulled the Mickey Mouse beany from her head with an irritated gesture, and laid it between herself and her husband.

"I'll fix it in place," Bruno offered.

"Fix what? This whole thing is just a little too much."

"We've got through the worst of the traffic," their daughter soothed. Iris was beside the chauffeur, her tall trunk erect in a stiff tunic representing the cone of an ice cream cone. A great round cowl, the ice cream, hid her head from her parents.

"Why don't you look at it as a little fun," Bruno told his wife.

Bruno tugged at the corkscrew he'd had fixed, one half on each side, to his head. It held. (That was his "optical illusion." Putting it on, he'd told Edmée: "People think I'm screwy"—he'd used the English word, relishing it—"but it's purely an illusion.")

She said now: "It's stupid, it's distasteful, it's untimely, and we're making ourselves a part of it."

"We're a part of it, like it or not," he answered. "We might as well *assume* the whole thing, and do it well."

She didn't answer, nor did Iris. As they sat silently the car drove into country. In a while, they saw lights dancing on the plane trees.

Marc had hired the local police to stand out with flashlights and indicate the last few turnoffs on the way to the château. Ahead, there was already a caravan of big sleek automobiles. Bruno's chauffeur slowed down a few cars behind where Gilbert de Wolfflen sat in his yellow Ferrari, with Cynthia Ashe beside him.

"There's the couple of the year," Bruno said.

"The year is almost over," Edmée said.

The last few hundred meters before the gate of the château were lined with policemen; behind them, a crowd of local people stood about three deep, peering into the cars. The caravan had nearly come to a halt—the cars ahead were guided into parking spots inside the gate. Long black vehicles were shuttling the guests the last kilometer to the château.

"Hearses!" Bruno observed.

"Too much," his wife said.

"Listen, Edmée," he said impatiently "we don't have any choice. It's Marc's wife. It's Marc—"

"You've become very resigned," she said. It was as if she'd thrust a knife in his ribs, and she regretted it the instant she'd said it.

He said with astounding calm: "Certain things can't be changed, Edmée ... I've broken my neck trying. Too many disappointments, all right?"

"I'm sorry," she said huskily, squeezing the muscle of his arm.

"I'm sorry," Iris said.

He leaned forward. "What the hell are you sorry about?"

"I'm ... not a son."

He was struggling with his anger to find an answer, to find his true target, when suddenly an empty wine bottle flew out from somewhere in the crowd and bounced off the hood of Gilbert's sports car, just missing the windshield. Gilbert bounded out of his car and tore his way into the crowd. Bruno could make out the cape of Gilbert's Batman costume flailing around. Gilbert was in a fight and with more than one person. Bruno jumped out of the Rolls.

Policemen came running by. Edmée saw them tear Bruno and Gilbert apart from the teenagers with whom they were scuffling. A handful of the police dragged the three boys off, behind the crowd, while some others formed a wall between the crowd and the cars. Two of the three had bleeding mouths, and the third a great welt on his cheekbones.

Bruno came back to the car whacking dust off his tailcoat. "Damn it," he said, "my handle."

Bruno and the chauffeur walked back to the scene of the fight. Gilbert was standing there, holding his elbows, trembling slightly, but his face was glowing with a strange and somewhat unpleasant look of joy.

"You all right, son?" Bruno asked.

Gilbert nodded, breathing heavily.

"You sure."

Gilbert took his cousin's arm, to lead him away.

"Yes," he said. "You all right?"

"God, yes," Bruno said, smiling. "... I lost my screw."

Some policemen pointed their flashlights on the ground, and in their light, the driver fumbled on his hands and knees until he found the handle to the Baron Bruno's corkscrew.

NINE

He'd been showered with happy birthdays. *"Bon anniversaire!" Happy birthday!* And now he felt sodden with them. For a full hour and a half, Marc had stood with Thérèse at the head of the ballroom stairs, receiving. Handshake after handshake, kisses, while the *boyeur* announced the names and titles of Thérèse's guests through a 1950's lozenge-shaped microphone. Marc estimated that there were a thousand people in his house. Presents were piled to the ceiling in the room below the stairs. Thérèse had revealed her gift before the guests arrived: another yearling. From America. "Getaway," it was called. A born winner, there could be no doubt, because in recent years, Thérèse had discovered she could choose good horses the way some people go around with a twig and find water. She didn't know more about horses than what a winner looked like—which was something she could not describe.

Thérèse was flushed with happiness. The last guests had dribbled in. All the people she had really wanted had come. Some had flown over especially from New York, among them "Suzy" and Felicia Hart, the columnists. Miss Hart, an indefatigable little woman in her sixties, had come as a New York City fire hydrant, and leashed to her, got up as a comic strip dog, was her photographer. Thérèse had promised there would be no press, but "Suzy and Felicia are friends, not ordinary reporters!" she'd argued. The French press, she'd insisted, was totally banned, and Felicia's photographer was forbidden to sell his pictures to any French paper. Marc had let the matter drop. No one could think of hiding this party.

The guests had made great efforts: "Pop-Op" had become an excuse for anything outlandish. They were going along with her in her folly, all the way. Marc could sense a bacchic excitement. Loosened inhibitions. Many of the women were dressed provocatively. Lili Manderes, the wife of the man who once ruled the Philippines, had arrived last, wearing only a black string bathing suit under her fox coat. To her navel, she'd attached a metal spiral rotated by a toy motor. Her optical illusion.

Thérèse was full of herself. Not at all wearied by the preparations or all the greetings accomplished through the awkward cage resembling a Vasarely that hung from her shoulders. Her makeup seemed to glow with an energy suffusing through her face. It had never before been more clear to Marc how much Thérèse enhanced her life by exaggerating it. Once she'd said: "I shall outlive several doctors!" That was years ago. Since which, Bern, the great heart man, had been done in by cancer of the prostate. Sorceress?

Marc realized that for years he'd got used to thinking of his wife with this assaying remove, his paternal remove. Maybe it was a way for him to cauterize the sexual wounds. Yet tonight more than ever he felt he could tolerate her folly with calm objectivity. And, at the same time, he could not condemn his own folly in having married her. He'd given her her head, catalyzed her role, made her a Baroness de Wolfflen, heiress to a history of extravagance. He'd helped her create herself. She'd been no mean creation—an exuberant work of art. The staircase was empty now. Before Marc could question why he was thinking in the past tense, Thérèse turned to him, and puffed out her thin cheeks in an imitation of fatigue. But her eyes burned with pleasure. She came up to him and crushed the cage with a hug.

"Happy birthday, treasure, happy, happier, happiest of birthdays!"

The orchestra in the ballroom had begun to play some tango. Marc recognized the voice of Tino Rossi. She loosened a clasp at her neck and the ruined cage fell to her feet. She stepped out of it and began to tango with him toward the ballroom. She pulled at the tail of his costume. "Bull," she said, laughing. After all the wild ideas she'd had for what he must wear, he'd finally held out for this simple thing, a bull with a tail made of painted ticker tape. For an instant, he wished he'd given in to wearing something more appropriate and at the same time breathtakingly insane. He decided to drink magnums of champagne tonight.

As he swept Thérèse into the ballroom, there was a burst of applause and good-natured laughter. Marc noted the sickly look of her little decorator, alone in a corner near the door, dressed as a package of Lucky Strikes ...

Godwin Laver, got up as a tube of toothpaste, was standing beside a short, heavy woman wearing just a ball gown and a blond wig. They were looking around at the billboards that hid the gilded ballroom walls. Laver smiled brightly at Marc when he spotted him, and Marc decided to use the man's smile as an opening. He came up to Laver and discovered that the person in the wig was Léopold's daughter, Léa. Her poor, homely face was heavily madeup in what he took for an imitation of Marilyn Monroe.

"Cousin Marc," she said.

"Hello Léa, Godwin." It was the first time Marc had seen either of them since he'd greeted them separately at the stairs. Léa had come with her American who was wearing a Nixon mask.

"Where's Nixon?" he asked Léa, with a calculated half-turn away from Laver.

She shrugged.

Laver interjected: "We've been arguing about advertising. Mademoiselle considers it a form of pollution."

"You mean I've been stinking up my house?" Marc turned again toward Léa.

"Oh, for one night it's a great joke. The trouble is, we have to live with it—"

"You've got a radical in the fold," Laver persisted.

"Home for the spring holidays?" Marc asked Léa.

"Yes ... could you have lunch with Jason and me, some day?"

"I'd like a crack at you too," Godwin said. "Lunch, or even a drink, Marc, just the two of us."

Marc decided to say nothing to Godwin now, to stay hard to get. And he'd had to somehow avoid the lunch with his young cousin. Right now, Léopold might suspect him of trying to play up to him through his daughter. He was struck by the realization that he'd become furtive . . . a man of stratagems.

"Let's call each other," he said, vaguely, to both of them.

Laver stretched his arms out. "The whole thing is too fantastic!" he exclaimed, as Marc stepped away. But Marc's mood had fallen the moment he stopped dancing with Thérèse, and he no longer agreed.

Pérou's billboards with real ads on them masked all the walls from floor to ceiling. The ballroom emptied of all furniture—there wasn't even a chair to sit down on—made Marc remember the *Vélodrôme d'Hiver*, where there were colorful posters beneath the bleachers. That was before the war. He'd gone there several times, mingled in the crowd that smelled of sweat and kerosene stoves, people who bought tickets to the *Vel d'Hiv* instead of eating lunch that day. The thirties. The Depression, which had simply grazed his life—the way the rough coats of those strangers had grazed his own. Later, when he was in London, the French police had used the *vélodrôme* to hold the Jews they'd rounded up, for the Nazis to send to Auschwitz. The past . . . and nowadays, Léopold had insinuated, Robinet would not help him for fear of offending the oil sheiks.

Tonight's crowd was made of cheerful figures out of ads and comic books. The billboards were identical to this week's crop in the streets: they vaunted men's trousers in a cloth you could lean on, a washing machine called Candy and the reliability of ITT when it came to building TV sets. All the ballroom's chandeliers had been removed, and in the center of the room there was a gray balloon the size of a small dirigible with "Goodyear" printed on it. Good year?

Bubbles the size of balloons were breaking over people's heads. Marc approached the cannon they were pouring out of, on which was written "G.I. Joe." An attendant, dressed in fatigues and with a cigar stuck in his bearded face poured liquid into the base of the machine. Marc presumed he embodied the comic strip hero, although behind him he heard someone call, tipsy, "Fidel! Fidel!"

He heard another voice say: "Compliments of Air France!" It was Thérèse, who'd come up beside him without his noticing.

At the buffet table near the bubble cannon, the junk food, which people had taken for a decorative gag—the mounds of colorful gelatins, hot dogs, hamburgers, and milk shakes—was being cleared, barely touched. But in its place, waitresses in blue stewardesses' uniforms were setting down nothing but trays—trays of airplane meals.

"That's all there is," Thérèse said. "They'd better line up for it, that's all there's going to be." Her voice was playfully vicious. Tino Rossi had begun to sing again. Thérèse held up her right palm in a signal to dance. Marc was brooding, but he responded. Tino Rossi. Marc had always thought of him as the Mediterranean ladykiller, but now as they moved past his little bandstand, Marc saw him as he was tonight, roughly Marc's age, fat and self-delighted, like a prosperous restaurateur. He was singing "Katerina," a jolly lovesong nearly drained of the languor of the tango.

"If they don't go for the trays, they'll get nothing," Thérèse said.

He's my age, or older, Marc was still thinking.

"We've saved a fortune on the food," Thérèse continued. "There's no big dinner. So there are no dinner invitations and no toothpick invitations. Just one big crowd. It's a pop democracy! You see, Marc, I *didn't* give a *lavish* ball, after all. Look at the decorations. Marc, you're not listening, darling. I've been very frugal. Austere—"

"It's hypocrisy!" he flung at her. "You've gone too far."

Too far. Now, quite calmly, he almost amused himself placing exactly when he'd perceived it, when it had hit him—after all these years—that she had gone too far. And he was sure someone else would laugh at what he perceived to be the last straw. Someone else would laugh, but that's what it was, the food. A moment ago he'd lost all tolerance. His house had been turned into a mess of deliberate junk—but the food was too much. Wolfflens—never in nearly two hundred years had they ever served their guests bad food. He wasn't dancing anymore. The music had stopped. Thérèse didn't answer, and just walked away and left him standing there alone. He felt it might not do him any harm to get drunk, even in public, and just blot all this out. Perhaps, he thought, he'd already drunk too much. At least there was champagne . . .

Gilbert de Wolfflen stood near the bubble cannon, alone, smouldering. His mind was replaying Cynthia's voice imitating the husky, crackly tones of his stepmother.

" 'There is something I have to tell you about Gilbert,' she said, 'I'm not at all sure he'll be happy spending his lifetime with a woman. I think his interests ... might lie elsewhere.'

"I said to her, and believe me it took an effort to find a tone that could quite match the acid in hers, 'A lifetime? A lifetime? Do you know of anyone planning lifetimes these days? I mean do *you*? As for your opinion about Gilbert, that hasn't *at all* been my experience.' "

Gilbert could picture that little scene Cynthia had recounted in the car. The bitch. That incredible bitch Thérèse. She had asked to see Cynthia in the middle of all her fussing for the ball, and Cynthia, poor victim, went all the way out to Bois Brûlé to see her. There was tea. So *comme il faut*. Who the hell does she think she is? She isn't even my mother.

"I went," Cynthia had explained, making her second trip out, beside him in the Ferrari. "I wanted to be the total *lady*, you see?" She'd forced a laugh. "But then I couldn't help it, whore to whore, you see, I said: 'If Gilbert is queer, *madame*, the way you go around saying, then he must be taking out his hatred of women in bed. He'll fuck you to death if you let him.'" She didn't blink an eye. Mind you, she was pouring at that moment, and she didn't spill a drop. Her eyes just brightened as she looked at me. I think for that one second she might have really liked me.

"Watch out though, dear boy, she'll be after your tail now ... But honestly, Gilbert, can't you see? She's the one inventing things about you. Actually she *wants* you to be gay. All her lovers are queer, don't you see. Oh, maybe they weren't in her prime. But that's her speciality now. She surrounds herself with emasculated men."

Well, Thérèse had had the best of that little meeting, Gilbert thought, for all Cynthia's smart talk. She'd pushed Cynthia far enough, and now he really had an ultimatum on his hands. Cynthia was asking him to stand up for her publicly now, to defend her formally. She wanted an engagement. But he wasn't sure she really wanted to marry him. And he wasn't so sure about that idea either. And now all evening Cynthia kept drifting away from him, as if she had already condemned him, passed sentence on him. Well sure, he might marry her, but not if she insisted on going on with her idea of the movies. She had to understand that he would not be married to a woman with that kind of career. Three months on this set. Six weeks on another. And what am I supposed to do, follow her and turn myself into a makeup man? And they all screw around, those actors. They get bored making a movie, and they screw. On one score Thérèse is right: being a Baroness de Wolfflen is career enough for any woman.

And there was Cynthia now, over there talking to Godwin Laver, giving him those eyes ... with Laver got up like a tube of toothpaste. Ultra-Brite. The fool ...

A couple danced by, blocking his view for a moment. It was little Alice Laver, with some young man. Dressed as Wonder Woman, she all the same looked so frail and vulnerable in her starry blue shirt, as she danced with her arms held stiff, as if to keep her partner from moving any closer ...

Léa was going to work for Ralph Nader while Jason was in graduate school.

Marc had come upon Léa again, as he returned to the bubble cannon to trade in his empty glass for another. The waiter had spilled champagne passing him the new glass.

"But it's not your country," Marc had teased, wiping his costume with an awful paper napkin.

"But it's our world, cousin Marc."

It had struck him just then how much she reminded him of Sara, his own dead sister. Her righteousness. Later, talking to Léopold, he'd learned that Léa and Jason would not have come home for the holiday—he had a good deal of cramming to do—were it not for Marc's birthday party. (It seemed they were already living together. And that seemed to be doing her good. She'd lost weight and lost that look of distress that made her even homelier.)

"She's terribly fond of you," Léopold had said. For Léopold, his daughter was a genius whose opinions were of exceptional value. Well, she was brilliant—*Sara* ...

Then Bruno had come up to them. And in a minute Bruno and Léopold were quarrelling. Accusations about family loyalty. Wild Bruno had started it. It was possible that despite the music, the people in earshot were managing to understand what the heart of the quarrel was. Marc doused the argument by pulling Bruno away for a drink.

"It's my birthday, damn you."

Over his shoulder, he looked back at Léopold with pained eyes.

Marc had hoped to get through the evening without the Cofra problem's spewing up again. But there it was. What could Bruno have possibly hoped to accomplish? The pleasure of venting frustration.

"It's my birthday."

So they stood there, he and Bruno, at one of the bars, and drank down a bottle of champagne, glass after glass, like cossacks. And then another. People nearly applauded. Bruno was finally so full of a strange energy that you couldn't tell his rage any more from hilarity.

And now Marc was at the point where you realize, with paradoxical clarity, that you're tipsy. Like someone dreaming and knowing that he is dreaming. Irresponsibility gaped ahead. But he was too tipsy to check himself at the brink. He looked around the room, surveyed the crowd gone part-crazy in his honor. At a bar near the *buffet,* Cynthia Ashe had just drained a glass of champagne and was holding out her hand for another.

"My friend," he told himself in the third person, "you have found yourself a drinking partner."

Tino Rossi had begun singing again. An incredible camp lovesong, and people were dancing and laughing at the same time.

Emma, Marc's first wife, still called Baroness de Wolfflen, herself a Wolfflen born, and Marc's friend for life, was all the same alone in a corner of the ballroom. Her escort, Philippe Arthaud, a gray person like herself, had disappeared completely. She'd last seen him with Pérou, the decorator. There was a plump girl, her head bent toward a tray in her hand, with her back to Emma. That's Léa. She went up to Léa, and to her relief found someone who felt as totally out of the mood of this party as she was.

"This is my father's bed," he said.

They'd wandered up the alabaster stairs, beyond the ballroom. He'd said he'd show her the house. They'd gone quickly through the part of the second floor of Bois Brûlé still kept open, and now, like children, they were exploring the rich ghostliness of the rest. He'd led her to Eveline's room, where fifty-nine years ago he'd made his surprising entrance into the world, on a weekend meant for killing grouse. Poor Eveline was not at the party tonight. She'd gone strange from the moment her husband had died, and was now nearly all gaga. Now they were in his dead father's apartment. In 1912, the Baron Charles had had this whole room done, down to the doorknobs, by Hector Guimet, who was immortalized by his lush, botanical-looking bronze *métro* entrances.

Everything here now was covered over in muslin. The undulating furniture under the gray-white cloth might have been twisted bodies bound together, knotted and bellowing. A mysteriousness hung in the air. They could still hear the music and a murmur of the noise downstairs. Yet here was 1912 left intact, but wrapped up, awaiting, like Sleeping Beauty, some sort of liberating prince.

Cynthia set down the red plastic transistor radio she'd been carrying under her arm. That had been her concession, her costume. She'd worn it for a while fixed to her head, but then she'd just carried it around under her arm, instead of a purse. Otherwise, she wore a Proust-period evening dress by Saint Laurent the color of bitter chocolate. Tiers of organza. She looked very beautiful.

She stared at Marc with her large eyes, and across the sagging barrier of his reason, they seemed to signal to him that so long as you are alive any dare is possible.

Inside his bull costume, he had tucked a bottle of champagne, a quarter empty. It had slushed around a little, wetting his chest as they'd climbed the stairs. He fetched it out. Under a little cover on the bedside table, there was a carafe and a water glass, with which Charles, dead Charles, used to take precaution against midnight thirst. Marc took the glass, filled it with champagne, and passed it to Cynthia. The champagne had got warm, and she drank it hesitantly like a child drinking a glassful of medicine flavored to taste good. He filled the glass again. And so they passed the champagne back and forth between them until the bottle was empty. Cynthia shrugged and began to walk away. He kissed her forehead when she turned back toward him.

Marc tugged at the sheet of muslin, and underneath, there was Charles' bed all made up forever for the night. Thin crisp batiste sheets and pillow covers with embroidered crests. Before Marc could even try to screen what was happening through his debilitated consciousness, their clothes seemed to have fallen away, and they were both in there, each drawing the other's body close. Marc felt as if he were drawing her to him across water, like someone he loved intensely he was trying to save. Their limbs grappled, and when they were finally locked together, it seemed to Marc that this sweet young thin body was not at all strange, but a body he'd known since he was old enough to love the feel of a woman in his arms.

He lowered his head between her legs and kissed her wetly. Then he was kissing her mouth. He penetrated her and held her for an instant perfectly still. Then with his hands on her smooth bottom, he began to rock her with his hips, plunging and receding but never leaving her body. She was silent, and then her breath became heavier and heavier. And for Marc, the room, the space they filled that moment, all that moment of his life became only their sounds, and her taste in his mouth, the feel of her body in his hands, and the warm moist pulse of her insides answering the undulations of his own body.

"Where—" Thérèse began to say. Cynthia had slipped away toward a cloakroom. "Everyone's gone—" she started to say again.

"I've been showing Cynthia the house," Marc said.

"There's no use in her taking inventory, Gilbert is finished with her."

Gilbert came toward them with a tear in his Batman suit, showing his chest. He glared at his stepmother. Cynthia came up behind them. "I'll take you back now," he said to Cynthia. Said or asked. His face was bleak. She closed her eyes and raised her brows, which said she was ready to get out of here. Marc held both her hands an instant as he kissed her formally goodbye on each cheek. He felt her squeeze his hands, but her hands were quite cold now.

"Don't overdo," Thérèse said to Marc, after Cynthia had gone off with Gilbert. Marc didn't know how much she'd meant to say. "Emma is stranded," Thérèse said. "Someone must take her back."

No, Thérèse had never been threatened by Emma. So she could always treat her husband's ex-wife as if Cinderella had a kind sister. Only Cinderella was past sixty now, all the more reason for Thérèse's patronizing.

"I'll drive her," Marc said. "I'll take the mini."

Marc had come out to Bois Brulé in the mini, after Thérèse and her decorator had been driven out early in the Mercedes to arrange the last details of the ball.

"Has *monsieur* Pérou gone?" he asked impetuously.

"He'll come back with me," Thérèse said.

"All right."

"Marc? They brought you out a telegram. Your should have let me know where you were."

She handed it to him. She'd already opened it.

"PROPOSE CONTINENTAL INTERESTS TAKE OUR SHARES. HAVE OFFERED OPTION IF YOU IN ACCORD. REGARDS HOYT," it read.

Continental Interests was Godwin Laver.

"Happy birthday, Marc," Thérèse said, but he couldn't decide what her tone said as well. She seemed finally tired. He felt quite sober now.

"It was a bit much, huh?" Marc asked.

"It was very untimely, you must admit."

"I admit," he said.

For the rest of the ride back, they said next to nothing to each other. "Are you feeling well, Marc, these days?" Emma asked at one point. "Better, yes. You?" She was well. In fact he'd been feeling particularly well recently. As if something inside him had unknotted after his meeting with Beauchamps at the bank. Tonight he no longer felt on a ledge but rather like a man who'd been let loose in a glider. He'd done things, and for the moment now, he couldn't exert any power over his situation, but he was still up there, planing, and the feel of the thin air about him was delicious.

She rode beside him in the mini, a woman five years older than himself, already totally transformed, physically, into the fag-end of a human life. Gray. The gray of her hair seemed to have spread over into her complexion, her eyes, her teeth even.

Mentally, she was still immaculate. She still played concerts to great acclaim. Her music criticism under her pseudonym, in *Le Monde*, was the best around. The little publishing house she'd founded was not just a prestigious venture, it even made money. She had the clearest mind and the most honest character of any woman he'd known, and she was the one person he hadn't been able to keep himself from hurting. Now that was an old, cold story.

She rode beside him, a kind of ghost embodying a portion of his life. And for all the kindness he felt toward her, her presence was stifling. Unconsciously, absurdly, he rolled down his window a little.

"Yes," she said.

Once they'd been intimate. For years they'd been intimate. Perhaps not *intimate*. Close partners in life. Once he'd considered her faint clean odor, the particular feel of her flesh to be things that would always be closely attached to his life. But physically they hadn't been intimate enough. Something kindness, fondness, respect couldn't repair was wrong with the contact. It had been a buried consideration. They'd married when he was in his midtwenties and then suddenly the war was upon the world, and there was the hardship of exile, London under the Blitz, and then he was going back and forth, and death at any moment was a very realistic possibility. So they'd been partners in hardship, stress, danger, and in that sense they'd been hand in glove. Her marvelous nature. He'd loved her then. Still loved her in that abstract way of admiration, respect. And until that day he noticed the Duchess de Flandres at a table in Maxim's, touching, touching the other woman's hand across her table, Marc had more or less resigned himself to the idea that the sensual side of his life would always be rather quiet. Then something in him broke loose. Just as now, something in him was breaking loose—although as for the young girl he'd bedded that evening, she, that—that was a miracle so integral, that incident, so enveloped in its own awesomeness, that he never hoped for any continuation, and oddly, felt no need of it.

But twenty years ago, he'd burned to possess. She wasn't that beautiful, Thérèse, her conscience was a disordered jumble of kindness and cruelty, because, depending on her mood, either kindness or cruelty could give her pleasure. "The Sorceress" Bruno called her behind Marc's back.

They'd fallen in love, he and Thérèse, but in too many ways, perhaps, he'd longed to possess and she perhaps, to conquer. He was a Wolfflen, which today meant more, socially, than a Flandres. Several titles down the line, he still outpointed the poor Duke. And finally she'd collected lovers like trophies. He couldn't count their number. And he was left, in the end, with another partnership, such as it was. Intimacy, he knew tonight, was just a miracle you couldn't work out, you couldn't even choose. It was luck.

"You've missed it," Emma said gently, as he drove past her doorway in the Rue de Seine. Gentle, gentle Emma. She'd never blamed him. And when Gilbert had become an adolescent, she'd sent him to him. A Baron de Wolfflen, she'd said, shouldn't grow up away from the house of his father. Gentle in the fullest sense. The last Lady left in this world.

"Oops."

He drove to the end of the one-way street and went around again. In the cobblestone courtyard in front of Emma's little eighteenth-century house, they kissed goodbye. She held his shoulders, and suddenly he remembered that far back in time, when his grandmother would kiss the boy Marc, she would steady herself on his shoulders just that way.

Luck. Win or lose.

The Mercedes was still not in the carriage house. Maybe she'd decided to sleep at Bois Brûlé. Pérou. It struck him that as Thérèse was getting older, her choice of lovers was going downhill.

Luck. The word was fixed in his mind. Where in this bull's outfit had he put his housekeys? Ah yes. Luck, he thought, as he felt the cold metal of the keys in his palm, was something he'd never given much consideration before. He'd never been a gambler. He was a man of responsibility, and a responsible man. But now the two irrevocable wild things he'd done struck him full in the face.

God, he'd cuckolded his son. And in the name of the bank, he'd taken a three-hundred-million-dollar forward position, against the going odds, dollars for marks—as an adventure.

TEN

Four-fifteen. Marc de Wolfflen was late. Godwin Laver watched a waiter finish setting the low tables for tea in the hall of the Plaza Athenée hotel. The chink of the porcelain sounded pleasant to his ears. For the length of the hall now, on the tables beside the stuffed chairs, there were embroidered napkins and floral cups and saucers set out beside handfuls of fresh flowers in glass vases. *Four-twenty.* The waiter left. Godwin, at the last table, which he'd discreetly chosen, was all alone in the long hall. Wolfflen was late. Two powdered old ladies came in with little dogs. The waiter returned with the pastry wagon.

Godwin realized that he couldn't identify any of the small flowers on his table, but he was pleased to look at them, and not being able to classify them didn't matter to him. What he didn't know about plants, he told himself, he knew about people, and about business. And that business was people. Your economic indicators and your company reports were useless unless you knew every time whom you were dealing with and what, among all the things the other person was seeking, was the thing he really needed. Was the real reason he was negotiating. Almost invariably, Laver could give the other fellow the minimum he needed by getting more in exchange. A lot of people were in business with funny ideas. There was a man he knew who'd disastrously tried to rescue a failing airline in the United States because he associated running airlines with a special kind of personal power. And Godwin knew a man in Paris who'd backed a couturier without talent because he thought it would give him a social entrée. And there were men driven by quirky dreams, men, usually engineers at heart, who fell in love with companies because of what they were making. But until now, Godwin Laver would be tempted by nothing in business except coming out ahead. He could walk away, without hesitation, from any deal in which his chances of coming out ahead were doubtful. In business, Godwin's clear and simple need was his strength.

But here he was with far from simple motives and wet palms, nervous, waiting for Marc de Wolfflen, a man the whole financial community considered pretty much at bay. Even at bay, Wolfflen was full of style:

"No, I cannot lunch with you, Godwin, you understand . . . I don't believe in business lunches. Neither does my stomach, actually. Hold on, Godwin, what do you think about a drink? No, coffee. Let's have coffee. How much time do you actually need?"

Godwin had thought he could feel a smile in Wolfflen's voice over the phone when Godwin mentioned the Plaza. He didn't seem to appreciate that Godwin had chosen a very discreet neutral place, above all very close to the club where he knew Wolfflen went for his midday squash.

Marc de Wolfflen's business career had become a string of mistakes, but Godwin, in all his ruminations about how to deal with him, couldn't bring himself to consider Marc as prey. He realized again the crazy awe he felt toward all of them, that family—an awe he could only explain by believing they got to him very deepdown, to what he believed was his essentially romantic nature.

They were nowhere in the financial world, now, another investment group, down the line behind a lot of other old money. Godwin Laver wished for the Wolfflens' sake that they'd stayed true to their own lights. That the Wolfflens had never bothered to ask themselves what the little man wanted to do. The consumers, the little investors, who'd since run away from Wall Street like scared insects, and who'd never come near the Bourse. The Wolfflens should have stuck to their own ways; their name had been built on finance, on calculations of strategy, on matching wits and power with men in their own world. On controlling what industry always needed, money, raw materials, energy—and letting industry worry about its consumers. Before Marc, the Wolfflens had barely touched any kind of manufacturing. They'd made their fortunes through coups. Strokes of financial strategy. Coups, not keeping a till.

Yet, there they were, still theatrical, self-assured, elegant, eccentric. And even if they were befuddled they still had—glamor. Glamor was a word people used cheaply now, but Godwin thought he had a feeling for its true meaning, and when he was with the Wolfflens he could feel their glamor fall on him like a blessing. He was, he told himself again, an essentially romantic person. And he believed that essence of his soul could finally make peace with his abstract drive to acquire, and make him some whole and better man, through a high friendship with the Wolfflens. A true partnership. That was all Godwin really wanted of them ...

Four-thirty. Marc de Wolfflen was a half-hour late. Godwin ordered coffee. He studied the pillars, the intricate moldings of the walls and wondered what it would cost to build a hotel like this one nowadays. Impossible. Could it be run at a profit? He seemed to remember, from some real estate research, that the Plaza had been finished in 1920. During the last and probably final classic revival. Godwin Laver would have loved living in 1920.

Marc de Wolfflen came into the hall, peering through the half-light hesitantly—a stranger to the place—until he saw Godwin. He looked impeccable. A perfect pinhead worsted suit, starched white shirt, a burgundy silk tie. A kind of prewar nattiness. He was smoking a cigar.

The waiter brought Godwin's coffee as Marc sat down.

"Will you have coffee?"

Marc nodded. "Did you say four-thirty?"

"Four," Godwin said, "it's of no importance."

"Well no, I'm terribly sorry."

Wolfflen took out a telegram, put on his glasses, read it for some reason— he'd surely read it before—and passed it to Godwin.

"Hoyt told me he'd telex you," Godwin said, looking at the message.

Marc's cigar was in danger of dying. He puffed at it energetically, looking at the end and then up at Godwin, "Personally," he said, "I've never had anything against you, Godwin."

"Bison—" Godwin started to say, but he realized immediately that he'd started to speak without quite knowing what he was going to say. His hands were quite wet. Marc's glance, through his spectacles, seemed oddly fatherly.

"I think I can be of use," he began again.

"Your name is poison to my cousin Bruno," Marc said quietly.

"There aren't many other people—" Godwin started to say. "I mean, there aren't many people able, or who are willing to take on—"

Wolfflen shrugged. "Bruno won't talk to you," he said. "He's my partner. He's my cousin. How could we do business?"

"I don't think there's any profound difference between us. You know . . . I think he'd find out he and I—well, are not dissimilar. It's a question of feelings. That could be repaired. I could see him directly if you saw fit."

Marc raised his hand. That would not be of any use.

"Cofra is in difficulty," Godwin insisted. "I'd like to make you an unusual proposal."

"Yes."

Give me . . . two weeks. I can prove to you beyond doubt that I can greatly help that company. I'm thinking of something unusual. If—if I do, then . . . you'll accept. Talk to Bruno. Make him understand. I'd like . . . a real partnership . . . I mean *an alliance*. I'm prepared to offer an option on a substantial share of Continental, as well, at the time of agreement. It will be a very attractive package."

"All right . . . we'll see in two weeks," Marc said. "We'll look into that, too. The whole thing."

Godwin put down the napkin he'd been crumpling in his palm. "What I had meant to say . . . about Bison—I'm deeply sorry, I want to tell you that I'm deeply sorry, Marc, that our first effort to do business together proved difficult."

Marc was standing now and offering his hand.

Godwin said goodbye to Wolfflen at the doorway into the lobby. He bought a copy of *Le Monde* at the newstand near the phones. He was tempted to call *her*, but he realized he was not in the right mood. As he pushed his way through the revolving door of the hotel, he had divided feelings about the meeting he'd just had. He'd got what he wanted, but for once he felt revolted by Marc's manner. He seemed insupportably superior ... but maybe that was a distorted impression. What the hell? They're all eccentric.

He decided to call. She was out. And he didn't call again until a week later.

In the meantime, his private plane got stranded on a remote airstrip in Western Nouwanda with a fuel-line problem, and they had to sneak him across an obscure border post in a Land Rover. Then he had to take a commercial flight home. He got out without a hitch, but it had been a messy trip. Yet he'd had to go. Godwin never did anything without knowing the people involved. He'd had to see the key person face to face. On the flight back to Paris, out of weakness, boredom or loneliness, he couldn't decide which, or in what doses each, he picked up one of the UTA stewardesses. He went home to her studio apartment for a night of cold, automatic, phoney sex. The next morning he felt like spending the whole day in his bath. But there was good news: his plane had got back out, too. The pilot had solved his problem.

Godwin got his nerve up and decided to call again. He owed himself a pleasure trip; not too far and not too close but somewhere very different. Someplace fresh *with a marvelous girl*. Marrakesh, he thought. It wasn't the perfect season, but it would be a very welcome change from the grime of Paris and from all he had to go through with those stupid Blacks ...

ELEVEN

"You and she," Thérèse had said to Gilbert, "you'd be a fascinating match. Alice Laver is one of the most beautiful girls on earth. And she's so young, my God, she's a pure little flower barely opened to the world. You could form her, Gilbert. Do you know how rare a girl like that is in this day and age? And afterwards, for a while if you like, you could both live here, for a while, and I could help her to learn about being a Wolfflen . . ." Gilbert had had an impulse to throw his lunch in his stepmother's face.

All the same, not for Thérèse's sake, Gilbert was spending the evening with Alice. He'd taken her to Maxim's for dinner. It was Friday night, dance night for the aged, and yet, he thought, it was just the kind of thing that would appeal to a very young girl. It gave her a chance to put on a long dress. She wore one of those nostalgic Rita Hayworth things. "Loris Azzaro," she'd said, blushing, as he looked her over. She read *Vogue*, apparently.

Cynthia had worn those dresses long before they were a fashion. They caught on after that Horne lady from New York saw Cynthia in one and had her photographed wearing that look for a big spread in *Vogue*.

Anyway, Alice looked a lot better in that kind of thing than Cynthia. She was younger, but she already had a much more womanly figure. Her breasts were impressive. Cynthia was really very boyishly built. Lanky.

It must be the South American influence, the Latin element. Maybe she'd grow fat after thirty or have to live on lettuce. Well, he wasn't yet looking that far ahead. Her face was thin, sort of ponylike, *une beauté attendrissante.* Not regular, but interesting, appealing, engendering just the faintest touch of pity for the faint touch of homeliness that seemed to linger, half-defined in the irregularity of her nose, the strange proportions of the whole face. *Vogue* won't be long in chasing after her. They always want New Faces. And then they drop them. Cynthia knew that—but she dropped them first. Well, Cynthia this and Cynthia that: what was the point?

"You look a little sleepy," he ventured. They were at Régine's now. They'd danced, and during the slow ones he was pleasantly surprised by the rightness he felt in the balance of her full body as he guided her. Now they were drinking scotch, and the cigaret smoke that seemed to cling in all the angles of the Thirties décor was oppressive. Actually, *he* felt a little sleepy.

"Who do you take me for," she said bluntly, "Cinderella?"

Yes, he'd put his foot in his mouth. "Pure little flower," all right, but she had frank opinions. Even if they might be just a caricature of what her father thought. Over dinner she'd gone on about how marvelous it was that Maxim's still existed, (yes, he'd made the right choice, all right) a place where you could still be served decently and where they didn't let just anyone into the right room, even if he tried to press a fistful of money on Roger.

"It can't last," she'd said. Paris was going to turn into some festering medieval city again, where you'll have to go round armed. That is, if the Communists didn't take over first. But who knows if even they could keep the mob down. The people had been spoiled.

"It's as if, you know, you feel like the Roman empire is crumbling and you're sitting here in Maxim's in a way, waiting for the barbarians to storm in ... All the worst elements are breeding like flies all over the world."

My God, at her age. She was barely nineteen. Gilbert wasn't sure that she was wrong. But what was the use in thinking that way? He never thought that way. The right kind of people do the best they can to promote their own cause and don't get into all that doom business.

"People like us are not exactly weaponless," he'd answered. "Your father isn't about to hang himself."

"I'm telling you what I think. Anyway, my father is sort of shoring up a fortress."

Useless talk. All things considered, Gilbert still believed that a free market economy was the most efficient possible, and that nothing would replace it nor the people who knew how to make it work. Even the Russians would wind up going back to it, if you want to talk about the long term ...

Well, anyway, then she was not entirely a little flower. Probably, though, she was pure. There was a good chance. She hadn't even really gone out much with anyone as far as he knew. The idea of her being a virgin frankly appealed to him.

He remembered what his father had said. He'd said she seemed to be like her mother—but he'd avowed he knew very little about both of them.

"What do you think of Alice Laver?" Gilbert had asked Marc the morning after the Pop-Op Ball. People had noticed how Cynthia kept avoiding him all evening. Part of why he asked was to suggest to his father that he wasn't just Cynthia's slave.

Marc had squeezed the bit of brioche he was buttering. He'd blushed. There could have been a memory somewhere that had troubled him. But he smiled and said, "Godwin Laver might have thought he could do some sort of Pygmalion act with her mother. The poor girl died before anyone could say how things would have turned out. They had a bad doctor in Ibiza. I hardly knew her. I knew her parents better, Fuertaga and his wife. But I think the girl might have had something in her harder to handle than Godwin thought. Alice strikes me the same way. A gentle surface. Some kind of animal strength. The grandmother, Alice's grandmother, was ... quite something."

Gilbert trusted his father's opinions about women, even if he'd got himself hopelessly involved with Thérèse. Marc really seemed to understand women, even if he didn't master them. All things considered, Gilbert believed, you were better off mastering them than understanding them.

"We're going," he announced to Alice. *Yes, there's a good chance she's a virgin.* He rose and as he turned toward the waiter he noticed Nicky Fallan with his inevitable camera standing at the bar. That creep. That tiring remnant of the sixties still in his stale velvet clothes, his crinkled Indian neckerchief. Becoming more and more of a nobody, despite his family.

For an instant, Gilbert recalled one precise reason he felt hostile toward Fallan, but he put it out of his mind.

As they passed the bar, Fallan raised his camera at them.

"Hurry up," Alice said, wincing in the strobelight. "He gives me the willies." She dug her fingers into Gilbert's arm.

A surge of pleasure ran through Gilbert then; he wondered whether deep down he and Alice had common instincts. He drove her home blazing across town in the Ferrari as fast as he could. Passing red lights. She clung to his arm as if she were scared. He kissed her goodnight at the door to her father's house in the Rue de l'Université very gently.

The following afternoon, Fallan's picture of them was in the gossip column of *France-Soir*. "The Baron Gilbert has dropped his American actress, Cynthia Ashe, for a new young English beauty," the column said, in its usual vulgar way.

But as for the facts, that was exactly how he wanted the matter to be cast.

TWELVE

It was past noon on a Saturday when Léopold called.

Marc had had a late breakfast brought to him in bed. He felt lovely there, propped against his pillow, sipping tea, poking a knife into little pots of honey and jam. His tea was perfectly smokey and redolent of bergamot. He felt positively lighthearted.

It seemed to Marc that he'd handled Laver well. As for Bruno, well Bruno, he believed, could at last be brought round. What would matter was that the Wolfflens hadn't gone crawling to Laver. Godwin was being put up by Hoyt to take over his minority interest. No one in the financial world would consider the Wolfflens other than mad to spurn Laver now. The way things stood, they would look totally irresponsible. There was no one else waiting on line with the money. And basically, Marc thought, there was really nothing wrong with Godwin. Bruno could be reasoned with. Laver was the suppliant, and he obviously wanted to get into Cofra badly. There was the piece of Continental to sweeten things. In the end, Laver would be right: the grudge would be buried over a few drinks. Laver was aggressive, you had to keep an eye on him, but there was nothing, Marc thought, basically wrong with Godwin Laver. He was clever. Maybe, give him his due, he was brilliant, as many people said. "Two weeks." He must know something about the copper market. Found something out. Marc would have to check around on Monday.

On Friday, the Deutschemark stood at 2.64 to the dollar and it looked like it would continue to get better. The Americans had published some very bad balance of payments figures and the Germans claimed to have cut inflation to 0.6 percent for the last recorded month. Marc felt buoyant. He felt lucky.

By the time he went downstairs, Thérèse had left for the hairdresser's. He went into his library, and out of impulse, had them light a fire. He sat there, looking at the flames and listening to Mahler on France Culture, until the phone rang, and they told him the Baron Léopold was on the line.

"Marc!" Léopold's voice sounded ghostly, paled out, scared.

"Marc, I have this from very good, very reliable people at the Quai. *I said the Quai d'Orsay.* Listen to me, Marc. Someone is up to something terribly dangerous and everybody seems to believe it's the Wolfflens. It's all we need. Marc, I know it couldn't be you. Please, I want you to call Bruno immediately. We're a very old and honorable family Marc—

"We're not ITT!"

Léopold went on for several minutes in that horrible voice Marc had never heard before. When they hung up, Marc called Bruno. No it wasn't Bruno. Bruno's reaction was a volley of curses. Marc felt an impulse of affection for his wild but undevious cousin and a tinge of relief. The feeling of relief didn't last long. He broke into Bruno's second wind of invectives and said goodbye.

Then he tried to get hold of Godwin Laver. It was no use, either at his house or his office. Nor at his London house and office. The servants didn't know where he was. None of the people who worked with him, whom Marc finally reached at home, knew either. That was all very unusual. And now, hearing Léopold's horrible tone again—Léopold has to watch himself, he should never get that excited—he felt his own nerves begin to jangle. Pain started to ooze and fill his abdomen, and he realized suddenly that it was simple: he'd never change his stomach until he got everything in his head all straightened out properly—until he could make his *whole life* tally. It was all that simple.

THIRTEEN

"Listen," Cynthia said, "I'm sure it would be positively dreamy, so long as we agree from the start that it's not going to be ... a shackup."

Godwin laughed into the phone. That hoarse laugh of his, that sounded at the end as if he were taking it back; an oddly engaging laugh. "Positively just an excursion!"

"I mean it," she insisted, "I'll hold you to that. I really will."

"Come on," he said. "Come on now, my poor baby, we're not the kind of people to think in that mean little way. I can't go without a friend."

She really did feel like getting away somewhere for a little while. Her head was all scrambled. It seemed to her that it was very possible she was not seeing the world in a normal way these days.

On the way out to the little field at Melun southeast of Paris, Cynthia reminded herself that she really did like private airplanes. Going somewhere on a regular plane had become such a dreary hassle. They felt you up and down. They went through your purse. Or they shot some surely unhealthy rays at you as you passed through. All the same you had a good chance of being blown up in the air or hijacked onto some hundred-degree desert where you'd have to beg for your life and sit and smell the toilets. And half the time they packed you into some bus like cattle, and then everyone stampeded onto the ramp to get just that seat he wanted. And lines. Lines. Everyone in the entire world was flying around all the time.

Godwin's twin-jet De Havilland took two and a half hours to get to Marrakesh. He had his rear seats arranged into a kind of little salon, all covered with chocolate-colored pigskin that looked very much like it had been done by Gucci. They sat there, and Laver tried to interest her in backgammon. She more or less knew the rules. "You're not very aggressive," he said, as he plunked around his buttons or whatever they're called. He made you think he was Rommel advancing on Cairo. "Honestly," she said. "I'm trying my hardest . . . but maybe we'd be better off reading."

They checked into two rooms facing the garden at the Mamounia. A haze hung over the pink city. The pool looked dim and unappetizing. This wasn't really a good time for North Africa. Godwin said let's go see the snow on the Atlas. They got a car and driver through Hadj, the doorman.

"Do you know what Hadj means?" Godwin asked. "It means he's been to Mecca. He made the trip and presumably it's changed his life, so he's changed his name. Hadj. He'll die holy now."

"Why don't we drive to Mecca?" she tried to banter.

He laughed that laugh of his.

Godwin slipped Hadj a handful of crumpled dirhams.

"Have you ever been anywhere that changed your life?" she asked in the car. They climbed a mountainside that already looked astoundingly like Switzerland, except for the clusters of Berber huts on the right side of the road.

He didn't answer but he didn't laugh.

She made him stop to look at silver. The tall, bald, grave Berbers looked much like they did the last time she was here but the silver had somehow gone junky. Maybe her taste had changed. The last and only other time she'd been to Marrakesh was way back on a shooting assignment for *Vogue* with Nicky Fallan. They'd shared a room in the second-best hotel, what was it called, the modern one, where the Ministry of Tourism had put them up.

"Doesn't he have anything in all that hardware that could ward off a hex?" Godwin said, while the Berber, who might have been seven feet tall, stood there silently beside the road, clutching about fifty necklaces in his hand. Cynthia shot Laver an embarrassed look. Maybe the Berber could speak English, who knew?

"I'm teasing," Laver said, with a strange, weak note in his voice.

Cynthia bought a slave bracelet she'd never wear, to assuage the Berber. She wondered what they'd do to a Westerner who bought one of those stone houses. And could you buy one? They were lovable, nudged into the hillside that was so very breathtakingly beautiful.

As she recalled, the ski resort at ths top wasn't much— Oukaïmeden.

People were going up and down pleasantly enough. There was no crowding. But it was all rather rounded out and dull once you got up there. They had some very hot mint tea on a terrace and headed back to the oasis.

They had dinner at La Maison Arabe because there really wasn't any better place to eat. The woman put them in the little room where there were tourists close enough to hear every word they said. But the *pastilla*, the sweet pigeon pie, was delicious.

Godwin had wanted to change the table, but the other room wasn't much different. More crowded. Yet it seemed that Godwin's dinner was a little spoiled, not because the table wasn't right but because he hadn't imposed the table. He kept shooting bleak little regretful looks toward the other room.

Several times at the hotel, he asked to see the latest paper in no matter what European language, but they were all a day old.

They drank in the lobby before going up. She ordered *ouzo*, somehow thinking foggily that it would be the right thing in a country like this. But the right thing of course would have been mint tea or maybe buttermilk. Godwin drank three scotches.

They spoke very little. They talked about people they knew and Godwin didn't have a trace of a bad word for anyone. They were all full of character, or full of spirit or full of fun, in his eyes. Even Thérèse de Wolfflen. She was all three. Godwin wanted Cynthia to get to know Alice. He seemed, as she'd expected, a man full of kindness, full of charming generosity. A great teddy bear, but someone who was also bright and powerful. He even seemed sincerely bothered that she wasn't happy with her drink. It bothered him that she wouldn't make herself happier by ordering something else. She didn't want to drink anything, she realized.

At the door to her room, he held her forearms tightly and looked at her a moment. His eyes actually seemed liquidy.

"Someone like you—" he started to say, and she knew she had to say something fast or he might just suddenly be hanging out there, exposing all sorts of sentiment she didn't care to hear.

"As I pointed out from the start—" she said, and thumped on his great chest.

"Tomorrow," he said, "we're having lunch with the King's brother."

There were an endless number of cloisters, it seemed, before you got to where the Prince lived. Long halls brought you from one to the next. Actually, as it turned out, the cloisters ended at three, and the last, a great white square with a fountain in the middle, looked like Peace on Earth itself. They ate in a corner. The Prince was tall and affable with youthful Parisian manners. He had his Irish golf instructor there for lunch, and his French cook had done wild asparagus and marvelous *tagines,* lemony stews in earthen pots. The three men got along very well talking about golf, and then their conversation went on to shooting. The Prince showed them all a room full of rifles and shotguns, a room just crammed with them, which wasn't the arsenal of his guard but all his gamehunting guns. They talked about all sorts of game. Chamois and things, nothing common. Godwin was very fond of shooting doves. He thought they were one of the best things to shoot of all. Cynthia closed her eyes and saw blood splash on white feathers.

Godwin said he had two matching Purdey shotguns but there was a tiny nick on the barrel of one, and it bothered him so much he'd let them both go for five thousand dollars. The golf instructor showed a polite and safely vague sign of interest. Bring them next time you're golfing at wherever it was in Scotland Godwin liked to golf, let me know, I'll come over from St. Andrews. The golf instructor seemed really too plainliving and matter of fact for exotic weaponry. His accent was good. He might have been courting Godwin as a customer, but the Prince seemed to take up a lot of his time. He struck Cynthia as someone with natural tact, who may have begun life as a caddie and quickly learned the ways of the rich, while never becoming a phoney snob himself nor overimpressed by anybody else. A man happy and confident with his objectively measurable skill.

As they left, Godwin said in the last corridor that the Prince liked to take friends shooting boar in the Atlas with a thousand beaters. "Incredible," he said, and then regretfully, as if in his mind he himself had actually formed an invitation and taken it back: "But of course, women can't come."

"Everyone has a right to his customs," she said. For the first time since they'd arrived, she felt the strain of trying to be pleasant.

He took her to the Agdal garden. There was a great square reservoir, where the Moroccans came to sit on the stone wall and look at the water. Most of them were in European dress; they seemed to have taken time out of their work day to come to the silent garden. The water was motionless.

"I took you here," Laver said "because I don't understand all the fuss. It's in the Blue Guide; but it's nothing. I mean, it seems hardly a sight to mention ... I mean well, do you understand it?"

Everyone has a right to his customs, she wanted to say again, but by then it would have really sounded sarcastic.

There was a blind man there with flies around his eyes.

Godwin said, "What could *he* possibly see in the place?"

"Maybe he feels something," she answered. "Maybe the place sends him a feeling."

"You," he said, "send me a feeling." He tried to make it sound like just banter, but oh-oh, she thought, she'd been crazy, this was no friendly excursion, Godwin was incapable of an excursion, his mind worked in terms of campaigns. He wasn't in Marrakesh to look at the water of the Agdal with her. Everything with him, she realized, was a project with a goal.

None of the papers back at the hotel seemed to have what he was looking for.

She made a phone call; she recalled that Federico Lammi, a scriptwriter she knew in Rome, spent a lot of time in a house he had in the palm grove outside of Marrakesh. Yes, what luck, he was there. She'd take Godwin there for dinner. It was someplace they didn't have to be alone together.

Freddy met them at the gate in a djeleba and bare feet. Godwin took particular notice of the glass beads he wore around his neck, his gray hair, and the belly showing under the djeleba. Godwin was very quiet through dinner. There was no one else there but the three of them, and Cynthia wound up talking to Freddy about movie people in Rome and movies done by people they knew or with people they knew in them. Godwin sat there as if behind a door. Maybe she should have made an effort to bring him into the conversation more than she did. She felt embarrassed for having brought him.

Godwin brightened when Freddy got out some hashish. He hadn't smoked dope in years, Godwin said, without any kind of pretension at all, and a strange, private note of nostalgia in his voice.

He was pretty high up there when they got back to the Mamounia. It had a strange effect on him.

Ten minutes after she'd undressed, he started tapping at her door. She pretended not to hear until he began pounding.

"That wasn't what we agreed on!" she shouted, and sounded so corny that she was furious with herself. *My fault*, she told herself, and finally she faced the truth about why she'd gone on this crazy trip. To get away from the other—from what had happened with Marc de Wolfflen; and that was *even more frightening*, more a threat than the wounded buffalo on the other side of the door, raring to charge between her legs. My fault, but too bad, she told herself, as she pulled a pillow over her head and decided not to do anything until he broke the door down. Then what? No, *in no case* would she lose control. She'd kick, she'd bite—

It sounded as if the boy in the corridor was running toward Godwin. There was a noise like someone being hit. The boy seemed to squeek suddenly, make an ugly noise of pain. Godwin turned the key in his own door and slammed it behind him.

Next morning her room with the gauzy view of the pool was stifling. She decided to have breakfast downstairs.

Godwin was already down there going through a batch of newspapers.

They said good morning and she ordered tea. He pushed the basket of rolls a little toward her side of the table and poked his head into the *International Herald Tribune*.

"My God!" he said suddenly. There was something that seemed to horrify him on the first inside page.

She looked at him.

"Nothing," he said, and he put the paper down. "People are

always dying of droughts or floods somewhere you can't pronounce." He seemed totally composed now, and so he said: "I'm ... very sorry."

Later she'd regret her vindictiveness, but before she could check herself, she said: "You're not a very happy man, are you, Godwin?"

"I'll get by," he said.

She felt sorry for him. Sorry for the cruelty in what she'd said, for the raw edges in the gap between them now, but just then all she really wanted was to be alone.

FOURTEEN

The day Godwin Laver left for Marrakesh Marc kept calling all the numbers for him he could get. The fire died in his library, the embers coincided with a pain glowing in his stomach. Once the houseboy put a call through to the library and he jumped up, feeling a sudden premonition that this time he'd reached him. It was Thérèse calling to say she was having lunch at Maxim's with so-and-so, he didn't quite catch the name, who was here from New York—he was barely listening—and they were going shopping afterwards, so he shouldn't expect her until late. He clucked gentle acknowledgments and hung up, further depressed by an awareness that his life with Thérèse had largely degenerated into a lot of petty details.

It was Saturday, he thought again, and the longer he waited the less chance he'd have of getting anyone useful at the embassy.

He asked himself again what he really owed Laver, why he felt obliged to reach him. Laver would of course try to talk Marc into closing his eyes. The thought that Laver might succeed at it flashed through Marc's mind but only for an instant. The right thing was to in any case confront Laver, first of all.

But if the Quai knew, doubtless they weren't the only ones. There wasn't much time.

Laver—and he had no doubt in his mind now that it was Laver who was involved—hadn't informed Marc; reasoning from that, Marc owed him no consideration. Marc could believe that Godwin might even have acted with a romantic knightliness toward the Wolfflens— he might have wanted to have kept them totally clean of the whole thing. But he was crazy. Yes, everyone must know and everyone must be blaming the Wolfflens. No, it wasn't even a question now of *informing*. It was a matter of exonerating the family.

And all the while he hoped to get Godwin on the phone, with the anguish almost of a man burning to reach his mistress, Marc wondered what kind of emotion he'd get out of him when he told him what he was going to do. Godwin would argue. Oh no, Marc told himself, no hope, not a chance in the world, answering another flicker of temptation to let things ride. No there's a line ... there are things we could never allow ourselves ... never ... otherwise we're monsters in a world of monsters.

And it was quite clear to him that one way or another Godwin had dirtied him, had forced him to react now, and thereby get involved one way or another in his intrigue. The idea of being a *mouchard*, an informer, repulsed him. But what choice was there? He hated Laver now, for having put him in this position. And from the bottom of his mind a dreadful premonition surfaced: there was a good chance that in the end, by the time the whole thing sorted itself out, *someone* in any case, was going to be killed.

Not Godwin. No chance. Laver wouldn't be on the scene. He was somewhere safely unreachable.

The phone rang again. He grabbed the receiver. This time it was Léopold's wife, Françoise. Léopold had what they thought was a bad case of indigestion. But the doctor was on his way. Meanwhile he wanted to call Marc's attention again to the matter they'd last discussed. There was a need to act quickly. Did Marc understand?

After she'd said goodbye, Marc paced the room a few minutes. Impulsively, he kicked a dying log in his fire, and it shot off sparks as if in complaint. Then he got out a phone book. The pain in his stomach cooled and swelled into a wave of nausea as he decided to call the Nouwandan embassy directly himself.

FIFTEEN

Home. Cynthia threw a pile of magazines off a chair and sat down. The word *excursion* came back to her, soaked in irony—well, it had been a real expedition of the soul, and she felt as drained and pest-bitten as if she'd trekked through a jungle.

Alone. There was the presence of other people muffled in the stack of mail the concièrge had saved, and the drip of her kitchen faucet for further company. And that was it. She was too tired to get up and jam a cassette into the mouth of her stereo. Fix it, she admonished herself about the faucet. Fix up, fix up your life, get it straight, start with as they put it *your environment,* if you need some way to get off square one. Decorate, then. This little apartment, under eaves on the Quai Bethune (a good view, but a long walk up. Good for the legs) had never taken on any of her personality. She'd left it largely as it had come, with the good fake period pieces, clean and dull. There was, however, a Miro lithograph she'd carried with her from place to place like a mascot. A wild array of color and emotion, which had become, without her quite consciously intending it, a kind of housebroken pet. Well, it seemed to be looking at her now and gesturing something funny, but insulting.

No, she had no intention of remaking her environment. Take it as it comes—everything except what's most important. No time.

She hurried through the mail until she came upon a telegram. Sydney Goldin. *Sydney Goldin.* Making a picture. A picture in England. Come if interested.

That was it! In the whole pile of—there was her life! Where she lived. Go? She'd run to be in a picture he directed. She'd swim the Channel. Her heart pounded as she hugged herself and strode up and down her living room, nervous with happiness.

The phone rang. And something got all confused and complicated in her head again, for something made her wish, irrepressibly, that it was Marc de Wolfflen.

It was Gilbert.

"I just want you to know that I had nothing to do with what they said in *France-Soir*—" His voice was very Considerate and Casual, and Friendly. And distant. "Your friend Fallan—"

"What?" she said, "what is this about?"

"You've been away?" he asked. For an instant he seemed to care about what he was saying. He seemed to want to know where.

"Yes. Away."

"Well, please, people will tell you things in the worst light, but I'm telling you directly and I know you'll believe me, I didn't ask for the publicity—"

"Tell me what you are talking about." She was as distant as he was, but irritated by curiosity.

"I can't now," he said, "I can't go into it. I'm on my way to the American Hospital. My cousin Léopold is in the hospital. He's in very bad shape."

SIXTEEN

"I died," Léopold said. His round head lay sunken in a mound of pillows. His arm was raised, as if in an act of prophesying, where a tube was dropping liquid into his vein. Beside the stand with the bottle, there was what Marc assumed to be the latest oxygen apparatus.

Two nurses hovered near the window. They beamed at Léopold benevolent glances, as if he were some newborn baby they'd helped deliver; Léopold, Marc noted, always made friends easily. Léopold smiled back at the nurses indulgently and waved them out of the room with his free arm.

"Ten minutes, my word of honor," he said. They left.

"I died," he began again to Marc, with a tone of wonder in his voice. "Don't ask me what it's like on the other side. I couldn't tell you. As far as I'm concerned I was nothing. Someone actually put his hand on my heart and made it go again."

Léopold's face was as white as the belly of a fish. Marc had been allowed ten minutes with him because Léopold had been insisting on seeing him with great anxiety.

"What did you tell them?" Léopold asked in a voice full of a grave, terrifying message of illness, which nothing it said could overbear.

"There weren't thirty-six ways to go about it," Marc answered. "I had to tell them what we knew. What everyone with any kind of sources must have known, since the Quai knew. I was nearly certain they already knew themselves ... As it turned out, they did. So we've kept the *beau rôle*."

He twisted his lips into a wan smile.

"I would have thought they knew," Léopold said.

"The *beau rôle*," Marc repeated. "I told them that we had reason to believe there was a plot against the life of President Kumbi and that our name was being falsely associated with it. That we learned this from diplomatic sources, but we had absolutely no names."

"They believed you?"

"I think they believed me. They hadn't taken counteraction yet. It was a stroke of luck, if you like, for timing. The next day there were forty arrests. It was in the *Herald Tribune* ..."

"And Godwin?"

"It looks like he's still clean. I don't know—"

"It was he?" Léopold asked.

"I think it was he."

"Using our name?"

"Oh no! No. I'd say no. Godwin really isn't ... that way. But what would anyone expect? We're what we are, Léopold. We've got a very high profile over there. And a big problem. Even the intelligence people would jump to what seemed obvious conclusions. Or suspicions, which would have meant the same thing."

Marc sat down finally, on a chair at the foot of the bed. He crossed his arms and legs in a faint gesture of self-protection.

"Besides," he said wryly. "Our ancestors left us a little vulnerable with their legendry. Haven't they? They were always changing governments, making emperors and things."

Léopold grunted. "Other people's ancestors pillaged Byzantium and massacred heretics. Does that kind of legendry smell better?"

"We're more vulnerable.,' Marc said quietly.

"Times have changed." Léopold said. It wasn't clear to Marc what he meant. But he continued in another direction: "Where does it all leave you with the mine?"

"The same... mess. I suppose."

"Marc," Léopold said, "I'm your cousin. I'll help you."

Marc didn't answer. Silence seemed to fill his ears like water. He turned away from Léopold. His eyes fell on the bottle and then on the serum falling drop by drop. He turned again and saw that Léopold's glassy gaze was fixed on that same point in the transparent tube.

"Don't misunderstand me," Léopold said. "Listen ... when you're where I am now, when you've been where I've been, it doesn't seem to matter to you who exactly you are, who you call yourself, beyond your being a still-warm individual. You understand? I don't want to rationalize. I don't have anything to justify, Marc. I just want the simple direct satisfaction of acting like an honorable human being."

Marc heard himself swallowing.

"I'll help you, Marc. I want to."

"Oh no no. No." Marc said, saying nothing, defending himself, his pride. He looked at Léopold's drawn features and recalled with a note of shock that Léopold was not yet forty-four. Léopold was talking at the same time.

"All our money ..." he was saying. But he paused, as if he were too tired to say all he'd have to say, or as if he'd begun to draw something only half-lucid from the back of his mind.

"We've always done good things with our money," he said finally. It seemed to Marc more like an answer to what he'd meant to say than what he'd really meant to say.

"No one could doubt that you have," Marc said. What did Thérèse call him? *A God in Israel.*

"The Wolfflen coup," Léopold said. "That's what they would have called it. Everyone. We're very vulnerable, yes, Marc. People would relish our disgrace. And you and I, we didn't choose to be born to be known as the richest Jews in the world. I don't even think we are the richest Jews in the world, are we?"

Marc shrugged. He smiled. "There are so many Jews in so many woodpiles," he said in English. "I suppose we've more than the Rothschilds, but there's a man in New York in the cosmetics business with more than we have in the Holding. There's a man who used to teach Hebrew, Riklis is his name—"

"There are Japanese and Germans and Americans whose ancestors were immigrants on the *Mayflower,* and little Calvinists in Switzerland with more than all of us," Léopold interjected. "It's always the same story."

"It's just that we're Wolfflens, Léopold. All that history."

"All in all, we can hold our heads up, Marc. The Wolfflens and the Jews. All in all."

Yes, but they were all unpleasant to Marc now, all those old stories, the old partisanships and antagonisms. He didn't want to have to think about them. What had Léopold said? *An honorable human being.* And there he was going on again. But who could deny he was right? What did it matter? Marc stood up and walked to Léopold's window. It was a very sunny day for early winter. Outside, in the little hospital garden, a small boy was hunched over tensely, reading a comic book, waiting apparently for someone being examined inside. A very old man, with a heavy coat over his pyjamas, was being walked around, near the hedges, by a middle-aged woman. She held his arm. His daughter? Almost as if she were trying to teach him to walk. A sunny day ... This same place. Marc closed his eyes and saw his father dying, dumb and motionless.

A hospital, too, it came to him suddenly, was like a casino. You go in not sure what your luck will be. You come out flushed, or just ahead. Or you come out broke, in a hearse.

"Léopold," he said, "I've done a crazy thing."

"You have?" Léopold asked listlessly. He seemed to expect to hear something trite. As if Marc could only be tritely, domestically crazy.

"I took a big forward position dollars for Deutschemarks. A number of two-month contracts. A number of them have already fallen due ... I've made about ten million dollars."

"You took *some position.*"

"Three hundred million dollars, all told. The way the dollar looks now, the odds are about fifty to one I'll make more than thirty million by the end of the month."

"The dollar is—"

"Two point four three today."

"What's crazy?"

"Oh no, I had a stratagem. Far from irrational. Everyone was looking toward a hard dollar. All those dollars people needed for oil. And the Americans were far less dependent on the Arabs than anyone else. But I thought people weren't paying enough attention to the total picture. The American payments situation was chronically sick, oil or no, and it just didn't seem to me that the Americans would have the discipline. I was right. A lot of people were wrong. A lot of people are in trouble—"

"What's crazy," Léopold repeated.

Marc looked at him. He felt a fear that his taking Léopold into his confidence, suddenly like this, came from some kind of selfish impulse to unburden himself. As if in some obscure way he was exploiting a weakness. And he felt that Léopold would never quite understand what he wanted to say. But he continued. Something in the mood of this room, of the moment, drove him to get it off his chest:

"The point is . . . it didn't really matter to me. All that money was just a lot of numbers. *The risk mattered.* Can you understand, Léopold, that in this crazy way I wanted to see whether I was capable—of a victory! I was testing my acumen, surely, but I put it all down to a kind of fatalism. I wanted to know whether I could win, as if . . . I feared I was predestined not to. You understand?"

Léopold merely grunted.

"The outcome hasn't been as conclusive as I thought. As if . . . as if the question were changed before I got the answer. No, now I'm not even sure of the question. That's not very clear, is it. The question I should have asked. In a way . . . in a way, I feel like a man who's crashed his glider and walked away unharmed. It's a relief. But it's hardly a triumph."

"Never mind all the sick talk," Léopold said with a sudden forcefulness in his voice. "It's all only money, is what it is. Money. Money. Money. Is only money. Why? Why is it?"—his voice sounded imploring now— "Why is it, Marc, everytime we get together all we can talk about is money—"

There was a knock at the door. Gilbert came in, looking grave.

"They want you to leave," he said to his father. "They've only let me in to say hello."

He went up to Léopold and took Léopold's free hand in both of his.

"Hello, cousin," Léopold said.

Gilbert turned to Marc. "Godwin Laver's been trying to get you several times."

"Can you handle him for the moment?" Marc asked his son. "Tell him ... that there's nothing meaningful I can say to him until I get back from Zaccra."

His son and his cousin stared at Marc with wide-open eyes.

"They've invited me to meet with the Minister of Finance," Marc said. "I guess there's only one thing to do ... and that's to go."

On the morning of Marc's flight, the *International Herald Tribune* reported on its financial page that Kyle R. Hoyt had left his roost in Las Vegas and flown to Costa Rica. The Justice Department refused to comment on whether its investigation of Dynamerica had led it to prepare charges against Mr. Hoyt. But an unnamed official pointed out that extradition from Costa Rica was a very difficult procedure.

Marc read the story over breakfast. He ordered his bags packed. For the moment, there was still only one thing to do, although, all in all, he didn't know what kind of face he could put on for them now.

SEVENTEEN

The Air Zaïre stopoff at Zaccra was at one in the afternoon, local time. Marc had a morning appointment at the ministry. He left the day before rather than try to change it. Oddly, he welcomed the full afternoon of dead time. He decided to use it to look at the city of Zaccra. He knew very little about Nouwanda as a place. He knew the minesite and a Zaccra hotel. In the plane, he felt calm and curious. Again he realized his life was such an embroglio, that his mind seemed to him to have fled for refuge outside the boundaries of his own life. For the sake of health, of sanity. The image of the ledge came to him again. Maybe his mind had called into play an old inner resource. Or weakness. In any case, he was calm, and he refused to stir his will into challenging his calm. Nothing to gain by it.

The dry season had just begun. As the plane banked and turned for a landing, he peered out at a paling grassland. It nudged in splotches into a city pocked with tall white buildings, built and half-built. The speckled grass swept around the city and turned into cane along a thin stretch of dried swamp. Now behind the green, eastward, he could see the land rise and turn into brush before the yellow savanah, higher up. And there, poking into the horizon was a mauve mountain. His father's mountain.

A haze coming off the cane blurred the edges of the airfield. Marc shielded his eyes as he stepped out of the plane. The first person he saw was a photographer. The man was taking pictures of him one after the other. The airfield was still, and through the thick hot air the sound of the photographer's automatic shutter whined at him like passing bullets. Then a band began to play.

A red carpet stretched from the airport building to the foot of the ramp. He advanced down the ramp and the band near the nose of his plane came into full view: tall men in red, white, and emerald uniforms, playing and marking time with a touch of syncopation in their legs. He halted on the carpet. And then an officer appeared and welcomed him in the name of the Nouwandan Republic and President Alexandre Kumbi. Behind him were rows of children with flowers in their arms.

The officer opened the door of a white Rolls Royce, in which Marc was driven to his hotel, alone, and left there.

The hotel, the same one Marc had used before, had been built by the French in the late fifties, a few years before Nouwandan independence. It was whitened cinderblock, functional and not at all conspicuous, no displaced château of stucco like the old colonial buildings. It seemed whoever built it might have already known it was time for his kind to pull in their horns. Inside there was the typical uncertain European taste of the period. Behind the reception desk sheets of plastic in a variety of colors and geometric shapes formed a tableau broken by a clock framed in a clutter of Venetian glass like melted candles.

Marc's entrance brought all the help in the lobby to attention, as if that moment had been rehearsed. The young man behind the desk, in a very Paris *minet* brown suit with wide, deep, flattened-down lapels, held out the room key like a gift, in the palm of his hand. His colleague took it and whisked Marc up to his room in a new elevator. The room was like any first-class hotel room in Lyons, say, or Düsseldorf, comfortable enough. The blue tiles in the bathroom gleamed and gave off a bitter odor of newness. The plumbing was also new. The French hadn't built theirs to last. The air conditioning might not have been redone. It gave off a clicking rattle each time the fan inside started up wearily with what sounded like a sigh.

It was a time for a businessman on a trip to study his presentation.

But Marc had no presentation. He knew all there was to know about Cofra by heart now, except for whatever *monsieur* Kumbi had in mind. For why he had been summoned. Yes, the Baron Marc de Wolfflen had been *summoned*. And here he was, kept waiting, where they wanted him. The rattle of the air conditioner sounded, just then, like a snicker. In any case, he had nothing to do but wait. Emptyhanded, with no presentation. He decided to nap. He took off his shoes and lay down on the smaller of the two beds, on which he happened to be sitting. He didn't wake up until the next morning. There was a message that his appointment was scheduled for that afternoon. He had a sudden absurd feeling of being kept prisoner. After coffee, he walked out of the lobby, half-believing he was doing something daring.

There was nearly as much traffic on the main avenues of Zaccra as on the boulevards in Paris. Marc was an observant walker, who knew intimate things about cities; for one thing, their particular smells. Different cities smelled differently—a function more and more of car exhaust, the effects of local gasoline on local climate. He could remember when cities in winter smelled of fires, wood and coal burning, an odor like phenol and bitter toast. But now they all smelled perennially of exhaust. The exhaust of Zaccra smelled oddly like Prague's, acid. The muggy weather turned the smell into a menace. He tried the back streets. Many of them were still unpaved, dusty, and potholed. But tall buildings were going up all over. They were made of concrete columns with thin, hollow brick tiles for walls. The cement work was thick and irregular, and some of the tiles on the unfinished buildings were already cracked.

So, again, was the wall near his elevator in Paris, he recalled.

He walked toward the glare of sunlight at the end of a narrow street. The street led back onto a boulevard, and now he saw that the sunlight had poked into the street from a great open square on the other side of the boulevard. Cars were stopped on the boulevard, traffic was backed up. A great crowd had gathered in the square and people were abandoning their cars to join the excited crowd.

Marc made his way gently through the crowd until he saw what had caused the gathering. At the foot of a fountain—the missing centerpiece of which, he recalled in a flash, had been, years ago, a monument in the likeness of the explorer Frédeau—there was now a heap of bloody flesh: the remains of a human being.

* * *

"It's the truck gangs," the Dutchman explained. The Dutchman knew a lot about Nouwanda. He was with the American Electronic and Communications Company that was going to install the new telephone system. He'd been sitting at the bar of the hotel when Marc came in.

Dizzy with nausea, Marc had broken through the crowd at the square and found a cab a block away that was able to do a u-turn and take him back to the hotel. By the time he'd arrived, his nausea had subsided, but he craved a scotch. That battered corpse, which only a while ago had been a man flaunting his share of life in a colorful sportshirt, the latest flared corduroys, had shaken him badly.

The Dutchman was having, as he explained, his regular prelunch sweet vermouth. "Are you all right?" he'd asked. Marc must have looked like a ghost to him. Marc told his fellow European what he'd seen.

"It's the truck gangs," the Dutchman said. The police had been unable to do anything with them. They had the police absolutely terrified. They would just pull up in trucks and break into places, houses, stores, and carry everything away. They were better armed than the police.

The Dutchman smiled as he lowered his head toward his glass. He looked like he greatly enjoyed finding someone else who could appreciate the interesting eccentricities of this place.

"Finally they brought in the army. Ah, but the army was very different from the police. Very tough. The army is the backbone of this country, as you must have realized. They began rounding up all the hooligan elements. The truck men—they beat them. They began to beat them to death one by one and then drop them off somewhere very public. As an example. I think they've got almost all of them now. And the total crime rate has dropped dramatically. No more truck robberies. I think the principle has been very recently extended to all burglars as well."

The Dutchman was a short, round-headed man with thick glasses that gave him a scholarly cast. He explained that he'd been trained as an engineer, but he was now a vice-president of AECC for Europe and Africa, and his sole job was contract negotiations.

"The first thing you learn is not to get involved in judgments about what they do among themselves. Personally—" his voice dropped to a whisper and he drew Marc closer to his barstool, "I know everything. I have ways of knowing everything, and you have to. You have to have an overall, up-to-date understanding of what's what, and who is what, because after all you are dealing directly with a government. For example I know that at least thirty thousand people who have been arrested were shipped up to Larmoua and fed to the crocodiles. Literally, my friend. The papers, I think it was the *Sunday Times,* talked about fifty thousand. They were at last twenty thousand too high. But all the same ..."

He took time for a sip of his vermouth.

"All the same in any case—" his voice returned to normal—"in any case the Africans are excellent for us, business-wise. They are excellent people to work with. First of all there's no trouble about money. They give us a promissory note backed by the Export-Import Bank. We write it over and get cash immediately. Cash. And the important thing, far from negligible, is you know when you're dealing that you're dealing with someone who can take action. Immediately. You don't get stories. Look at Italy, on the other hand. A place like Italy, the perfect example of the difference when you're talking with government people in Europe. If I had to do a deal like this one in Italy, we'd be talking for months. Years! God knows. Because the people you talk to half the time have no power to take action."

His drink was finished. He pointed toward Marc's glass and raised his eyebrows in a question. Would Marc have another too? He seemed unhappy with the refusal, but he continued:

"Here you pay—" He caught the barman's eye and tapped his empty glass with his finger.

"Here you pay and you get service."

The dead man in the square flashed back into Marc's mind. He winced, but he couldn't censor the image. Nausea racked him again, and he knew there was a good chance the image would come back again uncontrollably. He calculated that he had just enough time to go upstairs and make himself vomit once and for all before his appointment.

EIGHTEEN

They rang his room. The appointment, a male secretary said, had been changed from the Ministry of Finance to the Presidential Palace. He was to see *monsieur* Akkira first, in any case. The Finance Minister. There would be a car for him ...

A young man in a tight black mohair suit was waiting in a chair at the bottom of the double marble staircase of the palace, once the governor's seat. The entry room resembled the *pompier* classicism of provincial turn-of-century city halls.

"Akkira," the young man said, coming up to Marc, "I am Claude Akkira. We are going to see the President." He had nothing more to say for the moment and his voice was as neutral, as committed to nothing, as possible. Marc chose to follow him up the stairs equally silent, while the Cuban heels of Akkira's kid half-boots clattered on the marble.

The President was sitting behind a totally empty desk about twenty feet long. There wasn't even a pen or a lamp, or an ashtray. The top was a green marble slab and it sat on gold legs. The President did not get up as they came in. He pointed toward two

Pierre Paulin ribbon chairs in purple. He gestured for them to sit down.

As he sat down, Marc noticed a high building crane through the window to the side of the desk. Kumbi caught his glance. He pointed to the window with his thumb. "When we finish there," he said, "we tear this down. Right now it's just a hole." He flashed a smile. "But we have hired a man from Brasilia. This building—" He tapped his desk; "will be a lawn. With three levels of parking underneath."

Kumbi looked like he was made of leather. He was spare and small and his head was a long oval. Behind him on the wall was a picture of himself in a loose army tunic covered with medals. The President was about Marc's age, his thin wiry hair was nearly all white, and the picture, Marc guessed, was about fifteen years old. Taken about the time he seized power, not long after Nouwandan independence. Kumbi had been a captain in the Foreign Legion and he still had the sinewy look of a Legionnaire, although he chose to wear a nondescript double-breasted brown business suit. The fallen tip of his nose recalled that he'd also been a well-known lightweight boxer. For fifteen years he'd ruled Nouwanda with only two tremors of unrest—the student strike of 1969 and Godwin's botched coup. Godwin had set his sights on a hard target.

"Baron," he said, as if it gave him pleasure to say the title, to address a rare person such as himself. "We need not go into any details as far as your relationship with the Americans. With ... Dynamerica Corporation."

A barrage of sound filled the room. A bulldozer had started working again beyond the window. Kumbi pressed a button on the underside of the marble and the drapes moved together behind him slowly with a humming sound. He walked over to where Marc sat in that purple jersey chair and touched the top of Marc's hand, keeping him seated with the pressure.

"Nouwanda is nationalizing the mine," Kumbi went on. "The whole matter has been rendered very simple, you see."

So there it was. He'd done all the waiting for this. Marc suddenly felt very weary and full of disgust. They'd acted like children. They'd played with him; could they have that much contempt for him?

"Very well," he said. His hand froze.

Kumbi walked back behind his desk. "Listen," he said, "we are nationalizing the whole minesite, very simple. But I guarantee you that we will work out a fair price. This is a promise. And every stockholder will get paid bonds payable beginning in three years. Better than the government of France. The government of France, in 1946, when it nationalized the coal, an example of which you are aware, did not pay so easily as that. When it took over the Renault, it didn't pay anything. Not one franc. This I know. This isn't just talking."

"Renault had been working with the enemy," Marc said drily.

"And you," the President smiled, "have worked against our enemies... Listen—*Ecoutez-moi, Baron*—we make it very simple. We nationalize the mine and we pay everyone. Then you—" he pointed his forefinger at Marc—"you and I: we form an operating company. You and the people of Nouwanda. You can participate to the extent of thirty-five percent. That way, we both wash our hands of the Americans. My enemies were in the pay of the CIA. This I know."

"Really?"

"So you get your money and you keep your business. Not bad? What matters, frankly, is that you are the one with the capability. You have the experience. You built the new plants and you have the men to run them. Thirty-five percent. All right? We are not against foreign cooperation. We are against foreign domination. This I told the people and this they know. Nouwanda will do everything to ensure that the mine is profitable for everyone concerned."

"Taxes?"

"Not taxes, Baron, subsidies."

Marc could hardly believe what he was hearing.

"Now," the President said, "now please listen. I consider Akkira here as I would consider my own son. I can arrange everything with him. When you need something done and you don't see me, you will see him. Everything you need."

"Now," he began again, "this is my number." He wrote on a slip of paper from a little pad in his jacket pocket, folded the paper, and handed it to Marc. "Part of the payment is direct. You understand."

Marc unfolded the paper. The name "Pierre" was written on it and a series of numbers. The "Berne bank, Zurich branch." And underneath, in figures, $3 million

Marc looked up. "Direct," the President said again. Marc thought Kumbi had actually winked...

* * *

"You made an excellent impression," Akkira said, as he opened the door to an office down the hall from the President's. It was a bare room, except for Kumbi's photo, a yellow oak desk, and some folding chairs. The familiarity in Akkira's tone, the note of complicity, grated on Marc. His irritation made him think that this room might do for an interrogation.

"Excellent," Akkira said. *"Vous n'avez pas bronché.* President Kumbi likes people who know when to listen and not say what they don't have to." He folded his arms across his chest and stood at the other side of the desk from Marc. "I can feel that we will get along." Now he seemed to Marc totally impudent. Akkira wasn't even half his age.

He wrote on a paper and handed it to Marc.

"My number," he said frowning seriously, "for the negotiation costs. Two hundred thousand dollars."

Marc slipped the paper in his jacket pocket beside Kumbi's and kept silent. As Akkira led Marc down the doomed marble stairs, he withdrew something red from his inside jacket pocket. It looked like a passport.

"It's a diplomatic passport," Akkira said, beaming. "Take it. It is yours." He laughed. "You are an honorary representative of our country."

His voice dropped: "I will tell you something highly confidential. It cannot be long before the people of Nouwanda thrust a crown upon our President. At which time your name, if I have anything to do with it, will be on the list of nobles. You can be sure of being promoted to a duke."

Marc opened the passport. Inside, he was shocked to see, was indeed a photo of himself. Then he made out from the blur of background an open plane door. Yes, it was a cropped picture of him, taken when he'd arrived from Paris.

"These are bestowed on especially honored foreigners," Akkira was explaining carefully. His voice dropped again, to a confiding tone: "You can get through customs anywhere with that ... With anything ..."

Back at the hotel, the Baron tore his diplomatic passport into little pieces and flushed it down the toilet bowl. Then he got out some paper from his valise. It was Wolfflen paper, with the Beast on its hindlegs embossed on it. He began to write a letter to the President of Nouwanda. He had no secretary, no typewriter now, and as he wrote in ink, in his own hand, under the embossed crest, the letter began to look to him like an historic document.

He had it photocopied downstairs, before he mailed it and left.

NINETEEN

Godwin had remembered Wolfflen's cigar from the last time, so he filled his own little leather case with Davidoff Château d'Yquem's. They would smoke cigars and Godwin thought he'd even order brandy. Although he was in no mood to celebrate, Godwin wanted an old-fashioned, very civilized sporting mood to prevail. They would be two gentlemen in the same club, who'd played a long, important game of poker. He wanted Wolfflen to know that he'd nothing against him, although his winning had of course cost Laver a considerable sum. He hoped that Wolfflen saw no reason to hold against him the fact that he'd played as hard as he had.

Godwin questioned his luck these days. He'd had a call late last night from one of his partners in California. Rioters had attacked the site of "Open City." They'd burned the building shacks. His partners hadn't been able to sort out what exactly had stirred them up. They weren't even Mexicans or Blacks. They hadn't brandished any placards. As best his partners were able to guess, they had been "ecology freaks on the rampage."

Anyway, Godwin thought, as for Wolfflen, I wasn't really playing *against him.* The point is, I was working for everyone's good. And he was the one with the most to gain.

Nonetheless, Godwin felt a little nervous, as he discovered that Marc de Wolfflen had already arrived and was sitting exactly where they'd sat the last time, with a cup of coffee already emptied in front of him. Wolfflen's face was pursed as he stood up for Laver. He shook his head at the offer of a cigar. Godwin filled the awkward moment by lighting his own very carefully.

"What will you have?" Marc asked. The waiter was behind Godwin.

"Will you have a brandy?" Godwin asked.

Marc shook his head.

"Oh, a coffee," Godwin said, turning to the waiter.

"All in all," Godwin said, when the waiter went off, "I think you played it very well, Marc. You took your risks . . . and you did well. What do the mistresses say to each other in the cloakroom, to console each other their 'irregularity'? A share of a *bon coup* is better than title deed to a bad one. Thirty-five percent. Of a healthy company? It's better than all of a sick one."

"Where did you get that figure?" Marc asked abruptly.

"The whole thing has already been explained to a number of people over there," Laver answered. He realized he'd irritated Wolfflen. But he couldn't help but put a note of gloating into his information. He realized now that against his conscious will something in him was driving him to get the most ego satisfaction possible out of this meeting.

"They're all very happy from what I've been able to learn," he said. "I learned . . . from some French people. Our people . . . I mean, the Quai." By "our" Godwin had meant "white." He was not trying to dissimulate that he was English.

"Are you certain your information is up to date?" A smile seemed to flicker on Wolfflen's lips.

Godwin charged ahead: "I gather Kumbi's going to be sure there's profit if he has to man the mines with prisoners. A showcase operation."

Wolfflen crossed and uncrossed his legs.

"It has to do well," Godwin went on, "they're very interested in looking A-1 for all their credit guarantees."

Marc looked into his coffee cup and began to swirl the dregs around gently.

"Was it a tiring trip?" Godwin asked, avoiding the rejection, the tuning-out in Marc's silent gesture.

"No," Marc said "it all went very well. I have—a far better grasp of things."

"I should think." Marc irritated Godwin now. If only he'd open up, if he were to gloat, show some manly satisfaction for God's sake. The air would clear. They'd get on. "I suppose old Kumbi was really quite a reasonable person after all," Godwin continued, pushing Wolfflen to *say something*. "I think my deposit really went to the wrong account number. I must say, Marc, I really calculated it all wrong. There would have been so much less mess, if I paid the right person ... Even if it took more. He did—Kumbi—have a price? Godwin blurted now, impertinently. *Say something.*

"He gave me his number in Zürich ... or Geneva, I forget."

How much, Godwin would have asked, but he checked his emotion. Marc's evasiveness was like his whole mood from the start, a reproach.

"Marc," Godwin said instead in a conciliatory voice, "I did everything to see that your name was kept out of it. I deliberately kept you in the dark—"

"That was impossible," Marc broke in. "It was impossible to do anything like that in Nouwanda and keep our name out of it. For God's sake. It was ... gross."

The word fell on Godwin like a blow.

"But if it worked," he shot back, "it wouldn't have mattered."

"What wouldn't have mattered? Our name? *Our name.* And if it failed? If your colonel or your captain went ahead and fouled up? Just for the sake of conversation?"

"I am sure today as much as ever that he wouldn't have failed. He was already very hungry, Marc. All he needed was a little push, a little encouragement. It was a risk, everything is a risk—"

"Kumbi knew all about it in no time," Marc interjected.

"He didn't. I can't believe he did—" But Godwin's voice was losing its thrust of sureness. "I had the most competent person in that whole stupid country. He is—"

"He's going to be was," Marc said drily. "Kumbi will shoot him.

Or they'll hang pieces of him in the main square of Zaccra. Godwin, what am I here for? What do you think this appointment is all about? I came to tell you, in case you're still not aware, that you're a devious dangerous fool. That you're an unscrupulous bastard."

"Marc," Godwin said patiently, "the whole economic system of the Free World depends on men with courage, entrepreneurs, taking risks."

Wolfflen frowned, as if Laver had finally said something too stupid to counter.

"I'll tell you something you might enjoy hearing," Wolfflen said. "Yesterday I made six million dollars on the foreign exchange market. I expect I will have made something like thirty-five million by the end of the month."

"That's quite a coup," Laver said wanly.

"I went bearish on the dollar to the extent of three hundred million dollars over two months. Of course, I borrowed the money. I borrowed it for no reason than to exchange with some people who borrowed marks. They didn't intend to do anything with their loan outside of our transaction either. We borrowed and we swapped and in the process I'm taking thirty-odd million dollars extra from the people on the other end of my contracts. I won. They lost. Their investors. Their stockholders. Out of all this paperwork I've made a considerable sum."

"It's normal," Godwin said, diminishing slightly Marc's achievement.

"I didn't produce anything for the money," Wolfflen continued, "I didn't finance any trade. Doesn't that strike you in some sense as abnormal?"

"Happens every day," Godwin said, "some people hedge, some people speculate. There have to be some people there to make a market, you can't rely on the irregularity of trade ..."

Wolfflen put his hands on the arms of his chair as if he were about to spring up. "I just thought you'd like to hear the story," he said in a flat tone. "People will be talking about it in the market. As for me, may I tell you something very personal? I'm fed up with talking about money."

"Money," Godwin riposted, "is what people like you and me are all about!" Wolfflen had toyed with him. His attitude was finally insufferable. There was a manly note of indignation in Godwin's voice, but Wolfflen was already up and his eyes seemed to have gone out of focus. As if although he was facing Godwin, he was no longer looking at him at all.

Should I have told him everything, Marc wondered as he crossed the lobby of the hotel. The end of the story? He had intended to tell Godwin the end of the Cofra story, but a devious nastiness, not simple anger, had crept into their conversation. It was not really what either of us had wanted to happen—he granted Godwin his little measure of decency. But if people were judged by what they really wanted to happen, what they wanted to avoid but couldn't hold back, hell would be half out of business.

All things considered, he decided there was no point in talking to Godwin Laver again.

TWENTY

Thérèse was having her bags packed. She was going to Mexico. Marc came into her dressing room, where she stood before a mirror, lashing a brush through her long hair. Her arm moved with a fierce energy, as if she wasn't brushing her own hair, but something alien to her body, which had to be forced into serving it.

"There is something ... something has happened," he began, looking at her through the mirror. "I meant to tell you ... but so much has come up—"

"You're in love, Marc," she interjected. "It's all over your silly face. You never could hide it. You literally glow, my dear husband ... "

"Ah...."

"Ah ... who?"

"Well ... maybe you can guess that too."

"The mannequin, of course," she said. "I saw you coming down the stairs at your party. Your face ... oh Marc, your face ...

"Your beautiful face," she said. "Well, you have my best wishes, if not my congratulations."

"There's not much you could congratulate me on, I haven't even seen her again. Yet."

"How far do you intend to go . . . ?" she asked.

He felt oddly gratified that she had said something stupid.

"How can anyone tell?" he answered with exaggerated impatience.

"Marc," she said, turning from the mirror to face him. She took his wrist with her free hand. "Marc, nobody owns anybody. Don't expect me to recriminate. Don't come to me for your punishment. Do what you like. It's your life . . ."

He looked at the toe of his shoe and said nothing.

"You never recriminated," she said evenly.

She turned and began to tame her hair again.

He laughed inside—at what he was thinking just then. He was thinking that one of the important, defining things about his encounter with Cynthia was that it was something they hadn't *shared*, Thérèse and he. Once they'd set out to share everything. He'd gone off without her into the hurly-burly of business and she'd found a life to live without him, or almost without him. For even now, announcing, letting fall what he'd thought would be the last blow of the ax driving them apart, he felt the tie still there, whatever was left of what had brought them passionately together, not "need," he knew, not dependence, not passion anymore, but *complicity*. And it was a fruitless thing, now . . . But she was saying:

"The one thing I ask you, Marc, is that you think a while before we talk about a divorce. I'm a Wolfflen. You grafted me. You know, in many ways, I may have become more of a Wolfflen than you are."

For the first time, she sounded pathetic to him. He wished she hadn't. What was the point in getting down to the petty vanities of it all, the *legalities*, my God . . .

He said: "It doesn't matter . . . as you wish . . ." Imprecisely.

She pulled at a knot with her brush, wincing. She wouldn't accept his patronizing her, either. "That's the problem with you," she said in a punishing voice. "Nothing in your life, Marc, has mattered enough to you."

"Things have, Thérèse," he said evenly. "You have . . . you do. She . . . Cynthia"—he let the name fall—"I think she might." But to fend off nastiness now, he said something of clear use: "Will you be at Léa's party?" he asked.

"I think I'll have a better time at Las Hadas," she said. "Patiño is doing a big launching of the place. He's invited all the influential press and all the best people. It would be terrible for him if I didn't show up."

Marc realized that he'd married a woman from another planet. How many other men had known that kind of union? Maybe it had been a privilege. In any case, no one, he thought, could be blamed for the results. Or so he found it comforting to think, now, believing that blame, in any case, was of no use for the future.

"Do you feel up to the trip?" he asked, with genuine concern.

"I feel splendid. I'll outlive everyone!"

Something told him her boast would come true.

"You'll be very lonely, in that case," he said, trying to make it sound like a joke.

Well, the way things stood between Thérèse and Léopold, he'd hardly be shocked that she wasn't present at Léa's engagement party. Marc believed that Léopold might actually be happier if she wasn't there.

As he prepared for his own trip, Marc was relieved that he hadn't told Thérèse all the pathetic things he couldn't help rehearsing in his mind before he'd gone to her—all the too-much, thank God, he hadn't had to say. *You realize, Thérèse, that we haven't really lived together, not in a real sense, for a long time.* He winced to think of all that banality.

"Together." There were really too many kinds of together for the word to offer any instruction. What mattered was what you irrefutably knew: that there was an end to one thing, some kind of beginning of another. Thérèse too was entitled to another beginning. It was up to her to accomplish it.

On the plane to London, he went through the newspapers quickly. On an inside page of each one of them was the news that Alexandre Kumbi, having ousted thousands of opponents purportedly linked to the failed *coup d'état*, was having himself crowned Emperor of Nouwanda. Marc piled the papers on the empty seat beside him and opened his pocket appointment book out of habit. He couldn't recall when his calendar had looked so clean. For the day after tomorrow, he'd written "Herbert—Léa." Lord Herbert Wolfflen was giving the engagement party at Owen Glade for Léopold's daughter, Léa, and young Fullerton. Yes, Herbert's turn, by the rule of old Hannah: *All Wolfflen children are the children of each Wolfflen.*

The form survived.

After the day of the party, blank day followed blank day in his agenda, but for tomorrow he'd written: "London—C."

"C."

The morning after he'd arrived from Zaccra, he'd called her. He'd set his alarm, so that he could call her at seven London time. He wanted to speak to her before she went on the set. Would she see him in London? Finally, all he dared to do was to invite her to lunch. Would she be shooting?

She'd "take sick," she said.

"Hello, May?" he'd begun with clumsy wit, "this is January." A stupid thing to blurt.

"I don't think that's the least bit funny," she'd said, laughing from what he thought might be the pleasure of his call.

TWENTY-ONE

Rain was soaking London. The doorman of the Connaught kept running back and forth from the steps to the steaming black cabs, sheltering his guests under a huge umbrella. The revolving door churned in little drafts of damp air. Marc could feel them where he sat, in a chair near the entrance. But he wanted to see her come in.

Should a man his age be careful about drafts? Nearby, the manager was insisting to an apparently remiss hall porter that all lights in unoccupied areas must be turned out. You must check after a guest leaves his room. The old porter blustered about privacy. Nice old club of a hotel, the Connaught, but last night Marc had come in from the airport to a cold room.

"We are talking about a government order!" Mr. Gustav, the manager, said. "We are all being asked to do our share."

It sounded so much like 1941. Was there a kindly sheik anywhere who'd do his share to save London from this wet spring that felt like late autumn?

There she comes: Cynthia swept in wearing boots and a big peasant skirt, sweaters on sweaters under her loden cape. She kissed him on the mouth right in the lobby. Marc saw the concièrge peer over his stack of newspapers with a flash of curiosity. Then his eyes dropped: he was a servant, the other a guest. But they were about the same age. Cynthia's presence dominated the room like an enormous bouquet.

Stiff gentlemen looked up from their plates as she walked into the Grill with him. Every day, a hundred men must desire her. There were laws of statistics at work, he thought absurdly, not so absurdly. How could he prevent the day when the right young man would get the right response when he looked at her? But that whole scenario in his mind was absurd, he told himself. He was nearly nowhere with her. And for all he knew maybe he'd better stay there. Or be very careful of exactly where he went. January and May. January went blind and May romped with the right young man in the treetop over his head. Possession was to be excluded. But when he told himself that, he couldn't help but already feel a pain of loss.

She ate lustily. "They have this dreadful ghastly English canteen on the set," she said. "I feel like taking some of this roast beef back with me in my purse."

"How is Goldin?" he asked.

"A genius. And a prince. I think—Marc, I think he likes what I've done so far." She reached over and squeezed Marc's hand under the table. "You want to give him everything you have inside you. He really is so fantastic."

"Ah," he bantered—but it was a real twinge of fear that had stabbed his abdomen—"aha, you're in love with him. Hopelessly."

She lowered her eyes. "I think," she said, "we'd better call this meeting to order."

"All right."

"Coffee, sir?" the waiter asked.

"You must have a sweet from the trolley," Marc stalled.

"Marc," she blurted, "it's—I don't want it! Not the pudding, you silly ... I don't want you—no, I mean I don't want to need you! I'm going where I'm going *on my own*. I've figured it out. What matters most of all in this world to me is what I'm going to make of myself. My work—all right? I absolutely do not wish to be in love."

"Are you?"

She shrugged, blushing. "You keep me awake ... "

"Not with Goldin, then?"

"Don't be a fool."

"Don't be a fool," he echoed.

"That's what I don't want to be."

"Can a gentleman my age advise you?"

"Stop that—don't ever say anything that pathetic to me again. *Ever.*"

She looked up at him, and he turned away from the power of her eyes. Her "ever" spoke to him of a future. He went on: "I have absolutely no interest in stopping your work." He opened his palm and held it across the table. "Only, there's something here," he said, "if you feel it, as I do ... *I've figured it out* ..." He hadn't figured anything out.

"Do you want to be with me?" he asked.

She didn't reply.

"When you've really figured it out, let me know. I won't ask you anything. You let me know ..."

"In any case," he began, then he blurted: "Don't be tough! For God's sake, don't be tough, Cynthia. You're too tough—on the outside. It's your flaw. It can wreck you ... yes, I can teach you something: don't be a fool, the really strong people in this world don't carry weapons."

He walked with her under the doorman's umbrella to her taxi. The taxi door was open, waiting to enclose her and bear her away. She turned to get in, but then just before she plunged inside, she reached for his hands and kissed him again on the mouth, with open lips. She still had hold of his hand as she slid across the seat.

"If you're willing to see what can happen," he mumbled to the air as it turned out, for her cab had sped off. He turned away from the umbrella and decided suddenly to walk.

The rain hadn't let up at all. The doorman blustered something "... Sir?" Marc waved him away. He was all right. He had drunk three cups of coffee—they both had—trying to prolong the time she was there with him. Now he was almost shaking. He felt sweat on his back, soaking his shirt, despite the cold air. He walked. He went over to Berkeley Square, clotted with traffic, and he crossed it and walked to Piccadilly. He dodged the cars on Piccadilly and walked into the Green Park. He walked faster and faster. He felt an urge to sprint, though puddles splashed under his feet. He paused a moment opposite the Palace, as confusing cars swept, leftsided, around the Queen Victoria Memorial. He turned into the Mall, and an absurd sentiment of triumph welled through him while he strode on that wide imperial avenue. Behind him now he heard a band playing: the changing of the Guard. His manic mood was crazy, falsified, he thought. All that coffee. No, he said to himself, no, don't seek out the banal as a refuge. Past Trafalgar Square he walked and didn't notice where he was walking. The rain wouldn't let up. When he got back to the hotel, he was so thoroughly wet all over that the doorman who ran up to him couldn't notice that his face was also wet with tears.

TWENTY-TWO

He checked out in a hurry, although it was too late now to get to Herbert's before full night fell on the wet roads. He regretted that his frame of mind when he rented a car that morning, his buoyancy, had made him tell the concièrge not to bother getting a driver as well. Now he realized he was tired, felt a good physical fatigue that he knew, all the same, could turn into depression, given a little more strain. He resolved to keep all crucial matters tucked away in limbo during the drive. Without quite conceptualizing why, he brightened as he thought of spending a full day alone with Herbert before the party.

TWENTY-THREE

In Marc's mind, Herbert was forever fixed as an Older Boy.

Lord Herbert Wolfflen was a gray, stooped man of sixty-five now, a man of great distinction, covered with honors. Yet when Marc thought of Herbert, his mind would find reference less in Herbert's mature greatness than in a blurry admiration, a jealous respect Marc had formed when Cousin Herbert was eleven and Marc six. This attitude under the surface of Marc's consciousness, this frame for Herbert-ness, existed probably because those were the days he and Herbert had been the closest.

Now they almost never saw each other. Quite predictably, Herbert had taken "Emma's side," many years ago. Marc thought of the dinner at which he'd reintroduced them during the war. The "fatal" meeting that seemed more fated because in London, during the war, Marc had later eaten with Herbert only three times in the course of two years. Lord Wolfflen, the great brain of MI5, had worked night and day and lived like a hermit with guards at his door. After the war, Herbert got completely out of running the banking house. Now he lived nearly a hermit, at Owen Glade, having lost his wife to cancer in 1969.

Herbert had passed the operating control of the House of Wolfflen on to his son, Raphael. Raphael the cold fish, the smart-aleck, a man deformed perhaps by his father's aloof brilliance. Once Raphael had actually called the French Wolfflens "hopeless" in a conversation with someone in the City. The word had made the rounds of financial Europe. By then, Raphael had already gone out of his way to avoid cooperating with the French family. Maybe he wanted to be *the* Wolfflen in finance. Bruno would do imitations of his pudgy face whenever his name came up at parties.

At Owen Glade, Lord Wolfflen, Great Britain's modern Renaissance man, meditated, and wrote books on an array of knowledge from sociology to physics and extrasensory perception, and he prepared white papers for Her Majesty's government with rare and not always popular incisiveness.

But when Marc thought of Owen Glade, he remembered the fields and woods, the cool bright summers of those years when he and Herbert were little boys. Year after year, while the five-year gap in their ages still allowed them to be playmates, they used to spend their summers together, alternately at Owen Glade and Bois Brûlé.

Owen Glade. The name still tasted of sunlight, as Marc pointed himself there along a straight, dull, English motorway, while rainy gusts of wind blew across his hired Rover and tried to send him drifting.

The house at Owen Glade stood on the deep plateau short of the hilltop. The woods nestled the river below and began again higher up. The glade, the clearing of rich grass, wasn't manmade and the house at the head of it looked like something God had set down to call attention to his generosity in making this particular world. The Wolfflens bought it in 1820.

It was built for the Third Earl of Railford, cousin and a rumored lover of the Virgin Queen, at the end of the sixteenth century. The name of the architect and the reason for the name Owen were lost to history. It might have been designed by Railford himself. The light, fluid symmetry spoke of a mind of clarity and vigor combined with gentle grace; it recalled Railford's poetry. There were fine classical details around the gables, parapets, chimneys, and tall mullioned windows. The plan of the manor formed a great E, in mute tribute, perhaps, to Railford's illustrious cousin.

The Roundheads sacked Owen Glade in 1644. They destroyed all the paneling and furniture but the architect's shell stood nearly intact. Only the roofs were unsound when the Ninth Earl of Railford, whose family fortune had been precarious ever since the South Sea Bubble, sold Owen Glade to Noah Wolfflen.

As the tires seemed to lighten their hold with a gust, Marc had a slight sensation of being in a boat. Then suddenly a precise memory came to mind: he and Herbert were going fishing on the lake above the wooded hills at Owen. It was morning, before full dawn, and the light was a little like the light of this English afternoon's rainy dusk. Brown, the old gamekeeper, was accompanying the two boys.

"Do you know Brown?" asked the eleven-year-old Herbert. "Brown among other things has made some remarkable observations of the movements of colloidal particles."

"That I have!" said Brown, with a note of annoyance in his eager voice. He seemed to want to deflect the boy's impudence by cooperating enthusiastically in the joke. But he knew well enough he was the butt. Little Marc didn't any more know what colloidal particles were than old Brown did.

Brown carried two excellent rods. "Oh we don't want those," Herbert said, "we're going to fashion our own."

Herbert cut rods of willow and made hooks of pins. In the boat, he lost, patiently, three fine bass; each of them slipped off his pin because it had no burr like a true fishhook. After each loss, Herbert fussed with the angle of the end of his twisted pin. Then Herbert landed three more fish. As Marc recalled, he hadn't even got a bite. Had Herbert developed a technique for getting bites as well?

It was years before Marc learned about the Brownian movement of colloidal particles. He'd been too lazy to bother to find out what Herbert was talking about. Incurious. Over those years Herbert had already developed into an exceptional scholar.

Night had fallen. As Marc turned into the narrow road that would lead to the house between two rows of poplars, his headlights showed a high wire fence. There was a metal sign. He was shocked. He reversed over the glistening stretch of road, stopped the car, and read the sign between the moaning flashes of his windshield wipers. "Army Property," it said. "Danger. Keep out."

The fence ran alongside the road for a few minutes more as he drove, then formed a corner and continued away into the dark. Then there were just the poplars he remembered and, as the road took a remembered turn, the lights of the house came into sight. The lights of only a few rooms.

TWENTY-FOUR

Oh yes, Herbert explained over breakfast, they had taken four hundred acres. Paid for, of course, but it all seemed a low bit of spite on the part of the Minister, who somehow, Herbert thought, felt a mad need to seek out Lord Wolfflen and one way or another put him in his place. Oh no, Herbert assured Marc, he'd never looked for trouble, he'd never let a bad word leave his lips about any of those Socialists; above all, he wanted to be known as a man above politics, anxious to serve the country.

"Little men," Herbert said, "what can you do? I suppose I could have let my displeasure be known in the hope of some sort of *clemency;* it might have assuaged them for me to have asked for something. You see, I wouldn't. In any case, the next thing you know with something like that, there is a whole great exposé in *Private Eye* or somewhere: 'Lord Wolfflen kills Army Project Threatening His View.' They say the land is what they need for their tanks, or missiles or tank missiles. I can't see the fence from the house, but they do make noise when they start shooting things."

Marc raised his eyebrows in sympathetic resignation. He bit into a flakey, faintly chalky scone. They were still the same, although that pastry cook must be long dead. He decided to allow himself another.

Herbert poured tea from his lefthanded teapot. Herbert was too edgy in the morning to have people hovering around, serving. The two of them sat alone, opposite each other at a wide table. Herbert rose out of his seat to serve Marc tea. So that teapot did exist. Thérèse had learned about it somehow and made it into a joke, her conversation piece whenever the English cousins were mentioned.

Herbert was lefthanded and drank a lot of tea in the morning. He was said to have had that large pot made so that when he handled it with his left hand, the side with the family coat-of-arms, the wolf rampant, faced him. Herbert's desire to remind himself of his family every morning was out of keeping with the image Marc had formed of his cousin.

"So," Herbert said, "Raphael wouldn't go in with you on the copper." He clucked his tongue and frowned ruminatively. "Well ... this time, actually, you really mustn't blame him. He's got enormous problems of his own. This country is in an incredibly depressed condition. The only money in the City seems to be coming from the sheiks. They may well be bent on buying England. But they won't let their money come anywhere near the House of Wolfflen. Raphael can't even underwrite the big loans anymore. And they've created a whole climate. There are men who are running after them with all kinds of deals, talking like procurers, and who cross the street when they spy Raphael. The way things are heading, the House of Wolfflen and those of our fellow tribesmen will become the Warsaw Ghetto of the City of London ... God, that whole Middle East thing is such a bore!"

"Raphael will find a way out," Marc said. "Raphael is brilliant. His father's son."

"He's a puffed-up ass!" Herbert said. Marc couldn't quarrel with that judgment, but it shocked him to hear Herbert talking about his son as if he were some unlikable stranger. If Herbert had a simple human heart, it dawned on Marc, he might have been one of the truly greatest men of his age. At what? His heart would have told him ...

"Anyway," Marc said, "it's all right about Cofra. The crisis has been solved."

"The crisis has been solved," Herbert repeated after him—his way, a little arrogant, of asking for explanation.

"Solved. We've been nationalized. We've washed our hands of it."

"It's always good to have clean hands." Herbert's voice was slightly singsong, and he spoke with a faint smile that corresponded to the bittersweet irony of Yiddish humor in his voice.

"That's it," Marc asserted, "You've touched the heart of the matter."

Herbert waited silently for Marc to continue.

"Actually, they nationalized the minesite and at the same time, they offered us, exclusively, the opportunity to buy a piece of ourselves back. In an operating company. They liked our style. Also there was a matter of two bank accounts in Switzerland, three million in cash in the one and two hundred thousand in the other. Dollars. They prefer dollars, like your sheiks."

He buttered the second scone he'd allowed himself. "So I simply accepted the nationalization. I declined to be their partner. I wrote a letter to the future emperor before I cleared out of that horrible country. I thanked him effusively. But no, I said, we had decided to get out of copper mining and concentrate ourselves elsewhere. With all due respect..."

"They'll pay—?"

"Oh they'll pay. Unless I made the Emperor raging mad. But I really doubt it. They'll pay. You see they borrow all their money, and they don't want to look in the least unreliable. The terms for reparations were better than any the Fourth Republic gave. He knew that, Kumbi. He pointed it out. And he was right. There is a new policy of Enlightened Cooperation, the man explained. They won't have trouble finding someone else to operate Cofra for them. Kumbi wants to encourage more foreign capital to help the country move forward. They want the right foreigners to show them how to do things—so long as they don't try to run things—

"And," he added, "so long, I suppose, as they maintain a good flow of money under the table. You pay, and you get service."

"It all sounds so very promising," Herbert said.

Marc went on: "I wonder how he would have reacted if I told him the simple truth. For a moment I was tempted—"

"The truth?"

"If I said, sorry, but you know, there's a thing about the Wolfflens: we just don't do these kinds of things. No hard feelings. I couldn't have dared tell him the whole truth: that there are dogs we just won't lie down with."

Herbert put down his teacup and laughed. Marc was still talking: "Just don't—" He looked at his cousin. "Yes, the whole thing really is very funny, finally, isn't it?"

"Come on, Marc," Herbert said, "*you're* funny. Not our what? Isaiah, dear Cousin, Isaiah our hallowed forefather would have gone in with them without batting an eye. 'Wolfflens don't retreat,' he would have said. 'Always some ground for accommodation. Sensible men can always do business. Don't turn your back on history.' Isaiah, and Noah, Daniel and Benjamin, the three flames of his heart, and Hannah, the homely stoker God provided, full of blessings and counsel and remedies, *Familie über alles*—they all would have known what they had to do. They'd have gone in! Wolfflens come to agreements. And Charles, your father, and my father, in their hotblooded prime. Accommodations with power? Totally us!

"Come on now, Marc," he continued. "What you've come upon is just a bland sample of what goes on all the time, you know it, every day. Saunderson . . . do you know Saunderson, an old friend of mine in the City. For years. Saunderson went into an iron mine in Brazil with a group of Frenchmen. It was going to be the biggest source of ore, mind you, in this century. They started a railroad to their site, they were going to dig a port. They were very excited. A hundred million dollars they put in, to start; I think it was at least that. Amfer, you know, the Americans, Amfer Incorporated, the ones who had their fingers slapped in that antitrust case, American Ferrous? Well, American Ferrous found out about it in a hurry, and they went in there and spent I don't know how many millions of dollars but at least four or five, as I heard it, bribing every Brazilian official they needed, to put sticks in the wheels. They even had people *literally* sabotaging the railway. So then there was a meeting right away in the Hotel Ritz in Paris and they offered Saunderson and his friends three times what they invested. It was an offer, what's that phrase? An offer they couldn't refuse. They took it all right.

"Amfer stopped the railway, called everyone off the minesite, closed it, and put a guard around it. They didn't feel the market was ready yet for a vast new source of ore. You see?

"Oh there are rules, Marc, there are laws, but that isn't the way the big game is played. It never has been. You know it as well as I do. The big game is played to win, any way you can without getting caught, and it has always been played that way."

Marc looked into his cup. There were leaves. He tilted the dregs of the tea toward him and looked at the pattern the leaves formed, stuck to the porcelain. He fumbled for an answer, but then he lost himself, for a moment, in the leaves. People read futures in them; some readers were said to be truly remarkable at it. He recalled having read something recently on predictions, by Arthur Koestler. Herbert knew him. Herbert would be abreast—his own book on ESP. Herbert knew very interesting people and did interesting things ...

Finally, Marc said, making it sound as matter of fact as he could: "But let's just say, Herbert, if it won't make you laugh some more, that there are certain things *I* just won't do."

"Of course not *you*, Marc. Not Raphael either, my poor son. Nor Léopold, or even Bruno. You're all respectable, upright, honest. Proud of a name, afraid to stain it. You're rare. You're rare gentlemen. But you're all *decadent.* You know that, Marc. So you'll make your commissions. But there's no sense in talking any more about an empire."

"And you?" Marc couldn't help but believe what Herbert was saying, but he couldn't resist fighting back against the tone.

"Me? Well. Well, I hope Marc, that when my turn comes to mount the scaffold, someone in the crowd, some rare romantic trade unionist, himself decadent, might raise his hand and cry: 'Spare that poor bastard, for he tried, unselfishly, as best he could, to help save England.' But it would be bloody unlikely, eh? Me? Well, at the moment I am aiding a Socialist government to find energy where energy does not exist. A very important study. But maybe I too should make my little frank declaration. I should tell them that to the best of my knowledge energy seems to have gone out of the English soul. Me? Well, you know, Marc, I too, am motivated by foolish pride."

"We've always known that," Marc broke in, teasing now, affectionate. Yes, Herbert was a proud, disdainful, self-centered bastard. But Marc couldn't help but like him. He realized that people didn't need to please him for him to like them. He'd loved Thérèse, still did, in some blurred, peculiar way. He could enjoy other people's lives just the way they were. Was it a weakness, he asked himself, or a strength? And was that a criterion that mattered? Weak for what? Strong for what?

"I'm simply too proud to pass my time playing with money," Herbert continued.

Marc let the arrow fly by him. He wanted Herbert, the rare mind, to tell him more. "The scaffold?" he asked.

"The scaffold," Herbert said with a note of mock drama. "The guillotine. The block. The firing squad. Oh not really, of course. Not *really*. But who knows? *Something else* really is on its way, can't you feel it, Marc? Something's going to happen, and it can't just be some other Wolfflens taking over. The worst is of course possible. Chile, or Russia, God knows. When Rome fell, the world went dark for a while. That too, is possible. Ashes may fall on everything. The Arabs may be in Paris, not Poitou, with a clear deed to the place—although I don't think that's really very likely. Seriously, in any case, I don't think there's any point in dreaming the stale dreams of our fathers. Money, more money. Is there? Money couldn't buy a good drink of water if it's *all* poisoned, could it? All radioactive or full of mercury of something—I'm talking off the top of my head. I haven't made any *study—*" he pronounced the word study in a self-deprecating way. "But you do have the idea . . ."

Then what can I do, what shall I do? Marc's mind had suddenly turned inward and blurted to itself. What can I do, Cousin, tell me, I'm almost sixty and what is left for me to do? But he kept silent. And Herbert had already changed his train of thought. "Seriously, Marc," he was saying, "old cousin, I'm proud of what you did, if it matters to you.

"I think it took considerable courage." He stood up. Breakfast was over.

A Pakistani brought Herbert the morning's mail as they entered the library. "They're all Pakistani in the house now," Herbert said, after the little, thin man had gone off with astonishing noiselessness. "It's a little like living with cats. You know, they live alongside you, not really with you. You can't get English servants now. I know it sounds awfully patronizing, but they really did feel like family—you do remember Brown?"

"Yes. Oh yes."

"Marc!" Herbert's eyes suddenly brightened. "What would you say to the idea of going fishing?"

And so the two of them got into rubber ponchos and hats and boots, and walked along a pine-matted trail through the green-smelling woods under the morning drizzle. A groundkeeper, a sullen boy of about nineteen, went with them to row the boat. Brown, of course, was dead.

In the boat, the young man answered Herbert's directions without speaking. Herbert told him to row there, or there. But they sat in the wet boat until the rain increased, without a bite. Herbert kept changing lures from a big box he had, but it was no use.

They spoke little out there on the water. Marc tried to check the accuracy of his memory of the shape of that lake, but there were clots of fog hiding coves and points. Then, all at once, he said:

"Herbert . . . what do you happen to believe?"

"Ah?"

"In what do you believe?"

"Oh my . . ."

"Do you think," Marc insisted, "that after all these years since the last time we were on this lake together, we might just still be able to talk as seriously as children do, about the nature of the world?"

Herbert's smile faded. His hand sorted indecisively through his lures. "I believe: I believe in putting one foot in front of the other," he said. "One right thing at a time."

Marc smiled now. "You don't see a lot of things as urgent."

"Oh a lot of individual changes are urgently needed. What I mean to say is that we don't urgently need a new *system*. I mean we're not ready enough, each and all of us, to make any new system work better than what we have."

He found his lure and cast it just short of some lily pads. Marc sat there without taking his line out of the water.

Herbert sneezed: a little gust of spray was visible in the thick damp air. "Sorry." He wiped his nostril carefully with his handkerchief.

"No. No." He reeled up again. "This is fishing weather." He cast. "What do I believe? . . . Well, people want to believe there is an ideal social system—the single right blueprint for Order among us.

We assume this with the same faith we have in an ordered universe. But you know, we've had only such little glimpses of the order of the universe—and the more we learn, the more subtle that system seems. Nowadays, with each new glimpse, we change the textbooks a little. But until now, we've changed our societies with vast proclamations of new truth, and at the cost of many lives ...

"Imagine, Marc, a crusade without a cross, an army without uniforms and banners? There'd be an end to battles—and we'd *miss them*, you see. Little cautious changes don't inspire people, people want the New Jerusalem, on earth, in their lifetime. It's been a long time since men worked on cathedrals knowing they wouldn't live to see one spire in its entirety. But once you no longer believe in wonders worked from beyond this earth, you do want to believe in wonders worked on earth. One way or another, the world without wonders is unacceptable to mankind. Even though one stone at a time is probably all we can manage—one improvement followed by another, the right change for the right particular small situation—without making a mess.

"I believe that there are things in this world." Herbert went on, "worth doing for their own sake and that we know them. We know. So you sort out your likes and your dislikes, your 'value judgments,' and you esteem of these only what you like no matter what it does for you, no matter whether you are alive or dead. You say: 'I want this to be, because whether I exist or not, it should exist.' Then you understand what love is. The only worthwhile motive in the world. And love is the antithesis, as well, of chaos, the God of creation, or the force of creation, if you prefer, opposed to the force of destruction. But you see ... very few people have been healthy enough to look at the world that way. Most often the world changes through destruction. Revolutions destroy too much and so from the start prepare their own destruction. Extremes call to extremes, rage to rage. The greatest revolution would be the end to revolutions. Sincere reform. But there's little reason to believe it will happen. Reform doesn't excite people. And all excitement is a form of heightened living, a kind of pleasure. Rage, too. Killing, kidnapping, hijacking, warring are unfortunately acts that bring pleasure. Reform is dreary in comparison. And there are, of course, people who are very badly off, enraged beyond any patience with reform. They want their chance to be unjust. So what can *you* do? An individual cursed with a need to be lucid? Nothing very exciting. You can make one right step after another. As big a step as is in your power. We know what's right."

Marc remained silent. The rain had begun to fall heavily now, and the boy seemed anxious to get to cover.

"Home? he asked, "sir?"

Lord Wolfflen frowned at the sky, but nodded.

"I tell you what else I believe, Marc. I believe that some people are better than others, that this is blatantly apparent. And that we, you and I, because of history obviously, but no matter why, are in many ways better than most people. There may be any number of ways some people are better than we are, but it would still be a shame if we betrayed ourselves, and let all we have go down the drain. I mean, quite bluntly, if we let ourselves, in a profound sense, let ourselves *go vulgar.*

"Well, all this is very vague and pontifical," Herbert concluded. They were in shallow water now, and he reeled up his trawling lure to avoid the weeds. Neither had caught anything. In a moment, the boat struck the gray timber pier with a thud that echoed against Herbert's forest. They hurried to the house, where they ate a quick, spare lunch.

They talked about Léa over their cold roast beef. Herbert had a very high opinion of Léa, whom he esteemed very intelligent and sensitive. He was pleased that she was marrying an American.

"They are still a marvelous people," he said, "even though it's such a country of *excess.* Over the years, they'd got their greed and their morals all mixed up in a contradictory zeal, but they are still a very moral people. People like to fault the Americans because so much of what the world is like is their doing. So many problems, yes. And yet, I say there's never before been so benevolent an empire."

"I think the boy might be an opportunist," Marc said, "am I unfair?"

Herbert shrugged. He hadn't met Jason Fullerton. Herbert excused himself after some fruit was brought. He was working against time with his energy study. The Socialists thought it would help to have one ready if another election were to come soon. They needed a respectable energy program. Herbert thought the country needed one in a hurry, anyway. He excused himself, asked to have a little time alone before the party. Marc realized that the morning in the boat was a sacrifice for Herbert—and they hadn't even had a nibble. He realized that his whole idea of barging in on Herbert a day early had entailed a great sacrifice for Herbert.

Herbert thought Marc might want to have a walk. The sun had come up during lunch.

He stood now on the hill above the house, watching the long row of cars wind up from the crossing at the riverbed. There were eight ... nine of them in an accidental convoy, all on time. It was time for the party.

Marc had wandered all over the land until well past dark. He sought out landmarks, certain trees, certain great rocks, copses, and hollows. They were still there, but strangely the distance between points seemed to have shrunk remarkably. There had been three thousand acres of Owen Glade, and yet the ground he knew of it seemed to have shrunk.

Marc could make out the French cousins by their yellow headlights. Somewhere down there was his son, Gilbert, and Bruno and Léopold. He tried to distinguish their cars. All at once he thought of an American Mafia meeting he'd read about. A meeting up in New York State given away by the pack of expensive cars on the country road. Then the puppet features, red hair, and red face of Kyle R. Hoyt flashed into his memory. Costa Rica ... Well, he was done with all that. He realized he was still in boots, flannels, and a tweed jacket. And he had to bathe and change for the party.

He ran down to the house like a boy afraid of a scolding.

TWENTY-FIVE

Everyone expected had arrived: all the family except for Marc's old mother who could no longer voyage beyond her garden, and his wife. There was also a handful of Léopold's closest friends. The guests were drinking champagne and whisky in the music room when Marc came down. The room, unlike the landscape of his childhood, hadn't shrunk. He'd come and gone in a hurry several times, as a grown man, for ceremonies in this house. Gilbert had had his confirmation here, my God, seventeen years ago. The room was the size of the lobby of a grand hotel. It had been furnished by Herbert's grandfather, Lord Oliver Wolfflen, the mystical Lord Wolfflen, at the turn of the century, and it was still an Art Nouveau wonderland. Lord Oliver had been a moody eccentric who'd spent the twilight of his life trying to reconcile the Torah with the teachings of Professor Suzuki, the Zen celebrity. He'd been a financial meteor in his youth, and had mellowed into an introspective romantic by the time he was forty.

Since the sacking of 1644, no one at Owen Glade had felt obliged to make the furniture correspond to the house. Oliver, though he hadn't enough interest in decor to redo the whole interior, threw out all the Victoriana weighing on his soul in the winter parlor, and brought over Horta from Belgium to do the room, down to the doorknobs. Commodes, sofas, chairs, wood paneling, everything in the fluid, broodingly romantic lines of the period. Marc recalled now having read what Octave Mirbeau had said when he walked into his Modern Style hotel in Düsseldorf: "The furniture looked drunk."

Beneath a Dante Rossetti painting of thin women bathing at the shore of a dusk lake, with a peacock illuminating the foreground, there now stood a harp. The winter parlor had become the music room. Herbert had given the room a purpose. In summer, Herbert would bring some of the best musicians in the world here for a festival of chamber music. Tonight, across the room from the harp, an old Black was playing 1950's bop at the piano. Marc's son stood behind him with Alice Laver. They were holding hands as they listened; she was beaming. The fifties were the great new rediscovery of her age group. The good-time fifties. When Gilbert spied his father, he touched Alice's shoulder and went up to Marc alone.

"I have to speak to you, please."

Marc saw the anxiety written on Gilbert's face. He guided his son to a group of empty chairs.

"I ... ah ... had a conversation with Iris a moment ago," Gilbert said, shoving his hands into his jacket pockets.

"She is going to apply to INSEAD, to study business. I think she wants very hard ... well, to get Bruno to get her into the business ... if you can imagine ..."

"That sounds like a very good thing," Marc said.

"Ah? What do you think? A woman ..."

"I think Isaiah considered Hannah his partner."

"Well ... I'm not saying anything against it."

"It's new," he added, with a faint smile.

Gilbert removed his hands from his pockets and locked his fingers across his stomach. He was red faced, and he pursed his mouth before he was able to speak again.

"Father," he said forcefully at last, "I think that in whatever changes are to be made, I should acquire much more responsibility. Well, fifteen percent of our share is a bit risible.

"I'm thirty," he insisted, "almost. I'm not just a boy. Maybe I'm not even what people call young nowadays anymore." He turned his face from Marc's pained gaze and blurted: "And I believe I may want to get married ... finally."

"Alice?" Marc asked quietly.

"Yes. Do you like her? I'm not marrying *her father.*"

"She's extraordinarily lovely."

"She's impeccable," Gilbert said.

Gilbert married. Another milestone seemed to loom in Marc's life. And what would *she* do to him, Marc wondered. Alice. She was a beauty for Dante Rossetti. Small, ethereal, in her crêpe dress tonight. Over his son's shoulder, Marc saw her laughing with a strange raucousness at something the piano player had just said.

She projected frailty, innocence, yet at the same time, somehow, as with her laugh, total self-confidence. Gilbert will have to be strong. With her, and also with Bruno.

"As for Bruno," Gilbert was saying. "I've never known exactly how he feels about me. If I had more weight ... Something to run." He looked down, directly into his father's eyes now. "Well, do you see your way clear—?" Always at any moment I'll see my way clear for you, Marc thought, but if only I'd known and knew the right way. But now he knew it was too late. Gilbert wasn't a boy. He'd go on, his way, carrying his own character through the buffeting of time and experience. He'd have to heal himself, gain whatever health-bringing wisdom on his own. Marc had never been close enough to his son, and now there seemed to be nothing that could drive them together.

"Don't worry," Marc said, "I'll back you. Gilbert, I promise you you will be given important new responsibilities."

Gilbert looked at him, unrelieved but with curiosity.

"You can be sure of it," Marc said. He took his son's arm, but dinner was announced just then, and at the door of the banquet room, they each went to their distant places, where an immense horseshoe table had been set.

Fireworks!

Herbert, for whatever reason had tickled him, was being very fancifully ceremonial. For dinner, he'd announced, the menu was "an extract" from the wedding dinner at Owen Glade of Léa's grandfather, Saul, and Ariel de Vaunel. "An extract," Herbert had said, with the *bonhomie* of a man with some practice at scholars' banquets and government award-givings, "because none of us with our modern stomachs could survive the entire program."

Herbert was out of his shell, assiduously the host. He seemed moved, finally, by a sense of family. His manner was gaffish, but warm.

And the lamb could not have been more delicate in 1925 than it was tonight. The '45 and '61 La Garne were unforgettable. There was a bombe flavored with rose petals and champagne, exactly as it was on the old menu. Herbert had dug up the recipe somewhere. The *eau de vie* that followed the coffee had gone into the cask before the battle of Sedan.

And now fireworks.

The booming and the flashes at the windows sent the women rushing for their wraps, and the men went out with them and stood valiantly on the chill flagstone in just their evening suits. A wind had carried away most of the dampness and now the air was still and brisk.

Marc watched a roman candle burst into four parachutes of light. All gold. Herbert was doing the fireworks in gold instead of color.

A short man with a square jaw and his thin little wife passed in front of Marc. He'd shaken hands with them earlier. They were the Fullertons, the parents of Jason, Léa's future husband.

Mr. Fullerton squinted behind his glasses to examine more intensely the phenomenon of the fireworks. He and his wife wore the air of tourists.

"Gold," he said.

"What else?" answered his wife, with an old-country intonation that reached beyond generations of Pittsburgh.

Marc moved into the shadows and let them pass. He turned, and found himself face to face with Raphael Wolfflen. Herbert's son had a cigaret in his full, extended lips. He seemed to be wandering around now, alone, with great nervousness. He had a glass of whisky in his hand.

"You don't dislike me," he said abruptly to Marc.

"Oh no, whatever for?" Marc answered with embarrassment.

"Listen," Raphael said, "it was really very difficult for me. I really couldn't have helped very much at all. You must believe that. We've begun to go through hell in the City. If *they* have their way, they'll have us wearing yellow stars. You understand?"

"I'm sorry," Marc said, "I suppose when they look beyond the City we'll have the same difficulty. It can't be long—"

"Oh we'll manage," Raphael said. He pointed to his head. "It's our brains, you see, the others don't have. The whole world is still going to need Wolfflen brains. *Sechel*," he said, with his finger still at his temple. Marc had never imagined that Raphael knew Yiddish.

"We'll get around this thing," Raphael went on, "but I suppose if the Socialists make a go of it, they'll eventually nationalize the banks. And they'll nationalize just about everything big."

He lowered his head to sip his whisky. "You'll have it too," he said, and as he spoke those words he raised his glass almost in the gesture of a toast. "The Left as well. The Left on your side is more dangerous even than what we have. They're *madder*. After Robinet goes... I wouldn't be surprised; or in just a few years. I'd give them better than a fifty-fifty chance. They'll nationalize all right. Anything that dominates a market."

Raphael brushed his jacket where an ash had fallen. "I must say, Marc, you were frightfully farsighted. So *brainy*. You really were. Diversified. A little bit of a lot of things. You'll last longer than anyone."

He threw his cigaret into the grass and sipped again.

"Where *are* you now with Cofra?" he asked, knitting his brow.

"They nationalized us."

Raphael guffawed. "Nationalized," he said. He patted Marc's shoulder as if to compliment him on the joke and headed back inside, apparently to refill his glass.

"Poor Cousin Marc—" It was Léa, approaching with her fiancé. "You're a lonely bachelor tonight."

She wouldn't let Thérèse's insulting absence go unnoticed. He supposed she had a right not to.

"Oh ... yes." He faltered. Smiled. He wouldn't counter. Actually, he wasn't anxious to be thinking about Thérèse again.

"I'm teasing," Léa said. She spoke in French, but she had that open, frank, American tone in her voice.

"Sincere" and self-assured. In English, she reintroduced her fiancé. "Jason has met so many Wolfflens tonight it's as confusing as not being introduced at all."

"We've met before," Marc reminded her.

"Marc," Fullerton said in an emphatic voice, like a child who had his lesson right. "Originally, the Austrian branch."

"A French twig," Marc answered, smiling in self-deprecation.

In the embarrassing silence that followed Jason's error, the three of them could hear Jason's parents heading their way.

They were talking about the pagoda on the little island in the pond across the lawn. Marc looked at the pagoda and thought of his morning with Herbert, out on the lake, in the woods above, which fed the artificial patch of water in front of him now. The mood of that morning came over him again, but now he could decant it, understand it better. The clusters of fog on that lake came back to mind and inspired in him a dreamlike, surreal image—he thought of all of *us*, the living with the weight of their past like something material swaddling them, all suspended just above a dark smooth surface, the dangerous unknown. All of us, he thought, not just the Wolfflens, the whole world at this moment in time. Suspended, almost fallen.

"It's old," Fullerton *père* was saying about the pagoda. "I wonder if they built it here or if they brought it over."

"They must have brought it over piece by piece," his wife answered, "knowing them."

In what seemed an almost panicky attempt to escape his parents, Jason nudged Léa. The two of them broke away from Marc awkwardly, and headed in the direction of the house.

A vast star pattern of gold lit up the sky above the pagoda. The light seemed to echo, like sound, the gold of the roof. Near the lip of the pond, Bruno de Wolfflen was standing alone, looking at the fireworks.

"It's the Temple of the Golden Pavilion," he said as Marc came up to him.

He waited fruitlessly for Marc to answer, and then he said ruminatively, "I've been going through . . . I've been reading a little some of the books Iris left in the house."

"Yes."

"Yes . . . some of it is not so crazy as you might think," he said. His voice darkened. "But it's such a godawful jumble! The kids are interested in so many confused, conflicting things these days . . ."

"The times are confused," Marc assented.

"Very."

Bruno found a flat pebble at his feet, and like a boy, he sent it scaling across the pond. They could hear a flurry of *thwocks*, like the whirr of a whip, but the night blurred Bruno's achievement, kept them from counting how many times his pebble had grazed the sheen of the water.

"Marc," he said suddenly, "I've led a careless life."

Another rocket reached its apex and came down in balls of light whose tentacles gave birth to other balls as they fell. Marc didn't have a reply.

"Gilbert," Bruno was saying now, having fought back a choking sound in his throat. "Gilbert, Marc. I want to tell you that now I consider him as if he were my son as well as yours. I mean ... Gilbert is our future, all of ours. We both have to get behind him. He's got a good mind. He will make us all proud of him."

Marc took his cousin's arm. "Iris, too," he said.

"Yes, in a sense of course! But she's a woman ..."

"Let's not get in the way of history," Marc said smiling. "I mean it. You bring her in."

Bruno laughed. "God," he said "we're a couple of old men."

Before Marc could reply, one of Herbert's Pakistanis was there beside him, showing no signs of hurry, telling him in an unobliging voice that someone was asking for him on the phone.

TWENTY-SIX

"Ah here's where you are!" Léopold said as Marc hung up. Léopold crossed the threshold of the library and cast an assaying and awed glance at Lord Herbert Wolfflen's bookshelves. Léopold was holding a glass of champagne.

"I couldn't imagine where you'd gone, all alone." He sipped. "I'd never have forgiven you if you were getting ready to leave my daughter's party this early—were you going up to bed?"

Marc shook his head. "No," he said, "I feel like much more champagne."

"Stay with me," Léopold said, "drink with me." He beamed. "Think of it, almost the entire Wolfflen clan will be sleeping under one roof here tonight. So you see, big houses sometimes have their use."

Marc followed his cousin out of the library. Léopold's voice switched into a somber note: "Marc," he said, "I've had a talk with Raphael. He is in a very bad situation. We have to help him ... and we may have the same problem ourselves before we know it. We must all get together and do something as soon as possible."

"Yes." Marc was listening very thinly. His mind was still moored back a few moments to the voice on the other end of the phone. Léopold flushed and cleared his throat.

"Marc ... you know ... When I see all of us here, the family together this way, I get a very strong feeling. I can't help it.

"I look around at all these people, and I say to myself: look how brilliant they are, how much they do in the world, all these people, my relatives. It's a very strong, good feeling. Marc, you know I'm a sentimentalist, but I can't help it, and I say to myself: if we could only pull together, all in the same direction. If only we help one another more ... People are saying we're finished."

"Yes."

"People are saying we're finished, Marc. But I say if we all throw our weight in the same direction all the time, we could be incredible."

"Yes ... How do you feel, Léopold?" Marc was listening to the echo of Cynthia's voice in his mind:

Come get me. We're finished here. Please.

Count on me, he heard himself answer.

"What?" Léopold said, "I feel like a newborn baby is how I feel. I've come back from the dead and I feel like I'm just born, and we're going to do enormous things. *Together,* Marc. All of us, you and me and the others. And we've got youth, Marc. Gilbert has a brilliant head for business. Bruno wants to bring in Iris—and what's wrong with that? The same blood. The same *Sechel.* And Léa and Jason, why not? And Raphael's boy, after them ..."

The voices in Marc's mind faded. He blurted: "You're perfectly right, Léopold. I'm giving Gilbert my place."

They had walked into the great hall as they talked. The horseshoe table was gone now. There was only a bar with a little brown man in white standing listlessly behind it. Strains of music and the murmur of voices were coming from elsewhere in the house, but except for the barman, they were alone in the long room. The floor formed a gleaming empty space. like a body of placid water.

Léopold seemed at a loss for an answer. He reached out and put his hand on Marc's forearm, stopping him there.

"You're perfectly right, Léopold," Marc said again. "Only, it's time for the new people to find a new direction. It's up to them to show what they can do.

"You're a young man, yourself, Léopold. You'll help them. I'll be available. I'll be available if anyone thinks my advice will help. There'll be nearly forty million dollars more of Wolfflen money in the bank.

"But you see, Léopold. I owe it to Gilbert as his father. I owe him his chance. He's almost thirty and I'm nearly sixty. We're both of an age for a change."

"What . . ." Léopold started to say. He might have meant to ask: what will you do? And so he stopped himself. As if he knew that the answer was so fraught with import, possibly so shrouded with doubt that asking for it now, this way, was a merciless assault.

But Marc's mind couldn't help but take the cue. What shall I do, he asked himself. Thoughts came in a jumble. He thought of that American Justice of the Supreme Court, seventy or nearly, or more? Who'd married a girl Cynthia's age. Life was so short and this world so absurd, why should that seem more absurd than anything else? And beyond that, other than *her*. What? He had no program. Nothing came to mind. But after all, it all wasn't so hard. Money was power, power to create more money or create other things. He could think of numerous things worth bringing into being for their own sakes.

"I can't stop thinking of you, Marc, what am I going to do?"

"What *we* shall do," he'd soothed, "is to put one foot in front of the other and see where they take us."

No program. Except, tomorrow night, he decided, they would stop off at some country hotel with peat fires going. They would dine and go to bed and she'd be beside him all night and also in the morning—

"You've heard about Hoyt," Léopold was saying.

"Oh yes . . . Costa Rica."

"They found him," Léopold said, "I heard it in the car coming here. Then you must not have heard? They found him in the rear of a Cadillac on an empty lot in the suburbs of San José. With a bullet in the back of his head."

"What—my God!"

But Marc wasn't deeply shocked. It seemed natural. The way the world was now it was perfectly natural. Anything like that. More and more one would have to pick one's way through all that. Through danger to the body and danger to the soul. More and more. His century hadn't cured his grandfather's and now vultures were overhead. Marc could not sincerely grieve for Hoyt; he'd never known the human being in Kyle R. Hoyt.

They were walking again now, Marc and Léopold, toward where the others had gathered again in the music room. Marc became aware of an orchestra. The relatives were dancing. And at the same time he noticed the rhythm of their own steps, his and Léopold's which had fallen into the same slow and certain stride over the bright floor, a stride he recalled was a Wolfflen *démarche*, a family way of walking.

Suddenly Marc felt a warm and easy sensation of being in his place. It was something totally free of thought, and then it blended with an even stronger buoyancy. He felt oddly like a man who had just come into a fortune. For, as far as anyone could know in these unsettled times, he knew he never had to worry for money again.

U78-11452　　　FICTION

Dryansky, G. Y.

The heirs.　　　STORED

EUCLID PUBLIC LIBRARY

UPSON SCHOOL
490 E. 260th Street
Euclid, Ohio 44132

731-1151

PLEASE DO NOT REMOVE
CARD FROM THIS POCKET

PRINTED IN U.S.A.　　　Cat. No. 23 261